I'M NO HERO

By Sam Wicker

Copyright ©2024 by Sam Wicker

All rights reserved. No part of this book may be reproduced or transmitted in any form or by any means, electronic or mechanical, including photocopy, recording, or any information storage and retrieval systems, without prior permission from the publisher (except for reviewers who may quote brief passages).

First Edition

Printed in the United States of America

ISBN: 978-1-965770-00-9

Cover design by: Sam Wicker

Published by Carder Wicker Writing

www.carderwickerwriting.com

To Mom and Dad. You are the two people I love most, and I will forever be grateful to you for supporting and loving me.

To all who have stood by me, held my hand, dried my tears, and understood that anxiety takes hold and makes a monster of me. Thank you.

Chapter 1

Crashing and thrashing a boar of white shall emerge.
Threaten it will until The Hero makes the throw.
The Best takes the quests, but not The Hero of wills.
With heavy heart our Hero trembles, but hearten!
The Hero battles through.

"How many did you get?" His daydreaming expression fell to a blithe one as he called out to me from his perch on the wall after I cleared the treeline.

The old stone wall from an age ago stretched between the road, through the browned field, and into the forest, until it met a bubbling stream. Its once-white river stones were grayed and overgrown with weeds and moss. It crumbled in places while standing strong in others. Joni, his finger-length blonde hair shimmered in the noon light of the sun, sat on the end of it, at the road that would lead us home, or into Owlimount.

"Three." I held up my catches. The fur and feathers were smooth and soft, unbloodied by my expert traps. The forest behind me was a second home, but today something had been off. The birds, while few lived through the winter there, were silent. None winged through the branches of the naked canopy, nor chirped in those laden with green needles or jagged leaves. Even the trees stood quiet, not a hint of a breeze to clack their branches together.

"That's good." He said with a grin that always made the girls of the village scramble to catch his eye.

The string of two rabbits he pulled up from his side drew me from my thoughts on the quiet. "Same trap." He added as he let them fall back to his thigh.

I tried to smile. I wanted to go home. To shake off the oddness of the forest today.

Joni picked up his long spear as he stood. He was practicing with it before our yearly hunting trip in a few weeks. Unlike me, he didn't have to hunt every day to keep his family fed. "Town or home?"

"Ho-" I noticed a group of village children climbing up over the steep riverbank from the roaring Gala river. Something pricked the hairs on the back of my neck. "What are they doing out here?"

"See the older ones?" Joni pointed with his spear. He placed his free hand on my belt, his palm and digits easily spanning my hip, and pulled me close to his side, "They were teaching the little ones to fish."

I finally spotted the handfuls of fishing rods two of the older children had in their hands. Joni pressed into my back. All broad and hard, warming me against the chill of the lingering winter and the quiet. He wrapped his bulky arm around me as I watched the kids pause by a large naked tree. My still healing shoulder protested the added weight of him, but I ignored it. I scanned the area, the prickling sensation growing worse. Bumps rose on my arms.

"How many?"

"What?"

"I want four, at least." His breath was like a hot feather on my neck seconds before he nuzzled there.

"Four what?" I gritted my teeth, wondering what this dread curling in my stomach and making my fingers itch for my daggers meant. *Couldn't he feel it?*

"Kids." His arm squeezed, hard.

"Oh." I wriggled away. The trees were making noise now. Creaking and swaying as if in a storm, but there wasn't any wind. A pebble tumbled off the wall beside me and into the brittle grasses below.

"Chi…"

His voice grated on my ears like a knife tip dragging along a rock.

The racket in the forest grew louder. The trees swayed as if the ground under them erupted. *Was that a snort?* I dropped my catch to the wall, "Joni-" I started to warn just as something burst through the treeline in a spew of dirt, torn branches, and dead leaves.

The kids' screams broke through the second of silence.

The giant white pig- *white pig?* - turned its fat head toward the screams. The tusks covered in roots and dirt were as long as my forearms and sprouted from each side of a wrinkled muddied snout. This thing could probably wrestle a bear and win.

My feet pounded toward the kids before I knew what I was doing. Those tree trunks of pig legs started moving too. I felt Joni's fingers graze my arm. Then the thundering of those hooves shook the earth underneath my footfalls.

"Run!" I screamed, waving my arms high in the air as I did. My shoulder burned as I waved my arms higher and higher; part to distract the boar and part to try to get the kids to snap out of their huddle. I yelled again, my lungs burning with the effort of running and screaming at the same time.

A few moved, scrambling toward town. Away from the pig's trajectory. Fishing rods forgotten. Their friends forgotten, too. There were three that stood, their mouths as wide as their eyes, rooted to the spot by the old tree.

"Run! Move!" I screamed at them again. Panic ran up and clawed at my throat. I tugged at a dagger, fumbling the hold until it fit into my hand. I tugged another one free. I let the black blades fly, missing the pig's snout by a hair. Blood trickled down the white cheek.

The other thunked deep into the tree by the oldest boy's head.

That pig kept barreling toward the children.

I tugged out another dagger and let it fly. This one hit its mark sinking deep into a dark, white-rimmed eye. The pig gave a shrill squeal as it skidded to a stop on four stiff legs. Dust and dirt flew up in front and around it as it tossed its wide head. The dagger stayed in it. The one in the eye hadn't done what I hoped it would though. Any other animal and that dagger would have damaged the brain.

I had just made it angry.

My dagger, or the dust, made the eldest boy wake out of his stupor. He shoved the younger kids up into the large tree. The tree's trunk, as thick as the pig was wide, leaned over, long trailing branches tickled the deep Gala waters.

It wouldn't hold if that pig decided to ram it, no matter how deep the coils of roots dug into the earth.

The boar pawed the ground with another squeal, this one deeper, thunderous, and less a scream of pain. I threw another pair of daggers deep into the wide, low-slung belly. It screamed that high-pitched scream again, that large head turning to me.

"Gods." I skidded. I threw down my hand to grapple with the road sand as my old slick boots slid. It helped the change in trajectory to the river bank. If I could jump it, I could get in the deep part and swim away. Unless pigs could swim. *Could they swim?* Thundering sounded in my ears and reverberated through me.

At least my family would have enough pig meat to last a year or two once someone got it down.

"Nadachia!" Joni yelled to my left.

I dared a glance, his spear held high. I shifted toward him, arms and legs pumping, my lungs burning, trying to get the boar to do the same so Joni could have a decent shot. I still headed to the river bank, but it would take me longer.

I realized my mistake. The short rapids, shallow, were beyond the lip of the bank instead of the deep part with the slight whirlpool. I would either be killed by the boar or I would break myself on rocks that refused to bend to the river's will.

Out of the corner of my eye, I saw him take the running stance. I watched that familiar fluid motion in a blur as his spear began its flight. The pig had gotten too close. That spear would land right behind me.

I readied to jump in the next couple of steps. Only to have my foot slip into the soft sand of the pushed-up bank. Instead of leaping, I slid and half lobbed myself down the embankment. Sand sifted up over my boots as I tried to dig in for secure footing. I pushed at the bank behind me with my hands, trying to push further away and down.

Sam Wicker

Sand, dirt and a few clumps of grass showered down on my head as I slowed at the mud and small rocks beside the fast waters of the Gala. I whirled, looking up to see the pig skidding down the path I made. Joni's spear sticking up out of its neck. Blood and foam flung out of its mouth as it struggled to get back up, to stop from sliding. A small squeal sounded this time as it flung its front legs out and dug its hooves in the sand.

A cloud of dust and sand wafted over me as the pig emptied its lungs before splatter hit my face. I threw another dagger, the hilt nearly disappearing with the blade into the eye, right beside the other one. That last breath warmed me as we stared at each other. What could have been my death was the pig's last effort.

The world whirled slowly around me, the river switching places with the embankment. My backside ached with the landing on rocks and mud. I dug my fingers into the cold land, water eddying around them and into my palms. *The White Boar*.

"Nadachia! Chi!" Joni half slid, half jumped down to me. He grabbed my arms in long-fingered hands, "You hurt?" He swiped at the wet dribbling down my face, "Is this yours?"

His hand, covered in red and white foam, lifted from my face. I shook my head, the sky and land shaking with it. He puffed a breath, "Good." There was a pause before his hands were on my shoulders and he shook me, "You stupid girl, what were you thinking?! Of all the-"

"Helloooo!" A boy's broken voice called from behind the pig.

"We're alright! Get help!" Joni interrupted his own tirade.

"They're already coming!" The boy's head popped up over the edge of the bank. As far away from the pig as he could manage and still be within earshot.

Ignoring the now not-so-dull ache in my shoulder, I reminded myself to breathe normally. I didn't need the thundering heart in my chest to try to jump out or my brain to explode. With Joni's help, I pulled myself up out of the mud and sand. His newer brown pants now wet and caked in mud on his knees. The gurgling of the Gala was soft against the roar in my ears. Joni took a rag out of his back pocket and began drying off my back and butt. Each swipe near my shoulders drew a whimper up my throat until I bit down on my lips.

I pulled away, "Stop, it's fine."

As the world kept turning on me slightly, I moved toward my closest daggers in the pig. I reached for them, Joni beat me to it. He pulled them from the eye with a liquid pop. Blood splattered on his arm and shoulder. A pig leg thrashed, knocking me in the shoulder and I fell back into the rocks at the river's edge. My good shoulder plowed into the muddy soils before stopping at a rounded rock. I heard the crack before the lance of pain.

I had just gotten that shoulder to work properly from the fall I took last week too. Well, with a little leftover pain. The other one would always be a pain as it was my throwing arm.

Joni was on top of me, pulling me up before I got a mouthful of muddy water. I coughed, groaned, and coughed again. "Must've got a nerve or part of its mind."

I glared at my daggers he handed me, then at the boar. The White Boar. We wouldn't be hoping to find it on our hunting trip anymore.

He half-carried me back to the bank. I crawled up it, taking out my daggers from the cheek, then the two from the stomach of the pig as I went. I cleaned the red flesh and blood off the black metals as best as I could before slipping them back into my belt. Thanking the gods again that these were a family heirloom I hadn't sold yet. Sitting in the grass, I tried to get the world to stop spinning, my eyesight to stop tunneling, my heart to stop running away, and my stomach to stop clenching. I sat on my knees, watching the dust cloud rise from the eastern gate and head toward us.

The cold water of the Gala sunk into my clothes. They stuck to my back and sides, leeching what warmth my body had soaked up during the morning out. My teeth began chattering as my heartbeat quieted in my ears and eased its thunder in my chest.

I pulled myself to stand, then considered how terrible of an idea that had been as I stumbled drunkenly toward the kids who were climbing down off the tree. I leaned against the thick shaggy trunk once I made it there. I looked at each of their upturned faces. Their eyes were so wide I thought they might pop out of their little heads. "Are any of you hurt?"

One little girl showed me her hands, scuffed from the red papery tree bark. I went back down to my knees. It was safer being closer to the ground when it kept moving on me. The contents of my stomach, if there were any, wouldn't have that far to go either. I gently brushed her hands clean, "Just a little cut here and there, little one. You will be alright."

She nodded, tears welling up in her eyes. *Gods, would she ever want to go fishing again?*

Horses skidded to a stop beside us, spraying road dirt with their hooves. One snorted and tossed its head as if impatient to move along. I looked up at the shining armor of the two guards.

"Chi?" Edi dismounted, rushing over to me.

Ria right behind him asked, "What happened? The kids were saying something about a pig monster?" Ria's voice always amused me. As one of the physically strongest women I knew, stronger than many of the men and oxen in town even, her voice was like a songbird.

Edi, the youngest and best looking guard in Owlimount, scoured my face with sharp gray eyes, wiping away some blood and foam. His thick leather gloves were rough but warm. Once he grew satisfied, he stopped, his hands falling back to his sides. I must have shivered because in the next moment he had his blanket off his saddle and over my shoulders.

Pig monster. White boar. THE white boar.

A chill washed down my spine. I pointed to the bank. He had killed it. We all knew he would kill it. "Joni's with it."

Ria patted my shoulder, I tried not to scream. She shoved Edi toward his horse with her free hand, "Get her some water before the whole village arrives."

He obeyed, quickly giving me his canteen, "Drink slow, you went pale there for a second." He motioned to my face, "Since that's not yours, are you hurt anywhere?"

I shook my head as I swished around a mouthful of stale water. I swallowed and took another gulp, before answering, "Just my shoulders again."

"Again?"

"Gods! It's The White Boar!" Ria found her voice. Edi started over, then hung back, casting a furtive glance at me. Not that he couldn't see the rear end of the thing from the tree. Still, seeing it closer had an appeal now that it wasn't trying to run me over.

"Go." I waved the canteen at him. Another mistake as the bones creaked and cracked below my ear with the motion.

Edi reached Ria's side when the first of the villagers stopped around me, clogging the road and my view of the riverbank. Doc was first in his swift cart. A traveling merchant and a few villagers hanging on to the sides of the merchant's wagon stopping behind him. Doc hopped out as I gave the canteen to one of the kids to take and pass among them.

The mayor in his polished chase pulled to a stop next to the magistrate in his less glamorous and much older wagon. The magistrate had a woman with him. The girl beamed and sniffled at the same time when the woman dropped to the ground off the wagon and gathered her skirts in thick fists as her head swiveled between the tree and the riverbank. The girl started toward her, but Doc knelt in front of her.

"Ye hurt?"

The girl shook her head, her brown wad of hair on top of her head wiggling like a lid on a boiling pot as she hid her hands behind her back.

"Just scratches from the bark," I told him as he started reaching for her hands.

He nodded, "Go on then." He checked the other two kids over, talking with them gently in his lilting baritone. He waited until their parents arrived before allowing them to stray from his side. He then moved to me, going down on one knee with a grunt, "Look like a mess, Chi."

"You should see the pig."

He grunted, looking down at my legs and running his hands along them, but I caught the half-smile as he asked, "It's white, ain't it?"

I nodded, finding my mouth working dry again, but the children had put the canteen back on Edi's saddle when they left.

I cringed when he touched my shoulders and he grunted, "Got both of 'em this time? I ain't gonna tell ya to rest and expect it to happen. But I'm gonna tell ya and hope it happens. You need to rest. A good whole day, a week is better, a month or two would be best, of doin' nothin' but eatin', sleepin', and talkin' with your family. Yer not gonna have much time with 'em soon 'nuff."

"I'll try. It's just the one. Hurts worse this time."

He leaned over me, "I'm gonna have to set it again."

Grabbing a stick from the still winter brown grass beside me; I bit down on it and worked to keep my breathing even. Doc counted under his breath, but he pushed it in place at the wrong count.

I should be used to that by now.

Pain shot through my arm all the way to my fingers and tingled there. I moved them, making sure everything was set correctly, even if the pain worsened momentarily. He rubbed the area, easing the muscles and their attachments as best he could with his thick fingers. "I'll make sure Rossi gets the majority of that pork, but I'll have to cut ham off it for the celebration that's sure to come."

I nodded, knowing what would happen. Ever since Joni had grown into his large hands and feet, everyone knew he had to be the one. No Hero in our past had ever been scrawny according to the statues and paintings. Most had been pretty, like Joni, too. All had been from Owlimount, or the surrounding areas. The feast would be to honor him. To start his journey to the capital to claim his Hero status and start the quests with a cheer, gifts, and a belly full of food and drink.

They still weren't through butchering the boar and having a pre-emptive party at sunset. I nodded off against the tree every now and then. The vial Doc had given me for the pain worked its magic and made me drowsy too. Joni nudged me often enough that I got tired of it and told him to either move or he was going to lose his hands. He sauntered off with the crowd with a roll of his pretty green eyes.

I was having a nice dream about voices buzzing like white bees nearby when something started shaking me. I gasped in a lung full and struck out with a hand. Doc's hard chest stopped me, cracking my fingers and making my wrist hurt. "Sorry," I yawned, patting his chest where I hit him.

"Edi!" Doc called, "Take 'er home." He hauled me up to my feet, gentle with his hands on my sides rather than pulling me up by the arms.

"I can go on my own." I folded the blanket someone had given me at some point. No, I tried to fold it. I could barely lift the thing off the ground.

I dropped the waded mess with a gasp as Doc picked me up by a thigh and hip to deposit me on Edi's saddle. I glared down at him as he said, "Yer too light, lass. Gotta put some meat on ya."

Edi mounted behind me, his armor cool against the thin fabric of my mud-caked shirt and hunting gear. He chuckled, his breath warm against the shell of my ear and cheek, "A bit bony, but she's still got some curves."

Doc's look soured as it traveled from me to Edi, "Any funny business Edi of Tamanim and I'll make ya sing like a bird fer life! Understand?"

"Aye." His swallow was nearly as loud as his answer.

We were well down the road on Edi's sturdy dun steed before he took a big enough breath for his arms to loosen at my sides, "Doc's scary, ain't he?"

I giggled, "Only to those with bad intentions."

"Aw, come on Chi, you know me. I wouldn't do nothin'." He paused, "Unless a girl were willin' and we were in love and…ya know."

I leaned my head back on his shoulder. The moons above, although not full, were bright enough to see the road and surrounding bare trees well. I could tell it wasn't the shadows darkening his complexion, "Thinking about Seaghla?"

Edi shrugged, making my head bounce.

I sighed, closing my eyes, "I dunno if she's coming back, Edi."

"I know." His voice was soft, "Momma always told me that first loves are hardly the lasting, lifetime ones."

We rode in silence for a while. The clip-clop of his horse a slow plod against the gurgling and slapping waters of the Gala the road butted up against still. I was about to fall back asleep when he spoke up again.

"That don't mean you and Joni won't last though. Even when he goes off to be the Hero, he'll take you with him. He always said he would. Said he can't take down the big ones without you."

I snorted, "If he can take the big ones out at all."

Edi chuckled, "You both did a number on that boar. But Joni did give the killin' blow."

"Oh?"

"Yeah, right in the eye."

"Is that what he said?"

"Didn't have to. Part of the eye was still on him."

My face heated. That had been my daggers in that eye, not his. He didn't even have daggers. I took a deep breath. The boar had still moved after the dagger in its eye though. Joni had downed it with the spear. Blood loss. That was that.

Joni was the New Hero of the New Prophecy. He would have to go to the Capital and choose his team carefully. There, we would be given quests. Quests that would save people. He would be popular.

At least I'd have the Welkans and Taspe to help me keep my family fed.

"Looks like you have company."

Edi's voice drew me from my thoughts. Leaning against the gate, just outside the pool of lantern light hanging from our tree, as if my thoughts had summoned him, stood Taspe. He opened the gate for us, but Edi stopped just outside.

"You won't come in? At least water your horse and get some for yourself before heading back." I pulled my leg over the horse's neck. Taspe's long-fingered hands came to my waist and half let me slide down, half lifted me toward him.

"We'll be fine," Edi said as he patted his horse's neck, "'Sides, you got a story to tell. Taspe." Edi nodded at him.

"Edi." Taspe nodded back, "Should I lock her up or something?" His ebony hair hid his face from me, but I could hear the smirk in his bluejay raspy voice.

Edi chuckled, "Good luck trying that, and let me know how it goes if you live." He turned his horse and gave a wave over his shoulder before nudging the long-legged beast into a canter.

I slipped from Taspe's hands, leaning on the gate to shut it behind us. I turned, then I was captive. His hands cupped my face and tilted it to the lantern light.

"How did you get all this on you?"

His voice was quiet. The kind of quiet it took on before he got to the good part of the story. I swallowed, my mouth still dry as I avoided his gaze. Something in my hand pulsed hard, like my heart was there instead of in my chest. "We killed The White Boar."

"We?"

"Joni-"

His broad, cool hands fled from my face and he took two steps back, "I see."

"What? Why?" I lifted a hand, the pain shooting up my shoulder, I let it back down and tried with the other one, reaching for him. It didn't hurt as badly.

"I suppose he will choose you to be part of his Hero band to fulfill what the quests have unleashed? We've been hearing some rumors of odd things."

I watched him run a hand through his hair, the waves shifting with the pull halfway down his back before settling. It was all puffed like a beast bristling. "Maybe." I stepped toward him.

Toward the path home. "We've talked about it since we were kids."

"Yes, I know. Another grand adventure for the two of you." *Was he growling?*

Taspe turned and walked down the path before I could reach him again. His long legs made me have to run to catch up to him. My muscles screamed in protest as I jogged after him. I tripped over something, caught myself, and decided it wasn't worth another fall to catch up. "Taspe?"

"You're hurt." *Had he left my side at all?* I could feel the coolness of his skin as his hands came to rest on mine. So light, like feathers resting there instead of fingertips. Something as large as he shouldn't be able to touch feather-light like that.

The way he had said it was like he knew better than I did what I felt.

"Just some sore muscles." I looked up at him, peering into the moonlit face of my best friend, into his midnight blue eyes, "What's wrong?"

"You're hurt." He stated again.

I waited for him to bite the air. Something was in those words, in that tone, but I couldn't put my finger on it. The marks of his tribe and status glowed softly along his forehead, cheekbones and down his chin, like he held the blue moon, Sakon, under his tanned flesh.

He loomed over me. The darkness cloaked him as a cloud skudded over one moon and then the other. His eyes flashed once the cloud was gone, as did his teeth, "Will you go with him like this?"

I wanted to take a step back. I needed to make myself smaller, not a threat like I had been taught all my life when up against a bear or other carnivorous beast. At the same time, a flame flicked to life, daring me to go on my toes and square up with him. I wasn't scared of Taspe.

I felt my spine straighten. I tilted my head back and met that burning gaze with my own. I doubted mine was as intense as his. My eyes burned. Of course I wanted to cry now.

"Yes. Yes, I will go with him. He needs me. He can't do all that alone." I pressed my hands up onto that larger-than-life chest, feeling both sets of lungs working under my palms. He wasn't racing me, so why were both inflating? "I will go. You don't have to leave this time to get away from me."

His hands covered mine, warmer than moments before. He didn't back down, "You really think that's what I want?" He hissed, "I went to my uncle's to…to figure out what I need to do."

"You couldn't figure it out here? I couldn't help you?"

"No. You were-are part of the problem."

"Then I would've been the best to help you out!" I tried yanking my hands free, but my shoulders trembled and screamed lightning pain from the effort. So much for the medicine.

"You only make things worse," Taspe groaned. Each word he uttered made him diminish from the growling, fiery thing he had been a moment before to the boy he kept hidden inside. The part of him that always second-guessed himself.

There they were, trailing down my cheeks now. Those words he threw at me filled me and made me spill over. I slid my hands from a grasp that fell loose with the appearance of my tears. "Then you will be rid of me at last."

I sidestepped around him. My legs felt like they had boulders tied to them. The path to the house blurred before me, but I knew it by heart. I was going to crawl into bed and hopefully never rise out of it again.

Chapter 2

The Gods reign
The Stygra calm
The Welkan dance
The Human toil
The Rogue roar

"What do you mean you aren't going? You killed it; you have to go."

"I mean what I say." The fire crackled behind Joni in the river stone hearth as he turned from it to face me. "I'm not going."

I hit my knees, the wood floor creaking at the shift of my weight. The pain from landing heavily on my knees shot up and down my legs like whiplashes. "You have to."

What is it with my two best friends turning into opposites of themselves?

"Oh come on, Chi, get up. You're being dramatic." He rolled his eyes, grabbing my elbows and hauling me up to sit me on the only chair he owned. My shoulders felt like they would crack open, a burning sensation searing from them through my neck and upper arms.

He sat on the matching stool, and he placed his hands on my knees. His palms covered them easily. I felt like a child when he put those big hands on me. I watched his face turn away from me, toward the fire. The orange and red flames cast the side of his golden face in flickering shadows.

That face that I once knew better than my own felt strange to me.

"You..you were the one that killed The Boar." The cotton in my mouth made the words thick, quiet.

He sighed, his broad shoulders jerking before curling in toward his chin, "I didn't mean to kill it. Just scare it away from you. I didn't know it was *that* boar."

"It was white! There aren't any white boars other than *that* boar!" My heart leaped up and so did I. I stood over him, still not able to work any moisture into my mouth or any air into my lungs.

His hands hung limply between his knees, "It was instinct. That's all."

"Well, then, that just proves it! You are The Hero."

A log slipped in the fire, sending tiny tufts of sparks toward the edge of the ash-filled hearth. They shone in those bright sky-like eyes of his before he turned to narrow them at me.

He was the Hero. Had always been the Hero. Everyone in the village knew it. He was blonde, strong, blue-eyed, charming, and…there were other attributes. Big. Those were all the merits of the man or woman that would be heroes. He even had a smile that sent all the women, and some of the men, swooning.

He managed to tame the wild black stallion from the spirited herd in the Unforgettable Mountains.

After I tracked it. Got a rope around it and a tree so it wouldn't kill us and wrecked my shoulder. After I half dragged it and it half dragged me down the mountain to Joni's shoddy paddock. After I fed it mint leaves each day and night, talked to it until it greeted me with upright ears and a soft whicker after a month. After I rode it first, but he said he did.

"The rock it fell on is just as chosen as I am," he muttered, his eyes still on my face. Searching. Ghosting over my eyes. He and the villagers had found that a large boulder jutted up out of the bank and into the boar, bruising the heart and some of the meat.

"You threw the spear that made it stumble into the river bank."

"I only meant to turn it away from the kids." He threw his hands up, his body moving as if he was about to stand, but he just leaned on his elbows on his thighs.

The fear was quickly turning into the burn of anger. "You killed it, Joni. You have to take up the Quests." *You have to take me with you so I can gain enough money and notoriety to provide for my family,* I thought about saying, but stayed the words on my tongue.

Sam Wicker

His back bowed as he dragged both of his hands through his thick locks while still leaning on his elbows. "There's no such thing."

My mouth got dryer. My heart fluttered and seemed to bound all around my body while thundering in my ears. It took every ounce of willpower to get my jaw to work again. "How can you say that with a straight face knowing Doc is cutting the meat as we speak?"

I should've asked Doc to become his apprentice, like Father had suggested years ago. Maybe then our family wouldn't be in the straits we were in. Maybe I would wear many hats, like Doc did, by now. Doc was our healer, butcher and mortician.

Doc had more blades than the rest of the village put together, but I was getting close in my collection.

I had skill in butchering the small animals that I caught in my traps. I sold their fur, meat, feathers and claws to tradespeople, Doc, and anyone who showed interest in town. I should have done a lot of things.

"Chi?"

I blinked, my thoughts turning back to Joni after I reminded myself of the three traps I needed to check soon. I had to focus on something else. Anything other than the stranger before me. "You need to go to the Matron to get your first quest."

Another sigh sent ash skittering back toward the hearth from between his worn leather boots, "No, Chi. It was a mistake."

My body tightened, my fingernails digging into the palms of my hands as a gurgled mess of sounds poured from my mouth.

I had nothing else. That was it. My mind flitted between beating my fists into his pretty face or tossing him into the fire. I settled on whirling and striding out the door. I slammed it so hard behind me some of the thatch slid off the roof and into the cobbled path.

Part of me wanted to stomp down his pathetic excuse of a garden he started too early. I cringed at the waste of food, if it survived the last frosts. The stomping only hurt my feet and legs by the time I entered the Evergreen forest. A few hundred steps more and I stopped by a large gray trunk. Pressing my forehead against the rough bark; I breathed in the heady scent of earth, pinewood, and of dried, rotting leaves.

I hadn't asked him why he didn't want to go.

Yes, Owlimount was his home. He had never dreamed of traveling other than the hunts. His family had been in this part of the country for longer than the village had a name. His only dreams, that I knew of, were to marry a gorgeous woman and have kids in numbers that would rival my Father's orphanage. Ridiculous, in my mind. No one could feed that many mouths without giving up their freedom and sanity. Surely no woman would want to put her body through such torture as birthing umpteen children.

I ran my hands down the rough bark.

My mind tumbled over the possibilities. He was afraid. The time was finally here and fear was gripping him, making him say stupid things. Tomorrow. Tomorrow he'd be ready.

I trailed my fingertips over the trunk, making my way around the tree in a slow circle before I pushed away from it. I picked up a stick and set out for my traps. Following a deer path through the thick bare undergrowth, I tapped it along the numerous trunks. Giving anything not in my traps fair warning that I was nearby. I didn't want to kill anything.

Other than Joni.

I swatted at the head of a large pink late-winter flower with the stick. I hadn't noticed the white stinging bee on top of it until it whirled in mid-fling to land on my cheek and sink that barbed stinger into my tender flesh. I howled, smacking the fuzzy bee. It released, zig-zagging through the dense woods. I gently prodded my cheek with my fingers, pulling the stinger out and feeling my skin getting hotter with each breath.

I groaned. Then missed Taspe not being there to make a comment on that sound, and groaned again. I restarted my trek toward my first trap, stick forgotten. I didn't need to make another mistake like that again. White bees weren't as poisonous as the others. Just enough venom to make a swelling, puffy mess of the area it stung for a week or two if not cared for properly. Doc made a salve that would lessen the severity and time.

With a promise to myself that I would stop by Doc's to get the salve, I reset my first trap. It was empty. If the one iron bit in my pocket wouldn't be enough, Doc would just have to add it to my tab. Said tab was growing steadily with the magnitude of sickness kids seemed to breed and pass amongst themselves. Our poor orphans were building immune systems, but in the most expensive way.

Doc had a staunch rule: if you infected or harmed another, you pay their fees too.

After a few months of allowing everyone in the house the freedom to go where they pleased, we had added a significant amount to our medical tab. This was why we had all agreed to allow me, Father, and the two older orphans to roam freely as long as we didn't have any symptoms. Usually I was the only one comfortable enough to go into Owlimount.

The second trap was empty, but not triggered. The third held a small pheasant. I took the bird out, after checking to make sure it had killed itself trying to escape, before tying its legs with one of the leather thongs attached to my wide belt over my right hip. I ignored the pain in my shoulders with each move I made as best as I could. I knelt, pulling the bait out of the pouch at my other hip to reset the trap.

Moko would love the quills we could pluck from the bird. Her fingers were always covered in inks she made from berries, flowers and whatever she could find to write and sketch. Some of her poems, drawings and paintings sold for nearly as many bits as the pheasant at my hip would bring. With the right trader. Usually, only the capital traders bought Moko's wares. She was the closest in age to me, a few months older, but her being a Welkan made her look and act much younger than her age.

I turned and made my way to the village, picking my way carefully along a little stream until I hit the familiar trail that ran the length of the forest. I whispered to the trees, "If he would go, I could make sure Moko has enough inks and paints to do all the things she wished. They'd never go hungry. They'd all have a chance." Who I was whispering to, I didn't know. The gods never listened. If they did, there wouldn't be orphans.

We had ten orphans in our home. Moko, Detri was next in age, then CiaCia, Vey, Rosen, Aber, Biobi, Gretta and little Tokli. Detri was six months younger than I. His parents were killed in a fire on the village dock along with a handful of other fishers. He could weave a fishnet wide enough to go across the Gala in just a day and a half. Most net makers took at least two days. His skill with a fish spear was like nothing I had ever seen before. I was able to sell the fish he caught in our river in the village every day because of his skills. His new nets brought in more than a few bits too. He stayed with us at his age because he felt the need to pay Father and I back for taking him in. Without him, the others would surely starve.

CiaCia's blood ran green as leaves so all things natural loved her. Stygra had a way with earth and growing things, which was what CiaCia was. She was turning out to be a decent herbalist thanks to the books Doc loaned me for her to study. She sang to the plants on and around our little farm. They grew stronger with each beautiful note.

Vey, a Rogue, was the next in age, and the best worker I had ever known. I didn't know when he slept, or if he did at all. Having blue-gray shining scales in parts made him get cold easily though. During the harsh winter, he would slow down to where the rest of us could keep up with him in our duties. Vey never talked much about his past or where his parents were.

Rosen and Aber were found together after the flooding two summers ago. Their family had been washed down a ravine along with their houses and most of the surrounding land. Much of the mess the flooding created was still piled up in the ravine. Some bodies had been found and given proper rites, but there were still plenty missing. Those who could spare the time and work tried to keep cleaning up the area. Vey had taken Rosen and Aber under his scales when they came to us. The trio were inseparable.

Biobi was another Stygra like CiaCia. He kept to the woods and garden. He talked to the plants constantly, and if he couldn't chatter at them he would find one of us to listen to him. He even talked in his sleep. That took some getting used to for many of us. His mother had gone missing after his father died in a scuffle at our borders.

The only one that could be considered not an orphan under our care was my nephew, Tokli. My aunt on my mother's side had died some years back. Her husband had no idea how to raise a child on his own. He sent Tokli to stay with us last month. At least he had waited to be able to use a king's order for his presence at a border patrol as an excuse to send Tokli away. The child seemed to be getting accustomed to living with us.

Out of all of them, I pitied Tokli the most.

Gretta just showed up in the village one day. She never said where she came from. She never spoke of her past other than mentioning things she had fixed. Her little hands could fix anything broken. Tinkering was the only time she smiled.

Kentrim was caught in one of my traps two weeks ago. He was so starved he didn't care about being trapped, he just wanted the bait. We took him in, a little bird Rogue.

Six of them were under the age of adulthood. Mother, if she were to come to visit, would faint in shock. None of us had our own room. A year ago, she had taken my elder sister, Seaghla, to the capital. She was of age, well past it if my grandmother was to be believed, to find a suitable husband.

Departing the thick forest, I strode down the road toward the northern gate of Owlimount. Giving a nod to the usual guards, I made my way into the center of town. Doc's shop was two streets from the church and central fountain in the middle of the busiest portion of town, four streets from the North Gate from the Evergreen Forest. I walked on into Doc's shop. The smell of fresh meat made my mouth water.

Finally, some moisture on my tongue.

"Caught a bee in one o' yer traps, did ye lass?" Doc asked as he wiped his hands off on his butcher apron. He stood behind a slab of white marble, some of the boar meat on top of it, a wide blade set in a wooden handle buried in the pink slab.

"Better story than the truth," I muttered as I sat down on the stool in the back corner of his shop. The pheasant stared glassily up at me from my side.

Doc washed his hands off in a concoction of water and herbs that were supposed to kill illnesses carried by things like blood and innards at the large basin against the wall behind his working table. After drying them off on a fresh towel, he gripped my chin in his thick, rough fingers to peer at my swollen, and swelling still, cheek. I hadn't really noticed until now that the swelling was obscuring my vision. I couldn't see the palm of his hand or his thick wrist below my chin.

"Got the stinger out I see. Good." He prodded my cheek.

I whimpered like a pup.

"Ye'll be a'ight." He let go of my face and turned to look through his cabinet of jars, bowls and little glass vials. "Gimme that bird an' I'll half yer whole tab."

Moko wouldn't get new quills if I did. "Can I have two feathers off it?"

"Aye." He said as he turned to regard me with a small smile, a little tin cupped in his large hand.

"Deal."

He handed me the salve. "Don't let it dry on ye for the rest o' the day. Tonight, pack it on 'fore ye go to bed." He took the pheasant from my hands after I picked two nice wing feathers. "Ye'll be kissable again by mornin'."

I rolled my eyes as I twisted open the tin and covered the sting with the salve. It smelled of the blossoms of the pretty pink flower the bee had been on. "And just who do you think I should be kissing, Doc?"

His grin was wide, "Most'd say Joni. Ye've been wanderin' and huntin' together since ye were wee bonbons. But I's know better. One to treat ya right. Not have ye working when yer hurt nor worried 'bout ya when ye are. There be only one like that."

I studied Doc's face, looking between the soft brown eyes underneath graying bushy brows and the quirk to his thin lips on his rounded ruddy face. "Joni's gonna have some kissing with princesses he'll save soon enough."

"Aye." Doc nodded, "But the one I'm thinkin' just lies 'cross the river."

Sam Wicker

I waved the nonsense off as I stumbled up off the stool, not anticipating the sharp pain in my shoulder with the jostling. I tucked the closed tin safely into my pocket.

"Rest. Those shoulders need it, lass."

By the time I exited his shop, the sun was hovering a few fingers breadth over the village walls. I dodged people trying to finish their business and hurry home on my way to the East Gate. I didn't really have a safe place for the feathers, so I just twirled them in my fingers.

"Hey, Chi!"

I jerked my chin at Edi, not daring a wave like I had at Doc's.

"Didn't get anything but feathers? What happened to your cheek?" He stepped away from the gate wall and peered at my sting.

We stood still in the shadow of the thick rock and iron walls of our village. "Just feathers and a white bee sting today." I stood my ground, eyeing him as he seemed to get closer and closer to my face with his. "How ya doing, Edi?"

"Bored. How's your shoulder?"

"Better," I shifted back, but didn't take a step away yet.

"Kiss her now. When she comes back she'll be too rich and fancy for ya, Edi." His partner smirked from the other side of the gate.

I had never taken the time to learn his name. He was always greasy looking. Much older and rounder than Edi and I too.

"Maybe." Edi shrugged with a slight redness to his cheeks. He cleared his throat, "But I figure you're always gonna be Chi. Not too good to stop and chat with, yeah?" He gave me a wink, the redness not abating from under his coal brows.

"Maybe." I stuck my tongue out at him and started back down the lane.

23

The sun was sinking behind the trees toward the horizon by the time I saw the lit lantern above our gate. Each night Father lit it, letting orphans know the path to safety. Before we started taking in orphans, after Mother and Seaghla left, he lit it. I knew it was really for them he lit the way for.

Next to the path was our fenced-in garden. I saw the reflection of the lamplight in her dark green eyes. CiaCia put the land to sleep much like a mother would her children at night. It was a strange act to watch at first, but now it was our normal. I gave her a smile, and a nod, not daring another wave again.

Harvest will be good this year.

"Ah, there you are Nadachia!" My Father grinned from his place by the cutting board on the table before I could finish pushing the heavy panel door open. The children were arranged around the kitchen and lounging room next to it. Each one busy at some task that would prepare the family for supper.

The rich scent of vegetable and wild rabbit soup and baking biscuit bread sent my stomach growling ferociously. There were only crumbs left of the cornbread from breakfast. There were always signs of bread on the table, if not a fresh batch.

Moko gasped. Her kyanite gaze was trapped by the twirling feathers in my fingers, until she looked up to my face, "What happened?" Her accent was still thick with her native tongue of Welkan.

"Just a white bee. Got mad at me for disturbing its gathering. Doc fixed me up," I soothed and motioned for her to grab the feathers so I could begin pulling off my layers.

Untying the knots of my boots, Father's old boots, was deceptively hard. The laces were rotting and broke easily. I only had patience when it came to trying to save us money. From my seat on the smoothed river rock stairs at the door, I watched CiaCia from under my lashes. Her movements reminded me of the ghosts old-timers told stories about on harvest nights. Her pale skin shone in the remainder of the red-orange light where her thick black robes didn't hide her.

I tugged the boots off with a grunt each, taking out the packed bits of cloth stuffed at the toes and heel section. Each night I aired out the boots. I had made the mistake of leaving the stuffings in and a fungus had started spreading over and between my toes. I wouldn't have minded if not for the stench. That had been unbearable.

I sat the boots just inside the door on a broken trap so no varmints could crawl into them during the night. Although traders liked buying rodents at times, I just couldn't stomach the idea of putting my foot in where a rat had just been.

The thick belt Father and I had fashioned from a bear hide came off next. I could breathe. The cords, hooks, and other tools attached to the belt stayed put. My daggers also stayed in their sheaths sewed into the belt. In the village, there wasn't much need for weapons, but I never knew when something sinister would come up on me in the woods.

My dust pants were made from old sails of fishing boats. Father's were made from an old mill sail. I wore a pair of dust pants out every day over my decent clothes to try to keep them from getting too worn, or ripped from limbs and briars. Clothes had to last through a few people in our house now. I hung the dust pants up over my boots on my peg along with my skint up leather hat. The brim was just wide enough to keep the sun out of my eyes.

The door needed to be left open. The heat of the oven and fire made it hard to breathe in the house. Even if the winter cold crept back each nightfall after the sun teased us with spring during the day.

I took the clips out of my braid that held it in place on top of my head, under my hat. The plain dark brown braid slapped heavily against my back and butt when it fell. The pain in my shoulders made me grind my teeth to keep from whimpering again.

I washed my face, hands and arms in the deep metal basin at the back of the kitchen. A flash of memory of bathing in this basin as a child ran through my mind before I buried it. Father still made us be somewhat presentable at the table while we ate. Mother was the one that had truly cared about manners and cleanliness.

I added more salve to my cheek. Moko watching me closely as I did. I smirked at her, "Don't worry, I didn't kill the bee."

She scrunched her little nose up with a huff, "Does it hurt?"

"No, not really." I ruffled her soft white curls as I passed on my way to sniff at the soup on the fire. Biting back the need to groan with the strain on my muscles such an easy motion caused.

"Did you give Joni a good-bye kiss already or is he stopping by on his way out to get you?"

I toyed with the idea of grabbing the fire poker and using it on my own father, but thought better of it. The cowardice that Joni showed me today turned my stomach sour still. Even with the heavenly scent of the soup. "He's not going."

The knife in father's calloused hands stilled over the herbs he'd been chopping to add as a final touch to the soup. "Wh-when then?" Father's voice had a small tremor in it.

"No, not when. Never." My mouth was going dry again despite supper being so fragrant.

Rosen gasped, "But he died the boar!"

"Killed the boar," Moko corrected. She looked between Father and me, "What about the Prophecy?"

I felt my shoulders draw toward my ears, and they ached worse for it, "He doesn't believe in it." As I said it, I didn't believe my words. We talked about the Prophecy during our hunts together. Especially when we were younger, just babies learning to hunt and trap from his father, aunts, and uncles. Every child knew the Prophecy. All children hoped they could be The Hero. To go on all the quests. To be known to all.

Three generations of the last hero's descendants were still wealthy and respected lords and ladies of the kingdoms.

Princes quested to find The White Boar. Weasley lords and ladies made secret deals with hunters to hunt the boar for them. None had been successful.

Until Joni.

Until me, a small voice uttered in the back of my mind.

"You're joking, right, my Nadachia?"

I turned, staring into my Father's hazel eyes, the match to mine, "No. I wish I was." I sighed and then laughed, "I'll go."

"You will take his place." CiaCia said quietly from the doorway, highlighted in the beginning of the moonlit night, "You have to, Chi."

I stared at her. Her green eyes glittered in the firelight like emeralds as she stared right back at me. "I-I was joking."

She shook her head, "No, you weren't. It's what the True Prophecy foretells. When the Hero refuses, the Best will take the Quests."

Stygra and their riddles and different prophecies. "Best?"

"You are better than him at hunting. At everything."

I laughed, the sinking of my insides cutting my amusement short. "No, no I'm not."

Detri snorted from his stool near the oven. He watched the bread and licked his lips before stating, "You are. I've seen it. Everyone talks about it too."

"This family isn't everyone." I growled.

"The villagers that come here to trade with us do." Moko defended with a nod that made her short pearly curls bounce, "Doc says so too. Always saying you bring back the best."

Detri took out the golden loaf bread with large mitts and set it in the middle of the worn oak table.

Father said, "Let's talk about this more once we have our bellies full," his hands shook as he stirred the herbs into the soup.

Chapter 3

After two helpings of the soup and sopping up the juices up with warm bread, I made my way over to the hearth. I took Father's pipe, knocking the old tobacco from last night into the ashes and refilling it with the dried leaves he stored in a green pouch. The pouch was the final item Mother gave him before leaving for Galanesse. Our family sigil, embroidered on both sides, glinted silver in the firelight. A horse's head shield leaned on the Royal seal with a dancing pair of foxes on either side and spears crossed at the back wasn't the easiest subject to embroider, but Mother finished it within a few days.

I perched on my usual stool and brought the pipe to life. The embers glowed as I took a few puffs of my own. Mother blamed Father for me picking up the nasty habit, but he had told me she had smoked too when they courted. I handed the pipe to him when he sat down in his chair next to me, putting his feet up on the swept hearth.

"I'll go talk to him in the morning. If I can't convince him, I'll speak to the Matron in Galanesse to see what she suggests."

Father puffed his pipe, then tapped the mouthpiece on his chin, "Either way, you will travel to the capital."

CiaCia moved to undo the large plait that stretched down my back. I sighed, watching Greta and Tokli wrestle the empty cast-iron pot from its hook over the hearth. It had cooled during supper, mostly. A smile parted my lips even as my heart reached to the boy as Tokli crawled into the thing to clean it. He was still so small, too young to be away from his father for this long.

Quick, noisy slurps started at the table, again. I glanced back, earning a yank of my hair for me to straighten from CiaCia. I watched Moko feeding our little bird boy, Kentrim, from the smallest bottle we could find for a moment before straightening to look back at the fire. With the way he was eating, he would grow into the size of a human toddler in no time. He fit in the cup of my hand when I first found him. Now he was the length of my forearm.

"I figure our Matron'll tell you to take the title." Father's gray mustache bristled as he pursed his lips around the pipe.

"She will." CiaCia said as she pulled the comb through my dirt brown hair.

I rolled my eyes up to the ceiling, spotted a cobweb between two of the four large logs supporting the second floor above us, and glared at it for a breath. I looked back down at the fire, maybe that spider way up there would kill off some flies this spring. "Then I guess I will have to discover some poor saps to do all the hard work on the quests."

Detri chuckled, sitting down beside me to stretch his latest net out on the floor. I watched his quick fingers craft as he spoke, "Won't find anyone decent in Owlimount. Best be picking some folks along the way."

CiaCia made a noise in her throat, "Just make sure you get a couple brave, slow ones. Heroes always survive if they are with some slower companions."

"Cia!" Moko chided.

"Not nice, but it's true." Vey slipped in with a toothy grin, sitting on the hearth beside Father's legs. "Hero Catram wouldn't have died if she'd had some bumbling brute with her for the Huskybear to catch instead of her."

Joni would fit that description. Finding someone to go with us that was slower than him would be a challenge. Maybe I could weigh the next slowest down with equipment enough to allow Joni the speed advantage.

CiaCia replaited my hair after she finished grooming out the dust and tangles. We switched positions. Her silky dark tresses caught on the rough parts of my fingers and palms, but she had gotten used to the tugs and pulls they caused. Moko loathed me combing through her curls.

Father heaved a sigh, gray smoke pluming in front of his mouth in a wispy cloud before heading toward the chimney. "I suppose I expected this day would come."

I felt my brows rise, "You did?"

"Oh yes," he nodded, "I always knew you'd be Joni's companion."

I thought the same thing. I had even snuck away some of my earnings to purchase a pack and map instead of putting it toward the medical tab or food. That was before things had gotten as they are, with Father and I not eating as much so the others would have more. Guilt over that small indulgence had eaten away at me for the better part of two years. The knowledge I would make it back did little to help with the predicament we found ourselves in.

I hoped the rats hadn't broken into the chest Mother and I shared in the attic. No one ever went up there. It was a thick oak and iron one with cedar bits to keep the moths out. A relic of our ancestors. It was the best place to hide away the items.

The idea of going alone…

Detri stood, folding up his work neatly to put it in a basket beside the fire. He disappeared into the bedroom he shared with Father, Biobi and Tokli. When he reappeared, he held a slim package wrapped in sackcloth out to me. "I saved this for you," he said as his face and ears turned a darker red than I had ever seen on him before.

I rested the comb on top of CiaCia's head and took the crumpled package. "Detri.." at a shake of his head I swallowed the rest of my words. I opened it. Gently lifting out a small hoop net of shiny green strands.

His workmanship was of such high quality, I knew no slippery fish stood a chance of finding a way to escape. As long as there were fish, I wouldn't go hungry on my way to Galanesse.

"Thank you." I smiled at him, tugging him into a one armed hug before he could run away and withdraw to a corner. I wrapped the net up again.

Vey came up to me, his hands behind his back as he waited for me to stop messing with Detri and the net. I caught sight of him out of the corner of my eye as he shifted from one foot to the other. I turned to him. He smiled, barely showing his sharp teeth, then he thrust a pile of scales toward me.

As I took them, he said, "Mine aren't as hard as an adult's, yet. But these should protect you until you get rich enough to buy better."

Sam Wicker

My fingers smoothed over the polished flakes, sown together in long gloves that would leave my fingertips free but cover my arms up past my elbows once I put them on. I hadn't realized he shed so many. Along with the underside of my arms and across the bottom of my palms, I buckled the five leather strips. They fit perfectly, the undersides feeling cool and soft on my skin. But the outside was thick, buffed and made into overlapping points that shone blue-green in the firelight. Nothing should penetrate such a close setting of the scales unless it was a shattering blow.

"Detri and Moko helped me with the sewing and buckles." Vey murmured, watching me with a grin.

I didn't bother to take them off as I gave him a hug. He hugged me back, his long arms wrapping fully around my frame to give me a hard squeeze. His cool skin felt wonderful against my hot cheeks.

Moko tapped my shoulder, Kentrim still cradled against her. "It isn't much, but yours is so old.." She pulled out a package from under the table. Hiding something under there without it touching my knees, clever Welkan. I carefully opened the paper packaging to a pair of dusters of soft blue. She made them from the curtains we took down before winter to replace them with the heavier weighted linens to keep the cold out. She'd doubled the cloth and lined them in another fabric I didn't recognize.

I grinned at her, holding them to my waist. They were the perfect length, not two hands too short like my old ones. "Thank you, Moko." I gave her a hug, gingerly, not wishing to disturb little Kentrim in his belly-filled slumber.

"Everyone wants me to go?" I asked, hating the break in my voice as I watched Rosen and Aber come up from the cellar carrying something between them.

The crossbow's richly polished dark wood caught the firelight. They put it up on the table with a grunt each.

"How on earth?" I ran my fingers over the smooth carvings of hawks on either side of the stock. They also pulled out a leg sheath of bolts. "You didn't steal these did you?"

Rosen huffed, "No!"

Father and the others chuckled along with me at the indignation written over her pale, freckled face.

"Ros 'n' I sheered all old lady Kukoo's sheep and helped her feed 'em!" She had that bum foot." Aber's chest was about to explode or he was going to fall over from being on his tiptoes to puff it up so much.

"Lady Kukoo gave it to us," Rosen added with a nod that had her too long amber bangs fall into her eyes, "Said it was hard for her to pull. She got another one she said, easy for her." She grinned, "Got it from the same trader that gave her Milky." Milky was the biggest dog anyone in Owlimount had ever seen and the talk of the children for months.

As Rosen explained, I tested drawing it back. It was simple enough for me, with swallowing back the pangs of pain in my shoulders. I would just have to get better at crossbows. I hadn't been the best shot, ever. That's why I stuck with my daggers. I set the crossbow back down after releasing it to give the two a hug.

"Good work. I'm so proud of you." I told Rosen and Aber with a smile. In my mind's eye, I could imagine them working with the sheep, barely able to see over the animals even without the thick cream and gray wool on them.

CiaCia sighed and stood, taking the comb from the top of her head and placing it on the table as she waved Biobi over, "I suppose we are next."

Biobi ducked his head as he handed me a basket. It was flat on one side with straps of woven fibers with buckles to attach it to a pack or belt. Someone had tooled a scrap of leather into our family sigil for a lid. I opened it and gasped. Inside were tins and packets, clearly labeled in CiaCia's beautiful hand. Along the back were a few needles, small blades, and threads. A tiny mortar and pestle took up most of the room. Rolled and tucked into a corner rested a sheaf of wax papers.

"Your medical kit. I wrote instructions for things to do for what you might run into." She glanced at my face, I guess I should have added bee remedies too." CiaCia laid a hand over Biobi's shoulder, "He wove the basket and made the pouches. He helped me gather the herbs, dry them and grind them too."

I gave them both hugs and Biobi a kiss on the cheek that created a big enough grin to show me his two missing baby teeth.

Tokli tugged on my pants. I knelt and smiled as he blushed, "I wasn't able to do much. But Papi sends me bits." He held out both hands, his fingers looking pudgy and rosy compared to my pale, slender ones. His fists opened to reveal three silver bits and five iron. "I saved these for you. I gave the gold ones to Uncle Rossi."

"But Tokli…I cannot."

He nodded, "You take care of us." He smiled, shifting from one socked foot to another.

I kissed his forehead and hugged him as I slipped the bits into a pocket. "Thank you, my darling little Tokli. I will pay you back and bring you many sweets."

He grinned and sputtered as he moved away to give Gretta room.

I watched her sigh; it feathered a strand of hair loose from my braid so it tickled my stung cheek. She studied my face with a narrowed dark brown gaze as she pulled something from her large red apron pocket. She adjusted the straps on it and then pushed them on over my head. "So you can see in the snow, dark, and in the bright sun."

I shifted the contraption down over my eyes. She guided my fingers to the switches on either side of the glass parts held by metal rings. I pressed them and watched the tints change until a clear one slid into place.

"Wind too." She fussed about the goggles, her already calloused fingers adjusting the straps again.

I chuckled and gave her a hug. The burning in my eyes meant I needed to switch the goggles back to the dark hue, but I didn't. I stood from my crouch and faced Father. The tears fought free as I saw the moisture lining his eyelids. I pulled the goggles to the top of my head and swiped at the hot trails, cursing the bee sting.

He held a long box in his shaking hands.

I took it and popped off the lid. The smell of newly tanned leather hit me as I pushed the tissue paper off what was inside. Thick soled, knee high laced boots shone with a dark brown glimmer. I touched the supple leather and felt the waterproofing on them. "These are exceptional."

"They are not enough." My Father corrected me, his voice broken, matching the emotion in his gaze.

They all knew. Even the little ones who I thought were too busy playing and being children, as they should, to notice much else. They all planned for me. They kept their work secret because they knew I would protest. Guilt gripped me again, sinking my heart low into my stomach. They should have done something for themselves.

Father wrapped an arm around me, careful not to put much weight on my shoulders as the hot tears started sliding down my cheeks incessantly.

My family and I stood there together in the warm, fragrant kitchen. The fire crackling in the hearth was the only sound as we silently communicated the love and acceptance we held for one another. Only a few of us were blood, but all of us were family.

Chapter 4

My first set of traps that morning held two rabbits and a guinea. I whistled along with the songbirds hiding in the budding branches above me as I took the well-worn path to Joni's. Their song and my terrible attempts at mimicking them a needed distraction from the dread curling in my stomach. I knew what was coming.

Joni, repairing the thatch on his roof, seemed to not notice me. I peered up at him, cocking my old hat to block out the morning sun. The only thing I wore of my presents were the new boots. The leather had to be broken in, especially if I was to head toward the capital the next day.

"Come to help?"

I handed him a bunch of thatch coated in mud and treatment that would last through the summer and fall unless it was a wet one. "Changed your mind about being a Hero?"

Joni took the bundle and rolled it out, weaving and tying it down before patting another thick layer of sludge over it and the new joins. "Nah," he shook his head, "I can't do it, Chi."

I released a breath, my lungs burning from the effort of holding it so I could hear him clearly. I had to make him accept this fate. I handed him the last bundle. "I know you believe in it. We've talked about it all our lives. You knew you were the most likely to be chosen if the boar came out here."

"Just silly dreams to pass the season." He stood, carefully walking over to the ladder with his bucket of mud. He turned to look over his work from the new perspective before nodding and making his way down the wooden rungs that creaked under his bulk.

I fixed my hat, giving myself time to pick one of the many reasons I had laid awake last night to give to him, "Don't you want to have enough bits to pay someone to fix your roof?"

Joni plunged his hands and forearms in the washing trough just outside his door after putting the mud bucket down. "That'd be nice, but it ain't so hard."

"People will throw all kinds of bits and jewels your way when the Matron names you her Hero."

He snorted, draining the now muddy water to the trench by pulling the tar and sap plug from the base.

I watched the little stream of water skip and wind through the little river rock path that led it down the hill toward the small garden. There it would gather in another trough to use when the land grew dry. I remembered carefully picking the smoothest, prettiest stones with him from the streams. We hauled them all back in buckets slung on yokes over our shoulders.

My body had hurt for days, but the little spillway was beautiful, perfect, and one of the best things I had accomplished in my life. "People will know your name for generations, Joni. Your family will be provided for long after you're gone."

He looked at me over his stained towel, wiping the water off his face. He replaced the plug, and then began drying his hands, "I have to have a family to provide for first."

I snorted, "You will. One peek at you and all the girls trip over themselves to be near you." I knew, because I had gotten my fair share of dirty looks, elbows, and vulgar names tossed my way over the years since Joni had hit adulthood. I missed his gangly days.

"All 'cept you."

Laughing, I shook my head, "Yeah, cause I'm too busy trying not to tumble over your big feet in the woods."

Joni hadn't been clumsy in a long time. He was just as stealthy as he could be, considering his size and weight. If I had been as tall and muscled as him, I wouldn't be able to walk silent at all.

He ran a hand through his hair, making the damp strands slick back on his head momentarily before they fell back to his broad brow. He slapped the towel back onto the side of the trough where it belonged. "I can't go. I got too much going for me here. I'm about to inherit the mine from Gramps."

"You hate that mine."

"It will provide a livin'." Joni stepped toward me, "Enough for me, you, and our kids and their kids."

Sam Wicker

My mind caught on the 'enough' while my heart tried to catch the rest and bury it deep. "You will hate your life. And you will always wonder what would have happened if you had taken this up instead of leaving it to me."

His hands were halfway to my waist, but they stopped, "What?"

"What? You think you can just leave this mess alone?"

"You're going?"

I swallowed. *Was I?* "Yes."

"You can't go!" Joni's hands finally reached their destination. They squeezed my arms until I knew I would have fingerprint bruises over my elbows. "I've got all this figured out for us. We…we're together like we should be. Finally."

"Us… finally…" I stared up at him. Something stranger than the creature I saw last night was in his place. He wasn't Joni. That wasn't my friend I looked to understand all I worked for and wanted. He wasn't the boy I had thought of as a brother, the teen I thought was a partner in our little hunts and adventures. Joni was as dunderheaded as those girls that chased after him.

"Yes, us!" His fingers tightened and loosened, those forearms and biceps bulging. Pain eased, then returned in my arms as he flexed. "Us! Never apart again. With a family. Just like we always wanted."

Something had bitten him. Made him mad. He had fallen off the roof and hit his head before I arrived. *Had this been what I wanted at any point? Did I tell him that*?

Taspe's grin mocked me in my mind's eye.

I swallowed, no moisture going down my dry throat or working into my mouth, "Joni, I-"

He kissed me.

Those legendary lips were on my too thin ones. His hands moved from my arms to my back, crushing my body to his. This was familiar. His hunger and need warring to rip into me and spread me wide. It had been that way, our first time. Our only time.

My nose smushed into this cheek, and I strained for breath. I gasped as I jerked my head away. His hand cupped the back of my head and he pressed on. The breath I caught only opened me up to his tongue.

I used the heel of my boot on the bridge of his. It was a feeble move, the first one, then I got my bearings. I slammed my heel down onto his foot as hard as I could manage and shoved him away with everything I had. My shoulders screamed in agony as I growled through the pain and whatever he caused to boil up inside me. The new boot had a hard heel, and it benefited me more than I imagined. He stumbled back; I stumbled forward, then pushed off him again to stand on my own two feet. I filled my lungs, once, twice, "You-!"

"We're perfect for each other."

"You-you…" I kept stabbing at the words running circles in my mind, but none came to my mouth.

"We can build closer to your Papi if you like. We can help him out and he can see our kids whenever he likes. I'll work at the mines and you can keep trapping and hunting until you get with child."

He was reaching for me again. I flung an arm out and he stilled, hands open and in the air. His fingerprints on my arms throbbed in tandem with the shoots of pain in my shoulders. "No."

"What?"

"No. No. No. No." I shook my head. Once the word was caught, I couldn't stop saying it. *A wife to him?*

My future flashed in front of my eyes. Always tied to the house we built, but he got the credit for. Forever working, never resting, never feeling fulfilled. Taspe fading into the background. His Legacy grew as my hopes and dreams died. The orphans slimming to skin and bones as I couldn't do enough to keep us all fed and well.

The pity hidden in the smiles of the villagers.

But if i went, I would find bits and jewels to take care of it all. Happiness would jingle in my pockets as I fought for my life. My family would flourish. They would grow fat, healthy. Their dreams would bloom. They wouldn't have to settle for what was before them, but they could reach out and find more, anywhere. Seaghla wouldn't have to settle for some old lord of little more than we had. Mother could come back home.

I could build them a proper orphanage. I would build hundreds of them.

"No." I said again, my spine straight and straining with the word. I looked Joni in his bright blue orbs and I watched the narrow world he painted fade in them.

"I'm taking up your quests. I'm going to Galanesse. You can find someone else as dunderheaded as you to share in your dream." I spat the last word, and it hurt. The prick to my heart opened wider as he stepped back from me. His eyes burned into mine, and I knew he didn't know what he was looking at anymore.

Something we had in common, that moment of staring at a familiar stranger.

"You wanted this. We talked about settling down…"

"No, Joni, I talked about all the different girls that wanted to settle down with you. I made up stories of their fantasies. Fantasies of them with you. Not what I wanted." I had told him naught of my dream.

Welcome to the biggest mistakes of my life.

"I want to hunt. I want to explore."

"We can do that!" He reached for me again, coming toward me with that long-legged stride of his.

I swatted his hand away, not giving ground, and he stopped advancing, "Not with me being on my back all the time."

Joni's face paled, "You'll die if you go. Don't you see?" His jugular bobbed, and I heard his swallow. "Stay. Stay. If not with me, then where we were before. We're good together."

"Yeah, good. Friends or siblings are like that, Joni." I shook my head, "We should have never gone further." I turned on my heel and made my way down the lane to Owlimount.

His heavy footfalls didn't follow. I knew he would have some repairs to do after he calmed down.

I stopped in at Doc's after taking a few more trails around the village and by the Gala to cool off my head. The festivities of the White Boar killing were still going strong. Even if the two that had killed it weren't ever in attendance. I had to wade through the crowds gathered in the main streets. People from nearby villages were here already, news spread fast.

I had to wait until he completed Mr. Tot's order, "Hey, Doc."

"What's wrong, lass?" He canted his head to the side, "No boyo wanted to kiss ye even if'n the swellin's gone?"

"Oh, I got kissed." I said and swallowed the bitter words that dared to follow, "I'm taking the quests."

"He's not goin', eh?" Doc leaned on his marble countertop and looked me up and down for a moment. "Glad the boots fit. Rossi's had 'em for ya for a couple of years."

"He's not." I looked down at my boots, shame at having something so new, expensive, for myself washing over me. I slid the three silver bits across the counter to him, "I know that don't take care of everything…"

His meaty hand came down on mine, warming my chilled fingers in seconds. "Yeh can pay me back when ye rollin' in the bits as our Hero." He covered my bits with my hand and then released me.

I swallowed, willing the burning in my eyes and throat down with it, "Doc?"

"Yeah, lass?"

"Can you check in on them? Take care of them if you can, when you can?"

"Aye. Ne'er you fret."

"Thanks, Doc."

He nodded, looking away and fussing with wiping down his counter, "When ya leavin'?"

"Daybreak."

"You best stop in, no skirtin' us on yer way out."

Sam Wicker

I stepped back out into the cobbled street after giving him a nod. Doc enjoyed leaving his doors wide open this time of year and well into the summer and fall. The rich air of Owlimount, rank with people, but thick with yeasts and herbs and flowering with sweets, mixed with the scent of blood and fresh meat at his threshold. I breathed it in. The peppermint and pest root growing in barrels at each side of his stoop kept most insects away and out of his shop.

Carts jerked and squeaked by as they rolled over the stone streets. The smaller ones pulled by their owners, the heavier hitched to a horse, ox, or donkey. A carriage on thin painted wheels circled the fountain in the middle of town to my left. The large black draft with a white nose let me know the mayor and his wife were inside before I saw his sigil on the shiny black door.

The flower maidens were letting lilies and roses float into the fountain waters from their slender hands. Tomorrow was a washing day for many. If the festivities died down by then. The blooms always gave the clothing a soft scent over the earthiness of the Lyme in the harsh soaps.

Five other fountains were placed strategically, and would be treated the same as the one before me. The center fountain, in the square, would have flower garlands draped over and around it as it was never to be used for washing. That fount was for drinking only. From it Meandria's priests drew water for blessings in their weekly services and special occasions.

I had never witnessed the blessing by the priests. Having only attended one service, I remembered little; especially not anything about the words spoken or what they had meant to me. He pulled me to it.

Taspe.

A grin pulled at my cheeks as I remembered teenage-like Taspe hauling preteen me over his shoulder to go to the service. It had been something for the Welkans that the Priests had set up, but Taspe had toted me there, claiming it was for my own good. That I needed to be cleansed of my heathen ways.

That they were going to make me a Priest so I wouldn't be a woman anymore.

Gods were there. Around us. I had seen too many Welkans and Stygra use their blessings and powers to not believe the gods were real. I lived with Rogues, who were the creations of the gods. Recently too.

I just relied on my instincts and my abilities too much to rely on the gods. They had enough to watch. What was I to them?

I turned my feet down the familiar streets toward home. Villagers tried to stop me, asking when Joni was leaving for the capital. If I would go with him. I waved them off. Once out of the confines of the village walls and making my way down the road, I headed down another intimate path. It didn't matter that he had pulled away. I at least needed one of our places.

I made my way to the rock. In the bubbling waters of the stream flowing over the smooth dark rocks, I let them out. Those pesky emotions that impeded doing, of working. I let them fall into the clear water. I didn't watch them flow away.

Chapter 5

I tossed and turned so much in the night that Moko and CiaCia suffered. Gretta would wake, come over from her bed in the corner to mine against the far wall and hug me. I wasn't sure if it was to assure herself that I was still there, or if she was trying to comfort me. After the third time, I pulled her in with me.

All the girls, and now little Kentrim, slept in what was once the master bedroom of the house. We were on the second-floor, taking up most of the area at the top of the stairs other than a small closet and a bathing room. We each had our own bed, except for Gretta and Rosen, who shared one. CiaCia currently kept Kentrim at her side, keeping him warm during the cool nights until he grew enough to start regulating his own body heat. After I left, the little ones could have their own beds.

Long before the glow of dawn, I rose and dressed, trying not to wake Gretta. I took the stairs, avoiding those that popped when I could. I looked behind the curtain we always pulled across the kitchen to look in on Vey, to make sure the fire hadn't died down while he slept. Then I glanced into the second bedroom, where Father, Detri and Tokli slept in their separate beds. This was the bedroom that Seaghla and I had shared when we were young.

If Mother and Seaghla were to return, there wouldn't be room.

I ducked down into the musty cellar and walked the narrow length between empty shelves and barrels. We had a few jars of vegetables and fruit from last year's harvest. Enough for a couple of weeks as long as there was meat and bread to go with them. The barrel of salted bear meat had one slice of roast, as wide as my hand, down in the bottom.

Could they really spare me?

I reminded myself of the boar meat arriving that day. That would last a good, long while. It had to last.

At the back was a half door in the hill. It stuck often. It groaned in protest, the hinges wet with morning dew as I pushed it open with hip and thigh, trying not to worsen the ache in my shoulders. I pulled myself up the earthen steps and ducked out into the morning. Dew glistened on the thick blades of brittle grass under a light blanket of gray fog that rolled from the river. I ignored the freshly plowed field and made my way to the gray barn.

The grizzled plow horse stood with head hung low in his stall. His back leg held heat after he walked the fields or we worked him. "Just a little while longer, old boy." I murmured, raking my fingers over his shedding withers. He stirred to rub his velvet nose against my pockets.

I dug around in them til I found a little leaflet. I held it out in my palm and he lapped it up with his lips before hanging his head back down with a snort. Luckily, he was a horse of pocket-sized needs, a simple mint leaf made him happy. "We'll get you a young stud to boss and for you to show how to plow soon. Then you can rest and grow fat."

The old spotted cow, dried up, would provide more meat. Enough to tide my family over if the boar meat wasn't to come to us. The two chickens scraped their claws against the straw strewn packed earth and clucked. We had five until a little beast had taken off with two and the third had died of old age. The skin of the foxit had been gorgeous and brought me a silver bit just by itself.

If I died, the animals would hold them for a while. The plants would help in three month's time, I hoped. In the middle, they would struggle for vegetables and fruit.

Vey and Detri would have to check my traps. Moko and CiaCia might need to sell more of their work. I'm sure the many farmers of Owlimount would love to have CiaCia sing their plants into strength and bearing.

I hopped up on the fence and settled there. The first rays of the orange sun shot in a halo of weak beams over the mountain tops through the gray fog. Soon the sun would be strong and high enough to burn off the mists and dew.

The dangling windchime we made of broken utensils and pieces of glass tinkled from the porch corner in the light breeze coming in off the river. I turned, catching sight of my father in the window. My vision blurred as my eyes burned.

I could not go. Joni did that. Why did I have to?

I had to secure their chances.

Taking a deep breath of the morning air, filled with the scent of wet hay, moist earth, and fog, I stilled my grieving and fear. My stomach turned and ached, my throat burning right along with it, so I took another breath. I had scant time to get control until I had to go back inside.

I should have been on the path to Owlimount by now.

Father grinned at me when I entered the house. A grin that didn't meet the red rim of his eyes, but I smiled back, my lips trembling with the effort. We still showed some lies to each other. The kids were busy waking up, yawning and rubbing their eyes as they helped with breakfast preparation. Moko quietly gave Kentrim his first feeding of the day.

I escaped up the stairs to gather the gifts and place them in a neat row atop my bed. Gretta had made my bed once she got out of it. I then hauled myself up the attic via the crawl space and the small ladder at the end of our hall. Dust drifted into my nose and I sneezed after I brushed off the trunk. On the top of my other things was my map, then my pack.

The tissue paper was browning over the precious items underneath.

I didn't have the heart to go through my memories. Or Mothers. I was aching in my soul enough.

I put the things I would most likely need first in easy to reach areas, my skinning and butchering case, sewing and repair kit, and a cloth wrapped bar of lavender soap. All emergency items and Gretta's goggles were up top, just in case, resting on my shabby excuses for extra clothing, and a single but durable blanket. I grabbed the bolts, crossbow, and Vey's scaled sleeves after pulling my pack onto my back with more pain than I cared to admit before going down the stairs to deposit them by the door.

Everyone sat quietly at the table as we ate. I put what was on my plate into Vey's and Detri's. My stomach wouldn't let the food settle and there was no use in wasting it. Rosen burst in, panting, mud crumbling off his boots onto the floor. He was always the first to finish eating to go back outside. I opened my mouth to ask where he'd been when a shadow fell over him from the door. I looked up into the soft, dark blue eyes of my friend.

I stood, after a beat of silence between us, and started giving hugs and goodbyes to my family. After I drew on my new boots, duster, and settled my pack on my back I gave them another round of hugs. There were too many tears, too many trembling smiles, and too much burning around my heart.

"You be careful." Father gripped my hands, "Don't worry about us. We will make do." He tugged me into another bear hug. I took in his scent, pipe tobacco, fresh yeasty bread, polished steel and riverstones. I willed myself to remember it as he spoke our words, "My heart is your heart. Feel it. My blood is your blood. Know it. Strength of the smartest and the world with us, not against. Believe and breathe."

I managed a nod before tearing away from him and ran out the door.

I swiped at my cheeks, the tears not stopping.

"Here, Oulileah." Taspe pressed a soft cloth into my palm. He placed a hand, broad and warm, against the small of my back and I followed it as a guide down the road. I covered my eyes with the cloth, making it catch the waterworks as we trudged along the road.

About halfway between my farm and Owlimount, Taspe began. "I'm sorry. I'm sorry I make you doubt yourself and that I keep hurting you. I can't think, sometimes, and I have reasons. If you'd like to hear them."

I finally made the tears stop. I gave a last wipe with the cloth and held it out to him.

"Keep it." He tugged on my braid, then wrapped and pinned it to the base of my skull as we walked. A feat only he had ever managed. Then he took the crossbow from his belt and hooked it to mine. I had completely forgotten about it. Taspe then stopped me, and leaned in to press his forehead into mine, "I hate Joni."

"I know."

"No. I truly, really hate him. I was angry that you would let him touch you, take your first, instead of asking me to do it." He gave me a half smile, "Welkan males are far better mates than anyone else, especially someone like me. Then I got to thinking, last night, how asking me might have made you feel. I think I understand. Now. We were both born out of the slave times, but we still fear saying or doing something wrong. I'm sorry."

"What you're telling me is that you were, are, jealous?"

Taspe's breath puffed over my face, smelling birch brush fresh, "When you put it that way it's pathetic."

I smiled and wrapped my arms around his cloth belted waist, burrowing into his broad chest. The warmth of his skin through his tunic startled me a little, Welkans were usually cool unless they had sunbathed. At least this time, I didn't worry his lungs were working too much, as I could only feel one set working with each of his deep, calming breaths.

"I want to go with you." He said softly against the top of my head as he wrapped his heavy arms gingerly around me.

"I know."

"Promise me you will be careful."

"I will do my best."

"Once I have this uprising taken care of, I'll be as close as I can to you." Taspe pulled back, cupping my face. His fingertips rough against my tear warmed cheeks.

"You need to be careful too." I wrapped my hands around his wrists, not able to get my fingertips to meet around them.

"Always."

I sighed, "Who knew being the first male Welkan Legace would cause so much hatred?"

He nodded, turning and walking with me down the road with his arm snaking under my pack to curl around my upper arms. He took the weight of my pack off me, easing the pain from carrying it. "I think they just fear that it will bring more attention to us. That the laws will dissolve and we will have to fight for our freedom again. Others might think that since we've had women Legaces for hundreds of years, it should stay that way. They still see males as weak since we were the ones enslaved the most."

"You know… I thought about asking you, but I was afraid that if anyone in your tribe found out, they would kill me. Think I was trying to enslave you or use you. They're very protective of you." I poked his thick ribs through the soft gray of his tunic.

He chuckled, "They are quite jealous of you. My tribe knows me, they trust me. Some trust you. Love you. Just got to get the rest of my tribes to see me as they do. As you do."

I snorted, "So much jealousy. Why?"

Taspe cleared his throat and suddenly found something deep in the forest on his side of the road interesting. "Well, I might have done something stupid."

"Does this have something to do with you calling me 'oulileah'?"

"Sometimes I forget how smart you are because you're so boneheaded." He muttered, looking up at the sky. "Yes. I-" He grabbed my hand, ran a finger along the scar there. It was blue, like his blood, and it hadn't faded in the five years since that moment by the river well past midnight.

I had been waiting for him, sitting on a log. Once I caught sight of him, I slid down, but a few splinters jammed their way into the soft flesh underneath my thumb and into my palm. Taspe helped me pick them out in the moonlight, but then cut his own hand in the same place. He pressed his cut to mine while murmuring words, so low, I couldn't make any of them out at all.

Once he finished, my wound had healed into a blue scar, slightly raised, and always cool to the touch. Now and then, it would thrum as if it had its own heartbeat.

"This is a mating ritual."

I jerked my hand away, "A mating ritual?" I stared at the scar, swallowing so that the next time I talked my voice wouldn't be so stupidly high.

"Not like human mating. We… well, you know we have soul mates. A very human term, but our soul mates can be just close friends, those that we feel complete us. It doesn't have to be love, although, more often than not, it includes that." The words spilled out of his mouth, "We perform this ritual to show our bond to one another. As Welkans it also gives us an inside look at how the other is faring. We feel their fear, any emotion." He rubbed the back of his neck, then splayed his hand out, palm up toward me so I could see his matching scar, "You're my oulileah."

He was making this difficult. I glanced down the road. The tops of the tallest buildings and the walls were visible in the melting fog. I took a deep breath in, trying to wrangle my thoughts into something cohesive. "You can feel me now?"

"Yes, and I realize now that I should have told you years ago. I'm sorry." He shook his head, before saying, "All I do is confuse and torture you these days."

"I think I felt your heartbeat a few times."

His eyes widened as he pulled us to a stop. "I've wondered if humans could feel something from us." He shook his head again, "Now I'll know if you're safe when you're away. I think if you focus on the bond I might feel more." He sighed, "I wanted to tell you, quickly, just so you know that you have a way of communicating with home that won't take as long as a bird or messenger. And one that's safe."

My eyes started burning again. Safe. Home.

"I really want to go with you." HIs broad shoulders slumped as he placed his forehead on top of my head.

"I really want you to go with me too."

His eyes brightened as he pulled back and met my gaze, "I have some things for you."

"What?"

"You'll have to wait. Come on, we're already late." He slid his arm from around me and took my hand to pull me into a run.

As we neared, the noises of a crowd grew. The fog shifted around groups of people just inside the gate. Had they ever quit the festivities? Rich yeasty and greasy scents floated on the last of the gray mists as we stopped at the open gate.

"Nadachia of Silverequis!"

My heart jumped into my throat and hung there.

The crowd closed in behind us as Taspe urged me into the village. We walked through jostling, cries, and laughter. They placed hands on my shoulders and on top of my head, my pack.

Tears sprang into my eyes as my body began throbbing with each congratulatory pat.

Taspe wrapped his bulky arm around my shoulders, safely encasing them so that they touched him instead of me. I looked up, noticed how his markings glowed with the sun's light and how warm his flesh was, my words of thanks were lost in the noise, even to my own ears.

A priest met us at the eastern fountain, two streets in from the gate. It took me a moment to recognize the High Priest Gentri. He smiled and bowed before stepping off the fountain's side and down to Taspe and I. His robes were blue, like the rest of the priests wore in Owlimount. They dedicated themselves and our church to Meandria, goddess of the waters and mother to half the gods and goddesses of the twenty-seven our people worshiped.

"Welcome Hero!" he raised his arms high with a bright grin, "Let's begin the parade and then we can get to the celebration!"

He turned and led us down the streets so that we circled Owlimount, stopping briefly at each fountain. The one in front of the church, in the middle of Owlimount was our last stop. Somewhere between the second and third fountain, guards created a box around Priest Gentri, Taspe and I. We were no longer patted, but my friend kept his arm over me anyway.

"My people of Owlimount!" Gentri cried as he leapt up the church steps to the top one. He motioned us forward, Taspe nudged me to stand on the step to the right and below Gentri. He entered the church through the thick oak doors. I wished I could go with him. I let my gaze wander over the many wide-eyed gazes staring right back up at me. So many smiles. So many people. I never knew Owlimount held all these people. I couldn't pick out any of my favorite faces. Where were they?

"Our Hero accepted her quest yesterday!" Bile rose in my throat as the cheers did in volume. I distracted myself by counting how many teeth were missing in the mouths of my village.

"Today, she will begin her journey to the Capital to accept the first quest. Upon completion of that, Nadachia of Silverequis will be officially titled Hero of Lanpress by the Stygra Matron

Keandria." His hands came down on my biceps. He must have noticed the protective nature Taspe had over my shoulders. "Keep her in your prayers, my friends!"

Another cheer rang in my ears. A twitch started just above my right eye.

"As I know what you all are truly waiting for... go eat!" He motioned to the tables on the other side of the fountain. The white table cloths a stark contrast to the brightly and dull colored clothing of the people surrounding them. Mounds of freshly cooked delicacies topped platters of all shapes and sizes. That's why the village smelled more of food than anything else today.

Maybe the people actually washed properly today too.

The cheer that erupted as the villagers pushed their way to the tables was more deafening than any of the cheers before. Food. Money. Power. People were always after that. None of which I had or could give.

"Come, my dear, there is a separate table for us."

I turned and followed him inside the church.

They moved the long pews to make room for two tables in front of the altar. The food on these tables wasn't as abundant as what was outside, but it was still far more than I'd ever seen in one setting. Possibly more than I'd eaten in the entire year. The mouth-watering aromas only made my stomach churn. I imagined there was no escaping the smell, not even the tops of the stained glass windows would be a safe haven. Pork was the predominant meat. Candied and caramelized apples and apple pies were the next overabundant dishes. Eggs and flat cakes sat between jars of jams, pates of butter and bowls of creams. The food glistened on shining platters.

"Ah, you survived." I looked from the tables, following the sound of a voice as familiar as my own father's. The man reclined in his seat on a narrow pew, thick arm thrown over the curved back, "Am I to assume through the lack of screams that there were no casualties of the worshippers either?"

His son had the same bright blue eyes, but his always shone in mischief and intelligence. He stood, coming to stand before me. He reached up with a broad hand, knuckles snarling like knots in a tree root to smooth my hair from my face, "There, my girl, easy now. You're among friends."

"Village has to 'ave it's fun, lass." said Doc, his voice laced with a smile somewhere behind me.

"Since my son is too much of a simpleton to go with you, this now yours." Jahni flipped open an oilskin sleeve to display eight ebony throwing daggers with black and silver threaded hilts.

"Are you sure?" I picked one up, testing the weight and feel. Of course, it was perfectly balanced and light enough to match my own daggers.

"Oh, I'm sure. The coward doesn't deserve such weapons." Jahni muttered as he motioned for the next person to come up to me. He started slipping the blades into the empty sheaths in my belt.

Edi put down his plate and picked up a box. He grinned at me, "Well, I guess I won't have anyone interesting to talk to at the gate for a while." He held the little box out to me, "It ain't much, but seeing all your new ones it should come in handy at the least."

I took it from him, pulling open the cap and revealing a new whet stone that would fit into my palm easily, a honing bar, some metal restorer, polish, and two cloths. I closed the lid and drew my arm through his. "Moko's shy, but she'll come around. Detri, you'll have to tease him until he opens up."

I pulled away from the half hug, Edi's cheek held a pink tinge to their usual paleness as he gave me a sheepish smile. Jahni took the box from me and slid it into my pack.

The best baker in the world, Hano, smiled a toothy grin as she handed me a bundle. It was warm and a rich yeast smell enveloped me as I peered underneath the cloth. Sweet rolls the size of my fists and two golden loafs as long as my forearms and a handful of profex still steamed within. Profex was a hard biscuit packed with enough ingredients to serve as a meal. It was often a favorite of hunters, travelers and miners.

"Thank you, Hano," I signed as best I could with one hand while speaking the words to her.

She nodded with another smile. Hano didn't talk much, and could only hear sharp, highly pitched sounds from birth. The woman said plenty with her baked goods.

His smooth tanned hand grabbed the pouch of goodies from me and handed it to Jahni. His eyes were almost white as he looked into mine. Had he been sunning the whole time? "Taspe?"

"I said I had something for you," he said, his markings glowing a white-blue. His tunic was pulled open, revealing more markings on his bare tanned chest glowing like those on his face.

There were gremlins in his eyes as his lips peeled back to a lopsided grin. "What?"

"A blessing."

I stared at him. I knew my mouth was hanging open, but I couldn't close it. "You… you can't. I'm not-"

He shook his head, "Listen to me. You need it. I need you to have it and yes, you do deserve it. But," he paused, those eyes dancing again, "You need to tell me you accept the blessing that I'm going to give you, no matter what I have to take from you."

Since when did blessings take? "I- what is the blessing?"

"Protection from the elements. They will still affect you, but you won't get a cold or frostbitten, or any broken bones if you slip on ice. You won't have terrible things happen because of weather or fires, just…small things." He lifted a shoulder, "Difficult to explain, but once you're in those situations, you'll understand."

"I want it." I said, feeling my brow twitch as he grinned again. "What are you taking from me?"

I noticed then that another priest was hovering nearby. He was Taspe's friend, someone my Welkan used for council, too. "It's a kiss."

Taspe growled, shooting a look over his shoulder at the thick bearded man.

I laughed, "You made it seem like a huge deal." I glanced beside me, where Jahni chuckled and waggled his eyebrows at us.

His hands were warmer now, matching the heat in my cheeks as I realized this kiss was going to be watched. At least Father wasn't here to watch.

"Where do you want the mark?"

"My back, I guess."

"Wonderful choice. It's going to hurt, but the back is usually the least painful." He pressed his forehead to mine, "Close your eyes."

I did as I was told and listened to his raspy voice speak the words of the incantation, his breath fluttering over my lips. A searing heat flowed from his lips to mine. Melting into my mouth, solid as water, but mobile like air. It trailed down my throat, then bounded to my spine, right between my shoulder blades. A needle-like pain pricked, heated from a fire, and then dragged along the skin of my spine in tight circles and curls. I wanted to pull back, but Taspe kept his lips locked on mine.

The needle stopped, but a tingling burst from the design it had made and flowed over me. From the top of my head to my fingertips and toes, I tingled with heat. He shifted, pressing his forehead to mine again. His palms were cool against my cheeks. When I opened my eyes, I saw his normal shade of midnight blue again.

He chuckled, and looked at the scar on his hand. His eyes slid back to me, a curl to his lips as his gaze danced in as much mischief as before. "Interesting," he said, dropping his hands to his sides.

I caught Edi looking between me and Taspe before he asked, "T, how come when you gave me a similar one during the floods you just tapped me on the forehead?"

Heat creeped up my neck.

Taspe rolled his eyes, "Edi, love, I'll kiss you later."

Everyone chuckled around me. I shook my head, "I'll remember that."

My best friend grinned at me, "Think of it as two gifts."

Jahni sighed, "Oh the beauty of having a break from fending off all the girls and boys off Chi for a while. It'll be a blissful peace."

The heat made its way to my cheeks as I turned to him, "What?"

He just winked.

"Lass, come eat." Doc waved me over and handed me a plate.

"Yes, eat up!" Gentri cried, "You still have more gifts!"

After adding a few things to my plate, Taspe and Jahni adding more to it, I sat down beside Doc. At least he wouldn't add more to my dish. I hoped. He leaned over and put a small envelope by my plate. "Yer gonna pass through Dragotown on yer way. Stop in there, and find my cousin, Spacya. Give her this. She retired from hunting last year, but she might be good for a companion fer ye." He took a sip from his cup, then added, "She's rough 'bout the edges, but she's honorable."

"Thanks." I tucked the letter into my belt.

After talking and eating, I said my goodbyes. Taspe walked with me and the priests, Gentri and Blari, down a hall to what Gentri called the Hero's Departure Room. I figured it would be midnight before I got out of Owlimount at the rate we were going.

We paused at the door, Gentri looked to Taspe, then me, "We will be inside. Enter when you're ready." The priests left us alone.

"Your pack will weigh heavy. Can you manage it with your shoulders?"

I nodded, "I will make do."

Taspe sighed, pulling me into his arms, "I want to give you more, but I'm afraid that took everything out of me. It'll be another month before I can give another blessing."

His flesh was ice, and he had grown paler with each bite he took. "You need to get up to the roof. Lay in the sun." I hugged him tight, hoping the pressure of his body against mine would keep my heart from shattering like it was threatening.

"I will. I just want to make sure you're good. I know… you hurt. We'll take care of them and then I'll come take care of you when I can. They won't starve, Chi, I'll make sure of it still."

That word caught me, "Still?"

He cleared his throat, pulling away, "Need to get up to the roof."

I clutched at him.

He sighed, looking out the tiny slit of a window beside the door the priests had entered into, "I may or may not have put some animals in your traps. Some of my hunters do the same."

I swallowed the burning lump in my throat, "You buy Detri's fish when traders won't too."

"Yes, I knew you wouldn't ever accept my help outright. We just made other arrangements."

"So my traps are no good."

"Oh no, they are. Half the time they had something, we just made sure that at least one of them had an animal." Taspe chuckled with a lift of his shoulders.

I shook my head, "We'll talk. After. About all this." I patted his chest with my hands, the cold of his flesh bleeding through his tunic, "Go, get warm."

He pressed his hands to mine, "Oulileah, come back to me."

"I will. You too, come back to me."

"I will."

I watched him go. My chest throbbed. My eyes burned. This was it. Would I enter the room? Would I run away? Taspe's blessing would be a waste. The gifts I received would be wasted too. My family would still live on the edge of despair, scraping by when I could have them living larger than life.

I fisted my hands and turned toward the door. The pain of my fingernails digging in added to the burning sensation behind my eyes. I would not cry. I couldn't cry.

I twisted the silver knob set in the cherry wood door and pushed it open.

I faced statues. There was barely enough room for all of them against the narrow wall they took up at the back of the small room. Light filtered through the stained glass and around them, giving each statue the appearance of power seeping from them. All the heroes from before stared back at me, standing resolutely in front of the twenty-seven glass gods. All along the side walls were shelves holding books and scrolls. Copies of the great tomes of Heroes as I recognized the names of the heroes along their spines and ribbon ties.

"You may close the door, Nadachia." Gentri said, his timbered voice quiet. As if we were on more sacred ground than the church pew.

I looked down, only realizing then that my hand was white knuckled on the knob still. I moved into the room after closing the door, and flexing my hand. I sat in the curved leather chair Gentri motioned me to beside Blari.

Priest Gentri stood before the statues, behind a high table. On top was a wooden, oblong, squat box with braided silk for handles at the sides. It looked to be the perfect size to hold the little squeaking variety of water weasels that followed the trade ships down the Gala.

He smiled, his eyes shining, "Nadachia, I suspected it would be you taking up the quests. Your family has always had hearts and minds of brave, honorable, and sturdy mettle." He placed his hands on either side of the box's lid, "I'm afraid you will have a demanding set of quests. It has been long since the last Hero was born."

"Do you have any idea what my quests will be?"

Gentri nodded, "A little. Some disturbances reach us here, even as far away as we are. There is something along the coast that is attacking a town. I believe that might be your first quest. Any more information than that, you will learn from Matron Keandria upon your arrival in Galanesse." He opened the box, "Now, for the honor of bestowing these on you. Each village with a church gathers a few items together to bestow upon the Hero if one is chosen from their surroundings."

He pulled a letter from the top, yellowed and crinkled. Gentri began reading, "To the Hero and HIgh Priest and those worthy, welcome to the Day of Acceptance. You are, dear Hero, about to set out from our fine village of Owlimount upon the first leg of your quest to the grand capital of Galanesse. With you shall be your first companion, the Priest of Knowledge, Blari."

I smiled at Blari, who nodded at me, his dark eyes gleaming as his rounded body sat on the very edge of his seat.

"I suppose it could have been worse." Gentri grumbled, looking at Blari. He continued, "In Galanesse the Matron of the Stygra will see you. Treat her with respect, show us proud. She will guide you to your next steps toward fulfilling the grand honor of being our Hero. We, the priests and villagers of Owlimount, have gathered what we hope will be helpful upon this endeavor."

High Priest Gentri set the letter down as he pulled an embroidered blue cloth off the contents. Pulling out the first item, he stated, "This will give you rest at any Church along your travels. Just show it to the priest who answers the door. This Medal of Hospitality all churches must honor with shelter and meals for as long as you need them."

It was a small triangle of silver. It was filled with each symbol of the gods and heroes, most of them interlocking and overlapping to make them nearly unreadable. Cool to the touch as I took it in my hand. The chain slid against my skin like water. I passed the necklace over my head, not bothering to straighten up as I gritted my teeth against the pain.

"If your quests should take you to any countries besides our great nation of Landpress, show guardians of such countries this for safe passage. Even if you cannot announce yourself as Hero, you will be protected." Gentri pulled out a circlet of leather holding a bronzed clover. Etched in each leaf was a triangle of different colors: red, blue, green, black and in the center a dot of white. The colors of the known races of our world and the white depicting those unknown or not yet created.

I placed this around my neck too; the clover sitting between my clavicles while the silver one held still over my breastbone.

This was getting real. My mouth dried again, and the stones hanging upon my neck felt heavier than they should. I said I was going. Only death could change that now.

I was drawn out of my dreadful thoughts by Gentri's voice as he continued. "This pouch is enchanted by the former Matron Elspetha. You may carry all within its folds without bearing the weight of the items as long as you can fit it past the narrow mouth."

They made it of the softest waxen leather I had ever felt. The pouch's opening was as wide as my hand, and closed with a drawstring of the same leather. A flap then covered the opening. Upon it was a triangle filled with all the symbols of the gods burned into the leather, then stitched over with a fine silver thread.

"Last for our Hero, the Ring of Endurance. As long as you wear this, you and those close to you will not tire until dusk. Unless you are sick or wounded. For as long as your journeys be."

The thick iron ring was large and only fit upon my index finger. It covered from knuckle to knuckle in the first section. Some alertness returned, as I grew less tired from not sleeping the night before.

"For the priest who shall be the first companion and guardian of our Hero's story we give you three things. First, the Ring of Tongues. WIth this you shall understand through speech and the written words of all known languages of the known peoples. If you meet one unknown, listen carefully from dawn to dawn and you shall gain the understanding."

Blari took the ring of silver and put it upon the tallest finger of his left hand. I noticed how squat his fingers seemed compared to mine.

"Next is this dagger. Use it to protect your Hero if the need should arise."

I couldn't picture Blari stabbing anyone. I watched as the blade and sheath passed from Gentri to Blari and saw the bright blue gem set into the hilt. It was pretty. I might need to trade him one of mine.

"Know that only a priest of Meandria may wield it."

There went that idea.

"Lastly, we have quills, inks, and books. You must record each days' triumphs carefully. The written word is where we learn and honor those from before and your humble penning of her quest shall most honor the Hero."

Blari took the satchel and pulled the three leather-bound tomes out first. Each had a few empty pages. He looked up at Gentri.

"Gentri smiled, "Each will grow pages as the first fill. It's to help with the weight."

My companion priest nodded and pulled out three vials of the blackest ink in a pretty wooden box lined with white cloth. Next were five quills tied together. It was like watching a child during their yearly birthing celebration receiving their three gifts.

The High Priest then continued, "We bless you on this day for your bravery, dear Hero and Priest. May the gods protect and bless you for your remaining days until you join them." He folded the letter, then tucked it back in the box along with the embroidered cloth.

Other nations. Other languages. Monsters in villages that couldn't be taken care of by those there. Meeting the Stygra Matron. Entering the capital. My mind flitted from one unknown to another.

I clasped my hands together in my lap. The ring an odd companion and it made me focus on the now. One moment at a time.

`*Moments matter, and you can only make one at a time, Nadachia.'* Father's voice filled my head.

I stood, "It's time. I should have left long ago."

Gentri nodded and clasped my hand between his. "We have enough supplies for you to reach Dragotown, and a little after. So make sure the Church there refills your pack. All the food not eaten here is going to be sent to your family. Doc assured me that the rest of the pig he saved for them too."

My throat began burning again, "Thank you." I swallowed the flame down and blinked back the heat in my eyes.

Chapter 6

At least I knew my first companion. Not well, but well enough. Taspe trusted him with his secrets and asked him for advice on things. Most in relation to ruling a mass of people that might hold bitter grudges, while others loved him. I quickly learned why the first two nights.

His brain held many tales and wisdom those histories built.

Black bearded and curly haired Priest Blari could recall a story he read as a child with more clarity than I could remember what I ate for breakfast that morning. I knew this because he spent a portion of every night after we lay down to tell me stories in his smooth, warm tenured voice. It drew my mind away from the sickness roiling in my stomach. From me missing my family into a much older Lanpress with strangers doing remarkable things for one another. Of active, touchable gods. It made me have hope that I could do the same.

I had to do the same.

Often, I fell asleep to his voice. It cradled me like a blanket swing in that stage between sleep and alertness. Not because I wanted to. Exhaustion from the constant war and illness within myself wore me out. The ring helped with the walk along the Capital Road better than I expected. If only I had been given something to keep my mind from saying cruel things about me, of dredging up the worst scenarios for my family to go through while I wasn't there, of thrusting terrors long buried before my mind's eye for me to relive again.

Like the days I spent locked in Grandfather's cellar because the disease in his mind made him forget I was there helping him that week. Or the time Caterwalla stabbed me with the blade she'd just used to rip open the intestines of the pig I was helping her dress because she thought I was stealing Taspe from the tribe. The sickness and weakness my body went through after both instances was worse than the sickness I felt now, but I still felt horrible in ways I was not prepared to battle.

Blari's stories quieted my voice in my head.

Teasing him about writing and walking at the same time kept that terrible voice at bay during the day.

We reached Dragotown at dusk on the second day of our trip. I presented the necklace to the guards. One of them took us straight to the Church of the Goddess Beriaha.

A goddess of ripening, she looked like a beautifully shaped woman in all her paintings and statues. Meandria looked as if she would blend in with the eddies of waters at any moment. Dragotown was as different from Owlimount as Beriaha from Meandria. Squat buildings filled Dragotown instead of the slim tall ones I was accustomed to in Owlimount.

The church looked the same. A priest answered the door and I showed him the same necklace. He wore robes the color of berry jams and his shape reminded me of a strawberry. I followed him and Blari into the church and had to take a moment to look around.

The scent of wet earth and sweet fruit bombarded my nose. All the surfaces, even the pews, were covered in greenery. Pots crowded corners, down aisles, and hung from pillars and every spare space on the walls. Trees stretched to the vaulted ceiling of glass. Fruit hung heavy from their branches.

The church was warm, the air held a dampness that pressed my clothes and hair heavily onto me. Lamps made from balls of light that resembled the sun itself floated in place, lending light as the sun set behind the long, wide windows of stained glass. I smiled at a priest as she passed by, and she lowered her hood to smile back. A Welkan priest. Hence the magic of the sun lights.

"It's wonderful here." Blari murmured, taking a moment from writing to crane his neck to see how far a vine climbed up the wall nearest to us.

"Thank you for the praise, Priest Blari, may the gods bless you."

He led us down the hallway to the right of the altar. A few doors down, he opened a set with roses and strawberries painted on the white wood. "Here is the room we prepared for you, Hero. Does it please you?"

I looked in, then took a step inside. Strawberry plants were budding along the window sills of the two walls that had them. A large wooden bed squatted in the middle, holding far too many pillows to use. A door, slightly ajar, gave me a glimpse of the tiled washroom beyond, with rose vines crawling up the wall.

"Yes, thank you. You can call me Nadachia." I sent him what I hoped was a pleasant smile. Gentri or someone must have sent word along Capital Road to watch out for us if they had time to prepare a room like this.

He bowed his head, "Pleased to be of service, Nadachia." He motioned for Blari to follow him, "You are next door." I watched as he led Blari down the hall before closing myself into my room.

After a wash in rose petal laden water, I blended in suitably. A set of clothes and a pair of soft sandals were lying on a bench in front of my bed. I tried them on. The belt was wide and held the supple forest green tunic closed well enough. If it hadn't been for the thong between my toes, I wouldn't have felt the sandals at all after slipping them on my feet.

The clothes I had worn in and those in my pack were being laundered, according to the note, and would be back in the morning. I found my leg sheath and tied it around my calf before sticking two of the daggers Jahni had given me into it. The weight was odd compared to them being on the belt, but it would do. A strange town meant unknown people and dangers.

A soft knock sounded, and I pulled it open to look down into the upturned face of a child. Smooth blond hair fell to his shoulders, and his grin provided me with the sight of a bright half baby, half adult teeth smile.

"I'm Nikoi! I'm supposed to take you to the meal hall."

"Alright, Nikoi, lead the way." I said with a nod.

He kept smiling that big grin as he led me down the hall, across the main worship room, and down another hall to the dining room. Plants were everywhere. Three fire pits lined the far wall sand in between them were tables with benches. Two of the tables held an array of pots with sprouts, others held shrubs and some held herbs. At the front of the room, priests were already sitting, including Blari, on a table that just held them, their plates, utensils and candlesticks. Platters of food, mostly of the fruit and vegetable variety, covered the table behind them.

I sat across from Blari after adding a few things to my plate. The large golden rolls were too irresistible to pass up, along with the little bowls of fruit with a creamy glaze drizzled over them. As I ate, I listened to Blari and the other priests chat animatedly about Church practices and how the ceremonies between Beriaha and Meandria were different. I was glad no one seemed to pay me any mind, except Nikoi, who kept filling my glass with water. He also snuck an extra roll onto my plate and a slab of brown sugar ham.

As he slid a bowl of caramel apple slices beside my plate, I turned to him. His smile hadn't faded, "Nikoi, do you know where I can find someone named Spacya?"

The two priests beside me quietened as Nikoi looked to them as he answered, "She's..she's scary."

I smiled, "It's alright. She's a friend of a friend and I'm going to need her help."

He nodded, then looked across the table to a brown haired priest. His hair held a red tinge to it, and fell in waves to his collar. A wink shuttered a light colored eye when he noticed Nikoi looking at him. "Priest Kae, did you hear?"

"I did." Priest Kae smiled a little as he said, "I'll take her to old Spacya if she wants." His gaze flicked to me, before dropping back to his food, "Spacya is a special case. Few take the time to understand her ways. Most fear her, like Nikoi. And, well... she likes them to be scared of her."

She sounded similar to Doc. Rough until you get on the good side, or they know you a bit. I had an inclination to liking her already.

"I'll wait here." Priest Kae said to me as he stopped before a pub. The chained sign above the door sported a faded red rooster.

"The Rooster Den," he added with a twist of his lips, "Still owes me some bits. Spacya'll probably be in this corner." He pointed to the window at the end of the wall.

"Perfect." Blari snorted, "Always at a disadvantage going up to someone in a corner."

"Maybe you should wait with him. Get some supplies we might need."

Blari shook his head, "If you have to kick her, I need to write it down."

I stared at him.

He turned from studying the pockmarked door, then lifted a shoulder, "What? Taspe said you've kicked him plenty of times."

I turned to Kae, "Thanks. We can find our way back if you have things to do."

He grinned, "I do. Watching the show through the window here." He crossed his arms and leaned back against the support beam of the shop across the narrow street.

At that vote of confidence, I was glad I had my regular clothes on me. The laundress held Blari and I as top priority that night. I had all my weapons at my disposal, if needed. I swung open the door to the pub and inhaled the stench of watered ale, urine, and body odor. Why people loved these places I would never understand.

My eyes were slow to adjust to the dim lighting inside as I dodged a low bench just inside the door. It was the only one without a rear on it in the whole place. The nails sticking up out of it told me why.

The corner seemed streets away, I waded through, trying not to touch any of the patrons. Something slapping onto my thigh and holding nearly toppled me into a table. A low chuckle sent my teeth on edge. I followed the arm up from the hand that squeezed my thigh to a splotchy, crusted face. His grin was hardly cute.

I stared into his eyes, grinning back, "If ya want your had to be attached by the time I count to three, you best remove it from my person."

He chuckled again, and said, "Fiesty ain't my type." He removed it.

"Good." Then, under my breath as I moved further away I admitted, "Cause I'm not that either."

I found myself amid men and women in varying states of cups and dress after passing another table.

I glanced back at Blari, "Don't look."

"Too late."

His scribbles tonight were going to be interesting. I moved toward the back corner, the farthest from the bar. It held a small table, made for two, but there was only one chair and one person in it.

The window beside her was gray with grime, looking out onto the narrow street we had left Kae in. What I hadn't noticed was the riot of colors, faded from the grime, resting in a box along the windowsill.

She was staring out at it, watching a little green and red bird sip from a deep flower dangling off the corner of the box. Her hair was up in a mixture of braids in two wads. A few strands straggled here and there, but most were tamed into the buns. From what I could gather of her build, she was broader and taller than Doc.

A spear leaned against the window at her elbow. A thick bear's pelt made a caplet clasped at her shoulder with bear claws. Between them was a leather thong tie with three bear's teeth hanging from it. She wore a green tunic that had seen many years of wear, but it was clean, as were her pants of thick woven fabric. The sturdy cloth let me know she had money, but was practical.

She looked up when my feet cleared the invisible circle that separated her from the rest of the pub. I knew why most gave her a wide berth if they weren't deterred by the spear and bear parts. From her forehead, slashing down over her left eye, her nose, and her lips to her jawline were three jagged gashes. Near her ear was a fourth. The center mark was the darkest, but all were faded with the healing of a decade or two.

Her right eye was a rich green while the left was a faded, glistening thing of white. It was if the claws had drained it of color, perhaps of sight too. Her nose hooked, what remained of it. And her lips, perpetually pulled up into a snarl on the left side, were thin and pale. Part of her earlobe was missing, but even there dangled a bear claw that tapped against her cheek.

"Are you Spacya?"

She answered me with a narrowing of her eyes.

Blari leaned against my back to speak, and still I barely heard him over the crowd, "Not sure if we can run quickly enough…"

I stepped further into her circle. She took a sip of whatever frothy drink was in her tankard. The room hushed from the loud bellowing racket to murmurs and tittering laughter.

"Speak. Don't stand and stare, lass." Her voice bubbled from disuse and drink. The lilt Doc had was there, stronger in her.

I watched as her fingers and arm flexed toward her spear when I tugged the note out of my belt. I held the paper out so she saw it before completing the distance between me and her table, "Doc sends his regards."

She humphed as she snatched it from my hand. Her eyes swept down me, resting them on my boots for a moment, before she turned to the letter. After her gaze swept over it, her shoulders began shaking.

The half circle around us grew until Blari was out in the open too. I noticed more than one stare our way. I heard some of them finishing off their drinks in loud gulps.

Her chuckles made shivers cross the room like someone just opened the door to a blizzard.

Her hearty laugh had some scrambling for the door after slamming down bits on their table or bar.

She tipped the rest of her drink into her mouth, then smacked the tankard onto her table as she stood. My fingers inched toward my daggers as she grabbed up her spear. She tucked the letter into her belt. "What time we leave, lass?"

"The church is giving us breakfast at first light."

"I'll see ya then."

Spacya was in the meal hall by the time I entered it the next morning. Her equipment was next to her seat with five half spears lashed to the bottom of it and two longer ones leaning against the table beside her. Furs and leathers composed her attire, including her pack. I assumed her own hands made them, and marvelled at the strong, even stitching.

I sat across from her, placing my pack by my chair. I took a few steaming biscuits and filled them with red jam. At the first bite I discovered the jam was a sweet mixture of strawberries, cherries with a slight hint of apples. I washed down every three bites with the tangy orange juice Nikoi poured into my cup.

"Better eat more than that." Spacya leaned back in her chair, the wood creaking with the shift in her weight. She jerked her chin at Nikoi while pointed to a platter of smothered pork chops, the gravy a rich brown red. "I'll not be carryin' ya on this journey. If'n ye fall behind, I'll go on me own way."

Nikoi speared two slabs of the pork and slathered more of the gravy over them. He added a few pieces of buttered fish to the side and a spoonful of fluffy yellow eggs.

I ate most of it. The eyes of the huntress goading me to eat more even though I knew I would make myself sick later. There was a reassurance in that striking gaze. I had one tough to watch my back now, someone I could rely on to be smart about our travels, and to provide for Blari if something were to happen to me. The thought settled my roiling stomach some. The biscuits helped too.

Blari was the most talkative out of the entire breakfast group. There were plenty of other priests there, and I supposed he might as well get the chatter out. I doubted Spacya was a talker. I certainly didn't like talking half the time either.

After we ate our fill, we thanked the priests and loaded our packs with the extra food supplies they gave us. I put on Vey's sleeves, not sure what to expect on the road between Dragotown and Galanesse. In a few miles, I would be the furthest west I had ever been.

Dragotown was waking as we made our way to the gates and out them. A mist, light and feathery, skewed the fields on either side of the road from sight. I breathed in the warming scent of the earth and my body loosened.

I preferred the open spaces over any town or church.

Spacya set a pace I was used to. A silent walk of measured strides that put fields, vineyards and other towns between us and Dragotown by midday. Even with the ring helpingus all, Blari still panted a bit.

I could imagine the scribbles tonight berating one huntress for trying to kill him by walking.

When the sun rested its orange head on the treetops to the west, we broke away from the road to find a spot for the night. We came upon a small clearing with a tributary to the Gala giggling over rocks between the trees. Blari set up the tents, Spacya and I gathered the wood, water, and hunted for our supper. She brought back a couple of rabbits, and I found a few pheasant nests and took two of the four eggs in each for our breakfast in the morning. Always leave the wild things something, otherwise you'll want for everything.

We cooked together, a rabbit stew brewing in our biggest pot with some vegetables from Dragotown making it filling.

I watched the trees. The forest looked like it had stood for hundreds of years. It reeked of age. The roots running thick as the limbs rose high enough to brush the skies while growing heavy with new spring leaves. Bright green moss covered everything around us. Small animals rustled through the dead leaves and I saw numerous tracks and sign while hunting earlier.

"There're wolves and wild dogs here." Spacya spoke for the first time in hours, "The wolves won't be a problem. Wild dogs have no honor."

"I can take the first watch." It took me half the night to get to sleep.

Blari nodded, "I'll take the last to get an early start on breakfast."

"Wake me when Meandria's star reaches peak, lass."

I nodded, spooning the last of the stew between our bowls as they held them out to me. "Another full day of walking and we'll be at the capital, right?"

"Aye, maybe another night out. The last bit's crowded. Might have to walk beside the road fer the carts."

As my companions settled in for the the night, I curled into the crook of a large, low-hanging branch of a wide tree just out of the glow of the campfire. I began thinking of the forest and the traps back home. I wondered if Detri and Vey remembered to check and re-bait them. Both boys were good with dressing kills. Their skills with traps were a bit lacking, but they learned well enough.

Once I made money to send them, this would be worth it. This was for the best.

Chapter 7

Sleep eluded me. A drowning storm caused us to take an extra two days to get to the capital. By the time we reached the floating city of Galanesse, I felt soaked through and half mad from lack of slumber.

Galanesse. It was grander in person than the painting in the Mayor's office captured. It stretched further than I could see. Floating between the cliffs the power of the great Gala River had created before churning into the sea. Bridges of white led travelers into the city, polished from overuse, and wide enough for ten horses to march down without touching one another.

I stopped halfway over the bridge, and leaned against the shining white railing to look at the city.

I smiled a little. Noting the jutt of a rock underneath her. She didn't float, but the spew of the sea meeting the Gala hid the land underneath it well.

Even in the mist created from the fighting waters, travelers stared in awe at the shadowy Black Tower, the glistening spindly spires of the Royal Palace, and the Four Cardinal Towers of the Church. Nothing else in Lanpress was like them. Each building took decades to build. Sadly, only the Matron that started The Black Tower got to see its completion. The rest were enjoyed by the offspring or inheriters.

A Gala Keeper was called to guide us through the maze of streets to the Church. She wore a yellow tunic under a thin shirt of glistening blue chains over black breeches and yellow booties. Their jobs were to guide travelers to their destinations within the city, and I was grateful. Narrow alleys in Galanesse were like main streets in Owlimount. Buildings of similar colors and builds gathered between them, often representing the tribe, or peoples who lived there. But a few streets down was a similar section, and I began to wonder if we were not going in tedious circles as the Towers did not appear to be getting any closer, nor further away.

Then we were upon them, standing in the middle of the large open square they shared at their fronts. The towers gathered the sunlight so well that my eyes watered trying to see the tips they were shining so. I trailed my gaze over the statues of the twenty-seven gods that stood guard around the square. I could fit in one of their stone palms, easily. Each of them were as colorful as they usually were in paintings. If I didn't know any better, the stones were dressed in rich silks, but upon touching them, the robes were the smoothest of stone.

"Long ago, the Matron Pagevea gifted these statues to Galanesse as a symbol of unity when the Lanpress Administration was signed." I eyed the priest in rainbow robes who greeted the Gala Keeper when she knocked. The Lanpress Administration was a sore conversation for me. For those who ruled Lanpress were part of it, leaving the Welkans and Rogues out of power. When they were signed, Rogues didn't exist, and Welkans were slaves, but nothing had been done to add the races to the ruling party.

"I'm Nadachia of Silverequis-"

"I know." He interrupted me, "We have been expecting you and your first two companions, Spacya of Dragotown and Priest Blari of Owlimount. Come!" He motioned us into the church with a smile.

Blari shook his head at my look, and hurried after the priest, "High Priest, we are honored."

"Nonsense! It is I who is honored!" He bowed, once inside the doors that were just as tall as the statues outside.

I wondered how they opened and closed them, when I heard the grind of gears behind us and the doors click close.

"Follow me, I'm sure you will want to rest and wash up before all the festivities begin tonight in your honor."

Out of the corner of my eye, I saw Spacya's furs seem to bristle. Her breath sucked in through her pinched nose and I bit back a smile. She would not get any sleep tonight or the nights we stayed here.

I knew I wouldn't fare much better.

The front room, the worship room, was as tall as the building was. The pews looked relatively comfortable in this church, with cushions and wide seats. More statues of gods stood along the walls, watching whatever parishiners would sit on the pews during the services. These were just plain stone, not colorful like the ones along the square.

The High Priest led us down the hall to the right. Tapestries covered the walls between the long arched windows that gave a view of a garden and the back of the palace. Each tapestry was a different story. Some about heroes, others about gods and the leaders of our lands. Most were of the gods.

Toward the end of the hall, the Priest opened a dark oak door to his left, "Priest Blari, we have prepared these rooms for you." He motioned for a teen to come out, "And Vali will be of service to you." He moved to the door across the hall in six steps to open another door, "Spacya, these are your rooms, and Giera here will be of great aid to you." He grinned at me once the other two were within their room, "You are in the best rooms we have."

He opened the door at the end of the hall. "These, my dear Hero Nadachia, are your rooms. I hope they are to your tastes."

The smell of lavender and ocean tickled my nose when I stepped over the threshold. The room I looked into was larger than the three rooms of the first floor of my house put together. "I can take a smaller room."

"Nonsense! Only the best for the Hero!" The priest waved a hand dismissively, "This is Ida, if you have any questions or need of anything she is at your personal disposal."

He motioned to a slim girl just inside. Her head was down in a bow. At her name she straightened, brushing a few loose strands of her blonde hair out of her face before smiling brightly, "Come, Hero Nadachia, let me give you a tour."

I did as I was told.

Windows stained in almost imperceptable blues and purples made up the wall from above the clear glass doors to the ceiling, giving the entire room a soft muted hue that reminded me of an autumn night by Turquid Lake. The waters there held the bluest and clearest in all the lands, heated by underground vents. The area boasted of many minerals used for health, and of bright blue and soft green stones. .

This room held few tables, a desk, and a small collection of books in the corner shelf.

Ida led me out onto the balcony. I looked out through the trees and bushes toward the cerulean sea on this side. "That is where we keep most of our livestock for the kitchens." She pointed to a small clearing of green dotted with cows and a horse just beyond the trees to the far left. "There is a modest path you can walk down there, too. But the proper garden is this way."

I followed her around the outside of my room on the wide gray stone balcony. My rooms took up the end of the church until it reached the West tower. Below, the treetrunks gave way to green, manicured grass interrupted in splashes of color from flowers in neat beds that were every hue and size from all over the world.

Somehow, someone had shaped the trees within the garden. Some were in the shapes of former Heroes. White gravel paths led this way and that, often circling the shaped trees and larger flower beds. In the distance was a tall hedge.

"That's the garden maze created by King Heie and Queen Mada over a century ago."

I nodded, trying to place the names in the lineages I learned in Mother's schooling. I would have to remember all of that while I was here. It wouldn't do for me to shame my family by not being able to name all the royals when I met the current ones.

My stomach tumbled lower and sat like a rock. I would have to meet royals.

"There's so much more!" Ida grinned, clapping her pale slender hands together as she led me back inside.

The next room had a tiled floor of the same aqua stones as covered the bottom of Lake Turquid. Now and then, a group of tiles made a flower shape in a purple or darker blue. A sunken bath, the size of my attic back home, was in the center. My entire family would fit in it. Water seeped in from one side, then out through a grate at the base. Constant motion.

Such a waste.

All around the edge was a narrow line of coals glowing. Some were aflame with a low fire. I couldn't tell how deep the coal pits went, but I imagined they were as deep as the bath to keep all the water warm. Four tiled paths allowed for me or Ida to pass into the pool without fear of burning our feet.

Next to the bath was a copper tub fixed with a hose and head. A shower. Only the rich in Owlimount had one.

Ida pushed the narrow double doors into the next room. It was the size of the two bedrooms back home put together. In it were clothes hanging on either side. Shoes underneath them to match. Hats and wraps hung beside the three part mirror at the back of the room. A chest set in the middle, open to show rows of gleaming jewelry and gloves in sets.

"We will have to tailor these to you." Ida smiled as she twirled in her little green frock, "But these are all yours! Gifts from royals, the court, the King and Queen, and even our allied countries!"

"I-I can't wear all this." I trialed a finger along a dark blue flowing skirt to my right. The fabric softer than anything I've ever felt before, and my rough fingers snagged it. I dropped my hand.

"Of course you can!"

Ida giggled and led me back to the tiled bath, then through another set of doors. The bed filled this room. It had its own roof of dark, heavy wood. Carved in intricate vine patterns with leaves and flowers dotting it, four thick posts supported the canopy. In fact, each piece of wood on the bed had intricate carvings, including the pieces under the mattress and coverlet. Curtains tied to the posts equaled the blue autumn skies while the sheets matched the sky of moonless nightfall. Pillows of both hues and differing sizes took up the head of the wide, thick mattress.

Ten people could sleep in it, comfortably.

"They will send a tailor soon. She's the best, one who works closely with the Queen and Matron. You should undress and bathe first, she hates to be kept waiting, Hero Nadachia." Ida's tongue tumbled over my long name. She twisted a light blonde curl around her first and second fingers.

"Just call me Chi." I moved back to the bathing room and began undressing.

"Most feel cleaner if they shower first." She motioned to the copper tub once I got down to my underclothes. "Then they go to the pool to soak. But it is your preference."

I snorted, "My preference is a nice hidden pond or slow-moving portion of a stream or river."

She giggled before saying, "You really are from the country. Is it as green as they say? All woods and houses made of stone or wood you pull from the land yourselves?"

"You might say that."

Her eyes were so wide, I felt the need to cover myself. Not that I had anything to amaze her. Her reaction was like mine upon hearing of the capital.

After tugging off my underclothes I stepped into the copper tub, and she turned on the faucet, adjusting the nobs before holding out the handle to me, "Is this too hot?"

I passed my hand under the water, "No, it's fine." She helped me untwist my hair and rinse it. "We have a lot of houses made of wood, yes. Some are of stone, but nothing to impress, just plainly hewn. Some rich people have marble houses, or floors."

"I bet it's beautiful. All the trees and the wild land. All the animals you get to see too."

"Have you ever been out of Galanesse?"

With a shake of her head, she answered, "No. I was born here to my parents who are merchants. Then I was hired by Mrs. Brigandfor when I was eleven to be her maid. She lived to be over a hundred years old!" Her lips trembled, "She was the nicest lady, far nicer than my own mother to me. Then I've been with the Church since. I take care of travelers." She grinned, as she rinsed off the rest of my body, "Now I get to take care of the Hero!"

Once we finished, she turned off the shower and I stepped out onto the tiles. The heat warming my bare feet more than the water of the shower. I took the steps leading down into the water slowly, I sank into the hot bath, watching the steam rise around me. I groaned once I stopped, the water reaching my chin.

The tightness of the walk here seemed to float away.

"You like baths the best, don't you?"

"One of my favorite things in life." I said with a half smile, and watched as Ida worked my clothes, then hung them up on a special hook near the door. She put my belt, boots, and bag in the closet.

"The staff will take what's on the hook to wash each night. They'll dry and be back by morning." Ida informed me as she pulled out a large fluffy towel from a shelf in one wall. She placed it in a basket of dark wicker before pulling out a cloth of the same softness and three small bars of soap. She set the basket beside the stairs on one of the wider sections between the bath and coals. "We cannot keep the soaps near here or they will melt. The informants told us you like the smells of lavender, irises, and of sweet pine." She pointed to each bar of soap with my favorite scents. "These are the soaps the locals made just for you."

I eyed them, "I have my own soaps?"

"Of course! Once you approve of them, they will start selling them as your scents to the public. They'll make a lot of money off them soon." Ida's voice dropped as if she was afraid of being overheard.

She had a soft, mothering way about her. It made me wonder just how old she was. No lines marred her features, her hair was shining in the lights of the sun from the windows and candles, and she moved effortlessly. Her hands were rough though, years of work scrubbing and cooking.

"That's just ridiculous." I took a soap in my hand and noted the tiny petals of lavender set within the creamy colored bar. The scent sweeter than the soaps back home.

"Do you want me to wash your back and hair?"

This was a realm of the gods."Yes, please."

I moved back over to the stairs and sat on them. Ida's rough fingers worked the soap into my scalp and thick strands of hair with gentle, circular rubs and long strokes. Bathing was one of my favorite things to do, but it was someone else washing my hair that I wished for the most. A luxury I hardly received the older I got.

The last person to wash my hair was Mother before she and Seaghla departed for the capital. Three years ago. No, four years.

I wanted to see them. I smiled, wondering if they were on their way here to visit me. Or if they were allowed. If they knew I was taking up the Hero's tasks. Surely, they had Father's letter by now.

Ida began working on my shoulders and back, and I leaned forward to give her room. As she worked, I toyed with my hair in the water, watching it bunch and spread on the surface. My hair felt softer after her treatment. I didn't think something like that possible after a simple wash.

"Your hair is really thick. And so long. I can't wait to put it up prettily for you!" I heard the grin in her voice as she spoke. "Do you want me to wash the rest of you?"

"No, thank you." I took the cloth from her soap coated hands and began washing off.

"You must have siblings to be comfortable around me while naked."

I smiled, "Plenty of them. Eleven." I watched her eyes go wide.

"Eleven?!"

With a nod, I explained, "One by birth. We collected the others. Orphans. My nephew also lives with us, so I should probably say ten siblings and a nephew."

"That's very…honorable of your parents." Ida swallowed, a rinsed hand going ot her cheek. "You must come from a rich family."

"Not at all."

A rapping at the door had Ida rushing to it after making sure the screen partitions hid me from view. I heard two unknown voices chatting with Ida getting closer after a breath or two.

"If you would wait in the dressing room, I shall get her dry."

The rustle of skirts were accompanied by clacking heels on the marble flooring before fading into the rug filled dressing room. Ida peeped around a partition, "Are you ready to get out?"

I nodded, not really wanting to, but I remembered what Ida said about the tailor not liking to be kept waiting. I took the steps, slowly again, I knew how slippery rocks in the river were, so I wasn't about to brain myself in the bath before I ever started on a quest.

"What exactly am I supposed to do for the rest of the day?"

Ida's eyes went wide, "Oh, you like to know. Forgive me. Right now, you are being measured so the tailor can work on your clothing. She will modify a dress for you to wear for tonight's activities. Tonight is a dinner at the Castle with the royals and those specifically invited by the Royal Family. There you will also meet with the Matron. A dance will follow where you will mingle and get to meet those who might become your companions, or benefactors."

Pressure built up behind my eyes with each word she said. She was drying me off in quick swipes with the thick towel, and each was as sandpaper as my skin crawled with the idea of meeting royals and the richest and most powerful people in the lands.

"Then tomorrow is an all-day affair. A luncheon, then you will receive your first quest at the meeting with the Matron and her Council in the Tower, and then another dance with more lords, ladies and greatest minds of our time. There might be one or two pledges to become companions there. I'm not entirely sure how that works. That's more of a Priest question."

She twisted my hair up on top of my head in a smaller towel. Then pulled a light gauzy shift over me that hung down to the tops of my thighs. The warm tiles now burned my tender flesh as shivers of what was to come washed over me.

So much for the comforting bath.

I hadn't felt this badly since the time Taspe dragged me along to one of his Legacy meetings. Hundreds of Welkans were there. I was among a handful of humans present, and the great and mighty Taspe had invited none of them. Only me. The humans ignored me there. The Welkans literally looked down their noses at me. But each time Taspe grinned in their faces and introduced me as if I was a jewel, or the sun. I wanted to skin him alive.

What I wouldn't give to have him at my side during this mess.

In the dressing room was a stately woman. One that would bend a sword in half with a look. The slight woman behind her had some similarities, but her gaze was much more gentle. I swallowed as they bowed to me.

"Hero Nadachia, this is Madame Sira and her daughter, Willa."

"Pleasure." I managed around the bile rising in my throat.

"You must tilt your head slightly when saying something like that. Preferably 'a pleasure' or 'it is an honor.' The latter especially with a bow to those of royal blood and the Matron."

I wasn't about to bend to that tone, but I said, "I'll keep that in mind."

She had spider thin arms ending in long fingers from wrinkled age-spotted hands. Her dress was a misty gray, like morning fog, and it flowed around her as she moved around me, much as the fog they colored it after.

"You are very malnourished. Eat as much as you can, but be a lady about it. You must still be able to speak readily when spoken to at meals."

How many times had I ignored that growing up? Not that I was malnourished, but that I had to learn to eat like a lady. If they wanted me to speak, they would wait until after I chewed whatever I stuffed in my mouth.

"You are still rather pretty. No, beautiful." She said and smiled at me, her sunken eyes brimming with light for the first time since meeting her. "Yes, a little care, and you will be right again in no moment. You are already the talk to the city. So let's make you the beauty of it too."

Beauty? I choked on my words, "I-I'm just-I-"

"No need to be modest, dear. This is my job." Madame Sira raised a hand. "Willa, let's get started." She took a pad of paper out of her pocket, and a thin pencil out of her graying hair.

Willa moved toward me with a measuring tape, "Raise your arms, if you please." She raised her own, and put her heels together too.

I mimicked her, and she smiled. It actually reached her eyes too.

"Face is rounded. Brows need shaping. Just a light dash of color needed to hide the shadows in her cheeks until she can gain some weight. Hazel eyes. A perfect palette really, Mother, you have a gem." Willa smiled again, "Healing gloss for the lips before coloring them. Can I see you smile?"

I managed not to snarl at her, I think.

"A mint soak before bed, but they are strong. None missing." Willa continued, "Neck and shoulders are strong. Tan line along neck and forearms, though. Half-sleeve or full would be best to hide that." She then felt of my hands with her own silky ones and groaned, "Desperate need of trimming and smoothing. Do you claw your way instead of walking?"

"I need the calluses."

Willa and Sira both stared at me, lips parted slightly.

"I hunt and trap. Not just a doll for you to dress up."

"Right. Right. A Hero is a warrior too." Sira nodded, "Yes."

I could almost hear her cursing running through her head behind those cold eyes. "We shall glove your callusses and claws then. Just creams each night and a trim today."

Ida giggled from the corner. I glanced over at her and she grinned at me. I was going to like the girl.

"Breasts are full. No shame there."

My cheeks heated and I nearly dropped my arms to cover myself.

"Skin is good." She moved to my rear, "No padding. Good muscle tone."

My butt had saved me from some hard landings plenty of times.

"Better tone in the legs. Might need dresses to have a slit to show them off."

Using the measuring tape, she started calling out my measurements. Sira noted them. Willa stepped back and I dropped my arms, like heavy tree limbs.

Sira moved to the dresses and pulled three out. "These should do for tonight. Let's see which fits you best, and go from there."

After hours of trying on the dresses and Sira fixing them to fit, the woman finally settled on one for the night.

It was a white gown that faded into a green in the skirt that reminded me of being in a deep pine forest. The edges of the long sleeves matched the deep green at the end of the skirt. It fit tight in my chest and hips, and stomach after she altered it, then flared out into a cone al little wider than shoulder-width. The most important thing was I could breathe in it.

Chapter 8

Three years since my Mother forced me into the torture contraption that was being forced upon me again. With how well the dress had fit earlier, I didn't think they would make me wear the troture device. I was wrong.

At least this one was cloth and not leather and bone like Mother's had been.

The thin little shift, or chemise, I should really learn the name of these things, was silk. The corset was soft too. A breathable fabric. It still had bones in it. I grunted as Sira pulled my ribs in and my breasts closer to my collar bones with each jerk of the laces and cloth.

If I looked down and tried to breathe in deep I could smother myself. I wondered if any of these grand ladies of the capital had ever considered ending their miserable existences in corsets with that. Death by breast suffocation.

One day, these things would make us evolve to where our breasts were just under our chins. I shuddered at the thought.

"What's wrong? Too tight?"

"Of course it's too tight!" I snapped, glaring over my shoulder at Sira.

She humphed, "If you can talk that way, then you're fine."

Ida guided me to a vanity. I watched as she twisted and tamed my drying tresses. She braided three thin pieces at my temples and wove them through the rest of my hair as she pulled it all up top. The braids looked like they were playing the old children's game of peek out. Then Ida placed flowers, small ones, throughout. Soon my head looked like dirt with spring flowers dotting it. It wasn't bad, but nothing I would have ever done to my hair. She then pulled some tendrils loose to frame my face and tickle my neck.

After Ida finished, she beamed at me. I smiled back at her before Willa descended upon me. She had tools in her hands that I grew to despise in the matter of seconds.

I kept glancing in the mirror to see if I had eyebrows left. There were undesirable bits near my chin and lips too. After little skin remained on my face, she soothed my flesh with an unscented cream. Another cursory glance let me know I was being dramatic and still had skin left.

Her hands flew over my face with brushes and pads next. There were several floral smells to tickle my nose. I didn't have a chance to glance in the mirror until she was completed.

I was a different person with that stuff on. She used a light hand, making my skin glow rather than overburdened by false color. My eyes and lips looked bigger, slightly. Perhaps being feminine for a night or two wouldn't be the end of the world. If only I could relax in a dress like I could in my normal clothes.

They covered Chi and The Hero Nadachia stared back at me.

How would the Hero Nadachia act? Calm. Collected. Proper. Talking instead of listening. Smiles, lots of those.

I took a look at the shoes Ida brought to me and shook my head, "I better not wear those axe ends."

Ida paused, looking at the death traps in her hands, then back to me, "Axe ends?"

"Something's going to break if those are on my feet and I doubt it'll be the floor."

Sira made a sound in her throat, but nothing more as Ida pulled another pair of shoes out. A set of flat-bottomed lacey things that had straps to go all the way up my calves. At least I wouldn't die by taking a step.

As impressed as I was with the contraption with the ability to move in it, and not sweat to death, it still hindered large movements. Like touching my toes. Deep breaths. Running. Not that I'd tried running yet. If I couldn't pretend to be The Hero Nadachia, then I might end up seeing if I could run in the corset.

They finished with the last touches on me. A pair of fingerless gloves to match the green of the skirt to hide the worst of my callouses. A necklace of jewels shaped in tiny flowers with matching ear cuffs completed my transformation.

Sam Wicker

They stared at me. Nods of approval did nothing to settle the heart fluttering and my rolling stomach. I was being fed to a den of royals.

Ida led me out of the rooms and pushed me into the hall. There I met the dark gaze of Blari. His eyes grew wide with each step I took toward him.

"Taspe was right, you clean up well."

"What?"

Blari cleared his throat, "I just meant that you look nice. That's all."

"Nice is one thing. Able to do anything is another," Spacya said behind me.

She was wearing a fine set of clothing, too. A tunic and pants. "No dress?"

Spacya snorted, her brows ticking toward her hairline, "Do I seem like someone to wear a dress or would want to?"

"No. No, not at all." I sighed and I looked at Blari, who wore tight black pants with a tunic of blue belted closed with a thick sash at his rounded belly. The curls on his chest were the same thickness and shade of his beard and hair. His beard sported a few braids decorated with silver closures, but his mane flowed free to his shoulders in dark feathery waves.

At least they could still bolt.

My breath hitched as we started down the hall that would lead us to the garden, and then palace. My heart hammered with each step I took with my companions. Thunder sounded in my ears and I wondered if I was suddenly hearing the ocean below us.

Blari slowed until he was walking beside me. His fingers, cool and gentle, pressed against the base of my head and my bare neck, "Easy Chi. You're fine."

Father's words echoed in my mind. *'My heart is your heart. Feel it. My blood is your blood. Know it. Strength of the smartest and the world with us, not against. Believe and breathe.'* I'm not alone. I kept repeating Father's mantra, stilling for a moment. Blari stayed with me, turning his fingers over so they remained cool on me.

"You are Nadachia of Silverequis from Owlimount. You are a daughter, a sister, a friend. You need naught here. Nor do you owe a thing to anyone but yourself."

I looked over to Spacya, watching her twisted mouth form those words in a softened voice. She wasn't staring at me. Did she know this feeling too?

"Better?" Blari asked softly, dropping his now warm fingers.

I nodded, swallowing down the bile. It felt constant these days, that burning in my throat and chest. "Thank you, both."

"I wondered when it was gonna get to ya."

I looked at the huntress again, and she lifted a shoulder, "Once, I was brought here." She pointed to the scar on her face, "I killed a bear that got a taste for man meat. It'd killed twenty or more," a shadow settled in her eyes, "They paraded me 'round with that carcass. I's sick for months. The only thing that calmed me was tellin' myself who I was, and that I didn't owe nobody a thing." She jerked her chin to me, "Might help ye, too."

"Stand here as long as you need. Breathe." Blari added.

Spacya stood, watching, her eyes going between us. Her cheeks puffed, once, then twice, before she snorted, "The breathin' be for her, not fer ye to ogle, Priest."

His skin reddened above his beard. His gaze darted away once I met it, "I didn't mean to! I just- I wasn't..."

Spacya chuckled low, "Married to the gods, my white arse."

I giggled before I knew I wanted to, or had the ability. I patted his shoulder and started toward the door at the end of the hall. Given time, they would grow to be friends. Already a great help to me. I just hoped I would be to them too, one day.

A priest walked with us through the garden between the Church and the Castle. Being outside, seeing green things and feeling the crunch of pretty white gravel beneath my feet helped calm the flutterings and burnings within. She guided us into a wide expanse of polished gray and white marble I assumed was a foyer. She turned to me, "There is a powder room you may escape into if it gets to be overwhelming, just here." She pointed to a set of narrow doors just before the hallway began.

"Thank you."

She bowed and left as a guard came up to us.

The guard in glistening mirror plate sewn into a black shirt bowed low, a smile on her face, "Follow me! Please use the powder room as sparingly as you can. The royals and the richest of our land have arrived to see you. I cannot say what they will do if they only glimpse you through the night."

"Why bother to come see me?"

Blari looked at me as if I had suddenly grown two heads. "It's only been over a century since the last Hero was born. You are a rare breed, child. Monsters need to be taken care of, by you. Monsters that wreck havoc upon our world." Blari huffed in his speech, "You killed The White Boar. The first monster. Therefore, you are chosen and blessed by the gods. Blessed by them to help, to be our Hero, to help us earn our gifts from them. Why wouldn't everyone want to see one such as you?"

My jaw tightened, "I didn't kill it."

"You, I, Doc and Taspe know that you did. Joni doesn't use your daggers."

"Lets just get this over with." His words punched through me, doubling the torment inside.

We followed the guard down the hallway. The floor here held a pattern of interlocking diamonds of gray in white, while the pillars were a stark white against gray walls up to a high ceiling. It was painted in the scene of the gods laughing and playing in a field of green. I could scent the meal we were about to partake in halfway to the dining room. We turned to the left and entered a red carpeted room with a single large circular table covered in a black cloth. In the middle of it was a statue of white marble of the very first king and queen of our lands. Platters, plates, bowls and tureens of gold and silver covered every inch of the table otherwise.

All the people within were decked with more jewels and finery on them than were in the mines, I was sure. The guard stomped her boot, the sound echoing, and all turned to stare at us.

"May I present to you The Hero Nadachia of Silverequis from Owlimount, her companions Priest Blari of Owlimount and Huntress Spacya of Viyarey from Dragotown." The guard's voice echoed off the walls much like her boot stamp did.

They clapped. Smiled. They saluted me with glasses of varying hues of red, purple, and cream.

I just stood there. Willing my legs to move. To run. It was time to test breathing in the corset while running.

My legs turned to jelly. My knees locked in place, keeping me upright by some blessing of the gods. Blari took my arm. The guard turned back to us, "Please, follow me."

She led us, Blari half carrying me as I wobbled on my weak limbs, to a set of people in the center of the room, just behind the large table. Circlets on their heads let me know exactly who I was meeting before the escort could open her mouth again.

"May I present Nadachia of Silverequis to my Majesties Queen Azara and King Bahai and to Prince Tori." The guard bowed, and left.

Blari, Spacya and I bowed. I wanted to follow the guard. Did they not care to have another introduction to my companions? The Queen held out her hand to me. I took it in mine. I froze, not knowing what to do with it.

She stepped up to me, Blari moving away. Her grip tightened as she smiled, "Remember to breathe, dear Hero. All here are flesh and bone, just as you and I are."

Her voice was a gentle caress of warmth over my frozen thoughts. It held something behind it, power, a strength. As if she were accustomed to commanding hoards and beasts with mere whispers. To me, it held understanding, too.

"You and I, Nadachia, we are not used to being in rooms of glamour and power." She shuttered a brilliant green eye, "I too would much rather not be here. Alone on the prow of a ship, feeling the salty air upon my face and the warmth of the sun all over."

The king shook his head beside her, "My dear, we shall never tame the wild of you." He smiled at me, "We are not here to take you from the wilds either. But one must amuse the bits and jewels to make our voices heard."

"Bear it as you can. The wilds are more savory once you are free again." She released my hand with a final squeeze.

The next moments in my life were a blur of colorful fabrics, sodden perfume, and too many names for me to remember.

The final meeting was with a woman that had the darkest and longest hair I had ever seen. She swept in as the last set of the richest were making their introductions to me. Her pale flesh glowed against the black lace of her dress. It hugged her form, as if it was a second skin, until it got to her thighs, where it loosened its hold on her slightly. I wondered how she could walk.

I heard none of her footfalls, even though the room fell quiet at her entrance. Yet she did not stop until she was directly in front of me. Everyone bowed, I followed suit. The surrounding people disappeared, and a damp coldness seeped from her, like the caves near the base of the Unforgettable Mountains. Her hair fell nearly to the floor, flowing with her dress. The ridges Stygra were known for upon their heads, were points around the crown of her head. The guard appeared at my side again, "May I present to you our Matron Keandria to the Hero Nadachia of Silverequis from Owlimount."

Her head tilted in my direction slightly, and her thin lips pulled into a smile that did not show her teeth, "Welcome Nadachia of Owlimount."

"Pleasure to meet you." I smiled after trying to place what her voice reminded me of. *A stream? The sounds rocks made when they moved over one another in water, maybe?*

"Let's eat together, shall we? You must be hungry after meeting all these people." Her eyes were colorless. A small pinpoint of a darker pupil allowed me to see where she was looking, and it was directly in my eyes. Tingles. She caused me to tingle all over. She took my wrist in her hand, her fingers warm, but sharp. Like talons.

We walked together to the large table. Servants came up to us, each holding a plate. Keandria dropped my arm and smiled a little at the servant. "Ah, my dear, you know my favorite."

The girl in a frilly little blue dress bowed with a slight smile, "Of course, Matron." She turned and began filling the plate with golden and green vegetables, juicy orange slices, and a large slab of meat that gleamed in the lights of the surrounding candles.

"You cannot go wrong with any of the food you choose. All is cooked well and tastes glorious." The Matron said with another tight-lipped smile in my direction.

I nodded and turned to the servant waiting for me. I hadn't a clue what I could eat. My stomach tumbled. It all smelled so good, but it just wasn't what I needed right this instant. I wanted to get away. I wanted trees and quiet.

"Some of the potatoes there." I pointed and eyed the other dishes, walking around the table slowly. After not seeing anything else that caught my eye, I turned to the servant, "What are your favorites?"

The boy pointed to large sliced carrots glistening with a buttery hue and to an apple cobbler.

"Add those."

"Good choices." The Matron smiled as she took her plate from the girl. She waited until mine was full and motioned for me to follow her.

I hadn't noticed the benches set along the walls with little tables set at intervals along them. Some tables also had delicately carved seats with them too. The Matron sat in one of the wooden chairs and I sat across from her. Blari and Spacya joining nearby. We sat in silence until I finished half of my meal.

"I hope you don't mind, I found it interesting that your Mother and sister, Seaghla, live here. I invited them to join us later. They will have an open invitation into the Castle, Tower, and Church, if you wish."

I stared at the Matron for a moment, my heart leaping back into its original state from its perpetual home in my stomach since arriving, "I would like that. Thank you."

Sam Wicker

"You are welcome. No sense in you being here and not visiting them." She paused, placing her fork down beside her plate and dabbing at her pale lips with a napkin the girl presented her. "I want you to know, too, that you have free range here. Treat this as your home. Well, a home with some chambers that are off limits. I'm sure you wouldn't want to go into someone's private bedchambers, anyway." She smiled at me.

I shook my head, "Oh no, I wouldn't do that."

Her smile stayed, "I'll make sure you are given a tour of the grounds so you won't get lost."

We continued our meal, asking each other questions. She kept steering the conversation back to everyday conversation instead of things relating to Hero business. Taking the hint, I asked her about becoming Matron.

"Ah, well, the rumors are true, to some degree."

I frowned, probing my memory, "They say you defeated the last Matron. Killed her."

"I did. In order to become a Matron you must prove yourself the strongest. Yes, it's rather brutal, but such are our ways. Alas, I did not mean to kill her. We pushed ourselves so far during that battle, I didn't think I had that much strength left. But I did. It…my power got away from me in that last moment of her life."

Her frown seemed much more natural than a smile on her. The lines on her face were softer. There was something shining in her odd eyes I took to be the regret she spoke, though her voice was unchanged. "Have you been challenged since?"

"No, not yet." Keandria continued, "I'm still the most powerful, as none have challenged me. Enough of that. It was a while ago. You will meet the others, my council, who are formidable. They are powerful and knowledgable, and will gladly help you in any way they can in your endeavors. As will I. You just need ask."

"I appreciate that. I feel like I'm going to need a lot of help."

Keandria's lips turned up again, her face growing hard with the motion, "I'm sure the heroes before you felt much the same. They succeeded, in ways, so shall you." She looked up, then stood, "I must leave you so you can mingle. I'm afraid I'm getting frowned upon from the Queen. Don't worry, in a few hours I will tell you all I know of what you must do."

I watched her depart, her black dress swishing across the floor behind her.

I slid my food around my plate before Blari came to my side, "Come on, we should talk to some of them, at least."

"Do I really have to?"

At his look, I wanted to pull his beard until he gave me another answer. As I toyed with that idea, someone came up to us. I stood as Blari bowed so I could do the same.

"Prince Tori, at your service." The prince smiled, holding out his hand. His eyes matched the queen's, as did the rich black sunkissed to brown in areas hair that swept back neatly on top of his head, but was closely shaved near his ears and neck. His skin was as dark as mine, if not a touch darker, and he was the same height, perhaps a finger or two taller.

I took it, and before I could shake it, he brought my fingers to his lips. They were warm and soft. I jerked my hand back, and Blari cleared his throat. I glanced at him to see disapproval darkening his eyes.

"I've come to introduce you to some more people. Call me your guide to the strangers, if you will."

"Thank you," I managed, rubbing my thumb across where his mouth brushed.

He nodded and held out his hand again. I eyed it. He laughed, showing off pretty whites "Don't worry, I won't kiss it."

Blari made a strangled sound as Spacya chuckled behind me.

The chats with these strangers, all royals, were mostly kept to pleasantries. Most talked about themselves. That was completely fine with me.

I had nothing in common with these people.

Long lineages of wealth and never worrying about a thing surrounded me. Some had enough stomach to ask me if I was angry with my long dead ancestor for wasting our inheritance. I bit my tongue, shook my head, and smiled sweetly as I tasted my own blood. These people were more of a waste of air than my fifth-great grandfather.

I learned that many diplomats from other countries were here visiting. They came to see me. Most were here already, but the royals were waiting for others. Especially the pirates that conquered Iethyll, a country to our south border. A diplomat, or representative of that court, had yet to arrive, but rumor had it that the Prince was coming himself.

"Can you imagine? What will he look like?" A lady pressed her fingers to her cheeks while asking that question in the latest circle I found myself in.

Tori chuckled, "I'm sure he's a fine man."

"Oh please!" A princess from Angler scoffed. She had the finest golden hair I had ever seen on a person, "He's going to be all dried up, like an old prune!"

"And his manners! They can only be the worst! A pirate in our midst. What is the world coming to!"

All seemed to think the same about the prince from Iethyll. Poor guy, he wasn't even here yet and already judged unworthy. It made me wonder what they thought of me.

I straightened, pulling my shoulders back and down, "He can be no worse than me."

They stilled then, their eyes on me.

I smiled, "I'm nothing but a woman from the country." I lifted a shoulder, "The only reason I'm here is because of my luck in killing a large boar rather than it killing me."

There were some splutterings. Some gasps.

The Princess of Angler recovered the quickest, "My dear Hero, you are much more than that. Why, your breeding alone stands you above most others here. If only your great-whatsit hadn't lost all your titles and lands you would be as well known as Prince Tori and I. Maybe more!"

It was true. From the time the royals came to be, my family had a part in it. Whether they were advisors or generals, my family had their hands in the shaping and creation of Lanpress from the very beginning until that one fateful ancestor. The bitterness of these royals turning their backs on my family after the disgrace left a foul taste in my mouth, but it was to be expected of these types of people. And so long ago that none of these here were responsible.

A new arrival interrupted my thoughts. Much to the dismay of the others in the circle, it wasn't the pirate prince. No, it was a familiar face to me, though.

The pink-haired woman stood at the entrance to the room, her eyes carefully scanning each person until they landed upon me. Her teeth flashed in a grin and she swopped through the stilled crowd toward me, her men and women she brought trailing behind her.

Her gown was a mere swath of cloth around her chest and hips before wide swatches swayed between her thighs to her ankles. A smaller band of cloth hung down from between her breasts to brush the top of her flat belly button.

"There you are darling." Clara wrapped her arms around me, the bangles and bracelets jangling in her movements like tiny bells. I hugged her back, breathing in her familiar scent of adventure and sands. She pressed a kiss to my forehead. "You should have waited for me to come get you. I would have brought you here in style! Oh, this is pretty on you. I never thought I would see you in a dress again."

Clara, the Princess of Ecia, the country that bordered Lanpress to the east, lived but a day away from Owlimount. Father and the King of Ecia were great friends, having fought together in the war that occured during their youth, The War of Insurgence. There was some dispute on who had saved whose life the most still.

The king and his children often called upon Father and I for strategy and battle plans. Ecia was the line of defence against the war tribes of the Taviere Islands and Northern Countries Coalition.

"What are you doing here?"

The Princess from Angler stammered, "Princes C-Clara?"

Clara turned, the smile fading from her golden features quickly as she lay her rich brown eyes on the one from Angler, "Ah, Princess Symeia, always a pleasure to see you again." Her gaze flicked to the others in the now half circle around us, "Prince Tori, you too."

She twisted back to me, "I stopped in to see Rossi. I nearly beat him for not sending word you needed help. I can support you, you know. You only need to ask. I do not know what you lot go through unless you tell me."

Shame burned through me. We always went to Ecia, never allowing them to come to our home. It was not place for royalty. Her arm snaked around me. She was a full head taller than I was, even though she usually walked around in bare feet. As she did now. Most were realizing this as they came to terms with her entering the room.

"Princess Clara of Ecia, how nice to see you!" The Queen's smile was broad and her eyes shimmered with it, "It has been so long!"

Clara grinned right back, "Queen Azara, you are so beautiful. If I could ever grow to cut a figure like you, I would find my life fulfilled." She untangled herself from me to hug the queen tightly.

The queen's cheeks reddened, "Oh please! I'm too old for you to flatter like that."

Clara laughed, returning to my side, her arm about my waist again, "I had to come to make sure you were keeping a watchful and protective eye on my friend here."

"Oh, I didn't know you two had met before. I suppose it is far more realistic, your palace is only a day or two from Owlimount, is it not?"

"You are correct. My family and I have found Rossi's mind to be invaluable when dealing with some of the affairs of state. Sadly, they do not think the same of us, otherwise their grain bins would not be empty." Clara's glance sent a barb into my heart.

"You have a country to care for."

"Yes, yes, we do. A country you have helped. It is only fair you accept payment." Clara chided, tapping my nose with a fingertip.

The queen smiled, "I wouldn't mind picking Rossi of Silverequis' mind over a few topics as well. Perhaps I'll start a letter tonight to see if he's interested in helping me."

I swallowed, now seeing how this could endear me to these people for the rest of my life. At least, until a quest killed me. Suddenly, I hoped one would render me speechless, or horrid to gaze upon. Then I wouldn't have to put up with these people.

Chapter 9

The Matron pulled me to the side after Clara's arrival and told me she would talk to my companions and I in the morning. She wished for me to catch up with my old friend and to make new ones. It made me wonder what in the gods' I had gotten into after that many more hours with the royals.

Well before dawn I was up, roaming around my rooms. I felt each cloth, smelled every perfume, soap and the few flowers in the rooms, and peaked into everything that I could open. On a table in the sitting room, I compiled some books on the history of Lanpress and some legends. I picked out one about the last Hero and began my studies.

I must have dozed off reading the fine print. I woke to the sound of Ida saying my name. Her fingertips were pressing gingerly into the middle of my back.

"Did you get any sleep?"

"Some."

Ida placed her slender hands on her hips, "How much?"

I eyed her, wondering how such a small girl could look so threatening with a single motion, "Half the night." I shrank back into the plush chair, closing the book on the table.

She sighed, "Get into the bath. I'll be right back."

I did as I was told. Sinking into the hot water and about to doze off again when I heard the door open. The scent that preceded Ida into the room wasn't like the bitter coffee I loved. This scent was darker, richer, in some way.

Ida smiled as she set the tray down beside the bath. She began pouring from a long narrow spout and decorative pot into a cup of silver metal around clear glass. "I think you will like this."

I drank a sip. The dark liquid hit the back of my tongue before jolting down to my stomach to give me a warm embrace all over from there. My thoughts returned full force after I drained the cup. I both cursed, and welcomed it.

Ida dressed me in a blue dress. The color reminded me of the tiny flowers that usually grew in with the hay in the fields by our house. She tamed my hair into something presentable once I had another cup of the strong coffee within me.

I chewed on a mint leaf as I met Spacya in the hallway right outside her door. She eyed me up and down, "You're still too skinny. Once we hit a quest, you're gonna be a doner."

I cringed at the slang for dead that I hadn't heard in a while. "I'm eating as much as I can."

She grunted, "I know."

Blari and the priest that guided us last night joined us, and we progressed to the palace. The Matron waited for us at the large, open doors, a small smile on her face.

"How do you feel about taking a turn around the garden?"

"I think that would be nice." I was glad we had chosen flat shoes again.

"We have all day for you to mingle. The garden party, lunch, which they dressed you for, your dinner and the ball. I wanted to prepare you for the announcement section that will follow the party."

"Thank you." We turned, and I walked side by side with her down the path. Small flowers opened wide, to the dawn light, and their heads turned, seeming to follow the Matron as we passed.

The others flanked us, and she talked loud enough to be heard over the trickling water of a fountain as we passed it, "We will be on the grand staircase of my Tower when I make the announcement. Nadachia shall be at my side on the same step. Tori, as he is to become a companion, shall be one step lower at your side. Spacya across from him at my side, and Blari next.

"I will give a speech, all about heroes, of course. Then I will gift you a pin. You must wear it at all times during these gatherings, and when you re-enter the capital from your quests. I will announce your first quest. Here, there may be some that state themselves as a companion to you. You accept them, by taking their hand and shaking it as you would when meeting or completing a trade. Prince Tori among these. None have said anything to me about joining, so he might be the only one. Oh! Wait, I have to mention one of my favorite people will accompany you; her name is Sterla." The Matron's voice changed slightly, warming at the name, before she began again. "Next, there will be dancing in the square for all those that were not invited to the ball. You are allowed to mingle with them, but you must spend some time with the guests of the royals too."

"How long is this ball going to last?"

The Matron patted my hand, "All night probably, but you need not stay that long. You will meet me again in the morning and we will set you down the road for your first quest at that time."

"Any hints?"

The Matron shook her head, "No. That is not fair."

Spacya asked, "How is it not fair? We're the ones risking our lives."

"It is the drama. The play that people watch is now you and the quests you go on. We must show them your genuine reactions. You must be part of the parade, the principal attraction, for when you reenter Galanesse after each quest."

"We have to come back here? What if the next quest is closer to where we're at?"

The Matron shook her head and glanced back toward the castle, "Ah, they have found us out. It must be time for the garden party." She paused in our walk, turning to face all of us as we made a half circle around her, "You return after each. I have prepared matters for each quest. It is the way things are. Now, I excuse myself so that you can mingle with the others."

We watched her go.

Spacya crossed her arms over her chest and huffed. She leaned against a tree that had thick vines twisted all about the trunk beside the path, "That's ridiculous and a waste of time."

"If the next quest is dangerous, traveling back and forth could mean the lives of innocents," Blari added.

"Agreed. Maybe once we're out we can fix that." I lifted a shoulder, the twinge of pain less than when I left Owlimount at last. The very thought of going against someone as powerful as the Matron made shivers go down my spine.

"Chi!"

I looked up to see Clara in a flaming orange gown wave at me. Beside her was Prince Tori, and both were coming toward us. My shivers settled slightly at the sight of someone familiar to me.

Clara pushed a small plate into my hands. It held a cream-colored cake with smooth icing and fruit spread over it. "Try this. It's the best thing that will ever pass your lips and that includes a lover's tongue."

Tori stared at her, then shook his head, "Clara…really."

"What? It's the truth." Clara grinned at me, "Even if that tongue is a prince's or Taspe's."

Blari sputtered, and looked away as if suddenly interested in a flower hanging from the tree Spacya was leaning against.

I sighed, "How many times do I have to tell you we don't have that kind of relationship?"

"Several. I think you should." Clara grinned after she nodded sagely, her pink curls bouncing.

Tori asked, "Taspe? As in the Welkan Legace? That would make sense, he lives near Owlimount, doesn't he?"

"That's the one." Clara and I stated at the same time.

"Fer someone who claims to not be much, you know plenty of high people." Spacya said from her relaxed state, "The Legace to the largest Welkan Legacy, a princess of Ecia, and who else?"

"As The Hero, she gets to meet more of us… higher people too."

I lifted the fork off the plate and cringed as it clanked. I was still shaking, even with Clara there. No one else seemed to notice. Once I got a bite to my mouth, citrus scents tickled my nose. I let the piece rest against my tongue as the orange, lemon and cream flavors burst upon it. All my thoughts went toward the delightful flavor.

"What is this?" I asked, after chewing and swallowing several bites.

Clara beamed, her eyes bright, "That, my dear, is the gift of the gods called Citrus Dream Cake."

"It is a dream." I took another bite, and a sound broke from me.

Clara giggled as Tori cleared his throat.

"Well, I'm gonna find some of that cake." Spacya pushed off the tree and headed back toward the castle.

I felt my cheeks grow hot as I looked at Clara, "Did I really do that?"

"Yup. Now we know what notes you make when pleasured. Be careful, we'll have all your secret sounds before Taspe does." Clara winked at me.

I rolled my eyes, but kept digging into the cake. Once I finished, a server gathered my empty plate.

"Let's stretch our legs, shall we?" Tori held out his arm.

We walked arm in arm, Clara on my other side with Blari on hers. The sun caused her pink hair to glisten. She was always changing her hair colors, but this one seemed to suit her the best.

I glanced around. Some of the people I had met the day before, and many more, were watching us as they walked along the open garden paths as we did. If their eyes were not upon us, then they were on the King and Queen, to the back corner of the garden, or on their children.

I swallowed the bile that threatened the enjoyment of the cake. I was going to need to see a healer if this kept up. In this part of the garden, hedges were lining the paths, along with flowers. We passed another fountain on the way to the low rolling hill. Inside the reservoir were little fish with scales that shone in the sunlight in many hues. I was not familiar with this type of fish. I wished Detri were here so he could watch them with me.

"It's beautiful here."

"We hoped you would like it." Tori said, "The gardens ahead are perfect for dodging others' eyes as the hedges are taller. There's a maze too."

"We can tell you who is good or bad to talk to. Some of these people can be nasty, or just downright boring." Clara added.

We walked along. One of us would stop to marvel at a beautiful flower. Tori knew some of the names for them, or Clara, the others we guessed at. Making a small game out of it. The statues we passed were of heroes, gods, advisors, kings and queens and royals of old. There were a few priests too. Blari readily told us who they were, and fed us bits of knowledge about all of them if we asked.

We paused by a larger fountain to sit along the wide sunwarmed marble edge. The fish within tickled my fingertips with hungry little mouths and soft fins when I dipped my hand into the cool water. A breeze gently blew the scents of all the flowers together with the salty air. If only Moko were here to capture the pretty picture the garden made in one of her paintings.

At a call from someone nearby, Clara excused herself, dragging Blari with her. "I'll not deal with him alone. Besides, you need to mingle too."

Tori stretched his legs out, crossing his shined boots at the ankles. He plucked a small blue flower from a vine beside him and turned to place it above my ear, "Are you alright?"

I nodded, swallowing again, as if it would rid me from missing my family. "Just missing someone."

"Taspe?"

I laughed, "Clara's already gotten to you." I shook my head, "No, well, yes, in a way. Mostly my family."

"How about friends, do you have lots of those?"

"What friends I have became family long ago."

"I couldn't imagine having friends like that." Tori looked down at the toes of his boots, "I'm only close to a few of my family. Royalty, we're different I suppose."

I studied the angle of his jaw, his tawny skin, "In many ways. Rich. Haughty. Used to getting everything."

Tori's eyes narrowed when they swung back to me, "Some of us are. Not all. You like Clara well enough. Sure, she gets a lot of things, but she's also got a good heart."

"And you?"

He opened his mouth, only to shut it. After a moment he said, "I get my way, I admit."

"Now why are you sulking, Tori?" Clara asked when she bounded back up to us. Blari was still caught up in a conversation with the person who had called Clara over. "Rushed in to ask her to dance for the ball already, did you?"

"No, not yet." Tori said with a frown at her.

I looked down at the pool and saw in its reflection how they shared a glance. I changed my gaze toward the maze and stood. I took a step toward it, pausing as Clara clasped my hand. She smiled brightly as she swung our hands between us.

"Don't worry about Tori, he's not normal."

"You are the abnormal one, Clara." Tori stood and walked beside us.

"Not all can be broody like you."

"At least I don't act like a child."

Clara sighed before saying with a lilt to her voice, "A child is much better than being an old toad."

"I like toads though." I murmured.

"See, Tori, you might make a friend yet."

Chapter 10

Mother and Seaghla finally made their appearance halfway through the day. They entered just as the bells started tinkling from the North tower of the church, signaling lunch. Mother's grin was infectious, as were her watering eyes. Her grip around me was strong, and I burrowed into her graying hair. She felt much thinner than I remembered. The sweet scent of cinnamon and body powders tickled my nose as they always did when she was near.

"Oh Nadachia, how I have missed my heathen girl." She grinned, pulling away to hold me at arm's length.

I took her in as well. My mother had always been the picturesque lady. One that poems could have been written about. As I looked, I noted the gray strands feathering through her dark blonde hair and the paper thinness of her skin. Her once full cheeks, now sunken. She shook in my hands, as if she were chilled.

"Look how pretty you are!" Seaghla exclaimed.

I drew my gaze from mother to her, finding that not much changed there. Her golden tresses were longer, curled more. Her brown eyes seemed softer, more kind, or maybe knowing. I smiled and hugged her. "Never as pretty as you. Edi sends his regards."

Color rose in her cheeks as we ended the hug on that note, and she glanced away.

Mother clutched at me, drawing me back to her. "My girls have always been beautiful. One just took after me, and the other after her father." She squeezed my hand, "But even Rossi of Silverequis knows how to present himself."

Someone cleared their throat behind me, and I turned to see Tori.

"I don't mean to interrupt, but lunch is beginning. I am to escort the three of you to your seats."

As he spoke, Mother and Seaghla dropped into deep curtsies. She didn't let go of my hand, not even for the curtsy.

Sam Wicker

"Oh, yes, please." Mother paused, glancing at my hand in hers.

Tori smiled and offered her his arm. She kept a tight hold on me. I didn't think she had missed me that much. She was probably doing it so I wouldn't do anything odd or embarrassing. We walked down the path. Walking past the maze, we entered into a section of the garden that was corded off earlier.

The pretty little white tents had cloth under them to cover the grass and housed low lying tables with dinnerware set. In the middle were platters of fingerfoods and pitchers of fruity drinks. Cushions to either side of the tables looked plush and some of the royals were already sitting and partaking of the lunch.

Tori led us to where the Queen, King a few of the other princes and princesses were and helped my mother and Seaghla sit on the soft cushions before taking his place across from us. After the pleasantries with our table mates, they began telling me about their stay in the capital, especially when they heard I was the Hero. They asked me about home.

I told them about little Kentrim, the newest addition to our family. About Tokli finally opening up. It took him a while to talk to us in a relaxed manner after his father, my uncle, dropped him off with us.

"What about Joni?" Seaghla asked.

I speared a piece of juicy white meat with my fork, "What about him?"

"Why isn't he here with you?"

"Because he's a coward."

"Now, Nadachia," Mother began, "Joni is not a coward."

"If he isn't then he would do this instead of me."

"You got it though." Seaghla smiled, "Why would it be him?"

I sighed and shook my head. We made some more small talk about the family and about the things they did in Galanesse. Mother had taken up a job to help ends meet. She was one of the finest seamstresses in the capital, according to Seaghla.

After we finished eating, we roamed the gardens again. More royals, advisors, and people of note had arrived during the lunch. They wormed their way into our little circle.

One such charmer, couldn't get a hint. Somehow, he cornered me. "I could make it worth your while." His spotted digits curled over my hip as his breath floated down to burn my nostrils.

I peeled his hand off, a few knuckles cracked under my fingers, "What exactly are you going to make 'worthy of my while' again?"

Undeterred, he leaned into me and down to place his lips against the shell of my ear, "My bed, tonight, and you shall find out."

I jerked my knee. He whimpered, his body folding in on itself. I grabbed his nose, easily done as it was as large as a waterfowl's, and squeezed it before twisting hard. I felt the cartilage pop. He howled, and I let go of him with a shove so he fell, the gravel clattering away from me.

Tori was at my side, calling to a nearby guard as he picked the royal up and twisted his skinny arm behind him so he couldn't lunge at me. The prince passed the man to the guard. He wasn't some useless prince after all.

Mother pulled a handkerchief from her bosom and passed it into my palm. "Nadachia, I believe a simple 'no' would have sufficed, don't you think?" Her voice was light, mouth smiling slightly, but her hand clutched my wrist as if it would save her life.

"He wanted to bed me. Tonight." My lips twitched as spiders walked down my spine.

Seaghla, finishing her prim pouting routine at how Prince Tori had been torn from her side, scrunched up her nose, "What an awful old man."

"Well, my Hero, you have caused a stir again already." The Matron floated toward us down the path from the shadows of a grand tree with spring leaves just starting on its wide arrangement of branches.

Mother and Seaghla curtsied. I could barely manage a tilt of my head. *Was I about to be punished?*

Those dark eyes narrowed on me as she stopped in front of me. She flicked her fan of gossamer black lace and began gently fanning her face and neck, "Never fear. The duke shall not approach you again. He likes his women far more willing."

Duke? I might as well have broken a prince's nose.

"He certainly won't find willingness in me." I clenched my teeth to keep them from chattering. *What if he had friends here? What if they came after me like he did, but I was alone? Could I take care of them as I did him?*

Her fan fluttered, she changed the trajectory, so I was now getting air. The lace smelled of something metallic with a hint of citrus. It tortured my nose, and I shook my head to keep from sneezing.

She turned her fan back toward herself. "You realize you are now one of the most eligible women in Lanpress, yes? You are going to be flirted with, hit on, and pawed at by many. Some worse than he, some better, and some may even interest you." Her dark eyes flicked to the queen who was across the way, on another path, "Of course, she would have you marry within her bloodline. I have superior prospects in mind for you."

My mother's fingers tightened on my wrist. If my thoughts could focus on anything other than what the Matron said, I would have feared my hand would go numb from Mother's grip. *Marriage?* What an absurd notion. *Was everyone here under the feverish pheromones of spring mating?*

"I wouldn't dream of marrying my best friend. What makes you think you could make me marry a complete stranger?"

The Matron lowered her fan to show the serpentine curve of her lips. Her gaze flicked to my Mother and held for a moment, and then to Seaghla, before looking back into my eyes again, "For love, of course."

The fan snapped closed, with that metallic scent wafting toward me. *Blood.* My brain clicked on the odor at last. Not human blood, but Stygra blood. The deep metallic, earthy scent of Stygra blood was in the lace. *Why?*

Wait. For love?

Her gaze flicked to my family again, her lips curling upward a bit more, "One would think you would want the best for them, your loves. Even if humans have such brief lives." She paused, flicking her fan back open in front of her face.

Did she just take in a deep breath to scent the blood? Was it really blood? Was my mind playing tricks on me?

My blood ran cold as her words twisted and formed many meanings in my mind. My heart plummeted. My Mother's hand loosened slightly, shaking harder.

I stepped in between the Matron and my Mother. Me. A tiny human pulling my tinier mother behind me as if I could stop the most powerful of all Stygra from harming her. I wanted to laugh at my own foolishness. Surely, I was mistaken. Every muscle felt tight in me.

"For those I love, I will do anything to keep them safe."

"And happy?" The Matron asked.

"Yes, but the other always comes first. I will risk the happiness to make them safe."

Something darker flashed in those eyes, right above the lace of her fan, "You have a spark. I was wondering if you were at all worth anything."

Blari came up, his cheeks puffing out, "I have never had to talk so much in my life. Not even when I had to do all the sermons for two weeks." He grinned, then his lips twitched downwards as he looked between all of us.

The Matron made a soft noise, not quite a giggle, but not a snort either. A smileless sound. "Get used to it. It will only get worse from here." She tilted her head to me. "Until next time, my little spark of a Hero."

"What happened?" Spacya strode up to me and glared at the young royal or advisor or whatever he was who sat beside me until he excused himself. She settled in his vacated chair and grabbed a soft, fragrant stick of buttery bread from the basket between us. It was the only food currently on the tables.

I took a piece as well, tearing it into bits before popping them into my mouth. The butter made my fingers glisten in the candlelight. "I broke an old man's nose cause he wanted me to bed him tonight."

Spacya grunted around a mouthful of bread, "And after that?"

My gaze moved toward the Matron and then the royals at the head of the table. I was told to sit in the middle. None of them were paying attention to be at present for Blari was relating a story of some sort. "You and Blari come to my rooms tonight, after everyone is asleep. We'll have something to talk about."

She followed my gaze with her mismatched eyes, "Aye, that'd be best."

The flurry of hundreds of servers interrupted us as they carried out our first course. A blue soup. *Who ate blue soup?* I couldn't fathom what it would taste like, as it didn't produce that much of an odor.

Mother leaned forward from across the wide table, "It's a creation of the Royal Family, the second prince, Aphonse, to honor Welkans."

My brow twitched up. Now that I understood, it reminded me of the colors of their banners here. I spooned a sip into my mouth. At first I noticed the thickness as it coated my tongue. The sweet flavor seemed like I was tasting how the blue flowers smelled out in the garden.

"Not bad, if'n you like flowery thin's."

Mother smiled at Spacya, "It's become one of my favorite indulgences."

I turned as boots scuffed on the marble near me and met the gaze of Prince Tori.

"I wanted to be the first to ask you to dance."

My last mouthful turned to stone as it headed down. I covered my mouth, tried to clear it, and nodded. I couldn't trust the sudden frog in my mouth to not make a fool of me.

Something twinkled in his green eyes, "Is that a yes?"

"Yes, of course it is!" Mother cried behind me.

I sighed, the act releasing the frog and the stone slightly, "Yes, thank you." I felt a sting of realzation and added, "You will probably regret asking."

"Why would that be?"

"I'm not a good dancer. Shouldn't dance at all."

Tori chuckled, "No matter. My boots are thick. They're good enough for me to walk with; they should be good enough to support you too." With another bow of his head, he strode back to his seat toward the head of the table.

The unspoken retort on my tongue burned.

Seaghla whispered harshly, reaching across the table to dig her claws into my hand, "Don't you dare bruise him!"

I shook her off and bent back to my soup, "He's a grown man. If he can't manage a few bruises then he shouldn't ask to dance."

Spacya chuckled into her chalice.

They took away the first course, and the second was served simultaneously. The gentle clatter of delicate plates and utensils was more welcoming to my ears than the constant buzz of voices in the room. The vegetables added color to the little pile of herbs and lettuce greens in this dish. I picked up a fork, only to pause at Seaghla's gasp and Mother's lips pursing.

I looked from one to the other of them.

Mother casually pointed to the other fork with her pinky as she dapped the corners of her mouth with a napkin.

The muscles in my jaws were gaining a terrible workout today as my teeth clenched. I traded forks. When Mother gave a curt, tiny nod, I dug into the salad. The strong vinaigrette hit my tongue and nearly took my breath away. Maybe I should have made a show of stirring the greens and vegetables on my plate like a real heathen.

The rest of the meal passed with listening to the small talk of Mother and Seaghla to our neighbors. They knew the many things that occurred in Galanesse. The latest fashions. The rising stars of the theatre. The great singers of the time. New books.

I glanced at Spacya. Her eyes were as glazed over as mine felt. At least I wasn't alone in my misery.

Once others were finished, they made their way out and down the hall. Music drifted into the dining room from the dance hall. Tori appeared at my side and took the vacated seat. Spacya was still downing the deep red liquid in her chalice. I had lost count of how many refills she'd had.

The worst was how boldly Seaghla stared at the prince.

"How many siblings do you have?"

Tori smiled, "Ten and a half-sister too."

I blinked, and started to look to the queen, but she had already left for the dance hall. "Your mother doesn't look old enough, or she looks good, rather." I stumbled over my words and shook my head.

Tori chuckled, "They started early. Jesmina, the oldest, was born a year and a few months after they married. It was at least three years before my grandparents gave the throne to my mother. And the last two are twins."

"I heard a story that your mother and father actually love one another. Is that true?" Seaghla asked, a croon in her voice.

"Yes, it is a rare occurrence among royals. Especially those born to rule."

"It's rare to find love in any rank, I think." I downed my chalice too, thinking Spacya might have the right idea.

"I would imagine so." Tori said and kept his eyes on me as he asked, "Do you hope to find love? Or have you found love?"

My wine spluttered from my lips. I dabbed at my chin with the back of my hand and immediately regretted it as Mother glared at me. "I hope to survive. Don't have time or the luxury of dreaming about love."

"Nadachia," Mother said my name like a curse.

It wasn't my fault he asked a ridiculous question while I drank. I hoped my glare told her as much. Both Seaghla and Mother returned my glare, so I doubted they got my message. Theirs was always more important.

Tori's eyes darted between my mother and I twice before he looked toward the hall. I caught a smile changing his cheeks out of the corner of my eye. Bastard knew I was going to get into trouble.

"Come along. We need to change for the ball." Mother stood, her lips pursed. Seaghla quickly followed suit, as did Tori.

"This is fine. I need some more wine," I said. Drunk me wouldn't care how many feet I stepped on, and I wasn't anywhere nearing the level I needed to be.

"Nadachia." Mother said my name again, like a curse.

I groaned and stood.

Spacya chuckled and patted my shoulder, "There's more wine in the ballroom, I bet."

That was promising.

As large as the castle was, I didn't know why Mother, Seaghla and I were in the same changing room. Other than to allow her to lecture me on acting properly. Mother's voice buzzed in my ears. I closed my eyes, letting Ida work, and wished I had more wine. Something stronger would be even better.

"Are you even listening?"

"Of course, Mother." The years she'd been gone hadn't dulled my instant response time to the inflection in her voice. I even opened my eyes so I could smile at her.

She smiled back. Satisfied. The separation had dulled her intuition of my actions and responses. A minor gift from the gods.

"Do give me a dance or two with Prince Tori."

I felt my brow twitch. Mother and Seaghla were not changing. Something about it being a hassle to have their dresses sent here. But Seaghla did change her gloves to a nicer set. "I can't control him. You can have all the dances with him for all I care."

That caused multiple gasps around the room. At least the maids could cover their shock by completing their tasks.

Mother, on the other hand, had her mouth open in an 'o' shape. Her cheeks flushed. "Nadachia Wanya Dietra of Silverequis!"

They were going to have to find another hero.

"The Prince is the most eligible bachelor in all the country! No! Of all the allied countries. He is a precious gem that you WILL treat with respect. You WILL attempt to be nice to him. You WILL make an effort to engage him. And. above all else, you WILL endeavor to marry him."

Forget the chalices of wine. I needed a cask. I hated my lineage for being able to handle drink with ease.

"Of course, Mother, as you say." My jaw hurt from speaking through my teeth.

Clara breezed into the room. "There you are!"

I watched Mother as Clara grinned at me. Watched her lips go thin and press into themselves. My shoulders and jaws relaxed. She would not speak another word on the subject while the Princess was here. Nor would she kill me.

I was going to live long enough to die a hero.

"Don't you all look so beautiful. It's so nice to see you again!" Clara beamed at Mother, and Seaghla even as she grasped one of my hands.

"It is a pleasure, as always, Princess Clara." Mother bowed and Seaghla followed suit.

"Oh now, stop. No need to bow to old friends. Please." She fluttered her free hand toward them and smiled when Mother and Seaghla straightened. "There, that's much better. I'm going to walk with your daughter to the ballroom, if I may?"

"Of course." Mother answered with a strained smile.

Clara whirled us out of the chamber, "Now then, are you still breathing?"

"Yes, just."

The Princess of Ecia giggled before she said, "Oh, she can chill a room with a glance and a word. I always admired that of your mother."

I shook my head, not able to comment as she babbled on.

"Now, Chi, I know Tori has the first dance. I must insist on the second, if he will let you go. He is rather selfish at these dances. I believe he's already smitten with you too."

"I'm a shiny new thing."

"That you are." She smiled and squeezed my hand, "But after the newness wears off, they will see the true you and still be amazed."

I highly doubted that, but didn't say anything because it would start an argument.

"Green is such an excellent color on you." She plucked at the emerald swishing around my legs. "I can't pull it off very well. Red and purple are my best colors."

I could see that she was right about reds. She was wearing a dress that reminded me of the soft hues of a robin's breast. "You look pretty in anything, probably. I can't wait to get back into regular clothes."

Clara giggled, "Now are these clothes you speak of the half nakedness Taspe made you don that one time..."

Gods. No. I waved a hand in front of her glossy lips.

Her grin was toothy. "I figured it was Taspe making you do that instead of you. I know how you like your long boots and pants and all those ridiculous layers." She shook her head, and sighed, "I'm not so sure I can stand pants again on these quests with you."

I stopped. It was sudden enough that she jerked backwards toward me before being able to stop herself, "With me?"

Her grin became toothier, "Oh, yes."

"But you're the eldest!"

Clara patted my cheek with a soft hand, "An adventure with you shall be the most challenging and fun I will have in my life. Besides, someone has to smooth over your temper with the locals and who better than a born diplomat?"

"It won't be safe! You won't be safe!"

With a tilt of her head, she said, "I'm never safe." A darkened shadow fell across her eyes, "I might actually be the safest I've ever been in going with you."

I glanced around the hall. We were just outside the music room, ball room, whatever it was called. My fear for her gripped my heart.

"Trust me, darling. I can handle myself. I'll be a help."

I nodded, formulating ways to ensure her safety on the road with the four of us. She should be in the middle at all times.

"Besides, that new friend of yours can probably scare just about anything off with a look."

I grinned, "Let's hope so."

Chapter 11

As soon as there was a moment, I grabbed a slumbering Blari from the corner and made our escape. The gravel of the garden path between the castle and church bruised my throbbing feet more. My back and shoulders were killing me from keeping them straight and my arms up. I hadn't a clue who I ended up dancing with other than Tori and Clara, thankfully those two were several times over otherwise my sanity would have flew away long ago.

The festivities in the courtyard beyond the high garden wall echoed down to us before we shut ourselves into the safety of the church. Spacya opened her door when I knocked, still half dressed in her finery. Blari fell asleep leaning against the wall next to her room. "We'll talk after some sleep." For it was already morning.

She nodded.

After making sure Blari's aid took him in, I made my way to my room. Ida helped me peel the dress off, and slipped the nightgown over my head. It was cool against my heated and aching body. I waited until she finished tucking me in, gathered my ball things, and left before I slid back out of the bed.

My feet and legs protested with sharp pains up the shins as I hobbled over to the desk. None of the words I'd formed through the night were elegant. The letters were not going to be anything special either. I sat down, rubbing my calves and bare feet for a moment, trying to ease the aches, before I settled in to write.

Father,

It is the night before my party and I are to receive our first quest. I worry for you and my siblings. Keep them safe. Keep Vigilant. Know that I love you with all my being and will do my best to come back to you. To make you proud.

The Matron has ideas. Promises. So do the royals. Promises of things that I might have misunderstood, but I want you to know my misgivings. Be careful.

Mother and Seaghla send their love.

Nadachia

The quill's scratch over the thick paper soothed me, reminding me of listening to Moko's quills as she wrote her poems. I didn't know how far I could go in writing out the unspoken things that flitted around in my mind that still made my blood run cold. I didn't want my family to be in danger. If someone else should read it before my father, I didn't want people to get too much information.

Perhaps I was mistaken.

I slipped it into an equally thick envelope with silver trim. Addressing it in the most careful hand I could muster was a task nearly beyond me after dancing all night, but I managed. Then I began my other task.

If anything should happen to me: death, not of sound mind, the following is to be my will.

I, Nadachia Wanya Dietra of Silverequis, hereby give my father, Rossi Titsui of Silverequis and my mother, Wanya Dietra of Silverequis, the full right to plans and execution of my health, and burial rights. All my worldly goods are to be distributed to my family per my father's and mother's wishes, as named above. All that is to be paid and made to me by the capital, Galanesse of Lanpress, and its people to be decided by my father and mother as well.

Of sound mind, without inhibition,

Nadachia Wanya Dietra of Silverequis

I made a copy of my wishes, and started another letter.

Taspe,

Do not think much of the envelope I have enclosed. Once I die or become a burden, you must open it. Not before then. You know how greedy humans can get.

I hope this finds you well and you are not in another battle. I don't know if I said thank you for all you and your people have done for my family, so I will say it here. Thank you.

I also ask that you keep looking after them. When are you going to make a family I can look after?

Just so you know, Clara is here. She's going to be one of my companions. At least I will have someone at my side that I've met more than once. Someone I can trust. Maybe just enough. You once told me she was fierce. I've seen hints of it now.

Take care, please.
With all my love,
Chi

While waiting for the ink to dry and failing in getting the same sized envelope inside one another, I looked up into the faces of the two moons. It was a few hours until dawn, and I doubted sleep would come to me. I wondered if it was the same for the people in my heart, if they were looking at the moons with me.

Ida pried the quill from my numb fingers, "What were you doing?"

At her words and touch I jerked, nearly falling off the chair. I groaned and peeled the blank sheet of paper off my cheek and lay it back on the desk. "Couldn't sleep." My own voice sounded foreign to me.

Her brows were low over her eyes as she read the scrawl over the two letters. One within a makeshift envelope that I was quite proud of, considering I had to make it out of two. "Nadachia…"

"Will you make me some coffee?" I interrupted her, folding my copy of my last wishes and tucking them in a central desk drawer, making sure Ida watched.

She stared at me, her throat convulsing with a swallow, her eyes lining with tears. She nodded and went about making me some of the bitter liquid. I glanced out the window, the sun's first hues of orange hitting the ocean beyond the trees and gardens.

The girl made quick work of my coffee as I stood. Things popped that probably shouldn't in my body and I stretched my aching muscles as best as I could. Feeling old and broken was a great way to start off my first official day as the Hero.

Ida filled the bath with lavender petals as I waded into it after stripping out of my nightclothes. My muscles eased their tightness more as I floated in the hot water. I napped.

After my hands and feet grew wrinkled as sunned fruit, Ida pulled me out of the bath and began her ritual. By the time she was done with drying my hair and twisting it into a couple of braids to pin to my head, I finished the entire pot of coffee.

"We've upgraded some of your clothes." Ida announced as she led me to the dressing room. My boots and bag were the same. I had to wear a corset in my travels apparently. After she shoved me into it, Ida pointed out the daggers Willa had sewn into the contraption.

"Well if that doesn't make it more uncomfortable I don't know what will." I muttered under my breath as I tugged on my shirt. It showed off more of the corset than I liked, but at least it covered my arms so I wouldn't get sunburnt. Next was a brown leather vest with bits of iron in it to deter attacks over the forest green shirt. It wasn't the most protective piece, but it would help.

I would have to be half naked before I could touch the daggers in the corset. That was probably the point, last resort. At least I couldn't tell the difference between the daggers in it and the boning.

After Ida slipped daggers in all the places along my calves, boots, and two more on my thighs, I did a count. I held thirty-six daggers on my person. "I don't think I can carry much else."

Ida snorted with a smile as she helped put my belts on with the last of my weapons.

I placed my jewelry on, the ring already soothing away the tiredness the coffee hadn't with just a brush of my fingers over it. Hauling my pack up on my shoulder, I gave Ida a grin.

"See you soon," she said, "I'll ask the gods to bless and protect you every night until your return."

"Thank you. I'll need them." I was at the point where my nervousness and rolling stomach were constant. I moved to the desk and placed the letters in her hand, "Can you make sure these get to my family?"

"Yes." She hugged them to her chest. Her dark eyes drifted over to the desk, where I hid my will, "I shall see that remains safe too."

"Thank you." I blinked back the burning in my eyes and swallowed the fear back down into my stomach before I would cause a scene. I entered the main dining hall and Blari waved me over to the table.

The priest stared into my face as I sat across from him, placing my pack down at my feet. No priests were with us, just my companions and I. I could hear the cheers outside, and guessed where the other priests were.

"Did you sleep?"

I lifted a shoulder and poured myself another cup of coffee.

Spacya plopped some scrambled eggs and two pieces of toast onto my plate. She didn't take another bite until I did. I rolled my eyes at her and tried to keep the bites down. I knew I had to eat something. My body just didn't appreciate it.

A side door opened and I heard the patter of Clara's feet before a clunk of boots moments before she burst into the dining room. "Have you seen your horses?"

"They haven't been outside yet, Clara." Tori said as he sat down beside Blari.

"They're so pretty!" Clara's voice reminded me of a child opening presents. She sat beside me and grabbed a muffin.

Spacya's brows hitched over her one good eye, "We get horses?"

"Of course! Surely you weren't planning to *walk* all over the country." She glanced between us, then grinned, "Nevermind. You have horses!"

Tori cleared his throat before speaking, "After we eat, we are to ride a circuit through the city. The people want a good look at you." He smiled at me, "Then we meet the Matron on the Tower steps. Finally, we start our journey."

"It'll be midday." The huntress glared at the prince.

He nodded, "That's the plan though."

I finished what was on my plate, and stood. Clara shoved a muffin into my hand. I glared at it for a moment, before putting it on top of the things in my pack. "Let's get this over with."

Each step toward the tall, heavy oak doors brought the roar of the crowd outside closer. I counted the steps. Each one I wished that I was somewhere else with all my might.

The priests opened the doors with the gear and crank system. The sun was not bright in the sky yet, the mists of the ocean and Gala River not burned off completely. In the gray hued courtyard, a sea of people were held at bay by a ring of guards wearing the green silks of the royal court. Wide wooden pieces were attached to their arms, reminding me of fence posts, and they used them to create a human fence.

As I stepped out, my companions slightly behind me, the cheer became a roar that set my ears ringing.

"Here are your rides."

I paused on the third step from the bottom, staring at the horses. I looked at the members of my party. Two I had spent little more than a week with, one I'd known for a few days, and Clara, I had known for years, but not consistently. Couple that with beasts that didn't know any of us, except Tori and Clara.

This was going to be a disaster.

Horses were bred for their environment. The capital horses had evolved from their meticulous breeding into flamboyant beasts. Their claws were shorter, to not clack so much on the stone or paved roads, and the pads of their hooves were thick, calloused, to protect them from the heat of the streets. Tails and manes were as colorful as the plumage of wild birds in the deep forests.

Clara and Tori's horses were of this breed. The fancy breed of the cities.

My horse, was less ostentatious. Her coat was a mottled black and white with touches of gray-blue. Her claws were that of the wilderness horses, long and thick, perfect for protection and gripping earth and bark. Her tail and mane were iridescent, shining in the sun's light with many colors, like the wings of some of the river insects. She was gorgeous.

The stifling and obnoxious crowd faded a little as I stepped up to her. She arched her thick neck, her nostrils flaring as I placed my hand near them for her to scent me. Her velvet nose pushed into my palm. I caressed her nose, then the flat wide spot between her full black eyes.

"Her name be Unia, Hero." The servant who held her head spoke loud enough to be heard over the still cheering crowd.

Unia was armored, like the rest of the horses. Her claws tipped with silver to make them that much more dangerous. They covered her chest with a plate of the same color. They also fit the bone structure of her mane and tail with thin, paper-like blades and sheets of armor.

I mounted, not as graceful as I had hoped with pack and a blanket tied to the back of the saddle. Still, the crowd cheered even louder. Unia arched her neck and pranced in place. Showoff. At least one of us was happy to be in a crowd. The servant reached for my pack, and I gave it to him with a frown. He darted through the guards and toward the Tower, fading into the mass of bodies.

I should've held on to that.

Tori and a mounted guard led the way through the city. On every street, there were people surrounding us. They stood between us and the tall or squat buildings, or around the stalls of the market streets, or walked beside us through the narrower ones between houses.

By the time we completed the circuit, I was wondering why it wasn't dark yet. If not for the ring, exhaustion would drag at me.

Unia kept prancing along like everything was fine, but even she had a sheen of sweat. We dismounted in front of the black, shimmering Tower.

If only we had just crossed the courtyard to begin with.

The Matron stood on the top step. Her dress was a black gossamer thing that mimicked the starlit night stones of the Tower behind her. Behind her stood seven Stygra of varying heights, weights and whether or not they smiled.

The Matron lifted her arms once we arranged ourselves in front of her.

The crowd immediately quietened.

I looked up at her, and her black eyes met mine. They drifted. To a spot behind me. I turned my head and saw a small Stygra girl standing at the edge of my peripheral, between Tori and Clara. I turned back, something crawling down my spine, immediately followed by a chill that shook my body even though the sun was well into warming the earth.

"Good morning, people of Galanesse! Look upon them! Your Hero! Nadachia of Silverequis!" A cheer rose up, crested, and fell back to silence before she went on, "A Hero from a long lineage known to us for being kind, intelligent and honorable!"

She introduced my companions, leaving off compliments or comments of their lineages, which I thought odd. By the time she got to her speech, my head throbbed with my erratic heartbeat. Her words echoed in my mind with the roar of the crowd when they were allowed to cheer.

"Here is a map. It will show the paths of least resistance to your active quest and back here once it is completed." After I took the map, she continued, "We have a quest! The village of Columbri, just north of us, suffers greatly. Our people there have suffered a monster, a beast, attacking the fishing vessels and the village itself. A beast the size and strength that none have seen before. We call it the Misshapen."

My heart sank. I feared how many people had died while I was being paraded around like some prized animal. I wondered how many families were starving because it destroyed their boat while I tried to fight down a bite and wasted the rest.

"As tradition persists, Hero Nadachia, I am to give you a gift and blessing!" The crowd cheered the loudest at this.

One of her clawed fingers poked my forehead between my eyes, "I bless you Nadachia, Hero of Humans," did she sneer the word human? "With the gift of life. You shall not die, so long as you hero quest with the life I broker for yours."

Pain poured from her finger into me, swathing my body in a heavy ache. There was a small gasp behind me, and the Matron smiled in my face.

I blinked, and the sting faded. Only a lingering sensation deep within my chest remained. Not of pain, of something holding. Something there that was not mine.

"What do you mean?" I breathed, staring into those eerie eyes.

I imagined my life forever chained in service to her. Then I imagined watching those I knew and loved die without the grace of being able to follow suit. I imagined the pain, the suffering of lifetimes ahead of me.

She whispered, "Isn't it a wonderful feeling?" She looked out onto the sea of people, "Let's set our Hero and her Companions on their way to save the lives of our fellows in Columbria!"

I turned, seeking the origin of the gasp when the pain entered me. My eyes landed on the little Stygra between Clara and Tori. The thing in my heart pulled, as if there were a chain between her and I.

I swung back to the Matron. I wanted to scrape her face off with my own fingernails. As if she sensed my intention, the Matron smiled again. I held still in that gaze. Frozen like a small animal lost in the eyes of a predator.

"Sterla." She motioned to the girl. "I give you the gift of Sterla." She said as she placed her clawed hand on the little girl's shoulder.

Another tug.

Sterla bowed, and took my hand. Together we walked back down the steps. At some point, they drew a narrow wagon with a miniature horse hitched up beside our horses. Sterla dropped my hand as soon as we reached Unia, and climbed aboard the little wagon instead. She sat primly on the bench, and gathered the shimmering reins in her tiny hands.

My mind numb, still. I mounted Unia, and the horse had enough sense to follow Tori's out of the capital and onto the road. I slowed Unia, my mind forming thoughts again, until I was riding beside the wagon.

"It will be all well." Sterla's voice was soft, a slight lilt that made her simple words seem like a song.

"You want to come with me?"

"Yes, of course." Sterla turned to look at me. Her eyes were wide, and too dark in her slender, pale face. Her teins, the ridges on her head, were small and curled back against her skull. Her dull black hair hung to her shoulders, did not shine in the sunlight but seemed to soak it in.

"Sterla, my life-"

"Will be long and happy." Again that lilting song-like voice, and a smile that brightened her features. "The Matron has anointed you in the same way she keeps her blessing. You are so lucky!"

I looked forward, trying to figure out the spoken words. The tug in my chest when I looked at Sterla. Spacya's paleness. Blari not writing, but staring ahead blankly. Tori and Clara riding stiff in their saddles.

The life I broker for yours…

"Oh gods." I slid off the saddle, not stopping Unia. I tumbled to the ground and scrambled for the road's grassy edge. My stomach finally had the chance to empty.

A small hand fell on my back, just below my neck.

"Forgive my mess." I wiped my mouth off with some spring grass. I stood. Sterla was barely the height of my waist.

"Do you feel better now?" Sterla's face tilted, those wide eyes making her look like a fawn.

I nodded. It was partly true. My stomach no longer had anything to push up. It sat like a rock within me.

"Gods." I muttered again. I squatted, my head between my knees as my body heaved. Nothing came from it.

As long as you hero…

I had to get through this mess. Unscathed.

I heard in my mind each word come from the Matron's lips repeatedly. Remembered how her eyes looked, the curve of her thin lips, the tightness in her cheeks, the muscles as they moved to form the words. An ache grew in my mind.

There were tricks in there. She named no time. She could keep me until she tired of me, make me be a hero forever. Until she died. Or got bored. Could I live normally? Grow old? Die if my head got chopped off? How did that all work? No one could come back to life if their head was gone, right?

Bile rose in my throat. *How was that still there?* I kept it down. "Hero?"

"Call me Chi." It was an automatic response. I looked up at her from where I crouched.

In her pale hands was a canteen. I rinsed my mouth out. She got back in the wagon after I was through. As I stood I met Tori's gaze, Clara's; I knew they were trying to figure out what happened too by the tightness in their faces.

I took a deep breath. There were no perfumes to muddy the natural scents of the earth and sea. No smell of human inhabitants except for a faint hint at the capital behind us. We weren't half an hour out, yet on this road we could not see the capital's wonders for the cliff face. So be it. I welcomed this.

Chapter 12

"What we lookin' at?"

I'd halted Unia and the rest of my companions just before a bridge that led across the river to Columbria village. We were a few lengths from the sand beach to our left. The road for the past few lengths and up to Columbria held more sand than dirt in it.

That wasn't what stopped me.

Over the rolling hills barely big enough to be called hills, bits of debris dappled the gray beach. People were milling about, most wearing the many pocketed and hook marked clothing of fishmongers, and some stopped to shoo scavengers from smaller, darker piles. Bodies.

A pair of Columbrians pulled a cart and loaded the bodies onto it, further down the beach.

The stench of rotten flesh mixed with the salty sea air. The dank, dark scent of death constantly blew toward us off the ocean. It all looked gray. The sky, the ocean, the beach, even the people.

"Looks like they can't keep up with the damage caused." Clara murmured, closing her eyes and clasping her family sigil that hung around her neck. She often prayed with it between her fingers.

"Or it just hit." Blari said beside me, his wide sleeve held tight over his nose and mouth.

My horse shifted, digging her claws and flexing them in the sand of the road. A few of the villagers were heading our way, coming up the low dunes in quick even strides. They made walking in the loose sand look easy.

"You there! Who are you?" The woman leading the trio bellowed out as she paused in the middle of the long bridge.

"We are The Hero and her party!" Tori called back, his training as a prince showing in the pitch and carry of his voice across the expanse.

A brightness entered their countenances, one even smiled a little, as we moved to meet them. "Thank the gods!" Tears rimmed her eyes and glistened at the corners. "Come, I'll take you to our Priest Lindra, she will be so happy."

We followed the woman into the town. The two men ran back to the beach to continue their devastating work. I dismounted, choosing to walk beside her instead of riding, "What is your name?"

"I'm Mena, no one important." A grin broke her face as she looked at me. "We were about to take a meal break when we saw you coming."

"Mena, what did that?"

Her grin disappeared, her sun-reddened face going pale again. "The Misshapen is what we call it." She swallowed, her eyes drifting to the ground instead of staying on me, "It rises from the sea and grabs and smashes all it can with all its arms."

"Arms?" Spacya eyed Mena from atop her horse.

"Been hard to count all of 'em. But a kid said he counted twelve. Some have fingers, spikes, and still others just like a dishfish."

The only dishfish I had ever seen was a dead one on a trader's boat. He had told me they could squeeze into just about anything and had gotten their names from the line of dishes on their arms. They used them to suction to their prey and to help them in crawling along or in things. The legs were supposedly good to eat.

One big enough to do the amount of damage we saw on the beach would probably have the toughest meat ever.

Spacya, Clara and Blari kept talking with Mena. My mind locked on to odd thoughts. *I am here, The Hero. I'm supposed to be thinking of ways to save this village and all I can think of is some fishy meat? What was wrong with me?*

The grit of it settled in me. I had chosen this. I felt obligated to do this, and I had chosen to follow through. Come what may, my world had a hero, and it was me.

The village walls, made of dark pitch covered wood, were caked in white salts of varying degrees. The thickest were above the sands and in the crevices of the lumber. Most of the houses butted right up against these walls, made of the same dark, sea salt coated wood. A dampness presided over everything. Not even the fires in the many braziers along the roads could lessen the coolness of the damp air in the shadows of the walls. As we entered the square, a statue of Meandria welcomed us with open arms and a smile.

Blari immediately got off his deep chocolate brown barrel of a horse and paid his respects.

The church, not much bigger than the statue, stood in the center of the village. A priest opened the dark wood door and shuffled down the three stone steps. Her eyes were ringed with dark circles, her skin pallid, and the lines of her face deepened with the effort of a smile. "Welcome! We appreciate any help you may spare in our time of need."

"Lindra, this is the Hero's party." Mena motioned to us.

Tears spilled down her cheeks and Lindra fell to her knees before us, "Oh gods… thank you for your kindness! Thank you for sending us our Hero." When she finished, her eyes still spilling tears, she looked at all of us and murmured blessings.

I bent, taking her hands and pulling her back to her feet. A child scurried to Lindra's side. She motioned him toward our horses, and he and another boy took them. I dug for my pack in the back of Sterla's wagon, pulling it free before a man could lead it away.

Spacya lay a heavy hand on my shoulder, and I realized my pain was gone in it. "Learn what we're up against. I'm gonna help." She jerked her chin toward the beach.

I nodded as Tori claimed he would go with her. Clara, Blari and Sterla stayed by me. I looked back to the priest and said, "I'm Nadachia the Hero." Saying it aloud felt like a death sentence.

Lindra led us into the church. Barely moving bodies filled the pews. Most had a sheet or pillow, others had blankets piled on top of them. There were people milling about, some providing water with a bucket and ladle, and others gave needed care. There were some resting on the floor too, or sitting against walls.

Sterla spoke up, "I can heal. I want to help heal."

I nodded, and she took off into the pews before Lindra could say anything.

"You are already such a great help." Lindra breathed as she watched Sterla.

I couldn't tell if Sterla was really doing anything. Stygra magics weren't as flashy as Welkan magics. She looked tiny compared to the patient, a grown man with a huge gash across his chest, she spoke softly to.

"Come. I have an office that hasn't been taken over by the sick yet." Lindra led us down a narrow hall to the right of the rectory. "I'm afraid we will have to clear bedrooms for you. I didn't know when you were coming and…"

"No need. We will find a place to sleep." Even the hall held some of the sick and wounded. Some just looked green, as if caught with a cold, with no injuries showing.

Lindra followed my gaze before ushering us into her small office. "The monster spews water from its mouth. Those it touches end up like that. Sick. We have likened it to a poison, though we have yet to find a cure or manage to purge it from anyone fully yet."

"Poison and many limbs to smash and grab things. Does it do anything else?"

"Isn't that enough?" She paused, then tried to clear a place for all of us to sit around her desk. She had four chairs, all but one were full of half eaten food, papers and books, or medical supplies.

"When did it show up?" Clara asked.

"This morning. Dawn. The first attack was sixteen days ago."

If we didn't go to all the stupid dinners and dances we would have been here for this morning's attack. Maybe we could have made a difference. I motioned for Lindra to sit. "Please, you look exhausted. We've sat all the way here."

"Has anyone wounded it?" Blari asked, taking a seat in the chair he cleared, and began writing again.

"Yes!" Lindra brightened, straightening a little in her chair, "A captain and some of his crew here to deliver supplies. One of them blasted an arm and speared it before their ship went down. A sailor of the crew is here, sick with the poison."

"I would like to talk to them once we're done here."

"I can have him fetched. He isn't well enough to help at the beach, but he insists on making himself useful to the healers and patients here." Lindra stood and yelled down the hall for someone to bring her the boy from the monster limb ship.

She should really learn his name.

In a short while, after a few more questions were answered by the priestess, a pale, skinny teen stumbled through the door. I immediately finished clearing out the chair meant for me so he could sit. Clara pushed him into it.

"Are you the Hero?" He asked her, looking up at her with eyes rimmed in red and gray. His flesh was a light green and sweat coated it, as if he carried a high fever.

"No, I'm Princess Clara, one of the Hero's companions." She pointed to me, "That's your Hero, Nadachia."

His gaze stayed on me. I was measured as I asked, "Did you wound the monster?"

He shook his head, "No. The Captain and Harlii did. The Captain can create fire in balls and Harlii is the best with a harpoon in all the known waters." Something lit his eyes up as he talked, a strength returning to his face. "Blessed by some Welkans they were."

"Where are they?"

He shifted slowly in his seat, "I dunno. I lost sight of 'em when I went in. When one of those big arms smashed Toti, our ship."

I placed a hand on his shoulder, feeling the heat radiate from him through his shirt. He smiled a little, and I gave him a nod. I didn't know the words to say, but he offered me a nod back.

Sterla peered around the doorframe, then came in. "I think it's death."

I let my hand drop, "What?"

"What's in the spray it spits. The poison. It is death."

We all stared at her. She dropped her gaze to her feet, her hands twisting together in front of her. "I think I see a way to pull it out. There are a few other Stygra healers here, and I've talked to them. They aren't as trained as me, but I expect we might manage quite a few each day."

"Do it. Take all you need." Lindra cried, standing and placing both hands on her disheveled desk.

Sterla looked at me. Unmoving.

"Go," I told her, a little concerned at why she was asking my permission, of all people. "Do what you can."

She nodded and slunk out of the office. I turned back to the sailor. Lindra fell back into her chair. "Does it have a pattern? A way you can tell it's coming, or how it attacks, anything?"

Lindra rocked, her eyes squeezed shut and her lips moving, but no words came out. She blinked after a moment, then answered, "No, not that I know of."

She didn't seem to be much use with the actual monster. She was a great help with the people, I could see that.

"I bet if'n you can find Captain and Harlii they'll be able to tell ya."

"I bet they can too." I answered the boy. "Clara, you want to stay here and help, or do you want to come with me to try to find them?" I held a hand out to the feverish sailor, "You need to lie down."

Clara lifted a shoulder, "I'll take his place as errand master." She smiled at the boy.

"Just stay in here, boy. We'll both take a quick nap and then get on with it." Lindra smiled, putting her feet up on the desk and wriggling down into her chair as she motioned for the boy to do the same.

We left, Clara peeling off to start helping the healers while Blari and I made our way back outside. I spotted a gate that looked like it would lead directly to the beach and made my way to it. Once out, we met a cart hauling debris to a pit in the middle of the beach.

I asked the men pulling it, "Do you know where I can find the captain who wounded the monster, or a sailor named Harlii?"

They shook their heads.

"You plan on helping here at the beach, don't you?"

"Yes."

"You won't sleep will you?"

I shot a look at Blari, and then lifted a shoulder, "I'm going to do what I can. As much as I can."

A few people, and piles of wreckage loaded into carts later, we found Harlii.

His skin was sun darkened while his hair was sun bleached. He sported a wide bandage over his left side and upper rib cage. Harlii was sitting on a pile of rocks that jutted out into the water, plucking pieces of wood, metal, and other debris from a net. After seeing a man unwrap a bloated body from another net nearby, I knew they weren't trying to catch today's fish feast.

"Harlii?"

"Yeah, who's asking?" He paused in his work to look me up and down.

I began helping him pick the pieces out and tossed them into a cart just below the rocks, "Doesn't matter. I'm here to help with the monster."

"The Missapen," he said, his voice harsher than it had been when he answered my question. "Never seen nothing like nor had any nightmares that could match it."

"Heard that you and your captain wounded it."

"Lot of good it did. Still wrecked everyone and everything to get away." He said as we pulled out a heavy section of net from the ocean. Part of a sail tangled in with the thick threads.

I put my back into it, pulling it up close to him so he wouldn't have to. "It's something." I told him after I settled to help him untangle it.

His brow drew lower over his dark eyes, "I didn't throw well enough. It shoulda tore right through that arm the first throw."

"Why do you think it didn't?"

He shook his head, "The skin on it. It's thick, like a whale. Oily too. No, thicker and oilier than any whales I've gotten before."

I didn't have a clue how thick a whale was, so I looked at him. I could only build off his wonder and confusion. "What about the Captain's fire thing?"

His lips twisted, "That oil on it burns easy enough. I'll say that. That's what finally broke the arm off, his fire."

Sam Wicker

"The oil on the beast and not what your captain uses to create the fire?"

"Yup, lit up like the driest kindling you can find."

"If we fight it with fire, it'll go down."

He stared at me, his fingers stilling in his work, "I reckon so."

"Hero!"

I turned to see Sterla running toward me with an army of children and teens in tow. They all held baskets and buckets. She was grinning.

"Hero?" Harlii murmured behind me.

I focused on Sterla, "What?"

"Seaweed!" Sterla wheezed when she skidded to a stop by the rock, Harlii, Blari and I were on top of. "Need seaweed... takes out... poison."

Harlii acted before I did by grabbing a bucket off one of the kids and filling it with the seaweed plastered to the rock we stood on. "Have cap bellow it out." He pointed to a man hanging off what remained of a pier a few lengths away.

One kid started, but I caught him. "No, stay and gather what you can. That's dangerous." I ran toward the Captain, slowing as I crossed the boards placed over the broken pieces of the dock. He looked up at me as I neared, "Tell everyone the kids need seaweed to help stop the poison in the sick."

He whirled, almost slamming the handle of a hammer he was holding into my ribs. "What kids?" Then he noticed the little ones gathering what seaweed they could off the beach and rocks. He stood on top of one of the bare posts, stripped of the pier it once supported. He cupped one hand around his mouth, "Ho! Hi! Hey!" he bellowed out louder than the waves crashing in and the sounds of the hammers all around us.

My ears rang, so I placed my hands over them as he continued, "Weeds to the kiddos!" he shouted once all stopped their work and looked toward him, "Weeds to the kids to stop the poison. Weeds to the kids." The Captain pointed his hammer to the kids along the beach.

Soon the youngsters were scrambling back to the church with arms, buckets and baskets overflowing with seaweed. Two adults hauled a cart full of it after them too.

Soon, torches along the beach in even intervals were lit. The captain and those working on the pier came in. Not safe for anyone on the wood pilings as darkness crawled closer as the sun drowned at the edge of the sea.

Most gathered up the last remaining dead. I noticed then the pieces of broken pilings and timbers arranged around the beach. Some were higher than my head, but not by much. Each had layers of bodies lain out neatly over dried wood. Kindling was in the middle of each layer.

Harlii came up beside me, tugging on a shirt. "We cannot keep up with the grave digging. Sos we won't be spreading more disease, we burn most of the bodies. Tonight is the night for those."

I looked back to the path from the village. People trailed down it. White and gray clothing covered most of them to replicate the look of ash and dust to which the dead would return. As the fires were lit, we stood in silence, until Harlii broke it.

"So you're the Hero?"

I nodded, motioning to Blari, still scribbling in his book by a torch beside us, "That's Priest Blari, one of my companions." I pointed to Tori and Spacya once I found them still gathering debris off the beach, and told him of Sterla and Clara.

He nodded, "This is Captain Otteri." He hooked a thumb at the man on the other side of him, "The fellow who can set fire to just about anything he can lob a ball at."

Otteri's lips twisted up slightly under a large red mustache, "At your service, Hero. Pleasure."

"Thank you, but the pleasure is mine." I paused, watching the flames lick up the pyres. The wails of the families began. I caught sight of Priest Lindra, her arms spread wide, giving the last prayers to the dead.

"What exactly, in your opinion, can we do against this thing to keep from having to light more of these." I motioned to the pyres.

"She's thinking we can beat it." Harlii tilted his head, his eyes on me, but he aimed his words at his captain.

Otteri rubbed at the stubble on his chin for a moment, "We're gonna have to." He looked around and motioned for us to follow him.

A broken hull was pulled up onto the beach and we climbed in it to sit on the benches within.

I kept watch on the pyres, on the people mourning. My heart heavy for them. As Spacya and Tori stopped as darkness claimed most of the beach, even with the help of the torches, I lifted my hand so they could see me. The pyres were mostly coals. They burned quickly.

Music began playing in the village, low, somber.

I gave introductions once Tori and Spacya were settled in the hull with us. "The priest knew little of it, what have you found out about The Missapen?"

"Most say it's random," Spacya shrugged, "Another few says they think it might come out when the sea turns cold or it's causin' it to go cold."

"A lot of them talk about a fisherman named Nerii. Say he's been raving about the monster so much he goes hoarse. They put little stock in him as he's been drunk since the first attack, though." Tori paused to look out at the sea before adding, "His boy drowned in that one."

Captain Otteri grunted, "Sounds like just the person we need to talk to." He eyed Tori for a moment, "They say where we can find him?"

"Octo's Tavern or in a tiny boat on the north side of the farthest pier. Said his is called Popper."

"Might as well find him." I stood, and made my way out of the hull.

The two sailors led the way since they knew the beach better than we did. Tori and Spacya held torches up so we wouldn't trip over debris or large trenches I assumed were raked out by the beast. The further we walked along the beach, the less damage the monster had done. Only three piers remained intact on this side. On the last pier was Popper, beside the rocky outcropping that stretched as far as the torchlight allowed us to see.

What boats and ships survived were crammed all along these piers. I wondered if there were more boats than people could manage them after all the deaths.

We stopped beside a small fishing boat with a square cabin covered in nets and lines. A lantern hung out over the short deck from a lone mast. In the soft glow, sat a lone man in a shadow cast by the cabin. His back was to the side of his vessel, feet in the circle of light, and a bottle glistened in his hand resting on one knee. Gray smoke drifted from his lips after each slow drag on a husk pipe held tightly between his lips.

"Captain Nerii?"

A bald spot in the middle of graying brown hair caught the lantern light when he finally looked our way. His tunic was brown, like old rust, stained, and hung about him as if it was made for a more robust man. Nerii's pants held so many patches it was difficult to tell which was the original fabric. His feet were bare, gnarled and patched in callouses.

The weed in the pipe flared amber as Nerii took a drag before answering, the smoke snaking around the single word, "Aye."

"I'm Nadachia, this is captain Otteri, his mate Harlii and these are my companions: Spacya, Blari, and Tori. We're here-"

"To see a drunkard 'bout the beastie."

"We're going to beat it. But we need a plan."

He huffed, then groaned his way up to his feet. His eyes, rimmed in red, swelled with tears before he blinked them away, "'bout time."

We took our new friends to Nerii's favorite tavern so we could have some light and a table to sit around. He claimed the drink was good, and the food fair. Tori broke off to go get Clara and Sterla, or at least make sure they had eaten. The more heads the better the plan of attack. Or so I hoped.

The tavern was nearly empty. I could hear snores from patrons in the rooms upstairs and some weeping. The barkeep and owner said the rooms were full of the sick, and most of his help aided them while serving down here too.

His staff dragged their feet, as did he, but they kept our drinks filled even if the food was slow to come to the thick oak table. I looked around at the threadbare velvet chairs of reds and blues. The square pillars in even intervals through the middle of the room, were painted with scenes of fields, warriors and seas. The ceiling was a mixture of gods of the waters and winds, and numerous fish and legendary half-fish half-man beasts. As the first plate arrived, so did Clara, Sterla and Tori.

"Was it you who made it bleed?" Nerii asked, his watery gaze on Captain Otteri.

Both Harlii and Otteri nodded.

"Good lads." He leaned forward, holding his cup at them before taking a drink.

"I fill pots, clay ones, with oil and I put the fire in them for long throws or to put in catapults." Otteri explained, "For short distances I can just lob the fireballs at it. But I didn't want to put my ship too close to the beast. So we used the catapult. I hit it twice, once before Harlii threw his harpoon and nearly sawed the arm in half, and the other after. Between the three attacks we did, the arm came off."

"Where is it? The arm?"

"Bottom of the sea. Thing's too big to drag up." Harliii said around a mouthful of bread.

"We need to get all the potters and their apprentices making these pots you use." Tori stated.

"Gather up those that can be spared from the locals too." Spacya added.

"Are there any Welkans around here?"

"A few to the north," Nerii answered.

"We need to see if any of them can wield flames to help Otteri attack." Taspe and his tribes were too far away. It would probably take them a week to get here, if not longer. "Hopefully we will have a little while before it attacks again."

"I'll keep watch. The water always goes cold and stays that way the day before it attacks and lasts until a day after."

Clara's brows furrowed, "Colder? So it comes from the deep and churns the cold water up?"

The men nodded.

"Would warm water slow it? Is there a way to warm… no, never mind." I thought outloud. It would be too much work to try to warm an entire bay.

"Would probably kill what's left of the fish, so many temperature changes." Spacya added.

"Fishes are gone. That's a lotta sea to heat in a short time too. Would have to have Welkans here though. They's the only ones I know can heat up water." Nerii nodded, apparently liking the way we were thinking.

"What else can we do?" Tori asked.

"We should gather harpoons, nets, and make the people safe." Clara answered.

"Some of the sick can't travel yet. They'll have to stay." Sterla's voice was almost too soft to hear.

Clara nodded, "That's true. But what about adding supports to the walls, or spikes? I saw when we came in where the monster breached one area of the wall and it's not repaired yet. The locals are saying that's where many died and were injured."

"We need to gather a team to rebuild that and add spikes. Something to make it retreat and think twice about attacking the walls and town. Use some of the wreckage." I said.

"Debris is already usually spikey. Maybe add some harpoons and spears, axes too. Just so it'll get caught and be held in place." Otteri added to the plan.

Blari was scribbling so furiously I wondered if the quill would last.

Then Spacya asked, "What about a warning system? The villagers said it caught them unawares. Didn't have time to drop work and run off the piers or in the town."

"It takes forever for someone to get to the church for them to ring the bells," Harlii added.

"Whistles? What if we could make sure that enough people on the beach and those working on the piers have whistles on them?" I asked, "They're small enough that they shouldn't impede work or get lost."

Otteri nodded, "Agreed."

"We need a plan. Two actually. One for evacuation and the other for attack. Stations with warriors, for first aid, and supply chains in case the monster is at one or two of the stations and it's not feasible to be used." I paused, willing my brain to keep thinking along this track instead of delving down into the fear that made my body shake. *Just what did I think I was doing here?*

I looked at Blari, "What's our list, we need to break it up between us."

He read from his paper, "Clay jars and a timeline on potters making more."

"Otteri for that one, Blari, you too."

"Harpoon gathering, making, and set in needed areas." Blari read, while he made notes on the first item of the list.

"Harlii and Nerii since you two know most about the beach, and beast."

"Evacuation plan."

I looked at who was left, "Tori and I."

"Warning system set up and implementation."

"Clara and Spacya." I watched as all of them nodded or agreed to their tasks. "Once you are getting close to being done with these tasks, send word or speak with me. I have a feeling we're going to need to gather volunteers to help make the village ready and figure out shifts for building, sleep, and other preparations."

After they agreed I looked down at the platters on the table before us. What was it about there being so much food on this endeavor of mine?

Chapter 13

We found places to sleep in the barn. The hayloft made a warm bed, even if it was a bit noisy with Blari, Spacya, and Sterla snoring. At dawn we began our tasks.

The silence in the village was deafening. Children didn't play. The beast and the destruction it wrought shone in the eyes of every villager. Most wore the shawls of mourners hanging loose over their shoulders when not working, and kept to their vow of silence until their loved ones were properly buried or burned.

Tori and I dug through the maps of Columbria we found stashed in the Mayor's home. With them open and guiding us, we walked the streets, marking paths of least resistance to get out of the village. We made sure the catacombs underneath the village were clear and not caved in to use those too.

We also came up with a system to mark empty houses so no one would check for people during an attack. Tori and I helped some of the families packing up and moving out during our exploration and mapping. The main street was the best one to use for evacuations, and we marked the maps accordingly with our plan.

When we finished, most of our companions were too. We made our way back to the tavern. Nerii and Harlii were already there, and began their report.

"The beach is getting there. Most of the mess are in piles, ready to be made useful." Harlii emptied his tankard of water after he finished talking.

"The nets have been comin' up clean." Nerii added quietly.

Sterla sent word that she was staying at the church to keep healing.

Each team broke down what they had accomplished and brought up some other concerns. With the information we gathered, we created a rough timeline of what we could accomplish. A couple of weeks to prepare and stock up on more supplies would be ideal. I hoped the Misshapen gave us the time.

Clara said, "I think we need to separate the sick from the wounded. Sterla mentioned that earlier today when I checked in on her. She said something about infections spreading back and forth."

I pulled out a map, "These are empty houses." I pointed to a few toward the inland portion of Columbria. It was a bit far to move them, but that would lessen the danger the sick would be in during the next attack. "Let's move them here."

She nodded, "Guess that's our next step."

"That and buildin' fortifications," Spacya said around a mouthful of stale biscuit.

I nodded, "Two shifts, rest at night. A team to rebuild the wall. Another team to build some traps on the beach. And the last team to put spikes and spears on the walls and below them. Same break down for the sick and wounded. Figure out how many houses we will need for each. Three teams of healers and caretakers to work around the clock, not all the time like it looks like they've been doing. Two teams to move during two shifts, rest at night for them."

"Sounds like a plan."

We had been there for a week. Preparations were getting done. I was quite proud of us.

Plans were laid for the attack. Three of them. We had weak plans in case those three fell through. I hoped it didn't come to that, because the fourth plan was to run away and come back with a Welkan army.

The villagers that were part of the evacuation teams performed practice runs, and I was pleased with their timing. The makeshift hospitals were steadily emptying. Thankfully, most were walking free and not part of the pyres.

I was helping build another catapult when Nerii cried out from his little boat. I looked out at the end of the newly built pier and tripped-ran toward him. I fell to my knees, peering down at him in his boat.

He rasped, his hand wet from the ocean waters, and grew paler with each word as he spoke, "It's coming."

Everything stopped. I couldn't breathe. I couldn't hear my heart. There were no thoughts. Nothing.

"It's coming." He screamed again. "Here!" His hand shook, droplets of salty water splattering everything around him, including me.

Otteri came from no where, and gripped Nerii's shoulders, "Nerii? When?"

Nerii's head jerked back, as if the captain slapped him, "It's coming!"

"I know, when?" Otteri squeezed Nerii's shoulders so tight I thought I heard bones pop.

"Soon. Two days. It's not the coldest, yet." Nerii's whole body shook in Otteri's grip.

"Two days?" I barely breathed.

Otteri looked up at me, a nod his only answer.

I turned to look at the crowd along the pier and beach. I hadn't noticed them gathering. A woman began screeching. Men began murmuring. I swallowed and stood.

"We have prepared for this!" My fingernails dug into my palms. I felt the scar warm just under my thumb. "We have a plan! Work around the clock, remember your rotations! Remember to sleep! Remember to eat!"

The murmurs subsided, the screeching died a little as someone dragged the woman to the village. I recognized her as the mother of some fishers that had died on the beach in the last attack. Her sons and daughters had taken up their father's business when he died in the first attack. She had lost everything.

"You all know what to do!"

I hoped they did. I was at a loss. My mind was running in circles.

"Chi." Tori stepped up to me and held out a letter.

Sam Wicker

I stared at the mark of the Matron embedded in the envelope for enough time for me to take two breaths. I took it, remembering Father's mantra for me and taking a few more breaths to calm down. This was it. But what could this letter be?

Our Hero,
Return as soon as possible. There is much for you to attend. Marriage proposals, at least three, and more quests for you to take up. Make haste.
Matron Keandria

I crumpled the letter in my fist and snorted.

"What is it?" Tori asked, eying the wadded paper.

"We are to make haste."

"You can't leave now!" Nerii's skeletal fingers gripped my wrist so hard I was sure to have bruises in the morning.

"I'm not." The annoyance bubbling inside gave way to sympathy. For some odd reason, these people held their hope in me. Someone who had just walked from Owlimount to Galanesse to take the title of Hero. I had nothing else. Just my stupidity and stubbornness. "I will be here until we end it."

Whether that be my death or the Misshapen's, I had no idea, but I would be here until one or the other came to pass.

I had my list of things to take care of. So did everyone else. And we weren't ready.

Supplies from all over Owlimount had arrived, but it wasn't enough. I was glad of them. I was proud of my country for sticking together.

I wondered if the monster knew we were trying to be ready for it. Or if it felt the absurd rush the Matron was in for me to get back to Galanesse. I shook my head, heading to the taverns to begin my first task: rationing.

Nightfall on the second day, had me crawling to the lumpy bed in an abandoned house. The owners had given us permission to use it as they left Columbria for the safety of the village at the base of the mountains several leagues away. Clara and I shared a room, as we were on the same shifts, but different preparation teams.

"What are you doing?" I whispered, once I turned over and saw her sitting up in bed.

Clara looked up, staring at me for a moment, then she grinned. "I wasn't sure if you were in there or if it was all just a pile of blankets." She looked back down at her hands, "Mother wants me to keep practicing my stitching. I thought it was useless, but after seeing some of the wounds... it might actually help."

I grunted. It was an odd thing to do in the middle of the night via a single candle. I had to admit, I didn't know a single thing about stitching skin together, except for boot laces. That was dead skin. Would it work up the same? I shuddered at the thought.

"Do you think it'll come tomorrow?"

The princess paused, the cloth nearly touching her nose as she concentrated hard upon it, "I hope not." She stitched some more, "Part of me hopes it does. Just so we can get this over with. So we can live or die. And not live like this. Not knowing." Her hands fell back into her lap and she looked at me again. "Does that make sense?" She tilted her head, strands of her pink hair falling into her face and glimmering there in the candlelight, "Does that make me a bad person?"

I had been thinking along the same lines since entering Columbria. "I don't think so." It was what I wanted to hear.

Clara let out a puff of breath, "I hope there aren't any other monsters with poison in it like this one."

Silence reigned. I watched her stitch two more lines in between her rubbing her eyes. "You should try to sleep."

"So should you." She muttered back as she tucked the cloth and needle away in her pack at the base of her narrow bed. She lay down, swinging her foot off the edge, "Do you think it will come tomorrow?"

"I think so." I managed through a dry mouth. Nerii thought so.

I was in the middle of my next shift when a roar sounded from the beach. It shook the land underneath my feet. The tavern I was in groaned and shuddered like its dark wood planks would shatter like glass.

The whistles sounded. The bells began clanging.

My feet were like rocks attached to my legs. I stumbled forward, loosening the hold of fear as I broke into a lope, then a run. I took in deep breaths of the salty air, and released the fear out with them. The sun hung toward the white capped waters instead of the land. In a handful of hours it would set.

Would we be alive to see it?

Captain Otteri stood on the platform of the third station. Past him, in the deep water of the darkening bay, an oily skim formed on the surface between the white foam of thrashed seas. My breath puffed in clouds before me as I climbed the platform and began hauling the first box of pottery up with the pulley system. My eyes never left the ocean.

Something smooth, in a mixture of gray, green and black broke the surface. It kept rising. The sun didn't reflect on any part of that wet splotchy skin. Another roar from a gaping maw of jagged teeth in succession down the throat shook the ground again. I fell, hauling the box quickly up the rest of the way up to the platform with my clumsiness. The Misshapen blocked the sun from my sight.

Captain's Otteri's legs were wide. His hands fisted at his sides. He stared down the beast. A wild, odd fire in his dark eyes.

"Here!" Tori called out, setting the machine built much like a catapult, but smaller, to fit on ramparts. Or platforms. He set a pot into it as I climbed into the seat.

Otteri shoved a flaming hand into the pot and fire licked up around the narrow clay lip once he pulled away.

There was never enough preparation. I wasn't sure of my aim. My mind feared I was pulling the wrong lever seconds before my instinct took over and fired the pot toward the monster.

The wood contraption groaned. Ropes whirred and the large arm whooshed up into the air and let loose the pot. The clay broke apart over the white slitted left eye of the monster. Tar and oils mixed, the fire crawling with the liquids.

The Misshapen screamed. The many arms lifted, rubbing and spreading the concoction and the flames along its thick skin. The few Welkans, from neighboring villages, launched their flames. The two other machines whirred, releasing two other pots over it.

It screamed again and the world shook.

Harpoons launched, landing in the burning hide with wet thunks. Cranks pulled clacking chains taught, pulling the monster to the central, widest part of the beach. Toward the weapons and the strongest part of the walls.

I prayed the village nearest the beach was evacuated.

"Ready!" Tori yelled.

"Fire!" Otteri yelled a moment later and I launched another flaming pot on the monster.

The tar pooled over the arms and into the maw, flames following. The next cry was a gargled mess. A harpoon sank into the soft looking flesh between two rows of teeth.

The Misshapen lurched forward. A flaming arm raking across a pier to reach the beach. Two flaming Welkans fell into the freezing water. Their screams broke something in my chest.

The chains attached to the harpoons clanked some more as the villagers kept pulling the beast to the beach.

Two of the clay pots burst upon the arms, no flames erupted and slid. I eyed the other two machines. Another two pots launched, the tar spreading over the Misshapen. The limbs the tar fell on grew sluggish, the liquid sticking them to each other, and to the flesh of the beast.

"Don't use the fire! Not yet." I screamed back at Otteri.

"Done!" He bellowed back over the groan pouring out of the monster's mouth.

I changed trajectory, aiming for the arms raking over the beach, trying to pull out the chains. I pulled the lever, watching as the thick tar coated the arms. The machine jolted as Tori loaded the next pot. I launched it at two other arms along the beach.

Switching back to the body, I yelled, "More fire!" I kept my eye on the sluggishly crawling and warping arms on the beach. The flames along the arms and body made the once dark flesh pink and white. The flesh raw and seeping blackened, ink-like fluid I assumed was its blood.

"Fire!" Otteri yelled after another reset from Tori.

I watched as the pot from my machine seemed to burn longer. Deeper into the flesh of the monster than the pots from the other two machines lit by torches. I would have to ask Taspe about fire blessings. If I saw him again.

I would see him again.

The scar on my hand warmed as I launched another pot onto the beast. This one landed into the mouth, flames spilling down the throat, like I hoped it would. It didn't roar.

The Misshapen leaned back out to the deep. The cranks and anchors to the harpoon chains groaned in response. Its arms roiled in the sea.

"No. No." I screamed, changing trajectory again and firing pots along the back of the monster as quickly as they could reload and light them. The Welkans on the remaining piers shot fire from their hands and mouths at the back of the beast too.

Two arms wrapped around two chains, pulling and beating. Somehow they held. The villagers along the beach stabbed and hacked at the arms along the chains until the Misshapen pulled them away. It swept some of its attackers off the beach. Their screams tore into my soul, breaking it.

The fire at its back pushed it to the beach. The ocean surged up onto the sands as it dragged itself away from the fires. The water did not break the walls of bagged and raked sand, except for where the Misshapen's arms had broken them. I watched villagers thrash in the dark, inky water, peeling off the poisoned clothing while running back to the trench of clean water. They needed to wash off the poison as best they could.

The Misshapen's legs and arms unfurled like serpents stretching out from a nest. The legs were much thicker and longer than the thrashing arms had been. They stretched and gripped with large, platter-sized suckers.

Otteri barked orders to the villagers. They dodged legs. Dancing and weaving to hack with heavy swords between the suckers. The skin of the legs filleted out quicker than that of the arms and body. Once damaged or pierced, the legs and arms drew in upon themselves, curling around the source of pain.

Some blades were lost. A few villagers crushed.

The Misshapen screamed. The stench of rot poured from its maw. Many gagged, including me. I launched another pot as I wiped my last meal from my mouth, leaning over again to spit. This one landed in the mouth, the flames licking through and around the rows of teeth. The mouth closed, smoke pouring from folded nostrils I hadn't noticed until then.

I launched another pot at the open nares. Flames snorted down in a breath it took before they closed again. I prayed to Meandria for it to die soon. Surely we had gotten enough fire into the soft insides by now.

"Drink!" Otteri cried.

I looked down to a boy holding up a large bowl to me. I took it. Rinsed my mouth out, then drank down the rest.

He handed me another, "Drink up! I dunno how much we'll have left soon!"

I stared at him, "What do you mean?"

"The river, old Colimi, she be actin' odd. Gettin' all low, like she's not drawing enough from the Gala or mountains. She's been going backwards some, after spluttering like some fish."

I looked into Tori's eyes. He was drinking from another bowl, now it sat forgotten in his wide hand. "Ever heard of a river draining?"

"Not that suddenly." He shook his head.

I watched the Misshappen. The mouth was closed. The nares closed. How was it breathing?

"Stupid." I muttered, standing on the machine to look down into the water. Those sucker covered legs pressed to the cliff face just past the end of the pier, some of their ends disappearing into a darkened area. I assumed that was a cave. A cave system the Columbri let out at.

A cave and river system I ignored on the maps because they couldn't be used in evacuations because they were too narrow, or full of water.

I cried out, "It's pulling the water out of the river!"

"Why?" Otteri yelled back, then his face went white.

"To poison!" I wanted to scream, but I barely whispered.

"Pull it out!" I screamed with another breath. "Up on the beach! Pull it out!"

I half fell half climbed off the machine to grab the closest chain and pull along with the cranking mechanism. I watched Nerii and a few others get into boats. They circled the Misshapen. Harpoons launching from their boats. They sunk in deep, and they tossed the lines onto the piers and beach. Villagers grabbed them, pulling with all their might.

With the new leverage, I could see some movement. We were making progress.

Flames continued to be thrown on its back. The flesh was all pink now, raw with burns, some ranging deep like gulleys through the Misshapen's body. I couldn't see a single bone, other than the teeth.

Nerii and the other boats were pushing. Ramming their vessels into the back of the Misshapen, trying to push it onto the beach as we pulled. With each crank and ram of the boats, the beast was rolled up onto the sands.

Its arms and legs started flailing a moment before there was a great groan. It thrashed, raking its body and arms along the beach. Chains loosened. People were grabbed up or crushed.

It screamed. Black water and ink shooting out over the boats and into the waters of the bay. I could hear the softer cries of the men and women on the boats and pier as the wood disintegrated as soon as the inky poison touched it. So many lives lost again.

The body was up on the beach enough I could finally see the gills. Otteri released his hold on our chain and ran toward the pink undulating sheets of flesh. He threw as many fireballs as he could each time they opened. Villagers on the other side gave war cries as they stabbed at the gills with all they could find.

It screamed and shuddered. Thrashing and crushing all it could reach. Legs and arms seemed too heavy for it to lift with each fireball or thrust of a weapon.

Finally, the collosal beast shuddered and was still.

"Hold! Still!" I cried. Waiting for it to move again as the villagers watched the body along with me.

It didn't move.

A cry arose. A cry of joy. A cry of heartbreak. A cry of victory. It swept the beach and I allowed it to take my voice too.

Chapter 14

Cool water rippled around my fingers, reminding me the tributary was getting back to normal. No burns popped up on my flesh. Guppies and some smaller fish were swimming and feeding on the river. The peaceful mile-long sunny trek to the rapids just before the waters dived underneath the land and Columbri was something I needed.

It was quiet in the village.

No one had time to return from their evacuation. Of those that stayed, a quarter were in teh churches and inns, being treated for poison and various wounds. Children were still too scared to play. Fifteen died. Twelve were still missing.

Fifteen passed while I had been here. The Hero. I was to save people. Not let them die beside me.

The scar on my hand warmed, the coolness of the river seeping away from the blooming head as it spread across my palm. I sighed, rubbing a finger over it as I stood from stooping over the waters. The scar seemed to warm more.

'You saved some.' the burning scar seemed to say. There were those that were living and smiling still that might not have had my crew and I not been here. I should've done more. What more could I have done?

"Chi!" Clara had her hand raised above her rosey head as she waved it slightly.

I changed my course toward her instead of taking the path around the town to the beach. In her other hand were long purple flowers, lavender.

"I thought," she paused, looking down at the blossoms, then back at me, "I thought it might be a pleasant touch. Your touch." She held out the bunch of flowers to me.

They didn't grow around here. A delivery made it to Columbri. Another thing to be thankful for.

"Our touch." I said as I halved the bundle with her.

We joined several other villagers on the road as it narrowed to slant down the cliff face to the beach after going through the town. Down on the beach were the pyres for the fifteen. A silent hope that none of the others would join them.

The corpse of the monster, half cut up, and half leaning awkwardly upon the sands, shadowed the beach and the people gathering. The stench of rotting flesh undulated from being pressed into my nose from the wind off the sea, or being swept back out from the breeze from the land. Clara and I stopped at each pyre to add lavender to them. Spreading the sweet scent before it blackened in flame. I put the remainder of my bundle, double what I had put on any others, on Nerii's pyre.

Clara and I then moved away, standing in the back of the crowd curling in a half moon around the pyres on the beach with the rest of our comrades. Tori had been poisoned while hacking at the Mishappens arms on the beach. His arm was wrapped with seaweed and kelp, and he held it tightly to his side. Sterla looked as if she could fall asleep standing up. Other than that, my party were well.

After the rites were spoken to the rhythm of the waves crashing upon the sands, the pyres were lit. They burned bright, quickly going to flame and growing tall. The stench of burning flesh folded into the salt of the air.

A few hours after the pyres were lit, we said our farewells. While the road to Columbri had been mostly empty, now we saw a few travelers. I was glad they were returning to the little town. To live without fear of a beast.

"Does anyone know how many, total, died because of The Mishappen?" I asked quietly, not sure I wanted the answer to it even as the words left my lips.

"I think the count was thirty-four dead, and eithy-seven injured or poisoned." Sterla replied.

The population of the village had been around four hundred if I remembered reading the last census correctly that Tori and I had come across while looking for maps. It could have been much worse. Still, my heart ached at the lives that would never be the same.

"All for the gods' game."

"A test to see if we are ready, Chi. To see if one is worthy enough to stand for us and fight, with all of our best qualities." Blari murmured, his dark eyes sweeping over my face.

I snorted, "I have more of the worst."

"You do snore." Clara chimed in with a grin.

"Can't be as loud as Blari." Tori added.

Blari huffed, shooting Tori a glare, "Says the one that takes two hours at the water pitcher and mirror each day."

"He has to make himself purdy for the future Princess Tori." Spacya smirked, "Whoever she may be."

Clara grinned at me and I waited for her to say whatever she had thought of, but she never did.

"I don't think he's going to meet his princess in a village like Columbri." I shook my head.

Blari cleared his throat, "The Hero and the quests are to prove to the gods that we humans are ready for gifts."

The sorrow I felt at the losses in Columbri flickered into a flame. My teeth pressed together so hard my face and head hurt with the pressure. These things were made by gods that we worshipped. That we looked to for guidance, safety, and knowledge. We didn't look to them for tortures, harm, or death.

"You ever met a god, Blari?" My voice was not my own.

"No, no, I haven't." His horse shied away from me, and I wondered if it was sensing unease from the priest as he quickly looked away from my face at last.

"Pity. I want to meet them all."

The door clicked behind me, and I leaned against it, closing my eyes to just be for a moment. We snuck into Galanesse in the dead of night. None of us wanted to deal with the crowds and cheering idiots. We would make our grand entrance later, tomorrow. I wanted a bath. I wanted a bed that didn't reek of sea salt, sweat, and body odor.

"You're late."

The bluejay-like voice called from deep in my rooms. I opened my eyes, scanning, and I saw him. He stood in front of my bed, belting his tunic as if he had just pulled it back on. His grin was crooked, slow to grow, but his midnight eyes sparked with it before his lips stopped moving upward.

"Taspe?" My mouth was as dry as the road I had just been on.

"I'm real and here, Chi." He held out his hands to each side.

My heart flew to him before my sluggish feet could catch up. I hopped upon him, wrapping my arms around his neck and burrowing into him where his neck met thick shoulder. His chuckle rumbled against my chest and his breath feathered my hair over my ear. His arms wrapped around me, hands cupping my ass to pull me up further before sliding to my thighs to pull my legs around him.

"What are you doing here?"

He rested his cheek against my temple as he answered, "I came to see you." He purred, "If I knew you were going to react like this with just a few weeks away from me I would have held back a couple more to see what exciting things you would do then."

I snorted. Usually when he said something like that, I would wriggle free. Not this time. He was part of my home, and I needed it. My eyes began burning, and I squeezed them shut to keep from ruining the moment with whimpers and whining.

"Yes, I think next time a month and half shall have you grovelling at my feet to never leave your side again." Taspe murmured, the joy in his voice joined by something I couldn't quite put my finger on.

"You should stay here a few weeks, then. The Aghva would strip and lie down in a line to take a turn with you." I pictured all the single, and some married women, Welkan or not, doing just that. Or at least fawning over the beloved and awed Legace.

Taspe chuckled, "Perhaps I shall." He sat down on the edge of my bed with me. His hands went to my braid, undoing the tie and working the thick strands free. "I will only care for my Chi like this, though."

As the only male leader of a Welkan tribe since the Welkan peoples were freed, the entire world had their eyes on Taspe. His dying Legace, the title for Welkan leaders, performed a blood ritual over ageless tiles carved into Welkanese letters. The letters and blood spelled Taspe's name and moon of birth. The elders and Legace even performed the ritual a second time after a curse cleansing just to make sure the ritual still named Taspe.

It had.

He had to marry well. He had to win each challenge, growing his Legace with each tribe's defeat by melding them into his. After the tenth tribe fell to him, a Legacey was made. His Legacey. The only male to hold that many tribes, to have beaten so many Legaces, and to outsmart them and their battle hardened and often much older elders. He was young. They would have to put up with many decades, centuries, of him before his natural death.

"I need a bath."

"I sent your maid away a few hours ago. The poor thing was falling asleep standing up." Taspe helped me up off him. He started untying my boots and pulled them off me when I sat back down beside him. He jerked his chin toward the bathing portion of my rooms, "Funny how they have so much money here they can waste water like that."

I grunted, not willing to admit I had thought the same thing when getting here.

As I undid my belt, Taspe rose and went to the bath. The smell of chamomile and lavender wafted to me over the screens. He knew me well.

Taspe returned after I rid myself of weapons, belts and holsters; just as I was fighting with the last clasp of my corset under the thin, open shirt. He helped me, folding it, careful not to cut himself on the blades and placing it in the over-cushioned chair near my bed with the rest of the things I had flung at it. He helped me out of my pants that felt like they had became a second skin on the ride here.

He stood back, looking at my in my thin underclothes.

"Want me to commission a painting?" I fought the urge to cover myself. Barely.

He shook his head, not snapping back with any words. He took my hand, walking backward to lead me to the bathing room.

"I-"

"Let me do this." HIs voice was raspier than normal, deeper.

He pulled my top over my head after gently lifting my arms up, his fingers trailing over my skin on the way up, and again, silky soft, on the way down. He knelt, untying the cotton band before pulling the underwear over my hips, down my thighs, and helping me step out of them. His gaze raked up my body, meeting my eyes. Staring into my soul as I stood bare before him.

My breath caught as he stood.

He pressed his forehead against mine. I closed my eyes. I felt his fingers brush through my hair and then his cool hand was against the back of my neck. I wanted to lean into him. To cool the flame my skin had become at his touch.

"Will you allow me to bathe with you?"

I opened my eyes. I stared at his lips, the bottom slightly thicker than the top. He smelled of the wilds. All earthy and musk mingled with the sweet scent of lavender and chamomile. "Yes."

His lips curled into a gentle smile. His hands left me. They untucked his wide belt, and pulled it free. The thick red cloth pooled at his heels.

I lifted my hands to the rough band of braided ribbons of red and yellow along the hem of his smoke blue tunic. I pushed the soft cloth to either side, baring his broad, marked and scarred torso to me. His tunic fell to meet his belt with a soft swish of cloth against flesh.

His body was smooth, cool under my hands. His skin taught over thick muscles that were similar to humans, but numerous, woven tighter to make each movement ripple like rings of water in a lake. Each breath fluttered between both sets of his lungs like the wings of a bird.

Covering my hands with his, he pressed my palms against the center of his chest. The solid beating of his heart pounded against my palms. He then rid himself of his breechcloth, letting it fall to his feet in a pool of gray blue. He held my hands to his heart again. His eyes the color of a midnight sky as he stepped forward. I stepped back, matching his movements in a dance.

I did not fear the coals. His body guided mine in perfect synchrony to the lip of the bath. His hands slid to my bare buttocks and he lifted me. I wound my legs around his waist as he took the steps down into the water.

I floated, wrapped loosely around him. His hands left my body, one to grab the cloth in the nearby metal basket, and one of my soaps. Taspe unwound me gently, pulling me to float in front of him. I felt as light as the petals floating in the water around us.

He took great care to wash every inch of me, starting with my hair and then down my back. His fingertips were calloused from battles, weaving and fletching arrows and they scraped gloriously well over my flesh once he dropped the hindering cloth. Washing each of my extremities in torturously slow circles, soap slicked fingers and palms slid over my breasts then over my ribs down to my buttocks. Then back up, and over again.

He rinsed me off, and I grabbed for the soap. He smiled, placing it back in the basket. "I just bathed. This is all about you." His lips curled wickedly, "All that should have happened for your first."

Long ago, before the enslavement, Welkan males trained in the arts called Stayu would be hired through gifts or money to give a female her first mating. Taspe had been taught such practices of old, never intending to become a leader, much less a Legace. It still came in handy, apparently.

His lips found mine in a gentle claim. Taspe kissed my chin, then under it, trailing kisses down my neck as his hands trailed feather light over my flesh until they cupped my breasts. I gasped, pressing into his palms and lips. His thumbs, rough with small callouses, brushed slowly over my nipples and a moan ricochetted out of me.

"Gods. Do all humans sound like you?" Taspe groaned, nipping the tender flesh at the top of my breast.

Then he went under. Nipping there and I gripped his hair in my hands like a lifeline to more of his ministrations. I wanted him to suck on me. He obliged. Mouth on one nipple, suckling and flicking the hard nubbin with his tongue as his hands slid on down to cup my buttocks and pull me flush against him.

His hardness pressed against my thigh. Then it was gone as he slid further down into the water. Warm fingers spread my thighs and then I felt his tongue slip along the folds. Delving and licking until that tongue found another nubbin to pay attention to. I leaned back, floating in the water, thighs wrapped around his head. I bit my finger to keep from crying out. To keep from drowning.

Taspe sucked and licked, faster and faster. My body arched, heat arcing through me as I yearned for something. Then I went taught, unable to move as a cry broke through me before a sweet vibration of release. I felt sated. I wanted more. I needed more.

He pulled, fitting me against him. His cock throbbed twice against my belly as he licked his lips of me. I pushed his hair away from his face and then I tasted myself on his lips. Taspe walked to the edge, lifting me out of the water onto the edge and following me as easily as if he had just taken the steps.

I tightened my thighs around his hips, rocking against him. His cock throbbed again, slipping between to rub against my clit and the damp heat of me. I watched his smile, slow and lopsided as he pressed into me. A few quick, pounding thrusts of his cock against my clit and I was soaring again.

"Take me." I barely got out between ragged breaths.

"Oh, I will, oulileah." He murmured, detangling myself from my arms. He grabbed my hips, and rubbed his length all down my clit before pressing the fleshy, hard tip against it. He moved, rubbing hard and fast until I cried out again. Clawing at the tiles in my madness and release.

We stared at one another, the coals dangerously close to my head, as I gathered my wits about me. His smile was slow again, a glint in his eyes as he picked up my noodle-soft feeling arms and wrapped them about his neck.

"One day, I'm going to try something with the coals, my powers, and your body. But not today." He purred against my ear as he stood with me curled about his body like a frog against a tree. "Today I will prove to you why I should have been your first choice." He chuckled darkly, stealing a kiss before he peeled me off and tossed me onto the pile of pillows on my bed. "And why no other male will ever compare."

I ate up the sight of his body needing me fully for the first time. His tanned skin flushed with the heat we had created between us. His muscles rippled with each breath, and they were rapid. Welkan's mating organs were similar to a human's. Taspe's was as long as the full length of his hand at the moment. Erect and pulsing with each beat of his heart before him.

I moved to the pillows, laying back against the great number of them, and held my hands out to him.

He crawled. Taspe crawled to me on hands and knees across the bed. Something inside me pulled, hard, toward him until he lay his hands upon me again.

He ran his fingers up the length of my legs. His eyes followed his progress. He spread my legs and settled his hips on top of mine.

He kneaded my boobs. He suckled on them, one at a time, taking my hard nipples into his mouth and making them harder. Everything inside me begged for more. His back arched into my fingernails as I tried to draw him in. To me. Inside and all around me.

With each pulse of his penis against me, something inside pulsed in answer. I wanted them to meet. I reached between us. My fingertips grazed him before he grabbed my hand and pulled it back to our side.

I arched, wanting him to release me from the throb of needing him.

"Taspe." His name was breathless on my lips.

"Nhg gods…" he groaned into my belly as he worked his way down. His hands spread over my breasts. He squeezed.

A familiar sensation flicked that nubbin again.

My hips bucked into his mouth.

His tongue licked along one fold, then the other. He delved into the heat coming from deep within me. Then he touched it again, with the tip of his tongue.

I cried out, my body coming off the bed as something exploded down there.

I shook. I throbbed hard with each heartbeat. My heartbeat? His? I wasn't sure anymore. All I knew was that it was a release of sorts. But I still wanted more. I hurt for him.

He worked his tongue around again, teasing the nubbin for a few flicks and suckles. The throbbing inside me quickened again, and I whimpered with each move he made. I couldn't help it. I couldn't stop.

He moved his way back up. He left large kisses in his wake. On my hip, he suckled on my skin, biting it until I cried out. He then licked it, kissing it again before he moved his mouth to my breasts.

His cock was against my middle. I rocked my hips, begging him to move inside me, but he moved with me.

I gripped his ass with my hands and dug in. He moaned loudly, his head jerking up as his body lurched over mine. I pressed one hand between us. I moved my fingertips along the smooth skin around his cock. Then I wrapped my hand around, moving up to the tip.

His breathing hitched, his hips thrust forward, and my hand was again at the bottom. I smirked and moved back up to the tip, and his hips thrust again. I looked deep into his eyes. His eyes were wild and wide, and I saw myself in the deep blue and black of them.

I guided him with the next thrust. He moaned as the head of his cock entered me. His body shook, muscles so tight I thought he wouldn't move again.

Slowly, he sank into me. Deeper and deeper. His organ filled me, adjusting to my body. Filling the ache. Growing into my folds. His hips settled against mine. His cock kept filling, kept widening to where every inch of my shaft he touched. As he took in the heat from inside me, his cock began the second phase of changing.

When they mated, each Welkan male's cock grew ribbing over where the woman's pleasure spots were. So that each thrust gave the ultimate sensation. Welkan males were built for pleasuring females.

Taspe was no exception. As he drew out, that ribbing caressed my spot, and my body shook with pleasure. He thrust back in and I cried out. I wrapped around him. Needing more. This part he moved at the pace I set.

He thrust with the beat of our hearts. With each pulse of our bodies. Quick, hard, relentless. Another quake of release made my body go taut underneath him. He rode it out with more thrusts, not breaking a beat. I began moaning with each meet of our hips.

I lost all sense of time. Countless orgasms. I just knew each time I came, it drove him closer to his own release. A release he was desperately holding back with every fiber of his being.

I became liquid underneath him. My limbs were heavy and not my own. I was panting and moaning like an animal. "Taspe." I whispered his name through a dry throat, "Taspe…"

This time, his moan vibrated into my core. He covered my mouth with his and rolled us.

I got my heavy legs to push my knees under me. I pulled away. I rolled my hips. His fingers dug into my ass, his hips still plunging into me with each beat of our hearts. His eyes swept over my body.

"Permission." He gasped and propelled himself into me twice more before adding, "Give me… permission."

Another layer of warmth spread from my scar all over me. His eyes were on my breasts, watching them jump with each of his thrusts. I cupped my breasts, then ran my hands down myself to rest over his. "Taspe, release in me."

As soon as the words left my mouth, Taspe bucked into me, hard and deep. A heat spread in me. His entire body shuddered under mine before going lax.

His breathing was quick. His eyes half lidded. But a quirk of his lips with a deep breath in, and a sigh out, let me know he truly finished.

I lay down on his sweaty chest. His arms came up and over me.

❤

I woke the next morning with a rumbling in my stomach and limbs that didn't want to work. His flesh was cool against my cheek again, and I smiled at the sound of his deep breaths and steady drumbeat of his heart. I wanted to snuggle closer, by I just couldn't make myself move either.

"Sleep well?" His already raspy voice was deeper, more gravely.

"Yeah. You?"

He chuckled, "Always do with you by my side, oulileah."

His fingers trailed against my temple, pulling a tendril of hair from my face. "Ready for a massage or would you prefer another round?"

I groaned, torn between the two, then my stomach probably woke the whole church with a growl. Heat filled my cheeks as he laughed. "Food."

"I have to agree." Taspe grinned, turning us to our sides. He kissed me, "Starvation after breaking my record is something I should have considered before you woke."

"Record?" I asked as he stood.

"Twelve." He grinned at me over his shoulder, pulling a small, thin gray blanket off the end of the bed and tying it around his hips.

I stared after him, watching how his tattoos shifted with each movement of his rolling muscles as he loped like a predator to the door. "Are you really going to go out into a church with nothing on?"

"I'm decent." He gave me another grin and wink before going out into the hall. He didn't bother closing it behind him.

Spacya was walking toward her room with a plate and rolled her eyes to the ceiling as he passed her. "Gods, ain't anywhere safe from naked flesh?"

I bit back a chuckle as she slammed her door shut behind her. It was a good thing that Taspe wasn't a companion right now. She'd probably have murdered him by now. He wasn't fond of clothing. He came back, shouts following him, and a red-faced blustering Blari too.

In his hands he had a large platter, covered with a silver metal top.

"I'll have you know that in NO CHURCH is this acceptible! You may get away with it in Owlimount, basically because you're…you…and you've slept with all the priests! But here is a different matter!"

"Now, now, you're just jealous. It's your fault that I haven't bedded you. Keep turning me down all the time or running off with my oulileah."

Blari halted hard enough that I thought he was going to fall back on his ass.

Before the priest could say anything more, or think, Taspe kicked my door shut behind him. "I grabbed a bit of everything."

"Every priest, hm?"

He shook his head, his tangle hair falling all around his face as he set the tray in the bed beside me. "Not every priest, just one or two."

"So twelve?"

"You had twelve orgasms."

"Oh." I stared at him, watching him take off the lid. Steam rose from the variety of meats and bowls of candied fruits.

"Is it so many because of the bond?"

He shook his head, "No. Probably because you were manhandled badly for your first and only time. I took extra care." He held out a slice of ham for me, "You're gonna have to sit up."

"The bond, it's true, isn't it?" I asked before sitting up.

"Yes." His voice was low when he answered. "We are forever bonded, but not solely. Not meant for each other, but for someone else."

Something felt like it shattered in my chest. A small thing. Like a little vial of hope. "I do love you, you know?"

His hand not holding the ham cupped my cheek and his forehead pressed against mine. I stared into his midnight blue gaze as he stated, "And I love you. I know."

It was simple. He wasn't teasing. He wasn't speaking in riddles. Nor was he lying. Truth reverberated between us, healing the shatter. We would always have one another. A bond deep, but not a bond of mating. Or true love, as Seaghla called it.

He bumped his nose into mine, before pulling away. "Well, I hope that by now you know I am indeed a male. A virile male. An able and willing male to showt he physical form of our love for days. No, dare I say, weeks! With our only pause being for water, food, and a change of position or foray."

I pinched the only tender skin I could find, right below his ass cheek. I smiled as he yelped.

"Fine. A month. Plan it and I will gladly clear my calendar."

Another pinch. Another yelp.

Chapter 15

The loud rap on the door had Taspe, Ida and I looking up at it with held breaths. I wasn't sure what the other two dreaded, but I was dreading a summons from the Matron. Of having to be cast out of the comfort of the home Taspe brought to me, a new friend that Ida was, and into the role of a Hero that I was not.

Ida jumped up and went to the door, nearly knocking over her dead pieces from the game we were playing over in her haste.

Taspe and I glanced at each other, then back at her when she took something with a kind word and then made her way back to us. "It says you may have the day, but she's expecting you to wake in the morning to go with the guards outside of town. Only to return in like you were just coming back and do a parade."

I groaned, "What use is that?" The stupidity of the idea washed over me, making a tiny flicker of anger sputter into full flame.

"Chi, you're a hero now. You're supposed to be worshipped by the masses." Taspe crooned with a grin and waggle of his brows. "Like me."

I rolled my eyes. He'd taken to being the most popular Legace, no, male Welkan, like a fish to water. Everyone either wanted to kill him and take his place, or worship him in every way imaginable. A chill swept through me at going over what the next day would bring, sweeping the anger quickly back into a trembling flicker of light. Crowds. Loudness. Touching. All eyes on me.

"It's going to be alright." Taspe said quietly, reaching across the game board to rub my arm, then take my hand in his. "I won't be able to ride with you, but I'll be at the end, waiting. And Clara will be with you. Blari too."

I nodded. There was comfort in that. I had something to look forward to in the end of being made a spectacle.

"Besides, I already took care of one thing. At least for a little while." He dropped my hand, watching Ida move one of her pieces to overtake his on the board. He frowned at her, "Here I thought we were friends."

She giggled.

"What did you do?" I asked, eying him when he wouldn't look at me.

"Well…see…the bond."

I nodded, waiting on him to go on.

"I told her it was complete. Like I was going to marry you, complete. Not like the partnership that we have." He finally looked at me, a goofy grin plastered to his face. "She cancelled all the meetings with suitors she sat up for you in some little fit of Stygra rage."

I laughed, "Oh that's good."

Ida stared at him, "You should tell her the other thing too."

"Other thing?"

As Taspe showed his teeth at my maid, I sobered, feeling my grin fade quickly. "Now what?"

"I didn't come alone-"

"Father?!" I knocked over the board getting to my feet to run down the hall.

"No. Chi." Taspe said slowly, then sighed, "Joni."

I stared down at him. "Joni?" The anger roared. I clenched my fists, reminding myself that he'd made his choice. I'd made mine. "He changed his mind? I can go home now?"

"That's definitely not what he's hear for." Taspe muttered, grousing.

I watched a muscle begin feathering in his jaw beside his lips. "Then why?"

"I wanna know how you didn't kill him." Ida whispered, looking at her hands in her lap. Her face reddened when we looked at her, "I didn't mean to say that out loud."

Taspe groaned, "He wants to lay claim to you again. Take you home to marry you and pump you full of his seed."

My teeth clenched together so hard an ache started. I loosened my jaw, "He never had claim to me."

Taspe smirked, "Never."

Sam Wicker

I shook my head, "He's my friend. Was. Now he's just an idiot."

"He's always been an idiot."

Another rapping sounded at the door as soon as I settle back down. We began putting the game up, none of us interested in it to continue playing. I watched Ida go back to the door. She yelped as the door was pushed open on her.

"Good, you're awake. We need to go." Joni strode into the room.

Taspe was on him before I could brace myself to stand. He slammed the boy into the wall by the door, pinning him there with one arm as he reached gently toward Ida. "Are you hurt?"

Ida shook her head, rubbing her wrist where the door had been twisted from her grip, and her eyes going wide as she took in Taspe's swift attack.

Joni and Taspe were the same width in the shoulders, but there is where their similarities ended. Taspe was all lean muscles, battle scars, and swiftness. Joni was made of mining muscles making him thick in the shoulders and thighs, but he wasn't quick. Nor was he used to having someone fight back. Most backed off when he confronted them, just because of his size.

"Go where, exactly?" I asked, coming up behind Taspe.

Joni struggled to free himself, pulling on Taspe's arm across his chest with both hands and trying to wriggle out at the same time. His tanned face started a red shade. "Home. To Owlimount." He huffed, wide light blue eyes sweeping to me.

"I'm not going home for some time," I tried to hold back the emotion, but the tears of the truth behind those words made them break, "Because someone was too much of a coward to do it himself."

"You don't have to do it!" Joni growled, trying to throw an elbow into Taspe's ribs and kick his shins.

Taspe just sneered at the boy.

I hissed.

Joni stopped struggling again, his gaze swerving back to mine. "We can go home. Do like we planned."

"Taspe, I think he's gone mad. Maybe a priest can help him."

Taspe chuckled, "Cutting his prick off might set him straight. Not sure if they do that here."

Joni paled.

The Welkan tossed the human out into the hallway. Joni flew in the air for a bit, before landing heavily on his chest and knees in front of Spacya's door. The huntress didn't even bother to open her door at the noise.

"Make an appointment for tomorrow if you want to talk to me. Sensibly. Like about how you want to take up being the Hero, as you should've weeks ago. Otherwise, I will have the guards drag you through the streets." I slammed the door shut. I waited until I heard his stomping feet fade down the carpeted hall. I heard a door shut.

"He's staying here?"

"Yes." Taspe said, kissing the top of my head. "You're so bitter and angry with him." He rubbed a hand down my back in long slow strokes. "Still so raw."

"I can't. He's impossible." I shook my head, "Changes when it suits him or just can't think for himself at all. He probably didn't become Hero just because his little pack of friends wouldn't be allowed to join him. One of them is the brains behind all their operations."

"I cannot agree with you on the last one. I thought his plan for you was quite impressive." There was a dark laugh in that bluejay voice.

I rolled my eyes, "Is it the plan with the nineteen kids?"

"Ah, so you've heard of it."

I snorted as Ida stammered how gross and impossible that was, her little fists squeezing shut before she shook one at the door. "While I'm in labor I suppose I can dress my latest kill while he sits on his ass and claims it as his own too."

Taspe chuckled, "Both of you, take a breath and let it out slowly." He nuzzled into my hair. "That's fair. I would have you give me full body massages while your pushing out our child. Oh, and to cook our supper. Don't foget to wash the dishes and the lines our childbirth soils too."

"Not funny." I nudged him to the side with my shoulder and sat back down on the couch. Our game completely forgotten, halfway put up, on the table.

Taspe and I took a stroll through the large church after our evening meal. I remembered walking with him through our much smaller church in Owlimount, nearly a decade ago. He would stop in front of each tapestry that depicted Meandria, the goddess of waters, and tell me the story the woven threads showed him. Each tale grew in length, vulgarity or humor until I cried with laughter. To this day I wonder how he hadn't been struck down by the goddess for making up such tales of her. Maybe she enjoyed them as much as we did.

I stopped in front of a tapestry of Meandria pouring water out of her amethyst and sapphire pitcher for Glena, the goddess of learning and creativity. Glena was at a table filled with scrolls and paintings, while she wrote on a piece of parchment with a soft smile on her glowing ebony face. I cocked my head and smirked at Taspe.

He stared at the woven threads for a moment, then looked at me. He chuckled, "Oh gods, I don't know if I can be as entertaining as I was…" He cleared his throat, looking back up at the tapestry and sweeping his gaze slowly over every detail.

"Long ago," he began, placing a hand over his heart, "Our goddess Glena became so overwhelmed with the creativity of all the Welkan tribes that she could hardly transcribe it all, or keep up with herself. Our goddess sat down to create a system where all creative ideas are kept safe for future generations. But she knew she could not do it alone.

"She called for aid! Far and wide she called on her cousins and brothers and sisters to help her. Alas, only one answered. Her own mother, Meandria, but she did not come empty handed.

For before Glena was born, it was Meandria whence creativity and learning flowed like the waters of the deep Gala.

"Meandria gave her daughter the water of all life. The water that Glena drank at succor. And refreshed became Glena with each sip. And power flowed from her fingertips into her new system. So created were the God Scrolls of Creatives. No mortal shall ever see, but the gods and godesses keep them safe and read from them to us when we need art and learning."

I shook my head at him, biting back the smile, "You were right."

"Hm? I enjoy being right, but what was I right about this time?" Taspe lifted my hand and kissed the back of it as he turned to look down at me.

"You weren't as entertaining."

He scoffed, "Well then! Let's find a better tapestry! I can only be as entertaining as the threads allow!" He wrapped my arm around his before starting off down the hall.

After looking at a few more tapestries, he looked up and down the hall before pressing me against the wall with a grin. "I can't seem to find anything more interesting than you at the moment." His grin grew as I gasped when his hands drifted over my shoulders and down to cup my breasts.

"Taspe!" I managed a half-hearted swat at his hands. He kneaded them, and my body betrayed me by arching into his fingers.

"I think I've made a fair trade." He dragged his hands down my sides, curling them around to my backside to pull me flush against him.

"Trade?" I wondered if he was warm enough to take me.

"The trade of being entertaining to being able to make you gasp my name, need me and want me so badly that you don't care that we are in a semi-public area." He smirked and dug his fingers into my underside of my ass cheeks.

I felt my body flush all over. I moaned, pressing against him, and suddenly his teasing disappeared as his lust reared its head. A moment of triumph made me smile before I heard a throat clearing and a cough just down the hall.

Taspe and I both looked over his shoulder to see Blari grinning at us.

"I am happy to see you both out of the room." The priest kept that stupid grin on his face.

Taspe slowly released me, his hands moving up my pants to rest over my hips. "At least it is our normal priest of perversion watching us from the shadows."

Blari coughed in the middle of his gasp, "I do not know what you mean! I am not watching!"

I laughed, "You were."

"Only because I didn't know whether to run away or to tell you to go back to your room!" Blari held his hands out with a shrug.

Taspe chuckled, "Pervert."

"Whining Welkan."

"I only 'whined' to you once." At Blari's brows flowing up to his hairline, Taspe amended, "Maybe twice."

"Try at least once a week for nearly seven years."

"What did he whine about?" I broke in before Taspe could spout another retort.

Blari's smirk was half hidden by his beard, "About you mostly."

Taspe growled at the priest, turning and keeping me pinned to the wall with his back to me. "Not mostly her! There were plenty of other things I talked to you about. Need I remind you it was in *confidence*?"

I shoved at Taspe's back, making the Welkan stumble forward and freeing myself. I moved between the males, grinning at Blari I asked, "What kinds of things did he say about me?"

Taspe tried covering my ears with his palms, but I shifted away and swatted his hands.

"Oh, just that he would be alone for all eternity, because his love for you was just so immeasurable that he could never pretend with another. That you were meant for a stupid, lump of a human and deserved so much better. That he was going to…" his breath whooshed out of him as Taspe's shoulder made impact against his stomach.

The bare skin of Taspe's forearms squeaked against the stone flooring as he tried to pin the priest down.

Blari grunted as he tried to push the Welkan off him, "What in god's… Taspe! Get off me, you big, overgrown. Thing. Off!"

"Thing?" He paused, holding Blari's wrists above the priest's head. When Blari started bucking, Taspe grunted as well, trying to keep hold and stay atop at the same time.

"What I was trying to say…" Blari started after freeing a hand and roll both he and Taspe to their sides.

Blari forgot that with his hand being free, it also meant that Taspe now had a free hand to shove into his chin. That effectively cut all words off.

"Confidence! Doesn't that mean anything? Isn't that in your priestly vows?!" Taspe's eyes went wide, "Why is your beard so much softer?"

I stood, watching the two men's wrestling bout come to a pause as Taspe fondled Blari's black facial hair with one hand. My arms curled around my sides and I covered my mouth to keep my laugh from echoing up and down the corridor.

"Oh! The boy who takes care of me while I'm here introduced me to this oil. You rub it into the beard hairs after you bathe while it's still wet and let it dry. It makes it softer, and it doesn't tangle half as bad." Blari blinked, "He was planning ye…ow!"

That softer beard was tugged, hard, by a now glaring Taspe.

Blari forgot all about what he was going to tell me to focus on attacking Taspe for that low blow.

I couldn't breathe. I slid down to the floor, curling in on myself as I laughed so hard there were no sounds coming out any longer.

"Off. Off. Fff. OFF!" Blari kept saying, trying to get back out from under Taspe, who had regained his top mount.

"Stop. Saying. My. Personal. Stuff!" Taspe ground out.

It looked like he was trying to get Blari to eat his own beard. I wasn't sure though as my vision was blurry from laughing so hard.

"What in all gods and goddesses blessings is going on here?!"

The males froze.

I curled on my side, desperate for air, and tried to look innocent. I covered my face with my hands and looked through my fingers at the priest standing over the three of us.

"Separate! There will be no mating rituals in the middle of the halls!"

My lungs and sides burned as if I had run a mile, and I needed to pee.

Taspe sprang off Blari so quickly I thought Blari might have lit a lamp under him. He sputtered, "Not with him!"

Blari sputtered beard from his mouth and sat up, "Forgive our actions Head Priest. It won't happen again." He glared up at Taspe.

"As long as you keep quiet about my talks with you. For I knew you would never share them with another soul for as long as you lived." Taspe glared right back at Blari.

"What was shared in the confidence halls of any church shall be held in such outside it's walls!" The head priest barked as if he were a soldier giving an order.

I saw my bonded pale as Blari smirked.

"Of course, Head Priest. And all that is shared with us outside the hallowed halls shall be used at our discretion for the good of our fellows." Blari's voice held a note of triumph.

The Head Priest looked both of them up and down, and then his eyes landed on me. "I would expect more from our Hero."

I watched Taspe's hair bristle, and grabbed his wrist to help myself up. I brushed my sides off and tried on the haughty look that mother had taught us at a young age. "And I would expect that a priest of Galanesse wouldn't allude to the terrors of our dark past when Welkan males were kept for such dark practices."

I had the satisfaction of watching the man turn green as he stepped back. "I…I would never. I did not mean…"

"Have a gods blessed day." I muttered, grabbing Blari's hand and tugging both males down the hall, away from the capital priests. After we put a few halls between us, Blari pulled, stopping us, "That was dark, Chi."

"He was showing his ass."

"Still." Blari glanced back, then smirked, "Imagine if he had come across you instead of me."

Taspe shook his head, "Both of you are terrible." He canted his head to the side, as if he could hear the priests. "Do you think he was one of those?"

"He's not old enough, is he?"

"I don't think there are any humans still living that had slaves, Taspe." I murmured, "But he might have been from a family that did."

"The Matron had two, before the treaty. She released them, but one stayed with her until he died." Blari mentioned softly.

Taspe shrugged, "It's hard to believe it's only been a little over 100 years since the treaty. Some still think we need to be slaves. I can see it in their eyes."

"Now you're just being mushy." Blari rolled his eyes, "The capital has always been a bit... odd. The richest are here so they would be the ones that had the most opportunity to own slaves. The Stygra powers are here too, and we all know they owned slaves."

Taspe sighed, "My mother was a slave. She doesn't speak of my father, but I assume he was a slave as well."

"I didn't know your mother had been a slave." I had always just assumed she was tribal.

Taspe's smile was slow and small, "She was, but she was lucky. They captured her only two years before they signed the treaty."

"She conceived you while she was a slave, didn't she?" Blari asked, leaning back against the wall, "But she incubated you for half a century until she knew it was safe?"

Taspe nodded, "She knew I would be male after a month. She couldn't bear the thought of the treaty being broken and someone snatching me away from her. So she asked the Agigave and Ghiga to still my growth until it was safe."

"So you're really old."

Taspe's eyes narrowed on me, "I'm only 15 years older than you."

"Technically, over 80 years older if we go by when you were conceived."

"No one does that." Taspe poked my forehead.

Blari chuckled, "You are old and still act like a spoiled child. Understandable, with as much time as you spent in the womb."

The Welkan's blue eyes would have shot daggers if he had that kind of magic. "I never should have spoken to you all those years ago." He sighed, "But I took pity on the new priest as he was thrust into an unknown land."

"You only started talking to me because I asked for your help while you stood there watching me get screamed at by…" his eyes shot toward me, then back to Taspe, "A certain woman."

"Pretty woman, who had every right to yell at you." Taspe corrected with a dark smirk curling his lips as he drew me closer to his side. "Did Blari ever tell you about meeting your mother?"

"No, he didn't."

Blari's cheeks reddened over his beard, "Aren't you hungry? Shall we go eat?"

"Oh, nevermind your empty pit of a stomach, man." Taspe waved a hand in front of Blari's waist, "I'm surprised he didn't. You mother, is such a patient, loving, and welcoming little thing."

I snorted and eyed Blari, "What did you do?"

"Nothing!" He croaked, then puffed out his chest, "I have forgotten to tell you what you asked of me…"

Taspe showed his teeth. Blari smirked.

"Go eat. We'll meet up to go back out in a few hours so we can do this parade through the streets thing." I waved Blari away.

He nodded, "I have a feeling we will need to fill our ears with wax."

I groaned, "Probably."

After Blari left, Taspe and I continued to look at the paintings and tapestries in the church. Some statues were interesting too. I asked what Blari had been saying to my mother that first day.

"Your mother asked him to pray for a rich husband for both her daughters. He said it was foolish. She took it the wrong way. That's all."

I laughed, "No wonder she talked to other priests instead of him from then on." I eyed him then, "And your secret?"

He leaned back against the wall opposite the latest tapestry we were studying, "It's not really a secret. Just a plan I had until you took up this Hero business."

"What?"

He sighed, "I was going to marry you."

I felt my brows quirk, the left one more than once. "Why?"

"To get you away from Joni. He would make you wretched. He was making you miserable. I couldn't have that."

I nodded, knowing he was right in part. I would have settled with Joni. Settled because it was supposed to happen, he and I, according to everyone in the village. A tiny part of me was happy that the Boar showed up, that I took up the Hero tasks, and that I was free of him. "Speaking of Joni, has he left?"

Taspe lifted a shoulder, "One can only hope. Maybe he'll get lost on the one road that leads home."

Chapter 16

Guards lined the street, keeping the people behind a literal body wall. Or tried to. The crowd jostled guards into our horses and the wagon. Fingertips grazed my legs, sending fingers of unease and nausea through me. Flower petals, ribbons and colored bits were everywhere. The sound roared in my ears until I couldn't even hear my own thoughts.

Tori and Clara ate it up. Smiling, waving, and reaching down to clasp hands to make the crowd swoop in even closer. Soon the width of the road was the same width as my horse and two shield carriers. Every guard struggled to keep them back with sweat pouring from under their helmets, constant grunts and shouts.

As we got closer to the ivory palace, the color of the armor changed. From reds and greens to white and blues. Here the guards seemed larger than life. They stood shoulder to shoulder, the crowd kept an arm's length away from them. The sweet scent of flowers tickled my nose instead of the wretched stench of excited bodies in the hot sunlight.

My horse acted better, too. She pranced, her neck arched high and her hooves making music on the stones. I patted her, my shoulders loosened, just slightly, at the feel of her warm short fur under my fingertips.

On the palace steps were the royal family, front and center. Some officials and royals from other countries stood to either side of them. My gaze swept over the guests, looking for one in particular who should be there. Our eyes met, and I couldn't help the grin.

He was standing with a group of rich capital families and officials. His legs wide set, arms crossed, and a head taller than anyone around him. He grinned right back at me, and the scar warmed my palm.

As soon as we were close enough, we dismounted. They carefully instructed me on what to do at this point via a letter that morning. Me legs felt like trees. I dragged myself up the steps to the Queen, King, and Matron to kneel before them. Sterla brought a bag that reeked of dead fish and placed it beside me. I pulled the tentacles out of the bag, showing them to the gathering.

"We have bested the worst beast of the salt waters of our great country, my lieges. Please accept this as proof of our victory." I was supposed to add 'and as a toke of my right to be Hero', but I didn't feel it. I didn't want to be the Hero. They needed me, wanted me.

With the number of dignitaries and royals behind those of our Lanpress having doubled, I knew they had taken the time to spread the word of my victory. Drawing out more. Coaxing more money into the capital. More opportunity for their daughters and sons to make prestigious matches.

"Rise my Hero and her party! You did well!" The Queen's smile was wide, showing all her too white teeth. "With this task complete, you are by action, the Glorious Hero of Lanpress and the World. May the gods and goddesses bless you as you continue to save our people from the evil that has spread over our country." Her arms were wide, welcoming. That too white smile aimed right as me as I dropped the noxious tentacles back into the bag and stood. Slowly stood. If it hadn't been for Taspe's massage after we ate, I probably would have had to crawl the entire way to lay flat on the steps and carried in.

"Let us feast!" The king bellowed, rising his arms up above his head with tight fisted hands.

They cheered until it reached a deafening ring.

The royal family split, the queen motioning us to enter behind her.

A guard in blue and white picked up the pack of tentacles and gagged. My lips twitched on their own. It would stick up the castle. So be it. These royals knew nothing of what the people in Columbri suffered.

We moved inside. Only the royal guards, dignitaries and their families, and those chosen by the queen were allowed. Their numbers were up in the hundreds.

Sam Wicker

As we walked, some broke off in conversations with one another. As a beady eyed woman and man neared me, cool fingers slid agains the back of my hand. I turned my head to look up at him.

He smiled down at me. We entered the great hall. The man and woman deigning not to approach me with the big Welkan at my side. Servants passed drinks and foods from their little trays of glistening blue metal. Light music floated around in the room from a small orchestra set up in the center on a slightly raised dias. The talking was a quiet murmur compared to the ruckus we had escaped outside.

Clara bounded over with a giggle and grasped Taspe's wrist in a Welkan hello, "Next time, massage more. She looks like she's still on the horse."

"Oh? I hadn't noticed." Taspe drew Clara's arm into his, leaning into her as he talked.

It was going to be a long day. I sighed, only to straighten as I tried to remember everything mother taught be about being presentable. I couldn't shame her. "How about now?"

Taspe snorted, "Too stiff."

She laughed, "A little better. About normal for a place like this for you."

"Excuse me, Princess Clara, the diplomat from Ocrea desires to have a word with you." The servant bowed low as he spoke.

With a sigh she said, "Of course he does." She turned back to us with a smirk, "Ever seen a walking weasel?"

Taspe chuckled before asking, "Are we about to?"

The princess nodded, "You will when you see Ocrea's famous diplomat, Jeffi."

"Famous how?"

Clara smirked, "You'll know when you see him." She waved her fingers at us and followed the servant across the room.

It was difficult to see where she disappeared to, even with her pink hair. Even Taspe barely saw over the crowd. He reported that the man had shiny black hair, and it was far too close to Clara's pink for comfortable conversation.

"How are you feeling?" He whispered in my ear as he gavy my hand a squeeze.

"Sore. On a cliff's edge."

"I'll fix the soreness later. I'm trying to hold you from the edge with all my might."

I laughed and shook my head, "I know you are."

"It is nice to know that you can smile naturally."

That voice sent a spider down my spine. Taspe's hand tightened around mine and his body automatically shifted between me and her. Just slightly, to not draw too much attention. The protectiveness curled over me like a thick blanket.

"I smile natural plenty." I faced her.

She was wearing all black again. The difference between her hair and the dress was so slim they looked one and the same. Both gleamed a blackish blue in the sunlight spilling from the tall floor to ceiling windows of the great hall.

Her face tightened, "Congratulations on defeating The Misshappen. Tomorrow you will set out on your next quest. We have wasted much time already."

"Yes, I could use this time to prepare and rest rather than handing out my fake smiles."

Taspe's hand squeezed mine again, hard. He was gently placing pressure, trying to pull me back, but I stood my ground. I knew I couldn't do much. Words were it.

Before I left, early the next morning, Taspe and I talked.

"Is it still bad? The tribes wanting to kill you?" I stared at our joined hands in his lap. We were sitting on the bed, facing one another.

We would leave today. And not together.

"They have slowly come to an understanding with me and my tribe. They cannot argue the ritual, especially since they saw it with their own eyes the second time. For now, we are safe and at peace." Taspe pulled me in, resting his cheek on top of my head.

"Good. I would wait to see if you returned safely when I was still home."

"I know. You would also hunt for the elders and do some work that they couldn't and the warriors we left for them refused to do." He chuckled, "You made some of the wary, others angry, and yet more love you."

"I smiled and placed a hand on my side, "The angry ones I know about."

Taspe murmured something I didn't quite catch as he pulled back and lifted my chin with a gentle hand to look me in the eyes, "Please, be careful."

"Nadachia! It's time!" Blari called from the hallway.

I groaned. Taspe kissed me and got up, pulling me up with him. He held me for a few breaths, arms tight about me.

I had known him my whole life. I had daydreamed about us being together as a teen, some as an adult, but I always knew we were not meant to be. Together. Bonded in hearts and minds. "May the gods watch over you as if you were their own child," I said into his shoulder.

"And you." He whispered into my ear.

"You know…the sooner we go, the sooner we can get back!" Blari again, from directly behind the door.

Taspe growled, "Why does he always have a point to prove?"

I giggled, and he walked me out. The Welkan had to stop at the steps with the priests. His eyes warmed me as we mounted our horses. I looked back at him and we gave each other a smile.

Our little party kept quiet for most of the crowd cheering ride out of the capital. By the time we crossed the bridge and were on the road to Emleton, no one had the energy to talk. It was fine with me.

I glanced over at Clara, she had her bottom lip between her teeth.

I knew it wouldn't be long before she began chattering about something. I started counting the minutes, and only had to wait until eleven.

In a clearing, just off the road, we took a break. Something about the air out here made Tori sickly. Or maybe it was something in his canteen. I was washing out the canteen and replacing the old water with fresh in a creek, when I heard a twig snap to my right. I peered through the low undergrowth that surrounded the water, keeping my breath steady, and my body still. My leg muscles began to twinge in the awkward crouch I now had to hold for longer than I expected.

Clara was singing something by the horses, her voice smooth and a welcome sound. Though it distracted me from listening to what was in the woods. I hoped it was an animal. Something made the hairs on the back of my neck rise, though.

Out of the corner of my eye, Spacya moved through the tall grasses of the clearing, crouched low, speer ready at her shoulder. Her eyes were on the woods to my right. I knew then, something in me was right.

The princess' voice faded slowly, as if she was ending the song naturally. I wanted to smile with pride for her being so smart.

Nothing showed itself to my sweeping gaze. I took my time, studying every little movement, each stump that was an odd shape, the trunks of the trees to see if something hid behind them. Nothing. I glanced toward Spacya. She was crouched in the grasses at the edge of the clearing, her head moving slowly from left to right as she too tried to see what it was that had us both feeling watched.

Watched.

That's the feeling.

I twisted the cap back on Tori's canteen slowly, barely letting the sound of metal against metal reach my ears. I let my gaze travel up the tree trunks, looking for something unnatural. The hairs on the back of my neck felt like needles.

Sam Wicker

Something about the large, gray barked birch tree made me stare at it. The limbs were fine, nothing clung to them except a twisted vine. Not even a nest clung where the branches met.

A vine? A single vine with no leaves. My gaze flew back to it just as it grew taught. High in the tree a metallic crack sounded and something began fluttering. That flutter turned into a beating of drums as out slid an animal I'd only heard of in stories.

Six long tendrils hung from around its narrow thick lipped mouth that never closed. Six small blinking eyes were right behind that mouth and its body stretched out as long as I was tall, covered in tiny gray feathers up to those eyes and mouth. Around the mouth, it was featherless, its skin a glistening raw red. Even it was poisoned by its own spit from those tendrils. Eight iridescent wings beat in rapid succession, like a rabbit's heartbeat made ten times louder and in the air. Each of the four legs had two long gripping claws, used for both resting on tree branches and holding on to its prey as it ate them alive.

"Yever!" Spacya cried, flinging her spear up toward the gray feathery beast. The Yever screamed, sounding like shield against shield as her spear snicked through it's back right leg.

Its leg dangled from the spear stuck in the tree.

"Tori!" I yelled, "There's someone that trapped it and let it go. Find them!"

I circled around, pulling my crossbow. I wished I had taken more practice with the thing. I should have practiced instead of being with Taspe. But he was home brought to me when I desperately needed it.

"Clara, go with Tori!" Those two were nimble and swift on their feet. If someone was running in the woods, they could catch up to them easily.

Clara whooped, jumping back up on her horse to gallop across the clearing and dive into the woods.

"No!" I cried as the Yever dove for the loud thundering hooves and flashy mane and tail.

I made a mistake. This was my fault. I took aim, careful to sight the main portion of its body, and took the shot. Another mistake. The bolt flew through one of the wings. The Yever only faltered in mid dive.

It latched onto Clara, the claws digging into her shoulders as the tendrils dug for purchase through her thick pink hair. I could see the yellow dripping through her hair, melting it down to her skull as the Yever yanked her from the horse.

Clara's scream wrenched through the air and tore into my heart. I ran, surpassing Spacya's steady, but slow gait in what felt like years as another scream tore through the air. I dropped the crossbow, yanking out daggers into my hands. I let them fly and tugged out two more from my belt as the first two sank deep into the gray feathers of the Yever's side.

Pain shot through my thigh, before something solid pushed in and I tripped. Sprawling into the grass as my leg felt like it had a skewer through it. I screamed, covering the fang-like blade of black with no hilt with my hand to try to yank it out.

Spacya was over me in an instant, "Don't pull. Up!" She yanked me up to my feet, her body between me and the woods. The pain in my thigh disappeared as Sterla screamed from under the wagon where she hid. I whirled toward her, torn between Clara and the little Stygra.

Nothing was attacking her. Blari held her against him, rocking and soothing as she cried, long trails of clear tears tracking over her pale cheeks. I stumbled as Spacya pulled me along.

She threw another spear, pinning the Yever with it. The beast fell, the spear thunking into the ground and holding it there.

The Yever spun around the spear, wings flapping up clumps of grass and dirt.

Spacya yanked Clara away from the beast as I hacked off its arms, bending under the bombardment of earth and a few of its wings. It slowed, the frenzy of a feast lost as it had no prey to hold onto. It worked its way around and around on one leg before wildly trying to fly. At last it settled, and died. A pool of yellow acid and blood tainting the ground around it.

"Clara!" I cried, wanting to hold her close to me and reaching for her.

"Stop." Spacya said calmly, taking off her cloak and wrapping it quickly around Clara's head. She dripped with acid, holes from the tendrils maring her scalp. Only a few tendrils of her beautiful pink hair survived at the base of her neck and one of her temples. "We need to get her back. Only Stygra can fix this."

"I'll take her!" Tori was beside us, Clara's horse tossing its head beside him. He jumped up onto the horse, "Hand her here."

Spacya lifted the princess, careful of the claws sticking through her shoulders with dangling arms of the Yever and of the acid that was already eating through her cloak.

I pulled the canteen from Clara's saddle, dumping it over the ruined cloak and Tori to try to still the work of the acid. "Go."

We watched him spur the horse into a breakneck gallop.

Spacya turned to me, gripping the bolt in my leg. She jerked it out.

I yelped, then bit my cheek against the pain. I covered the hole with one hand as Sterla screamed again. I stared at her, feeling the hole grow closed under my bloodied palm. "What…what…why?" I couldn't breathe. I looked from Sterla down to my thigh, pulling the cloth away enough to see the hole closing.

I give you the gift of Sterla.

Those words stung in my memory. I could almost hear them again in her dark, sneering voice.

"No."

Spacya grunted, "Blari's got her. We need to find who did this." She held out the bolt, my blood making the black darker. "Stygra bolt."

I swallowed, staring at one of the many powers that Stygra could posses. The ability to make threads of black and weave them together or thicken them into metal shafts. Why would a Stygra attack us?

I peered at the woods, "Let's track."

Hours later we found a fresh print a mile from our little clearing. Spacya followed it, just like she followed all the little signs of someone running away. Tori's trail threw us off for a moment, but we soon realized it once it met up with the hoofprints of Clara's horse and turned back. We followed the slender deer trail weaving along another creek bank, through the thick ageless trees with dark sticky bark.

Smelling smoke, we fanned out, surrounding the little fire with two hooded figures crouched around it. They talked so low among themselves that I couldn't pick up on their words. Just heard the murmur, and then one laughed, making a yanking motion with both of her pale hands.

I prayed to the gods that they were young and foolish. I couldn't take on a full grown Stygra who was in her magic. I watched Spacya for a signal. She waited. The one closest to me lay down with a heavy sigh. Spacya waited a beat more, before she wriggled her finger at me.

I ran and lept upon the Stygra lying down, pinning her down with my body. I rose up, grabbing the crossbow and bringing the butt of it down hard against her temple. As soon as she went limp, I jumped up, looking around to Spacya and the other Stygra.

Spacya grinned up at me, sitting on the Stygra's narrow ass as she twisted the female's arms back and up. She pulled a cord from her pouch on her belt, "Let me teach ya how to tie a knot."

I rolled my eyes, and bent to the task of tying up the Stygra. "Why did you attack us?"

The female spat at my shoe. I wound the cord around her upper arms and wrists, pinning them to her back as Spacya gagged her. "Guess we go back to the capital too, hm?"

"Yup. Let the guards handle asking them questions." Spacya patted the Stygra's head as she wriggled and said something against the gag. "Can't hear ya. Not sorry."

The two prisoners were tied to my saddle, slung over my horse like sacks of meal. Tori's horse and mine were tied to the back of the wagon, Spacya led Blari's by rein while he drove the wagon. I held Sterla in the wagon, putting pressure on the wound in her thigh. The exact place I had mine. Or should have mine.

Tears kept falling down her pale face, mine matched hers.

"I'm so sorry," I said for the thousandth time. "I didn't understand."

Sterla sobbed, "It's okay."

"No. No it isn't. How do we break this? How do we stop this?" My heart felt like it was about to crack open.

The little Stygra cupped my cheek with her slender hand covered in her dried blood, "I die."

Chapter 17

The road back was too short. Filled with me failing to plan a way to break this curse on Sterla that tied her life to mine. Dear curled heavy in my stomach with each bump in the road back to the capital. A few miles outside the city, guards met us, stating they spied us from one of the watchtowers. They led us down a side-road where we entered the caves underneath the capital.

I thanked them for showing us the way. Trying to map the path through the dark caves lit with flickering torches in case there was another instance like this one where we would need to find a way back without the ruckus of crowds impeding our every move. There were many twists and turns, paths that led elsewhere, and I hoped Blari managed to draw it out, or Tori knew the way.

Unia did not like the caverns. Thrashing with shrill whinnies against the rein tied tightly to the wagon's edge. One of the guards untied her and ran with her ahead so she wouldn't end up overturning the wagon with us in it. We followed them out, entering the gardens at the back of the church. Blari drove the wagon right up to the Black Tower.

The waves thundered below, and gray clouds scuttled to settle over the beaches and the tallest buildings of the capital. For once, the weather matched my mood. The guards took the prisoners away, leading them into the tower before us.

Blari carried Sterla inside, a handful of Stygra meeting them and immediately cooing soothing words to Sterla. I watched them lead the priest down the hall to a door under the smooth black staircase that swung upward toward the glimmering glass ceiling of dark obsidian. I debated asking after Clara. Then I followed the boards down the stairs, watching them drag the prisoners with ease.

The metal of their thin armor echoed through the narrow corridor, bouncing off the stairs up and down the spiral walls. Torches of green light lit the stairwell like moonlight from the full moons. One guard, bringing up the rear, paused to look up at me with wide eyes.

"I want to see where you take them."

She nodded, continuing down after the Stygra prisoners and her three companions.

I took another pause, studying a vine crawling up the wall through the cracks between large square stones. Tiny black flowers opened and closed, as if they were breathing for the thin dark green vine. Beautiful, but it unsettled me.

The stairs emptied into a hall and the guards turned to the right. Tables of trinkets and books in glass display cases under the green torches lined the walls between support pillars covered in the same vines that crawled into the crevices of the walls. The crashing waves sounded as if they were beating the walls. My head thrummed and my stomach churned.

Cold sweat popped up on my flesh as I tried not to focus on how narrow and dark the hall was.

The end held a black door, as wide as the door and carved into an oval. The vines didn't touch the wood. As the other guards stepped through the door after opening it on silent hinges, the last guard took up her stance just inside, holding the door open for me.

My boots met silty earth, smoothed to a shine and smoothed.

"Ah, Hero, I didn't know you would join us."

Her smooth voice startled me, the urge to run spiking through my limbs. She closed a door behind her with a snick. She slid a bolt into the wall and secured the thick wood with a chain of silver that seemed to glow of its own power. She rubbed her fingers after touching it, as if burned with cooking oil.

In the middle was a small table with a tome and a single candle on it. That candle was one of the three in the circular room. The darkness tried to swallow me, but it was cool to the touch, pleasantly drying my sweat.

"Matron Keandria, I thought it best to see where the prisoners were being held. Maybe ask them a few things."

She nodded, a small smile touching her lips. Her pale face seemed to glow with that little light there was in the chamber.

"Appreciated, but unnecessary. I'm sure you are exhausted. The amount of stairs you just climbed down will not help with that."

Her gaze shifted to the guards and the prisoners. "Bring them to the desk, I must have their names."

Keandria turned to the desk and took up a purple quill and dipped it in a silver inkwell.

"Do you take in all prisoners personally?"

Her hand paused halfway to the book lying open on the desk. There were more pages to the right, crinkled with use, than to the left, flat with their blankness. "Yes, I have. Though it has been rare. I like that it has been uncommon. So did the matrons before me."

Each prisoner stood before the desk, giving Keandria their names, titles, and lineage. She wrote them down; her strokes precise and even. Far different from Blari's wild scrabble to write everything at once. She put her quill up and looked at the prisoners.

"For what deeds you have done, we shall know. For what your reasons are to break the codes of our people, the beliefs and our solidarity, we shall know and judge you worthy of our disdain. You will reside here, until justice is served, until we learn all you know, and until the council and I decide your future."

The prisoners bowed. Keandria led each one to a thick wood door and locked them inside. "Your trials shall begin tomorrow." She stated after they were behind their respective doors.

I studied the room, trying to see how many doors were in the dim light. "Are there Stygra in any of these cells?"

"Empty. But the two."

"Isn't this a gift to be held in this darkness?" I didn't understand what kept them from pulling from the darkness, the source of their power, to escape.

Keandria smiled, "We give them a day in here. Then we take them to the true dungeon of the Tower. I'm sure you have noticed the higher tiers are all glass?"

I nodded.

"It is a special glass. One that holds, refracts, and brightens any light, but especially sunlight and fire. It was a gift from

Welkans ages ago, the top of the tower. That is where we hold prisoners after the initial day."

"Why not go ahead and put them up there?"

"Down here, in this comfort, sometimes it is more torture than the light. Do you not, each night when you lay your head on the pillow in the vast rooms that were given to you in the Church, feel guilty that your family cannot enjoy the same?"

It wasn't just at night. "Yes." For I did. Many nights I did. Many days when I ate so much I could burst, I felt guilty. I wanted to send all these things I enjoyed home.

"That is what these rooms accomplish."

Keandria moved passed me, motioning for me to follow, "Come, let's get you back on your way."

We walked a few floors in silence. She broke it with a question, "How far did you get?"

"Not far at all. Only a few hour's travel." I paused before adding, "Clara's hurt. As is Sterla."

She halted on the next step, bringing her feet together. The guards stopped behind us, throwing the narrow corridor into silence. I managed another step before I realized I had moved alone.

"That is unfortunate. How badly is she hurt? I shall send my healers to her immediately."

"She was attacked by a Yever."

The Matron clutched at the smooth wall at her side. She shook her head, long fingers going up to press against a temple, "This may be a political disaster waiting to happen. I shall have to visit the Queen."

"I can talk with the ambassadors from Ecia."

Keandria looked at me, "That's right. I heard rumors that your family aids Ecia's royal family from time to time. That's why they won against the raiders a few years ago and lost naught an inch of territory, nor a life."

In her voice there was a bit of something, a hiss, or a growl. Whatever it was, I wasn't sure what it was aimed at. I kept quiet, wanting her to go on.

"I think that would be best. Smooth things over."

"I will do my best. Then be on our way."

She shook her head, "Stay. I'm sure they will arrange parties to keep the dullness that is injury out of our minds. The beast can wait. It has done little damage thus far."

Again, there was something in her voice. Though her words flowed freely, something was behind them that sent the hairs on the back of my neck to stand. We entered the gardens after our feet echoed in the hall of the Tower. Following the sound of giggles that had my skin crawling, we entered into a small drawing room toward the end of the western hall of the castle.

Tori and Clara sat around a small table, playing some board game I didn't recognize. The ambassador that reminded me of a hairy toad whenever I saw him had his arms crossed over his rounded chest as his reddened throat bobbed with each heavy breath he took through his open mouth.

The Queen had her hands delicately folded together in front of her voluminous skirts, but her chin jutted. Spacya sat next to the game table, a biscuit halfway to her mouth when she spotted the Matron and I. She grinned at me, giving me a wink with her clear eye.

"This is ridiculous! This is an attack!" The toad ambassador spat, pointing a thick finger at Clara who just gave that high pitched, careening giggle.

I shuddered, before I could control it. Straightening I mentioned, "Attacked by a beast." I said as I came to stand beside him, "Hello, Antri."

He sputtered, his eyes bulging, "Nadachia! I–"

"Was just about to calm down and have some of that…is that tea?" I pointed to the little table beside the game. Tori nodded. "You're about to have some tea."

He nodded, the skin on his neck wobbling, "Yes, Silverequis. It is an honor again. May I say that your plan to draw those raiders through the pass was magnificent?!"

For the thousandth time in five years, each time he saw me he had to remind me of the plan my father and I hatched to rid Ecia of the army or raiders from the islands.

The Queen smiled, her jutting chin softening, "I have not heard this. Do tell me what this plan was all about."

"Why! Your Majesty! This young lady here, and her Father, ran all the way to Ecia to aid us! Raider beset us. Thousands of them! Brigands! Pirates! They came upon our land! But the Silverequis family had already been to work among them! They spread rumors of treasures and riches in a few mansions just on the other side of Fairmount Pass. Our people helped to, of course, but it was their quick thinking that had these ruffians fall right into the palm of our hands!"

He paused to suck down some tea from a porcelain cup a servant handed him, "You see, Fairmount Pass is barely wide enough for a three-horse team. And long enough for hundreds to be in at the same time. Just three by three, maybe four at the most!"

He had no idea about Fairmount Pass. Once the raiders entered the kingdom he and many of the nobles hid themselves in the closets of the castle while the royal family, generals, and my father and I handled the plans and battle. Antri only stepped a dainty silk covered foot outside of castles to step into carriages to get to the next one.

"The Silverequis family laid out a brilliant plan that allowed our army to trap them all in the pass. ALL the ones that came upon the land! Brilliant! Not a life on our side lost! Minimal damage to our lands too! They scampered away like pups being scolded! Never to return!"

"That's not all!" Clara chimed in, her voice pitched high to ring across the room wildly bouncing against the walls and making the chandelier tinkle. "They won't come again for the monster will eat them!"

I laughed, fearing I would cry.

"Monster?" Spacya asked, another biscuit in hand and crumbs along the furs at her neck.

"In the pass are mechanisms to move rocks from slides, they happen often there. We used the way the pass carries echoes to make louds growls and howls. Then we threw boulders down upon them from up top. All the while some of the villagers from nearby were whispering about the rock monsters that ate people in the pass. Not once did the raiders see a human, Stygra or Welkan from us up top. So they believe it was all the monsters that attacked them."

"Oh, my dear, wonderfully done." The Queen smiled.

"Yes, it is indeed." Keandria murmured, her dark eyes upon me.

I felt a chill crawl up my spine at their attention. "It's nothing."

"Nothing?! It was everything!" Ambassador Antri cried, spilling his tea on the carpet with a grand wave of his meaty hands.

I was sure that if given the chance, one of the others would have come up with a better plan. I knew there was no use in arguing with one prone to excitement like Antri, so I didn't bother again. I began what I needed to finish, "Ambassador Antri, Clara will be fine. She's already sitting up, an improvement." Although her laugh and the voice she used disturbed me, and had tears burning behind my eyes. "I'm sure she will be fine, sooner rather than later. Only her looks will last longer than we can hope. And those are rude to speak about, are they not?"

Antri nodded, a sigh parting his thick lips. "Yes, I suppose you are right. Devastating, to be sure. Now we must make sure she is properly cared for at all times."

"I have my finest healers ready." Keandria motioned, and four Stygra swept into the room from the hall.

"I gladly welcome such a gift, Matron Keandria. Thank you!" Antri crooned.

"She shall have every comfort here and she may stay here as long as she wants." The Queen smiled, a motherly look crossing her features as she watched the Stygra guiding Clara to her rooms. "Now, go get washed up, Companions! We shall throw a ball to honor Clara's sacrifice!" The Queen smiled and clasped her hands.

I wanted to groan, and nearly did, but Antri gushing about the hospitality and wonderful ideas drowned out anything. I slipped from the room, heading toward the church. Bootfalls echoed in the hall a second later behind me. "Chi, a moment?"

Sam Wicker

I paused, letting him catch up which only took two strides, and then continued a little further down the hall with him. We stepped into a small alcove and Tori looked around as if shy about there being someone near. He then looked at me, a hand raking through his dark hair which had grown a few inches since our first meeting.

"I want to pass something by you before I make plans. If Clara is… is beyond repair, do you think it a good idea if I offer to marry her?"

I felt my brows twitch upward. I shook my head, it was the one thing Clara detested about being a princess. She hated that diplomacy was tied to marriage for her. They seemed to get along well enough, before. I studied him, "I'm not sure what her father will want to do now. I don't think he will turn down the offer though." Considering. I heard the echoing giggle Clara had now in my mind, and felt my skin crawl.

It was honestly, a good idea, if they liked one another. Which they did. In a way. I supposed. I wouldn't speak for Clara though, not if she could speak for herself.

He nodded, "It's a thought I had, while getting her back here. I want to make sure she is still going to be important to her people and taken care of for the rest of her life."

"You don't have to worry about that. We'll both make sure of it."

He smiled, "You are going to be a good friend, I can see that already." He turned on his heel and walked back, taking the stairs to the bedchambers.

Chapter 18

Ida grinned when I stepped into my rooms, "Wait, you're back so soon?"

I told her what happened.

"Poor Princess Clara! Poor Sterla!" Ida wrung her hands together, her face pulled into a frown with a deep line between her brows. "Pure evil! Stygra live such long, peaceful lives. To put one through a trauma at such a young age is complete, true evil."

I floated in the bath, having stripped down with Ida's help as I told her the short, but profound story of the attack. It was true. It molded the being, trauma changed them for life. I knew that. I had seen it more than once. I had it, once, or twice. Still, mine was nothing compared to others. What happened to Sterla would torture her, would be remembered by her well after I was dead and gone.

The water suddenly couldn't warm me enough as the thought of something ending my life. It would kill Sterla too. The thoughts tumbled through my mind. Attacks of all kinds killing me, but not. Killing Sterla instead.

"You alright? You're pale. Nadachia?" Ida held my shoulders, gently shaking them.

"I'm- I need to lie down." I needed to break this. Surely Keandria would see reason now. Now that she saw Sterla hurt. No human was worth a Stygra life. No life was worth a child's life.

If she knew this could happen, how could she have tied us together?

Evil.

Ida's word filled my mind in an instant. I didn't want to believe it. Keandria didn't know the spell, the tie well enough. That was all. Now that she did, it would be dissolved. We would find a way.

Ida helped me out of the bath, and dried me off. She slipped a long shirt over my head before I crawled into the plush bed. I sat back against the many pillows stacked against the headboard and watched as she tidied the room.

"You want me to partake in gossip?" Ida crossed her arms over her chest after setting the lunch tray down.

"Yes. Partake. Speak it, listen to it, toy with it all to your advantage." I said with a reminder to myself of my plan. I shoveled a spoonful of juicy orange slices in pudding into my mouth. The realm of the gods was in that bite.

"I can't talk to you when you look like that."

Ida's cheeks were red when I looked at her. I chewed and swallowed most of it before asking, "Like what?"

"Like that Welkan is inside you." Her hands came up to cover her mouth as her eyes bulged out of her skull.

What I left of that last bite tried to go into my lungs as I cackled. That wasn't paradise at all. My cackles turned to hacking coughs before I got a little orange piece free and down the right tunnel. "Ida…it's okay. That's the best thing I've heard in a while." I giggled and shook my head.

"But it's slanderous!"

"Only if it wasn't true."

Ida's hands slid to her hips, "Chi!"

"What?"

She shook her head and huffed, "I'm not going to bother with teaching you anything." She grabbed an extra spoon and took some of my orange pudding for herself. "I'm to mostly focus on the Matron, right?"

I nodded, trying not to pull my pudding out of her reach. "The Matron and anything with what she may be doing. Or those around her. Like the council." Maybe it was one of them that convinced Keandria to tie Sterla to me. Or maybe it was Keandria who was evil and up to something. There was a piece of the puzzle I was missing, if not several.

"I can do that. You know, she is highly secretive, right?" Ida eyed my pudding, licking her spoon.

I eyed her eying my sweet deliciousness, my fingers itching to grab the bowl and run. "I know. That's why I think starting a few rumors will start some more. The truth will eventually get dragged out."

She nodded, her spoon diving from my tray, but she took some of the shepherd's pie instead. "What kind of rumor were you thinking?"

I wasn't sure how a rumor started exactly. I figured it had to begin with one person running their mouth. Ida was going to be that start, "How about one that claims she has a lover? Another about how she was the one behind the attack on us. And another about how she secretly experiments on the children in the Tower."

Ida's brows rose, "Any of those true?"

"Maybe?"

"Maybe is enough. If she has a suitor she won't go around stealing kids."

These orange pieces in this pudding would rather find the bottoms of my lungs than my stomach. "What?"

Ida plucked a piece of crust off the pie, "She steals kids. All those girls aren't orphans." She snorted, "There're not *that* many Stygra deaths."

"Sterla?"

Ida shrugged, "I think her father is still alive, but her mother died giving birth to her little brother."

How did I not know that? Had I even asked? No, I had assumed because she called herself, no, Keandria called her an orphan. I sighed, "Breathe some new life into that one too."

"What are you planning?"

I studied the food on my tray for a moment. My stomach was still deciding if this discussion warranted more food, or for what I had eaten to evacuate. I didn't want to tell her. The less she knew, the less danger she would be in. "I just want to see what dark secrets she has. See how much I can get away with as the Hero." I lifted a shoulder as I added, "If she already steals children, what else does she do to her people? What do her people have to allow because she's the Matron?"

Ida's face softened, "I'll help you out."

That evening, Blari, Spacya and I talked. Mostly about Clara and Sterla, and how they were faring. From the news Ida had gathered, both were healing remarkably well.

"I found some things." Blari blurted, his ink stained fingers squeezing the arm of the plush chair he sat in. He rose, going to his desk and picking up a thick tome that looked aged with dust and time. "I had some time and looked through the library and discovered an archive of two Matrons. I've been reading them today. Before Keandria took over, the former Matron lived here, in the church."

"Why?"

Blari smiled, "See that's what I found interesting. Keandria couldn't The Church kicked her out."

Spacya chuckled, "Good for them."

"They noticed she was buying children. Messing with their powers."

"Buying children?" I swallowed the bile that flowed after the words.

"Yes. She paid Stygra families for their little girls. Taking them and calling them orphans. She performed rituals on these orphans. The head priest at the time found a dead orphan, and that was the last straw." Blari flipped the pages filled with neat handwriting until he found what he was looking for.

"Here. She tried to place blame on her own mother." Blari pointed to a passage as he handed the book to me.

I was too stunned to read more than a few lines. This wasn't made up. Not like the rumors I wanted Ida to start. This was much worse.

He continued, "Some fanatics in the capital found out and beat Keandria's mother to death, thinking that Keandria was telling the truth." He swallowed, "She killed all of them for the murder."

"They know that and she still lives?" Spacya leaned forward, placing her hands on her knees, her knuckles growing white.

"No, but the priests suspected. Each one involved in the beating died within a cycle. Most caused by nature or natural causes. Nothing to use as proof. Just suspicion."

I curled up on the soft couch, Blari's rooms having the most comfortable furniture out of the three. I felt chilled. I placed the large tome beside me, carefully. "Anything else?"

"No, not really. The next high priest only wrote Keandria's praises." Blari took the book and closed it, "I want to look for more. Because…" He glanced at my leg.

"Please do." I nodded, "If she's still buying children, we need to stop her."

I had seen far too many ripped from their homes and lives. Being bought and taken, I couldn't imagine what that made them feel like. Unloved? As if they were nothing more than a thing to be bought? A slave?

"This isn't going to be easy, Chi." Spacya said as she ran a finger down the scar that rested just below her eye. I noticed she did that from time to time. A tell. "She's scary power."

Blari's brows drew low over his eyes, nearly enclosing his face in bushy black hair, "Are we truly considering doing this? Going against the Matron?"

I looked to Spacya, after a moment she nodded. I then looked at Blari, "If she's harming others, I don't see how we can't try to help the victims. Isn't that what we're supposed to do?"

The priest rubbed his beard, "Yes."

I felt the coil of sickness in my stomach, "I've enlisted some help. Ida."

"She can be trusted?" Spacya asked me in a low voice.

"I think so. If not, we'll find that out too."

Blari's cheeks puffed out, making some hairs in his beard stick out. "Pity the priest that wrote the first half of this isn't with us any longer." He patted the book on his desk, "We could've used someone with enough iron to kick the Matron."

"We have enough iron of our own."

"Your beard could hold a goat."

I glanced at Tori as we paused just outside Blari's open door. That had been Spacya's voice. The princes' head canted slightly to the side as he listened too.

"My beard is luxurious and vibrant!"

"Full o' crumbs and slick with gravy more like."

He scoffed, "Oils! My beard has been and is being treated with oils! Not gravy."

"Same gods' blessed diff'nce you prancin' horse."

"I will have you know, woman, there is a huge, significant difference between an oil to treat the hair and gravy slop. I-"

"Yeah, one is necessary while one takes up space and adds weight to a pack."

"If someone couldn't burn the biscuits, the gravy wouldn't be necessary!"

"If someone'd shave or be less of a prancer, the oil wouldn't be needed at all!"

I barely heard the next sentence from the priest: "My face gets cold."

Spacya huffed, "I'll sew you a beaver pelt face cover for yer cold face, you prancer."

"I'll have you know prancers work hard too."

"Oh, I respect prancers. Just don't understand why you insists on packin' three full tins of oil in your pack only to complain the whole way we have to walk. And get out of breath because of talking and carryin' extra. And complain some more."

"I don't complain that much."

"Then how do I know that you have five blisters on your feet at one time? Or that your pack must weight as much as a horse?"

"I...I..." He started, then huffed himself, "Fine. I'll take two tins this next time."

"Oi." I stepped into the room.

Blari grinned, "Ah! My saviors!"

"Let's get going." I said, ignoring the way Blari happily trotted out his door and watched Spacya roll her eyes after the priest. At least one of us was happy to go to the ball.

Chapter 19

The dress Ida had poured over me at least had pockets and I had daggers. And pants. The pants were a wonderful feeling. Nearly as welcome as anyone from my family being by my side at that moment would have been. Something about having four daggers on my person comforted me.

I was about to enter a den full of royals. I'd rather enter a den of bears and river lizards. At least with the animals I could tell an attack. The people, I couldn't tell a truth from a lie when it poured from between their shining teeth.

"This way, Hero." A guard stepped forward, from the castle as his blue adornments on his chest plate and arms gave him away.

I glanced at my companions. Only Tori had a smile, a gleam in his eye. The other two looked just as confused as me.

We followed the guard out the front doors of the church, instead of going to the castle through the gardens as we were prone to do. The thick castle walls and doors held back most of the roar of the crowd outside. The bright sunlight burned my eyes and I had no idea the vastness of the number of people in the courtyard until I was well in the midst of them.

Like during our return parade, guards flanked us with shields, keeping the crowds at bay. Fingers of complete strangers still brushed my bare shoulders. I shuddered, my heart leaping into my throat and pounding louder than if I was the waves upon the rock cliffs below.

Father's voice whispered to me: My heart is your heart. Feel it. My blood is your blood. Know it. We are as one. Strength with strength and the world with us, not against us. Then his voice timbered, stronger in my mind until it too roared beside the thundering of my heart.

A guard caught my eye to my right. He leaned in and yelled to be heard above the crowd, "We have you, Hero. It's all just a walk. All this noise is whatever you imagine it to be. Push it out. Quiet it down. You are safe with us!"

Had I said Father's words aloud?

I nodded to the guard, thankful for his care. Safe. I was safe. I refused to look over the crowd. I focused over the shoulders of the guards ahead of me, including the one that had gathered us at the church. A small part of me felt bad for ignoring the people. They had come to see us, after all. To see me.

Before long, but too long for my strength to bear as my heart palpitated harder than ever before, we stopped at the third step below the Queen. Her smile was as glorious as the sun as she addressed the crowd. "My people, we celebrate our Hero's safety! Villains attacked her and her party! But they won! They are well and safe!"

A deafening roar rose. A word formed in the roar. "Justice!"

"The Hero and her companions captured their attackers! We will deal with them post haste! Justice shall be served!"

The roar erupted into nonsense again.

"The time has come to bequeath land to our honorable Hero!"

What? I stared up at the Queen, and she continued.

"Upon signing the deed and in time of her assessment, her land shall be open, as she sees fit, to trade, work and for families. I'm sure she won't keep you or her new people waiting for long for her decrees!"

Decrees indeed. The Queen grinned at me, looking feral to me. That's when I realized she had just settled a hook in me. I had land. Not only was I Hero, but now I was a Lady who governed people. I would have to make appearances at court for the rest of my life. I would have to follow the rules and suggestions of the Royals and other rulers.

I took a deep breath. My mind pounding in time with my heart. Part of me had always been glad our family had fallen from notice, from grace. Now, I had to deal with this added nonsense.

"Feast and drink away my loves!" The Queen raised her arms, dismissing the crowd.

We followed the royals up the stairs; the guards keeping the now partying throng at bay until we were safely behind the closed castle doors.

Sam Wicker

Keandria appeared at my side as I barely stepped into the corridor after the Queen. "You will now have something more for suitors to appreciate."

Her words made my steps falter as my brain stumbled over them. "Suitors? I don't have any more do I inte-" Seaghla. I swallowed, interrupting my own words, "Seaghla has to marry first. Tradition."

"Not necessarily, but yes, she will have better chances now too." Keandria's voice was cool like a trickle of water over river stones. "You must do what is beneficial to the people of your lands and for your family." Her eyes shifted to me, takin in my face before returning her dark orbs to bore into mine. "I invited your Mother and sister to our festivities today. Many suitors are here now. Perhaps, one day, the rest of your household shall join us too." Her head tilted, hair flowing like silk around her face and shoulders with the movement, before she turned and made her way down the hall that would lead her to her Tower.

Spacya stepped into the space the Matron just left, "Everythin' good?"

I could barely hear her over my own heart, and the pulses throbbing at my temples. I nodded.

"Hm." Spacya placed a hand in the middle of my back, where a strap of cloth was, "Breathe."

Blari was already talking to some group of people, and Tori had disappeared nearly as soon as we entered. I let out a breath. Then took another deep breath in and released it slowly. The throbbing at my temples eased slightly. Hadn't I been wishing to see my family? Why did the thought of them being here make me so uneasy now?

They could be in danger. Playing the games with the Matron that I hadn't a clue of the rules or consequences. My family, here, in her grasp. What if-

My stomach plummeted. Breathing caused sharp pains as if I had run a mile or two. What if the Matron tied CiaCia to me as she had Sterla?

"Hero! Forgive the forgoing ritual, but I had to meet you and your companions." The voice, gentle, came from a slim woman

205

who stopped before me. Her gown shimmered as starlit fire. Her blonde hair pulled back, folded and tucked into a bun on top of her head where little paper butterflies held it in place.

I tried a smile as she curtsied before us, "Please to meet you." My voice sounded like a tree frog's.

Tori was at her side, appearing as if knowing I needed a buffer. He bowed his head slightly as he offered an arm to the woman, "Nadachia, may I present to you the Archduchess of Iethyll, Liade."

The thundering in my head made my thoughts march slowly. *Iethyll? Wasn't it just conquered? Something about pirates?* "You are a long way from home, Archduchess." *What was an archduchess again?*

"As are you, my dear Hero." Liade smiled, "I would have been here for the first ball and your introduction ceremonies, but I had some matters to attend to concerning a certain pirate overlord plaguing my country."

I watched Tori stiffen a little, but his smile never faded. Movement behind him caught my eye. I watched a stumbling Clara and Sterla escaping down the corridor, heading toward the staircase to the royal rooms. Both of them were smiling, and that warmed my thundering heart to slow down a beat or two.

I returned my attention to Liade and Tori. Spacya dropped her hand from my back and looked around. Trying to find an escape too, I imagined. "I'm sure that was a horrific deal."

"Yes! It was. That pirate killed everyone in his path and then some. Only I and a few others managed to get out of the court in time! We are gathering forces to take her back, Iethyll. To free our people."

I glanced at Tori; he gave a slight shake of his head as his eyes caught mine. With Father, that would mean to keep my mouth shut. Did it mean the same for Tori? Diplomacy. I tried to form a few sentences that would hopefully sound right before I said them out loud.

"I hope we can discover some way to settle these matters." Tori interjected for me.

I was probably taking too long.

"Well, allow me to find some other distraction. I shouldn't keep you to myself for too long." Liade curtsied, "Prince Tori, may I ask for your accompaniment for a little while longer?"

"Of course."

I watched them walk off.

"Nadachia?" Mother's voice squeaked out my name.

I turned, met her gaze. Her eyes were red rimmed, her face a shade or two paler than normal. My heart flew up into my throat. I didn't know it had left there to run up it again. "What's wrong?"

"The royals and Matron have taken an interest in Seaghla." She swallowed before clasping my hands and leaning in to speak low, "They plan to choose a husband for her. They have been prancing your sister about in front of rather…distasteful… I dare not say any more."

I held Mother's chilled hands in my own. She forgot to put on gloves, strange for her, even in her state. "Have they said anything specific as to why they would start this?" The throbbing in my temples doubled down.

Mother shook her head, "I only overheard something. They were speaking about how Seaghla and I might become a distraction for you. That you would only half-heartedly perform the quests just so you could get back for us."

Flames fanned my cheeks and neck. A distraction? My family was my life. These little quests were the distractions. A means to an end. A way to save them.

Mother's words spilled from her lips, but I had to strain to hear them as there was barely any sound behind her breath. "They keep saying that you approve of these choices. They are the worst. Like the merchant who- while rich, is said to steal and kill for his trade goods."

What was the meaning of this? There had to be a reason to risk my anger. And a scene or two. For the life of me, my head throbbing and the fire burning in me slowed my thinking. "Where's Seaghla now?"

Her fingers tightened over mine as her eyes flowed past the corridor and into the ballroom, "There."

I followed her gaze. Somehow, I had an unobstructed view. Seaghla's dress was the color of coals where it wasn't sheer. Her breasts were only half covered, each shallow breath she took threatened to bare them to the room fully. The cloth stretched over her body down to the midpoint of her ass and hips. There it grew sheer. Her pale thighs visible down to the boots that halted at the base of her knees. The heels on those boots made her a hand taller. Her lips, painted a thick bright red, stood out against her pale flesh.

Beside her, with her spidery hand splayed on my sister's bare back, was Keandria.

Seaghla was rod straight. Her lips strained against her teeth. She shivered enough that I could see from across the room.

A man grinned. He was thick, neck corded in muscles and his hands were as large as Seaghla's head. He reached up, brushing some of the loose, tousled curls off her bare shoulder.

My sister's jerk away was hindered by the Matron's steadying hand.

"No! Don't-" Mother's voice was behind me. The distance between my sister and me was just a few strides in my rage. My pulse thundered in my head as I took two of the man's thick fingers off my sister's shoulder and twisted until I felt them crack. I continued twisting until something split underneath his rough skin.

One of my daggers to his chin cut his yelp short. His eyes widened. He was a good head taller than me. The thickness of his arm did not fully register until he had me off my feet. The other hand had me by the scruff of my neck, and he hadn't uttered a grunt when lifting me. He didn't strain. He just held me there, inches off the ground.

I pressed my dagger harder. Blood skimmed over the blade's edge before a droplet started down his thick neck toward his white shirt. He lifted me higher, stopping when I was eye level with him.

"Put. Me. Down. Gently." I slid my blade ever so slightly. Fresh blood bubbled and spilled onto the shining metal.

His hazel eyes, a shade lighter than mine, flashed. "Take the blade off me." He might as well have growled at me. He sounded like he was talking from a barrel.

"You seem to have a nasty habit of touching women." A smirk curled my lips. *Where had that come from?* "I have a habit of teaching lessons that need to be taught." *Since when?* I tilted my head, my flesh and hair in his grip pulling painfully with the action. I wasn't about to let go of his broken fingers so he could get that hand on me, too.

"Nadachia." Seaghla's breathy voice drew my attention for a moment.

She was pale. Paler than Mother. I doubted she was getting any air with that ridiculous dress on.

"Yes, Hero, put your weapon away. You are causing quite an unnecessary scene." Keandria stepped closer, putting herself between me and my sister.

That was fine by me. One more person between her and this beast that had a hold of me. I turned back to the man. I caught sight of something, no, someone behind him.

"Nah, she needs to be put on her feet again first. Then she can put her little blade away, if she wants. If it were me protecting my sister, well, there'd be a bit more blood to clean up already."

The man was tall, behind the ugly beast that had hold of me. The stranger's skin was dark, reminding me of the dark ships of Columbri, his hair shone a blue-black, and it spilled over one shoulder to stop in the middle of his chest. His clothes were on the fancy side, soft and pliable looking, but not as embroidered or silky as the royals and other members of the court. His voice was something to behold, and I wanted to hear more of it.

The molester ground his teeth, "You will place my blade back into its sheath or she gets splattered against that pillar."

It was a wide and tough pillar. Splattering would happen with his strength I was sure, and I pictured it perfectly. I bared my own teeth, mocking him, "You do that and your head will be off your shoulders before I hit."

"Not to mention you will miss a kidney." The man added, "Oh, hi. Correction, you won't have your skull or either of your kidneys." The darkened hero turned to Tori beside him, "You must be a prince. I like that knife of yours, much fancier than his. Care to trade?"

"I am. No. You must be Prince Austere."

"Ah! My reputation precedes me then. It's a plea-"

"Enough!" Keandria stomped her foot. The sound echoed behind her voice in the now too quiet hall. "Put her down. Gently." The last word was ground out between millstones. "Nadachia, remove your dagger so he can do so without you skinning him."

I eyed the giant of a man holding me off my feet. His eyes narrowed on mine. Then he nodded, ever so slightly. I pulled my dagger back. He lowered me, only letting go when my feet were firmly planted.

I let go of his fingers too. I then stepped back. Seaghla's chilly hand snaked around my wrist, while her scent, that familiar smell of oleander, washed over me. The throbbing in my head gentled with her perfume. "Wanna touch my sister again?"

Tori's eyes rolled to the ceiling as he stepped out from behind the mountain of a man. The other stranger, the pirate prince, stayed put.

The man chuckled, taking a handkerchief out of his breast pocket with his unbroken hand to press it to his bleeding neck. "I'd much rather have you now."

The dark Prince came around, making a show of studying the short sword, like a needle, in his hands. "Yes, yes, I do like the Prince's blade the best. Above all, my own, but I am partial to them." His grin was a flash of white as he slid the short blade home into the bleeding man's sheath, ever so slowly.

"You like the idea of trying to tame me, do you?"

He chuckled, his eyes never leaving me even as the dark prince talked to him. "I do. It might be fun."

I smiled, like I was just showing my teeth at him again. I flicked my dagger, the blood, his blood spattering onto his finely embroidered coat and white shirt. He frowned at the now ruined clothes on his person as I said, "I don't think it would be for you."

Sam Wicker

I noticed the guard standing at the ready beside Tori. I wondered if they were here for me. The guard met my gaze before asking, "What shall we do with him, Hero Nadachia?"

"Give him a sleep in a cage somewhere. Maybe for a couple of days."

Keandria made a noise in her throat, but nothing more. I didn't care to even look at her as I watched as the guard, and another he called over, each grab one of the man's arms. They dragged him away. After some ruckus, a third joined, holding the man at spearpoint. He didn't struggle after that.

My head thrummed. My neck throbbed. I took Seaghla's hand, drawing her away from the Matron. After she was behind me and a few steps away from Keandria, I asked, "I really like the dress you chose for Seaghla. Got one in my size? Maybe in a green?"

Whispers bounced off and around the pillars and walls. People were skulking closer, slowly, now that the brute left, and we put away the blades. They would have had an easier time hearing us if they would stop talking amongst themselves.

Keandria's smile was tight, "I'll have one made for you."

"Good." I smiled again, or tried, "Do you want to reassure our guests that they are safe?"

Keandria blinked those eerie orbs of hers before she glanced around. For the first time, I saw her eyes widen and back stiffen. I had the sudden urge to create another, bigger scene. Seaghla's trembling hand in mine made me hold the desire down on a tight leash.

"This color doesn't suit my sister. I'm going to escort her home. I'll be back after she's able to change into something more her style."

Keandria nodded.

I turned and found the Queen moving toward us. I met her, as the crowd parted like I was in a poison bubble. "Go. Spend some time with your family. Just make sure you are back for the feast and dance tonight."

Music started at the end of the hall. I glanced at the musicians and saw Liade began her own ruckus. Tori was at my side.

"I shall escort you."

"Thanks."

Outside was chaos. I stood in the shadow of the large double doors of the castle, staring out into the courtyard before us. People were everywhere. Tables were everywhere. Children darted in and out, between tables, chairs and adults alike, giggling and laughing. Some held little sticks that crackled. We called them Flickers back home.

I wondered how long it would take the children to set someone on fire.

Tori cleared his throat, "I would call for the carriage, but I do not think that they could make it through."

Mother put a hand to her chest, "Oh gods, we have to walk that?"

The courtyard wasn't the end. Beyond, I could see people dancing in the streets too. The stench of alcohol, sweat and greasy or overcooked food filled my nostrils as I took a deep breath in. I squared my shoulders and started to the bottom of the stairs so we could begin our push through the crowd.

After a few feet, I needed to come up out of the swarm for air. Seaghla had ripped her hand from mine on more than one occasion to push people off her or Mother. Tori did his best to protect both of them. Somehow, I was the lead.

"Straight, the road there!" Seaghla pointed over my shoulder before placing her hand on it.

"If we can make it out of the square, I think we shall be fine." Tori's voice carried over the music and laughter to me.

"Heeeee join us!" A couple of men and women with hands full of ale casks pushed a frothy mug toward me.

The stench of ale curled my stomach. I pushed it away and said nothing. I felt like I was wading through the mud of the Gala's banks, hip deep in it.

I held my hand in front of me, pushing people away before I had to shoulder into them. It worked better that way. For a while.

The old shoulder wound started back up with a dull ache. In the center of the courtyard, I glanced back to make sure Mother and Tori were still behind us. I was reassured by Mother's pale nod and Tori's half grin.

Then, my world turned red.

Hands were on my breasts and lips on my neck. The stench of ale engulfed me as a tongue darted out to lick my flesh, that had been sucked between those strange lips. Before I could think, I had my daggers in my hands and I pressed them to the neck.

"Back up." I managed through my teeth.

She held her hands aloft, "S-s-sorry."

I put them away and placed my hand on top of Seaghla's on my shoulder and pressed through the crowd. We got to the street and through the thinner crowd there. A few more buildings down and Galanesse looked like a quiet little town, if you ignored the loud music coming from the courtyard.

I stopped, breathing in some air that didn't have the stench of too many bodies on it, but it wasn't truly fresh by any means still. Seaghla's hand dropped from my shoulder.

"Are you alright?" Mother and Tori asked me at once.

I turned, giving them a nod.

Mother's eyes were wide, her face still pale, "Are you certain? How is your stomach?"

I felt as if I had no true insides anymore. It had created a knot instead. "It's fine."

Her brows rose slightly toward her hairline, "I suppose being a Hero gave you a stomach of iron."

If she only knew what I had seen in just one quest. I bit down on the shiver crawling down my spine at the thought of what I might see in the quests to come.

"Come, let's get home so you can go back and enjoy the party."

She walked so briskly, I couldn't catch the look on her face. She had to be mad to think that I had changed so much in such a short time to enjoy such things. Then again, that was mother's way.

Seaghla smiled at me, taking my hand again, "Thank you."

"For what?" I asked as we began following our mother.

"For saving me from being pawed by that man."

My jaw tightened until my teeth hurt. I loosened my mouth by licking my lips before I answered her. "Don't let anyone paw at you again. You have a choice, no matter what they say."

She shook her head, "No, Nada, no I don't."

I looked at her, "How long have they been meddling?"

"Since you became the Hero. Since the day I was allowed into the Castle."

"Use your voice. I know you have one. How many times did you tell me no or stomp your feet at me?" I squeezed her hand, "Talk to them like you would me."

Mother hissed, "She best not."

"If it means that she can wear tasteful dresses and find a good husband, she can do what she wants!"

Tori cleared his throat, "If I may…" His eyes widened as we all turned toward him in the street. He then continued, "While we are here, we can keep an eye on her. While we are not, I can ask some of my younger brothers and sisters to help in this area."

"Oh, you shouldn't put anyone out because of us, Prince Tori."

I shook my head, "Thank you, Tori. I truly will appreciate this."

Mother and I stared at each other for a bit, then she turned and started toward their house again. It was on one of the outskirt streets. Farther from the courtyard of the three largest buildings in the capital than I imagined it would be.

This section looked old. The houses leaned against each other. Some had shops on the ground floor, but most were narrow homes. The one Mother and Seaghla lived in held three floors and they lived on the top one. We reached their door by a series of crumbling, steep stairs set on the side of the building. I looked down at the alley below, wondering how badly it would hurt to fall that far down onto the broken stones that made the streets.

Once Mother unlocked the rusty latch, we entered something smaller than our home back in Owlimount. It was narrow and held a small kitchen, dining space that doubled as a living space, a bath separated from the rooms by a battered screen and a single bedroom with two small beds on either side of it.

Tori closed the door behind us and I moved so we could all stand in the apartment. Seaghla promptly squeezed into the bedroom and closed the door and Tori suddenly found the framed embroidery made by mother's hand along the walls to be interesting.

"Would you like some water or tea?"

Tori smiled, "No, thank you though."

Mother looked at me, "We will not be a bother to Prince Tori, nor to his siblings."

"I assure you, Madame, it will be no bother. We deal with much worse daily. It shall be a privilege, honor, and a break for us to see to the protection and state of your daughter. And you." Tori added the last bit quickly.

Seaghla entered the room. Her dress covered her from neck to floor and she wore a smile. "I think I want to burn it."

"I wouldn't blame you." I muttered, then shook my head, "Sell it."

Mother gasped, "No!"

I looked around at the apartment, "Mother, you know you can afford a bigger residence now, right?"

She smiled at me, "Darling, that is your money. We are fine here."

My teeth ground and my hands clenched. I took a deep breath, then released it, "I'm doing this for you. Take the money and buy whatever you need. I can't spend it all."

Tori was still looking over each stitch of Mother's framed embroidery. He liked the red floral one especially well.

Mother stared at me. Her eyes, where I got mine from, bored into mine. She then swept her gaze over my face, my body, then back up. I saw beads of tears at the corners of her eyes when I met her gaze again.

"You have always wanted to take care of everyone. Especially us, your family, but also every person and thing you came across. Even when you are not able. Even when you can't take care of yourself." She looked down. She never looked down when speaking. Especially not to me. "Nadachia, remember to take care of you, too. We will be fine."

I walked over to her and wrapped my arms around her. I was heavy. Like something huge weighed on my shoulders. When I was with her, when I soaked in her warmth and breathed in her scent, that weight shifted a little off me. She smelled like home.

At one point, I thought I hated my mother. I thought she hated me. As I got older, when she left to take Seaghla here, to Galanesse, I found I didn't hate her. She just wanted what was right for me. For all of us.

I wanted to be that way, too. I wanted to make sure that everything she wanted would be right at her fingertips. That Seaghla could have a choice. I glanced at my sister, and she smiled and hugged us, too.

Tori stopped looking at the embroidery.

I laughed and pulled him into our little family hug. "Best get used to this. You're part of this now."

He grunted, his body stiff, then he relaxed a little.

"Oh, gods... we're hugging the PRINCE!"

I rolled my eyes as Mother laughed at Seaghla's exclamation. Tori grew stiff again and pulled away.

Seaghla whimpered, "What would the girls think back home?"

Tori's voice had a whine to it, "I-what would they think?"

"That I'm so lucky!"

I snorted. Mother smacked my shoulder. The hug broke.

"We should get back. It's going to take us until dinner time to get back through that crowd in the courtyard."

I nodded, "I'll see you later. Just stay here tonight. I don't like that there might be more... of that type waiting for you."

"Be careful. It's not only Seaghla who is single."

I gave each of them one last hug before leaving with Tori. The stairs going down were far more treacherous than going up. I could make them into a quest.

Chapter 20

We had fewer distractions on the way back than we had coming out. I would have thanked the gods when we entered the hall, but I had no time. Ida was on me in an instant and pulling me down the hall to a dressing room.

It still amazed me how each room had one particular purpose in this castle.

She stripped me down, washed me off, and pulled fabric off a hanger. "What is that?" I asked as she held it out for me to step into. "And why do I have to wear it instead of the one I had on?"

"A dress, of course." Her voice held a note that made me feel like an idiot.

"It doesn't look like a dress. It looks like a wrap."

"Put it on and we'll see if it's a dress or a wrap. It'll do you well to have a change of outfit after that fiasco."

It was a wrap.

The green silk hugged my hips, and thighs until it split. The split grew wider the closer it got to my ankles. Most of my legs were bare, ready to be seen by the public. It was drafty. I was wearing a long silk loincloth.

Two strips of fabric wound around my top half. Barely holding and covering my breasts. Bits of my side and nearly all of my stomach and back were bare. Where had I seen this before?

I racked my brain and saw it. Clara. On a visit to Ecia. Many times there were women wearing dresses like this.

"Why am I being put into a style from Ecia?"

"In honor of Clara. For her sacrifice and trouble she has gone through for us, for you."

I suddenly felt truly small. Clara had gotten hurt because of me. Here I was worried for her, but I also ran off with my family and hadn't thought of my dear friend for a few hours. Shame heated my cheeks as Ida began the finishing touches of doing my hair and re-painting my face.

The heeled boots Ida wrestled into place, they appeared much like the ones Seaghla wore that night. I slipped a dagger in each. I tied another set to my thighs. Just in case the brute got out of the dungeon or there was more like him.

Ida pretended she saw nothing, but I saw the shake of her head out of the corner of my eye.

"I'm going to break my ankles, and my neck too, in these things."

Ida laughed, "You won't have a chance, I think."

"What does that mean?"

She looked at me, dead in the eyes, "All the eligible bachelors have been patient thus far. But tonight, you don't have the distraction of your family, and you do not have Clara around to distract them from you. Nor Taspe. Blari and Spacya have already been in deep conversations with those that interest them for a while now. I doubt they will think of saving you, or notice that you need it."

"I shook my head, "What does that mean? I can still break my neck and ankles without them."

"You'll be dancing. You'll be dancing Ecia dances."

I thought back to the few dances I had hidden from in Ecia. Shame no longer made my cheeks hot. I chilled all over. "This isn't good. Tell them I'm sick."

Ida shook her head. "You had to make that scene earlier…"

I always ended up screwing something up. Now I was going to make myself sick. My stomach decided to no longer act like it had disappeared by emitting a loud gurgle before it became a rock.

Ida pushed me out of the room. "Eat something, will you?"

I turned to go back, but she slammed the dressing room door in my face.

I debated on running in the opposite direction, but I couldn't remember what was down the rest of this hallway, but I wouldn't mind finding out. I eyed the door across from me.

"Don't. Come."

I turned to Blari. He was smiling at me from down the hall.

"They sent me to make you follow me. I shall be your leash until everyone else gets you under their claws."

Sam Wicker

I turned to glance down the opposite side of the hall. I sighed. Another time. I had to start thinking quicker on my feet.

"Come on. They have Ecia food. I heard you like Ecia food." His voice had a tone like he was taunting a child with candy.

I did like Ecia food. Especially the caramelized fruits. "Can't you bring me some?"

"No. Come on or the priests and Queen will have my head."

"If they can get to your neck through that beard," I muttered under my breath and made my way to him. He placed my hand on his arm, and he steadied me until we reached the banquet table.

At least it was far enough away from the music and dancing that I had no danger of being asked.

I never said I wasn't naive.

Liade was beside me, "Ecia fashion looks good on you." .

"Where's the rest of the thing?" Blari muttered from behind me. I turned when he tapped my shoulder and he shoved a goblet of wine at me.

I took it and downed it.

"Who would think a priest would induce one of his friends into getting drunk." Liade smiled, shooting a look at Blari.

Blari smiled, "Either she is tipsy, or she's going to kill someone."

I looked over the table. Before I could make a choice, Clara's handler, a boy she leaned on, handed me a small plate filled with caramelized apples. I hugged her while I took the plate. She wore a pink dress, and had her head covered in a silken wrap of matching material with a jewel of white pinning it closed.

She giggled. It was tinged with the same pitch as her cackles in the recovery room, but the gleam wasn't high in her eyes. She was returning to herself more.

"How do you feel?" I asked her.

She draped an arm over my bare shoulders, "I'm better. I think. I think I'm fine."

I nodded, "You are. You will be." I ate a few bites of my apples and Blari got me another goblet of wine. As I ate, Liade wandered off until Clara, Blari and I stood alone.

An ambassador and another priest came up and involved Blari into a conversation.

"I remember how to dance."

I nodded. I wanted more apples, but for the life of me, I couldn't find them on the table anywhere. Where had Clara gotten them?

"Let's dance."

I looked over at the Princess of Ecia, and she grinned at me, "I remember how you love to dance."

Sarcasm. Of course, she would remember how to torture me. I sighed and put my plate and goblet down. "Fine. But you best get me more apples afterwards."

She giggled with another strange lilt to it that reminded me of the cackle. Maybe her giggle would always hold that now. It was going to take some getting used to.

We walked arm in arm to the dance section of the hall. It was a corded off section of the hall in front of the musicians. It was full of couples and groups dancing in Ecia's style.

Clara took my hand in hers and stepped into me, our bodies flush as her free hand slid to the upper curve of my buttocks. That's when I figured out I had bare skin there.

I placed my free hand on her shoulder, as the other dancers were doing. Well, at least the ones that weren't plastered to one another.

"Up on your toes, and follow me."

I lifted my heels, and we were off in a tight circle. As I picked up on the steps, Clara moved us faster, keeping with the rising tempo of the music. At the end of the longest song I had ever danced to or heard, I was sure I was going to pass out. I felt like I had run a mile.

The music stopped. Clara peeled herself off me with a grin, and we clapped for the musicians. "I'll dance with you again before the night is over. Or you escape." Clara's golden skin was pale, and soaked while she breathed heavily and with a slight rasp.

"Go rest, please." I motioned for her handler to help Clara to a seat. I whispered to the boy, "Try to convince her to lie down in her room."

"May I have the next dance?"

I followed the direction of the voice and met the King's eyes. "Yes." Who was I to deny the King?

"You are making quite the stir this time." The King began. The song started and was much slower than the last one. He led me along the dance floor in a glide. I stumbled after him. "At first, I thought you would be a whisper in our presence. One who keeps to corners and all that rude behavior of an unmannered, backwards sort." He paused, his eyes boring holes into mine. "I was wrong. You voice your opinions. You dare to be bold. I believe you may have some secret agendas."

I smiled, widening my eyes as I had seen Seaghla do so often to get away with everything less of murder, "I'm far from bold and my agendas are known. To survive while doing my duties."

The King smiled, but his eyes narrowed, "Not all can be saved, no matter how well you may plan or fight."

"True, your majesty, but some will. It's that few that are saved that keep people like me going to save more. Perhaps one of them will save someone, and so on, and so forth until we can become our own salvation."

The King's stern eyes kept on mine. "You speak like a priest, but your words are Stygra and your actions are like those of the Welkan warriors. Do you not want things for yourself? Do you wish to sacrifice everything that is you?"

"I want plenty of things. One is for my family to be taken care of. I want to go home. I want to lie in a meadow and sleep all day and not worry about a single thing. Finally, to be fully, undeniably happy each day of my life. And yes, if I have to sacrifice parts of me to get that, I will."

"Very well and honorable things to want, Hero. I wonder what pieces of you they will leave once you enjoy your wishes."

My thoughts faltered. I wasn't sure what to say that would keep me as me in this conversation. Or that would propel me toward the bold warrior I needed to be. "The pieces that need to be there. The pieces that are important to those I love."

He smiled at that, "Indeed."

We danced in silence for a little portion of the song.

"I will have you know," he started, "That I appreciate your kindness toward Tori."

He seemed genuine, but I couldn't be sure. I had liked the Queen before too. Now, I had doubts about everyone. "It's the least I can do. He deserves the world."

"Yes, I agree. All my children do."

The song ended. I curtsied and made my way to the buffet set up. My stomach felt like burning rocks now. I picked up a piece of cake.

It looked like snow on top of the sunset. The icing was a pale cream that melted on my tongue and moistened the luxurious citrus flavored cake more. I had two forkfuls in my mouth and was about to wipe off some icing at the corner of my lips when he stepped up to me.

The callous on his thumb scraped my face, somehow making me raw there. "You should eat some meat. Your strength must be kept up during these shows of power and fortune is necessary."

He sucked the icing off his thumb. His lips looked unreal to me. Perhaps they were painted. The dark hue of his face doubled with the stubble all along his chin, jaws and upper lip. I met his eyes. They gave me pause more than the darkness of his flesh.

They were red.

Red blood eyes. I had never seen red eyes before.

He chuckled, "I didn't mean to startle you."

"You didn't. How do you have red eyes?"

His face dropped the smile as he looked away. "A curse."

"Oh. I didn't mean to ruin your mood."

His shoulder lifted, and he smiled. His mouth had more pull to the left, making it crooked. "It didn't change my mood. I am used to those questions."

"Guess I should thank you."

"Do you now?"

Sam Wicker

I took another bite of the cake, finishing the tiny slice off. "You came to my rescue with Tori. Even stole the brute's dagger."

"Oh, that. It looked like fun."

I snorted, "Maybe for you."

He smiled again. "I'm Austere, from Iethyll, most people call me Stere."

"Prince Austere, isn't it?"

He tilted his head back, his lips curling upwards slightly as his eerie red eyes shone bright, "You have heard of me?"

"You have been the talk of the court for a while. They were all waiting for the arrival of the pirate turned prince."

"Not you though, Hero Nadachia?"

My name on his lips sounded odd in my ears. The burning in my stomach had lessened with each tone that spilled from his lips until I felt soothed. I had to admit to myself that I had been curious about him, about his family. "No, not really. I have a lot of things to think about. Are you going to steal things here?"

"Hard to say." That smile he showed me this time had a couple of dimples added to it. "If I'm not careful, I might have something stolen from me."

"Prince Austere!"

He deflated with a sigh. I couldn't stop the giggle from escaping me.

"Thanks, Terithi." Austere stated as the man barreled up to us.

He was about my height, on the skinny side, and had a mop of blonde hair he brushed back from his face with a wide hand. "What'd I do now?" He looked at me and gasped, "Hero Nadachia of Silverequis! Oh! I-um…" He bowed. And stayed bowing.

"No, say nothing. Just leave him like that." Prince Austere held up a hand when I started to tell this man to not bow to me.

Terithi slowly straightened, his face as red as his Prince's eyes, "I'm sorry. I'm new to… all this."

"Obviously." Stere muttered.

I racked my brain on the history of Iethyll. Didn't they have a war?

"Yes, is probably going to be the answer to what you're going to ask."

"What do you think I was going to ask?"

"Either how long I've been a prince, or if there isn't still a war brewing over if I'm a prince or not."

"Not quite. Were you truly a pirate before, or were you a lord?"

Before Terithi could say anything, Austere answered, "We were definitely pirates."

I wouldn't have believed him if his friend hadn't turned as white as the icing I ate. "And you stole the kingdom?"

Austere chuckled, "Yes."

I snorted before I could hold myself back. He raised a brow at me over his drink. "You went from one way of stealing to another. There is no difference really."

"Ah, you speak of taxes. Yes. Legitimate thievery." He eyed me, "Please, eat. I wasn't kidding about needing your strength."

I shook my head, but still took up some juicy, sticky duck. "Why are you insistent that I gain strength?"

"Because you are going to dance with me."

Terithi stammered incoherently before he managed, "You should ask nicely!"

"If I ask, she might say no."

"If you ask, I might say yes." Where had that come from?

Those red eyes glinted like jewels, "May I have the next dance?"

"Yes." I finished the bites of duck and took a warm, damp cloth from a waiting servant. I took Austere's offered hand after cleaning the duck juices and spices off my fingers.

His hand was twice the size of mine. Under the bright lights of a million flickering candles in chandeliers over our head, I finally got a good look at the rest of his features.

His black hair was dark in the middle, and underneath the thick mass. It rested over one shoulder in thick straight lines and sometimes shone with a blue or gold tint, depending upon the light. He had some lighter strands and areas on top of his head, at his temples, and some of the thick strands looked bleached from the sun and seas. There were tiny scars on his face. The largest was a scar under his chin, that was about the thickness of a blade's edge, and ran to under his right ear.

The music started. It was slow. So, very slow.

He pulled me into him, flush against his towering body. I felt like a child. I also became in tune with how much of a man he was against what I was as a woman. He had hardness about him. He wasn't broad with the muscles like Taspe was, but tall and lean. I tried pulling back, but with one of his large hands splayed low over my back, he held me firm.

"Relax."

His deep voice washed over me like warm bath water. I could almost feel its rumble in my skin. Who was I going to get entangled with now?

"I would feel better if I could breathe."

A chuckle was his first response as we kept moving to the thrum of the musicians. "Breathing is the least of your worries, Hero."

"What do you mean?"

"Do you know how many people talk about you? Do you know the reach your name has now, in this short time?"

I wondered where this conversation could go that wouldn't get me into some sort of trouble or match of wits. "No."

"The citizens of the Capital do, they constantly have your name on their lips. The members of the Court say your name at least once an hour from what I can time. Do you know why?"

For someone to have held a title for as little time as he, he liked the sound of his own voice. Not that I could blame him. "Because I'm the Hero."

"Yes."

He paused in his words; the hand holding mine came to rest those long fingers of his under my chin to tilt my face up. I met his gaze again. His eyes flickered like flames.

"With that title you gain the world, but there are some that would want that power, that renown for their own."

"I don't gain the world."

His eyes narrowed, the flames brighter within them at the threat of them being shuttered, "I'm going to have to see how much you actually know."

"What do you mean?"

"Darling, in Lanpress alone, the title of Hero means you are just under the Queen and King, The Matron, and the High Priest. You are equal to a Princess or Prince and a member of the Stygra council. You can state something you want done, and the rest will have to do it. Did you know that?"

Not that I had any plans to exercise that kind of power, "Yes."

"In the allied nations you hold the same position as you do here." His eyes were on mine, as if trying to bore the knowledge he was trying to share with me through them. "All the allied nations."

Five nations were allies with Lanpress, all the nations within the walls that bordered the north and south of the isthmus. It hasn't always been that way. Lanpress had been at war before, many times, but we were at peace going on a few centuries. The last war had only been about fifty years ago, against the Rogues under their ruler Asphmiri. Asphmiri thought the Rogues should rule all from wall to wall.

"Of course, there are checks and balances, as there are with anyone who holds such power these days. But I wonder how someone who is friendly with the greatest Welkan Legace since the beginning of time would have to listen to such things. Or one who has befriended a Captain who is called King of the Trades as he holds most of the best ships and trade between us and the mainlands. She's also friends of the Princess who shall rule Ecia, one day, if she regains herself completely from this latest accident."

My stomach reappeared with a heavy flop before churning. The taste of acid burned my nose. The captain, who could… Otteri? He just happened to be at Columbri.

"There it is. There is the Silverequis brain I have read about in books. It works behind those glorious eyes of yours."

"What do you know of my family?"

"Enough." The smile that had his lips twisting to one side happened again, "I have no more to say to you. Shall we talk about the weather or how every man in here is in a pot to bed your sister the quickest?"

The world went silent as those last words he spoke replayed in my mind again. My body went stiff of its own. He moved me along. I stumbled to catch up.

"Well, not every man. I do not believe your companions would enter such a thing, nor your good friend, Taspe. I am not sure if the King has his name in there or if he automatically gets first call."

I gripped his collar, my knuckles straining under the hold, "You lie."

"No, darling," something softened around his mouth and eyes as he spoke, "I'm not lying over this. Your court is overrun with power hungry serpents who will do anything to destroy you."

"Why?"

"If you are anything like your ancestors, your great-great-great-great grandparents who made the name of your lineage, then you know why. Silverequis clipped out the weeds of a dishonorable court within a month and set into motion centuries of honor and peace. Your grandmother from that long ago single handedly gathered the nations together as allies except for five. Her husband slaughtered every liar and power hungry royal, council member, and advisor in three lands with his team of assassins he trained himself. In the other three countries, he gave ultimatums, which they met."

I shook my head, "Th-they had help. They were following the great leadership of Vesta, who became Queen."

Austere laughed, the sound louder than the music. "If you were to read the history as told by the people, not by the royals, you would know Vesta was your grandmother's best friend. She only took the throne because your ancestors detested the idea of being rulers."

He dipped his face down, close to mine. His warm breath feathered along my chin and cheek.

"You are like them. You want what is good to have a greater place in this world than lies and evil. You see the darkness and your reaction is to crush it with all you have within you."

"No. No, I'm not like that." I gritted my teeth after saying it.

"Liar."

"I'm not like that at all. I'm-"

"What? Just fulfilling a prophecy you don't understand?" The pirate's head canted to the side, his hair feathering over his shoulder.

"You do?"

"Someone else killed the White Boar, didn't they? Or so people think?"

"Yes." *What was he on about?*

"The best will take the quests. That person wasn't suitable."

I must have made a face because he continued after a pause, to study me.

"You were suitable. You are chosen." He loosened his hold on me, but didn't let me go completely.

I realized then the music had stopped.

"I want to dance with you again. I promise not to fill your head with any more than you can handle."

I don't remember if I nodded or said anything. I know he swung me into the next dance as soon as the music started up again. That song was much quicker. His hands on my bare flesh felt like I was burning there. My mind was too much of a spinning top to focus on that sensation and what it meant for the time being.

"Your sister is single, correct?"

My head had tried to go one way while my body another as I focused on his question. "What?"

"Seaghla? That's her name, right? She is available to be courted, yes?"

Heat rose into my cheeks as I glared at that smile.

"I am a little confused. I mean, you tried to kill a man for just touching her hair earlier…"

"Not to you. Not to anyone unless they are worthy."

"Ah, that hurts." Prince Austere dipped me and he pressed my hand to his chest, "I would say it hurts here, but the pain is mostly lower, much lower."

Not a single witty thing to say came to mind. He still held me in the dip. I swore my breasts were going to come out of the dress if I took a breath, so I held it.

He chuckled, "I suppose I could charm you then."

"Hardly." I managed as we straightened and continued dancing.

"Pity. I'm going to have plenty of time if you allow it."

"Allow what?"

"I wish to become a companion, to you, my dear Hero."

How many times was he planning to make my head spin in two dances? I could not keep up. Companion? A pirate prince as a companion.

His knowledge of the sea might come in handy if we have something crop up in the next quests, like what happened in Columbri. Or if we have a greater distance to travel along the coastline. He seemed to have a grasp of history, albeit rather twisted from what I was taught.

"Why would you want to do that?"

He grinned, those dimples winking again, "To help. Besides, I think being next to you would prove to be an adventure on its own, even if you weren't going on quests."

The music stopped. He allowed me to pull away. "I will think about it. I'll have to talk it over with my other companions too."

He kissed the back of my hand and smiled up at me from his little bow, "Of course, my darling."

With that, he turned me loose and disappeared into the crowd.

♡

There were a handful of other dances. I had enough of a break to warn Tori, Blari, Clara and Spacya of a pirate prince wanting to join us as a companion. None of them had any real qualms about the man.

I danced with Prince Dolfi. He was the next in line to the throne, the second eldest. He was the wisest of the children of the Queen. According to most.

"Seems as if you are finally having some fun with us." His voice was nowhere near as soothing as Tori's. It raked through my ears and set my teeth on edge.

"Of course. Dancing, food and wine, what more could I want?" I barely kept the sarcasm from my tongue.

"A husband? For the quests to be over?"

My smile fell before I could school it into place. I tried again, making it sweet, "After all this is over with, yes, I shall find a husband."

"Anyone in mind?"

"No." Although, the list was probably growing in Mother's mind.

"You should consider a few. You have plenty of options." His hand slid low, too low, "You could be the first Hero to turn Queen."

I tapped his elbow, his hand shooting back up to a reasonable position on my back. Though, that part was still bare to his touch, too. "Far too much headache to be a ruler, even as a Hero. I'm having difficulty with what little I can do."

"My poor dear, shall I help you?"

"I don't see how."

His smile, blinding like his father's, fell. "You are harsh."

My brows twitched as I tried not to grind my teeth with each word he uttered. His voice was terribly lilting. "I do not mean to be."

He proceeded to vividly recount his first hunt and kill. It must have been his only one for him to remember such detail. I couldn't remember my first kill that well. I remember it had been a pheasant. His was a rabbit.

"Well, Dolfi, you successfully bored our Hero to tears. Allow a real prince to lift her spirits again." Austere took my hand in mid clap after the song and spun me away.

"You're gonna make so many enemies with that mouth of yours."

"I have. I'll make plenty more. But I'll make as many lovers, or more, with it too."

"Not if I cut your tongue out."

His lips pursed as his eyes flashed, "That will make plenty of lovers cry, but I'll manage. Don't cut it out before I've had your lovely sister, though. I want her to experience all I have to offer for at least a full night and day."

I slammed my heel down; he jerked his foot back just in time. "Do you want to become a companion, or not?"

"Why? Is it based on whether she gives an excellent review of my efforts?"

I reached for the dagger at my right thigh. His hand slid down with mine and covered the handle before I could. He dipped me back. My blood simmered in my face and head. "I'm really going to enjoy taking your tongue out now."

"You seem to have a fetish for it." He drew me back up, sliding his hand over mine and dragging it away from my weapon. "Trust me when I say this, I know how to use it best. It won't do you any good without it being attached to me."

"I'll take your word for it."

"Ah, is this a true bond, then?"

Before I could react, his lips were on the scar Taspe made. It thrummed in response and I wasn't sure if that was me, or if that was Taspe.

"Oh, don't look like that. Anyone that pays attention to something other than your breasts, ass, thighs and eyes can see it." Here he smirked, "most don't get past those admirable traits though." He dipped me again, "And Taspe is betting on that. Otherwise, if he is protective, he would insist on you wearing pretty little gloves."

"You're impossible." Breathing came a little easier during the dip this time. Or perhaps I was beginning to not care whether or not I showed more skin at this stage.

"No, darling, I'm completely open and willing."

I wasn't witty enough to win with him. He knew it too, because the dimpled smile returned.

"Welcome to the crew."

He chuckled, drawing me back up and flush with his body. "Who knew that flirting with you was all one had to do to get into a prestigious group?"

"Sounded more like threats to me."

"If you're into that, sure."

"How do you hear so many rumors so quickly?"

"Now darling, I can't reveal all my secrets on our first night together. We must have a bit of mystery and foreplay."

I reached for my dagger again.

He sighed, "Tongue?"

I nodded.

"Very well. You are determined. I like that." His brow quirked over his right eye and I let go of the hilt. "Every decent thief has a network of those he can trust."

"And?"

"Foreplay," his grin flashed.

"Ass."

"She name calls! I'm in love."

"I lied. You're not a companion."

Austere chuckled before saying, "Fine. My network is numerous and vast. Father started it, I expounded upon it. Call them spies, but they are much more than that to me." He eyed me, "I will not put their lives in danger by telling you more, unless it becomes necessary. Besides, I have to protect and use my network for my gain. I hardly know you."

"Fine." I mimicked his tone from earlier. "These rumors spread quickly."

"As rumors do."

"How can you tell which are true and which aren't?" Because it was difficult with so many people I didn't know.

He pressed his cheek against mine, his breath hot on the shell of my ear, "My dear, all rumors have some basis in truth. You have to pluck out the kernel from which the lies or stretches of the truth sprung."

Sam Wicker

The rumors that I had Ida start, if they had some truth, they would probably spread like wildfire in a drought. If they did not, then those would be the ones that had no truth. It was a start. I had to figure out the puzzle that was this group of royals, advisors, and council members.

"You're thinking too much in a place that is not safe for you to do so. Smile or blush, something to take that thinking look off your face."

I scowled.

"Better. I would have much preferred a smile, but I shall take it." He pulled back, and the music stopped. We clapped for the musicians. "The next dance is mine."

"Why?"

"Don't you have more questions?"

"I do, but won't they-"

"Let them," Stere interrupted, "The more pots you have your hands in will keep them guessing about how much you know or don't know. This is all a game for them. Lives do not matter. It is power and knowledge."

Perhaps it was his height, or how different he was to the rest of them, but no one came up to us during the brief interlude between dances. We started the next dance without an interruption.

"If you are going to be smart, you need to play to the enemy."

"What do you mean?" I was better than this, but my thoughts wouldn't solidify on anything but the crowd and his hands.

"Don't just dance and talk with those you trust." At my snort, his brow quirked again, "Or that you think you might trust in the future or downright need. Dance with the other princes, the king, gods! Dance with some of The Matron's council and the priests if they ever show up."

"Not a bad idea. I could get some information too." *Maybe.*

"Exactly."

"How old are you?"

He stared at me, his smile slowly spread, "Finally interested?"

"Of course." I purred like I had heard Seaghla do with Edi a few times back home.

"We might need to work on that. Impressive try though."

I wanted to gut him.

"I'm twenty-eight."

Only five years older than me and he was already a prince and worming his way into the position he wanted. Taspe wasn't much older than Austere either. Where had I gone wrong?

No where. I wasn't a Hero's companion, as I had planned. I was The Hero.

"How old are you?"

"Twenty-three," I answered before thinking.

"Ah."

Something crossed his features with that sound, "What?"

"You look older than that."

"Thank you?" *What could I accomplish with all this madness? How much older did I appear to him?*

"Good childbearing age."

"Um-hm." My thoughts trailed off. If Keandria was a victim, how could I help? If she were the villain that started a mess, how could I defeat her? She was powerful. She was dangerous. I was a mere human, a child compared to her. Worse. A beast. Even Stygra children had magics.

"Could get started on a child with me. Well, at least the act." His voice buzzed.

"Right." If I could gain her trust, then I could truly know what was going on. She and the Queen. Luckily, with the royals, I had Tori and Clara. Clara, definitely. Tori, well, would he rally against evil if his mother turned out to be evil?

"Next time, Taspe can join us."

"Um-hm." I blinked as Taspe's name on his lips was an odd sensation for me to bear. "What?"

"You agreed to make passionate mating rituals with me for a week. The next week, Taspe can join us and together we could probably summon ten gods to do our bidding."

"Is everything about sex with you?" My head hurt from returning to his topic.

"No. Sex is a tool used to get what one wants, like a smile and a witty comment. And a dagger." His gaze dropped to my thigh as he spun me out, back again. "It's easier to act with my penis while I work out my plan to take over the world."

"One bedding at a time?"

"That's the spirit."

"Do your eyes glow in the dark?" He couldn't have bedded many if they did.

"You make my head hurt."

"Better that than your manhood."

"Thwarting my plans already, I see."

"I shall do my best."

"No, at least not that I know of. No one screams and runs away from me in the dark. Then again, they are usually out of their mind with pleasure."

"Are you part Welkan?" Because no one else had that kind of ego when discussing sex.

"No."

"You brag like one."

"Naturally."

The song ended. Austere grabbed my hand and kissed the back of it again. I swore I saw at least three ladies swoon in my peripheral. While scanning the crowd, I vaguely remembered who went with what country or business from the previous dinners.

I spotted a familiar face. I moved over to her, making my way through, and smiled at some who turned to bow or curtsy to me as I passed. She was one of the few that Keandria or the Queen had introduced me to during one of the first gatherings I had as a Hero. Foendaria, the Anglarian princess, was wearing a pale blue half cut cape over an Ecian style dress. Both pieces shimmered in the candlelight. "May I have the next dance?" I asked once the conversation paused at my approach.

"Of course, Hero Nadachia." She took my hand, and we walked to the dance floor.

We had a faulty start. I expected her to lead and she, in turn, expected the same of me. I forgot that in Ecia, and most lands, the one who asked to dance was usually the one to lead it. After I gave her a sheepish smile, she took the lead.

"I didn't think you would get away from Prince Austere."

I shook my head, "I know."

"He's rather handsome. All the eligibles talk about him and how they want him. But I think nothing will come of it. They are still unsure of how his standing will go in court because of his background."

"I'm sure he won't mind giving them more to talk about."

She blushed, "Some have stated such things as…well…in vivid detail."

I giggled because I couldn't help it. He had to be part Welkan. "He will enjoy that."

"What do you mean?"

"He thinks highly of himself is all."

"Oh my. I'm not sure if that makes him less or more appealing."

"Less."

We shared a giggle. We talked a little more about some people at court. She asked a few questions about the quests, especially interested in the monster of Cambria. I tried my best to do it justice in my description, but I feared I failed. I told her she should go to Blari and ask him, because his words were of a true storyteller.

As the song ended, we left each other to our own devices.

"May I have the next dance? Or are you still busy trying to find your next beast to attack?"

I turned and took Tori's hand, "Are you sure you want to dance with such a troublemaker?"

He smiled, but it didn't reach his eyes. "I'm sure."

We started promptly on the first note. "What's wrong?"

"Did you already tell Austere that you would take him on as a companion?"

"Yes, but I don't see why we can't change our minds. Why?"

"He's a pirate. A-He's… cursed."

"Cursed?" Someone overheard him telling me.

He nodded, "No one knows the details. It's a rumor. It might not be true." He cleared his throat, "From what I've heard, his father was a pirate. But he was…an odd one. Austere too, is an odd pirate. They stole, yes, but they also gave a lot to poor islands and started trade routes and the like to help bring money and transport to them. Austere though, some say he is more of a-"

"A rake?" I tried helping as Tori's face turned red with the strain of trying to find a proper term.

"Yes." He eyed me for a moment, "I'm not against it, him being a companion, but we should be wary."

"Yes, I think you're right." I didn't have the heart to tell him I was still wary of him half the time.

"You're already planning on using him, aren't you?"

"I know he could be useful. His knowledge of the seas alone." I was about to mention his spy network he claimed to have, but something held me back.

"Spacya has been saying there are too many men."

I laughed, "It's even now, unless Clara wants to quit."

"I know. I think she would prefer Austere, or even me, to be female."

"We might need to pack a keg from now on."

Tori's brows rose, "Whatever for?"

"Spacya and I might need it in order to put up with his wit."

Tori chuckled, "I'll see what I can do."

The song ended too soon and Tori shuffled me off onto a lord I knew I had met. I remembered his overwhelming scent of tannery chemicals and leather. Not that I could see he ever truly worked the leather himself.

The teeth he had left were blackened and his skin paper thin. From what I could remember, he was from Crea. I knew little of that country. I didn't plan on learning much more about it if the people there smelled and looked like him.

He was at the height when he dipped me, he could rest his head on my breasts. After the first time, where he licked me, I slipped a dagger out and held it against his neck. I hid it well enough in his overflowing collar. Only people who dared to dance too close to us could guess it was there. He sputtered apologies multiple times after I placed the blade.

He didn't dip me again until the end of the song. It was respectable. Before he pulled me back up, I caught the red eyes next to me and slid my gaze down to the dimpled smirk before returning my gaze to the Crea man. A deep, throaty chuckle let me know that the bastard pirate prince was also laughing at me.

I slipped my dagger back into its sheath. My next dance partner, I remembered even less. He was young, with sweaty palms and blushing cheeks. One glance at his red-eyed advisor told me all I needed to know. The poor boy had been shoved at me.

"Hey, breathe."

"Sorry." He said around a gulp.

I brought my hand up to the back of his neck and rubbed my fingertips against his damp skin in small, slow circles. "I'm not going to eat you."

His laugh trembled like fall leaves in a frost bitten wind, "I know."

"Have we met?"

"No. My name is Pitrini, Prince Pitrini from Iethyl."

"You're Austere's brother?" They looked nothing alike. This poor boy was nearly as pale as a Stygra with reddish hair and freckles.

He nodded.

"How?"

Pitrini flushed more, I hadn't thought it possible until I saw it. "After his father took over, they adopted me."

"They did?"

"I've always been a prince. The youngest. In the battle my Father and brothers killed themselves instead of surrendering." He looked away, eyes rimmed in dampness. "King Jespar, that's all he wanted, was a surrender. He didn't kill many. Just knocked most of them out."

Rumors seemed to hold some truth, after all. "Do they treat you well?"

"They have. Stere treats me more like a brother than my actual… then… then they did." He cleared his throat, looking at anything but me, "I've already learned so much about sailing from him." He blushed and looked down, only to avert his gaze back up to my face, "He's disappointed though."

Sam Wicker

"Why?"

"I can't flirt."

I laughed and kissed his cheek. He started looking like a wide-eyed tomato. "You don't have to flirt. See, you have gotten a kiss from me. He nor anyone else here has gotten that much."

His shoulders dropped away from his ears, and he smiled a small smile that showed off a brilliantly straight set of teeth. What was in the water in Iethyll to make them so tall? He couldn't be more than a teenager, and he was already a few inches taller than me.

"In fact, don't take flirting lessons from him at all. He will ruin your natural charm."

"I-I-don't have that!" He laughed, stumbling a little in the dance.

"If he tries to teach you, tell him I forbid it."

"Can you order him around like that?"

I nodded.

The poor boy's eyes bulged. It made me smile.

"He said he's going with you. Is that true?"

I nodded, but had to ask, "Is that how he worded it?"

Pitrini's face turned red again, "Not exactly. Not in those terms. He-er… I shouldn't say."

"That bad? Do tell."

He nodded, and swallowing loudly, he looked around for Austere. Satisfied his adoptive brother wasn't too close, he stated, "He said he was going to ride you more than his horse."

At least he hadn't given the poor boy details. "I see."

"Do you like him?" The words spilled out of his mouth like water from a geyser. "I mean, he's a good guy and a prince and rich and I think he might settle down if he has someone firm and you seem really nice. I mean, this entire time, you've been nice to me. You've been rubbing my neck like that and it's so good and calming. Thank you for that. It really is nice. I think you would make a good sister, too. Stere is really nice. He flirts a lot and acts like he's all tough and deadly, but I once saw him help this old lady walk through the market cause her cane broke on her. He swore her to secrecy and threatened to kill me if I told anyone, but I don't think he'd do that. Do you? Everyone likes him. Even the women he's bedded and just bedded another one. It's like they don't care and think he'll come back around or something. I dunno about all that stuff, but he says he'll teach me about it when I get flirting down."

He finally took a breath.

"Why are you shaking? Are you laughing? Oh! I'm talking too much!"

The dance ended, and I wrapped my arms around his neck. "Thank you, Pitrini. I needed you tonight. Please don't be nervous about talking to me."

He stammered a thank you while his hands fluttered all over my back and shoulders.

When I kissed his cheek again, I thought steam would come from his ears. I turned him, nudging him towards an open balcony door. "Get some fresh air."

"Congratulations. You made sure I will not get any sleep tonight."

Something tugged on the hairs at the back of my neck. His long fingers passed through a few strands of my hair that came loose. "You're welcome."

Those red eyes gleamed through slitted eyelids as he slid them from my hair to my eyes, "You kissed him. Twice. What did he do to deserve that?"

I thought of the night Taspe and I had shared. The heat quickly rose in my body, especially my face and neck. I fanned myself with one hand, "Oh, we discussed his likes and dislikes..."

"What?"

"I held my hand to a lord nearby. From what I could remember, he had been stiff, but respectful the last time. He strode over and took my hand with a bow. I smiled, "You know... between a real man and a willing woman..."

The lord swept me away. Austere stood alone, still, for enough time for me to get a good study of his face. His mouth hung ajar. A couple of ladies swooped in and blocked my view.

Chapter 21

"Matron wants to see you."

I dropped my hand from over my eyes. Her head and shoulders were a shadow over me, and I was glad of it. "They sent after you to summon me even though I'm closer?"

Ida shook her head, or there was some movement. I couldn't tell, really, with the halo of sunlight around her. "I was watching you, making sure you didn't bake yourself too much on this bench."

I sighed and sat up, "I'm going."

Footfalls crunched on the gravel nearby. A path over, I saw the tall pirate prince. "Yup, definitely going now."

The grin spread over my face as I grabbed Ida's hand and made a run for it toward the Tower. He would just have to stew some more over whatever Pitrini came up with to tell him. Ida left me with a Stygra boy we met there. He led me within and down a midnight-like hallway to a grand room of windowless arches around paintings and statues of Matrons past.

Keandria stood behind a spacious desk of ebony and alabaster. Upon it a map. Worn and aged yellow with a few twisted pieces and vials on top of it. The script on it was delicate, curled, and in the old script of our ancestors, the language the gods often used for us.

"Ah, there you are."

"Am I late?" I moved closer to the desk so I could get a good look at the map.

"No. Honestly, I'm surprised you're up after you danced so much last night." She smiled when I turned my head to the side and gazed at her, "I was told this. I retired early."

I nodded, because I knew I hadn't seen her for the last few hours of the dance. I dropped my gaze to the design again. There was a large black dot on Columbri. I scanned and found a red dot near the Rogue Mountains. "What's there?"

"A monster."

"Of course it is."

Keandria placed her hands on the edge of the desk and leaned on them. "I have something to say."

"Go on."

"Your sister will marry. I have taken it upon myself, as the Queen has, to find her a proper husband."

My fingernails were painful in the palms of my hands, "She will marry a good man. Not one that paws at her while drooling."

"She will wed who I see fit for her to marry!" Her words were biting and echoed off the black walls of the room.

"Why does that matter to you?"

"Because if I have you, I can sell you to the highest bidder. Unless you want that bear to break out and somehow find where your whimpering sister lives, you will dance and flirt with whom I say. As shall she."

Her words struck my heart like hammers against an anvil. Each stroke hardened me. I had thunder in my ears. My daggers slid into my palms. As I released a breath, one dagger zinged from my hand with a flick of my wrist.

The thunk of metal sinking into flesh sent a chill down my spine. Dark green blood spurted from her shoulder, just over her heart. The chill shook out into a shock of victory.

She hissed, and with a snap of her own, I slammed into the wall. My hands curled around my throat. The other dagger slid down my chest out of my hand and clattered to the floor. My fingers squeezed.

I tried pulling away. My muscles strained and pulled, twanging against each other as if obeying two minds. They loosened, only to regrip harder. With each loosening, I gasped in much needed air.

"Look at me!" she screamed, rounding the desk.

Something in me warned me not to look. My hands moved like hers. Squeezing. Clenching. Finding a better grip. Squeezing again. I looked up.

Those black eyes crinkled in the corners with her large, toothy smile.

My muscles no longer fought. My hands squeezed my throat steadily. I couldn't move. I couldn't move them away.

Sam Wicker

"Matron!" The scream echoed from down the hall. Rushing feet pounded against the polished floors. The door flung open. It banged against the wall with a loud wood on stone crack. Two Stygra teens dragged a smaller body between them.

She was gasping for air. Her pale lips turning blue-green. Her face a green hue. She clawed at her throat. Thrashing to and fro to get away from the invisible threat.

A shriek tore through the office. It rang in my ears. It rebounded off the walls. I had never witnessed a cry like that before.

I gasped for air. What little I had gathered spent. That bit of air had another echoing, shrill scream erupting into the room.

Keandria's eyes never left me. The two teens placed the little female at her feet. They had tears streaming down their faces. Words fell from their lips onto deaf ears. They tried keeping her hands away from her throat. Blood already beading from the scored flesh.

I managed another breath, "Sterla."

Her eyes, all popped vein filled, slid to me. I stared into them. Her mouth moved, opening and closing like a fish's gills once you place the thing on land. Her face was turning into a deeper hue.

Another breath, "Stop!"

Her arms and legs grew limp in the teens' hold. She was still.

My hands tightened on my neck. My head came forward. I looked to Keandria before pain splintered through my skull and the world went black.

I was split in half. Or my head was hollow in the back. My lungs filled and emptied through the fire in my throat. My hands and arms ached nearly as much as my head. Cold. So cold.

"She's finally coming around."

The fire spread from my neck to the rest of me as that voice stabbed my ears. I opened my eyes and stared at my reflection on the polished black stone under me. I turned my head. It throbbed with each breath and beat of my heart. A tunnel started to close my vision, but I blinked it away.

Candlelight was so bright, it burned me. Rough hands grabbed my arms and hauled me up. Each movement sent the room to whirling and my head throbbing harder like three people were slamming their boot heels into it at once. They got me up on my knees. My eyes finally focused.

Her face was still a green-purple. Her eyes were huge and bleeding black. That scream echoed again. I jerked from those hands and landed on her.

So fragile in my arms. So cold. Colder than the floor. No breath moved her little form as I held her. No smile. No slight crinkle at the bridge of her nose, at me being too close to her. There was nothing there.

Something dark and cold within me stirred. It reached out to her. To the tiny body in my arms. Familiar and strange. It touched her, through me, but recoiled to curl deep inside me again.

"How…" the word tore my throat open, "could you?"

"How could I, what? My Hero, you did this."

Everything shook. My hand shook so badly I barely brushed a dark strand of Sterla's hair from her lips. I pulled her close. I breathed her in. The soft earthy scent mixed with peppermint and youth. I kissed her forehead. My useless shaking hand closed her eyes after a few tries. Was it even mine anymore?

My muscles barked, and my vision sought to close on me anew when I struggled to stand. I curled around Sterla's body. I tried again and got my feet under me. I cradled Sterla to me. She weighed nothing. She crushed me.

"No argument? Good." She pointed to one teen who had moved next to the door, "Come here."

She ran to Keandria's side. Her cheeks were wet, her dark eyes lined with unspilled tears. Her body was curled in on itself.

Keandria gripped her elbow and moved to my side.

"Don't." My voice cracked.

"I didn't hear you."

I turned to get out of the room. Hands grabbed me again. They ripped Sterla from my arms. I thrashed, but black threading wrapped tightly over me. It pinned my arms to my sides and my legs tight together.

Keandria gripped my face with her spidery digits. She pulled my head down. The black threading led from my body to the fingers of a female. Her face was half hooded, but her lips were moving.

I jerked my face away. Her fingernails raked into my chin. A warm dribble began and I smelled the tang of blood.

Those dreadful words that haunted my thoughts spilled from her lips. Everything in me bucked and thrashed. The pain doubled. My vision blurred and closed in on me until I just closed my eyes and fought against the threads. They didn't budge.

"No!"

The teen fell to her knees, clutching her head. Sobs shook her.

Mine stopped. The throbbing gone. My throat stopped burning like I had lit a fire in it. It erased the tang of human blood from my nose.

"Have you learned your lesson, or shall we see how long Eilse lasts?"

"Release me."

Keandria's eyes bored into mine. "A moment longer." She moved to her desk.

The other teen took Sterla's body from another Stygra that had a hood on. He wept over her, holding her to his chest as he walked out.

I looked at what I assumed to be a guard. He stood still. Stiff. But a small flicker of a smile curled one corner of his lips upward. Turning back to the map, I studied the familiar lines of the Gala River flowing through our country all the way to Owlimount.

"Take Eilse after them. She will want to say her goodbyes. Call a healer to her."

The guard sneered as he strode to Eilse and lifted her to her feet. He pushed her out of the door ahead of him.

"Now then, let's learn about your next quest."

I finally shoved my knife back into its sheath after stumbling into the light. The one I had thrown into Keandria. The one who had tied me up in black thread had been kind enough to put my other dagger away for me. Keandria… she had made a show of cleaning my dagger as she talked about the next quest I was to go on.

She placed it in my hand as those threads loosened, then disappeared.

The gravel path dragged at my feet. The maps crinkled in my fist. I covered my mouth, biting my fingers to keep from screaming. The bright sunlight only added tears to the flow down my cheeks and neck.

One foot in front of the other. The crunch of gravel ground into my soul. Her wound was gone. Only a bit of blood stained her dress on her shoulder. That was all.

That dagger in her shoulder never happened.

I entered the gardens that belonged to the castle. Laughter floated to me on the breeze from the sea. I stopped. How could anyone laugh? What right had they to be happy?

My feet became less heavy. I rounded a corner, then another to turn down a path that led further into the gardens instead of to the Church. I followed the sound of that tinkling laughter. Two voices, one male and one female, reached my ears before another one of those hideous giggles erupted.

They strolled arm in arm. No, not arm in arm. His hands were helping her undergarments hold her two small breasts. His lips dipped to their tops. She was fully dressed, but I doubted that had been the case minutes before. He said something. She laughed again.

A sob tore out of me.

Sam Wicker

She gasped, her eyes alighted on me. She had the decency to blush before running in the opposite direction. I watched him watch her. He looked around to me. That red gaze aflame.

"Nadachia?" The flames in his eyes softened, darkened into something different as he strode towards me. "What's wrong? Is that blood?"

His fingers were on the few droplets that dropped from my chin to my shirt earlier.

"She's dead."

"What? Who?" He gripped my shoulders, bending to be level with me.

"S-Sterla." I killed Sterla. My hands choked her.

Austere shook his head.

How could he not know Sterla? I slammed my fist with the maps into his chest. He didn't budge. Nothing gave. He didn't back down. The pirate prince just bent to swoop me up into his arms.

I gritted my teeth, burrowing my head into his shoulder to keep the sunlight from burning my eyes more from his towering height. I kicked and bucked. His arms were like vices, holding me in place against his chest. "Put me down."

His long legs made quick work of the paths. In seconds we were at the Church's side door and he pushed it open with a shoulder. "Which way is your room?"

"Put me down!"

"If you don't tell me, I'll kick down every door in here until I can find someone who can, or I discover the room full of your daggers. Stop squirming."

"Put me down!"

Austere stared at me. He loosened his hold, but didn't release me. He sat on the floor with me and pressed my back against his chest. One of his palms splayed over my stomach, while the other rested over my heart.

"Breathe with me." His voice was gentle, but still rumbled through me like thunder.

He pressed gently with his hands, "Breathe with me. In."

I breathed in, his chest swelled behind me with mine.

"Out."

His body softened as I too released the breath.

"In, a little deeper."

I did. I killed her. A sob broke my breath.

"Easy. Try again. Breathe in."

I tried. I shook. The feeling of my own hands around my throat. Around her throat.

He lifted me and stood, cradling me like a child as a priest entered the hall. "Room."

The priest stopped in his tracks, and pointed to the end of the hall, "To the right, the end of that one."

It seemed to only take him a second to reach my door. He swung it open and kicked it closed. I was in the bed and he pressed my head to his chest as he knelt before me on the soft mattress. He was all around me. There was nothing else.

"Hear that? It's steady. That heartbeat. So is yours."

The patter of feet made me look under his arm. She blurred in my vision, but she had a fire poker in one hand. "What are you doing to her?"

"She's shocked. Is there anything that helps her focus or come back?"

"A bath."

"Make one."

His voice rumbled deep in his chest, thundering over the sound of his beating heart.

Large hands started pawing at me. I swatted them away. I wasn't about to be held down. They would not throw me into a tiny closet.

"Nadachia, I'm not going to fight you. Put the papers down. Help me take your clothes off."

Taspe was here. No. He wasn't here. Not yet. No.

"It's bath time, darling. Help me."

A bath sounded nice.

The papers fluttered from my hands. His fingers made quick work of my belt before moving to the laces of my boots. I pulled my shirt over my head. A bath. I was about to have a bath. I needed one.

He had both boots off before I had the silly thin undershirt off. I stood, loosening my pants and kicking them off. His hands shoved my underwear down and I stepped out of them. I couldn't find the hooks at my back.

He did.

"Where's Taspe?"

"Gone." Was he having a hard time breathing, too? I looked over my shoulder at him. He folded my corset and chemise, placing them neatly on my bed. What was I going to do?

He studied me, saw me staring, and lifted me back up into his arms.

Bath.

Ida loved to pamper me with a bath. He placed me down on the top step of the bath and held my hand until I walked down into the water.

It was exquisite. I wandered forward. Slowly sinking into the filled tub.

"Behind the screen, mister."

That little lady had the fire poker pointed at one of those weird eyes. He held up his hands and backed toward the screen that separated the bath from the rest of this vast room. They were saying something else. The rushing water filled my ears, as did silence.

I wanted to bury myself in the warmth. So I did. I folded my legs and sank to the bottom. The tiles were rough against my backside and thighs. Something burned my eyes, so I closed them. The bubbles from my nose tickled.

I killed her.

My throat and lungs burned.

Something huge disturbed the water. Hands were on me and pulled me out of the warmth. The warmth poured from my nose and mouth. The burning emptied from my lungs. My body shook. Those powerful hands held me against wet clothes.

"Find out what in gods' realm happened to her! Now!"

So commanding, that tone. There wasn't any room in that sentence for questions or arguments. A door slammed. It sounded so far away.

I was so cold. Everything was deafening. My heart was too loud. My breathing made my ears hurt.

"Nadachia."

My name thundered through me. I covered my ears, pushing at the wet clothes against me with my shoulder and elbow. The vices around me loosened slightly. Something shook all around me. I shook.

"Nadachia, can you hear me?" That thundering voice was softer now.

I nodded.

"I'm going to wrap you up in a towel."

I nodded again.

He moved away. I opened my eyes to watch him drag my towel from the edge and into the water. He soaked it before wrapping it around me; tucking the ends between the cloth and my flesh, he wrapped his arms around me again.

It kept me from shaking out of my skin.

Stere guided me to the steps, he sat down. He curled me into his lap as if I was a child. He pressed me firmly to him, wrapping all around me like he was a towel himself.

I held my hand up; the scar thrummed and burned.

"Nadachia?"

My head was so weighted it took me forever to see his face.

"What do you smell?"

I breathed in deeply, "Lavender, chamomile, water. You."

"What do you see?"

"Your face."

"What do you hear?"

"You, my heart, water against the tub walls."

"What do you feel?"

"Towel, water, you."

His odd colored eyes were on mine, "Are you here?"

My brain was like snow slush. I tried concentrating. I could see, smell, and hear all those things. Feel them too. "I am."

"Tell me my name."

"Austere, Prince of Iethyll."

"Now, how sexy am I on a scale of one to ten?"

I groaned and tried to push out of his lap.

He chuckled and held me firm, "I'll take it you can't count to infinity." He moved, unfolding from around me until he sat beside me on the steps. "What is your favorite flower?"

I rested my heavy head on his shoulder. "I don't have one really, like them all too much. If I have to go with flower scent though, it's lavender."

He nodded, "Good." He opened his mouth as if he was about to say something else, but he didn't. Instead, he reached down and started tugging his boots off. When he pulled the first one out from under the water, he eyed it. "Well, let's see how leather smells after we have soaked it in lavender bath water, shall we?"

I rested my head on my arms after pulling my knees up to me. "Have fun."

He tossed the boot to the side and pulled off the other one. He looked at me after tossing it in the general direction of the last. "I'm going to have to stand. Are you going to drown yourself again?"

"No. That wasn't what I was... did I?"

He placed a hand on my head, the callous on his thumb brushed against my temple, "Don't think on it now. Watch me undress."

I groaned.

He chuckled and stood.

His jacket was thick and had to drag at him. He shoved it off and started squeezing water from it. Austere also threw it toward the boots. He peeled his shirt off.

There wasn't any bare skin on his back. The phases of the guide star stretched down his spine, linked by a long arrow that pointed to his skull. The phases of each moon formed an X, where each of their full phases melded with the full phase of the guide star. Intricate swirls and lines curled and flowed around each until joining with the other designs started around each celestial body. They flowed over his whole back, spreading slightly over his sides and hips.

He turned, walking up the steps. I could see under his thick mane of wet hair another design on his neck. This one in blue.

The mark of the curse. It was more intricate and beautiful than the one on his back. Shapes formed and shifted within the blue ink so well that one Welkan letter could be used for three of their words.

He grabbed another towel and began drying off.

Winged creatures stretched over each collar bone with tails and wings unfurling down to his dark nipples. They inked a smaller star phase down the center of his abdomen, between the muscles. This time, the compass point disappeared into the band of the low hanging, drenched pants. Lines of Stygra and Welkan phrases curled over and down the inside of his hips to disappear into his pants too. They looked like claws, the lines of words.

He wrapped the towel around his hips before fighting with his pants to get them off.

"Are you with me now that I've given you something magnificent to gaze at? Or shall I show you my other tattoos?" His hand stayed on the towel, but he tugged it gently.

A beautiful, fat, scaled pair of fish curled around the calf of his right leg. A male and female pair of Rogues embraced on the right one. The ones from the legend that I could barely remember. Surely he wouldn't have anything on his ass cheeks.

His brows rose, "Well, fine then." He pulled the towel free, holding it in his hand so it wouldn't drop to the floor and soak up all the water at his feet.

The symbols for Meandria, the goddess of waters, intertwined with the symbol of Minna, the goddess of air, above the short hairs on his right hip. The symbols of Gonzen, the god of emotion, and Hoala, the goddess of storms, were on the other. Stretching from his waist to the short hairs was another design that surrounded the symbol for Arca, the goddess of travel. Intricate and expensive blessings for a pirate to have. I guessed they were given to him by a Welkan lover, or lovers with how close they were to his penis.

He wasn't just tall.

He turned. I noticed then that the skin of his backside and intimate parts were the same shade, if not a touch darker, than the rest of him. He was born that way. No sun had darkened him.

Unless, and he was the type, he lay out naked for the sun to bake. It was beautiful and flawless.

Curled along the curve of his ass cheeks started another design of blessings that ended in straight points at his waist, above the crack of his ass, and in the center of each thigh. I could pick out a few words, but there were so many lines. I wasn't sure what were part of phrases or words and what was just design.

"Done."

He wrapped the towel around his waist again before sitting on a dry edge of the bath. He let his feet dangle into the water. His hands clasped as he leaned on his knees.

"I will not ask you a silly question. One, because I want you to stay alert, and two, because you will tell me your story when you're ready. As soon as your firepoker servant gets back, we will both know the story everyone else will know. Whether or not it's true…" he lifted a shoulder, "you will have to say. Only when you're ready."

He paused, moving his legs in small circles in the bath, "Now what might help to bring you further to yourself is more distraction."

He was talking slowly. But my mind stumbled along, grasping at his words, "What distraction?"

"Usually when someone sees all of me I explore all of them." His eyes flicked to my towel, or the water in front of me, or somewhere. "But I rather like my distractions to be fully in the moment and not suffering from something. I will have to come up with something else."

"I have to tell them." The thought hit me like a bucket of cold water.

"No. Not yet. You're not ready yet."

"I have to-"

"It can wait." His voice was a barking command that made my head throb. "It's fine. It can wait until you are more yourself." That last sentence had his musical voice soft again. "Ask me a question."

"The scar on your left, over your ribs, where did it come from?"

"What is it with women and scars? I have all this design on me and they ask about scars."

"It's from an arrow, isn't it?"

"Good guess, but no. When I was sixteen, another pirate, Dread, attacked my ship." His sigh was deep and long before he continued, "My first ship. She was a beaut. Named her Mieasia. It translates to Wind Raven for you common language lot. This," he pointed to the puckered skin tinged black, "Is from one of her splinters. As is this, and this." He poked two more scars, one a long and wide scrape on his arm and the other another pucker of skin on his thigh that he had to pull up the towel to show me.

"I thought the Dread left no survivors."

"She doesn't." He smirked, leaning back on his hands, "She slayed me every day and night until next port."

I frowned and looked at the blessings. Was one of those blessings something that wouldn't let him die?

He snorted as he caught my gaze shifting, "Bedded. Mated. Sex, Nadachia, sex!"

A gentle heat feathered over my cheeks, "But you said you were sixteen."

"Aye. Sixteen-year-olds can be just as skilled as any grown man or woman. More than some." His brows drew low over his eyes, "How old?"

"Twenty-three."

"No, how old were you when you first had sex?"

I gritted my teeth and willed the heat in my cheeks to go away, "Twenty-three."

"He is patient. I will give him that much." Austere said after a low whistle.

The door to my room clicked open.

Austere was out of the bath and slipping along the floor to his clothes pile, where he grabbed a blade.

Ida rounded the screen. Her eyes were wide, puffy and red as she stared at me. She swallowed, clasping and unclasping her hands, which were turning red from the abuse. "There was an

254

accident. The man from last night, that you put in the dungeon, escaped. He followed you from the garden to the Tower and attacked. Sterla, she met you at the door. She-she tried to protect you and he killed her. Killed her before the guards could get him subdued."

I shook my head.

"Who then?"

I pointed to myself.

Silence filled my rooms. I stood. Those moments in the Tower played through my mind. I saw it as if I wasn't part of it. As if someone else had controlled me and I was just helplessly watching. An observer of my body.

"Keandria." The name fell from my lips like a stone. "Sh-she choked me. I choked me. Sterla died. I choked her."

Ida whirled on her heel, "I'll go get you some of your clothes, Prince Austere."

Nothing was in me anymore. Just pain. I was dead. I should have been dead.

A hand dropped in front of my gaze.

"Come out of there, Nadachia." His voice was soft again, almost like a purr from a huge cat.

He pulled me up. My towel slipped. He pulled it off and grabbed a dry one. With long, slow strokes, he began drying me off. The towel and his hands were far away. I watched the scene in my mind. Sterla coming in the door, thrashing in their arms. My hands around my throat. Her skin going from pale to blood filled. The veins in her eyes popping. Her lips moving, working my name and a few other words.

What were they? Those other words.

Naked. I was naked in front of a man. He saw me naked before. Held me naked before. No need for modesty now.

How could I choke myself? How could I choke Sterla? She was so tiny.

"Here, darling." His voice was a whisper compared to what it usually was, but not quite. He helped me into some underwear. He pulled a thin little chemise over my head. Then he took my hand and led me to the bed. "Sit."

I did.

The bed shifted with his weight.

Puppet. I was controlled. That wasn't me. How? Puppet. She made me look at her. She flung me against the wall. No. I walked to the wall.

Something brushed my temple, and I pulled away.

"Easy."

"Sorry." My voice wasn't my own.

Slowly, he brushed the tangles from my wet hair. Long strokes with the brush from scalp, all the way to the ends. Something about his actions slowed the replay of Sterla's death in my mind. Something about my hair being brushed eased my thoughts into a slowness.

Ida ran back into the room and thrust a pile of clothes and large boots at Austere, "Please put these on now."

A sigh, and the sound of the brush going through my hair pulled me out again.

"Must you ruin my progress of keeping her calm by being so obnoxious?"

"Sorry." Ida said in a whisper.

"Care to help me dress?"

Ida would make a good strawberry.

"I have considerable difficulty with the buttons of those particular pants you have there. And in tucking my shirt into them."

"Please don't scare her any more than you already have."

A tug at my hair made me tilt my head back. I met his gaze, and watched a lazy smile curl his lips, "There you are, darling."

After another hour, I felt more myself. I flexed my hands. I still shook some, but not as much as before. When spoken to, I concentrated on what was being said and thought of an answer.

"Ida, please go get Clara, Tori, Spacya and Blari?"

Her eyes darted to Austere sprawled out on my bed behind me, "Are you sure?"

"This needs to be done." They needed a day, like me, to grieve, before we set out for the next quest.

"Want me to braid it?"

"Huh?" Maybe I wasn't myself yet.

"Your hair."

"I figured that. You, a pirate prince, can braid?"

He was off the bed. He dropped his towel and pulled on his pants, "Wanna know what else I can do with these fingers?"

"No. No braid. And no I don't."

He frowned, "To think that, for once, I wasn't going to be lewd."

My brow quirked up at that.

He tugged his shirt on and tucked it in before buttoning and buckling everything else. "I was going to say that I can rub some oils on some pressure points to help. Make you smell good too."

"Are you saying I stink?"

"No, but your scent is rather tame." He waved a hand dismissively, "I'll teach you about that later." He sat down beside me. Of the whole bed, he made sure he was close enough that I warmed from the heat off him. "We'll have plenty of time to learn one another." He said, while pulling his boots on.

I got up and pulled on a shirt and a pair of pants. I didn't bother with anything else. Besides, his eyes were telling me he was picturing me naked, anyway.

Ida came in and held the door open for my companions. She looked Austere up and down with a narrow gaze.

"She's going to be a lot of fun." Austere's lips stretched after his statement.

I took a deep breath, feeling my resolve quake with it. I dropped into a chair. Seeing them, watching them watch me, made me question whether or not I could do this at all.

"Did something happen with Clara?" Blari asked as he sat down next to me.

I shook my head and looked at Ida.

"She was sleeping, and the healer told me they had completed an extensive round. I didn't disturb her."

"It isn't Clara." My voice sounded weak, even to my ears. "You're going to be told something different, but I'm going to tell you what really happened. What I think happened. I can't make sense of all of it."

Starting with Ida summoning me to the Tower, I told them every detail I remembered. Every word that was said. Everything I saw. Everything until I blacked out. Until I died. I finished with walking out into the garden.

Everything felt so heavy again. I dropped my head onto the back of the chair.

"She tied another to you?" I heard the tremble in his voice, his quill pausing over the page.

"Eisle." Spacya said with a bite to it. I was glad she was sitting. Otherwise, I didn't think I would have the energy to stop her from attacking the Tower.

"Gods, we can't let you get hurt. Not again." Tori's voice had too much breath behind it, "never again. Not until we fix this."

I agreed, but knew it would be fruitless to try. We had to leave for another quest. Who knew what Keandria could do to us in one day?

I was her thing. I was her Hero. Nadachia was something she controlled and used to control others. How was she going to sell me? Was she already selling me?

I rubbed the heels of my hands into my eyes. More tears burned there. Sterla was gone. She died because of me. I wouldn't see that sheepish little smile anymore. No chance of getting to know the real her.

"She was so young. I killed her."

Blari was on me in an instant. His ink-stained fingers around my wrists pulled my hands away from my eyes. "You didn't kill her."

"What you hold choked her to death."

"Look at me." He demanded.

"Look at me!" her scream replayed in my mind.

Sam Wicker

I stared at my palms. Plenty of things had died with these hands. Some were young animals. Never a child. Never someone that could live for hundreds of years. Not someone who could do this world so much good. I looked up into the priest's eyes.

"Yes, these hands are yours, but they were not in your command. You were not in control. You did not kill her."

"Keandria killed her."

Blari's voice was gentle. Coddling. Spacya's a rake across loose stones. Unyielding.

"Next time we all go." Tori leaned on the back of the couch to my right.

"Agreed." Spacya swiped at an escaped tear on her good cheek.

"I shouldn't have provoked her."

"You didn't. Not there, at least. At the dance, yes, but not when you met with her. In that room, she was poking you." Austere said as he toyed with a fruit I didn't know the name of. He had taken from the bowl on the table between us. "I don't think there was any way you could have left and Sterla would still be alive."

"What?"

"I think she wants to break you. She's cracked you. Maybe she thinks she has crushed you. You need to act like she has broken you."

I looked back at Blari and watched him nod.

"That shouldn't be hard to do."

Chapter 22

The day passed by too quickly. I climbed up on Unia, all my gear on me or tied to her this time. The crowd still clapped and cheered. They called out their hopes for our success. The only difference was that the people that lined our path held fronds of black, white, and red flowers to lie at our horses' hooves as we passed.

Behind me were my comrades. Austere, a hulking addition to us on his huge black stallion who pawed the ground with breathy snorts. Eisle too, riding on a small mare with a green and brown coat. They replaced our usual cart with a single horse of sizable width led by Tori.

Behind Eisle, who had taken the end position of our little party with Blari, was a four horse-drawn funeral flat. Upon it, Sterla lay.

We would take her to her final resting place in her old hometown called Emleton. It was on the path. As if I would have it any other way.

Keandria and the royals made a show of putting flowers around her. The leather of my reins threatened to crack in my hands as my knuckles turned white around them. In this crowd, would she kill me? I would make sure I killed her. One day.

Austere was at my mare's hip. He slowly rubbed a hand down his stallion's mane, speaking gently, but loud enough for me to hear. "Easy. There is a time and a place. Today is for Sterla. Tomorrow, is ours." His horse shifted, his warm nose bumping my hip. "Breathe," Austere added.

After they finished with their sorrowful show, we started forward. The pace was slow, allowing the people to show their respect for a child they hardly knew. They believed the lies. Sterla was a hero for coming to my aid against the mad Lord Ducarii. He had a name now that he was dead.

I gutted him after he killed Sterla, according to the lies.

Soon enough, I found myself on the bridge, crossing over the watery boundary that separated Galanesse from the outside world. We were on Capital Road. If I followed it to its end, I would be home. The urge to gallop until I reached home was strong, almost irresistible.

In a small grove of trees that held a tiny house, we met a priest. With him was Pitrini. The priest was to cover Sterla and join us until Emleton to help with the burial rights. Pitrini, though, was a surprise.

Austere slid off his horse and strode to his little brother. Without all the calamity of the hall around them, seeing them together revealed how truly different they were.

"What's going on?" I asked as Austere placed a large hand on Pitrini's narrow shoulder.

He waved his other hand dismissively in my direction.

I moved Unia closer to the brothers' huddle.

"…up the Gala. Dock at Emleton and wait."

Pitrini nodded before getting up on a bay horse. He smiled at me, nudging his horse beside mine. "How are you?" He leaned toward me, speaking low, "I know this is not my place, but each day makes the pain a little easier to bear. Until a bad day happens. You're entitled to bad days. Remember, you are strong, and when you're not, you got plenty with you to lean on."

I hugged him. It took a breath for him to hug me back. Here he was, a boy who lost everything, and he was comforting me. I wanted to adopt him.

"Isn't it about time you returned, Piti?"

I pulled away. Pitrini's face was nearly as red as Ida's was last night. I looked to Austere, his eyes were flicking between the two of us. "Piti?"

"One of many nicknames he has for me." Pitrini rubbed the back of his head before nudging his horse back toward the capital.

"I'll see you in a few days' time." Austere called after him as he walked toward my horse. "What is it about you that has my little brother stammering and glowing red?" His hand slid down my mare's neck, then stopped on my thigh.

"Sometimes kindness can make a person react in ways they normally don't." I watched him, watching his brother ride away. "He's going to meet us in Emleton?"

"Aye, I never go anywhere that I can't reach my ship in under a day's hard ride. Why?" He looked up at me through his lashes.

I patted his hand on my thigh before pushing it off. Unia moved back into the road and we watched as the priest and driver finished covering Sterla. "I'm going to miss him, is all."

Austere hauled himself back up on his stallion and caught up to me. "Miss him?"

I nodded.

"You get attached easily. I'm glad to know you would miss me if we ever part ways."

I shook my head, biting back a smile at Blari's snort on Austere's words. "Distance from you would not make me grow fonder."

Austere opened his mouth to say something else.

"Neither does proximity where you are concerned."

His teeth clicked when he shut his mouth.

With the wagon in tow, it took us a full day and a half to get to the next large town. Pariadiso was a bustling town, as were most that grew straddling a crossroads of two heavily trafficked roads. Mostly composed of taverns, inns, and a decent market, but a few necessity shops dotted the streets in between them.

We had only stopped every six hours to give the horses a much needed break. Most of us slept while riding, so I pushed us well into the night. I found a decent-looking inn that had large rooms, as the Paradidiso church was under repair. Spacya, Eilse and I would have to share a room, but the guys would only have to double up in theirs. One got his own, and I allowed them to decide who got that luxury.

Sam Wicker

We stabled the horses. Tori, Eilse, and Spacya retired to their rooms. I gave my pack to Spacya and began walking around the town.

The salty air of the sea was gone. In its place were the scents of drink, grease, sweat and waste. Underneath all that was a hint of what we were heading toward, large pines and snowy mountains.

Most taverns had tinted windows; giving them an air of privacy and mystery that I figured they didn't need to spend the extra coin on. Everyone knew what happened in taverns, even children. The inns, the ones that didn't have a ground floor dedicated to a tavern, were all dolled up in lace and frilly things.

I counted five of them on one side of the main street alone. I didn't bother counting the others. Thankfully Owlimount wasn't as bad, I wished for home. We at least had the decency to only have three taverns per street, some only one.

I turned a corner, the inn we were staying at well behind me, and started down another sidewalk. I followed my nose along a scent that sent my stomach to rumbling deeply. They painted large white letters in a block script on the window that stated: Crossroads Bakery. In smaller font: Owned by the prettiest girl in all Lanpress.

I smiled, opening the door to a tinkling bell sounding over my head. I let the juicy, yeasty smells wash over me and breathed them in deep. Large rounded rolls, golden and shiny with butter, steamed on the first rack.

"Hello there!"

"Hello." For the life of me, the origin of the voice evaded my sight. Breads and sweets were everywhere. Little tables dotted an area to the side where a handful of patrons were eating or slurping tea. No one stood at the bit box at the end of the long counter that wound around the back of the shop.

"Here dearie." Out from behind a pair of swinging doors popped a woman holding a tray of cookies. "Welcome to Crossroads! What may I get you?"

I smiled as I took in her salt and pepper thick hair tied in a tight bun. She sported a few flour fingerprints at her temples and cheeks. The lines of smiles and happiness darted her bright blue eyes and bracketed full rose-red lips. She was gorgeous.

"I would love one of your fat rolls there. A bag of those cookies, and give me an assortment of eight muffins and eight of those… things right there." I pointed to the curled bits of glazed dough with fruit poured over them. The door behind me tinkled as I talked.

"Oh my, of course! You must travel with a large family." Her eyes darted to my hips.

An arm came around my shoulders. I reached for a dagger, my fingers stopping on the handle as the smooth tenor tickled my ear.

"Don't let her size and demeanor fool you. She's given me plenty of rides to make enough."

The woman blushed as a few of the patrons chuckled, "Well, with you to ride, I don't blame her!"

"You're a pleasure and definitely the prettiest lass in Lanpress."

That blush deepened on her cheeks as she set to work gathering my order. "Oh, that was ages ago, sir!"

"No, that's today, love."

She ducked behind her racks, working on my requests with an enormous smile on her reddened face. She tittered as she worked.

Part of me wanted to pull the dagger or pinch him in a tender spot. The raw part of me wanted to lean against him. "Why'd you follow me?"

"That's a silly question, darling." He murmured close to my ear, "Blari and I are taking turns keeping you in our sight. The poor priest isn't used to such extreme exercise so I'm holding the day for him."

"How sweet. It's not needed."

I took a big roll from the rack, making sure the lady baker saw before I bit into it. The crust was perfectly flaky and gave way to the most tender, moist bread within. It made my knees weak. I moaned.

"Gods. I'll buy the whole rack of these to hear that sound again."

I tore a piece off and held it out to him.

He took it from my fingers with his mouth. He moaned. I felt like I should bathe.

"You silly ducks." She laughed, "You two must be famished to react in such a manner to simple bread."

She handed us the rest of our purchase. I gave her the bits and an extra two irons because I didn't think she charged enough for her gods'-realm goods. We made our way back to the inn, juggling the boxes as we finished the roll, and another.

"I'm going to move her to Iethyll. Right into the castle." Austere said as he licked the butter from his lips and fingers.

"No. She's staying right where she is so I can enjoy her goods again." I felt a pang of guilt for cheating on Hana with another baker.

"You can live in the castle too." He turned his head, suddenly interested in watching something across the street so his next words were barely audible to me, "Gods know that you and Piti get along swimmingly enough."

"Why Piti?"

"Pitrini is a little long to yell when you're in the middle of a squall."

"That's cute."

"Of course it is." Austere rolled his eyes. "The single room is yours tonight."

I shook my head, "You're bigger, well, all of you are bigger than…" I stopped before I insulted someone, "One of you should take it."

"I'll bed down with the baker. Take it."

I rolled my eyes this time, "She's married."

"And? I'll bed with him or her too. He might look like dirt and feel like mud and it'd be worth it to eat some of this fresh in the morning."

"Is that all you think about?"

"Bread? No. Pleasure? Yes."

Once upon a time, I thought pleasure was all Taspe thought about too. I was mistaken. I had been a distraction from everything else in his life. Flirting with me helped me too. A diversion from Mother and Seaghla leaving and us having little bits to care for ourselves.

"Nadachia, here."

I stopped and turned. How had I missed it? Austere held the door open to the inn for me.

It didn't have much lace in the windows as others did towards the middle of town. The inn was warm, with large chairs to lounge in. Candles placed on tables, a fireplace and the windows kept the shadows at bay, but wasn't bright enough to make the eyes burn either.

We set out boxes on the dark, smooth wood of the bar and had the barkeep bring us some plates to distribute the goodies per room. He also gave us some trays so we carried the plates easier.

"Maybe I should bed down with you." Austere said as we took the trays and plates up.

"No."

"Nadachia, you walked past the inn. You'd still be walking if I hadn't called out to you."

"It's fine. I'm fine."

His cheeks puffed out as he blew out a breath, "Fine. Sleep with the girls and I'll bring something to my lonely room."

"Can you not be alone for five minutes?"

"Yes, I can. Are you jealous, darling?"

"Hardly."

I bumped my elbow against the door to the priest and driver's room. They were groggy, but gladly put a pause in their sleep to eat on the goodies we brought them. We then moved to Tori and Blari's room.

I heard Blari's snores. I hesitated on knocking, not wanting to wake him. Austere just opened the door.

Tori stood near the middle of the little room, his hand reaching for the hilt of his sword. When he saw it was me and

Austere, he reached for a shirt instead. His hair was slicked back and dripping down bare shoulders and chest.

"Didn't think you'd be up, but glad you are." Austere's deep voice was a tumbling purr.

Tori glared at the other prince after his shirt settled into place. His nostrils flared as his eyes slid to the trays. "What's that?"

"Presents."

"Gifts for showing off that pale skin of yours for once."

Tori took two of the plates, setting them on the little dresser between the narrow beds. "Thanks." He turned and looked straight at me, "Get some rest too."

"I will."

"I won't. All doubly hot and bothered now." Austere claimed before tossing a smile Tori's way.

I nudged him back out of the room. "How have you survived this long?"

"My actions are far greater than my words."

"There needs to be a means to make you turn off for a bit. A whip? A button?"

"The first suggestion is exciting and I'm willing, if you are. I'll definitely show you all my buttons if you show me yours."

I shoved open the door to the room I would share with Eisle and Spacya, "No."

"You know where my room is if you change your mind."

I shut my door in his face with my foot.

Spacya chuckled before she started eying the tray in my hands. "Told you we have too many men."

"Agreed." I handed her a plate, then Eisle, before sitting down on the edge of my bed. "You're not tired?"

Eisle shook her head.

I knew Spacya could go all night and then some if she had to. Eisle, on the other hand, was young and seemed close to Sterla. I hadn't a clue what her normal limits were.

The huntress picked up a cookie and bit into it, "Good." She said around her mouthful before stuffing the rest of the palm sized cookie in her mouth.

"I'm going to take you there in the morning for a roll, both of you."

"That good?" Eisle asked shyly.

"Better."

Spacya gave me a curt nod, biting into the fruit covered thing. Her eyes rolled back in her head.

"Sterla would have liked these. The chocolate cookies, or anything chocolate, were always her favorites."

Eisle's voice was so quiet, I had to strain to hear her over my chewing. I hadn't known that. If I had known, I wouldn't have purchased the cookies to save Eisle some heartache. Tears were being wiped away by her slender fingers as she ate a cookie in dainty bites.

"Sorry, I didn't know."

"No. It's... I like them too."

When we finished, I rounded up the plates and the tray up before Spacya or Eisle thought of doing it. Most of my companions were asleep, so I gathered their plates as quietly as possible. Tori didn't snore half as loudly as Blari, but he slept half naked. I saved the worst for last.

I knocked and hoped he would be out.

"Enter."

I pushed the door open, mentally cursing myself as I tried balancing everything on my hip.

He lay sprawled on his bed. Boots kicked off, shirt untucked with the lace that held it closed loose to the middle of his chest. He had a book in his hands, only looking up when I just stood there. Or he had found a decent stopping point.

"I'm taking the trays and plates down. You done?"

He picked up the last bite of cookie and put it in his mouth. He lay the book open on his bed before pulling his boots back on. He placed his on my tray, then tried to take it from my hands.

"I can handle it."

"I know. Grab the other one." He stated, pushing past me.

I had to let it go to him or risk breaking all the plates when I fought with him. I grabbed the empty tray from his nightstand and shut the door behind us. "What were you reading?"

"Quill Child, read it?"

"No."

"It's about a Rogue being adopted into and cared for by a human family, but things aren't… quite what they seem."

"How?"

He smiled down at me, the dimples winking into existence, "I'll loan it to you when I'm done." He paused at the top of the stairs, "That is… can you read?"

"I can read."

He smiled again, "Of course you can."

We gave the plates back to the innkeeper, but Austere held on to the trays and pointed to a list behind the bar. "What drinks do you think we should get for them?"

I lifted a shoulder, wondering why I hadn't thought about drinks before. I was parched, as I hadn't dug out my water like Spacya had while she ate. "Tea?"

Austere wrinkled his nose as his lips curled, "How about some warm milk with cinnamon and a dash of cream instead? Eight, please."

"That's to get children to sleep."

"Works on adults too. Plus, it goes well washing down sweets and breads." He drummed his fingers on the bar top. "I've been meaning to ask you something." He said after a few moments.

Why had he paused? "Go on."

"Aren't there any eligible families your sister can marry into in Owlimount?"

This again. "Most of the high rank have already married that are Seaghla's age or older. Why? Wondering if you stand a chance?"

He grinned, "I have nothing to worry about. What about ones your age? I just find it odd that your mother traveled all the way to the capital to marry off her daughter. Usually, someone of such high standing would have the beaus come to you."

"The richest and numerous are in Galanesse."

"Ecia's capital is closer. They have lords and royals just as rich if not richer than those in Lanpress."

I didn't like his tone. "We don't have a house in Ecia."

"Ah, you have one in Galanesse then?"

"Yes. An old inherited piece that was split into two smaller homes."

"You rent the other side?"

"Sold it. My great-grandmother did."

"I see. That makes a bit more sense now."

I leaned toward him on the bar, peering into his face to see if I could read it. My chin jutted out. Mother hated when I did this. "What were you thinking the reason was?"

"Just curious is all." His gaze didn't stray from mine. In fact, he leaned in closer, our noses nearly touched, "Nice to know we have a house to hole up in, if need be."

"Hide in? It's no secret."

"Ah, but I believe it is. Seaghla would not have been forced to change into those dresses when she arrived. They would have sent them to her. She would have ridden in an open carriage for all to see. Why would Keandria have missed that opportunity to show off your sister?"

"What of it?"

"Always have a secondary plan, meeting point, escape route, everything. Sometimes a third too."

"Are you always so careful with your dallying?"

His hand cupped my cheek. Warmth spread over me as he said, "Darling, this ensures that you can live."

The innkeeper set the cups on a tray, muttering something about silly lovers not knowing when they should do things in private. I pulled away, paid the man, and started to grab the overladen tray. Austere did so before I. I wouldn't admit it, but I was glad he did.

"Think the keeper wanted me to touch his cheek like that too?" The pirate prince asked as we made our way up the stairs.

"Austere, he probably just didn't want us to have sex on his bar."

"Ah! Progress! The word sex and my name in the same sentence uttered from the Hero's precious lips! Soon. Soon, I shall be able to give you the full experience that is I."

I asked the priest to pray for Austere's survival on this trip when we gave him their refreshments. Both men were awake when we cracked the door open to sneak in. Blari and Tori were still fast asleep, I left their drinks on the nightstand between them.

The pirate prince came into mine with me. "Three ladies in one room, what is a man to do?"

"Go to his."

Austere's frown was clownish as he held Spacya's mug just out of her reach. "My darling huntress, surely you don't mean that."

That scarred smirk would have sent me running for cover. "Yes, boy. I do mean as I say. Especially if you keep me from that mug."

"Should have held the cinnamon in yours. You're spicy enough." He stated as he handed her the mug, giving her a wink.

Eisle's eyes darted back and forth between the two of them. They grew wider with each word and expression the two shared. She reminded me of a child watching her parents have a fight for the first time. I started to say something to soothe her, but Austere sat down beside her. He took her hand and pressed the warm mug into it.

She blushed.

"Don't you dare. He's a womanizer. Don't you blush at him." Spacya wagged her finger in front of Eisle's face.

I giggled for a moment before I tried to settle Eisle's shocked expression, "It's alright, Eisle. Just know that he works on all women and men the same way."

He shook his head, but had a small smile curling his lips, "I see I will get nowhere soon with you three." He lounged back on the bed, propping up on an elbow as he nursed his mug of warm spiced milk, "Are the three of you going to be comfortable in here?"

"Been in worse. Her and I." She nodded to me.

"As have I." Eisle added in her trembling voice.

"I tried convincing Nadachia to take my room, but she won't." He held up a hand at a glare from the huntress, "I would be good."

I snorted, the sound echoed by the other two ladies.

Austere's breath came out in a huff before he said, "Gods bless me, this is going to be a long trip."

After a Crossroads Bakery run, we set out again. At the slower pace, we would reach Emleton just before nightfall. At least, that was my hope.

"Serve me an inkwell and I'll buy a pint. Don't go a tellin' my song for me." Blari stopped when I looked at him, "Sorry, been in my head for two days."

"Now you want it stuck in everyone else's?"

"No." He sighed as he glanced back at the wagon behind us. "We're going to stay for the funeral, aren't we?"

"It's the least we can do."

"Chi, how are you feeling?"

I pulled out a small smile with too much difficulty. Riding had become my torture. I was left with my own thoughts too often while on Unia. "I'm fine."

"I need a description."

"You're not putting my emotions in your book, Priest."

"Not for that!" he scoffed. "Besides, I'm your friend."

I shook my head at him, "I'm not good with words."

"Try."

Feelings. I knew exactly what I had been thinking. I knew each flop my stomach made and how my throat burned with the tears I held back. It was sadness. Guilt. It was those doubled and tripled at times.

"It replays in my head still. I want to go back and fight harder, or sew my lips shut so it won't happen. I want to tell her I'm sorry I killed her. That I didn't mean to, but it's my fault she's not here. It's my fault she's not humming that silly song with you. I killed her."

Blari's hand cupped mine over my reins. We rode, side by side, for a while. Silence between us. He broke it with his next words, "I'm going to tell you this until you believe it. You didn't kill her. You did not kill her." His hand squeezed mine, "Sterla wouldn't want you torturing yourself in this way."

Eisle's voice drifted to us, "You didn't kill her. Matron did."

Blari and I both looked back at her.

"I was there. I saw what was happening. She knew your love for her. She saw it."

The burning in my throat crawled up to my eyes. Allowing the tears to fall, I let my eyes and throat burn with them. I allowed myself an ugly, spine curling cry as I lay on my mare and let her mane catch my tears and sobs.

Blari's wide hand rubbed my back in slow strokes, patting now and then. I coughed up junk and more tears.

"We should stop." Tori's voice cracked on the words.

"No." I forced the word out through a sob. "No, we keep going. She deserves to be home."

We kept moving. Something cool and slick grew within me. It eased the burn in my throat, the need for me to cough lessened. I became more aware of it. The same feeling I had when I held Sterla in my arms. This time, it didn't recoil. It just rested, low along my spine and stomach, waiting. Between my sniffles as I finished sobbing, I heard another quiet crying. Something in me, that cool slick feeling, knew it was Eisle.

I wasn't sure when I stopped crying. My mare's mane was soaked underneath my wet face. My mouth and throat were a little raw when I breathed as my nose was uselessly clogged.

Blari passed me a cloth he pulled out of his sleeve.

I wiped my face off with it and blew out my nose. "I'll wash it before I give it back to you."

"Wash it, but keep it. I have another."

I sat up. Grimacing at the pain leaning on the front of the saddle caused me. It faded, quickly, as Eisle started rubbing her stomach area where I had hurt. I picked up my canteen and rinsed my mouth out. I watched Blari wipe his eyes off on his sleeve out of the corner of my eye.

"Did that help?"

Empty. It was the second cry I had in three days' time. Part of me was always a little lighter after a cry like that. "I think so."

"Good." Blari smiled and reached over to squeeze my knee. We rode beside each other until Tori called for a break.

Our party moved off the road onto a little path that ended at a small field by a stream. It was barely big enough for the flat with Sterla on it, but we managed. I slid off my mare and went to work, rinsing out her mane where I had ruined it. She dipped her head, taking a long drink before slowly wandering toward the lush grass of the field. I followed her. Calm and solid, that was my Unia.

"You look horrible." He leaned against her beside me as he took a swig from his canteen.

"That makes me feel much better about crying in public, thank you."

"All the things you have done in public and you think we care about you crying?"

I focused on her mane, trying to ignore the obnoxious thing beside me.

"You're among friends here, Hero. There's no shame in showing emotion with us."

"Even if two are strangers, one I've only known for a few months, and another a few more weeks than the last one, and the longest relationship I've had between these here is a priest and I did not go to church regularly?"

"Even then." He chuckled and shook his head, "I've seen you at your best, naked, and at what you may think is your worst. While being naked, I might add. We're friends, you and I, not strangers."

"I don't know you."

"You've had a grand start." He began twisting a tiny braid in my mare's mane.

"You can flirt, but let her eat too." Spacya called from the packhorse.

Austere heaved a sigh before saying, "Thwarted, again."

I took a swallow from my canteen, finally satisfied that her mane was clean.

Sam Wicker

He took it from me, "Go. I'll fill this."

Chapter 23

Emleton sprawled across Rogue Road and the Gala River before the white-capped peaks of the Rogue Mountains. Another trade town full of taverns, inns, and a large market along the docks. The only difference between it and Paridiaso was Emleton had a huge permanent population.

Homes stood side by side along roads that led to the mountains. Some were white, but most were vivid shades of greens, blues, reds, and yellows. Shops had colored glass windows and chandeliers made of gems of all hues. The richer shops had candles with different colored flames on their tables where patrons ate.

The smells were crisp, and the air always held a hint of snow. Pines stubbornly grew between houses, along the roads and river, and covered the area outside the city all the way up to some of the mountain peaks.

Guards kept the peace and were out in the open, seen, active and mingling with Emletoners. Not hidden in corners like Galanesse had them. Like in Galanesse, all the races walked out in the clear. No fear nor judgment and certainly comfortable in their city.

While my Owlimount had much the same, we hardly had any Rogues to stay for long. They traveled through. Emleton was home to many of the Rogues.

We stopped in front of the Church and were welcomed in. This one had rooms for us, plenty of them, so none had to share. Although, I was sure one would try. We placed our things in our rooms, and some took a moment to ourselves. I washed and dressed in a nicer set of pants and shirt.

I walked to the main worship hall. Sterla lay amid fresh flowers of white, creams, and blacks at the altar. Wrapped in gray and black linen, her body seemed even smaller than when she was alive.

Sam Wicker

A female in white knelt by her. Three children, a girl and two boys, like stairsteps in height, just behind her. To not disturb them, I knelt by a pew a few feet back.

Their sniffles and soft words of grief ripped my heart anew. This cry was not as harsh. It was a great wash of sadness, but the rage was held back. The guilt still mingled with the pain.

"You."

I looked up at the voice.

"You were with her."

I saw Eisle had come in with Spacya. The woman in white was looking at me, though. I nodded, keeping on my knees as she stood over me, "Yes, I was with her."

"What happened?"

Eisle's breath hissed between her lips in a harsh intake. I knew the story I was told to tell; the one everyone else would believe. I looked into the dark eyes of the female Stygra and saw Sterla in them. She had taken after her mother, then.

"The Matron tied her life to mine. Keandria killed me." Sharp pains shot through the palms of my hands from my own fingernails. A reminder I was still in control of them.

"She killed my Sterla, through you?"

"Yes."

"My baby girl is somewhere in you?"

I stared into her face. Ash made the pale skin dark and added gray to her black hair under the white hood. "She… she died."

She moved. So slow, so smooth I thought she would float along instead of walk. "You felt something, didn't you? When she passed. A darkness, a coolness around your heart and stomach. You still do, yes?"

Grief did a lot of things to people. "Yes." How did she know what it did to me?

Her hand slid out of the long sleeve of her mourning robe. The mother's nails blackened, fingertips darkened and hand gray from the ash. She lay it against my chest. Spacya stepped to my side, stopping just behind me. She had no weapons.

"Only one in every million can tie lives, souls, powers together. So rare are they among us, that little is known of our gifts."

"Our powers?" My mind was tripping over each word that came out of her mouth.

She nodded, ash falling as flakes of snow onto her shoulders and the dark blue carpet between us. "Keandria is the daughter of one of my aunts. Odd how there are two of us living at the same time. She had hoped when Sterla emerged, she would be a third." Tears ran down the ashen tracks on her cheeks, "But we shall never know. Not until you accept her power in you."

"She's human, Momma." The eldest looking male spoke, "She can't have Sterla's power even with that. Can she?"

Sterla's mother's flat hand curled into a fist upon my chest, over my heart. "She does. I feel my daughter here."

I must have weaved because Spacya's knees pressed against my back to support me. She told me to breathe.

Cool fingers cupped the side of my head and began rubbing small circles along my temples. The scent of ashes swept up my nose. "I'm glad my daughter lives on, in part, in you. You need not worry. You need not miss her."

"Why? I'm the reason she's dead. She died in my place."

"That's not how we look at it. We die so others may live. That is our life. My Sterla did that for you."

"I wish she hadn't gone to Galanesse."

"We had no choice! It's Keandria!" The daughter's fists clenched at her sides. Her slender body shook.

"I'm the one that convinced her to go." Eisle sat beside me, "Keandria came and pulled all the children together to see who she would take. She gave Sterla a choice, unlike the rest of us. I asked Sterla to come with me."

I stared at Eisle for a moment, "It's not your fault." I knew it wasn't. It was mine. My mind rolled around the new ideas, trying to make sense of them. I should have spent more time studying Stygra, but Welkans were more interesting and readily available. Selfish of me.

"What do I do?" I asked as I turned to look back at Sterla's mother.

Her eyes closed for a long moment before she answered, "When we bury her, just know she lives on in you. The rest will be learning to use her talent."

"I'll help." Eisle stammered as she wiped a tear from her cheek.

"Will Keandria know?"

"Yes, she will. She cannot feel the type of power until she tries to tie it to something. Until then, she may think you have Sterla's healing gift. Which you do. If you accept her, her coming of age power will awaken within you."

I stared at the ash covered face, picking out features Sterla had inherited from her. She would have grown to be magnificent and beautiful, as her mother was before me. "I'm sorry."

"Your sorrow is not cause for apology." She turned her head away, and then said, "I must go now. I must cry mine out, so she may rest."

I watched her stand and move back toward Sterla's body on the altar. Her children followed, not one of them looked at me again. I was thankful for that.

We held the funeral during the darkest hour of the night. They lowered Sterla, face down, into a deep chasm. Two Stygra and the Priest from Galanesse spoke words over her. I could not bring myself to focus on them. I only listened to the thing within me. Sterla.

I sensed her weeping.

I watched as the blue and green flames of Stygra power enveloped her little body in the chasm. She joined the others of her race and those that preferred to be buried this way of Emleton's past. Once the Stygra taught their funeral rights to the other races, many wished to be buried like them. Others desired the Welkan way, while yet others kept the rituals of their ancestors.

Choice. It was always about choice in this life. Sterla had her choice taken from her.

I placed a hand over my heart to aid me in focusing there. Her essence swelled like dipping into chilled waters. I pictured my soul opening to the darkness, to Sterla, and allowing her in. I imagined her finding a home within me, not to overtake me, and I not to swallow her, but to form a partnership.

Some box opened in me and I felt a warmth with cool edges spread and take hold. I looked into the face of the moons overhead. Sterla smiled from there for a moment, then faded.

Spacya, Tori, Blari, Austere and I made our way back to town. The Stygra had further rituals that were private for family members and those chosen to stay by them. The priest and driver walked with us. They would leave for Galanesse in the morning.

"Has your brother arrived yet?" Blari asked as we explored the streets.

Emleton was mostly empty at this hour, except for a few tavern hoppers and drunks.

"He will be here tomorrow, probably. I didn't give my crew much warning before they had to make way." We entered the Church, and he added, "We could stay on my ship."

"No. Nope. Never." Spacya shook her head, her face growing pale.

Tori chuckled, "Finally, a weakness!"

"Don't do ships, love?" Austere asked with a cheeky grin while leaning in close to her.

Spacya's hand splayed over his face as she shoved him away, "Not a weakness. Just don't like 'em is all."

"Sickness?"

She shot the man behind her hand a look, "Aye."

"Even on a river?"

"Aye. Not as bad."

"Well, there goes that idea."

"What idea was that?" Tori asked.

Sam Wicker

"I take all of us back to Galanesse when we're through with this mission."

Spacya shook her head, going from pale to a shade of green.

"We have horses for a reason. Let's use them," I said, not wanting Spacya to get sick on me at the thought of getting on a boat.

"Anyone care for a quick nightcap? I know a grand tavern just around the corner." Austere paused at Blari's door. His room was the first of ours down the hall of rooms.

Blari yawned and shook his head, "We should get to bed. Got a long day of riding and talking ahead of us."

Tori nodded, watching Spacya go into hers further down the hall without deigning to answer Austere. "Agreed." He then turned to grin at me, "You two have fun."

Austere wrapped a heavy arm around my shoulders before I could think of an excuse. "How about it, darling?"

It wasn't like I was going to sleep anyway. "Fine, but I'm warning you, only one or two drinks. No more."

"Famous last words."

The light was way too bright behind my eyelids. There was a roaring in my ears that set my head to thumping like a madman on a drum. I groaned, trying to turn away from the glow.

Something lay around my chest, another at my hips, and another over my lower legs keeping me immobile. I knew it was going to hurt to look. Sheets and pillows should not feel that heavy.

The heaviness on my chest turned out to be a slender shoulder and arm of a dark, rich hue. A slender hand with pink painted fingernails lay amidst my loose hair at my side. Her hot breath caused light tender-bumps to rise over the tops of my breasts.

At least my shirt was still on. In a fashion.

My head was as heavy as a boulder. Those tattoos were getting too familiar for my tastes. I blinked, trying to make sense of limbs, hair, and bedsheets. His head was on my stomach, closer to my hips, face turned away from me.

I couldn't see past Austere's hulking back with its too interesting tattoos. Unless he was a contortionist, which I couldn't rule out, there was someone else lying across my knees. I let my head fall. I groaned as my brain bounced with the movement.

I think I still had underwear on. No pants, though. The person on my legs gave off heat like a low burning fire.

I couldn't imagine a way out of this mess of bodies. I couldn't fathom how to pull together enough strength to have a go at a try. Talking was out of the question. My mouth felt like sand. The sweet wine grew sour overnight on my tongue.

How did I even get into this?

After the funeral was a blur of me trying to drink and think over Eisle's information on drawing powers. Alone. I had told this braggart over my hips hundreds of times to leave me alone. Which drove me to drinking more, to put up with him without slicing his throat open.

Therein had been my mistake.

I rolled my hips.

Austere jerked, moaned, and then licked the skin above my belly button.

I growled.

The lady rolled off me.

I smacked Austere on the back of his head with a tingling hand. I hadn't realized she had been lying on my arm. "Up!"

"Ow! Gods." He twisted to his back, pinning me under him on the bed. "Are you always so violent in the mornings?" His hand slid over a pair of sizable breasts. I guessed that was where some of the new grumblings were coming from.

"Get off me. Him too." I finally got a decent look across Austere at the one sleeping on my legs. Shimmering scales lay smooth as skin all over him. The one hand, I saw, was webbed up to the knuckles, but not on his thumb. His hair was slick, like reeds more than hair, but was a natural black. He was lying in the path of the most direct beam of sunlight.

He could heat the whole room in all that sunlight.

"Just a few more minutes." the scaled one's voice was gravelly. He rolled, grabbing and pulling and curling against the other female near my legs. She turned out to be a redhead. Her skin freckled over her shoulders and back.

Austere shifted as well, nuzzling into my breasts. I shoved his head back.

"You weren't this mean last night."

I wriggled my feet. The Rogue male chuckled, "Just ask nicely."

"Get off me, please?"

He sat up, and crawled toward me over my legs. He stopped, hovering over Austere. Another inch and his nose would touch mine. His eyes were blue, cloudy, and too large for his narrow face. "Don't let him lie to you. You were plenty mean enough. We all had to settle for him while you slept."

"Settle?"

The Rogue grinned, showing sharp, jagged teeth. "Drink doesn't make anyone hard of hearing." He bumped my nose with his, "Come now, girls." He called softly after sliding off the bed. Gathering clothes off the floor he tossed them to their respective owners. Except my belt. He lay it gingerly, almost reverently, on a chair.

The women got dressed with yawns and soft grumbles.

The Rogue finished dressing, and he shot me a wink as he said, "Any need you have for pleasure, come find me, love. Anyone who can fight off this many while drunk will be Gods' realm level of fun sober and wanting it."

"I'll keep that in mind." I flopped back down from where I had propped myself up on my elbows to study them. The realization of my mistake when my head hit the pillow again arrived with an earth shattering throb.

They all left. Three different states of dress among them. I smacked Austere again. And because it made me feel better, I did it anew.

"Would you stop!" He groaned, smacking my hand away before I could do it again.

I took stock. Shirt and underwear were still on. A little damp down there, but not if I had sex wet. My lips weren't feeling it either, so no kissing, much, if at all. Taspe was going to roll around laughing, upon hearing about this.

If I could remember what happened.

He stood and finally started pulling on clothes, "You should thank me."

"Why would I do something as ridiculous as that?"

"Because for a whole six hours you didn't worry or cry or think at all."

"Congratulations. You made me drunk for six hours."

He shook his head with a chuckle, "When is the last time you let go?"

"A month, or so, ago."

"Really?"

"Don't be so shocked."

He pulled on his shirt. "I'm impressed. There aren't many people I misjudge."

"Glad to be on more than one of your short lists."

He chuckled again. As he sat down on the edge of the bed, he asked, "What other list of mine do you think you're on?"

"The one with people you haven't had sex with yet. The one of women who don't swoon at your feet." My mind whirred, but there was nothing else there, "I can't think right now."

His head tilted slightly, as I met his gaze, and he said, "You are on the list of women that have been through too much too."

I snorted. My brain throbbed with the noise. Why wasn't Sterla healing this? Could I use her power to heal this?

Oh. Oh, that was wondrous. My head stopped pounding and cleared. It was as if I had a full night's rest and bounded up in the morning. I sat up and slid into my pants.

"If you cry and shut down every now and then, or just let go more often, I think it would be well deserved."

Sam Wicker

"I need to do better." I moved to the opposite side of the bed, closer to the door. He was dangerous if he could get me to drink that much.

"Agreed. You need to share the load. Why else do Heroes have companions for?"

"I have got to take a bath," I said as I stood. I opened the door and saw I was at the end of the hall. I turned back to glare at him, "You could have told me this was my room."

He chuckled as he pulled on his boots. "I'll go get us some breakfast. Wonder if there's a bakery like Crossroads here."

I listened as he walked down the hall and watched until he rounded the corner before shutting the door. I locked it, just for good measure. Without a servant or maid, I was alone. At last.

I opened a window to let the stink of all the things Austere had done with the three last night out. Part of me was angry. The broken part of me hoped he had meant well. I breathed in the crisp pine and fresh snow scent that came in on the breeze. Soon enough, we would be in the middle of those mountains.

After my bath and getting dressed, I packed my things that I had taken out of my bag. Thanks to the bath and the open window, the room smelled more like me instead of the others. I heard boot laden steps outside my door before the doorknob jiggled. A muffled curse and a thunk before a knock came.

I debated on keeping still and quiet. Maybe they would go away. That was until I heard the scrape of metal on metal coming from my door. Palming a dagger, in case it wasn't who I thought it was, I pulled open my door.

Austere crouched, a set of small lockpicks in his hands, as a piece of buttered bread dangled from his mouth. His dark hair gleamed wetly, but his clothes were fresh and perfectly fitted to his body.

He put the tools away in the pockets of his vest, "Well hello, darling. Thought you might be drowning again." He said, after dropping the bread into an empty palm. He split the roll in half, handing it toward me, "Glad to see you haven't."

I turned when something scraped against the window.

"Gods! Next time just kick down the door." Blari huffed from my window as he tried to pull himself up into it.

"She well?" Tori's voice drifted up from somewhere below Blari.

"She's good. Coming down. Don't put your hand…" Blari finished his sentence in a scream as he disappeared from sight. A few moments later, he called from below before I could get back around my bed to the window, "I'm fine!"

Austere placed the bread in my hand. "We're to meet with some witnesses that came to see us. They have a meal for us."

"Am I to ignore that the three of you tried to break into my room just now?"

"Yup."

I shut my window after sheathing my dagger. I took a bite of the roll and fervently missed Crossroads and Hana's breads. It was rock hard. I closed my door and half ran, half trotted to catch up with Austere.

"We weren't sneaking. The priest said he knocked a few times, but got no answer."

"When?"

"I suppose just now."

Spacya smirked, leaning against the door that led to the dining area. She held out her hand to Austere, "Told ya she was jus' fine."

Austere dropped two iron bits into her palm.

We sat down at the table laden with food. Two priests were there, the high priest and the one that greeted us when we arrived. I needed to get better with names.

"After we eat, we will adjourn to the drawing room. There you will meet with the witnesses, one by one."

"How many are there?"

"Only six."

"What are we facing? We haven't talked about it at all." Tori asked before biting into something that crunchy while being iced.

I felt the heat rise into my cheeks from my neck, "Sorry."

The High Priest interjected, "Allow me, if you will." At my nod, she continued, "It calls itself Cotkit. It lives somewhere in the mountains, near the Alban Wastes."

"Wait, it calls itself?" I leaned over my plate. Keandria hadn't told me that the thing talked.

"Yes, it speaks. Quite well, from what we have gathered."

"What has it been doing?" Blari had one hand full of fruit while he wrote with the other. His plate buried beneath the book.

"It eats people."

I eyed my full plate, regretting putting anything on it. "How many?"

"Thirty-three as of last night. We haven't gotten another report yet."

"Thirty-three people?" Austere's fist lay on the table with a thud, "What has been done?"

"Most of the dead are the effects of what we have tried." The High priest cleared her throat, "I have exact numbers, if you want them."

"Yes."

"Three human children on the first sighting, a boy and two girls. One Stygra female aged twenty-one on the second sighting about three days later. Two Rogue males of the Bird Tribe on the third sighting, another three or four days later. A band gathered to attack, numbering five. They did not see it again for a week after… after dismembering the band…" The list went on, varying in numbers and races, but usually every two or three days. Until a band got together to attack, and failed, then it wouldn't attack again for a week, depending on the size of the party.

"That's enough." Tori stated, leaning back in his chair.

"Where have these attacks been?" Blari had stopped eating as well. Only Austere and Spacya seemed unaffected.

"Mostly in the mining camps in the foothills, some along the road, others were pulled or attacked on the outskirts of this very town."

"Has any attack on the Cotkit worked? Wounded it in any way?"

The priests of Emleton shook their heads, "We are not entirely sure. Those that get close rarely make it back to report to us. What little information we have gained is from those that have been nearby during the attacks in the camps."

"One man said he thought he saw a sword sticking out of its leg, but no one else has remembered seeing that." The other priest added.

A miner that saw it is an artist. She drew this." The High Priest took a small piece of paper from her robes.

I took it, unfolding it once. At first glance, it looked like the legendary fire bird, the pet of Dani, the god of fire. On closer inspection, it was so much more than any of the artwork that depicted that legendary bird.

It had too many eyes in a straight line down either side of its skull. Those would make it difficult, if not impossible, to sneak up on. "Are these scales or short feathers?"

"Scales."

"Gods." Austere breathed over my shoulder, "Nothing will ever penetrate those if she is a talented artist."

They were thick, overlapping tightly over one another thicker than a fish's scales. The neck, chest, head and legs were covered in them. Feathers or protrusions of some sort came up from the center of the sharp beak, growing larger as they ran the crest of the beast's skull and down its long neck.

Wings, twice the size of the body and numbering four, came out of its sides. Underneath them were more of the tightly overlapping scales. The wings themselves looked sharp and shaped like a curved sword of the Ecia people.

I passed the drawing to Austere after taking in the huge talons at the end of each of the four toes. It even had a spur talon on the back of each leg.

They had sent two sets of soldiers to kill this thing. None of them had returned. Highly trained, armed men and women of the guard defeated. My companions were not all trained that well. Gods, two of them were not learned with weapons at all.

Sam Wicker

After the drawing made it around the table, my companions and I sat, listening to the priests. None of us ate. I hoped that someone would enjoy all the food left.

"All six that are here have been told to keep it relevant and give you as much information as possible. We know that your time is important."

I raised a brow at that, "What else would they talk to us about?"

Austere chuckled and shook his head, "Plenty of things, love."

Thinking back on all the things he has said to me over the course of a few days, I knew he was right. Surely no one else was like that, though. Well, other than Taspe at times.

"Let's go meet them."

They led us to a room set off to the side of the meal hall. I caught sight of a few people in the room next door, as the door had been slightly ajar. They were whispering among themselves. No laughter came from that room.

We sat down, a table between us and the townspeople. I felt like we were to be protected from something other than the Cotkit in this setup. The High priest stood at one side, and the other stood at the entrance. She nodded at him once we were all settled. He let the first person in.

The woman could have been the redhead's mother from last night. This morning. What time was it? Her dress left little to the imagination, but it covered her, mostly. Her back must hurt constantly with what she had to carry on her chest.

She bowed. Austere leaned in his seat next to mine. I had the sudden urge to smack him even though he had said nothing, nor really done anything.

"Oh… Gods you are here." She beamed up at us upon straightening. "You are as beautiful as the stories say."

Spacya snorted, and I bit back a smile.

"No, really." She grinned. At the High Priest stepping forward, she licked her lips. "My husband and I work at the Blue Mining Camp, just north of here. About two weeks ago, the thing came. It was in broad daylight, not scared of us at all, not even hiding. It

289

swooped in on these huge wings and started grabbing at people with its claws and beak. Landed right in the middle of the square, crushed our fountain. We went without fresh drinking water for a week before we could clear all the rubble and fix it." She breathed slowly, putting a hand to her chest.

Blari was scribbling furiously as she talked, but he paused, and I noticed his eyes were on that hand. I shook my head. It was spring. That was the only explanation. That and the thing next to me who always spoke of sex. He was proving to be a bad influence.

"My dear Heroes, it grabbed up two people. I didn't learn until later who they were. But it flew back up, carrying them in its feet, as if they were nothing but twigs." She sniffled.

I placed a hand on Austere's knee to keep him in his seat.

He glared at me. I glared right back, before turning to her, "It didn't... eat... anything while it was there, did it?"

"No, not that I could tell. There were only the two missing too."

"Is this the first time you have seen anything like it?"

She nodded, "It was the biggest creature I have ever seen. It was bigger than most of our housing put together, my Lady Hero."

I cringed at the title, "Is there anything that you can think of that was strange...well, other than it. Any smells it gave off? Any sounds?"

She thought for a moment, wiping her cheek clean, "I... I don't think so. It was so loud with the screaming and the buildings being torn down by its wings and tail that I don't remember hearing anything. All I remember smelling is... well, dust and things you smell when things are being turned over and destroyed."

"You mentioned a tail. Was it feathered like its wings?"

"Oh no, scaled like its legs with a hook at the end. It... it reminds me of a white bee stinger, actually."

I could only hope it was as small as one, but I knew that was a foolish thought.

"Anything else you can think of?"

She cast a glance at the high priest, and then moved toward our table to bow again, "Thank you for coming. You are our saviors and if there is anything… anything at all you need, my husband and I would be glad to provide you-"

"Thank you, next."

The High Priest motioned for the other priest to come forward. He ushered her out and brought the next one in on his way back. This one was an older man. He held a gray stained cap in his hands, which he turned round and round in his gnarled fingers. His skin was pale, but looked stained in the wrinkles and along the edges of his clothes. They only looked like that when they had spent most of their lives in the dark mines.

"Hello, sir." I said with a smile, already liking him.

He bowed his head, a sheepish grin showing me a snaggle tooth. "Hello, heroes." He said with a bit of gravel in his voice, "I'll get straight to the point so you can ask questions that'll help you. I'll do the best I can." The hat ran faster through his fingers as he spoke, "It was about midday, we were all comin' up for lunch cause they gave us a long one that day. The mine boss has a set of twins, ya see, and it was their birthday, so boss always lets us have an hour for lunch on those days with some cake and tea. There were only a few of us up. I was on the second ride up, I love that cake, ya see." His smile was more of a frown, "Just got off the lift when I overheard someone ask 'what's that?' and I looked around. A great big shadow passed over, fast, like a big cloud when a terrible storm is blowin'."

He paused, the hat working so quickly in his hands I wondered if his fingertips were burning. "It landed. On the mountain. Rock and trees fell. We ran, trying to get away from the mountain. I think it took advantage of it. You know, showering us with rock and debris. Cause it reached out with one leg, grabbing and it grabbed with its beak too." He swallowed, his head bowed, "It took us a long time to get the rock away from the lift. Took us longer still to see who 'n all was hurt and who was missin'. It landin' on the mountain made the lift get off its gears, and we had a shaft collapse."

We all waited for a beat or two, the old man's hat slowed in his hands, and he didn't continue. "I'm glad you are safe." I said, "I'm sorry we couldn't come sooner so this wouldn't happen."

He looked up at me, eyes lined with tears but none fell, he gave me a nod, "Sooner might not have done much. It was the second attack we know of here. 'preciate the thought though."

"Is this the attack where four were taken?"

Both the High Priest and the miner nodded.

"Did you see which way it flew when it left?"

"Toward the desert, the Wastes. We're only a ridge back from that evil place, our camp is."

"Do you think it came from the same direction?"

The old miner's fingers stopped, then started turning his hat again, "Dunno for sure, but I would think so. The mine mouth faces the Wastes and unless it circled, the shadow started from that direction and moved to the mountain."

"Did it do anything with its tail while it was attacking?" I leaned forward, an idea stirring in my head.

"No, it was all curled up over the back. Didn't even really see it until it flew off."

"All four wings used in flight?"

"Yup."

"Did it drop the ones it grabbed with its beak into the feet claws before it took off?"

"No, it carried them there." He paused, "I always thought it odd that it didn't eat while it was there... why not eat and carry extra back?"

I nodded, "I'm thinking the same thing. Some birds carry back to a nest to feed their young."

I realized my mistake as soon as the man's knees went all wobbly and the priest grabbed hold of him. "I mean... and some have to... they carry back to the nests because they eat peculiarly."

I saw Austere turn his head out of the corner of my eye toward me, his eyes narrowed, "Good job, Hero, give the poor man a heart attack."

"I didn't mean to." I muttered, then added louder, "I'm sorry."

The old man held up a hand, "It's alright. Truly."

"Was there anything else that you can think of? Something that struck you as odd?"

The old man humphed, "Other than the creature itself? No."

"Thank you for talking with us."

He smiled, and bowed, "Thank you for listenin'."

The next one made me want to cry. The little boy was no taller than the priest's waist. He sucked heavily on a fist, the first finger's knuckle deep in his mouth. His eyes were wide, a beautiful green. The priest stayed by the door as the child was led in by, who, I assumed, was his mother.

"Hello there." Austere leaned forward, his tenor soothing and open, "What's your name?"

The boy looked up at the woman; she urged him closer to us with a smile. He turned to us and pulled out his fist. He wiped it off on his pants and marched right up to the table. "It's Niji, sir."

"Niji, it is nice to meet you. Do you have a story to tell us?"

His bottom lip shook, and he nodded, "Momma says I gotta tell sos you can get it before it gets anyone else. Says I gotta be good and brave."

"You are brave, Niji." Austere smiled and stood. He moved around the table and sat down beside the boy. "My name's Stere. Wanna tell me what happened?"

Gods he was still taller than the boy sitting flat on his ass.

"Yessir. We were out playin'. Me, G, Runk, Vaya, and my little sister. We were out in the fields, out by the road tuh Minervaton. We were findin' funny rocks that comes off'n the mine wagons sometimes." He brought his fist up as if he was going to start sucking it again. Then he straightened, his chest puffing out as he took a deep breath, "It landed right on top o' Vaya, sir and it grabbed up G. I grabbed my little sister and ran for the trees. She's heavy, but I got her and ran, sir." He looked down, "I didn't see much. Vaya didn't scream, didn't yell, but G was. She can scream, sir. Peoples heard her clear into town and they came runnin' . It grabbed up Runk too." He hung his head, "I didn't know what to do. I just hid. I didn't look, until I heard it."

"Heard what?"

"It talked. It said 'I thought there were two more' like it was Momma huntin' for cookies we snatched on holiday."

"What did you see when you looked?"

"It was big an' orange an' red. Its legs were shiny, like a fishes. That's all I saw. I closed my eyes cause it stirred up a big dust pile when it flapped to lift off. It was taller'n the trees. Trees are mighty tall."

Austere nodded and smiled. He ruffled the boy's hair, only to smooth it down, "You did a good job, brave Niji. You can go back to your Momma now."

"He saved my girl and himself, my little Niji did." The woman beamed, holding out her arms. She caught him up when he ran to her and held him. Tears streamed down her cheeks, her nose and eyes were red and looked like they had been that way for a while. "We weren't that far away. We came running as soon as we saw it pass over us. I thought it was God Dani at first. You know, finally visitin' again. But then I heard the screams."

She shook her head, "There was no blood on the ground. As soon as we got there, it left. We couldn't see from the dust it stirred up from the field. Just tilled and sewed it. We were at the next one, past the road and the stream."

She sighed, "We were too far away." She hid her face against her boy's chest, her body shaking. Little Niji hugged her.

"You did what you could. Don't be guilty anymore. You had no way of knowing it would come." Austere had stood again and placed a hand on her shoulder.

If he so much as flirted, I was going to skin him alive.

She sniffled before looking up at him. Her eyes went slightly wide. I feared she was going to hurt her neck as she looked shorter than me. "Th-thank you." She wiped her face.

Austere smiled the dimple smile.

"Go rest, lovely lady. You, brave Niji, you be careful and keep taking care of your Momma and little sister."

The boy nodded. The priest led them away.

"Get back in your seat, flirt." Spacya muttered.

"Why Spacya, do you need me to come comfort you? Are you jealous of the attention she got?"

Sam Wicker

"You come near me and I'll tear out yer heart, pretty boy."

He clutched his chest, "She thinks I'm pretty! You! All of you heard it!"

Spacya growled and shifted in her seat.

I giggled and patted her shoulder, "Don't let him get to you."

"I'm gonna say the same to you every day."

Austere sighed, "Now what are you two whispering? Should I be worried?" He sat in his chair as they showed in the next person.

"Yes." Spacya answered for me.

The next two were much of the same. They described the Cotkit just like everyone else. It landed, picked and was gone in five to fifteen minutes. In that time it damaged enough lives that I dreaded the day it might just decide to nest in a town.

Chapter 24

Austere led us to a tavern a few buildings and one street over from the church. I vaguely remembered it from last night. As we wove through the patrons to ask the barkeep for a private room, I caught sight of a familiar duo.

The Rogue and red head grinned at me. Maybe it wasn't the bar that was Austere's favorite, but those that frequented it.

"Hello, my feisty goddess." The charming Rogue purred in my ear after sauntering over to us. "Gonna be a bit more friendly tonight?"

"Afraid not. Got business."

"Well, come see me when it's done." His eyes drifted over my companions. "Wait…six of you and you're staying at the-" He laughed, throwing his head back, it nearly drowned out the other patrons. "The heroes! Of course! I should have known Stere would worm his way in!"

I grabbed his elbow as Austere still talked to the barkeep, "You know him well?"

"I've known him every time he came through my hometown. Eight years or so. Well enough you could say." He toyed with a dagger hilt on my belt. "Why?"

"Is he trustworthy?"

He snorted before answering, "Asking a stranger about a man you travel with. Odd."

I rolled my eyes.

His fingers were rough, scaled, like the rest of him as he pressed them to my chin. He held my face like a lover. His cloudy eyes searched mine. "You are the Silverequis?"

I wondered if I should answer, "Yes."

He smiled then, "You are The Hero. The Silverequis of the family that takes in all kinds and aids them in every way possible, no matter their story or aims." His hand fell from my face to take up mine and bring it to his thin lips.

"He is dependable. As trustworthy as they come with lives under his ward and doing the right thing. Just don't let your heart out of its cage for him. Oh, and I wouldn't let him out of your sight if you care about riches. He has a knack for finding a better home for bits and gems."

"I'll keep that in mind."

"Thank you."

"What for? You're the one that helped me." I slid my hand free of his.

He shook his head, "Twenty years ago, your father nursed a bruised ankle on a Rogue female traveling from Ecia to Emleton. That was my mother."

I shrugged, "Just doing the right thing."

"Not many do."

"Coming?" Tori placed a hand on my shoulder and jerked a thumb to a hallway that Blari disappeared down when I looked.

"Coming." I turned back, "Thanks." I trotted after the prince. The hall was narrow, but well lit. A few doors led off at even intervals down the sides. They led us to one of the middle rooms.

Austere was already walking the walls. By his actions, I assumed he was checking for holes. More so that he could watch what was going on next door than to preserve our secrets. The room to the left of ours sounded like they were having his kind of fun.

"Both platters, a pig of ribs, and keep ale and sweet wine flowing." Austere paused in his assessment long enough to order.

The barkeep nodded and left us, closing the door behind him.

A low table was in the center, but toward the back of the room with eight chairs around it. A couple of couches were crammed together at the front. Pillows dotted all other spaces between.

A strong acidic smell and a bit of metal with tubing coming out of it on the table told me what they usually used the room for. Tori took the mechanism from the table and placed it in a corner. The couch hid the mechanism well, and the smell followed it.

"Taller than trees, bigger than two inns put together, and as tall as Ward Mountain. Exaggeration aside, how big do we prepare for this thing to be?" Tori pulled out a chair at the table and sat down in it.

"It landed on a mountain, so that last one we can ignore. Taller than trees and inns are about the same so we will go with those."

"Big 'nough to carry seven grown people," Spacya added, "I think that sounds about right."

"Do we hunt it? Can we look at it then come back for what we need? Make a plan? They say anyone that has gone looking for it never comes back." Blari leaned against the wall opposite the noisy room, and rubbed his beard with one hand.

It had to be getting darker, his beard, with all the ink stains on his fingers being rubbed into it.

"Scales. Claws. Hooked tail and sharp beak. How do we fight that? That's how we prepare." I sat down across from Tori.

"Feathers. Fire or something hot and sticky to slow it down or keep it grounded." Eilse talked with her head down, looking at us through her lashes from her perch on one of the couch arms.

"Tar or melted metal. I'm not sure which we could get a lot of on such short notice. We will have to figure out a place, or find its home." Tori pulled a map out of his pocket and spread it on the table. There wasn't much detail around the wastes. Not a lot of mapmakers enjoyed risking their lives between desert and unforgiving mountains.

"Get to pour deadly stuff on to it while avoiding it ourselves, plus the Cotkit's killing bits, too. This is gonna be fun."

"We could explore the mountains. We find its home, we find the path it takes the most. Along that path surely there will be a cliff face or something we can use to our advantage." I sat down beside Tori, studying the map.

"Here." Austere had leaned over the back of our chairs to look at the map, too. "That looks like a canyon. If we can't discover its home or its path, maybe we can lure it in there."

Tori took a quill from Blari and made a small 'X' on the canyon and wrote the word 'trap' beside it.

"What if these scales just let the sticky or hot stuff slide off? What then?" Blari took his quill back so he could write our conversation in the book.

"Go for the eyes. All animals have their brains right around or behind their eyes." I took out the picture and flattened it out on the map.

"Agreed." Spacya added, "There are plenty of them. Surely we can hit at least one hard enough to count."

"What did the others try? The soldiers?"

"The High Priest got a copy of their orders." Blari searched his pockets as he spoke, "Ah, here." He pulled two letters out and paraphrased them. "The first squad was told to search and gather information. The last report the captain received from them stated they had tracked it to Claw Caverns."

Tori studied the map, and sighed before saying, "Hardly anything is labeled on here." He looked up at the barkeep when he entered with pitchers and pint glasses, "Sir, do you know where Claw Caverns are on this map?"

"That's just a bit o' dried up river bed. Right here." He pointed to where the canyon we had been looking at met the desert. "Why?"

A few platters followed him, carried by barmaids and boys.

"We're looking for a gully or canyon that's deep or a set of cliffs nearby."

"Hmm," the barkeep wiped his hands on his apron. "The old Craggies might hold something you can use. They're about a mile south of the Claws." He pointed on the map, then moved his finger further down the line that depicted the canyon, "There's a plateau here."

Tori quickly marked the two spots, as neither were labeled on the map.

The barkeep straightened, "I know who you lot are. But I gotta say this, you'll be killed going after it. No one's even hurt it."

"We know. We will do our best." Spacya waved him off. "Might at least wound it for the soldiers."

He jerked his head at our table, "Drinks on the house for you." He turned and strode out, barely dodging another platter of food coming our way.

"That's what I'm here for." Austere muttered as he poured himself a pint.

"Tomorrow, let's go out and look at these two areas."

"What if we run into it?" Eisle's little voice again. She was quieter than Sterla, at times.

I smiled slightly and lifted my shoulder, "Then we run into it. We're going in blind enough as it is. The least we can do is have some knowledge of the area. Maybe think up a couple of backup traps as we go along."

I paused as a thought occurred to me, "Those of you that don't want to come along don't have to."

Austere sighed and plopped into the chair between Tori and Spacya. He said after taking a large gulp from his pint, "Since you asked so sweetly, darling, I'll accompany you."

"I'm going." Spacya tore off a few glistening ribs. "Dawn?"

"Yeah."

Tori and Blari said they were going at the same time. I eyed them. Did they share a brain now?

"I want to go."

I smiled at Eisle, and motioned for her to come eat. "The more eyes we have, the safer we will be."

"And the better the ideas we can build." Blari added.

We ate. Tori looked over the map that he had pulled into his lap as the platters kept coming in. I tossed a bit of cheese into his lap. It sounded like a paper drum being tapped when it landed and rolled a little. "Got it memorized yet?"

He pushed his hair back from his eyes before popping the cheese into his mouth, "Just about."

"Why memorize a map when you can carry one?"

"Just in case things go bad. Do you have time to pull out a map while running for your life?"

"No." Austere canted his head, his eyes on Tori. "Memorize away my friend."

"What do you want me to write about this meeting?" Blari leaned close to me.

"You're asking me this now? Everything."

He nodded and settled back in his chair. A plate of food and book and quill balanced in his lap as he used both equally.

"Do you write everything down? Every little detail?" Eisle peered at the book, leaning over the arm of her chair after she finally sat down with us at the table.

"No, not everything. The basics, some details. When I get time, I put it all together and make it a bit more readable."

"He writes in code now," Spacya said with a twist of her lips, "Probably cursing the lot of us for his bad luck at being stuck with us."

"I do not!" Blari's plate almost toppled. At least his precious book was saved. "That code is shorthand. So I can get everything down!"

"Um-hm."

"What exactly do you keep in there? I mean, do you add nightly escapades in? Moments where you see your friends here bathe?"

I groaned.

"Yes, of course."

"What?!" I smacked the priest's shoulder.

"What? I don't… watch you and describe it as he thinks I should, I'm sure." Blari shot a glare at Austere, "But I have given some particulars of some of our daily lives for the sake of history."

"History? People aren't gonna be interested in hip measurements or what scent of soap we used. They'll want the excitin' things. The battles and the like." Spacya glared at Blari over a rib bone.

"That's not true." Eisle squirmed and added, "I read books that have some of those details and find them very interesting."

"Hip sizes?" Tori smirked at our little Stygra as she squeaked.

"Not… not exact numbers, but yes."

Her pale skin wasn't ideal for this conversation. A dark, almost black tinge started on her ears. It quickly spread to her cheeks at Austere's next addition.

"Ah, you read those scandalous books. They don't measure by numbers, but by handfuls and mouthfuls, right?" He held out his hands as if he was about to juggle a couple of melons.

"I…I… the ribs are really good."

We all laughed at that.

"Austere, leave the poor girl alone with her lascivious books."

His eyes darted to me, "Big word of deliciousness."

"Don't."

Tori cleared his throat, "I agree, the ribs are fantastic. We should come back here and order some more tomorrow or the next day."

"You know what ribs lead to, Prince Tori?" Austere leaned toward Tori, with his mockingly whispered question.

"Uh… more ribs?"

"Breasts."

Blari's drink came back up out of his nose as Tori's face went pink.

"Is there anyone who you haven't made blush yet?"

Austere grinned, "No, but I do like seeing it."

Spacya cast a look at me over the rim of her pint, "Shoulda went through with the threat."

"Is it the tongue one?" Austere stuck his tongue out at her.

"Spacya…don't…" I warned as I saw her fingers twitch on her pint glass, "We won't be welcome back to the ribs if you test out a pint against a tongue."

I woke the next morning with a fuzzy mind, but only the sheet and quilt over me. I thanked the gods I hadn't gotten too drunk last night. After my usual morning ritual, complete with a bath, I was about to put my boots on when something tickled at the edge of my awareness.

"Morning."

I jumped, throwing the towel I pulled off my head toward the sound. Then cursed before asking, "What are you doing? Can't you knock?"

He tossed it back at me, "Wanted to catch you getting ready and knocking defeats the purpose." He sprawled over my bed, fully dressed, and sighed. "Yours is perfect."

"What?"

"The bed in my room is too short."

"We can switch."

"I'll just move in with you."

I rolled my eyes and continued to squeeze the excess water out of my hair with the towel. I settled on the edge of the bed, by his feet, to brush it out. It was getting long. I needed to cut it soon.

"In case I don't make it, but you do, I want you to give this to Pitrini."

I turned, forgetting about the brush being halfway through my hair at the moment. He held a thick envelope in his hands above his head, flipping it back and forth by opposing corners. There was a wax seal on the flap that I couldn't focus on with all the movement. "Why me?"

"Because you have Eisle tied to you, therefore you're the most likely one to live out of all of us." His gaze flicked to me, "Will you do this favor I ask?"

"I will, but it won't come to that."

He sat up, swung his legs off the edge and stood in one fluid motion of impressive agility for one his size. He placed the letter on my dresser. "Good." His gaze drifted back to me as he asked, "You don't have anything for me to pass on in an unlikely event?"

"I left them with Ida."

"Smart."

I quickly braided my hair. A few slips of my fingers made me grit my teeth. I wasn't used to having a red-eyed audience. He'd witnessed everything else I held private, why not this too?

Finished, I hid his letter in my extra bag I was leaving at the Church. The priests assured us no one would enter our rooms while we were gone except maids to dust. I grabbed up my hunting pack and hung it over my shoulders before fastening it to my belt, too. We would have to travel most of the way on foot to the two areas after reaching a stable. Horses, while more adept than they were a century ago for mountains, still didn't do well with shale rock.

Unless it was a wild stallion of the Unforgettable Mountains. I should have stolen that horse and brought him with me. Joni didn't deserve him.

We were just about to leave when a breathless yell caught our attention. I turned to see Pitrini waving wildly as he ran toward us. A couple of men were with him. Somehow, they all still carried the scent of the sea.

"You made it." Austere grinned, reaching down to ruffle his kid brother's hair.

"Did. Where you- going?" Pitrini gulped for air between words.

Austere pointed with his thumb over his shoulder, "Going to check on this gigantic monster that eats seventeen-year-olds. Wanna come with?"

"Just seventeen-year-olds?" Pitrini's narrowed eyes on Austere had me biting back a smile. He tried brushing his hair back down in his next breath.

"Yup. Prefers males too."

"Right. I'll go." He peered around, "I need to borrow a horse and get some gear. Can you wait?"

Austere glanced toward me. I looked to Spacya, Tori and Blari. They all just shrugged. I answered Austere in the same fashion. He rolled his eyes skyward before getting off his stallion. "Hurry. Get your gear, I'll get you a horse."

In ten minutes, Pitrini was back, his breathing so heavy that it startled the horses. He dropped his pack and rested his hands over his knees, "Hooo… that was a longer way than I remembered."

"What took you so long?" Austere handed the boy the reins to a pretty dun colored mare with blue stripes, mane and tail.

"Oh, you know, just running to the docks and back." Pitrini picked up his pack again and got up on the mare, "Not anything close to a mile and a half. No."

"I coulda done it in five minutes."

Sam Wicker

"You have stilts! Of course you can do it in no time." Pitrini waved a hand toward Austere's long legs.

I nudged Unia forward, Tori at my side, as he was now as good as any native guide with his mapping memory bank.

An hour later, full of bickering brothers, we reached the end of the road. The stable within the mountain pass was the last place we could keep the horses sheltered. We paid the man well and headed to what the barkeep called Old Craggies. The path was narrow. Mountains of blue-gray rose steeply on one side and dropped to a roaring river on the other. The jagged peaks seemed to touch the sky. Each step we took disturbed a pebble or rock which set off more around it. I felt that walking on wet grass would give me a better foothold than anything here.

I led the way, Tori behind me, Eisle behind him, then Pitrini, Austere, Blari and Spacya brought up the rear. I didn't like us being in single file, nor spread out as we were.

Once, I made the mistake of looking over the edge of the path. I had to lean against the mountain until my vision stopped making me swim around and around. It seemed the others were perfectly fine taking a break to breathe too.

All talk had finally died down to only what was necessary. Spacya was the most surefooted out of all of us. During our pause, she took a moment to sit on the path and let her feet dangle over the edge. It made my whole body pull in on itself.

"Should be around the next bend, the trail will split. Go to the left."

I rounded the bend and saw the trail to the left we were supposed to take. I doubted anyone with any sense made that trail. It looked like some small fuzzy animal had made it instead of a human. I peeked over the edge again. The cliff the trail edged didn't stop for at least a thousand feet. With the route split, there was some room for all of us to gather.

Tori whistled quietly, so it wouldn't echo through the mountains, "I knew it would be bad, but I didn't think it would be that bad."

Eisle groaned, not deigning to look over the edge. "I don't think I can do that." She sat and wrapped her arms around herself and shook her head, "No, I'll wait for you here."

"Is this the worst of it?"

"Until we get to the plateau."

Austere put his hands on his hips as he stood at the edge of the drop. "Why would anyone take the time to carve a path to something called Craggies?"

Blari sat down beside Eilse, "To be alone?"

"Heard a story once, 'bout the Craggies." Spacya studied the path, "They say Aul will meet anyone who calls to him there."

"Well, there's a reason good enough for me." Pitrini grinned even though his face shone with sweat.

Austere looked down at Eilse, "You can't stay here, dove."

"I can't cross that."

The pirate prince took off his pack and handed it to Spacya. "I'll carry you then, but you got to hang on to my back."

She shook her head.

"It'll be fine. Just close your eyes and hum. It'll be over in no time." Blari added with a small smile.

Eisle swallowed. She looked from Austere to Blari, then to me. "I'll try."

"Tori, you go first. Austere behind him and Spacya behind them. Try to steady Eisle…" I didn't finish the thought for the fear Eisle would back down again, "Pitrini, you're after Spacya. Blari, and then I'll bring up the rear."

Austere knelt in front of Eisle and she climbed onto his back, hanging tightly to his shoulders. He stood as if she weighed less than his pack. After he shifted her up, he had to adjust her stranglehold on his neck. He wrapped an arm around her hip and bum.

She squeaked, and he chuckled.

"Austere." I gritted my teeth.

"Just takin' her mind off it."

"Don't."

"Yes, darling." He muttered and started down the path after Tori. Spacya was close on his heels. Her hands free with his pack shouldered on her front.

Somehow, we made it across with no trouble. Eisle hadn't hummed, so Pitrini sung a wildly inappropriate tune about a woman and a man of the pleasure trade taking over a pirate's ship. One by one, each pirate fell to their wiles. So drunk with pleasure were they all that the ship ran aground and they were never seen again.

Of course, Austere added some details.

I wondered if Pitrini was as innocent as he acted, or if he was as bad as his brother.

Blari cleared his throat, "Well, that was a lovely song."

"One of my favorites." Austere called back. I could hear his grin.

"Of course it is."

"Wanna hear it again?"

"No!" the word came from at least three of us and it bounded off the mountains surrounding us. I stopped and listened to its echo. That was all there was. The sound of my breathing, of my comrades making their way down the path, and the remnants of that single word.

No wind stirred our clothes or my hair. No birds sang. In fact, I hadn't seen a single nest or hole where anything might make a home since about an hour after the stables. I never knew an area could be untouched.

"What is it?"

I looked down the path, Blari had stopped a few feet down and looked back to me. "Nothing lives here."

His brows drew down low over his eyes, "Nothing?"

I watched him glance around and wondered if he thought he could spot something before me. "Nothing."

"That's… rather odd. Isn't it?"

"Yes."

He shrugged, "Probably a reasonable reason. Come on, we need to keep up."

The path spiraled up, weaving around the mountain, before a ebony bridge suspended with black threads stretched across a chasm between our mountain and the next. Spacya called for a break, and I wholeheartedly agreed.

We rested, and Austere allowed Eisle to slide off his back. The Stygra teen scurried over to hunker down beside Spacya. I wasn't as sure as she was that the huntress could protect her from Austere's wiles.

I felt my body relax as soon as I sat down on a small rock outcrop that jutted out onto the path to the bridge. Taking a swig from my canteen, I nearly choked when Pitrini appeared at my elbow with a grin.

"You gotta try this." He thrust a flat, white, crispy thing at me.

"What is it?" I took it and sniffed. It did not hold a scent.

"A cake."

"Boy, I feel for you. Once we get back to civilization, I'm going to make you a cake or buy you one. This is not a cake."

"Just try it!"

I bit into it. After the shell melted on my tongue, a sweetness erupted. Icing. It was like eating icing in a hard shell of sugar. "It is a cake." I laughed and shook my head at the both of us.

He grinned, sitting down beside me. "Told ya. There's a lady who made these famous. She wanted a better meal on board than biscuits, beans and gruel. She's made up all kinds of things, but I think this is the best one."

"First thing I'm gonna do is make a trade agreement with her for Owlimount when I get back home."

"Better come up with something good," Austere cooed, "They are going to be in high demand with how that kid shares them around."

I broke off a piece of mine for each of the companions.

"Thanks, but I don't think I can eat anything for a while."

Eisle still looked pale. I wondered if her greatest fear was heights. CiaCia couldn't even climb onto the roof without shaking like a leaf and getting nauseated. I nodded to the bridge, "That's Stygra work, isn't it?"

She nodded, "My grandmother's."

I blinked and stared at it for a moment. "That's right, you're from Emleton." Those black strands that formed together to make the bridge and its supports looked all too familiar now that we were closer to it. "The one in the tower-"

"My mother. Council member Ryelda." She looked over at me, "I have it too. So when you die again, you will have it. Unbreakable threads."

I swallowed, looking down at the now sticky mess on my fingers.

"What?" Pitrini looked between Eisle and I.

"Don't worry about it." Austere waved his brother off before grabbing my fingers. His hot breath melted the sticky sugars more as he spoke, "It won't happen."

Then he put my fingers in his mouth.

I wanted to toss him over the bridge. Blari and Tori held me back. I managed a nice kick to his shin before they pulled me away.

Chapter 25

At sunset, we barely saw where we were going as the path moved to the east side of the mountain. It widened into a flat area that had a small overhang just as it became impossibly dark. No fire tonight. Granted, I had seen signs of life again; we didn't want to attract the Cotkit to us. Not yet.

The three torches we had were bad enough.

With seven of us, the shifts were short, even with two being awake at the same time. In the morning, we ate a quick breakfast, basking in the brilliant oranges, reds and purples dancing across the mountain peaks and the clouds hugging them. Puffy clouds were quickly burned away, leaving a bright sun to warm us on our journey.

A few hours after dawn, we met The Craggies. Rocks of shale, blue banded white stone, red shoots in pressed sand all intermingled together. The rock jutted up and out of the mountains. They hung over a deep canyon with a small river winding through its bottom to disappear under another mountain decorated the same way as the one we were on. Some glistened with gems here and there.

The odd rocks jutting out reminded me of the drawings of monsters the kids would make. Jagged teeth and claws everywhere.

Pitrini grinned and called out, "Aul!"

The god's name bounced along all the outcroppings and broke into a thousand Pitrini voices. I grimaced. If it didn't bring Aul, it would certainly draw the Cotkit. I hoped we were still far enough away that it wouldn't call the beast.

I leaned over the edge, stepping out, gingerly, onto a jagged finger. If it was as big as a mountain, this place might work. I looked at all the rocks. Spikes. Dangerous where they were, but if dropped...

"You called, young one?"

I scrambled to keep my footing as a rich, booming voice sounded. I felt a large palm steady me, splaying across my stomach like I was a child under my father's protective hand.

I peered up into the toothy grin of a stranger.

"I didn't mean to startle you, Nadachia."

"Y-you know my name?" He pushed me gently back into the path before removing his hand.

His skin glittered with gems and sands, his nails black like the polished volcanic stones of Ecia. "Of course I do. I know all your names." Another white-toothed smile. He shifted, not walking or moving as a human, but part of the mountains themselves.

He had felt solid enough. I bowed low, as did most of the others. Pitrini kept standing, frozen, mouth hanging agape and eyes wide.

"No need for that, children." Gravel in his voice, but it was soothing like thunder from a distant storm. "What brings you here to seek me?"

Did anyone have words?

Blari stood, "We came here on a quest. There is a monster that, well, you probably know it. Anyway, we were thinking of luring it here, so we would have height advantage."

"I see." Aul smiled again. "You are smart, but the Cotkit will not come here. For I am here, and it fears me."

"Do you… can you help us? Is there another area like this where we will have an advantage?"

Though Blari spoke, Aul's shimmering black eyes moved to me. "There is no place. If you attack at the plateau, all of you will die. Should you attack at the Fox Gully, six of you will die. If you do not attack at all, thousands will die. If you attack it at its home, only two will die."

"You can't help, can you?"

He shook his head, slow, methodical, "We gods created these tasks to help you grow in wisdom, technology, and in the faith you must have in yourselves. We may guide you through words, vague ones, or through a gift, but that is all."

"If we go there to scout, we will have to fight it, won't we?"

"No. Only one can get close on the north side. The rest of you must stay back a mile."

"I don't want to ask too much, but may we have a gift to go along with your words?"

Aul chuckled, turning his shining gaze to Austere. "I am god. I make my own rules on what I may give and take from you. But on this…" He faded into a mist, only to come back to his glistening shadow of a form. "I have found a way."

Seven items protruded from him, shooting out to stop at each of us. "Only one of these shall prove useful in your current quest. The rest will be in the near future. That is all I can share on these."

Ten bolts in a quiver were in front of me. They glistened like his skin, and the holster was black with blue and silver intertwining shapes down the sides at even intervals. I took them in both hands. The leather was so soft; the bolts cool to the touch, and a feeling of power zinged down my fingers and up my arm. My heart warmed with it. I felt rested, soothed, and oddly hungry.

"It writes itself!" Blari cried, holding open a book.

I thought he was going to hug the god, but he hugged the tome instead.

"It will never run out of space either, but you must place it on top of another, empty one, after each quest so that it may fill it."

"I will, thank you!"

Eisle clutched a vial as wide as her palm, but tapered at the top. The liquid looked black and shimmery, like Aul's eyes. The god and the Stygra teen said nothing to one another, but shared a long look. Something chilled my heart when watching them.

Tori took a sword. Aul told him it would always come to the aid of his bloodline, no matter how far away they may be from it. Spacya held a cloak in her hands, before unfastening hers and putting it on. It caused her to blend in with the mountains behind her. And also Austere, who stood beside her.

She laughed and shook her head as she put her cloak on on top of it. At least then, the cloak Aul gave her just made her blend in with the cloak on top. That was going to take a while for me to get used to seeing.

Austere held a necklace in his hand. After he studied it for a while, he smiled to himself before slipping it on over his head. It was on a gold chain and looked like some kind of compass.

To Pitrini, the god gifted a small satchel that he looped onto his belt. Of course, the boy opened it and pulled out a sandwich. "I was just thinking about how hungry I was!"

We stayed the night with Aul, talking to him about all he has done and seen. He was fond of telling stories. He also had a feast laid out for us, moving some outcroppings together so that we would be comfortable. As we ate our fill, one by one we succumbed to slumber.

When we woke, he was gone.

I stacked a few rocks. It just seemed fitting, though it was nothing special.

We stopped a little over a mile from the Claw Caverns. I double checked my map against the one in Tori's head and smiled. During our ride to Faladin, he had shared with me his odd talent for being able to memorize a map of an area fairly well after about an hour or two of studying it.

I listened to the boys and Spacya discussing who would go as I ate. They proposed drawing straws, though there were none to be had. Just some scraggly plants I stopped them from plucking because they had already proven themselves hardy enough to grow on all this rock.

"I should go, I have the mental map, I can run pretty fast too."

"On flat ground." Spacya pointed out, "It should be me. I have the best feet for it, I can track, and I've hunted in and on mountains for longer than most of you have been alive."

"Yeah, you're wise and useful. If we lose you, then we will have a hard time surviving." Blari growled, not even putting himself in the running for going to see the Cotkit.

As they talked, I finished my brief meal and slipped on out of our makeshift camp. There wasn't a pleasant path bridging the peeks between our encampment and the Caverns. So I picked a path carefully. In these mountains, the shale had mostly given way to sturdier fare. I half climbed, half walked my way around a mountain and onto another, before I stopped to check my progress on my map.

Keandria had been kind enough to tie each of us to our maps, so we were all little dots moving about. I shut out the nagging thought of how she had gotten droplets of our blood to do the dot spell to make them. I didn't need that panic and suspicion clogging my mind at the moment.

I smiled as the others milled around the camp and figured they had finally realized I was gone with the agitated movements. Relief flooded through me as my study of those dots revealed that none of them were coming after me. *I will receive more than a couple of earfuls when I get back.* That was fine.

I started again. Making sure my footfalls were quiet and wouldn't slip as I drew closer. The heat sent sweat dripping down the middle of my back, especially under my belt of daggers. I never realized sand had a smell until I pulled myself up onto an overhang and looked out upon golden, shimmering sand. Heat rose off the desert in waves, making it impossible to see if there was anything actually growing or scurrying about on it.

Have I miscalculated?

I began to my left, my eyes focusing from the rocky base of the mountain to its top, back down, sliding over, and doing the same repeatedly. After studying the three rock faces, I took off my crossbow, laying it down before I lay on my belly, shifting around the overhang to peer over the edge. The wind, riddled with heat and bits of sand, blasted my face. I practiced the same tedious searching technique. If the map was to scale, the Caverns should be rather large.

"Oh." I froze, barely breathing, focusing on the odd thing jutting out from far underneath me. It looked like a stinger on top of a full leather bag, bulbous and shiny and attached to another bag-like segment. It lay still, partly buried in sand as the wind kept right on blowing this way.

For something that carried away people to eat, I had to wonder why there wasn't the scent of rotting flesh or just death. I caught only the bouquet of sand, and rock, and fresh hot air.

Perhaps it stashed the remains deep in the cave. Still, there were no boots, no bits to be seen underneath me at all.

Smart. It was smart. It talked.

An icy chill crept over my back and arms, making me feverish in the heat.

The caverns had one outlet, the same as the entrance, and it sprawled in it, right underneath me. I thanked the gods for the wind, even though it was sandblasting me slowly and baking me to the path. I pulled my shirt up over my nose, my throat tickled with the sands. I knew if I coughed, I would probably be dead. Slowly, I dragged myself closer to the edge, taking my time, holding my stomach up off the rock so my hilts wouldn't scrape against it.

I stopped when I got my shoulders over the rim. I squeezed my eyes shut as my brain conjured the image of a large beak closing around my head and biting it off. *Not going to happen. No.*

I opened them again, half expecting to see that beak coming for me. I let out a shaky breath when all that met my gaze were rocks, sand, and that tail. If the rest of it was as deadly as its tail looked, we were doomed. I saw tips of large feathers, orange and red, blending together to seem like flames in a bonfire. They were gorgeous.

I would have to tell Blari to describe them in his pretty words to Moko so she could paint them.

Slowly, I pulled myself more over the edge. More feathers. Something in me told me they must be the wingtips. Slightly curved toward the tail, large and thick, with no gaps between. I would not get a good look. Not unless I was fool enough to drop down and say hello.

I slid back.

The overhang was generous, but I doubted it would adequately cover the entrance if we made it fall. We were in a mining center. I knew explosives were available readily, but hauling enough of them here… that was going to be the greatest challenge. That and not alerting the damn beast to our actions. I stood and stepped back. All I needed was a pebble to bounce on that tail, because it would with my luck.

The wind battered me and I settled my shirt more firmly over my nose, looking out at the desert. That wind. It was perfect for a big bird like this to lift up into the air. I looked up, studying the gouges in the sides of the mountains I stood between, and the rocks that had fallen…

It does just that. Catches wind and pulls itself further up using these mountains.

I didn't dare pull out the map. I didn't know how well it heard things, but I wasn't about to take the chance of rustling paper being one of its peeves. If I remembered correctly, the mining camps, the ones that had been attacked, were straight ahead. Simple. Easy. Almost lazy of the beast.

I studied the sides of the mountains again. An expert climber might get up to those gouges and send more rocks down with blasts. I wasn't sure how explosives worked really, but I knew the miners could set them and be at a safe distance when they made them go off. Joni was the miner, not me.

If we trapped it in the cavern mouth, or even on this little open area between the two, we might bury it. I needed a miner, an explosive and mountain expert to be here, right beside me. I wondered how many that would kill?

"What shall we do today, hmmmm?"

My heart stopped. The pebbles and rocks at my feet shook slightly with that thunderous voice. It echoed deep in the peak; it bounced around under me.

I looked around, and back toward the desert. Nothing. No one was there. *Was that it? Was that the beast talking?*

"Should we go see if we can find Daddy again?"

Daddy? This thing had a daddy?

I felt the little I had eaten rage against my throat. I pressed a hand over my shirt on top of my mouth and begged myself not to be sick.

"Daddy should have never lost us. Is he looking for us, do you think?"

Sam Wicker

Had I found the right one? What if it was the daddy that had been attacking and not this one? Killing this one would be useless, for now, if that was the case. It would prevent it eating in the future…

"We're hungry again. Do we have any left?" Scraping of hard things against rock underneath me felt like they were scraping against my spine too. "No, no, nothing left."

As it scraped some more, I bolted, grabbing my crossbow and half ran, half skidded down the path. *There was a crevice, a gulley, something to hide… yes!*

I slammed in behind a large boulder, throwing my back against the mountain and aiming my crossbow up. Right above me was a gouge. A sliver of sky peeked between the boulder and the jutting rock overhead. I cast around, looking for anything else that could hide me while providing an opening to shoot.

Bright orange feathers jutted up over the edge of the overhang I had just been on. The beak was longer than me. Where it met the head, it was wider than I was tall. A pair of nostrils opened and closed, blowing air as hot as the one coming in from the desert down the gully I hid in. Eyes of gold started a handsbreadth from the top of the nostril, smallest first, ranging along the ridge until the largest at the end, the size of the fountain in the square of Galanesse. The pupils were beads within each eye, black as Aul.

It tilted its head back, the wings, all four of them, flaring out behind it and shaking. It stretched like a chicken. I shifted, leaning around the boulder slightly to take in all the Cotkit's glory. The overhang was at least 600 feet over the desert floor, and I clearly saw its head and part of its neck. With the crest of feathers, it was easily 800 lengths tall. This thing was that tall… just how big was the daddy?

It turned, that tail curling up with the sticker up over its back as it walked out into the desert. The heat waves and wind filled with sand whirled around its wings. Its footprints were large enough to crush buildings, but the sand shifted, covering them up in minutes. The head bobbed, slowly receding, until I only saw the tops of the crest.

I leaned out some more, trying to get a better view, to not let the thing out of my sight. But then it rose. Those wings stretched out, then flapped and that immense body tucked up in under them with the claws snuggled in the soft-looking feathers of its belly. Higher and higher, it lifted into the air with each labored flap. It turned, I instinctively ducked and pressed against the rocks with all I had. It shot toward me, a great big claw grasping at the side of the mountain gully and pushing off. Rocks and pebbles skid skipped down from where it had gripped.

It flew over me, so close it would be easy to reach out and touch a claw if I had dared.

Another grip and push, and it fired up into the sky with one powerful flap of all four wings. It circled, shoving off a mountain peak nearby. I knew then my suspicions on the whereabouts of most of the mining camps were correct. It headed true, a straight line from where I hid. I pulled out my map, it would be there in no time at all. I shoved it back into my belt.

I ran for the outcropping and looked down. The mouth of the cave was large, curving outward from underneath me in craggy rocks and boulders. On one side, to my right, I picked out a path. I skipped down it. I had to see.

I eased around the mouth as soon as my feet hit the sand and sunk into it slightly. It was like snow, so loose. I moved a little further into the cave.

There it was, the stench. I recovered my nose, breathing in the scent of my own breath as it clung to the dampness of my shirt. Bits of clothing, bones picked clean, and groupings of skin, bone, cloth, and furs in piles were scattered on the cavern floor. It ripped apart what it could, ate it, and then had to throw up what it didn't digest later. It ate like a hunting bird, while it stretched and flew awkwardly like a chicken.

I was kidding myself by trying to compare it to something normal.

The cave seemed solid. Just as well, the only time we could get down here was when it went off hunting again. The cavern narrowed instead of getting bigger the further in I went. I didn't dare go in too far.

Sam Wicker

I scrambled out, my heart thundering in my head. I picked my way back up to the outcropping and ran down the gulley between the mountains. Hooking my crossbow back at my hip, I hurled myself onto the mountain and began climbing to my companions.

Breathing hard, the panic of being found had just subsided when a shadow passed over my head. I pressed into the side of the ridge and looked up.

A flash of orange.

The feathers covering the belly were thick, but I spotted the same shimmering effect underneath them as what covered the legs. Scales. So much for a soft underbelly being our saving grace.

Two bodies dangled from the claws, one in each.

"Give Daddy something to be mad about and he'll come get me! Punish me! Come find me!"

Its voice bounded off the sides of mountains. I watched the snowcap from across the way crumble and slide down in a cascade of white and gray rocks amid the clean snow. At the top of my mountain, the snow there seemed to hold steady. I breathed again.

As soon as the beast disappeared, I started my run to my friends again. Only one other mountain in my purview, had snow tumbling down it. Neither seemed to affect the other mountains around them. That must be the grace of Aul watching over us. I spotted my little group right as I crested the last hill before sliding down to them on the loose rock.

"Don't ever do that again!" Blari rounded on me.

I blinked up at him, not expecting that he would be the one to lecture me first.

"Do you know how worried we were? Do you know we couldn't do anything because of what Aul said last night? What if something happened to you? You're the Hero. The Hero! Are you listening to me?"

"I am. Nothing happened, don't worry."

"Oh... Gods... keep my sanity for I'm about to lose it." Blari threw up his hands, "Someone else deal with her."

They looked at one another. Spacya was the first to speak, "See anything interesting?"

"A few things."

Tori's breath puffed his cheeks out before he started, "Chi, come on, you should have at least told us you wanted to go and joined in on the drawing."

I shook my head, "I can't put all of you in more danger than I already have."

"That's you coming up with an excuse so you don't feel guilty." Austere tossed a pebble at my boot. It tapped on my toe, then bounced twice on the path before settling.

"You've done similar things plenty of times so you would know." Pitrini said, while pointing to his brother.

A long, thorough glare at his kid brother and Austere grew satisfied. He turned back to me, "What did you see that was interesting?"

I launched into the path I chose, how long it took me to get there and back, everything I saw and heard along the way. I didn't add my fears. They had their own, and I needed to bear mine as they did theirs. I wanted to hear their conclusions first.

"It really talks." Blari sat down heavily on the side of the mountain. Closer to leaning that sitting.

Spacya rubbed a whet stone across one of her spear heads with a grunt. "I wanna know what Daddy looks like. If he is alive or dead. If or when we will have to deal with him killin' off people too."

"That is what I'm most concerned about too."

Austere pushed himself up to stand and started pacing a little off from the group. I guessed always being in motion on the ship made him need to keep moving on land, too. "We could get some explosives."

"Maybe we sail upriver, then follow the foothills along the Wastes' edge?" Tori looked to me.

"The only problem with that is it takes longer, it's the deadly wastes. And if we come up on it walking out to lift off we're its next meal. Not to mention our scents will blow right to it."

"Then we take some explosives with us and we all blow up together."

Austere stopped pacing to stare at Spacya. "Bait."

"We can't use live people."

"I'm not saying that!" He shook his head, "Meat sacks! Put clothes over meat and explosives in skins."

"How do we detonate them?"

"The miners will know best how to do that. Or we can shoot fire arrows at the sacks."

"Leads," Spacya said, "But if this things talks, what if it's too smart to be fooled? Or it sees the lines from the explosives to the switch?"

"Then we set up backup plans." I said and then reminded them of the gouges in the mountain and the overhang of its home. If we topple both mountains onto it, surely, it would die. I didn't think the citizens of Emleton and the mining towns would mind losing the caverns if it meant they were safe.

"Two groups then? One to come up this way and the other along the edge of the desert?"

"That would be best."

I glanced up at the sun. "Let's head back to Aul's spot and spend the night there again. A good walk will give us some more ideas." I wanted to get away from the Cotkit's lair and into a safe zone.

"I'm still mad at you." Blari's eyes were sharp on me.

"I know." I would find a way to make it up to him.

Tori led the way back. Blari right behind him. I wanted to keep a distance between myself and the priest for the time being. He lecturing me with nowhere to run to sounded less appealing than the fear the Cotkit would bring if we sighted it.

"You know, I don't know who wanted to go after you the most." Pitrini mused.

"A tie between Austere and Spacya, I think." Eisle said, and I almost heard a smile in her tone.

"I didn't try anything that would put me in danger. Besides, Aul said we would all be fine if only one of us went."

"I know. I'm not upset." Eisle spoke softly, "But most of them were. Do you always do that?"

"No."

Spacya snorted at my answer.

"Maybe a few times."

She didn't snort that time.

Austere sighed, "What have I gotten myself into?"

"Told you. You shouldn't fall into a group just because of the stories."

"What stories?"

"Pretty princess and handsome prince and the pure Hero." Pitrini crooned as he stepped around me with Austere nearly bowling me over to get to him.

"What?" I sidestepped the boy, pulling him behind me so I was in between him and Austere.

"They said that Princess Clara or Prince Tori was meant for you. So there're all kinds of stories about your romances in between and during your quests."

"Romances? Like book romances?"

"Probably plenty of them out now, or in the works." Austere muttered under his breath.

I tried to wrap my mind around the idea of someone writing about my life in that way. "Don't people have anything better to do?" I remembered reading one of Seaghla's books. It had been about the Prince of Ecia's mistress and wife actually falling in love with each other and running away together. Ridiculous. The prince of Ecia was only ten years old.

"Of course not, darling. People live for stories about their hero; whether they are true or not."

"Where is Princess Clara?" Pitrini asked.

"She needed a break." I blurted.

"Oh, I hope I can see her soon. I heard she's the prettiest out of the princesses."

"She is." I didn't hesitate, for I believed it of my friend. She was safe. I hated to leave her behind, and she detested staying behind, but it was for the best, until she got better.

I brought my mind back to the task at hand. *How did miners set the explosives safely? Was there a way to move around the Cotkit cavern and the mountains above it without alerting the beast to our presence? How many was I going to kill or hurt in this quest?*

Part of me wanted to plan a way for my friends to stay in Emleton. The other part felt guilty for being willing to put strangers' lives at stake instead of my companions' that signed up for this. Every one of us had someone that cared for us. Some of us had someone to care for, too.

Chapter 26

Aul didn't come when we called that night.

The next day, the stable owner seemed surprised to see us. At least our horses were still there and well taken care of. We helped him saddle them before setting off. He hadn't heard where the latest attack had been yet.

"Can we bring down a mountainside?" I asked after we were far enough away. "Without damaging too much or costing lives or livelihoods?"

"I don't see why not. The only thing we will hurt is the Cotkit, I would think. I doubt there's anything brave enough to live in the caverns with it."

"I'm still more concerned about this 'Daddy'. What if we kill this one and the parents show up?"

"Then for the first time in our history, a Hero fails within the first year and they give another the chance."

Blari's words made my heart sink as I glanced toward Eilse, riding behind me. Had she found peace with what Keandria did to us, or was she burning with rage underneath that blank expression? "It won't come to that."

The rest of them nodded, and I had to sigh. It was the only way to relieve the pressure in my shoulders and chest. I hoped their resolve would give them the sense to get their asses out of there. Knowing them, they would end up doing something stupid. We were all too much alike in that. Except for Austere and Eisle. I wished, when it came down to it, they would save their own skins.

"How far apart are the mountains that are next to the caverns?"

"Their peaks are, but they come together at the bottom with just a little sliver of a path in between."

"I wonder if we bring down one mountain and save the other for when the thing it calls Daddy comes along?" As he spoke, Tori twisted in his saddle to look at me.

"Should be possible. There'd be some debris from the shakes." Spacya nodded, "And a good explosives handler will know how to control the blasts best."

"Let's do that then. If neither of those work then we set up another trap at the Craggies."

"Or clear a mining camp and set a trap there."

I cringed at the thought of endangering their homes. It would be worth it if it saved hundreds of lives. It would work, though. A camp it hasn't hit yet, or the one it kept hitting. I wondered where it attacked yesterday.

"What about the sticky substance? Can we somehow set that up with the explosives? If it doesn't get caught in the rocks, maybe some of that stuff will spray on it to slow it down. That way we might find a weakness to use."

My group fell silent for a while.

"First plan of attack," I started, "We set up some bait in all the mining camps. Hopefully, it takes those instead of the people. While the camps do that, we set up explosives, and possibly some substance around the caverns and mountains. We try to just destroy one mountain out of the pair in case the parent or this 'daddy' thing shows up." I took a breath, shaking in the saddle, "The second is to set up a trap at one of the smaller mining camps, and lure it there. We will probably have to rely on the bait tactic. Since The Craggies are probably not going to be traveled by it unless we lure it, a setup with explosives there is the back-up or final plan."

"I think I would feel better if we could have a backup of some harpoons, too. Tie it down."

"The scales and the wings…" Blari sounded like he was thinking out loud.

"Take the harpoons to the wings, tail, or head and neck. I would be better with the body, but we're going to have to aim for those instead."

"None of us have the great aim with them like Otteris' second had." Tori said with a small smile.

"Harliii. Someone in Emleton might." I glanced at Austere.

"I'm a pirate, not a fisherman. The only time I use a harpoon is to kill something on another ship."

"Fine. We'll ask around."

"The big thing here is how do we get all this stuff to the traps?" I felt the beginnings of a harsher headache. I kept them these days.

Austere's stallion tossed its noble head and stomped a few times, "And what if the Cotkit has better hearing than say, oh I don't know, a rock?"

I frowned at him. He was right, though. So many echoes in the mountains. The sand was going to be near impossible to get a wagon through with all that wind. Even if we dared, wagons made plenty of noise. Not to mention the smells.

Dividing supplies among pack horses would mean we would need a lot of them. If the Cotkit had a decent sense of smell, with the way the wind blew, we were done for before we got started.

"How does one bring supplies over the desert?"

"Sleighs."

"Of course." I smiled a little at learning something new. "We still have to mask all the smells because of that wind."

"Travel at night, darling."

I stared at him, waiting for him to explain further.

He lifted a shoulder, "The gale off the Ailban Wastes stems from the sun baking the sands, or so they say. The air is stagnant after it cools off until the sun is about halfway up in the sky."

"Then we wouldn't have the wind covering the noise either."

"One or the other, as this is not a perfect world, Silverequis."

What happened to him calling me darling?

"There are horses bred for the Ailban Wastes." Eisle spoke up again, "The only smell that comes from them is their dung. They don't sweat because it makes them lose water."

"Those will help." I ticked off on my fingers, "Explosives, Wastes horses, sleighs, at least two harpoons, meat sacks for bait, sticky substance like glue or tar, and an explosives expert. Anything else?"

"A god that will actually help, a hundred Welkan warriors, and at least twenty Stygra who can create weapons with their powers."

"Eisle, you can do the web stuff, can't you?"

"Yes, but I cannot make a lot of it if you want it to be unbreakable. I can produce a lot that withstands about seventy-five pounds of pressure, but truly unbreakable…I can make enough to cover a door."

"That should be enough. You can help spread the sticky stuff or help make it immobile."

Her hands tightened on the reins, "I have to be close to do that."

"I… you will be protected." Out of all of us, I had hoped to keep Eisle in Emleton, but I had to open my mouth with something that just occurred to me.

"Most ships that travel up rivers do not have harpoons on them."

"Surely you have two on your ship."

"I have one."

"Then we will borrow yours and hopefully be able to find another." I wouldn't mind finding twenty of those to go along with the hundred warriors and twenty Stygra. "We need to ask for volunteers. I'm not putting people at risk who don't want to help or are scared to help because they have families. This isn't like Columbria."

"I'm sure there will be plenty of volunteers." Blari tried to assure me.

"Especially if you get up in one of those fancy dresses and ask sweetly."

I made a mental note to train my mare to bite and kick on demand. "They'll just have to settle for me asking sweetly."

"I'd join!"

"No." Austere and I said together.

"But…" His smile fell into a pout.

"I'm not putting you at risk. You are to stay with the ship. Gotta make sure they steal nothing else off it like this one is going to steal the harpooner."

"You'll get it back!" I turned, glaring at him.

"Maybe." He smirked, "You'll have to pay me back otherwise."

"How are we gonna set up at The Craggies? Or the camp?"

"Since we will have to split into two companies and have enough resources for each; the attack at the caverns should happen first. If it fails, that will give the camp and Craggies' team time before it flies for food again." I swallowed, realizing what I just stated on a deeper level. It would not come to that.

Aul said only two would die.

But gods said things that twisted all the time. He might have meant two hundred. Or that two eras would die before the Cotkit was defeated. I hoped it was only two of us.

When we arrived, Tori went into his bossy mode. He asked the priests to bring the captains of the city guard, two explosives specialists, and to send someone to find out if any of the ships at the docks had harpoon machines. He also asked about any shops or factories in the area that made excess sticky liquid or things that would solidify once thrown on something.

We quickly learned there wasn't a glue factory for fifty miles, that was all imported in.

We washed up and ate. By the time we finished, the priests had completed all of Tori's requests. They impressed me with how quickly they worked.

The captain of the guard, two ship captains, a rather rounded man, and a jumpy man, joined us at the table in the dining hall of the Church. While we talked, the bread, cheese and wine never emptied. We began outlining our plans for the Cotkit attacks. The captain nodded regularly while the skinny man with more than a little gray hair kept leaning more and more forward in his chair. The ship captains kept eying Austere, who, in turn, just sprawled out and smirked at them.

"You're wanting to collapse a mountain on the Claw Caverns which houses the Cotkit." One of the ship captains spoke slowly. His collar had two stars on it and his hand stayed on the hilt of his sword at his side. "You have planned four attacks, is that correct?"

"Yes, simply put, but yes." Austere purred, his smirk deepening as the man's hand grew tighter on his sword.

I kicked him under the table. His sprawl shifted. He finally looked from the officers, to me, still keeping a lazy smirk on his face. Something in me told me that this smirk was entirely different from the ones he had given the captains.

"Describe the area again." The jumpy little man had his wide brown eyes on me.

I did, giving him as much detail as I could.

"Good. Good." He nodded, pulling a pad out of his shirt pocket and a pencil as I talked. He licked the tip of the pencil each time it lifted from the paper. "The mountain on the right of the cave mouth, you say its base comes out further than the cave?" After I gave him a nod, he continued, "Care to give a measurement? Your best is fine."

"At least thirty feet."

"Good. How tall is the same mountain?"

I shook my head, trying to think, "As tall as the Tower."

"A little over 16,000 feet." Tori stated.

"Good. And the other mountain, how tall?"

"Another two hundred feet taller, I think."

"Good. I've been to the Craggies. Those are gonna be tricky tricky." He nodded as he wrote and talked. "Hm hmmm… Ah, that should be enough." I didn't see his figure, but the captain of the guard's eyes widened with it. "Strategy for the Craggies, my dears, strategy of placement."

"Do we know if Emleton and the camps have enough?"

"That is if we go with these plans." The large man stated with a slight huff. "That many explosives are going to be scarce. Expensive. It might put mining operations at a stand-still until more are made. This means families starve if they can't work."

"If it comes to that, I'll get them food." I studied him, "Do you have a better plan in mind?"

"Wash our hands of it and let you deal with it. You are the Hero."

"If you believe one person can defeat a monster after my soldiers and our people have failed, you are a fool!" The Captain slammed his fist down on the table and stood.

"Why are you here?" Austere asked the large man.

He spluttered, his face turning crimson in the cheeks, "I'm the mayor! It's my business to be here."

"Sure. A mayor who protects his communities at all costs? Who has their welfare in mind and ensures it at all times, hm?" His voice had a bite to it, reminding me of Spacya's.

"Of course!"

"Then why wasn't your fat ass out there making the Cotkit look at you instead of the people it took?"

His mouth opened in an 'o' then closed again.

"That's what I thought. Keep it shut until you have something of use to say."

The wary captain dropped his hand from his sword hilt.

I didn't know if I wanted to kick Austere again or reach over and kiss him. I looked to the mayor and tried to be gentle, "Make a plan for your people in case this all goes awry. The Cotkit doesn't hunt at night, or it hasn't yet, so tell everyone to keep outdoor movement to a minimum during morning and daylight hours. Make them plan hiding spaces or ways to get away if it attacks again."

"I can do that."

"Does anyone here have any ideas? We are still open to them."

I watched as the captains looked to one another, then to the explosion specialist. Why was there only one? Hadn't Tori asked for two?

"I propose three squadrons, one for each group for each plan."

The jumpy man snorted, "How ya gonna get 'em to the Craggies? They gonna stretch for a mile and then they will take up too much room at them. Might be in danger with the explosions if they stay back too."

"I appreciate the offer, but I would rather ask for volunteers."

Sam Wicker

The Captain smiled, "I see. I can promise that many of my men and women will be part of the volunteers. I will gather the townsfolk at the square for you. What time?"

I looked over at the men, "No one else has a plan?"

"How much damage are we talking about here? Dust and debris in the air, how far will that spread to the town and camps?"

Now the mayor talked like someone who cared.

"The mountains should contain a majority of the debris and dust. Avalanches will start, but all mining camps have preparations for those. None should affect Emleton."

"Roads from the mining camps?"

"If damage occurs, then I guess you will have to clear them."

The captain of the guard sighed as he sat back down, "I hope this works."

"We all do."

In three hours' time, the captain had gathered a large crowd in the square. In that span, I had emptied my stomach twice. I stood on the Church steps, looking out at a sea of people and I was going to be sick again.

My teeth should have been clacking together; I was shaking so badly.

"Nadachia, breathe. Just say what we practiced." Blari placed a hand on my shoulder.

"Shoulda brought that little dress you wore at the dance. You could have asked them to kiss ass and they would do it if you were in that."

My eyebrow twitched, "You're not helping, pirate."

"Should I tell them about your fetish with tongues?"

"People of Emleton!" I stepped away from the pirate prince. My voice strained, and I didn't think they would hear me. "I am Nadachia of Silverequis, Hero chosen by the Gods. You have

331

been ravaged by a beast too long and we are here to help stop it! We plan to bring it down, but we need your help!"

Cheers erupted. I held my hands up, trying to urge them to keep quiet. All we would need is the Cotkit to get curious. I swallowed down the bile, "We have a plan. It's dangerous. It will involve going to The Craggies or through the desert to the Claw Caverns. We need volunteers. We do not want to order our guard, even though we know they would go with us as they worry about their families. Volunteers would be better so that people are not forced to leave their loved ones."

I expected some murmuring to start. Some hands shooting up. Not another round of cheers. As the crowd cheered, men and women came forward to stand at the bottom of the steps. I lost count around thirty, too amazed by their readiness to carry on counting.

"That's great. That's good. You are all such good people!" Tears burned my eyes. "Those of you that have not volunteered, please stay for a message, a plan of action from your mayor!" I should have asked him his name. "Those that have stepped forward, please follow us to the Hall. Thank you for your time and commitment!"

"Yup, next time, that little dress and we will have enough volunteers to go do these quests in our place." Austere leaned in to murmur in my ear as he held open the door for everyone. I stayed by his side, thanking the volunteers. "Would you call yourself Queen, Empress or Goddess?"

"Don't be ridiculous. They're just tired of living in fear."

Tori took over, explaining the plans. He and the Captain organized them into teams. I found my way to the side of our lone explosions expert. "Why is it you are the only expert here?"

"Ah, there are two others, both are at their mining camps."

"Only two?"

"We had five, but Joslina and Doki became one with their work." He placed a hand over his heart.

"Oh, I'm sorry for your loss."

"Quite alright. It is part of the job. Doki was getting up in age and had been talking about the way he wanted to die. I believe

Joslina did a small miscalculation. It happens with our way of life."

He was so calm about it. Death. Dying by exploding.

"Will one of them be joining our groups?"

"No, my son will go to the Craggies."

"He's an expert?"

"Near 'nough." He didn't even turn to me when he asked, "Who do you think'll die out of the crew?"

I stared at him, and he smiled, "I overheard some of your companions whilst you were speech makin'."

"What did they say, exactly?"

His shoulders jumped up and down, "I'll tell ya when we get through this."

That didn't set well with me. "Why not now?"

He chuckled, "Well, dear Hero, none of them want you to die and they are plotting ways to keep you from the action. That's all I will say."

"I see."

On the second day of gathering supplies for our plans, I started growing antsy. The Cotkit was probably getting ready to feed again. When would it strike? Which camp would it attack? The last time it, when it flew over my head, it had taken two grown men. Would it head here because of all the noise we were making?

I ran my fingers over the smooth wood, worked and polished until it gleamed. The ship still smelled of the sea. I looked out over the back and took a deep breath in of the fresh air. The scents of the docks and water mingled with that of the market. Spices being unloaded from a ship nearby tickled my nose.

The Sea Dreamer, Austere's ship. It wasn't as big as I had imagined.

My unease doubled as the scar in my hand thumped hard, like a quickened heartbeat. I kept telling myself he was just playing that game he liked, the one with the hoops. The fear still curled around my heart with each thump the scar made.

The ship creaked. Some wood groaned and ropes whirred through pulleys as the harpoon mechanism lifted off and onto a wagon on the dock. I turned, watching the process at the ship's bow.

Austere steadied the bulk of it along with three others. Four ropes had three men on each of them. Two men worked the crane. The pirate prince barked out orders the whole time. Some curses flew out of his mouth when the mechanism dipped as a rope slipped.

Of course, his men cursed him right back.

"I'll never get used to that."

My heart jumped in my throat. I looked to my side and found Pitrini there. "What?"

"The way they talk to one another. At first, I thought there would be a mutiny before we got out of the bay. But that's just how they are."

I nodded, "It suits them. Besides, he needs people around him who won't give in to his wiles and fall on his feet all the time."

Pitrini grinned, "He's still trying to figure you out."

"I'm not that hard of a read. Pretty simple actually."

"Doubt it."

"Oh, yeah?"

"Yeah, someone simple would have fallen at his feet already."

"No, not necessarily. Simple in mind or emotion, yes, but not simple to figure out. All there is to know about me is I want to do right by my family and those I care about. I want them to be well, and find happiness. If I can help them with that, it will fulfill me."

The young prince leaned back against the ship, "That's not simple."

"But simple to figure out."

"There's got to be something else. Otherwise you wouldn't be this far away from home, would you?"

Sam Wicker

"I came for the money to help us. Now, it's become an entwined mess. I've created a mess, found messes to fix and I need to clean it all up or else…" *my family might be in danger.*

"You have help, you know."

I nodded. So simple. So complicated.

The loaded harpooner was on a miner's wagon. It was the only thing wide and low enough to carry it and still be steady on the dock. Three more were being offloaded on other ships. As I looked between the docks, to the wagons being loaded with the mechanisms, I wondered if we had a chance. With so many people and animals heading toward it, it would be a feast.

Pitrini's name was called, and he trotted off. I turned back to the river, leaning on my elbows on the beautiful wood. My head thrummed, with the pull of my hair heavy.

I plucked the pins out, letting my wadded up braid fall. My head still thrummed. I unbraided my hair and let it loose in the wind. The weight subsided, and the thrumming lessened, but was still there.

I leaned over again and watched a merchant ship being unloaded on the wide dock next to ours. They checked each item over before being recovered and loaded onto a cart. A few barrels were rolled down a gangplank that led from an opening in one of the lower decks.

I moved down the bow to where I could look out across the Gala waters. I looked east, following the flow of the large river. To cross over it, flow with it, all the way home, tickled my imagination.

What was wrong with Taspe? My scar still beat erratically.

Had we overlooked anything? What was the Cotkit's daddy?

My thoughts crashed into one another and scrambled together. I couldn't see how I would survive the next meeting with Keandria. I couldn't think of how we would beat this monster.

I spread my fingers wide over the sun-warmed wood. They tripped over something and I looked down. The mark was deep, but smoothed and polished. A protection blessing. I ran my fingers over the familiar swirls curling into the Welkan words. Like reading a letter from home, my thoughts made sense again. I took a deep breath of the Gala air.

Everything in me settled. That was, until hips pressed against my lower back. Large hands splayed over mine as if they owned my flesh. A thick torso leaned into my back.

I pulled my elbow back, sharply.

A hand blocked it.

Hot breath feathered over my neck and he, for it was definitely male, pressed lips there and breathed in deep.

I twisted, bringing my leg up to slam my heel down, hoping to catch a foot.

One of those large hands slid over my hip, then down to the inside of my thigh. Wood met my bootheel.

I grabbed two long fingers, bending them back, trying to pull them away, and I bucked my hips.

He just shifted with me. Those fingers twisting to grip my hand in his fist. A knot rose in my throat. My thoughts became erratic again as I struggled to dislodge myself.

"Easy love," that tenor washed over me as his lips moved with those words against the shell of my ear.

I sank against him, mostly against his ship, but as he was determined to share the same space as me, "You ruined my peaceful moment."

"Ruined?" His nose was in my hair. "You belong on this ship."

"Do you use that often?"

"Hm?"

"What you just said. If you get someone on board, you let them wander, get comfortable, and then snag them to deliver the 'you belong on this ship' nonsense, right?"

He chuckled, "Only a few times. I don't find many attractives boarding my ship."

His grip loosened on my hand, his press against me softened until we might have been lovers enjoying the scenery instead of a man forcing himself on someone. "So you say. If I ask a member of your crew, would they tell me a different story?"

"Of course they would."

"Austere, you know it's never going to happen."

"It will. Especially now that you said that one, lovely, paltry word."

"What?"

"Never. Never is a word that is always broken." Austere kissed my temple. "I honestly just came up here to see what was going on. I haven't seen you take your hair down, not outside of bath time."

He didn't move away. His arms still encircled me, hands on my hips, his nose still in my hair, and his pelvis pressed to my backside. So I stepped back into him, away from the unforgiving wood of his ship, into his forgiving hold. "My head started hurting is all."

His hands shifted, something in his body changed, and it made my skin prickle. Want. That was desire, wasn't it? I moved to the side, stepping away from him once, twice. His hands slid away. I was free.

Except for the fingers now toying with my hair.

"Having it up like you do can do that. Better?"

"Some."

His dimples flashed, "Come now, just some? I distracted you from thinking too much."

Taspe's scar had calmed. I hoped it was a nightmare. Or a game. My head still hurt, but it was a dull ache. "I need to think sometimes."

He stepped closer, putting me in his shadow. He wrapped some strands of my hair around his fingers. I couldn't tell which was darker, his skin, or my hair. "You are admitting I distract you."

I rolled my eyes and felt his hand flow through my hair to the back of my neck. "Don't."

"Don't what?" He began working his fingertips over the base of my skull and top of my neck in small circles.

I closed my eyes as I pressed back against those glorious fingers. The pain seemed to release from my head with each circle he made. My eyes flew open as something brushed against my forehead.

"Easy. Relax."

His thumb pressed one temple, two fingers against the other, and he started rubbing there too. I closed my eyes again. My head felt so small in his hands this way. For once, I didn't want the pirate prince to stop his actions.

"Sometimes traveling to new areas can cause some pressure to build up there. Around the nose and ears especially. Yours is mostly stress, but I imagine some things around here might not agree with you too." He chuckled, "Therefore, Hero, you need to take time to relax. At least once a day. While I think you are majestically beautiful with your hair down, it isn't practical, nor conducive to other's work."

"How is it stopping others from working?" Talking seemed stupid at this moment, but there he was, running his mouth.

"You're being stared at."

"You are. I was just standing there. You're the pretty one. Pretty, tall one with giant hands holding my tiny head."

"If that's how you describe me, no wonder you think nothing will happen between us." He stopped, those long fingers ran through the hair at my temples. Then he cupped my face, gentle, the calluses on his thumbs scraped against my cheekbones. "Whether or not you are pretty, you are the Hero. People are looking and will continue to notice as long as they know your importance. Besides, you are not hard on the eyes."

"Not as pretty as my sister."

"She's not the measure of beauty, Nadachia."

"She is to me."

He growled.

I opened my eyes to see the face he made with such a sound. Something caught me in his gaze. Dark, fierce, and something else I couldn't put my finger on.

"How can someone so famous still be as blind to themselves as you are?" He pulled on the lobes of my ears and stepped away.

"You're stupid." I had more insults than that, some in another language, too.

"You are."

Sam Wicker

"Now we're children calling each other names and lying to one another about looks."

"You ready to go?" I watched his fingers dance over the wood where I had found the carved blessing, "Or we could stay on the ship. Together."

"Best be getting back." I was already halfway to the ramp that would take me to the dock.

"Don't think about it too much, or anything." I heard him mutter behind me.

The doors flew open and slammed against the walls, "It's attacking!"

"Where?!" I whirled and maps fell to the floor to roll from where I knocked them off the table.

"A mining camp just north of us. A mile away."

"How many hurt?" I started toward the door. Spacya grabbed my elbow and shook her head. There was a look on her face that made me feel like a child denied play time.

It wasn't like I could run there and save the day.

"Dunno. Just saw the flare."

"Flare?"

The man rolled his eyes, "Yeah, yannow, the flare system the old Captain what's-his-face told the mayor to implement in all the mining camps and towns sos we can keep track of the monster's movements."

I glanced around at the others. All of them looked as surprised as I did. "Let us know as soon as the reports come in."

"Will do." He bowed and left.

"He best not be coming in here like that again. These doors will break."

"And Chi will run off to…where exactly were you going to go?"

339

"Hush." I picked the maps up I threw on the floor and put them in an empty wooden chair. "We need to decide who will go where."

"I have to go with you. I think Spacya needs to go with the group to The Craggies as she is half mountain beast." He paused, "I think you need to go there too."

"No. I'm going to the Caverns."

"Why?"

"Because that's where the Cotkit is and I'm the Hero. Wouldn't it be odd if the Hero wasn't where the monster was?"

"I think you should play it safe this time."

Here it was. The part where they tried to keep me safe. I took a breath in and let it out slowly. "No, I don't think so. Aul said only two will die. We will have twenty-five people with us, my odds are good."

"That isn't... your odds would be even better at The Craggies." His hair was a mess, a tell the prince had when something wasn't going his way.

"Don't make me cut straws."

"Go! We'll decide while you're gone."

I glared at Spacya, then at Tori. They were the ones being obstinate and vocal. Blari and Austere weren't. While odd, I took it as an insignificant victory. "I'm going to the Claw Caverns, Blari is with me. At least two of you should be with the team at The Craggies. Who's it going to be?"

"I'm going with you." Eisle's voice was small, again.

"As am I." Austere smirked.

"It's settled then. Tori and Spacya, you're going to The Craggies."

"Now wait-"

I held up a hand, "Tori, I'll be fine. It works out this way. People listen to you. People fear Spacya, one of you will get the point across."

Spacya looked between Tori and I, "Let Tori go with you. I can handle the smaller team at The Craggies."

"No, two to be safe."

Sam Wicker

"Fine." Tori added, "Spacya and I will have your back at the Crags."

"I know you will." I smiled at them both, placing my hands on Tori's shoulder and giving it a squeeze.

Out of the corner of my eye, I saw a look pass between Blari and Spacya. I knew then my fight was hardly over. A knock sounded at the door, soft, hesitant.

"Enter!"

"Excuse me," a woman said as she pushed open the door, "I have a report from the attack."

"Go on." Tori stated.

"Four taken, adults. Its thrashing tore the camp down. They are still sorting through the rubble to see how many are hurt and dead."

I swallowed, it was getting more violent. "Thank you."

"I'll let you know more when we hear more."

I watched the woman go and sighed. It had taken four adults. That meant we would have at least two days. I hoped we would have two days. Its attacks didn't have a pattern. Not a set in stone one. Usually, there were two days free of attacks when it took an adult or two. It had to be two days.

"The teams are ready to leave at midnight tonight and the other at dawn, yes?"

"Yes, everything is prepared." Blari answered.

"We double and triple checked the numbers and supplies, yes?"

"Of course." Tori answered that one.

"Medical?"

"We have a couple of healers per team and medical teams on standby far enough away if it attacks either team, but stationed close enough to be of use in case." Blari said.

"The son and the father, are they ready?"

"Yes, and each has a backup explosives trainee in case something happens with them."

"There's nothing we are overlooking, Nadachia." Austere's voice was low, the words forming slowly in the room. "We have been over this several times, yesterday and today, with several sets of eyes going behind to check it again. We're as ready as we shall ever be, darling."

I nodded, "I just- I want to make sure."

"We know."

"Take the rest of the day to do what you need to do. Spacya, Tori, good luck."

They nodded, and Tori added, "You too."

There wasn't any use in me trying to sleep. All I had managed was to wallow in the bed until a few hours before we had to leave. I was down by the docks, ready to leave. I left my pack in the stables with my gear and horse. Not Unia, but the sand mare that was loaned to me by some breeder in Emleton.

The Gala sparkled under the moons. Waves lapped at the docks and the sides of the Sea Dreamer in a steady rhythm. The same beat that they made against the dock and ships at home. Soon the water that passed here would pass by Father, Taspe, and the children.

I ran my fingers over it. The blessing that I had found on his ship. It was mine. The pulse in my palm was steady, strong. I leaned on the balustrade and whispered to the Gala waters, "Tell them I love them. Ease their pain. Bring them smiles."

"Do you often talk to nothing?"

Of course, he was on the ship too. I should have found an empty dock. If there was one.

"Couldn't sleep?"

"I slept for a few hours. It comes to me better after a good long bout of sex. You should try it. Soon."

I fisted my hands, something boiled inside me, "Don't. Just don't, for once." I just kept my eyes on that water below that flowed homeward. If I asked it of him, I knew Austere would wake his crew and take me there.

Sam Wicker

I wanted to ask. The words burned holes in my throat. I couldn't breathe for them.

His hands dangled over the side as he leaned on his elbows beside me. "You know, the written records of the past three heroes are all that remain of their trials?" He paused, "none of them tell the struggles, only the bravery and fearlessness. It's all lies. You know, for a fact, that there is fear and doubt. You know better than anyone else what they went through. Yet those words written for them lie and dishonor the sacrifices they truly made for us. Yours won't."

"Blari let you read some?"

"The word 'let' isn't the one I would use."

"You stole it then?"

"Borrowed."

"What did it say?"

"Many things. What kept me reading until he found me and took it back was you. The you he sees. The fact that you wanted to stay home, but you didn't. That you had moments where you wanted to turn back, but you didn't. You keep rising to face these challenges with that thick head of yours. You defeat it, destroy it, and turn to face the next one. Even though you are breaking and broken inside, screaming to be released, you do it. You fight for us."

His words repeated in my mind. They tainted my tongue with bitterness. "He should write more truth then, and not such lies. I'm only strong because those around me are carrying me like the sack of useless that I am."

"Gods, Nadachia, are you ever going to see the truth or will you always believe the lies you poison yourself with?"

I laughed, my head shaking, "You should ask that question about your thoughts of me. Someone has sold you sweets when they were sours."

"Who has told you that you are weak or not pretty your whole life?"

I lifted a shoulder, "No one. No words were plainly spoken like that to me. I just know. Truth is truth, whether it is spoken aloud or not."

"We're gonna have to form a team to erase those thoughts of yours and bring you truer ones."

"Then those would be their truths. Not mine."

"Gods, keep me from shaking this woman until some selfishness and sight fall in her."

Chapter 27

Two days. Two days of sand blasting one side of me while the other baked. Or froze, depending on how late we started out or how early we stopped for the day. My left eye continuously leaked tears. My face burned as if I had fallen asleep in the sunlight. Which I did, but in a tent.

Each time I awoke, I thought I could touch the sun as it sank behind the glowing sands.

The third night of travel had me lying on the back of my horse, backwards, so that the remaining winds before they calmed would batter my other side for a while. The sand mare had proven to be a steadfast, protective creature. Riding her was like riding a bed. It was too cold of a night to sleep. Too hot during the day to try. I determined to get a little shuteye in the hours where the sands cooled off under the watery moons while traveling. But by the time the twin globes were up over the mountain peaks, my teeth were chattering so hard my jaw, neck and head hurt.

The extreme heat to the extreme cold had my body revolting in ways it never had before. Fevers and chills switched places with each other often, and with little warning. Water either ran through me so quickly I swore to pee while drinking it, or it came hurtling back up as soon as I capped the canteen.

According to the natives, I had Foreigner Illness. It was normal for those of us born in other climes and weather to go through this. Although, Blari, Priest of the Gods, was immune, as was the great huntress Spacya. Austere didn't count as he had traveled far and wide. Eilse was right at home here.

We stopped for our lunch on our last night of travel to The Claw Caverns. I shucked off the fur cloak I had bought in Emleton for these nights. It was black, perfect for blending into the shadows of the mountains. Sweat beaded on my brow even as it threatened to freeze there.

Eisle shoved the pelt back over me, "Are you sure you're not pregnant?"

Blari got a face full of whatever Austere was drinking.

"I'm not pregnant." As she wilted, I whimpered. "Sorry, I didn't mean to sound that way."

"It's okay. You're sick." She smiled at me, "I was more disappointed that you aren't. I think a baby made between you and Austere would be the cutest thing."

Blari ducked.

The pirate made a strangled sound as he covered his mouth with a hand. *Was his face pale from the moonlight or if he was getting sick, too?* I think I heard him snort. Moonlight, then.

"I've only been with Taspe."

"Oh, right. Austere should be your seeder if you stay with him."

"Seeder?" Blari kept a wary eye on Austere, staying low to the rock we were currently using as a table to share our dried meat and fruit meal.

"Father of the baby for them since it is difficult for Welkans and humans to breed." Her cheeks shone darker in the pale moonlight.

"Oh, my darling Eisle, you are brilliant." Austere's voice flowed with a chuckle.

I shook my head, willing the chattering to stop, "Not going to happen."

"Never say never, seed bearer."

"Gods," I groaned. "What kind of endearment is that?"

"Time!"

We stood in unison. One of our volunteers was a beautiful woman who trained the new recruits for the Emleton and surrounding camps guard force. It was she that kept this train running smoothly and on time. We were a few hours ahead of schedule, thanks to her. And praises to the gods for blessing us with clear weather and lack of equipment issues.

I caught little snippets of sleep here and there while riding that night between fever bouts and chattering. I'm not sure if it was the dreams or the fever that had me picturing a babe with the chubbiest of cheeks that made its eyes squeeze shut when it smiled or if it was my own imaginings. Seaghla and I both had chubby faces when small, but we quickly outgrew them.

The captain of our envoy halted us before we rounded the last mountain fully. My teeth clacked so viciously I barely heard her, but my horse understood the order. The woman turned in her saddle to find me before sliding off.

"I'm going to scout ahead, see if it's there. The rest of you make camp. If I'm not back in an hour, don't come after me." She was off with two others in tow before I got any words through my banging teeth.

Someone set up a low fire in the depths of a crack that ran up the side of the mountain. It made the smoke go further up into the sky, and toward the south. He waved me over after I basically fell from my horse, "Sit. Stay warm."

It was the scaled Rogue that had spent the night with me. I sat down, too tired to fight through the chattering. The fire burned the raw skin of my face, but it felt good as the warmth from it soaked through the cloak. In a few moments, a wisp of steam came from the pot and he threw in a handful of green things from a pouch at his side.

We were too close to the Cotkit to risk many fires. Everyone else prepared their meals of dried fruits and meats and thin breads after they took care of setting up the camp. The next waft of steam from the vessel was fragrant.

"When I open it, lean into the steam and breathe it in as deep as you can."

"What is it?"

He smiled, "Something that will help." He lifted the lid.

I leaned over the pot and breathed in deeply. None of the essences were familiar to me. I closed my eyes and kept breathing in deep, long breaths. Earthy and rich were the only ways I could describe the scents.

I didn't know when my teeth stopped chattering, nor when my skin felt somewhat normal against me again. When he told me he was going to cover the pot after my next breath in, I took stock. I heard the soft clank of the lid being replaced and I sat back. I rubbed the condensation off my face with both hands. My cheeks were warm, damp, and soothed of the wind burn.

"Thank you."

"I meant to treat you with this last night, but I couldn't find the right herbs yesterday in the healer's pouches. So I had to mix it from scratch. Guess they figured no one would get sick on this trip."

"What were the ingredients?"

He just smiled again, "In about four hours, you need to do this again for you to fully recover. But I don't think we're going to have the time."

"We won't. I feel better."

He nodded, "Go, the brilliant planners of our troop probably need to talk again."

I looked over to the main tent, and true to his assumption, the little band had formed of leaders there. I sighed, my body loose for the first time since stepping into the desert. My boots sank into the snow-soft sands. I stopped between Austere and Blari, facing the explosives expert whose eye whites shone brightly like the moons. Today was going to be an interesting day.

I stared at the mountainside as they talked. They were just working over the steps for the millionth time. I watched something appear, crawling along the rock. I stepped in front of Blari and wished I had night vision.

"What are you staring at?"

"Did he put something he wasn't supposed to in that?"

"Drugs? She's drugged?" Blari grabbed my elbow.

"No... what is that?" I pointed, and then realized. "She's back already." That's when I saw the other two moving right along after the first one.

"Oh. Already?" Blari squinted at my side, rubbing his long beard with the hand he had used to grab me. I saw sand shake out of the thick strands out of the corner of my eye and onto his robes.

She approached us and took a minute to catch her breath. It plumed out in front of her, but quickly faded into the cold air. "It's there. Muttering about being hungry."

Sam Wicker

Did the thing sleep? Better yet, it hadn't attacked again yet. I couldn't believe I was hoping it would attack anew. With it gone, we could set the charges freely, not just outside the cave.

"Good. We have time to set up a bit. Let's get the plan rolling while we still have some darkness left." Our little group disbanded. Each of us had a job to fill.

During the worst heat of the day, the Cotkit emerged from the dark mouth of its cavernous home. It ran out, stretching all four of its massive wings. As it ran, it made a wide turn deep in the desert to run back to the mountains. Those wings caught the air like sails on a ship. Up it bound with a flap, then another. A gangly landing at a run and it jumped again. This time it stayed up, one claw pushing its large body further up.

"Go!"

We pulled our gear out of the sands as we ran from whatever crevice and shadow we could find. We dragged and pushed the harpoon machines into their spots before a team cleaned the sand from each one so the gears wouldn't stick.

I bolted to the cave. To each side of me, ropes with hooks flew up and caught on the sides of each mountain. Men and women yanked to make sure they were secure, before scaling those ropes and the mountainsides faster than I ran to the cave mouth. Something bloomed inside me.

"We might have a chance."

I set my groups of explosives according to the map, where our expert thought they would have the best impact. All around the mouth and a few deeper inside. There were others in there with me, setting their own charges.

I had prepared them and myself for this foray into the darkness. I made each of us a cloth to cover our noses, with sprigs of smelly herbs and florals. It was bad enough I had the crunch of bones with the slick of blood and gore beneath my boots. I still smelled the rot, but it was manageable.

Double checking my work, I made sure all the lines and sticks of the stuff were secure and wouldn't dislodge easily. I took the leads from the others as they ran out to find their hiding spots or to finish another task. I braided all the leads together into a thick rope and pushed it against the side of the mountain. Another woman, a volunteer, made the lead even less conspicuous by shoving some rocks in front of it or making a hill of sand beside it. We didn't think the Cotkit would notice the line, but just in case.

I was more worried if it picked up on the odor of live people around the cave or not. From what I remembered Vey and Detri saying, birds didn't have the greatest sense of smell, though. Just eyesight. I was probably worried about the wrong thing.

The expert was taking care of several placements of explosives and giving instructions to others as he went. He would lay three to their one. Once he finished, he zipped back down the mountainside and joined me. He made quick work of the lines by splitting and weaving them into two. If one didn't make the charges, then the other would.

"Right then, I'll go to the other one." The lines of the smaller mountain, we kept separate from the one I was standing beside. The backup collapse. I took a deep breath in as I walked the lines back to a safe distance from the mountain and the cave, as calculated by the experts. I handed the lines over to the guy in charge of the box. He attached them to it, carefully, and then wiped the dripping sweat off his dark brow.

I took up my position nearby. During the night, we dug several gullies and covered them with canvas, which we hid in a light coating of sand. Well, the winds were doing a better job of covering the canvases than we did.

I was in the one closest to the cave, next to the charges by the mountain. There were five with me, including one of Austere's shipmates. Austere hunkered down next to the farthest harpoon. Oddly enough, it wasn't his. Blari was in the small bushes and shrubs with the guys with the charges.

With another deep breath, I hoped the lavender in the cloth against my nose would help calm my ravaged nerves.

Dread curled in my stomach and sat there like an oily rock. I continued to scan over the people who came with us, making sure they were hidden and at the ready. Maybe something was already wrong. Maybe the Cotkit wasn't coming back to the cave. Maybe the Cotkit had seen our crew at The Craggies and was attacking them as I sat here on my ass. Maybe it was lying waste to Emleton instead of just making a meal run.

It could fly to Galanesse for all I knew.

I was about to push my way out of the cover and do... what? I didn't know, but I heard something that made me pause. Was that a blast?

I swallowed, lifting the corner to the cover slightly to stick my head out. A low rumble and the earth around me shook. I looked up at the mountains. They hadn't moved. Not these two, at least.

The earth kept shaking.

"That The Craggies team?"

Plumes of dust and debris filled smoke rose over the peaks. I was about to climb out when one cloud burst open. A flash of orange and red stretched out its wings and flapped. It dipped and twirled, flapping harder, all four wings going at different times. Smoke trailed it.

The Cotkit slammed into a mountain. Rubble tumbled from all around it. It pushed off, only getting one leg under its monstrous body.

A keening sound erupted from somewhere. It grew louder until my ears rang with it and still it increased in strength. I covered my ears, thinking my head would explode from the noise. Then it stopped as quickly as it had started.

I looked out again. Right above us, the Cotkit scrambled along the mountainside. Rocks rained down from its efforts. A leg looked blackened. One wing smoked as fire still crackled along its feathers. It held it out, shaking it. The feathers all along the underside of that wing were all but gone. Some scales remained, but they appeared cracked and uneven.

It circled in front of the cave mouth, flapping and ruffling the feathers of its wings and chest. Its beak was wide open. Words flowed, and sounds, but I couldn't make out what it was saying. Each stomp of its one good leg sent sand flying up to meet the debris cloud.

Finally, it wedged itself into the cave. It moved, shifting and rolling and fluffing feathers still. The sunlight fractured off the feathers in the cave's darkness.

No blast?

I looked toward the charge and gasped. A large rock, about the size of a horse, had landed on the tent. A few men and women were trying to get someone out from under it.

A great thundering sound ripped through the air. The second mountain crumbled. Rocks burst out and down in a wave of roaring and tumbling thunder.

The Cotkit bellowed.

I was up out of my hole, sprinting for the mountainside. Someone screamed my name. I saw the beast trying to back its way out of the cave. The second mountain's rubble bounced off its back, the dust catching up and covering it until only little clearings showed me bits of orange and red feathers and scales.

My flint with the switch strike was in my hands in mid sprint. The dust reached me. I barely saw my foot hitting the ground beneath me. I flung my hands out. Pebbles pummeled me. The dust burned my eyes and made them water. I barely got air into my lungs.

My hand smacked into the rocks before I slammed into it. My eyes burned more, tears streaking hotter than the soot down my cheeks. I slid down the side, pawing for the lines.

They had to be right there.

Something whooshed over my head, clearing some of the debris for a moment. I didn't question what it was. It was what I needed. I hurled toward the twisted leads and grabbed them in one hand. The switch flicked once, twice, and a flame flickered to life. I put it to the lines, and it sparked and then flared. The flame sizzled and popped its way down the lines.

Another whoosh, only this time, something soft and red caught my temple. Then I was spinning as a couple of claws squeezed my middle. I was flying, for a moment, until my back hit the sand. What little air I had stuffed into my lungs behind the mask whooshed out.

I was up again. Then slammed down. No air was in me to escape this time. Two large wings formed a tent around me. I stared into the open beak. Rows of jagged teeth in circles around the darting tongue, had my sanity running. Then it closed. Those golden and red eyes blinked at me. All of them. All at different times.

"You do this to me?"

Its breath was hot on my face, neck, and chest. I grappled with the talon curled over my belly. The scales over its skin cut into the tender flesh of my fingertips and palms. I managed a gasp. I bucked, kicking, trying to find purchase with my boots in the shifting sands. I had to get out. My lungs burned. I finally breathed.

"Yes. All me!"

"You must be the Hero then. Chosen by gods, like me. Are you tied like I was?"

"Tied?"

"By the black blood that smells of death and power. Tied to her like puppet toy."

I thought I had shifted an inch out of its grip. Then weight pressed me further into the sand. I managed a pant. Puppet. "Who? You are controlled now?"

"No. Before. Held back until she released us. She stole us from home. Stole us from gods. She kept us back. We are way past time."

"Why?"

"Don't care. Just want home now. I want to be me again. I want to be with Daddy again."

"What were you before? Who's Daddy?"

If I kept it talking, I could get out of this. I had to get out of this.

"Bird of flame for Daddy, the god. Yes. For you, Hero. For humans to have a power in the world to balance. Black, Blue and Made blood. Do they not teach this anymore? You are the Red, Red must find balance."

"Teach me. Let me go."

The wing tent disappeared. It curled back its neck, its head going up into the dust laden sky and it laughed.

I dug at its skin and scales. I kicked and flung my legs and body about. It lowered its head. That beak pressed into my sternum.

"No."

Dagger. I had daggers. I twisted and bucked some more. My blood slick fingers slid off a hilt. They gripped it again, and I pulled one out. I hacked and hacked at the leg above me. The toe, the talon. The metal just clanked against the scales and flesh.

I arched, slamming the blade up and into a nare above the beak as it flared open.

It screamed and lurched back.

The grip on me loosened. I scrambled back, scooting and sliding over the sand. Rock shot out at me before the sound of thunder turned into a high-pitched ring.

The world heaved. My feet flew over my head as more rock and dust pummeled me. That claw caught me. Dragged me back. A pain in my shoulder drew my attention to the blood-soaked talon in it. Something slammed into my skull and I knew no more.

Chapter 28

I was swaying. Was I being eaten? The thought had my eyes opening, and I stood. On a bed. Not rock. Not sand.

The whole room was rocking. It was a nice one. All wood of a dark grain, natural with some coating on it that made it shine with the light a little. The bed was attached to a wall. Built wide enough for two, and it had four pillows on it and just as many sheets, but no covers. There was a desk fixed to another wall by a door that was closed. A chair hung on a hook next to it. A pencil rolled to a book and back toward the edge. It was the only sound in the room, other than my own breathing.

I lurched up and sat on the bed.

A dresser squatted under one of three windows. I hoped I would find some clothes there. If I could make it. This shirt was covering, but it was only over some flimsy underwear.

Sounds. A lot of sounds. Water lapping and splashes. People called out to one another all around and there were bird melodies. Strange bird sounds, and a flute answering them, or it was someone answering them. There were also more than a few pairs of bare feet moving along the wood flooring outside this little room.

I planted my feet, bare, on the smooth wood and tried standing again. After a few tries, the bones in my legs were noodles, but held. I stumbled to the dresser and leaned on it.

On its top was a mirror, and I dared a glance.

Purple skin around my eyes explained the pain along with a bandage over my cheek and another at my temple. My hair had seen far better days, but at least it didn't hurt.

I pulled on the knobs. It took me too long for me to figure out the hook mechanism over each knob. I hoped I would never have to admit how long. I found a few of my clothes in the top drawer, the important ones at least.

With the rocking and my noodle legs, I learned to lean against the dresser to put my pants on after slamming into it more than a few times. I sat on the bed to pull my boots on after stumbling, then crawled back over to it. I wasn't about to take any chances, and I buckled my belt of daggers over the long shirt and stuck another in my boot.

I tried the door, and it swung open. The bright sunlight made me want to tear out my eyes. After a few blinks, I focused around the tears. Directly across from me was a wall, but to the right was the ship's deck. A few sailors were on it. One sat on a barrel just under the mast, a flute in his hands. The birds on the shore sang with the music coming from him. Past him, holding the wheel, was Pitrini. He lifted a hand high above his head. I waved weakly, my hand not reaching much higher than my shoulder.

The door down from mine opened, drawing my attention from the boy. He smiled, his smooth hand resting on my shoulder gently, "How are you feeling?"

"Hurting. What are we doing on Austere's ship?"

"Good. I'll let everyone know you're up, then we'll all talk about it."

That didn't sound promising. I frowned at Tori's back as he turned and rapped on the other two doors further down the hallway. Taking my elbow in his palm he said, "Come on, Austere's room is probably going to be the best place."

I nodded and found that to be a mistake as my head throbbed with each movement. I stumbled, only to be caught and held steady by Tori. That hand on my elbow disappeared, only to reappear at my side as he wrapped an arm around me. We walked across the deck.

Tori knocked on the door of the captain's cabin, and I heard that rich tenor answer. I wasn't sure I was going to be able to take his wit or humor. Or whatever we were about to discuss.

The prince led me through. Spacya and Blari crowded in close behind us.

The huntress moved to where she stood nose to nose with me. She looked me over, her eyes sweeping before she met my gaze again. Her lips twisted toward the scar in her small smile, and she gave me a nod. Something eased in me with that familiar look.

Then she was pushed back. He cupped my face in large hands and I looked into the bright red eyes I was getting too used to seeing.

"Thank the gods. How do you feel?" He wrapped me up in his arms.

I wondered how I had gotten this familiar with the pirate prince so soon. Right. Dancing, then nakedness. That's all it took for him.

"I'm fine." I tried pulling myself away and caught Blari's raised brows from over Austere's shoulder.

"You don't look fine still."

"Where's Eisle?"

They all got busy. One found me a chair and helped me into it, another started making tea, and the other shuffled papers on his desk. No talon through my shoulder, or remnants of it. My middle from the slamming and pinching claws didn't hurt. My head wasn't smashed in.

I don't know why I asked a question I already knew the answer to. "Where are we?"

"On the Gala." Austere answered as he hooked a knee over a corner of his desk.

"Why didn't we stay in Emleton and why aren't we going toward Galanesse?" My brain was figuring out things quicker than I thought. We were heading down the Gala, toward home. Not back up it.

"We will tell you, after you tell us what you remember." Blari stated as he handed me a steaming mug.

I told them everything I recalled after the Cotkit arrived. Even every word it said, too. "Did you set the charges in The Craggies?"

"We lured it there." Tori leaned in his chair beside mine. "It circled back from its usual route to the mining camps because we started making a bunch of noise. It landed in the wide part because we had some of those fake people, the meat sacks, set up there." He shook his head, "we set the charges just fine. Somehow, it survived. It beat off most of the rocks. It caught on fire and it didn't pause at the flames. I think its tail was smashed too, but it still didn't stop."

"How many?"

"What?"

"How many died?"

"Three. A couple more were injured."

Had Aul been wrong? "What happened on our end?"

Blari rubbed his beard, "It thrashed around so much that it cut a lot of the cords." He sighed and gave me a look, like I was about to get a lecture, but he continued with the story instead. "After you charged in, we tried shooting it. Those scales are, were, impenetrable. The first blast didn't go off and the inner blasts didn't either. The peak from behind didn't have enough to reach it. We relied too heavily on the first mountain and the inside explosives."

"They finally exploded, because of your fool neck running out there and lighting them." Austere interjected, staring me down from across his desk.

"You were caught. We heard talking. Nothing worked. Until the blast. It buried you with it."

Blari paused in the story, his voice growing soft, "We knew, as long as Eisle was alive there was a chance. We tried to dig you out." He shifted in his chair and shook his head.

"Then, it rose. It was a fireball coming up out of the sand, rocks, and debris. The firebird of legend, the god Dani's bird. It cleared all the rubble. It hovered for a while and then just… disappeared."

"We got to you. You took a breath, and Eisle took her last one." Austere added, his voice low, when Blari couldn't finish.

After a pause in their story, Blari began again. By that time, the hollow inside me grew.

"We stayed for two days. We had the funeral for Eilse, Emleton had a feast in our honor. The god Dani stopped by to have a chat. He gave this to me to give to you when you awoke." Blari pulled a rolled piece of parchment out of his robe pocket. Scorch marks along the ends made me pause in taking it. It was wrapped with a black and red ribbon, softer than any I had ever held, when I finally took the thing.

"We received a letter from a priest of Owlimount. We headed there. You have been asleep for three days, this is the morning of the fourth since your second death." He held out an envelope, and I took it too.

"Read the scroll first, darling."

I glanced at Blari, who nodded. Untying the ribbon, I began reading the letter. The ink seemed to glow like embers in a fireplace. The smell of rich wood smoke filled the room.

"Read it out loud," Austere urged.

If they hadn't opened it, why did they want me to read it first?

Nadachia and Companions,

I wanted to wait until you woke, but alas, I have a naughty animal to get back to punish and spoil. I think she did well in her duties as a quest, don't you? Although, I think she was overdue. Perhaps I got the era wrong.

Once you finish reading this letter, you will each be given a way to contact me. I will suit them for each of you. One of my last gifts like this turned into a small whistle the owner could wear around her neck. It was quite beautiful.

I will ask that you use these wisely and call me rarely. Know I cannot raise the dead nor prevent anything that is a step in your destiny. What I can do is give you advice, wisdom, comfort, and aid you in minor ways such as transporting you to another place, light a fire, or something of that nature. These items will work seven times, and seven times only; keep that in mind.

Also, be in an open area or where smoke will not heavily affect you.

Thank you for your service in giving humans something of power to help balance the world.

Your Fire God, Dani

One ribbon pulled away, floated between us, and broke into five separate pieces. Each piece moved to hover before each of us. Tori was the first to touch his. It flared bright orange and red in his fingertips before he held up a clasp shaped in the fire bird in a golden hue. He placed it on his cloak at his neck as a soft, male voice said: To call me, tap on the beak three times.

Austere's turned into a pocket sized spyglass and the instructions were to unscope it quickly three times. Blari's turned into a feather pin, golden orange like Tori's clasp, and Blari's instructions were to dip the tip, like a quill, in liquid three times to call the god. Spacya's was another feather, smaller than Blari's, and tied to strips of leather. She tied it into her hair with her other adornments there. Her instructions were to wrap the leather around the feather three times.

Mine. Mine was a tiny dagger shaped like a feather. The blade glowed like fire. I was to prick my thumb or forefinger with it to call upon him. I tucked it safely into my belt, into an empty holster.

Without prompting, I unfolded the other letter.

Blari,

I hope this finds you quickly and well, brother. They attacked the family of Nadachia this past morn. We have made arrangements to secure them with the Welkan tribe. Taspe has been injured, but he has ordered his people to form a hunting party to try to recover those taken: Rossi, CiaCia, and Detri.

As of this moment, we have had no word from the recovery party.

Do as you wish with this information, as you will know best. I will send word again with any fresh news as I receive it.

Yours, Glari

During the reading of the letter, I had stood at some point. My knees hurt from being locked in place. "How long?"

"We will be there in a day and a half," Austere told me in a soft tone.

Sam Wicker

I looked at the date on the letter. Two days ago. Who would attack and where would they go? Someone who wanted to hurt me.

Keandria.

Galanesse then. The quickest way was the Capital Road, as the Gala flowed in the wrong direction to make travel back to the capital via it difficult unless it was a rowing ship. "Have you checked other ships as we pass them?"

Austere's lips curled up at the corners, "Yes, love, we have." He looked at Blari, "Her mind is wondrous, isn't it? Any other woman would wail and thrash."

Blari snorted, "Her panic is planning or solving puzzles."

A cry sounded from the deck, high above it, "Ship!"

Austere rose, and flung open the door, "Hail and Board!"

"Hailing, Captain!"

He stood there, waiting.

"She answers! We are allowed to board!"

"Pull alongside!" He waved us to come out. We moved to the deck and stood to the side.

Feet pounded, they took ramps to the starboard side and hooked onto the ship as we anchored side by side with it. Austere turned to me, "Stay here, I'll be right back."

Tori grabbed my elbow and held me with his iron grip. "Chi, if this is it, you don't need to be captured too."

I stilled, thinking about that for a moment. It was true. But this was my family.

Austere hopped up on the ramp and strode across like he owned both ships. Three other sailors crossed with him. As one talked with who I assumed to be the captain, Austere and the others checked the deck, and below. No board was left unpounded, no barrel unopened, and no cabin not cleared. Austere came up to the two men after finishing and shook the man's hand before they all came back over. We unhooked and were on our way before Tori let me go.

"Nothing?"

"Merchant ship. He had some pretty silks and some jewels from Ecia. He hadn't seen or heard of anyone being captured or

361

attacked, either. His last port was Walla. I checked his papers, and he told the truth. He hasn't been down to Owlimount in a month."

I turned, watching the ship row away behind us. Fishing boats were few, as there were no towns nearby.

I sat down on a step that led up to the front of the ship and rubbed my temples. Pressure built just behind my eyes. I had a god that I could use. I looked at the clasp on Tori, debated, and shut that thought down. What would happen if they weren't in any real danger? Or if this was part of some destiny thing that a god couldn't mess with? Ridiculous. Humans should make their own destiny. I honestly didn't really believe in destiny anymore. Why would I be here if it was destiny? Joni would have taken up this mess if destiny had such power over our lives. My thinking was going off on a tangent.

Keandria. The King. The Queen. An unknown lord. They would take them to Galanesse. More than likely, they were taking the road or we were behind them. On this ship, there was no way I could reach them before they entered Galanesse.

Once there, where would they put them?

The Tower or dungeons were the only options there. Probably. Most likely. Or would they think I would think that and put them elsewhere? Would they be that clever? Would she think I was that clever?

I honestly didn't know what the Stygra Matron thought of me. Or the royals. If they thought I was smart, they would take certain extra measures. Otherwise Keandria wouldn't have told me so much or given me so much leash.

She had kept the Cotkit. Somehow, she had kept that beast trapped until she needed it. A beast of the gods. Had she done something to the gods as well? Was that why Aul and Dani couldn't do much for us or why Dani had seemed confused why his animal had been kept so long?

"Chi!"

I looked up.

"Didn't you hear us?"

"What?"

"Your nose is bleeding. Let's get you back to your room." Spacya held out a hand.

I dabbed at my nose and covered my fingertips with blood. "I'm fine." The words were coming out of my mouth as the sky tried to become the floor.

Strong arms wrapped around me and lifted me. The sky still didn't right itself. It kept turning; the trees twisting round and round over our heads. I closed my eyes, my stomach mimicking them.

"Easy. Breathe for me. Chi, you're going to make yourself pass out."

I breathed. It came in slow, but escaped in a whoosh that I couldn't stop. I was flipped up and leaned over the edge of the ship as the contents of my gut, mostly just water, emptied into the Gala and the wood. He pulled my hair back from my face. Those callouses scraped gently against my skin until most of my hair was away from my mouth. He patted my back with the other hand, holding me steady.

My stomach heaved a few times, nothing coming out. Some blood spattered along the smooth wood planks below me. "Let me up." I murmured, my throat raw.

Austere helped me stand, keeping a hand in my hair while his other arm wrapped around my waist. "That blood has me worried."

"Probably just where she breathed in all that sand and dust." Spacya said as she wiped my face off with a damp cloth.

"Didn't think about that." Austere murmured.

Blari snorted, "Not to mention she was crushed under a mountain, revived with dark magic, and is now on a ship in the middle of a river where she has learned they attacked her family. Come on, few can still stand with all that going on. A little bloody nose is nothing, I would think."

My knees and legs shifted more into the noodle territory with each word spoken. As soon as Blari finished his scoffing, Austere had me back up in his arms because my noodle legs just couldn't hold me up any more. For once, I was thankful he was so grabby. If I had gone down, I doubted I would get up from the deck.

Everything hurt. My stomach kept trying to empty a jar that was already bare, my head throbbed right along with my heartbeat, and my throat burned.

Was I really this pathetic?

Two girls had died for me, and I was being carried back to my room like a child. My family needed me. This may be the fastest route, it wasn't being helped along by my hands. It should be. I should row or make the sails catch more wind, or feeding or bringing water to the sailors who were far more adept at such things.

"Give me something to do."

Austere snorted, letting Spacya open the door to my room before he deposited me on the bed. "Rest."

"No." I dropped my feet to the floor so I could stand, but he held my leg still. He pulled the sheets over my legs and up to my waist.

"You will rest."

I shoved at his chest.

"Nadachia, listen, you have to rest to get up enough strength for when we reach home."

Blari. His words made sense, but something in me seethed, then snapped. I punched Austere as hard as I could in the chest. My wrist cracked and his breath whooshed out, making my arm hairs stand and tickle my skin. His body weaved back, but he stayed standing.

I shoved at the sheet, trying to untangle it from my boots and pants and from around my legs. It held fast until I kicked. I watched my kick, my leg barely lifting off the mattress even as it should have lifted completely off with the force I mustered together.

Austere was back on me, sitting beside me in the bed, blocking my escape, as the sheet was under his large frame. "That hurt."

"It was supposed to."

He frowned, "Lie down."

"I want to be useful."

Sam Wicker

"Tori, go ask Grill to make some of that special tea we usually reserve for Pitrini."

Tori nodded and escaped.

"Tea?" I glanced between the door and Austere. Since when did Tori do errands for the pirate prince?

"I'm gonna go learn some more about fishing off a ship." Spacya grabbed my wrist and placed the cloth she had used to wipe my face earlier in my hand. "You, rest. If I see you out, I'm gonna to spear you."

I wasn't entirely sure that she wouldn't put a spear through me, so I nodded.

Blari sat in the chair he pulled up next to my bed and heaved a sigh that made his whole body rise and fall. "Look, Chi, you have got to learn to let things go. You can't do everything."

"If she would learn not to run headfirst into danger, she might get to do more things." Austere nudged my shoulder.

"Are you not going to explain what the tea is you give Pitrini?"

"I don't think she thought about that last one. I mean, she usually wouldn't put another life in danger, and seeing as how there were two lives... hers and Eilse's, I really believe that was just instinct."

"So now we're gonna talk about me like I'm not here. Perfect."

Austere leaned over my legs, placing his shoulders against the wall and smirked at me. He lazily rubbed my thigh with his fingertips, "Perhaps if you would stop doing stupid things we wouldn't have to talk about you all the time."

I swatted his hand away, only to have him bring it back. I glared at those long fingers as both Austere and Blari chuckled. "Just wanted to make sure that everything goes okay. And... yes, I just ran. I didn't think. I saw what happened, and I wanted to fix it because we needed that Cotkit beaten. People were being killed every few days."

"I thought so," Blari said, "That's why you are the Hero. According to Taspe, you have always been that way."

"Not a bad way to be, but there should be some self preservation in there too."

"There is. At least, I think there is."

Austere shook his head, his brows rising as he looked at me, "No, there isn't."

"Maybe she fell too much as a kid or something. The fear that most of us have at getting hurt was just beat out of her by her little adventures as a child."

"How much has Taspe told you?"

"Everything," Blari groaned with a look skyward.

Tori came back in with another mug. Small wisps of steam rose over the edges as he closed the door behind him before holding it out to me. His eyes were on Austere's hand, "She can't rest with you molesting her."

"She won't be still if I don't."

I glanced at Blari. He was rubbing an ink stain on the back of his hand. If I could sense the change in the two of them, surely he did, too.

I turned back to Tori and smelled the chamomile coming from the mug he held. So they used this tea to put poor Pitrini to sleep. "Not gonna drink it."

"It'll help. You should." Austere urged with a gentle smile.

"Might help if someone wouldn't molest her, as Tori said."

Tori chuckled before saying, "See, even the priest agrees with me."

"He agrees with everything."

"I do not!" Blari's chest expanded and that long beard started wriggling with his working mouth.

"He didn't agree with that."

"What's going on with you?"

"What?" Blari and Tori asked simultaneously.

Austere just took a moment to look innocent. "Why is it you three are acting all friendly and nice?" I looked between the three men. Austere was a master flirt, Tori able to avoid subjects and worded his answers so they weren't answers at all, and then Blari. Nice, gentle, wordy Blari. I rested my glare on him.

"Are we not usually nice and friendly with each other? Do you not like us anymore?" He slid his hand up closer to my hip as he talked, but his tryst wouldn't work.

Blari was already glancing at me and then away. "You are, but not usually together."

Tori moved out of my peripheral vision. I could sense his eyes on me.

That hand rose higher, "We are just concerned. You have been asleep for three days…"

I pinched the back of his hand; I didn't turn my gaze away from the priest. Blari was sweating.

"Fine! Spacya has a friend that lives a few miles back. We made a stop and he is currently on his way to Galanesse via his fastest horse. He breeds fast horses. Pretty. The fastest on the whole isthmus, he says. I don't know how true it is but-"

"What is he going to do once he gets to Galanesse?" I interrupted his rambling.

"Try to stop them from getting into the capital. Because once they get put in the Tower or dungeons, there will be no getting them out."

"What resources does he have? He can't stand against them alone if they overtook Taspe and my father."

"He is to contact Clara. She will help him. Discreetly. I hope."

Austere sighed, "I knew I should've made you leave or go with Spacya."

"Why are you hiding it?"

"Because we didn't want you to get your hopes up."

I closed my eyes and made sure my breathing was regular. Before I could say anything though, Austere started talking.

"See how it feels to be kept out or to not have a say in things that matter most to you?" Austere sat up and pulled me further down on the bed. He uncovered my legs to unlace my boots. "Some things you cannot do alone. Right now, you would still be in Emleton if we hadn't taken action. Just so you know, I wanted to go to Galanesse. They are the ones that knew you would want to go to Owlimount."

I preferred to go home. I needed to know what happened and that the rest were safe. Most of the people in Owlimount knew we had plenty of children, but the letters hadn't mentioned Moko or the others. If Taspe had been injured… whoever attacked was powerful.

"We need to find out who attacked and why. I want to see how everyone is and any details they might have." I ran a finger along the only scar I cared about. His heartbeat was strong, but a touch fast.

"We needed to head them off ourselves." Austere shot Tori and Blari a look before he pulled my boots off. He covered my legs back up after taking off my belt. "Now, you need to drink before I force it."

Surely he wasn't suggesting that he would hold my jaw open and pour it down me like I was an unruly child. I shook my head, "I don't want it. Or need it."

"Stere, maybe she should try sleeping naturally."

"I've slept long enough."

"Obviously not with the way you were too weak to walk."

"Ever thought I might need some food? It's been a while since I really ate anything, hasn't it?"

"She has a point."

Austere sighed, "I'll-"

"I'll go. I want to see how Spacya's fairing." Tori grinned before he whistled out the door after depositing the mug onto the desk.

"They'll be alright." Blari glanced down at my hands, "How is he?"

"It's strong, his heartbeat. Faster than normal, though."

"He's healing then," Austere said as he leaned back against the wall, lying over my legs again. "Welkan functions always work with more speed when they are in the processes of healing and making babies."

"Been meaning to ask you… scorned lover? Did you piss off a female warrior or leader?"

Austere's grin was slow in growing as his eyes rested half-lidded, "Both and then some."

"Fool."

"Can't help having a bit of fun." He lifted a shoulder, "They knew what they were tangling with when they romped with me."

Sam Wicker

"Did you know?"

"Of course."

I raised a brow, my eyes trailing to the hint of the tattoo on his neck that I could see under his thick hair.

He then cleared his throat, "Mostly, then."

Blari heaved a sigh, "Being part of this party means that you must act with a bit more decorum in the future. You must think of what your actions will reflect upon us."

"Yes, Dad. For your information, I have calmed down since becoming a prince."

Blari blinked at me, and I could almost hear his thoughts. I was having the same ones. Meeting him before would have scared me. I probably would have killed him, or tried, by now. Blari would have sworn off his priesthood.

"How are you still alive?"

"I'm willing to show you my exceptional skills in the bedroom if you would like a demonstration, Priest."

Blari shook his head, "I prefer women."

"A man is just as good."

"With that, I shall take my leave." The priest stood and looked down at me, "Good luck." He opened the door right as a woman was about to knock. She nearly rapped on his chest.

"Oh, sorry, sir. Someone ordered room service like a queen."

"Easy, Cookie. Behave."

"Shoulda known it was you Capt'n." She placed the tray over his lap and then her hands were on her broad hips, "Capt'n I know ye be linkin' 'em willin' but ya gotta let the gal rest. She came aboard 'alf dead already."

Blari's laugh echoed down the hall.

"I haven't!" He snapped his mouth shut and glared up at the cook. "You know good and well that I don't take advantage."

"Ye might not think ye are, but who can resist yer purdy face for long, eh?"

"Me. I can."

She snorted, "We'll see, lass. Eat up. Ye'll need it."

With that, she slammed the door, and I was left alone with him. Again. At least I wasn't naked. Why was he always underfoot these days?

He began opening the covered dishes and smiled, "You're in luck. She cooked something special for you."

The rich scent of cooked creamed potatoes wafted to me first, followed by a yeast and the savory smell of a soup. Fattening, soothing food that I hoped wouldn't go to waste. I reached for the soup.

Austere lifted it into his hands, "It's best like this." He sipped it straight from the bowl, then handed it gingerly to me.

It was earthen, and so warm to the touch that it nearly burned. The warmth spread over my fingers and hands as I took a deep sniff of the rich steam. Cookie cut the noodles into small bits and they floated in a thick, creamy broth with herbs and tiny bits of onions and fowl.

My stomach let out a small growl.

That had to be a good sign. Hopefully, it would hold it. I took a sip and moaned.

Austere chuckled. I refused to pay him any mind. I had every intention of drinking the soup down slowly, but before I knew it, I was wiping my mouth off on the back of my hand and putting the empty bowl back on the tray.

"I'm a horrible host. I should have brought you something to eat and drink as soon as I heard you were awake." He eyed my stomach as a little gurgle sounded, "Good?"

"I think so."

"Eat the potatoes a little slower. They're from last night, not fresh, but warmed."

I took the bowl from him and held it for a moment. "We were distracted by a ship, so you aren't a terrible host. Just need some polishing."

"Tell me how you truly feel." Austere smirked.

"I do my best." I glanced at the cup, forgotten on the desk, "What do you drug your little brother for?"

His face twisted, "That's not a pleasant way to put it, but it's true." He sighed and lifted a shoulder, "sometimes he acts out.

It's only been a month since his way of life and family… if you want to call them that, were destroyed. He doesn't sleep much during these sessions. So, we give him that. He sleeps through the night and is mostly himself when he wakes. The shakes and thoughts are calmer after a solid sleep."

"Are you calling his sadness over losing his family 'acting out'?"

"No. I'm not as selfish as that." Austere's brows drew low over his eyes, pain flashing in the red depths. "One doctor called them nightmares during the day. Sometimes he relives some things of his childhood, other times it's crazy things like winged things attacking him."

He ran a hand through his loose hair, pushing it back from his face and holding it where his shoulder meets his neck. "That kid's had a terrible life for most of it, probably just as much as that bastard king's subjects went through. Maybe worse. Because he feels guilt that his people were put through all that too. Like he could do anything to stop it. He barely talks about it. When he does, he has an episode soon after."

My heart went out to the poor boy, "Is that why he's with you? To get him away from something that triggers the episodes?"

Austere let his hand drop, his hair fell back around his face, "As a distraction, yes. I suppose. He was having a tough time at home. Cleaning and, well, he needed to get away I think."

I ate some potatoes slowly, "Maybe it will get better as time passes."

"I hope so." Austere sighed.

"Could you look at something else?"

"No."

"Anything else?"

"Not a chance."

"Why watch me eat?"

"Not watching you eat, per se, just watching your mouth."

"How is that… nevermind. Shouldn't you be running your ship?"

"Ships don't run."

I flicked mashed potatoes onto his face from my spoon. They splattered over his cheeks, lips and chin in little globs of white. A waste of food. Shame burned inside.

His lips twisted up into a smirk, "Now lick it off."

"What?"

"Lick. It. Off. You shouldn't waste food."

"You lick it off!"

"Darling, my tongue can do many things, but I cannot lick my cheeks. Besides, I can't see where it landed."

I thumbed some of the potatoes off his face. He stilled, barely breathing. I took another finger and scraped some more off, mostly off his chin.

He grabbed my wrist. His eyes on mine, he put my finger in, licking the potatoes off with his tongue. His mouth on my bare flesh sent something damp and wicked through me. His teeth scraped off the food on my thumb.

I wiped his saliva onto his face, rubbing it in.

"You are an odd one."

"Do I really have to tell you again?"

"Yes."

"Never. Never going to happen."

That grin he flashed me had the dimples out in force, "That's my girl. The more you say never, the closer I get to making it occur."

I rolled my eyes and ate some more potatoes.

Chapter 29

"You're concentrating too hard. Your smile is supposed to be relaxed. Easy on the eyes. Welcoming. You're looking like you're about to growl."

"I would like to growl at you."

"Only if you promise to bite me in lovely places too, darling."

The sound of flesh smacking bounced off the cabin walls as he blocked my hand with his. He pulled my fingertips to his lips and then kissed them. I jerked away.

"You're still reacting on instinct. You've got to pause it, and react with intent."

"Maybe it would be easier for me to practice with someone who has no intentions for me."

"Everyone you meet is going to have intentions for you. At least I make mine plainly known."

"Do you really, or are you distracting me with false ones to get something else out of me?"

"Oooh, there's my girl." Austere grinned, "What does your instinct tell you?"

I looked into those red eyes, and then at the dimples in his cheeks. "That if I let you, you would have your way with me, but not hurt me in ways that matter."

"Good way to word it, I suppose." He paused, before asking another question, "Now, what do people want from someone like you?"

"Knowledge to use against me to get what they want, to bind me somehow to control me, or to gain my trust to get what they want."

"Which is the easiest to gain?"

"Knowledge."

"Therefore?"

"I have to not give any more of myself to them than I already have."

"What do we do with the things they already know about you?"

"Empower it so they cannot use it, make it not seem useful at all or that it's too much work to use."

"Good. It helps to keep those in mind so you can keep acting properly in situations that call for it." He canted his head to the side, "Have you ever witnessed a Welkan drama act?"

"Yes, they're gorgeous."

"Did you notice once they pass the feather over their faces, their actions and countenance change?"

"Yes, that's one of the key points of their dramas to show the power of emotion or action without words."

"Right. Think you can do that?"

"I…" *Could I?* In court or social settings, could I switch from an action or emotion to another with a mere drop of a feather? "Easier said than done, but it makes more sense to me than trying to read through the same layers of other people."

"Just to keep them uncertain and second guessing their understanding of you will help you keep yourself and your family protected. I hope. I can't promise it will always work, but it's better than nothing." He toyed with my fingers, "This way you don't have to think too much and that instinctual reaction time of yours can still be useful. Somewhat. Just try to downplay a lot of your facial expressions and jerks."

He stood, "Now dance with me."

I snorted, staring at his outstretched hand. I slept for almost nine hours and was awake for two. Now he wanted me to dance?

"Come on. You need to get your muscles working again and I'm bored. Besides, you need a few dance lessons so you can be the one making your partners breathless."

"Can't we just walk around the deck?" I pushed myself up off the bed. My legs weren't wet noodles today, but now they felt stiff and brittle.

"After a dance or two."

"How far out-"

"A half hour closer since the last time you asked." He pulled me into his arms.

"There's no music."

The hum started and stayed deep in his throat and chest. It wasn't the most beautiful sound I had ever heard, but it was a close fifth or sixth. "Better?" He asked in time with his humming.

"I think so."

"Gee, don't hurt my feelings or anything."

"Taspe sounds better when he hums."

"He probably sounds better doing a lot of things," Austere muttered.

"Are you jealous?"

"Why shouldn't I be? He's a Welkan male, a leader of a powerful Legacy and he's grown up with you at his side. Not to mention his voice is apparently amazing, and he has a body everyone at court talks about and drools over." He sighed, "Keep more weight on the balls of your feet. Turn them inward."

I did as I was told, "His voice is unusual. His mother thinks it was because she held him for so long."

"Oh? How long did she keep him in her womb?"

"Over seventy years."

"Gods." Austere shook his head. He moved my hands and elbows, "Loosen your hips too. Make me drool."

"I don't want to see you drool."

"Just imagine I'm Taspe or someone you want and you're trying to get me hot and bothered."

"I don't want to strip either." He stopped, and I ran into him.

He groaned, running a hand through his hair. "We have a lot of work to do."

"Gee, don't hurt my feelings or anything."

"Funny." He pulled me back into a dance, "You know that it's just not skin that turns heads right?"

"It's the most effective."

"Can't really argue with that. You and Taspe… you've been intimate, yes?"

"Once, yes."

"Study what he does to make you think he's willing."

I pictured Taspe, that easy grin. He reached for me that day, or night, and there was a heat in his eyes. It warmed me.

"Try one of his moves or looks. More than one, even."

I swallowed, rolled my shoulders and tried Taspe's easy grin. I then imagined us together like that one time.

"That works."

"What?"

Austere pushed me toward the mirror, "Do it again and see for yourself."

I looked absolutely ridiculous. "That's not going to do anything for anyone."

"That's a lie."

"Why would I do this again?"

"It's called flirting, and it gets you what you need. Do you want a pretty necklace? Find an unattached, gullible thing with money, flirt, oooh and aah over that necklace and then you will find it around your neck without spending a single bit for it."

"That's called a gift and I don't have time to get to know someone well enough for them to spend money on me."

Austere's hand smacked against his forehead before it slid down his face with a heavy sigh deflating his body, "I'm not giving up, but you have to be the oddest person I know."

"I'll take that as a compliment."

"It wasn't meant to be one, but by all means, take it as you will."

I turned away from the mirror and watched him for a moment. "I learn best by doing and watching."

Austere's arms crossed over his chest and he rocked on his heels, "You do realize what that means, correct?"

Unfortunately. "Yes."

"No, Nadachia. You're giving me permission to show you how to flirt and manipulate those we come in contact with next."

"Yes…" A little curl of warmth started in my belly.

"Your friends and family."

That curl sank, "Just don't do anything that will make me skin you in your sleep, Austere."

He grinned.

The ramp was barely in place before I was down it and taking slim, doe-eyed Moko into my arms. "Are you hurt? Are you well?"

"I'm fine. I'm so glad you're home."

I pulled back, holding her at arm's length. She had grown. Her hair was longer too. Tears stung and I saw the same in hers. I had been gone too long.

She wiped at her eyes with the heels of her hands before hugging me again with a giggle, "I have missed you, Chi."

"I've missed you too."

I heard footsteps pounding rapidly along the dock. My name was being called. Moko stepped to the side, and they wrapped me up.

I tried my best to hug all of them at once.

"Gods, are they all her family?" Tori's voice came from behind and slightly above.

I looked past my little group to see the shore filled with familiar faces. My cheeks grew wet.

"I told you to stay behind the planks of the deck." Moko's tone sent the little ones cringing.

"It's alright." I kissed each of them on the tops of their heads. Vey was taller than me now. His scales flashed blue and green and his eyes matched. Aber, Biobi and Tokli were all the same height now, and wide eyed with grins to match. Little Greta, willowy slender and with a tight grip on my arm, was nearly up to my shoulder.

"Let's get to the shore so the rest of them can get off the ship." Moko ushered the kids back. "Let the rest of the town have their hugs, too. We can't be selfish."

Even as she spoke those words, she and Greta stayed glued to my sides. I kept waiting to hear Father's gentle chuckle and see Detri's flashy smirk and be calmed by CiaCia's sweet demeanor. My heart burned and cracked with their absence as it swelled and warmed with being with the rest of my family.

Doc's meaty armed hug made up for not having Father there. "There's our girl. Haven't they been feedin' ya?" He squeezed my arms before letting me go.

"They have, don't worry." I turned, hugging a few others. Once done, I asked Moko, who was still somehow right at my elbow, "Where's Taspe?"

Moko shook her head, "Healing."

A quiet settled over the town and my family. They were all looking between me and my companions who were now on the dock.

"Might oughta give a little speech, gal." Doc murmured, patting me on the shoulder.

I stepped back up on the dock. It made me as tall as the tallest members of the town who came to greet us, at least. "Thank you for greeting me. Us. I really appreciate seeing all of you here, it brings me such comfort and happiness. It makes this seem as if we are meeting again under better circumstances. The attack on my family, our town, our people… I don't know what to say. I know that you have probably pulled together to help my family out a lot. Thank you. Owlimount has always been a large family. I don't know what we would do without your love and support all these years." I paused before adding, "I want to introduce you to my companions, and I hope they too will become like family."

I turned going to each of my companions, "Blari, you know, of course, he has some stories to tell and I'm sure will not hesitate in doing so." He and the crowd chuckled before I went on. "This is Spacya of Dragotown, the greatest huntress I know and one who has become a great friend, if not sister, to me. This is Tori, Prince Tori, the bravest and most selfless man I know other than my own Father. Last, but not least, in more ways than one, is Prince Austere. He's the newest addition, but has already proven himself invaluable in just one quest."

My town and family clapped for them, and then for Pitrini and the rest of the crew as I and Austere introduced them. Doc took care of the shipmates by taking them into town for food, company, and rest. Pitrini joined us as we began the stroll back to my home. We had to dock the ship in town, instead of at the dock on my lands because of how narrow the Gala was there. The large ship would have blocked all traffic.

"More introductions. Spacya, Blari, Tori, Austere, and Pitrini, this is my sister Moko with the pretty white hair, my brother Vey with his new shiny scales," I grinned as he blushed, "and dirt king Aber who is surprisingly clean today, Biobi with that spikey black hair and always smells of wildflowers," I grinned again as Tori made a show of smelling him. "This is Gretta, the queen of fixing broken things and building useful machines, and my handsome nephew Tokli, who learns everything so quickly he's like a sponge soaking it all up." I paused, looking at Moko's pockets, then Gretta's, "Where is Kentrim? I didn't see Edi, Jahni or Joni either. Where are they?"

My little family fell silent. The young ones wouldn't look at me. Moko shared a look with Vey.

"Edi would have been here, but he left with a few warriors, including Jahni, after Father, CiaCia and Detri."

Moko's mouth worked for a moment before words started spilling from her lips, "Joni was with the... he-he helped them."

I stopped, "He helped Edi and Jahni?"

"No, he helped the attackers."

Moko's fingers tangled in on themselves. Vey wrapped an arm around me, pressing his smooth scales at his forehead against my temple. Here he was comforting me when I should comfort him.

"How? Why?"

"He wanted all of us to go with them. They sent him in first. Talking to us about going to visit you in Galanesse." Moko started.

"When we wouldn't, he went back outside. Father, he picked up on something, or saw them. He tried to get us to run." Vey filled in a little more.

"Gretta and I got the little ones and ran. Taspe and two others were in the new field. There were some yells and screaming." Moko continued, going so pale I thought she would fall to the road.

"Father and Detri killed three of them." Vey said, watching the smaller children as they took it upon themself to walk ahead. "I ki-killed one. Taspe got Joni good when he ran back after getting Moko and the others to safety. He killed another one too, before they jumped him and…"

"There were eight strangers and Joni." Moko broke in before Vey said anything else.

"Impressive." Austere murmured, "If it had been any other family the damage would have been much worse."

Joni's actions were unfathomable. Why had he become the enemy? What made him hate my family so?

Austere's words ran through my mind. And again as I imagined the worst.

Soon enough, we were across the line that marked my father's property. A light shone in one window, peaking above the hill in the road. I climbed, following the children, Vey beside me as the others talked quietly. Austere, Spacya and Blari were asking the questions I could not think of at the moment. Moko, Vey and Greta readily giving answers and filling in each others' information. A cohesive unit.

At the top of the hill, I stopped. The house waited for me. It hulked behind the fence and gate, watching over the gardens and other fences all the way to the river. It seemed so much smaller than what I remember. Still, the comfort of being home spread over my heart and through my mind and body like a warm blanket wrapping around me on a chilly day. The hot tear slid down my cheek before I knew it had even formed.

There, on the gatepost, the lantern was lit, lighting my way home.

I swiped at my eyes, "Next time, everyone will be well, and here."

Austere stood beside me and took a long look at home. He smiled, "Looks like you." He started down toward the house, opening the gate and, with a grand wave of his hand and a bow, held it open for us.

Spacya nodded, "I agree with the pirate for once."

Greta gasped, "Pirate?"

Tori pointed at Austere when Greta's wide eyes flew between all the strangers among us. She shook her head, "He doesn't look like a pirate."

"Don't tell him that," I muttered.

"He'd probably cry for a week." Blari added, patting me on the shoulder. "Go on. Go home."

I walked through the gate and took a deep breath in. Home. The Gala flowing nearby lending a few musical gurgles and the ever present water odor on the light breeze that rustled the leaves of the trees surrounding our property and dotting the fields. The big old willow leaned over from the river, hid a bench and table where Taspe and I had many long talks. Rich land, fertile, and planted already in neat rows jutted from two sides of the house. A small fence penned in a couple of cows, fresh faces, but they were the ones staring lazily at me as if I was the stranger.

The door creaked open. My heart rose in my throat, knowing I should see Father filling the frame. Grandmother stood there instead, frail and squat. A bundle of feathers in one hand while she held a long piece of wood with nails stuck in one end in the other. She turned slightly, putting the piece of wood down when she saw us.

I ran to her, nearly tripping over my own feet. I took her in my arms. She shook in them. So thin I could wrap my arms twice about her if I tried.

"Thank the gods, Nadachia. You're alive. Taspe thought you had died. Died…died twice…he told me…"

"I'm here, Grandma."

"I didn't say anything to anyone else. I couldn't bring myself to. I just hoped it wasn't true. I prayed so hard."

"I'm sorry, Grandma."

She jerked back, wiping her face off on her sleeve as she straightened her back, "Come in, come in! All of you!" She waved the children in and toward the back of the kitchen. "Give them some space, they are guests you know."

My heart broke at not being hugged anymore by Grandma, but it also warmed, seeing her run the house. I looked around, expecting to see evidence of a fight. As it stood, the table had a new leg, there were three new chairs, the mantle had been replaced, and there were fewer knick-knacks upon it. A dark spot under the table peaked out from under the rug there.

I let the others in behind me as I set my pack down in its usual spot. Habit had me reaching for the ties of my covers, but they weren't there. They were already on the hook. I sat and took my boots off, placing them on my usual drying stool. Austere and Spacya readily sat down beside me to do the same.

"Oh, you don't have to…"

"Lady Silverequis, it is truly a pleasure to be allowed into your home. We do not mean disrespect, but if you would treat us as one of your family, it would be a great honor to us all."

"Here, here." Austere grinned up at Tori.

"I-you-but you are all lords and princes and ladies…" Grandma wrung her hands together. The feather bundle in her arm fluffed, and a bright black eye peaked out before disappearing back into the feathers again.

As soon as Austere had his boots slid off and by the door he moved and pulled out a chair for Grandmother, "Don't fret. We mean it. We all think of each other as family and wish to do the same for you. All of you. Please sit and rest. You have been through so much already."

Moko stirred then, her mouth clicking shut. She began by starting some tea. Vey jumped into action next, checking the pot and the oven to make sure nothing was burning. Greta pulled out silverware and plates for everyone, handing them off to the shorter Aber and Tokli and then pulled out bowls for Biobi to set.

I knelt before my grandmother and talked soothingly to the bundle of feathers. Kentrim, upon hearing my voice, peaked out again. His feathers smoothed, and a grin showed me his new, blunt white teeth. Feathers covered his fingers on the top, but his palms were smooth when they brushed over my cheeks as he cooed at me.

"Didn't think you would grow to be so big, little Kentrim."

He cooed again.

"He grows an inch every day." Grandmother huffed, running her gnarled fingers over Kentrim's feathered back.

"Thank you for coming down and staying with them."

She scoffed, "They are my family. What else would I do? Leave them to fend for themselves?!"

I grinned as Grandma muttered. I kissed her cheek, and she stilled her grumblings. She looked to our guests, "Where are you all going to stay?"

"We can stay at the Church."

A soft knock sounded at the door before it opened. Taspe's cousin, Lave, entered. "I couldn't help hearing the last bit. You are all requested to stay in the village. Every luxury has been prepared for you there."

His grin was as easy as Taspe's, but not as warm. He moved and hugged me before I stood to greet him properly. "Hello, Ma." He grinned at Grandmother and kissed her cheek. To my shock, her pale cheeks turned a little pink.

"You must eat first, please." Moko said as she motioned to the table.

Lave declined the meal and left to go tell his people we were taking them up on their offer and to wait for us. There was an awkward moment as I noticed CiaCia's chair taken by Spacya, Detri's by Blari, and mine by Tori. The head of the table, Father's, was left open. For me. I swallowed and sat in it. Grandmother reached over and patted my knee.

Vey served us all soup while Moko poured some of Grandmother's famous berry juice for everyone. I took a sip, letting the sweet beat out the tang before swallowing.

"Are all of you getting along together?" I eyed each of my siblings. Only Gretta and Biobi squirmed in their chairs. That was better than I expected. "Good."

"How…how are you?"

I looked into Moko's eyes, and tried a smile.

"She does well, Moko," Blari started. "A bit stubborn."

"Doesn't ask or like help at all." Austere added around his cup of juice.

Grandmother chuckled, "That's my girl."

I stared at her for a long moment. I picked out her traits she had given to Father, and then me.

"My baby girl will get my son and her siblings back." Grandmother smiled, her lips trembling slightly.

"We will be there." Tori nodded.

"Her cost is our cost. Cause is ours too. So is her family as ours." Spacya's voice broke on the last.

We talked for a little while, just as long as the meal lasted. There was a fuss over who would do the dishes between Tori, Blari and Grandmother. It was Tokli and Gretta's turn, but the two weren't in any mood to argue their way into chores when someone else was willing. In the end, Tori and Blari won out.

More suds and water ended up on the floor than in the sink.

"Nadachia, before you go, would you start up your Father's pipe?" Grandmother looked over to me, "The smell, I miss it."

I stood and took his pipe and pouch from the mantel. After knocking the old out on the hearth, I tucked in a bit of new weed from the pouch. I took a small stick from the kindling in the fire, made sure the end was lit, and then held it to the bowl until the weed began to smolder then grow to the correct smoking heat. I breathed in the scent with Grandmother and the kids, and we all smiled.

Perhaps it was the months of not having any, but the smoke tickled my throat and lungs more than it used to. We settled in. My heart swelled larger and warmer than it had in ages. I smoked the pipe some more, the tickle doubling, but I didn't stop. Not until the weed burned out.

I placed them back on the mantle, "I'll be back in the morning." I told Grandmother before giving her a hug. I hugged and kissed each of my siblings.

"I'll go with you to bring the boat back." Vey said, pulling on a pair of sandals that had too many knots in them.

"Take some money and buy you some new sandals, Vey." I poked him in the ribs once we were outside.

He frowned, rubbing his side and looking down at his wriggling toes, "But these just got comfortable."

I rolled my eyes.

Sam Wicker

"Can we take a moment to talk about how smoking is bad for you?" Blari shot a narrowed look at me.

"Nope."

"It smelled sweeter than what I'm accustomed to. What's the weed?"

"It's rabbit tobacco, grows all over the banks and hills to the mountains."

"Might have to get my father some. He likes the pipe every other day or so." Austere looked out toward the riverbank.

Blari sputtered, "No. No. No. Bad for you!"

Spacya clapped a hand over the priest's shoulder, "So's bein' a Hero, but yer not tellin' her to stop that, are ya?"

Blari's mouth hung open in an 'o' before he snapped it shut with a short blast of a breath through his pinched nostrils.

"This path is well worn." Tori mused.

"Aye, well worn indeed." Austere added.

"Don't." I shot Vey a look when he opened his mouth. His eyes went wide a little before he shrugged.

"Cute little boat too. Wonder if all of us can fit in there." Tori stopped, rubbing the stubble along his jaw.

"Sure, she can sit in someone's lap like she used to do with Taspe all the time."

I smacked Vey's shoulder, "You can swim across for the boat."

"She can sit in my lap." Austere waggled his eyebrows at me before climbing into the boat. He sat down on the narrow bench at the bow and patted his knees.

"Spacya, be a friend and sit in his lap. He looks lonely."

Spacya's mouth twisted into a grin, "Be glad to."

Austere's grin turned wide, "Bout time you grew to love my charms."

"Keep yer pants on, nobody wants ya that way here." Spacya sat beside Austere. The two of them so large they both had to lean a bit out of the boat to fit their shoulders side by side.

Vey climbed into the middle with Tori and took up the long pole we used to guide the boat across. I got in beside Blari and took up a pole to help my brother.

385

I looked down at Blari as we started, Vey was strong enough to do this on his own now. "Thank you for worrying about me."

He huffed, his shoulders rising to his ears before they dropped again. "It's not that it's just..." he sighed, "Yes, yes I must worry."

I smiled, helping Vey, but he truly had command of the little boat.

"You look better. Not as tense. Even with all this going on."

"Must be because I'm home. I still feel tired and like I'm about to snap into a thousand shards."

He smiled up at me, "They will be diamond pieces, for you have been forged and reforged stronger yet."

"You might need to give some lessons to Austere, that was a good line."

"I heard that." Austere muttered.

"I should become a pirate priest."

"Savin' souls and sailin' seas." Spacya spoke with a chuckle.

"Singing of Heroes and besting storms," Tori added.

"Yes! Yes, a pirate priest I shall be then."

Austere groaned.

We landed on the bank and hauled ourselves and our gear out. I grinned at Vey, giving him a tight hug, "Be careful."

"Always." He waved me off. He moved to the center of the craft and used both long sticks to 'walk' it back across to our dock.

My heart left with him. I needed to see Taspe.

His heartbeat had quickened again. Soon, I thought as I ran a fingertip over the scar. My head jerked up as I heard a footfall behind me.

"Easy. I came to escort you, Chi." Lave held his hands up with another grin. "As I must each time you arrive these days."

My brow quirked up, "No need really."

"I see that." He sized up my companions and before I could say anything, he shook his head, "No need for introductions. I know all of you by name."

"How?"

He just smiled before saying, "Follow me."

He led us into the village. A path I knew well, but Welkans thought humans forgetful, perhaps. He stopped and motioned to the medical house, "Taspe is in there, but please, put your things away first."

Tori grabbed my pack off my shoulder, "Go."

I nodded and pushed through the flaps. I had to blink twice to get my eyes to adjust from the light of dusk outside to the brightness inside. Welkan sun globes and candles filled the space.

Gurgled breathing sounds caught my attention, and I followed them to him. I pulled the curtain back that separated his treatment area from the others. My feet grew to the ground and my heart sank into my belly.

Crackles laced each breath in. Each out laden with gurgles. He lay on his stomach with a thick sheet draped over his midsection. His hair was wet. I wasn't sure if it was because they had just washed it, or if it was from sweat. His skin was glistening in the bright lights, too.

"I can feel you staring at me, Chi,"

His voice was only as loud as the gurgles that accompanied it. He patted the bed above his head. "I won't lie, but I am not as bad as the fear in you thinks I am."

I let the curtain drop as I circled around the bed to where I caught his gaze. I then lay down with him, lifting his arm to drape it over me so I wouldn't cast a shadow over him. He needed the light to heal.

Herbals, sweat and the faint odor of dried mucous overpowered his usual musk. I kissed his forehead, and the chill that met my lips spiked my worry higher.

"Breathe with me." His hand splayed over my back, "I will be fine in a few days' time."

"I should have never asked such a favor from you."

"Don't."

"I need to keep all of you safe."

"Chi..."

"You got hurt because of me."

"I got hurt," he took a shallow breath in, "Because people attacked me," another breath, "Not because of you."

I shook my head, but said no more. He was already working so hard to just breathe. He didn't need me adding to it by making him talk. It was a conversation that would never have an end.

"You died."

I nodded.

"Twice. Explain."

I told him the short version of both instances. I then asked, "What did they poison you with?"

His lips twisted, "We call it nowhanv ama." He pulled a cloth over his mouth as his body heaved up more mucus.

"Domination water?" That stuff hadn't been used since the slave times. They would automatically kill anyone in possession of it, no questions asked.

I lifted the sheet to look at his wounds. The healers covered them in the herbs whose pungent odor filled the building, but I still saw the dark stuff oozing out of the lines in his flesh to the herbs. Arrows. They hadn't wanted him getting close enough without being weakened by the poison.

"Yes, good." He breathed in a few more times, each breath becoming noisier than the last. "Joni attacked."

"I know."

"No." He coughed some more into the rag. "Willingly."

I shook my head, dropping the sheet back into place. His free hand slid out from under his temple to cup my cheek, "Jahni said he found traces of the people that attacked at Joni's house. They were there for three days."

It was planned. Joni had never been a strategist. Like a bull, he just forged ahead with whatever came to mind first.

"What can I get you to help?"

His bright eyes blinked at me a few times, his peeling lips pulling back slightly, "You're here."

I sighed, pressing my forehead against his, "I'm here."

"All I need."

Sam Wicker

Something in me swirled and filled every crevice that was close to his body. It cooled and shifted, trying to get to him. I knew it had to be Sterla. How dare I forget.

I stared at his chest. Each time he crackled and bubbled within his four lungs, I wanted to reach in and scrape them clean. I could feel the poison covering each little branch in them. I knew it burned him.

With each breath in, the branching things in his lungs strained and stretched and some spilled blue-black blood into the growing pool settled in his lungs.

How did I know that?

Blood is power. Blood is life. Sterla.

Her power within me stirred as I pressed him back to his side. My hands slid to the cooling flesh of his chest. I concentrated, picturing what I wanted to do as Eisle had taught me in one of the few lessons we got in before our deaths.

"What are you doing?"

"I think I can help."

"How?"

I pressed my forehead to his lips. One, I could feel his breath, two, he would have to stay quiet. *Could I do this?* I had to do this.

I imagined the pools separating, creating the tiniest of droplets that fit through the formation of his lungs, muscles, and skin to come outside. I pictured them moving, coming toward my hands and the bed. Fantasizing raining the tiny droplets of poison out of him, harmless once they were in my control, not to do any further damage.

I had to keep it flowing. Keep the poison drawing out of him. If I stopped, the poison would stop and be in a new place to do that damage there.

A coughing fit overtook him. His whole body shook the both of us, and in my concentrative state it shook the world. He turned his face to the bed to cough there. My heart ached for him.

Slowly, the blue-black of the poison and damaged blood filled the bed between us. My hands burned and itched where it touched them. I didn't dare stop. Not until I knew I had it all out of him. I knew his poisoned lungs would make more, but with the thick coating and pool of it gone, he should be able to cough what it made new out.

Especially if it would be sunny tomorrow.

"Nadachia?"

That ancient voice washed over me and nearly broke my concentration. The old healer's hands covered mine, but didn't pull them away, "Oh my." She said with a gasp.

"Almost there."

Taspe nodded. His eyes were closed. The sweat poured steadily. His breaths grew deeper as the gurgling lessened. It was working.

Still, fear of failure pushed me to keep going. I gritted my teeth, concentrating solely on drawing it all out. What I drew, I focused on it not harming any other portion of him. It needed to be encased in this magic as it flowed out of him.

Her hands disappeared, and the cool night air hit my back. "There, dear, draw in the night. Replenish yourself and your work."

It reached for me like fingers searching in the darkness. Candles and sun globes were being snuffed out until we were in gray shadows. The dark of night curled around, then pooled into me to join the magic.

The night in me lapped at the poison like a beast with water, it gained something from it. My hands, his skin, and even the bed between us grew dryer as the night eased my exhaustion and aided me in taking it out of him.

Sterla was in that darkness, siphoning and sponging, honing her magic within me so I, a mere human, wielded it.

The darkness guided me to pull the poison from the tree branches of his lungs and the sacks at the end of them. It wanted it all. Demanded it all. With it, I found the sources, the wounds at his lower ribs and the one on his hip. There I drew out more of the poison, feeding it to the night.

But it wasn't me. It was Sterla. Somehow, she taught me, worked her power in me as if she were her own being. I shared my body with her.

His breathing deepened, grew soundless. Exhaustion beat into me like I had worked on him all night. The night licked the last of the poison from my hands. It swam about in me, curling in little corners here and there, stretching, then retreating, pawing at the powers in me until it finally left.

"Done?" the old healer asked.

I nodded.

She closed the night out and relit a few of the candles. It was low enough to where we could find sleep if we needed to. I looked down at my hands. They were red from pressing against his flesh for so long, but that was all. I studied his chest and saw my fading handprints there.

Taspe rolled to his back. After I got up off the bed, the healer and I stripped the bed of the sheet under him. The healers here layered sheets. While the top got soiled, some underneath would be fine for a while.

The healer then checked his breathing by simply placing her ear against his chest. "You're clear. Tomorrow we will put you out into the sun. It shall be clear." She then pulled the sheet over him away and the bandages. After she wiped away the herbal pastes, I saw nearly healed wounds.

"Hm. Hm." The old lady nodded. She then turned to me, "Hands."

"I'm fine."

"Hands girl or I'll cut them off and study them that way."

I held them out to her, palms up. She studied them, muttering something about a salve, before she dropped them and returned to the main room. I sat beside Taspe. He draped an arm over my lap.

"Sterla?"

"Yeah, she did it. She pulled and fed the night."

"Careful, Chi, allowing free flowing power like that can eat your insides. Control is key." I must have made a face, because he continued. His voice was weak, nearly a whisper, but he talked without gasping for breath as much. "A watering can allows things to flow through it. Eventually they wear out, and some things put into it can damage it more than others. We must make the vessel a specific way to handle certain materials. Stygra power in a human… I am not sure…" His voice faltered, and he pressed his lips into a line.

"I will be careful." I lay beside him.

His arm came up around me, before it jerked back, "Gods, do you sleep armed now?"

I watched his skin turn blue just below his elbow in an agitated welt. A giggle slipped. He had been at death's door and was now whimpering about a minor scratch. I sat up and pulled my belt off, draping it over a chair at our bedside. "Better?" I asked as I lay back down with him.

He wrapped around me, "Yes." Before long, his breathing was deep and steady.

I was home. It was the same. I was the strange one. What had I just done?

Chapter 30

Two days and nights was such a short time. I watched my family and Taspe disappear around the bend in the river. I wanted to jump over the ship's wall, it felt like a cage, and return to them. Father needed me. CiaCia and Detri too.

Owlimount faded away. The Gala was swift. Swifter than I wanted it to be.

In just two more days, the spire of the Tower rose above the treeline along with the sharp edges of the castle and church towers. They stopped the ship before it entered the rapids that led to the ocean. The machines along those waters had a mechanism that shot across the water to slow it and fill one section of the rapids up at a time so the boats safely reached the ocean, drew my attention for a while. If I were to be honest with myself, it scared me to find out what happened to my family.

A deep breath of the forever tainted salty air and I moved down the ramp, my pack on my back, and my daggers ready at my waist and legs.

"You know yer not goin' alone this time, right?"

Just another thing for me to worry about. I wasn't sure if the power of tying lives stretched to tying humans together or if there had to be a Stygra involved. I wasn't too keen on finding out.

"Should we just go straight there?"

I looked at Tori, then at the others. "What do the rest of you think?"

"Might be good to see what others have seen. Where they took your family, and who has them. Plus, grab Joni and figure out what in Gods' realm made him so stupid!" Blari snapped.

I wasn't sure who was going to beat Joni to a pulp first, me or Blari at this point.

"I agree with Blari." Austere added.

Spacya nodded, "Same."

Tori looked at me and lifted a shoulder, "Don't sneak off, deal?"

Did I sneak off that often? "Yes, I know. Not going in alone." I paused, "We should always have a partner around us, or three of us together at all times."

"I agree with that too." Blari nodded, "Spacya and you stick together."

"Me too." Austere smirked.

I sighed as Spacya said, "Useless as tits on a bullduck."

We all got a chuckle from that, even the pirate prince.

"Fine. Austere, Spacya and I all in my rooms. Blari, you and Tori in your room." We all nodded in agreement. "No running off alone for any of us, no matter what."

"Baths are going to be interesting."

"There're these things called screens, pirate." Spacya spat.

Austere frowned, "Ruin all the fun, love."

"My work is done." Spacya said with a smirk.

Toward the town, I noticed crowds had already gathered around the port. People were standing on the limited beach and along the road that curled through the cliffs. Cheers were belting down upon us from above.

"So much for things being normal when we return."

"I guess someone's been spying on us."

"Nadachia!"

My neck cracked as I turned my head to find the carrier of the voice. I had heard it most of my life. The beach, to the right side of the pier. My feet were carrying me down the wooden slats before I caught sight of him.

There. With a hand raised high and that goofy grin on his face. The one that used to be my best friend. The man that I thought I would have to settle with for the rest of my existence. My eyes flowed around him. Hope died in my chest when no other familiar faces appeared.

No, but he was being followed closely by two Stygra in long black dresses.

"Nadachia!" He called again.

Austere caught up to me, his boots thudding deeper on the wood beneath us. "Easy. Don't cause a scene. We need to use him."

"Right." My vision was clouded with red. I dug my fingers into the straps of my pack. He was now at the end of the pier. The two Stygra flanking him.

A grin. I fought one to my mouth. Trying to pretend. Trying to play the game already.

His smile faltered. But I wrapped my arms around his neck, arching my body up to reach him. My knee went into his groin, and I just pressed it there. "We have to talk. Lose your babysitters."

My grin relaxed as I saw my threat upon his pale face.

"The Matron wishes to see you immediately." One of the Stygra flanking Joni stated once I had pulled away from my former friend.

I nodded, "Of course she does. Are we not going to parade ourselves through town like we normally do?"

"Yes, but after you see her."

My eyes narrowed.

"It's a surprise! One that you will love!" Joni grinned through the paleness of his face.

He had no idea. None. I glanced at my friends along the pier. The sailors working behind them. I turned back, hefting my pack higher on my shoulder, "Looks like we have an audience with the Matron, Companions."

"Just you."

"Afraid that won't work." Austere crooned, "they cursed me to stay by her side."

The Stygra that had spoken first began wringing her hands against her black dress, "That just won't do. A curse? Really?"

"That's right. Welkans just dislike me." He tilted his head, the tattoo peeking out from beneath his hair and over his shirt collar with the movement. "So we all go, or we don't go at all. Your choice."

"Very well." She motioned for us to follow.

Joni and the other Stygra fell in behind our group. I supposed he was too afraid that I would rip his throat out if he were near me. Or too confused why I had threatened his manhood with pain he wouldn't be able to bear.

It was probably the latter of the two. May the gods curse him with more than a pea-sized brain in their realm. Maybe Aul would take him and throw him into a rock enclosure to melt stone for the rest of his life.

We made our way up the winding path through the cliff face. It was slow going, even for the most fit of us it was a bit of a strain. No wonder the horses that carried the cargo were huge. Not to mention the towering fixtures along the cliffs that pulled up crates and flats of goods so the people and horses wouldn't have to break their backs too much. Galanesse was a proper city, with many technologies that aided them in taking care of their great number of people in one little area. Not little, by no means, but people were packed in smaller houses all over the city. All so a handful of people could take up most of the room in sprawling houses with rooms they never entered or used. It was always one extreme or the other in Galanesse.

Some found comfort. Others tortured. Only a few living their dreams.

We entered through a back gate. The thick walls of the Tower garden, with its enormous fountains filled with mosses, lilies and other water-based plants. It was more like an enclosed Swamp. The doors swung open once we reached the bottom step.

Joni stepped up to my side, "I can't wait til you see."

My brow twitched, then it jumped with each pulse.

A hand came down on my shoulder and squeezed. I looked at the ink-stained fingers and nodded. They were with me. I was not alone.

"Wipe that stupid grin off yer face boy, before I do it for ya." Spacya growled.

Joni stepped back, that golden face of his going pale again. He stared at the woman, the stranger, who dare threaten him. Then he looked at me. Was I supposed to do something?

I smirked and walked into the Tower after the Stygra. I could barely hear the echoes of my footfalls over my rapid heart. Was I going to see them well, unharmed? Or was I going to see them drained of life? Something in between?

"Breathe." Austere murmured at my side. "Breathe in with me." He took a deep, noisy breath in, "And breathe out." His breath came out in a loud moan.

"Gods, stop that noise." Blari whimpered.

Austere chuckled, and it echoed off the dark walls of the hall we entered.

"I see now why Welkans do not adore you, Prince Austere. Perhaps you should know when you are in a sacred place and act like it."

The Stygra held her head a little higher as she spoke. Prideful. I glanced at the other, still wringing her hands. She wasn't as sure as her companion.

They led us to an all too familiar room. Dread curled and bubbled in my stomach. This could not be good.

My heart thundered as they pulled the doors open.

I looked in. A gasp parting my lips. Red splatter, pale skin, black droplets, candles flickering and the harsh voice of The Matron bidding us to enter.

No, not us, just me.

Austere stepped in before me, taking my hand and dragging me along. "As I explained to your friends here, we come too. Cursed to stay by her side, you see?"

The Matron huffed, "Can you not do any better than that? Asking for such a thing to be put upon you so that you can protect her? Pathetic. All of you, pathetic."

I rushed over to Father.

He kneeled at the desk, one hand on the edge, his head resting against the dark side of the thick wood. He grunted as I knelt beside him. His shirt collar appeared to be splattered with red. When he turned, I saw dried blood over his upper lip and some remnants on his chin. He was so pale. So cold to my touch.

"Nadachia." He breathed, his hand dropping from the edge of the desk to the top of my head. "My baby girl."

"Father, what happened? Where are you hurt?"

He shook his head, "I'm not terrible hurt. Joni brought us here." His eyes narrowed slightly as he stared into my eyes, "He said you wished to see us."

"I did. I do. But not like this. I wanted to see you at home." Never here.

"I see." He nodded slowly, his gaze flicking to the desk, then back to me. "Help an old man stand."

He wasn't tied.

"Chi?" CiaCia's soft voice behind Father reached me before I saw her peak out from the corner of the desk.

My lips trembled, "CiaCia." I breathed her name as I helped Father stand.

"See! Part of the happy family reunion!" Joni cried.

I wanted someone to punch him as badly as I needed air. "Where's Detri?"

"I'm here." His voice was not his. It was soft, sounded like something caught in his throat. Or he had been coughing for hours. I glanced around, finding him in a lone chair in front of the Matron's desk right beside me.

He slumped in it. Like clothes thrown into a plush chair. He looked up at me. Pale as well. More blood splatter on him than Father.

"Are you alright?"

"Be better when I'm allowed to kick some ass."

"Language!" The Matron barked out. Her lips pulled back to the right of her face, her fangs showing in the flickering candlelight.

"Let them go." I shot back at her, my fists finding the edge of the desk. My knuckles cracked on that dark wood.

"They are as free to go as you are."

My eyes narrowed on her, "Meaning?"

Her lips softened into a smirk, "As I stated."

I glanced back at Blari; he shook his head at me. "Then we will go after you tell me my next mission."

"Oh no dear, I'll brief you on your next quest, then you must do your capital proud by walking the circuit for the crowds. Your family will be fine here."

"Let me take them to the Church so they can get cleaned up and rested."

"Oh, they can do that here. I have agreeable rooms set up for them."

Father gripped my elbow, his fingers digging into my flesh as he pulled. He had only ever done that to me when I was running away at the mouth, but he didn't want to cause more of a scene by scolding me. I glanced up at him.

His lips pressed, he slightly shook his head from side to side once.

Not the right fight.

"Fine. What's our next quest?"

"Near Ocrea's borders are great orchards that feed many fruits to all the lands. A significant portion of those orchards have a sickness that cannot be eradicated through normal means. You are to go there and solve the puzzle that is the detriment of our fruit supply before it devastates us."

That was it? "Fine."

"Oh, I hope that Eisle's family held their heads up proudly during their daughter's funeral."

Father yanked my elbow down so I wouldn't hurl myself across the desk at the Matron. Instead, I ended up doing an odd half step and kneed the desk.

"My, I see you miss having that kind of bond." Her voice sounded like bees in my ears, "I believe CiaCia, your dear sister, is ready to become a companion."

Ice flooded through me as my gaze flew to her, "No." I croaked.

"That won't be necessary, Honorable Matron." One of the Stygra that had come in with us stepped forward, "If it pleases you, I would like to go see the orchard and be a companion for our lovely new era and hero."

I couldn't take my eyes off CiaCia.

"Very well, perhaps CiaCia may join next time."

"No." I croaked again. Father pulled me against him, his arm wrapping over my shoulder and pressing me to his front.

"Breathe." He whispered in my ear. "Hear that heartbeat. Our heartbeat. My heart is your heart. My blood is your blood. Our hearts and blood are one, you and I, remember?"

I nodded, that familiar hold. The warmth of his embrace and words flooded through me and calmed the crackling and zinging ice. Father had always known what to do, what to say, and how to handle things. He had a plan. He had to have a plan. Because I was lost.

"Go. The quicker you go, the more time you have to spend with your family. You will have one day's rest before I send you to the orchard."

Father patted my collarbone, "Go. We will be fine. It isn't as bad as it seems."

I nodded, swallowing. Collarbone meant threat, but no damage.

"Remember, my heart is your heart, my girl."

I nodded again, pulling away from him even though everything in me screamed to stay. I looked back at him, his eyes shone. My eyes started burning, and I strode to the door and out of it. My companions following at my heels.

The crowds were more unbearable than ever before. They pressed in on us at every step. Their yelling and cheering a constant roar. Did they not notice Sterla and Eisle were not with us? Did they not have any respect for our dead?

I let my mare do all the work. I smiled and I waved now and then. How was I going to get my family to safety? Could I use this chaos?

They were as free as I was. What did that mean? I wasn't free at all. She told me when to go and where. I had come back a different way this time. I hadn't come directly back to Galanesse this time. That was a little freedom.

As soon as we entered the castle at the end of this parade, we would be shoved into a party.

The Matron would disappear into the recesses of her Tower, or spend time with the royals she loved so dear. Wait.

Surely she wouldn't parade my family out during the party for us in the castle. No. No, CiaCia would not be treated as Seaghla had.

I had my Father's strength, his knowledge, his cunning. He taught me well. As did Jahni, Taspe, and Doc. Spacya, Blari, Tori, Clara and even Austere were at my side too. I wasn't alone. I wasn't useless.

I straightened my spine and took a deep breath, smelling the salt and all those bodies around me in the air. I would not be beaten. Again. No, not again.

I had once. Twice.

My spine curled again.

My heart is your heart.

What if it isn't? What if I'll never be as strong as my Father? What if I wasn't as smart as my family and Taspe believed me to be? What if…I died?

I had. Twice.

I needed to stay alive. Especially if the next one was going to be CiaCia. My heart sank. I had to prevent that. At all costs.

We slid off our horses. The ride seemed short when I stayed in my head. The Queen and The Matron did their usual speeches. I kept my eyes on my family.

They were in fine clothes. Their faces and hands washed, their hair neatly done. All except Detri's, as his hair was never to be tamed. Father was resplendent.

His chest was out, showing off the sash that had our family crest shining brightly in the sun right over his heart. The layers were white, black and green, our family colors.

Your heart is my heart.

CiaCia stood beside him in an elegant black dress that skirted her collar bones with lace and flowed down in silks, lace and satins to pool around her hidden tiny feet.

Detri was in a suit much like Father's, but he had no sash to bear a family crest. A spark of anger ignited in me. He belonged to our family. Our crest should be on his chest instead of just a plain green vest.

I breathed in and out, slowly. Perhaps they only had one in the archives. Our family wasn't all that powerful or notable any longer. Only after I completed these quests would Silverequis rise in notoriety again.

They ushered us in. They gave each of us a changing room. Ida came bounding up to me with a pretty green dress that matched my family's colors exactly. I nodded. She helped me bathe quickly and get into the dress. She did my hair up prettily, leaving a few spirals and twists dangling about. Then I was off.

A fat meal lay along the long tables in the center of the room. Smaller tables, round for intimacy, dotted the room around the center one. Father, Detri and CiaCia were on me the instant I emerged.

I hugged each of them, not willing to let any of them go, but I had to in order for there not to have suspicions raised among the other guests. Too bad it would be detrimental to the game of royals if I were to cause a scene.

"Are you really well?"

"Nothing is broken except for our pride." CiaCia clasped my hand.

"And noses." Detri added with a huff.

"Mostly pride." Father added with a twist of his lips.

"How are you? You look pale and tired." He tilted my face up with his calloused fingertips under my chin, "Although, I'm glad to see you seem to have a healthy weight now."

I stared up into his face. Each line was familiar around those eyes, but they seemed deeper and darker. The flesh of his face was pale around the purple spots on his nose and around his eyes, which were covered in makeup, but from this close I witnessed them. "I've been eating well."

His brows arched closer to his hairline.

"I have!"

"Good. and how often?"

I squirmed, my fingers curling into the skirt of my dress, "Enough."

He puffed out a breath and let my face go, "I need to remind myself that you are no longer a child, but a grown woman now."

Sam Wicker

CiaCia squeezed my hand and whispered quickly, "Taspe said he felt you die. Twice! What is that about?"

"It… it's complicated."

"Is it what the Matron mentioned earlier? The tie or connection thing with CiaCia until that other lady stepped in?" Detri's eyes darted around the room, never resting on anyone in particular, just watchful. He was wary. Wary was something Detri never was.

"Yes. She binds the life force of a Stygra to me. So instead of me dying, well, I die, but then their life is given to me and they take my death instead."

CiaCia sucked in a breath through her teeth, her hands clamped down so hard on mine that my fingertips grew colder. "Only twice?"

"Not… it seems so small when you say 'only' like that."

"I don't mean it. I'm just trying to make sense of all this. Why didn't you write to us about this? You made everything seem fine."

"Because I didn't want you to worry, and I wasn't sure what would get to you." I shook my head, "Honestly, I didn't want any of you to be mixed up in this. I wanted you all to be safe, at home, far from the capital and their reach as possible."

Father grunted, "Nadachia, Matrons have long arms and hands, so do those with money and status. No one shall be safe if they put their minds to destroying us."

That didn't sit well.

I must have paled, because he shook his head, "Truth. My heart is your heart. We will get through this." He paused, "There are parties everywhere in the capital still, yes?"

"Yes, you need to use them to get back out."

"That's what I was thinking. Is there a place where we can hide in plain sight?"

I blinked at him, "What?"

"You need help."

"No, I need you safe. I have more help than I know what to do with."

"More like you don't know what to do with the help because you never need help." Detri muttered, stepping in front of us as a pair of royals came a bit too close. His grin was more like a snarl, and they skirted around us..

"Father, please. What I need you to do is keep everyone safe. I can't... I can't plan to keep you safe while figuring out how to best this situation."

His eyes narrowed on me.

CiaCia shook her head, "That's why you need us. The powers the two had. What were they?"

My mind whirled, going from one panic to solid facts, "Healing and the unbreakable black strands."

"Ah, that's good. You can feel powers, right?"

"Yes."

"And the strands, have you made any yet?"

"No, not really."

"Practice them. Only you can break them, or your death." She peered at me, her eyes hard on mine.

I could hear her voice in my head, *Use that, Chi, use your head instead of letting your emotions beat you down*. That was far easier said than done. Especially now that they were here and not safe. I had a moment where I looked at the good of this. The three that were here were the strongest mentally.

The capital wouldn't break them.

"During this next quest I will have plenty of time to practice." If I died again, would that mean that yet another in my possession? Was my blood going to turn black?

"Good. You need it."

"The one that volunteered, do you recognize her?" I glanced at CiaCia and Father.

Both shook their heads.

Sterla nor Eisle had volunteered. They had been thrust into this because they were voicing concerns about the Matron and her ways. At least, that is the conclusion I had come to. Why would a Stygra, fully grown according to how tall she was, volunteer?

Maybe she was already dying. Or she had a plan for me. Everyone had plans for me.

"Learn what you can about her. Keep plans and thoughts to yourself around her until she can be trusted, if she can be. Are your companions truly that?"

"Yes."

"Clara, we are acquainted. The young prince, Tori, wasn't it? It is said he is honorable and brave."

"I don't like the way the one long-haired boy looks at you." Detri muttered.

I caught sight of Austere laughing with a few royals at one table. "He's harmless."

"They say he's a pirate." Father's brow rose, "He can't be harmless."

"Let's go. We will look less suspicious if we eat." I led them to the long table and told a server what I wanted from the dishes there. Gods forbid any of the rich and powerful get their hands dirty serving themselves. Detri and CiaCia balked at the idea of someone else touching their food, but they allowed it. As soon as we sat down, my companions, including a much more vibrant and healthy looking Clara, joined us.

"It is an honor to meet you Master Silverequis." Austere bowed deeply before sitting down.

The honor is mine," Father bowed his head. "I thank you all for keeping my daughter safe."

I hated how we had to pretend to be someone else. A family get together like this would have been far less formal under normal circumstances. Father would have already figured out if he liked my Companions on his own through conversation he'd pointedly lead. He probably would like all of them. Austere might take him some time.

I still wasn't certain if I liked him.

I glanced at Detri. His gaze kept flicking toward the Matron and higher royals and then back to Austere. I reached over and ruffled his wild hair with a grin.

"What's that for?"

"My protective little brother, all grown up."

His cheeks reddened, and he failed to smooth his fluffy hair, "Dunno what you're talking about, Chi."

"The way you're glaring at me is you being protective?" The pirate smirked as he leaned back in his chair, "How sweet of you. You are in just as much danger from me as your sister is."

Blari sputtered on his sip, "Austere! Down!"

The pirate prince rolled his eyes, "I am down, but I can be in any position at any time if we're ready to have some fun."

I sighed, his eyes were on Detri the whole time.

"Huh?"

"Detri, wanna get another plate?" I asked, before he questioned more.

"Will that be alright?"

"Of course." CiaCia stood, "I'll come with you."

Father leaned onto the table with his elbows and looked Austere over, "My kids, sir, are to be treated with respect at all times."

"Yes, sir, I understand. And they are." Austere smiled, "Just giving them every option of joy they deserve."

I rolled my eyes, "Father, it's fine. He's harmless, really."

Spacya snorted, "I wouldn't go that far."

Blari nodded, "Agreed. Even the sparring matches he holds with his shipmates are brutal."

I pinched the bridge of my nose. It was going to be a long night. I still hadn't figured out what to do with my family yet.

Father tugged gently on a loose curl, "Nadachia," he spoke my name with a soft tone, "We will get through this."

"I need to get you home. I need you to be safe. Do you think you can stay in the Welkan village?"

"We can't abandon our farm and depend on others."

"Yes, you can. If it means that you won't be attacked again, that you will be safe, you can."

He frowned, "I think the only reason they got the upper hand was because we were not prepared. I-it's my fault."

"No, I wasn't clear enough in my letters. I didn't think they would attack you. I mean, we are the farthest from the capital in the country."

He chuckled, "You must have really hit a nerve or made them scared. Something."

"I doubt it." I shook my head, "That's besides the point. A way out, for the three of you, and Mother and Seaghla."

"Maybe we need to stay."

What little I had eaten threatened to come back up, "No, no you can't. You're in too much danger here."

He eyed me, "If I'm in danger, then you are too. How am I to leave you in danger?"

My eyes burned, and I took his hand, "Because I'm grown. Because I made this decision. Because I wanted to improve your life. Now I've created a mess, made your life worse, and I need to fix it. You need to let me fix it."

He sighed, squeezed my hand and looked down at our joined hands. "You didn't need to do this for us. You need to do this for you."

I stared at him, "No, I did this for you." My heart seemed like it wanted to sink to the floor and melt there. "I did this all for us."

He smiled, "I understand, my heart. But you are going to survive this by doing this for you."

"Then, I should just go home."

Tori shook his head, "Don't you understand that if you do that, you'll end up turning around and heading right back here to finish it? We haven't known each other that long, but I already know that about you."

Detri and CiaCia sat back down. Detri already had his mouth full. He looked at me expectantly.

"You're coming home?" CiaCia asked.

I looked at everyone. Studied their faces to memorize them once more. I then sighed and shook my head, "No, I'm not coming home yet."

She nodded and gave me a small smile, "I know, you gotta finish what you start."

I sat back in my chair. The weight of the decision I made on a whim resting on my shoulders heavier than ever. What had I gotten myself into exactly? I was unstable for willingly taking this on.

I noticed some people wandering into the grand hall and sighed. I stared at the rest of my plate. There I was, wasting food again. With fewer people to pick up on our conversation, though.

"Tori, you have horses ready for them, right?"

"I do."

"Where exactly?"

He drew a circle on the table, tapping the back end and pointing to us, he then pointed to a position on the east side of the circle. "There's a great little herbal place called Gala's Herbals. You should go there." He pointedly looked at my father.

Father nodded, "We shall go in the morning then. I would like to explore the capital's wares." He smiled, "Maybe watch the party outside too."

"Well worth it." Austere smirked, "In fact, if you would like to go now, I think we can sneak out."

My eyes started burning again, but they needed to go.

"What about Joni?" CiaCia leaned over Detri, who was still stuffing his face, to ask in a whisper.

"I'll take care of him." I watched her eyes grow wide, and then she nodded.

We all stood and wandered around through the alcoves and made our way out to the garden. Nothing unusual. After all, the gardens were open to guests during these parties. As soon as we made sure the area was clear, I hugged my family tightly.

"Don't stop until you absolutely have to."

"What about our clothes?" Detri plucked at the finery.

"Sell them here or in the first town." Tori answered. "I can lead you to the horses and your family. I had a man go get them ready as soon as we landed."

"That would be appreciated." Father nodded, "It has been a while since I have been here and it has changed, greatly."

Tori smiled, "I imagine so."

I hugged Father one more time. "I can hire someone to go with you."

"No, we'll be fine."

CiaCia clung to me for a moment, "Nadachia," she spoke softly, "Please, be wary. The Matron has turned… evil. I can feel it. Please practice everything that has been given to you, too. It will help you come back to us."

I nodded, "I will." I kissed her forehead, then hugged her again.

"Come, let's go. Just tell those that ask that I'm giving them a grand tour of the gardens and the church to give them some fresh air."

I nodded, "Be careful."

"We will be." With that, I watched my family leave.

"They'll be fine." Blari assured me, finally turning from watching my family leave to eyeball me.

Joni met us as we entered the dance hall from the feast. The urge to rake my fingers from his hairline to his chin to skin him with my fingernails was overwhelming. I stopped, keeping him at some distance so I would be less likely to act upon the urge.

The smile on his golden face faltered. "I just wanted to say hello and ask you for a dance."

"Are you truly that daft?" Austere grinned at my side.

I placed a hand on his elbow. The pirate paused, looking down at me. He kept staring even as I dropped my hand. My dress was going to have so many fist sized wrinkles tonight.

"Daft?"

Blari groaned and stepped toward Joni, "Listen, boy, and listen well. You are an idiot. Daft. Daft to your core. Do you have any idea what you have done?"

"I-I am not! I'm making sure she's happy from now on out!"

"I'm gettin' drunk just by listenin' to him." Spacya eyed a serving girl with a tray of ale.

"You haven't saved me. You attacked my family. You hurt them, scared them, damaged my home and then brought Father, CiaCia, and Detri here into further danger. How does that make me happy? How does that save me?"

"That's not what I did."

The fabric in my hands made a distressed sound as my fingers tightened more in it. My knuckles ached, but if I let go, I would cause a scene. I had caused enough of those. I needed to not draw attention to the fact my family was gone.

"What do you think you did?"

"I brought them here to spend time with you. I didn't hurt them." He paused, "The others were rough, but I protected them from the ones who held them hostage."

"You held them hostage!" My voice bounced along the pillars and a hush started through the crowd. Austere grabbed two women by their hands and started a maddening dance with them. Laughter started, and the quiet was short-lived.

"No. I brought them to safety. I'm sorry we couldn't save more of them for you." Joni stepped toward me. His eyes wide, his hands open, palms out.

"Who was holding them hostage?"

"Taspe!"

"The Welkan Tribe?" Blari's teeth were showing like a predator's smile, "Think Joni! For once in your miserable life have a portion of your brain work!" The priest shook his hands in the air in front of Joni, "Don't you think the tribe would have noticed Taspe being brainwashed?"

"N-no."

"When do you want me to take 'im to the garden and plant 'im?"

Kill him? No, I wouldn't do that to Jahni. Somewhere deep and covered by all this rage, I still cared for this fool before me. No where near what I used to as a kid, but still some feelings. He had a goodness that I couldn't conjure up an instance of it in my memory at the moment. He had done good things. On his own. Without prompting. Right?

I shook my head. Spacya cursed under her breath and stalked off after the ale. Perhaps I should let her. How did I deal with Joni for so long? Was I just as stupid as he was?

"How are you saving me?"

"I'm taking your place. I'll be the hero. You can relax."

Something bubbled up and out. My laugh surprised Joni as much as it did me as he took a step back. His eyes were on his toes.

"Good!" I threw my arms out. The skirts of my dress sticking to my hands and flaring out before flowing to settle around me, "Take it! Take it all!"

"Nadachia," Blari's tone was deep, soft.

I moved, jerking out of Blari's reach as I went toe to toe with Joni. His breath was hot on my forehead. "It's about time you held up a deal, a promise. It's about time you did something right." I laughed in his face. His pretty face with golden skin, too big pores, and hooked nose and dull, lifeless eyes.

I blinked, trying to take the film off my vision. When had his eyes gone gray? They never looked that dry. Was his skin gray too?

That grin spreading over his lips wasn't his type of grin.

His breath, while hot, smelled. Smelled of rot.

The power of Sterla leapt up in me, then recoiled with a chill. I stepped back. The Stygra at his side, always at his side, had that same grin.

"Convincing, isn't it?" The words spilled out of Joni's mouth, "Just act like a stupid human. Easy to do. Easy to convince other, stupid, humans too."

"How long?"

"Long enough to get the job done."

I heard Blari gag behind me, "Oh Gods," His voice broke. "The attack?"

"You're getting there." The Stygra paused, "he put up a decent fight. He stayed alive up to three days ago, too."

There was a long pause as my thoughts tried to process what I was seeing. What I was hearing. What truly happened. My friend, the idiot that he was, was dead.

"I must admit, I was surprised your family fought. Galanesse is the place to be!"

"Where is Jahni, and those that helped him track you down?"

"Where do you think?"

Something speared around. It searched for Jahni's familiar being. His strength and warmth. Nothing.

He was not here. He wasn't underneath or in the Tower. Nor the Church. Nor was he outside. Everything shook in me. How was I doing this? Sterla?

Jahni. I found nothing.

"He's dead."

My heart ripped. The shaking and searching halted. Everything drew into me, swallowed by a hollow darkness.

"No."

"Of course he is. You are smarter than that. Or you should be, as you are descended from humans that were known for their minds. Perhaps the line has become too diluted." The sigh that came out of Joni's mouth was not his. "Pity, we hoped you would be fun."

Fun. This was fun to them? Killing off those I loved. Those that were innocent. Those that had nothing to do with my mistakes. Hurting my family.

It was obvious to me now. Joni stood oddly. The smell. His *feel* off.

No other human had a Stygra kept close to them. My emotions had blinded me yet again. The game had kept me from using my sense. Everything was a distraction.

"One day, you will be at my complete mercy, or lack thereof." Joni grinned the Stygra's grin, bowed his head slightly, and walked away.

Blari had his hand at the small of my back, helping me steady my wobbling, "Do you need to sit?"

I needed much more than that. I nodded anyway. CiaCia's words came back to me. She had known. They had a double meaning to them.

"Aww I thought you said I could dance with the other pretty man."

Perfume punched my nose. My eyes watered as I tried to focus. Austere brought his new toys over as soon as Joni left.

"Go after him. He's just over there."

How could the Stygra make him dance?

"Oh! There he is!" They sauntered off. The perfume trailing after them.

"You're pale."

"Joni's dead." Blari's voice pitched low so no one else would hear him.

"He's right there. Standing and talking."

"The Stygra."

Austere's eyes bulged, and he swallowed as he stopped looking at Joni. He stepped directly in front of me, his face in mine, "Are you with me?"

I nodded.

"No, Chi, I need you here. Focus. What color is the perfumed girl's dress?"

My mind blanked. I dug around, my eyes trying to look past him toward the woman. How is he so big to block every line of sight I have except to him and to my peripherals? Blue? No. "Cream with some yellow or green bits."

"That was her friend, but good enough. Hard to tell where the cloud of perfume comes from when they are so close to one another." Stere straightened, "He wasn't normally that stupid then?"

"No. Not entirely. Well, yes, sometimes." I raked a tickling strand of hair away from my neck. He was dead. Dead, but still walking around. What more would these evils do?

Chapter 31

Spacya, Tori, Austere and I were at the Tower as the sun broke over the walls of the gardens. Dew glittered on the leaves and thick blades of grass between the gravel walkways. The wind, for once, was light and from the mainland, carrying with it the scents of bakeries and stables.

Tori had ridden with my family for half the night. I thanked the gods for him and swore I would pay him back for protecting them for as long as he dared. I watched his jaw crack with another yawn for the second time this morning. "You should have stayed in bed."

"You need me, besides, Blari was having a nice snore."

"Ah, there you are, with your entourage I see." Keandria stood in front of her large desk, pale hands folded primly at her waist. "Where is your family?"

Nothing was in that grating voice. Not even the bite of annoyance. Chilled, invisible fingers skittered down my spine, "Aren't they here with you?"

Her lips pulled into a frown. Something flickered between her eyes and brow. Was that her second guessing herself?

"You know where they are." Her hands flattened against her stomach.

"You have lost my family?" I took a step forward, clenching my fists. Game. I could play this.

"You sent them away, didn't you?"

I shook my head, "No! I did not. Where are they? What have you done with them?" I took a few more steps toward her while trying to get the blood to drain from my face.

"Do not talk to your Matron that way."

She came out of the shadows to my right. Her hissing voice sent anger roiling through me. I couldn't remember her name, or if I had ever known it. At least she wasn't puppeting Joni beside her anymore.

"You tell me where my family is then!" I whirled on her.

"Gone. Obviously."

"What?!" Keandria's teeth bared when I turned back to her.

The Stygra puppeteer waved a hand, "What do we need humans underfoot for, anyway? Nothing but a bother. They aren't worth-" Her eyes bulged.

Keandria sucked in a slow, deep breath. Her fingers moved as if gathering twine from a spool. "They are worth more than your life. How dare you. Do you think you know best?" Keandria's laugh grated along the stone walls, "Your mind is as small as a human's."

The Stygra stumbled, then fell to her knees. She grasped the air, grabbing at nothing. "No," she rasped, "Please. I'll find them."

"Find them?" The Matron snorted, "You can't even watch them."

I saw it then. No, I felt it. Smoke, black and liquid curled from the puppeteer toward Keandria. It drew around her fingers, bunching, narrowing, threading within them before slipping under her skin. Power.

Taking the soul, the life of her companion as if she were drinking water. My feet froze in place. Something in me slunk and pulled away as far as it could.

She deserves it! A small voice in me cried. She deserves all of this for what she's done!

"No." I shook my head, trying to shake that voice from me, "Stop it. It wasn't her fault."

The power drained in her pause.

"What was that?"

"I let them go. I helped them escape."

"Did you? How clever. How very clever indeed." Keandria frowned. The power yanked toward her. The puppeteer slammed to the floor, gasped twice, and didn't move again. Another Stygra in the room, or it was one of my companions, choked on a sob.

Keandria's shoulders rose with her sigh. She turned to me, "Don't be heartbroken, Nadachia. She lost them on her watch."

I glanced at my friends. They looked like I must have. Useless, weak, scared, and angry all at the same time. They were all around me, battle ready, protective.

"Let's get this over with." Keandria began speaking the all too familiar words.

The power weaved in with mine. Slick, cold, flowing as the deepest waters of the Gala. Sterla's and Eilse's power met Randia's. She stood so close to me at that moment, I felt as if we might blend together then.

This was my new normal.

Accepting wrongness. Welcoming destruction of what I knew and cared for. Allowing things to be done to me and my family. My friends. A tear started down my cheek before I swiped it away.

"Go. Fulfill your duty. Do it quickly for once." Keandria waved toward the three maps folded on the desk. "And you, pathetic little Randia, may your death be as useless as your life."

Austere scoffed, "All life is worth living unless it be with the likes of you."

Keandria's eyes narrowed slightly, and then she smiled, "Trying to insult me with such sentiments is vulgar."

"I suppose it is, but it makes me feel better."

I followed my companions out. Randia was at my side. Her head was high, eyes bright, and a smile upon her lips.

Just what did she have planned. She was happy with this? How?

We got on our horses. Unia pawed at the street, her hoof making a deep clicking sound that mimicked the beat of my heart.

A poisoned orchard. The land that produced fruit and vegetables for most of the country, no less. Of course it was. She wanted me to fail or to succeed. She had a plan for both. I was certain of it. Which did she actually want to happen? That was what I had to figure out and see if I could do the opposite while still making sure the people didn't suffer.

We rode through the street that had most of the market on it. Glancing through the stalls and shops, I realized there were fewer tarts and pies. The baskets that were usually overflowing with brightly colored fruits held a handful, or stacked, empty against a wall.

I paused by a stand which had plenty of empty ones. The woman was mending them. "Did you get your supplies from the orchard that is poisoned?"

Her eyes widened when they drew up to my face, "Y-yes, my Hero."

"Have you any news on its status other than what the Matron or Royals have stated?"

"Yes, from traders. Would you like me to share it?"

"Please."

Austere and Blari rode up beside me. Spacya eyed the crowd a few lengths ahead of us as people started drawing nearer. Randia canted her head to the side as she stopped the cart. Tori watched from behind, tossing a few iron bits to some children who dared come near him.

"They say the trees grow black, the leaves and fruit falling off them with this sickening stench. Rotted before they ever hit the ground, Hero." She swallowed and shook her head, "I have never heard the like before."

"Has anyone told you what they think it might be?"

She glanced around, stepping closer to my horse. She rested a gnarled hand against my mare's neck, "They say it's a Stygra curse," she whispered, "only Stygra control the deep dark and the rot. But why would they do something like that?"

"Indeed." I murmured, knowing one who would do just that to see the world starve. I smiled and took her palm, putting the bits purse I had on me in it. "For you and those that may find themselves in need until we can fix this."

She brought her other hand up to cup the bag, her eyes growing wide before brimming with tears, "You are truly a Hero. May the gods bless you for all your years without hindrance."

"And you as well." She stepped away, and we started on our way again.

"Well, it looks like you are going to be drunk to tonight." Austere murmured as he handed out some of his bits to those as we passed.

"All of us are. Shame that we cannot share the wealth we partake of in the Castle and Church among the less fortunate." Blari muttered.

"I'm sure we are going to run into worse as we near the orchards." Spacya warned over her shoulder, "Might wanna spare some for those that'll need it most there. Here they've some resources."

I frowned. She was right. Here, the Church held meals for those in need daily, twice a day sometimes. The royals could be partitioned once a week, too. The villages that we would pass through farther out would not have that luxury.

I hadn't thought of that. The repercussions of some of these fights and horrors. I knew Columbria was getting help. What of the carnage and fear the Cotkit had caused? I looked over at my friends, "What's been given?"

"Pardon?"

"What has been done to help those that we couldn't aid in time? The destruction and the death, how are the people being compensated?"

Blari glanced back at Tori, "The Prince would know best. From my research, they sent supplies to help rebuild, costs of funerals and medical attention the royals and the church take care of, I believe."

Austere cleared his throat, "A system of checks and balances are always in place with a government as refined as this one. Don't worry your little head about that. The people are being taken care of the best the government sees fit. You should worry about what you can change."

A prickle of irritation made me snort, "Fine. If you have so much trust in our Royal Family, and the Matron then you deal with them from now on. I'll catch up on sleep."

He chuckled, "And not get to see you struggle to socialize. Never. You're still going to 'deal with them' for the rest of your life. Or theirs." He muttered the last under his breath with a glance at the guards as we passed through the gates onto the Capital Road.

Sam Wicker

We had been three days upon Capital Road and had made it to Dragotown finally. So close to home. Spacya seemed loose as she rode into her hometown. Plenty of people greeted her, she scowled at them. Some things were not supposed to change.

Spacya insisted that we all stay at her house instead of the inn, but we argued. She, Blari and Tori stayed in her house, on the outskirts of the village, west of the gate while Austere, Randia and I stayed at the Inn. I wanted to get more news on the orchards since we were close. And of home.

"Did an older man, a Stygra girl, a pink-haired woman, and a teen boy pass through here a day or so ago?"

The innkeeper frowned, "Seems I saw some that fit that description. They didn't stay here." He jerked his head to the lodging across the street, "Stayed there though."

"Thank you."

"My rooms are better."

I knew it to be true, Spacya had stated such. "I know, we will stay here, but I need news."

"Understand. That be three?"

"One suite." Austere put the bits on the counter, "Preferably one facing the main street."

"That be our only suite. Only got two beds though."

"That's fine."

Randia sniffed. I had learned over the past few days that was her note of revulsion, the polite sound of disgust. Thus far, she had managed not to room with Stere. Now that she was faced with it, her nose went high in the air and she wouldn't look at us at all.

Austere grinned at me.

I groaned. It was going to be a long night ahead of us. We took our things to the room. Randia stayed there, claiming the smaller of the two beds while I went back out, Austere tight on my heels.

"You know, I can go alone."

"No, you can't go anywhere alone."

I rolled my eyes, "What's gonna happen? She's going to send someone to kidnap me back to Galanesse? Kind of defeats the purpose of sending out a hero to do the dirty work, don't you think?"

"Darling, there are more dangers than just the Matron. These backwood towns hold people of opportunity."

"You would know."

His chuckle was short as we crossed the narrow dirt street to the other inn, "Hence, why you should listen to me."

"And trust you?"

"If that makes you feel better, yes."

"Wouldn't that make you better?"

"Hmm." He leaned on the counter, his breath hot on my neck, "Yes, I say it would."

Ignoring him, I smiled at the innkeeper, "Did you have an older man about this height stay here with a boy, a pink-haired woman, and a Stygra girl about a day or two ago?"

The innkeeper's eyes were watery, and they narrowed as they looked me up and down, "Don't give out information 'bout my tenants unless you the guard."

"I'm the Hero."

He snorted, "No Hero would grace these parts."

I showed my teeth, "Nadachia of Silverequis." I brandished my family emblem that I had sewn onto the collar of my new jacket, "Hero."

He swallowed, "Er... beg ya pardon, Hero. Yes, I had them stay here two nights ago. Arrived late in the night and left before the sun was up."

"Good." My muscles eased about my shoulders, "Were they... well?"

"Er...well?"

"Were they hurt?"

"No, Hero. They were unhurt. Tired and pale, understand, but not hurt that I's could see."

"Thank you. Did anyone else ask after them other than me?"

"No, Hero."

I nodded, my muscles relaxing even more. I took out a gold bit, "If anyone other than me or my party asks about those travelers, you say you never saw them. Got it?" I slid the gold bit over the counter, pressing my fingers over it until he nodded. "Swear it on your grave. If you speak, I will come collecting."

"I swear it. Won't be no need to collect on it."

"Good." I turned and started out of the inn.

"Miss Hero!"

I paused, looking over my shoulder and past Austere to the innkeeper.

"If'n they come by here again. If'n one mentions yer name or shows me yer emblem, I'll care for 'em like they be my own family. No questions asked."

I smiled, "Thank you."

"Well, you have done nicely." Stere stretched his arms up over his head once we were back out on the street.

I paused, looking up and down for a place to grab some good sweets or breads. I followed my nose to the right, down a few buildings, and entered a pastry shop and breathed in the yeasty aroma deeply.

"One could say that you have a better knack at threatening and making an impression than you do at flirting and playing into some games."

I sighed, "I've always been good at threats. All I have to do is skin a small animal in front of them and they turn around and do anything for me."

Austere laughed, "You skinned nothing in front of him though."

"No, my title took the place of that."

I watched him tilt his head to study me in the reflection of the glass counter I was looking into. I pointed to the cream-filled pastries once the baker's apprentice finished with the other set of customers, "Six of those please and a dozen of your best cookies."

"Maybe I was wrong to teach you to play. We should concentrate on how to threaten royals into doing as you want."

The steady hands of the apprentice shook at Austere's careless words. My brow rose as I looked up at the pirate's face, "I kept trying to tell you I'm no good at games. I don't enjoy lying. It makes me nervous. I forget what I said even as I say it and liars need to remember everything so they don't get caught in it."

He shook his head, a hand raking across the back of his neck, "Sorry. I should have listened to you."

I stared at him.

"What?"

I gawked at him some more.

"What are you…oh for the gods! I make mistakes and I own up to them. Often. Don't stare at me like I've grown two heads!"

I giggled and took my prizes, paying for them with a few bits. I passed Austere a cookie as we turned down the street to explore some more. Near a small gathering of men and women in front of a shop that had a few benches under the windows, we paused. They were speaking in not so hushed tones.

"The orchards should just be replanted."

"Fool! It'll take years for the trees to mature enough to bear and then the fruit will be sour until they age well into sweetness. We'll all starve!"

"Import. I'm sure Iethyll or Ocrea would share their wealth."

"Neither of them has the amount to feed all of us. They can drive the prices too high too. None of us could afford that."

"The Hero needs to hurry and solve the problem. Has she already left?"

"They said she left a few days ago. She should be nearby."

"I heard she's here."

"Here! Where?"

Austere grinned and opened his mouth. I stuffed a pastry into it. He coughed, tearing off a bite to cough some more. A few looked over at us. I patted his back, trying to look the part of a concerned friend.

"Praise gods if she is here. She'll fix it."

"It's taken her months to fix the others, though. Or almost a month at least. Does she have enough time to figure it out before we see starvation come in?"

Sam Wicker

"We got grains and meats still. We won't starve."

"You are still a fool. If we have no fruits or vegetables, the meats and grain prices will go higher. We won't be able to afford them much longer."

After I overheard that, I walked around them. I needed what was happening at the orchard and the theories circulating. I had learned with the last quests that being a bit more prepared would work in my favor.

I was a slow learner.

After we walked for a few minutes, we stopped by another group of people. Each one of these was resting on boxes and barrels in a narrow alley between two large buildings. I assumed they were taking a break from loading what they were sitting on into the tavern. I took out a pastry and bit into it. The cream slid sweet over my tongue and I would have moaned, but Stere's presence reminded me to be reasonable with my sounds.

As it were, he was in my space, leaning on a shoulder, his arm draped along the wall over my head. I quirked a brow up at him.

He smirked in return, "Care to share?"

I tried to juggle mine while opening the box for another, but he grabbed my hand. He took a bite from mine. What exactly was that supposed to accomplish other than taking my food?

I kicked his shin.

The thick breading muffled his curse.

I took another bite of my pastry and listened.

"Pops says it's gonna be hard winter if'n we can't get enough for us to jar. Be all grains and meats. No vitamins to keep the cold at bay."

"What could make a tree turn dead in the middle of growin' season?"

"Dunno."

"Gotta be some kind of sickness."

"Old man Joe says it's the Stygra."

A hush fell over the crowd. The woman who said it sniffed before adding that it was just what she overheard.

"Careful," one man glanced around, the whites of his eyes flashing in the shadow of his raggedy cap, "They might do the same to you."

When had Stygra become so feared? I was believing Owlimount and my family were odd compared to the rest of the country in how we treated the other races. Was it scary to treat everyone equally? Without judgment or prejudice?

"I ain't scared." The woman shook her head, "Done lost my boys. Nothin' else to lose."

Another quiet moment settled over the group and had me nudging Austere back the way we came. We crossed the street, and entered a shop. I couldn't quite place my finger on the scent that tickled my nose until we were inside.

Spices. All kinds of ground and whole herbs, sticks, beans, and barks. Glass and clay jars, all neatly labeled, lined uniformly in shelves along the walls and in those that stood back to back in the middle of the shop. Dried and drying branches and roots hung from the open rafters above our heads. Barrels stood in rows, some full to the brim while others were at varying stages of empty.

"Ah, welcome. Come in travelers. Come see. Refresh yourselves." A Stygra male shuffled out of the back, drawing a beautiful flowered pattern curtain closed behind him.

Austere breathed in deeply. He moaned. "I would never have dreamt something like this could be so far inland."

He prowled. I stood watching my tall, dark companion begin his inspection of the store wares. He carefully sniffed, looked over the grains, commented on scents and coloring, asked about how each was prepared and all with bright eyes and an easy smile. I thought I knew of my companions' hobbies.

There were the obvious, of course. Spacya and her hunting, Blari with writing, Austere with sex, Clara had a penchant for fashion, and Tori with map making. Over our time together, I learned pieces here and there about them. We were thrown into odd situations so much that our knowledge of each other was all wrong. Most people learned the hobbies, likes and dislikes of one another before learning how the other acted under duress.

"Nadachia, love, come. Try this."

I walked over to him. He poured a couple of drops on a piece of plain bread. Austere held it to my lips. Because of that smile on his face, one I hadn't seen before and the gleam in his eyes that lifted the shadows that were usually lurking there, I took the bread from his fingertips with my mouth. I didn't have a free hand, anyway.

His eyes widened. I realized then I had finally gotten him, once.

The oil grew into a buttery, spicy thing on my tongue, and my face or eyes must have changed because he grinned. "I knew you would like that." He swept a strand of hair from my cheek to behind my ear with gentle fingers.

"What is it?"

"A cooking oil." I narrowed my eyes, licking my lips for more of it before he continued his explanation, "It's made from olives. Different breeds of olives and ages lend different flavors. They use mostly these oils here for cooking. Other oils have been used for centuries by many peoples for skin care or making a room or person's odor pleasant."

I looked over the barrels, shining in the candlelight before us. Printed neatly were the country, orchard, and year each came from. The one he had let me sample was from Iethyll. "People like yours."

"Yes. Families of Iethyll have grown and bred olives for generations to make flavors that are special and lovely."

"You are from Iethyll, good man?"

"I am."

"Have you any news of the pirate king? Is he horrid?"

Austere's back went straight. He grew interested in another oil as he answered, "The former king was the horrible one, sir."

"Oh yes! I agree. But one wonders if a pirate can be any better or if poor Iethyll has gone from the ravine to a cliff side."

He sighed, his fingers sliding down the smooth surface until his hands dropped to his sides. He rocked on his heels, "Iethyll was drowning in debt, and death. The last king drove people from their passions and into devastating hard labor that not only crushed their spirits, but caused them to physically and mentally weaken into disease. In the months the Pirate King has been reigning, color has returned. People sing again. Trees and other plants that were neglected for the mines are strengthening. Sickness and death numbers have gone down." He sniffed, looking down at the Stygra male even though he was about the same height, "Yes, Iethyll is far better suited to a pirate king, I think. What say you?"

The Stygra took a step back, nodding his head, "Yes, good sir, I would have to agree."

Austere studied the Stygra for a moment before asking, "You have family in Iethyll?"

The shopkeeper's head jerked back around, his eyes widening a little on Austere before he could collect himself, "Yes."

"You haven't heard from them?"

"Not in a month."

He nodded, then blew out a breath, "I have connections who are well versed in gaining news of persons. I can send them the information of your family and they will send a message to you once they find them so you may have the knowledge you seek."

"Will they be harmed? How much will this cost me?"

The frown etched Austere's face as the light faded from his eyes, "Nothing. I know what it is to not have news from those you care most about. They will not be harmed, just searched for and well being gathered."

There was a long pause as the male tore more bread pieces off a loaf to put in a basket, "Very well."

Austere took all the information he needed from the male.

The shopkeeper gave us a small vial of some oil each. He clasped my hand and leaned over to whisper, "Your man is kind. This oil, use on your skin and he will love you like he never has before."

Heat bloomed in my cheeks.

The pirate prince made a few purchases of spice pouches before we left. He chuckled as we walked down the street, back to our lodgings.

"What?"

Sam Wicker

"Did he give you instructions?"

I'd cooled my cheeks a little until that question. "Not exactly."

Austere's chuckle grew deeper, "That oil will never see the light of day again, will it?"

"No."

He stopped me, wrapping an arm around my waist and tipping his lips against the shell of my ear, "It's meant for the night, darling."

I shoved him, getting out of his hold. I quickened my pace away from the still chuckling pirate.

Chapter 32

My family was out of Galanesse.

I was entering another quest, riding upon my sweaty mare on a strange road. So close to home I could nearly scent it. Almost see it in the jutting peaks of the mountains to our right.

I wondered if Father, Mother, Seaghla, CiaCia and Detri had made it home yet as I stared at a particularly high snow-capped peak. Clara had promised to send word. The princess had snuck out with them, riding home with them. Another body to protect them, even if she was still on the weak side.

A stench alerted us to our arrival near the orchard before we could see the rows of trees over the next rolling hill. We crossed a low, narrow wooden bridge over a small river. The water looked like smoke.

"This must be the start."

The smell didn't come from the tributary, though. It blew in on the wind, over the hills. I slid off Unia. She pawed at the wooden slats as I leaned over the edge. There weren't any dead fish floating, nor rodents. It was just gray, like it was reflecting heavily laden storm clouds.

To reassure myself that it was indeed the bright blue I knew it to be overhead, I looked up at the sky. I took my pack off and rummaged around in it until the familiar rough fibers scraped against my fingertips. I unwrapped the net Detri gave me.

I watched the pretty green netting sink into the gray waters.

"Mud? Are the trees falling into it upriver?"

We would have to check on that.

"Well, I know one thing, if you catch any fish, I wouldn't eat it." Tori watched from atop his horse. "Water as dirty as that can only ruin them."

"I shall pray to Meandria. Perhaps she doesn't know some of her waters perish."

"That smell... it isn't the river. Is it the orchard itself?"

Seeing that the horses weren't going anywhere, Tori joined me at the edge. "Could be, have to see." He watched the net with me, "Food or testing?"

"Both?" I smirked as he made a face. The net jerked and waggled. I gave it a few moments before closing it and pulling the shimmering strands back to me.

Tori helped pull the small catch in. Four flopped upon the slats. Three were small minnows, but the larger one was freckled with an enormous mouth.

I picked up each one, studying each fin and scale and opening their mouths. There were no discolorations or abnormalities that I could see. I was loath to waste meat.

Tori, sensing my hesitation, grabbed a minnow and began dissecting it. The insides were normal shades of pinks and reds. Its stomach barely had any contents.

"Definitely not the river." Austere straightened from leaning over the neck of his large stallion. "Those minnows would show it."

He wasn't wrong. Still. I emptied the net out; the fish plopping back into the ruddy water with small splashes. Tori threw the gutted minnow up on the bank. I eyed the flow. Skimmers darted along the top of it. The banks were thriving with plants and algae. It wasn't the river.

As I stood, I heard more than felt my back pop. My hands automatically rubbed my sore ass cheeks before I turned and caught Austere's gaze on me. I pulled myself back up on my mare, "I don't want a massage, nor a smoother or rougher ride, thanks."

I looked back at Randia, our new Stygra companion, as she made a gagging sound. I reached over and took Tori's kerchief from his pocket to take to her. "Here, need me to tie it for you?"

"No, thank you." She pressed the square of silk over her nose after tying the two corners together under her dark hair. She tucked the loose ends into the high collar of her dress. "Much better. Forgive my weakness, I have always been sensitive to smells."

"Nothing to forgive." I waved her off as I turned back around.

"I think the river is murky from the spotted fish, Nadachia. When they move, feed, and migrate they tend to stir up the bottom a lot."

"Oh, I didn't know that."

"I'm not saying it couldn't be something else too." She added quickly. We rode in silence, the rolling hills not changing much in our plodding walk. "Keandria warned me you were her pawn. I saw your fight." Her hands squeezed the reins until they squeaked, "I know not her plans for you, but I will tell you this: she is a fool tying us to you one after another."

"Why would you say that?"

Randia's eyes turned to me instead of her hands, "Do you not feel them?"

I swallowed the knot in my throat before I answered, "I do. Surely Keandria does too."

She shook her head. "No, she doesn't. Or if she does, she doesn't realize what it means. My sister, Wyla, has been hiding and dimming the powers that you have gained each time you enter the capital."

"Why?"

"Because you will become her end."

"I'm weak."

Randia laughed, but as she saw I thought my words were truth, she sobered. "You are untrained, far from weak." She looked ahead again, "Humans have the gift of adaptation. You are proof."

"How many Stygra have been tied to humans?"

"Only a dozen or so, I would think. But yours, ours, are the only ones that have been done unwillingly. That I know of."

"The others, did they absorb powers?"

"I do not know." There was a pause. I bit back my disappointment. "They gave their powers to you. You did nothing wrong."

"I put myself in danger."

"That is a given of your profession. I think it is as you always have been. You protect others over yourself."

"Have you known many humans? Most of us here would do that."

"I have befriended some." Her voice lowered, "You say that, yet you are the only one who has died."

I looked ahead at my companions. They had done plenty, "Perhaps that is my foolishness."

"That is why you're the Hero and they are not."

Tori cleared his throat, "She's right. I see something or someone and I stop. I think about the choices. You act. Just act. No thinking, or pause at all."

"Very true," Austere added, "It's that action that saved the world from the Cotkit. If they had left it to us, it would have gone on a wounded rampage and we would all be dead."

I glanced at Spacya. She had been in the wrong place. She would have acted and gotten herself killed. I was glad she hadn't been there. She nodded at me. I sighed and muttered, "I'm just a fool, that is all."

"Fearless when it matters." Blari smirked, "Hard headed enough to get us through this."

"When I teach you, you can add unique and powerful to that small list." Her eyes crinkled at the edges and I knew she smiled under that kerchief.

We crested the ridge of hills and looked down on neatly curving rows of trees. To our right were red apples as far as the eye could see. To the left were green, but halfway down the hillsides the leaves and fruit were gray. They appeared to have ash covering them, pouring down upon them for days and sticking wetly.

The stench of decay made my stomach heave. I put my hand over my mouth and nose. A breeze blew in from the right, a reprieve with the sweet scent of the healthy apples and trees.

I watched the wind play through the leaves and branches of the green. As the breeze reached the graying ones, it stilled. It didn't touch the ashen twigs. It didn't stir the rotted fruit. The breeze didn't ruffle the gray grasses as it had the green.

A bird flew across the road, following the current. It stopped, fluttering along the edge of the ashen area. It turned back, landed on a good tree, and sat there.

"It looks like someone just drew a line."

I followed the edge of the gray grasses and trees. The line wasn't straight. It curved with the shapes of the hills. It plunged forward to take in a tree that leaned before curling back into the curve of the next slope. If a branch was within that line, then the whole tree became ashen.

The ashen edge stopped at the crest of the hill we were on. Green grasses waved at their gray counterparts below them. Only an artist could show us such a contrast if we weren't there to see it ourselves.

"What could do this?" Blari breathed, standing in his stirrups to see with a hand over his brow shading his dark eyes, "Who could do this?"

"Something of the earth fires?"

I looked to Austere, "How so?"

"There are volcanoes and geysers on some of our land in lethyll. As they erupt they sometimes poison the air and places. Things die from the volcanic breath."

As a child, I read in books about such things, but only remembered them as he mentioned them. "When new ones appear, does the land look and act like this?"

"I-I don't know. I've never seen a brand new one. The odor is similar, but not." He shook his head, "That is of no help. The ones I remember smell of the powder we used for the explosions for the Cotkit."

"Sulfur." Spacya aided.

"Yes, that's it." Austere nodded.

"Do you think the smell will do harm to us or the horses?" Randia asked, a hesitance in her voice.

"I hope not. Let's find some people to see if it does."

We followed the road, assuming that it would lead to a house or at least to the tower that we saw peaking over the next ridge of slopes. We found the tower, along with low barns, three small houses, and a large frame residence. They all sat in a wide valley between the hills. As far as the eye could see, behind the mansion and barns held fruit-bearing trees, bushes and vines in neat, uniform rows.

"Huge house." Spacya muttered, eyeballing it as we approached.

It was. It wasn't as tall as the castle, but it crawled over the land as much as it did. A woman peaked out of the open barn door nearest us before walking out to greet us. She wiped her hands on a scrap of cloth that hung from her wide belt. A large-brimmed hat perched on top of a thick sandy colored braided thickness.

The lines around her mouth hinted at a lifetime of laughter and hard work stood out in the tanned color of her flushed skin. She couldn't have been much older than my mother, if I guessed correctly. Her eyes were sharp. She took in all of us with a sweep of her gaze.

My companions stopped, giving me room to move between them. With the ground under my feet, I started my spiel, "I'm Nadachia-"

"I know who you are," she placed her hands on her thick hips. "Been waiting for ya for a week. No one else would come help without you getting here first."

Her voice lay heavy in the rotten air. It was commanding, more so than the men and women who worked the guards in Owlimount. She stood like them, too. Straight back, shoulders squared, and a way of looking pissed without moving a single muscle in her face.

"Forgive our late arrival. It was unavoidable."

"Word is as such." She nodded, "Can't imagine coming back from the dead or fighting a beast of the gods."

She held out her hand, finally, "Kodola, it is a pleasure to meet you."

We clasped wrists; I noticed then that she wore bracers, like an archer under her sleeves. "The pleasure is mine." I turned, "These are my companions," I said before I introduced each of them.

She nodded, "Come down." A sharp whistle from her and a few bodies came out of the barn.

One just grinned as he took Unia's reins, "Don't see many fancy horses." He took hold of Austere's stallion too, "Especially not like this one, huh, Ma?"

"These are two of my boys. The loud one is Hari, the other Kienri and my baby girl is Parha. I have two others and a slew of other family, but they're out in the fields. The man behind me, who just come out the door, is my husband, Chefi."

Hari kept grinning through the introduction, "Don't worry, I'm the loudest until mealtime." He waved us away when we grabbed at our bags, "We'll take them into the rooms for ya."

"Fair enough."

"Follow me, unless you have some pressing matters to attend to before the tour." Kodola jerked her head to her home after she finished speaking.

No one made a move toward the house. "We're good, lead the way."

She led us to the barn and through it. There were four horses, not tall like Austere's stallion, but wide, who greeted with snorts and stares over their stall doors. I patted the velvety nose of the nearest, most friendly looking one.

"Any of you scared of heights?" She asked curtly, as we started up a hill.

I looked up and noticed we were approaching a massive wooden framed tower. "After the mountains, I think all of us will be fine. Right?" I glanced around at my companions and then studied Randia for a moment to make sure she would be alright. She shrugged her shoulders. She wasn't like Eilse then. I turned back to Kodola, "Do you use it often?"

"Constantly now. We've been measuring the spread of this disease or whatever it is."

"And before?"

"Only for hunting, picnics, and marking progress during planting and harvesting times." She mounted the stairs that zigged back and forth in the middle of it.

It was wide and made with thick planks of good, sturdy lumber. Most of the steps barely creaked with my weight and only a little with the heavier friends.

"When did you notice the spread first?"

"About three weeks ago. It started with one tree in the eastern lower, I'll show you once we get to the top." She glanced over her shoulder, "You'll be able to tell without me pointing it out, probably."

That didn't sound good. A shudder ran through me, and I thought I heard the lightest tingle of a bell nearby. I shook it off. "Have you been to the spot?"

"Plenty, at first. We ran our own tests and tried to stop the spread as best we could figure how. Nothing worked. We sent messages to other orchards and farms, but they don't have this. We all studied our books from generations past for anything similar. Nothing comes close to the growth this thing has, or its actions. It looks and smells like a blight or rot, but what we normally use to treat those won't even slow it."

"How do you deal with the smell?" Randia asked with a slight groan.

Kodola's shoulders stiffened slightly, "You get used to it after it makes you good and sick." She sighed as we reached the top of the tower and spread out on the large platform. A banister ran all along the edge, there were some benches and barrels placed along it and beside the opening we just came through. A water spigot poked up from one corner with a bucket and dipper underneath, but both were empty.

We were so high up that the odor had faded some. We were above the treetops, the barn and the house. As far as I could see were neat rows of trees and rows of vines resting on their wooden stakes. One side of the tower showcased beautiful fruit filled green trees, while the other exhibited the ashen trees and grasses with black husks instead of ripening fruit.

I moved to the east, searching for the spot. It didn't take me long. Three ridges over was a clearing. It looked like a pile of the darkest coals of a silent fire. From it, the ground was almost as dark as it, and it spiked out like a black star.

"Is it sunken in?"

"No."

"It's just there, on the surface?"

"Yes. Before you ask, the reek is less there. It's strongest near the edges. Once you get past the remnants of trees and grass, it isn't as strong unless it comes to you on the wind."

"What makes it so black?" Randia asked as she stood beside me.

"Don't know. My best reckoning is just rot. Death."

"I would like to go there."

"We will, first thing in the morning. It's not good to go through the rot at dusk or dark. In fact, you all would be harmed if we catch you wandering around at night out there." Kodola looked at me, "The rot or death spreads at night. It takes all live things."

"How…how did you figure that out?"

"I had six children before this came. Now I have five." She turned and started down the steps. "Stay and study as long as you like, when you're done, go to the main house. There my husband will fill you in on the tests and actions of this stuff further."

"I am sorry for your loss." She was already down the stairs when I managed to utter the words. I hated that she possibly hadn't heard them. I turned back to the ash and coal land.

Like all the other quests, this was beyond me. All I could do was speculate. I remembered one blight that struck Owlimount. That year was particularly hard for everyone. That was the year I learned to trap from the Welkans so we could get by. I was eight years old.

"Anyone seen a blight before?" Spacya leaned on the top rail, looking toward the starting point of it.

Most of my companions shook their heads.

"I saw a small one. Affected the Hardberry. Made their leaves change colors and the bark to flake off. Killed 'em slow if they were older trees, quick for the younger."

"From what I could gather, blights usually hit one or two of similar trees." Blari threw a hand out toward the orchard, "This is everything."

"Not a blight. Poison, then?" Tori paced the platform.

"Maybe. Has to be in the land. The river water was fine and it wouldn't be with it being so near to this affected part. Right?" I was stabbing at something tiny and mobile in the dark with this mystery.

"If it's in the soil, how did it kill her kid? Why does she make it sound alive at night?"

"Death. She made it sound like a living thing." Austere sighed, "And I don't blame her. It killed her child and is taking over her land."

"What about outside the orchard? The forest beyond or the hills that way? Has it touched them?" I pointed, thinking that the area toward the mountains would be too rocky for trees.

Austere took out his glass and looked. He shook his head, "It's going up the mountain's sides." He passed it to me.

All the shrubbery and grasses along the base of the mountain range were ashen. The ones that managed to survive on the rockiest face were being overtaken by whatever this was too. Such sturdy plants fallen ill with this. I passed the glass to Randia.

"So it isn't something directly affecting her. It's not revenge or something stupid that's creating this." I murmured under my breath.

Randia snorted, "Would humans do such a thing?"

I glanced at her, "Any race would do such a thing. This doesn't seem to be the case. Other than ourselves, is there another country that benefits from this orchard?"

"All our allies." Tori answered quickly, "Ecia, Iethyl, Ocrea, all of them."

Unless they wanted to damage their own people, or had another way to gain fruit, then those countries would not be behind this. What was I thinking? Probably no one was other than Keandria and the quests. The gods. Whoever made these destructive things.

I rubbed at the tension in my temples, "We need to go down to talk to the husband. What was his name again?"

"Chefi." Tori and Blari both chimed at the same time.

"Right." I looked at all of my comrades, "Any new ideas or thoughts right now?"

Tori opened his mouth to say something, then closed it and shook his head as Austere cleared his throat.

"Don't take this the wrong way, but do either of you feel anything from it?" He was looking at me and Randia.

I hadn't tried that. I searched wildly through my body, searching for those odd feelings that I knew were Sterla and Eilse. Nothing was reaching out to the dark spot or the ashen remains. Recoiling. I studied it, turning it over in my mind.

Knowing the difference between Eilse and Sterla within my own body set my nerves and mind reeling, but I clamped down on it. I had to keep level. My heart and my blood were still that of my family, my father and I.

"It's…they are trying to get away."

Randia nodded, "The same. There is something there, but I cannot reach out to it with my own power to study. It's like I'm reaching toward a bright light."

I hadn't tried that yet. Did it feel like this? I tried to remember anything I felt in Taspe's healing room, but I had been too focused on him. "Let's go down."

"Wonder why she doesn't want us going out there now. It's just midday." Tori glanced up at the sky as he allowed the rest of us to go ahead of him.

"Perhaps because of what's going on, dark comes early?"

"Another question for the husband." Austere added.

A smirk tugged at the corners of my lips, "Are you sad? Afraid you can't get any action here?"

He snorted, "I can get action anywhere."

"She'll string you to the tower before you can get it out of yer pants, boy." Spacya muttered, pointing to where Kodola was coming out of the barn leading a team of stout horses.

"Just have to charm her first."

Austere was the only one not laughing at that.

We entered the main house and were greeted by Chefi. "Hullo there, I'm Chefi, welcome to Sweetarbor House."

"Pleasure to meet you." I gave him a round of introductions much like I did his wife.

"My boys and I have taken the liberty of taking the things off your respective horses up to your rooms. I would like to show you around this old house, then allow you to wash up or do as you like for a few moments while I finish lunch up. Does that sound good?"

"Yes, thank you."

He nodded with a smile that showed a missing tooth on the right side of his right canine. I wasn't sure if it gave him some charm or made him look untrustworthy. "This is the entryway. This first door is to the living area as we call it." He slid the doors back into the wall and stepped back.

The room within seemed as long as the house was wide. Plush chairs, couches, pillows were everywhere. There were three large fireplaces along the center wall. Paintings and tapestries hung on the walls, leaving little of the wood underneath to be seen. Only the middle fireplace burned low and a couple of lamps on scattered tables gave off light. The drapes along the front were all closed.

"That door at the end we will come through later, I like to show you the center first before we make our way around and down the halls."

These people were rich. I had guessed it upon seeing the house, but witnessing all the paintings, all the finely crafted chairs and rugs just solidified it in my mind. I had an intense worry that I was suddenly going to break something.

He shut the doors behind us, then led us to the next room, "Here is the office." He slid these doors open. The walls were covered in shelves filled with books. The large desk in the center back of the room was tidy. A leather folder held some papers in the middle, a stack of envelopes with seals broken beside it, and a wooden holder of pencils and quills were on it. The papers and writing utensils were watched over by a carved and painted statue of a white owl with orange eyes.

"I know where Blari is going to sneak off to every chance he gets." Tori chuckled, nudging our priest with an elbow.

Blari nodded, his eyes wide as he turned a slow circle after stepping into the room, "There are even books above the door."

Chefi grinned, "It is my favorite room other than the kitchen. Please read whatever you like during your stay here. I only ask to put them back as you found them. I have them in a particular order that took me months to accomplish."

"You married into the family then? This was not yours?"

"I did. Kodola's family has run this orchard for as long as there was a word for it, maybe before that. I have often wondered if they were the reason why orchards came to being." He smiled, not showing his teeth. Again he closed the door behind us and led us to the next, "This room is a bit…odd." He opened the doors.

We were met with bright sunlight as the entirety of the room had floor to ceiling glass along the outside walls. Frames built wide and squat held plants of every type. Our little family garden would fit in this chamber three times over.

"You start the plants in here?"

"Yes, exactly." He grinned at me, "You must live on a farm."

"Yes, a small one." I nodded, with a smile.

The next series of rooms were all larger than my whole house combined. The kitchen looked like something from a fantasy as there were marbled counter tops and two barrel-belly black stoves. My room and the attic could fit into their cellar.

"Darling," his voice was soft as his breath made a hair tickle the back of my neck, "I do believe you can build a home like this if you want."

I snorted, then thought about his words. The payments from completing the quests were still being sent to my family. I wondered how much it was. In my head I added the base number of bits that the Queen had mentioned. I swallowed, "I could."

His fingers trailed along the shell of my ear, "I could build you a house like this, bigger, if you want."

"Is that another line you use with the ladies that won't give into you so easily?"

He chuckled, "No."

Sam Wicker

"Words like that mean a long term commitment." Chefi smirked over at us as he leaned on the banister of the wide staircase.

It was the first time I saw Austere go pale.

We were led to our rooms and allowed to freshen up.

As we ate lunch, I marveled at the jam made from the apples slathered on the sweet bread. It had a hint of spice to it. The ham was juicy, and according to Chefi, cooked with apples too.

"The tests we conducted were for normal things that one would find affecting plants, especially fruiting ones. We've seen blight before, in our apples. Thankfully, we caught it early enough that it didn't spread over all our trees that time. This one…" Chefi shook his head, "We noticed it in three trees, the next day it had twelve and the next thirty-five. Somehow, these past three days, the growth has slowed down some. Only ten to fifteen have been added each night."

"Any explanation as to what could be the cause of the slow down?"

Chefi stated with a frown, "I'd rather wait to say that until after you finish eating."

My stomach rolled.

"Any of the landowners around have an idea of what this could be?" Tori asked after finishing off his last sandwich.

"We all have ideas, but nothing we can prove." Chefi grumbled with a lift of his shoulder.

"Has there been anyone suspicious lurking around before this began?" I noticed all eyes turned on me at that question.

"No, not that I can recall."

I ate another piece of ham as Blari fired more questions at Chefi, and our host readily answered them. No one knew anything. Everything was a guess. The people who had dealt with this the most were just as clueless as we were as to what it was, but at least we knew what it wasn't.

It wasn't normal.

It was probably made by the gods just as the Cotkit was. Part of me still wondered if the Misshapen was a pet of one of them when I laid awake at night reliving my mistakes. My mistake. I couldn't blame them on Joni anymore. He was dead. That was my mistake too.

The ham turned to ash in my mouth.

"We will go see it in the morning. Hopefully, I can tell something about it from there or Randia can." I added into a lull in the conversation around me.

"Being the Hero gives you powers?" Chefi asked, his thick brows nearly meeting this thinning hairline.

"No, just being in the wrong place and getting on the bad side of something."

Chefi's mouth opened, then closed without a sound passing between his lips. Austere shot a look at me. Blari cleared his throat and found his nearly empty plate fascinating.

"Forgive me, it's a long story. One that would bore you to tears." I gave Chefi a small smile. "I truly enjoy your jellies. I would like to purchase some to send home."

Chefi gave me a nod, "That would be an honor to have your family enjoy our sweets. If you are finished eating, I can take you back to the cellar so you can make your selections."

I stood and followed him, Blari close on my heels. He tugged on my sleeve and I stopped.

"I thought he was teaching you diplomacy."

"It didn't take."

Blari sighed and shook his head.

Chapter 33

The house was so big that we each had a room to ourselves. I was missing the tent tonight. I lay on the curve of an old straw mattress. It had fresh added to it. Still, it hugged me to the center. I had my arms out straight, my fingertips dangled over the sides. Two of us could fit comfortably in it unless one was Spacya.

She needed her space to toss and turn at night.

I needed to talk. I needed to listen to someone talking. Something. Staring at the white-washed ceiling would not lull me to sleep.

I rolled, my feet slapping against the wood floor that was so smooth with polish and age I had to grip with my toes to keep from slipping. I moved over to the window and drew the heavy curtains back. My room faced the north. I had to twist to see the edge of the ashen trees and land.

I sucked a breath down into my lungs, readying myself.

There in the darkness, the land moved. It rose and fell in even increments. Every rise brought the craggy, thin trees closer to the sky, standing stark against the night field of stars before falling again.

My breath fogged the glass in white, it blended in well with the grayness of the breathing land.

Breathing.

I counted each move up, began the count again with each fall. They were not even. Breathing wasn't even unless you concentrated on it. I turned, shoving on my boots as my spine tingled at the idea of turning my back on such a thing.

I pulled on my coat, then put my arm through my belt of daggers. Boards creaked under my feet, and I inwardly cursed with each step as I made my way to the next room. I peeked in after I scratched the smooth polished wood with my fingernails just above the doorknob.

Tori crouched behind his bed, sword level above it, and pointed toward the door. He stood when he saw it was me. I mouthed the word: Tower. He nodded, and I walked to the next door.

Spacya was always the worst to wake up. Luckily, she was just as awake as I had been. "Do you always sleep in your boots?" I whispered loudly as she moved across the hall to work her magic on waking Randia and Blari up.

She just grinned.

I reached the next and cursed. I looked over my shoulder, but Spacya had just ducked into Randia's room. Why was it I had to enter the whore's room?

I prayed to the gods no one was naked inside.

No, don't let them be acting upon nakedness. Sleep nakedness I might handle, but… gods… what had my life become?

I stepped into the room, pulling the door shut behind me so that I wouldn't wake the rest of the house, just in case there was more than Austere inside.

His musk tickled my nose. No other scent. The rumpled white sheets came into my view as my eyes adjusted to the near complete dark. Why hadn't I brought my candle from my room with me?

Just sheets?

I set my teeth.

Then there were fingers sliding around my left hip before I was pulled against a warm, tall body. My hands smacked back against warm flesh, thick with muscle. Thighs. Gods.

—"Up just a touch more and you'll find something interesting." His breath was hot on the shell of my ear.

His other arm dropped to his side, I saw a flash of metal in the pale light of the moon coming in from the sides of the window ahead of me. "You alone?"

"Not anymore. I was wondering when you would come to your senses."

Something twitched against my backside.

I pushed off him and whirled as I put two steps between us. He chuckled.

I growled, and I cursed the pirate, "I have seen far too much of your skin!" At least I still had enough sense to whisper.

He shook his head, "Seen, yes, but you have yet to partake. You need to touch as much as you have seen."

"Now is not the time! We need to go to the tower. Something is…moving…out there."

"Something is moving… in here." He gave a pointed look at his groin.

My eyes followed, and it twitched again. The ceiling of his room was just like mine. The air was quite a bit hotter, though. Mustier too.

"Put. Clothes. On. Now."

"So demanding. Am I to take it that if now is not the time, there will be a time in the future?"

He moved toward me. The hand that had been trapping me against him just moments before reaching for me again. I reached for a dagger, and closed my eyes.

Rustling cloth sounded. I cracked open an eye. His smirk met my gaze as he shrugged into a shirt. He picked up his pants from the chair beside me. How I hadn't run into it in my mad three step dash, I hadn't a vague idea. After he pulled his pants on, he didn't bother to button them, but he placed his large hands over mine.

"Come now, darling."

I side stepped him, brushing one whole side of my body against his. This room was not big enough for the both of us. I had seen him naked too many times. Taunted by him too many times. I was far too frustrated and needy to be here. I desperately wanted my family, Father, or Taspe at my side each day and I'd be damned if I settled for something less at the moment.

"Tower." I stepped out into the hallway and breathed in the non-Austere scented air.

I hurried down the hall, trying to keep quiet. Hopefully, whatever the land had been doing it was still doing it. I hit the side door and threw myself down the first three steps before the air hit me.

The crisp chill of a night under the mountains dug through my loose nightclothes to reach my skin. The gooseflesh rose before the first shudder racked my body so hard I nearly missed the next step.

"Careful." A muscular hand grasped my elbow. I shuddered again and dared a glance back. He had clothes on. More than me. I eyed his jacket.

He let go of my elbow and brought my jacket from the crook of his arm forward. "Here."

"How…"

He smirked, "Long legs, love. They propel me quicker than your nice-"

"Thanks." I interrupted before he could bring the heat back to my face. I shrugged my jacket on with some difficulty, getting tangled in my belt as I bolted down the stairs the rest of the way. His chuckle made another chill run up and down my spine as I finally put everything in the right places on my person.

At the top, the others waited. Along with a member of Kodola's household. I couldn't remember his name, but he wasn't a son of hers. A cousin or nephew.

To the east, the land heaved all at once. It didn't roll, but swung up all together with the middle being the highest point and sloping down from there. It then sank back, the edges being the first to settle as the heart came down to do the same seconds later.

"It is breathing." I breathed, my lips cracking in the cool air.

As it rose again, I looked for any of the edges to have any plants that sucked in. As it dropped, I searched for a plume or ash or dust, anything. Nothing.

"It's been doing that since it started. All of a night. Here in about an hour it will start lurching."

"Lurching?"

The man nodded and gripped the butt of his gun he had resting on his shoulder tighter, so tight his knuckles were white. "About every sixth breath, it comes forward. On all sides."

Blari yawned so big that I heard his jaws crack beside me before he asked, "Like someone moving under a blanket?"

The guard stared at him for a moment, "I… yes, that is a good way to explain it."

Sam Wicker

We watched the large breaths of the earth. I separated us into groups, watching different spans of the infected or infested area before us. Austere had his glass to look through, so he got the farthest swatch of ashen land, the nephew or cousin the next, as he had one too. The moon's bright silver light washed over the ash and black gnarls, interrupted by the scudding fingerprint clouds. The breathing, as we were all calling it, made a mockery of death by making the trees and grasses look as if they were coming alive.

My imagination kept creating grotesque images of whatever was underneath the land. What beast or magic could lift entire trees over such a large area as if they were dust on billows? Each image grew more and more insane. The cold gripped me harder and harder with each my mind conjured. I couldn't tell where one shudder ended, and another one began.

"Why is it so cold here?"

The man looked at me after taking his glasses down from his eyes, "Dunno, miss. It can get cool at night during this time of the year, but never this cold. Not since I've been alive or anyone else on the farm here."

Another cloud shot over the moon, the darkness only lasted for a blink. The wind was incredible too, but only for the clouds. Barely a breeze tickled the chilly air further into my clothes, even at this height.

I wrapped my arms around my chest and watched the edges of my section. I swept my eyes between one gnarled apple tree to the edge of Blari's section over on the next ridge. No breath was escaping. Maybe it wasn't breathing.

Mine feathered out in front of me.

"Idiot." I muttered to myself, "The gods gave you an idiot for a hero." I shook my head at myself and walked. There were only a handful of beasts that had air expulsion right next to where their lungs were.

"What?" Blari's eyes watered from biting back another yawn.

"Our mouths aren't right on top of our lungs." I pulled my coat tighter around me.

Nothing was coming up out of the ground in my line of sight. "Austere?"

"On it." He circled in place, his glass glued to his eye.

"Er…"

I glanced over at Randia; she pointed up.

I followed her finger to a point far into the night sky. A cloud formed. It was small, white, pooling in place before shooting off. Each of the other small clouds was doing the same, running across the sky from that point in every direction.

Austere was beside us in an instant, scanning the ground. "There. I think I see a hole."

He bent his knees, making himself level with my height before handing me the glass. He pointed to what he saw. "See it?"

I looked, squinting even with the glass. It couldn't be bigger than a barrel, and at this distance it was like trying to find a mouse's tooth on the floor without stooping. "Yes. Let's go."

"Wait!" the man cried, "You can't! It will change you, dry you up like it did the trees!"

That was right. Kodola's warning rang in my head. "How much time until it spreads?"

"Should be any time now?"

I looked up at the position of the moon. It had been over an hour, at least, since I first noticed the land breathing. "How long has this gone on tonight?"

"Three hours." The man jerked his chin to the closest edge, "Look."

We turned, I walked back to the edge. Right before my eyes, a thriving tree with hundreds of apples weighing the thick limbs down curled in on itself on its backside. The leaves crumbled to ash, the apples split as their skins turned from silvery green in the moonlight to gray, then black before bits shed off, until only the wilted cores hung from the branches if they didn't fall to the graying grass below. Heavy limbs lifted as their harvest weight lightened before the thin new growths crumbled, the twigs gnarled, and sections began peeling off their barks. The timber grew naked and old. We watched the long lifetime of a tree pass in a few minutes. That tree would have outlived me under normal circumstances.

The guard shook his head, "My great-grandfather planted those trees."

My heart sank. He voiced what everyone on this farm was thinking. The work of generations undone, disappearing in seconds after decades of care and love.I watched as the grass under the tree started the same show. It wasn't as beautiful in the despair, but it was still painful to watch as the sickness crawled ever closer to the farmhouses.

"You should go back to bed. I appreciate the company, but I'm sure Kodola has plans for you at dawn."

Austere groaned, "Yes, come on. Thank you for watching over us and helping."

"Thank you for coming to help." He hissed in a breath, "We could use more."

I started down the stairs and made my way across the yard to the house. I looked up, on a whim. Kodola stood on the bottom step, watching us. Before we could reach her, she disappeared back inside.

"Bit of an odd one, isn't she?" Austere murmured behind me.

"How would you act if everything your family worked for was turning to ash under your watch?"

Austere sighed after a moment, "Probably be drunk all the time."

I snorted, "Well, this is her drunk."

Dawn arrived too early. I finally got some sleep after counting the dips and cracks in the wood of my bedroom ceiling. After a hearty breakfast, we headed out. To the East, the bright morning sun burned spots into our eyes as we walked. The first step into the diseased circle the grass fell to ash, coating my boots with a light dust.

Dew didn't land here.

The ash was drier than the desert sands. I began coughing as we walked. It wafted up with each person's steps. I pulled a scarf out of my bag and tied it around my nose and mouth. Tori had on one of his fancy handkerchiefs over his face, Spacya her shirt, Blari used his wide sleeve, Randia's still had the one Tori had given her yesterday, and Austere had a checkered cloth tied to his face. I dug around for a spare anything for Blari, but Kodola beat me to it by handing him a kerchief.

I glanced behind us. Like walking through snow on a windless hill, we left a trail of footprints and scuffs in the ash. It took us an hour to get to the area where the thing started.

No movement. Even the music of the songbirds seemed muffled, growing quieter with each step until only the crunch of ashed grasses and twigs under our feet sounded. The breathing from last night was gone. No plume rose from the area into the soft blue sky, growing from reds and oranges as the sun burned away the morning fog hugging the mountains and nearby waterways.

Was it truly ash?

It didn't stink like it, but it acted like it.

I kneeled, running my hand over the grass, the fibers gave way to powder. I brought it up to my nose. Nothing. Only me.

I pressed the tip of my tongue to my index finger. I let the ash roll around before spitting it out. No flavor. I didn't know there was such a thing. Ash had a spice. It didn't even taste like grass.

I curled my hands, letting it sift through my fingers. From what I could see, each grain was the same size. A little bigger than the white sands of the desert, but smaller than the fertile, dark soil of a garden. Even the pyres we burned at Columbri had different sized ash.

I stood, running to catch up with the others. They stopped a short distance away, probably only realizing then that I was behind. None of them were talking.

"Are we praying?" I asked, not wanting to break the silence, but not wanting it to go any longer either.

Blari smirked, "Always."

Stere snorted, "Speak for yourself."

Kodola shook her head, "I thought a heathen like you would not pray. I was right."

"Heathen?" Austere tilted his head slightly.

"You reek of salt and sea." Kodola waved her hand, "Whether you're a merchant or a pirate, all they care about is coin, a godless life."

That was a first.

Austere chuckled, "Pirate, but a prince now too. Not to mention I'm a companion to the Hero. My godless life has given me many gods-given blessings, wouldn't you say?"

Kodola's eyes narrowed as she looked Austere in the eyes. She sniffed, "Wouldn't say that for you. But maybe you are part of the plan to help save one of them."

We started on, following Kodola as she trudged toward the center, to the blackness ahead.

Soon our feet didn't crunch newly ashed grasses and what remained of bark and limbs. We walked through the ash like it was the sand of a dried riverbed. It was darker here, charred looking. I knelt again, trying to get some sense from it. Still no taste, now there wasn't an odor, either. The grains were larger.

If they were larger, why did the smell go away?

I rubbed my hands off on my pants, leaving ashy handprints on the dark canvas. We finally made it to the center. The last few feet was a downward spiral into the side of the hill. An odd sensation of half climbing and half sliding to it, as I had never had to get into a hole in a hill before. It reminded me of crawling into a hidden cave on the side of a mountain, but without a narrow opening.

"What have you been figuring out?" Kodola asked, standing over the center of the hole where a large, black boulder shaped thing protruded.

"It has no taste."

Kodola's eyebrows sketched, "And?"

"The grains are the same size. All of them. But the darker ones are larger than the ones on the outskirts. No flavor for them either though." I poked the boulder thing with a finger and jerked back.

Black goo stuck to the end of my finger.

"You're acting like a child." Tori cleared his throat, "What if something had attacked and bit your finger?"

"Then I would have a short finger." I shrugged.

Spacya chuckled, scooping up a handful of the larger grains around the rounded boulder and letting them sift through her fingers. "There's a bit of an odor here."

I sniffed the black goop and nodded. I didn't rightly recall what wet charcoal smelled like, but that had to be it. "What's in the boulder?"

"Can't break it open. We've tried axes. Tried digging it up so we could throw it off the tower to bust it open, but each time we were about to lift it out, it burrowed down again."

"It moves?!" Blari stepped back, his scribbling pausing for a second as he stared at the thing.

"It's not hot or cold. Should be cool, the sun hasn't hit it yet." I muttered, more to myself than to anyone else.

"Nadachia, use your feeling." Randia whispered at my side.

I glanced up at her, having to squint as the sun was directly behind her head. I nodded and looked back down. The boulder swam in my gaze with the sunspots. Nothing.

"Everything that moves has an energy. But not this."

"Let's get the shovels and dig again. Chi, you think you can wrap and pull this thing up with your threads?"

I glanced up at Tori, "We can try at least."

"Threads? What are you talking about?" Kodola eyed me.

I stood, meeting her gaze, "It's a long story, but I'm probably more of a heathen than any merchant or pirate you've ever met."

Austere's laughter made the rest of the group grin if not chuckle a bit. All except Kodola. She shook her head, "Whatever gets this taken care of so I can save my family."

Only Spacya and I had brought our packs. Neither of us had a decent shovel, but I had a rather large metal plate, and Spacya had one just a little smaller than mine. Tori and Austere set to digging with them around the moist rounded thing. Spacya and

Kodola helped by pulling the dirt they dug out away from the area. They dug slowly, so the boulder wouldn't start moving down on its own.

"Breathe." Randia murmured, moving into my line of sight. "You need to concentrate on where you are putting these, otherwise you may cause more harm than good as… well, we don't know what this is."

I nodded, "Of course." My only concern was how deep this thing was. How was I supposed to know when to curl the strands up and around? Did I have that much control yet? I was going to screw this up.

I'd only practiced with the threads for one hour each night before bed. The healing portion was far more useful and interesting to me. I had made the wrong choice of concentration.

"About ready?" Austere and Tori paused in their digging and scooping. He looked up at me, those red eyes flashing orange in the morning light.

Randia moved to my side. I swallowed the extra saliva pooling into my mouth and rubbed at my sweaty hands, smearing the ash in streaks over my fingers and palms. I reviewed the little training I had received over the course of the… how long had it been since I killed Eilse?

Pin pricks of heat formed at the corners of my eyes and I shook my head. I had to concentrate. I had to do this.

"It's curved all around I think." Austere's steady voice reached my ears as they burned, too. I opened my eyes to look.

He was right.

Where they had scooped it out, you could see the ash covered bottom edge curving just like the topside did. If I could just follow the curve, somehow, I could at least get it in the strands. I met Austere's eyes, below them I saw his lips curl upward at the corners, before he looked back down at his work.

As I was taught, I concentrated on myself. The power I needed to use. It was like reaching into a well without knowing where the bucket was or how deep to the bottom. I felt it. The slick sensation that was neither fear nor comfort.

The power of the strands from Eilse was like water made of threads. Thick, but enveloping and giving. I imagined the threads flowing towards my fingertips from deep within me. I imagined them flowing from there toward the egg looking thing.

Kodola gasped.

I nearly dropped my concentration, but the power did not waver. It knew my intent and followed through. They became an extension of me. I felt the grit of the ash as the threads pushed through it and the dirt around the large black thing.

They gingerly touched the gooey underbelly before drawing away and pushing into the earth further down. Down they slithered, following the curve of the boulder, or egg, thing, until they pushed back up and around the backside. Up and out of the ash and dirt, back in on themselves until the threads became a nice, thick sack.

The threads snapped into place. Austere plucked a single strand with his fingertips. It sounded a deep timbre and took a while to still.

"Randia, help me pull. If it goes under, I might need more help to hold it."

Blari stopped writing and switched with Tori. The prince came to my side and filled his hands with the strands.

"Ready?" Austere glanced up at us.

I nodded.

Blari and Austere dug and scooped quickly. Spacya and Kodola stepped out of the way as more ash was flung than carefully placed. Tori and I were pulled forward as it shifted.

I realized the folly of our plan then.

I quickly wove new strands together into three thick poles. "Put them under."

Spacya grabbed one, shoving the end under the edge and using it as a lever. Kodola did the same after watching Spacya. Randia stopped pulling and grabbed the last pole and put it in the earth beside Spacya's.

"You're getting better at this." Randia murmured with a small grunt following.

Tori and I pulled. The thing weighed as much as a horse. Until it inched forward.

I glanced at Kodola as we pulled the thing up on my makeshift poles. She drew her brows down to her nose and her lips were in a thin line. This was going too easily.

Spacya, Randia and Kodola kept angling the poles so we could draw and pull the thing up on them. Austere and Blari stopped digging and grabbed the ends the three had set in the earth.

Once the thing was up onto the poles halfway, I used more threads to lash it to them. I didn't want the thing rolling off once we started moving it. If we did. What would happen if we moved it to a green spot? Would it kill everything there?

"I don't like this."

I glanced at Kodola, but her back was turned to me. She was looking down at the place the boulder used to be. "What?"

Austere shook his head, "It's uh… if I didn't know better… I would say we hadn't moved it at all."

I shifted so I could see past the thing on the poles to where I would imagine a large hole in the earth being. It was still on the ground. The one on the poles we'd worked so hard to get up and out, gone. I willed some strands of the sack I had wrapped around the thing away as they hugged only air.

Ash sifted through the hole I made, making a little heap beneath the poles.

I sat down where I stood. My eyes were on the black thing. Did we just all imagine the same thing happening? Some of us were even breathing heavily from the exertion.

I heard the scratch of Blari's quill on the page. All else was silent in our little group.

"Illusions. Some form of trickery."

I glanced up at Tori. His hands were in his hair. The strands stuck up between his fingers. "That would seem to be the only explanation."

"No power." Randia whispered. She cleared her throat before continuing, "I didn't sense any power being used other than Nadachia's."

The black thing had some significance to this mess.

I stood, pulling my crossbow from the bottom of my pack. I pulled a bolt, set it and aimed. Kodola and Randia jumped away from the black thing, and Austere just sidestepped. All eyes were on it as I fired.

The bolt thunked against the center of the boulder's side, held its place for a blink, and then fell to the ash. It was whole. The point didn't have any of the goo on it.

"I had to try."

Kodola nodded, "We did too."

"Can you make a bolt?"

I snorted, "I'm no blacksmith."

"Out of your threads, darling."

I sighed as heat crawled up my neck. At least it was getting warmer. I formed a few strands, twisting and lengthening them together. When I fit them in the crossbow, it was too thick. I frowned, and it grew too thin. I bit the inside of my cheek.

"Breathe." Austere murmured beside me.

I wanted to stick my tongue out at him. I didn't dare. He would probably take that as some type of invitation. I could have shot him with the crossbow.

I took a deep breath. I concentrated on what I wanted the threads to do. The bolt fit into the bow with ease after a few more steadying breaths. It wasn't the perfect fit, but neither were some of my bolts. The beauty of having everything made by tradesmen and women was that each had a uniqueness to them. My strands were the same way it seemed. I took aim again, willing the bolt to fly true. At least it wasn't a moving target.

I flicked my gaze to Austere, wondering if I should make this first one a moving target, but I refocused on the thing on the ground at our feet. I loosed the bolt. It flew true, if not arcing down a little at the end. I hadn't thought about the weight distribution much, but I figured the power had taken my intention well enough.

Like the wooden bolt, the one made of my strands thunked against the side and held. Only this time, after two blinks, it still held. Austere stepped forward and studied the area around the bolt. I waited for his words. He jerked the bolt out, showing me the tip where a glob had attached, and stayed.

"It looks like there are some cracks around the hole. Come closer. Can you tighten the string?"

"I can, but I won't be able to set it." It was difficult for me to pull back to begin with.

"I can do that." Tori held out his hand.

I gave him my crossbow, and he ratcheted up the pressure, then pulled and set the string with a grunt. "It's not healing itself, is it?"

"No, not that I can see." The pirate prince stepped back again as I took aim.

I fired, the crossbow sounding louder in my ear than it ever had before. It surprised me the old thing could take so much force and not snap something. The thunk was noticeably louder, too. The crack afterward was new.

Austere grinned as he watched the bolt, "Good. Another. This one is deeper, and it's made a crack." He yanked the bolt out. Some of the goop and a few pieces of the black thing bounced once on the curved side, picking up more goop as they slid down before falling into the ash. Both were covered in the little ash cloud they created before everything settled again.

"Can you see anything inside?"

He shook his head, "Like a rock. It's more of the same substance on the outside, just under the sticky parts."

"Can you hit the same spot?" Tori asked, as I handed him the crossbow.

"I'll do my best." Kodola's eyes burned into me. I took the crossbow back and made another bolt out of the threads Eilse had willed me of her powers. With a dagger, I could hit that spot again. But it wouldn't be as hard of a hit.

I took the shot. It landed below the first bit I had taken out. The break was larger, and took a chunk out. It was acting like a rock now. A rock couldn't cause six people to imagine it being lifted out of the hole when it hadn't moved at all, though.

This chunk was larger, but it hadn't made the progress deeper. Just wider.

I shot five bolts into the hole; some shots better than others. On the sixth, the bolt sank through until an inch of the back tip was the only bit showing.

"Gods!" Kodola rushed to the black thing. "Is it real or another trick?"

Austere dug at the end, but couldn't get a good grip on it with the goop all over his fingers. He smiled, "I think that this might be real." He jerked back and flung an arm across Kodola to make her step away.

Out of the cracks and around the bolt appeared a dark green, almost black, thick liquid. It wasn't as thick as the coating on the outside, but it was close. It spat once, splattering the thick green over the black hide and ash. Then it began leaking down in a slow column of paste. It suddenly reminded me of the time I had squished a large green caterpillar under the toe of my boot. It had oozed greenish yellow insides like this.

"Oh, gods…it's not an egg, is it?"

I looked over at Blari, his face stark pale against his dark beard. I wove some strands, hooking them to the inside of the hole. Handing a handful to Austere and Kodola, we pulled.

The thing cracked open from the bolt protrusion. More of the thick paste oozed out, turning lighter in color as it splatted heavily upon the ash. The shell was as thick as two of my fingers were wide. The middle slowed in flow. As we moved some of the shell shards, some plopped into the little mudhole we had created at our feet.

Gingerly, I dipped the tip of my finger into the dark liquid. It didn't burn, but it was warm, unlike the shell. I tapped the goo on my finger with my thumb. Tendrils of the stuff joined my two separated fingers like melted cheese over two pieces of bread that had been pulled apart.

"Look at the color of the middle. It's kin to green apples."

Kodola would know. I hadn't put that together. "Isn't this portion mostly green apples?"

She nodded. I was glad it hadn't been red. I released the strands we had used to pull it apart. What magic or trick that had made us believe we had lifted it seemed to have given up once we cracked the shell. What magic would not take action at this stage? Was this an illusion, too?

Madness. How was I to know what's real anymore?

I pulled a bolt free and poked the goop in the middle. Solids bumped against the bolt as I dragged it through the soup. I flipped and pulled the bolt upward, hoping to make whatever was bumping against it float to the surface.

What I saw next had the ash filling my lungs as I flew back and away, twisting as I tripped over Kodola's foot. I landed on my forearms and knees. I sucked in a deep breath before my stomach emptied.

Long fingers dragged the loose strands of my hair away from my face before they rested coolly against the back of my neck. Someone pulled the rag off my neck that I had used to breathe through on the way here and gave it to me to wipe off. I wiped my mouth off, and cheek. I watched my hands shake like leaves against the first hint of the winter wind.

Why do you disturb our dead?

"What is it? What did you see?" Austere asked, his palm trailing down my back to pat gently.

I saw Spacya and Tori move toward the shell. "No. No don't look!"

Why are you doing this to us?

Was no one else going to answer that? I looked around. I met Austere's eyes, his brow hitched toward his hairline as he stared at me.

"I saw…it's…"

Our dead. You desecrated our dead.

"Stop!" I growled, yanking my body forward, scrambling toward Kodola, Spacya and Tori. "Move away. Do you hear it?"

Spacya and Tori looked at one another.

I looked at everyone else. "Who… who keeps whispering?"

"Darling, what do you mean?" Austere was on me, helping me stand. His large hand cupped my cheek, his eyes level with mine. His hand was steady and warm against my flesh. Could he feel how I shook from the inside?

Touch them with your pinky, little human.

I reached up, placing my hand over Austere's against my cheek. The goo squished as I pressed my fingers against the back of his hand. His free hand came up to rest on my neck and jaw. My pulse beat a fast thrum against his palm.

Humans. Always touching what they ought not.

Austere's eyes widened slightly. He whispered in a language I did now know. It was fluid, like music instead of words. The little thing that was whispering laughed in reply. Austere sighed and moved to the base of the egg, boulder, thing. He took a bolt, dipped it into the goo that was resting in a small pool atop the ash. He kept talking in that language as he touched each companion and Kodola with the bolt.

We know the common tongue, boy. Your friends do not know ours.

I stared at Austere. Our tongue? Just who or what was he?

"Forgive me, I was trying to make amends for our grave mistake." He fell to his knees after touching the bolt to Randia. "I hope you can forgive us."

The young often need experience to learn. There were suddenly many voices speaking in the same language Austere had earlier. Only one kept to the common tongue with, *We shall forgive if we gain your aid.*

Chapter 34

Tori knelt on his knees, then Blari. There were plenty of discussions going on in the language that I did not understand. Mostly with the things, the beings, whatever was speaking. I swallowed the bile that was rising dangerously again.

At a lull in the musical discussion, Austere spoke, "That is why we are here, Natural Ones. How can we help?"

"What are we talking to?" Kodola asked, her face pale, as she too knelt beside the others.

Sometimes they sounded right by my ears, then some as if they were bouncing along the hills. If those had been their dead, my gaze swung back to the black egg. I wasn't sure if I wanted to see the living ones.

I moved to my knees. If I was going to throw up again, I might as well be nearer the ground. Randia knelt beside me. I buried my hands in the ash to concentrate on something other than the thoughts and images in my head. "I am sorry. So sorry."

"Child, will you help?"

That voice was right beside my ear. "Yes." My gut wrenched with the word, then settled. There was no malice in the voices. Something reminded me of the power of Aul, but this seemed older. Somehow.

"Our home is being eaten by a sickness, a plague. We have done everything in our ability to stop it. To free and dissolve it, but we have not managed it. Our suffering has caused our homes to rot and ash to abound."

"Wait." Kodola's eyes were all whites as she swallowed loud enough for me to hear it. "Your homes?"

"The first patriarch of your family gave us care and homes after we moved here from our homeland across the seas. As time and gods changed, we have stayed a hidden constant."

She let out a small strangled cry, "Th-they're real?! They were just bedtime stories!" She wrapped her arms around herself, "Can I- can we see you?"

"Yes, you may only after I ask this. We must ask for your forgiveness. We could not get to your son in time. The sickness destroys all in its path and we have been pushing it from the soil each night so that it may not be irreversibly destroyed. The harvest this year was a sacrifice we chose to make, but not a human life. Never a human life."

She turned her head away from us, looking back towards her house. "The harvest for the land to grow again?"

"Yes."

"I think I understand."

"And our forgiveness?"

She nodded, "I could not get to him in time either. I am still... I am still grieving."

"We understand." A shimmer began before Kodola.

It shone white before becoming pin pricks of blue light. White fur, mottled with gray, long and fluffy, appeared. Four large black eyes with long lashes blinked over a narrow muzzle tipped with a triangular nose. Slender arms with three joints each ending with ten-fingered webbed hands with sharp curved claws. They had two longer legs, tipped in the same way, and looked like they would jump instead of walk. A tail took up most of the fluff and could easily cover the body like a blanket. On the tail were three thicker shafts of hair that ended in three tiny indigo lights.

It shook its tail, the bulbs of light jingling softly as rounded, fluffy ears perked forward at the top of its head. *"Your ancestor said I was the spokes beast and named me Jingles."*

As it spoke, the mouth did not move. The tail flicked and shuddered; the bulbs producing the musical voice.

"That he presumed to give you a name and title must mean you were great friends." Austere smiled at the little thing floating in midair.

"Yes, if I may ask, why are you in this place? You know our tongue and look like the humans of the islands, our original home."

"Like you, we have explored and settled in different areas. Our numbers and need for adventure have sent many of us to distant lands and waters. I am here to make my mark as a companion to the Hero." Austere motioned to me with one hand.

"*Ah yes, humans are given the chance to prove themselves worthy every generation or so. They have yet to succeed?*" The little beast turned its dark eyes on me. "*This one may yet.*"

"She will."

"I will do my best." I didn't feel the words, but I had to say something. "How can we help?"

"*Our powers are limited to the earth. The disease we fight has cost us much. All of us are at starvation, weak, and sick. We must get the disease in the air, where it will die.*"

"How can we help you do that?"

"*You must dig. We are too few now and too deep to get it out properly. It is much worse than we anticipated. We were not permitted to show ourselves before, but as the Hero is here for the humans, we feared we must now.*"

"How much should we dig and where?" Kodola asked as she stared at the little beast.

"*All along the west. We have a vent there; it is a natural one that the gods blessed this land with, but we need it widened, otherwise I fear that the disease will move around and continue escaping our efforts.*"

"Consider it done. How wide on each side, Natural One Jingles?" Austere asked.

It was odd to have that name attached to someone, a being that has apparently been around for close to a thousand years, if not longer. There was no telling how long Jingles had been alive before Kodola's ancestor gave it a home. The little beast still had his eyes on me, but he was not near me.

"*I am old, yes Hero, you are correct. Jingles is a title I have grown to enjoy. The tail flicked and the little balls tinkled a laugh. We would need it to reach at least half the length of the width of that side. The plague is large and reaching farther each night and day.*"

"You were the ones creating the breathing sensation in the land last night, yes?" Blari jotted some things down.

I wondered if he was going to illustrate this one, too. He was a terrible artist, while being an expert writer. It was a shame, really. While his words were enough to paint a picture in one's mind, it would have been fulfilling for him to draw them, too. He grew frustrated with his drawings, even though I knew they were far better than anything I could try. Moko would have already done a perfect little drawing.

"Yes, that is how we get it into the air to kill it."

"Is it the moonlight that kills it, or the actual air?"

"Air. We only performed at night so as to not scare our human benefactors."

"What do you get from the land, and us, other than a home?" Kodola again.

Behind her and all around, I saw shimmers turning into these little beasts. They were far more pretty, fluffy and cute than the skeletons in the shell gave them credit for. I suppose even things such as these had a vast difference between their bones and their flesh, just like humans and other beasts.

"Other than a home, we gain food and all we need. Humans provide us with nutrients by planting fruit and vegetable plants that give off the gases and nutrients in the soil. The soil gives them what they need, and they give us what we need in return. Your ancestor was keen on planting potatoes, but we convinced him that apples and other fruit trees would be far more beneficial and lucrative to both of our needs. We build our homes from dead bark pieces within the root systems deep below the surface. Human waste has a way of providing nutrients for us as well, although we need to bury it and break it down some more. Your pile of waste of food and the like over by the north barn is most beneficial. Thank you for keeping it in one place rather than just tossing things about here and there for us to hunt down and carry. Now we have a system… I am getting ahead of myself. Do you think you can manage a wide trench by tonight?"

"I will go tell my family to begin now." Kodola turned, only to freeze upon seeing all the others.

"Do not be frightened or scared that you will step on us. We are quite agile."

She nodded and began walking.

"Will you walk with us?"

"If you allow me to ride upon your shoulder or in your hand, I shall not walk."

Austere chuckled, "You certainly differ from the ones over on the islands. They would not allow us to touch them, too proud."

"That is part of why we left. That faction is too full of themselves. They do not realize that we are the same, all of us. The Depth Ones, the Sun Eaters, the God Breeds, the humans and us are all the same. We all must live on this earth and provide for our families and ourselves the best we can."

"The Sun Eaters? God Breeds? The Depth Ones?"

"Welkans, Rogues, and Stygra."

"Much of what was made and what was common knowledge has been lost along the generations. It is why we disappeared so easily. We became stories for adults to tell children so they wouldn't run about at night or poke their little faces in our burrows. One mistook a burrow for one of ours, but it was a poisonous thing, and from then on we were something to be feared. Fear is such an overwhelming oddity that causes all to lose common decency and courtesy."

Without asking, Jingles came over to me and began riding on my shoulder after crawling up my arm. Others crawled all over my companions, but he was the only one on me. "I see what fear can do. It is a terrible driver, but it is an instinct."

"Yes, my child."

Two paws rested on my cheek. *"You have done many things to rid yourself of your fear, but alas, you only made it worse. Tamping and trapping such powerful emotions shall never cure you of it. Facing those things that cause you fear, now that is how you tame the beast. You must come into yourself, my child. That is going to be the only way you shall win the hearts of the gods and the gift for all human-kind."*

If I proved us worthy. Hundreds of years had passed since the first human Hero, and each had failed. I would probably fail too. I was not any better, nor any different from any of them.

"Ah, see, there is that fear you hold again."

"She fears her ability." Austere murmured as we marched behind Kodola and the bounding Natural Ones ahead of us.

"Somewhat right, young one. She fears relying on others and having others relying on her and failing. You love her, help her with this."

I spluttered, the heat in my cheeks beat into place with my pulse in moments.

Austere laughed, at a higher pitch than I ever heard it before, "I adore her, but I would hardly call it love."

"Ah, ignore that then. I did not know you two were in the awkward human stage of not admitting your feelings to one another. I shall not meddle."

"That's rich!" Tori chuckled, "Austere pretends he loves everyone and Chi is oblivious."

"Humans and your idiotic ideas of only being able to love one at a time."

"How do you know our feelings?" Blari and his amazing questions.

"We pick up on what you call pheromones and your chemical responses in your mind and bodies. It is as easy as when you read a book. I enjoy reading books too."

Blari nodded, still walking and writing at the same time with more Natural Ones on him than there were anyone else. It looked like they truly enjoyed reading.

"Wait, Austere loved me?" I glanced back at Stere.

He watched his feet. His hair formed a curtain between me and his face. That he wasn't joking about what they had said made my heart skip a beat. We made it back to the house in a shorter time than it took us to get to the shell.

"I am sorry for what we did. After we dig this trench, I would like to help to repair the damage for your dead."

"My darling, caring child, it is enough to express your remorse. We are already repairing the damage. We are sorry we made you all question your sanity."

"That was impressive. Do you do that often to humans?" Randia seemed a little too excited for the answer as she grinned at the Natural One on her arm.

"Only when we are discovered. We know that seeing something you do not know often causes fear, so we will it away or erase it from your minds."

"Understandable."

"We do it to the Depth Ones too, little one."

Randi seemed to settle after that comment.

"How old are you, exactly?"

The jingles tinkled a lot, *"Before The God Made were created, and The Sun Eaters and The Depth Ones were but children and dreaming of gods."*

"I… you're old."

"That's an understatement." He was back to his old self it seemed.

Kodola made one of her sons ring the bells to call people in. They handed out shovels and picks. Chefi and two other men dragged out an old machine and pulled it to the vent with a team of four horses.

We followed the machine. Kodola barked out orders and placed her workers and family members in stations, as well as us. The Natural Ones stuck with us, helping. Here, the land was rocky and bare. The vent gave out whiffs of a strong, rotten egg odor and, around it, yellow powder covered the soil and rocks. The disease had already taken what trees grew, but it didn't reach any further than the vent. If the fluffy gods had tried another way, most of the orchard would be ash.

I found myself between Austere and Spacya. We dug with our shovels. The younger kids came by with barrows and carted off our dirt piles we created on sheets and tarps. A handful of the other kids carried buckets of water from the wells nearer the house to give us drinks at regular intervals. We stopped for a small meal and began again.

I had forgotten how accomplished I felt after finishing a project such as this. By sunset, Jingles figured we had opened the vent enough. A large chasm was open to the depths of a narrow, long cave. Within, the earth looked yellowed and grayed. Unnatural in every sense. The smell kept waffling between rotten eggs and death.

"Everyone must get away. At least back to the house. Keep indoors. Please put blankets and things along any openings to the outside. We shall work hard to rid the land of this, I do not wish for some stray strands to find their way into the house and harm one of you."

The distance between here and the house was great, but I wasn't about to argue. If Jingles thought we might be in danger, I would follow his suggestion. "Is there anything else we can do to help?"

"Pray to the gods, child. You had their ears since birth, though you rarely use that."

I blinked, Jingles tail flicked outrageously even as he patted me on the cheeks with his paws before running away and running down into the chasm.

"How are they not affected?"

I looked, and it was one of Kodola's sons. He was leaning heavily upon a pick, his bare back and chest glistening in the fading sunlight, "They grieve more dead than you do. Trust me."

He swallowed, "Sorry, I didn't mean..."

I nodded, "A loss of a sibling must be hard. They regret they couldn't stop it, they said so to your mother earlier. I'm sure your family and the Natural Ones will have plenty of time to talk things over when all this is through."

I was doing nothing and its weight was irritating.

We walked back to the house. Kodola and her husband herding their family and workers into their houses and giving them orders to cover and stuff all cracks and holes that they could find. We made it back to the main house.

Jingles appeared before me again. *"You might as well sleep for the night. We shall wake you early in the morning, or if something goes wrong. Do not forget to pray, though."*

"I won't." I sighed, stepping inside and helping to stuff the window curtains into the corners and around the glass panes as best as we could. We took blankets and stuffed them around the door frames. They shut chimney flues. We covered the cellar doors with thick rugs.

Sam Wicker

All the while, I spoke to the air under my breath, naming all the gods I could and asking for their help, their strength and protection for the Natural Ones. I begged for them to destroy this disease. I pleaded with them to protect all living things, but especially those little beasts and this beautiful family.

I marched up the stairs and toward my room, after a bath in the communal bath house. Austere's heavy footfalls right behind me. I made it to my door and paused, my hand on the knob. He leaned against the wall beside my door.

I looked up into his eyes; he stared into mine.

I nodded, then he did the same. I opened my door and let us both inside.

"Where are you from, exactly?" I sank onto the bed. He lay on it. I leaned forward, trying not to get into his space too much. He wrapped an arm around me and pulled me back against his chest. We settled comfortably. I rested my arms along the length of his thighs. Why did this feel as right as it did with Taspe?

"To the right and below the south mainland. I was born on an island called Dorant in the common tongue. It is the beginning of the Natural Ones' domain, their home island too."

"What language was that?"

"The language of the gods is what the Natural Ones called it. They taught me when I was a boy. I was taught the common tongue long after that. It's more natural to me than the common tongue, honestly."

"You don't have an accent."

Austere chuckled, "My mother taught us. She saw the way my father spoke as heathen even if it curled her toes of a night."

"Your father was always a pirate?"

"Born on a ship in the middle of a gale, he says. He's been on the seas ever since." He sighed, "Are we not going to talk about what the Natural One said?"

"That you love me?"

He snorted, "That you love me."

I shook my head, "He said both."

"It. They are both male and female."

"You're still changing the subject, even though you broached it, pirate."

He sighed, "I will admit this: I hold a deep respect for you and I find myself doing things, and considering things with you in mind that I have not done for another. Not even…" he cleared his throat as if clearing his thoughts.

"Not even…who?"

"The one I thought I loved."

"What was her name?"

"Darling, I would rather deep dive into my feelings for you with you now than talk of her at the moment."

"I feel guilty. There's someone else I should talk to about this first."

"Taspe?"

"Yes. The last time I made a decision like this… it didn't go well. He was…"

Austere's fingers paused in my hair, "This isn't going to be that big of a deal. Love," he chuckled. "Though, the last time we met, I spoke with him."

I twisted, so I could look at his face, "About what?"

"About you."

"What was said?" My heart sank to my stomach.

"He told me about your tendency to never ask for help. Even asked me to help you, especially if you didn't ask for it. He said too that your powers were like none he had ever witnessed. He worries you will fall under more criticism, or be in pain over them because of how you had gained them. He loves you deeply and it's strong. I know, because the worry on his face exceeded his weakness and sickness. If you hadn't pulled that out of him, he would have died."

"Not something I want to consider." His death meant darkness in my world. "What do you think our gifts will be? With the Stygra and Welkan able to do as they do… what is left for us?"

"It would be something to give us an even footing. Stygra and Welkan would be evenly matched if they were to fight at their prime times of the day cycle." Austere lifted a shoulder, "I cannot imagine what that would be like. To hold power. It still surprises me every time you use the strands or the healing power."

"How can I prove we are worthy when I bear the powers of others?"

"Chi, they willingly passed their powers to you upon their deaths. Yes, they shouldn't have died, but they gave them to you." He trailed his fingers over my scalp, "Stop saying it like that. You dishonor their sacrifice."

"I don't mean to. I'm not."

We sat in silence for a while. Words formed, and thoughts, and I had to speak some of them. "If we love one another, we do not need to hurry this, right?

There was a long pause before he answered. "As you wish."

For Austere, it was probably just me being the Hero. I was a conquest and he would tire of me soon. For me, I knew the love of family and dearest friends. Yes, I had a romantic moment, or two, but mostly it was the comfort from another I desired. I wondered what Taspe would think.

"What are you pondering, darling?"

"Nothing much."

"Liar."

"I'm wondering if the Natural Ones, as you called them, will be alright doing this alone tonight."

"The Natural Ones used to be gods. Still are in some cultures. They will be fine. They just needed a little help. I'm actually surprised they are living underground here. In the islands they live in the waters and tree branches. They really like kelp beds and coral reefs."

His fingertips brushed my cheek, "I'm sleeping here tonight."

Of course he was. "I could just go sleep in your room."

He chuckled, "You could. I would just follow."

Another comfortable silence. "Do you get jealous?"

His question made me jump. He chuckled. I pinched his wrist, "Yes, I do."

"Ah… so if you ever admit feelings for me, I cannot flirt anymore then?"

"I… probably not."

He chuckled, "That's going to make my life interesting." He began nuzzling down into my neck and shoulder and rested there, "He told me about one of his villagers stabbing you. Said you would have died if you hadn't been in the village with one of the best healers he knows."

"Yeah, she cut into an organ we don't need much; it's called a gallbladder or something, but it holds poison. So it poisoned me as it was cut."

"He said he wanted to kill her, but you wouldn't let him."

"That's extreme, isn't it? Killing someone over a stab wound?" I turned, facing him.

He lay his arm back around me. He was so warm. "Perhaps."

I snorted, "It is."

"Welkan law states that you only harm an enemy, not a friend. Harming innocents is punishable by death to them. She knew what she was doing when she stabbed you."

His eyes caught what little light there was in the room and shone with a fiery tinge, "If she is that in love with Taspe, then I am her enemy."

"I…" he sighed and chuckled, "That is true."

"Besides, she is a fine warrior and he can't afford to lose any of them."

"Mmm. Here, sit up for a moment." He moved his arm under me, wrapping more around me as I lay back down. "Better. Is it comfortable for you?"

"Yeah, but won't your arm go to sleep?"

"Worth it. He's still being challenged, isn't he?"

"Yes."

"Word travels far. I heard about the Welkan male who had inherited a powerful Legacy long before I became a prince. First male leader in centuries. Well, except for the ones on the islands and mainlands. They were never enslaved like your Welkans were." One of his hands was trailing a light path up and down my bicep as he talked.

He still had a hint of seawater to him. "You are odd."

"Should I take that as an insult?"

Sam Wicker

"You're lying here, in bed, with a woman you claim you love…"

"That I must love."

"And you are talking about the male she spent most of her life with freely. That's odd."

Austere chuckled, "Darling, I know enough about you that anything I say against Taspe will only make you hate me. Besides, what little we conversed, he's a good guy. I like him. In fact, given some more time, I could learn to love him too. Maybe even more than I love you. I'm sure he's not half as prickly of a morning as you are."

"You're impossible."

"Now that is a compliment."

I giggled and shook my head.

"I like that sound."

"What?"

"You, giggling or laughing."

"I… what am I supposed to say to that?"

"Nothing, unless you want to say something about it."

We spent some time in silence. His breathing being a little uneven, and how he kept running his fingertips along my arm or thigh or hip let me know he wasn't asleep yet. Maybe he wouldn't sleep.

"Austere?"

"Hm?"

"How is it you know so much?"

He took in a deep breath, then let it out slowly, "The curse."

"What of it?"

"It… it has a hole in it. Some riddle to solve it and lift it without her having to release me from it. If I'm able to do it on my own, then I get a blessing, if not, then I must wait on her to see me worthy enough to release me." He stopped trailing his fingertips over my thigh, "You see… her curse has given me a rather… odd tie. I possess some of her knowledge, actually it's the knowledge of a few generations of her family. She really wanted me to earn this."

I snorted, "You mean you made her angry enough to pull that much power that she tied you to her unknowingly, probably."

He chuckled, "You should have seen me back then. I was barely a man, but oh I thought I was one." He chuckled again, "There wouldn't be any of this. You would be sated and I already moved on to the next woman in the house."

"Hm, I would have never guessed that about you."

"Sarcasm isn't good in the dark, darling."

Those glowing eyes closed, and he shifted closer. His forehead rested against mine. We began sharing breaths.

"More knowledge of the Natural Ones came from her?"

"Some of it. I grew up on their home island. I learned their language as I did my own. Our house was… it wasn't really a house. It was a shipwreck made into a house and a cave. Rather hard to explain now that I am trying."

I smiled, "I can imagine."

"Right. Our house was so close to the beach, close to their coral reef that most of them lived in, that we were family. It was mostly just me and my mother. Father was off doing what he must until I was old enough to board a ship. Then it was the three of us, some of the Natural Ones, too. We spent our storms at the house, some winters too."

"You had an odd childhood, but it sounds like it was a good one."

"It was. I wouldn't change anything of it for the world." He sighed, "This is difficult."

"What?"

"My new training."

I leaned my head back, his eyes glowed again in the dark, "What training?"

"Not wooing you or making moves."

"Go to sleep then."

He laughed, "I will be tonight, but you are going to make sure you exercise me well tomorrow. Maybe we can fill in that ditch and it will tire me out enough."

"You could sleep in your own room."

There was a pause before he said, "I can't sleep alone."

I sighed, "Pathetic."

"No, it's the truth."

"Fine."

"From now on?"

"Sure you won't miss torturing Blari and Tori?" I placed my forehead against his again. I wondered if his feet were hanging off the end of the bed.

"I get to do that plenty during the day. Besides, if I'm going to have any fun with you, I must know you better." Another pause, "Can't wait until I can get to know you thoroughly."

"Don't make me kick you. You have large targets."

"That's harsh, but true."

"Sleep, Mister Pompous." We lay there a while until something clicked, "They used to be gods?"

"Didn't you want to sleep?" he stretched, shifting us again, so that I was tucked into his chest. "Yes, they were, still are."

"Then… they can help us."

His body grew tight as his thoughts processed what I just said. "Yes, they might." He pulled me back, reached over and lit the candle. He sat up, cross-legged. "They don't enjoy meddling in our affairs, but since this is a gods given set of quests… gods they don't like much, I might add, we could persuade them to help."

"How?" I sat up, leaning on an arm as I ran my free hand through my hair.

He watched me, I was about to repeat my question when he finally answered, "We tell them that this happened because of the gods that are worshiped here." He waved a hand to the window, indicating the land, "That there are other things that are happening along the isthmus or in Lanpress that we could use their help so the gods won't overrun us."

"But… Jingles said we had to prove that we were worthy. How do we do that when we get their help?"

"I… well… isn't that the power of humans? We are weaker than everyone else, so we lean on our brethren of other races. Our power comes from working together. I… that's weak." He sighed and shook his head. His hands came up to rub his eyes, then his face.

I went through my lists in my mind. I reviewed the past quests, the information we had gathered about Keandria, what I knew of the gods and goddesses and what I knew of the former heroes. It wasn't much, but somewhere in it was a key to gaining the help of the Natural Ones.

He reached for my hand. His fingers toyed with mine, plucking them up off his knee, rubbing a knuckle or twining his through mine. He measured the length of his fingers against mine.

"Did the other races prove themselves in order to gain their powers?"

"From the way Jingles said it, yes."

I shook my head, "But they made the Stygra and Welkans before humans. I don't even know how Natural Ones were made. If they were gods or are gods, then where did our gods come from? Were they made by the Natural Ones?"

Austere shrugged, "I always thought gods came into being when someone believed in them."

"If that's the case, we made gods, not the other way around. Isn't that proving us enough?"

"You would think so." He squeezed my fingers.

"If we were to stop believing in them, or worship something else entirely, then the gods would disappear."

"Are you saying we should threaten the gods with their own demise?"

"Yes."

I lay back down, pulling the covers up to my chin. He stayed sitting up, his eyes on me. I almost turned to my side so I wouldn't watch him watching me. "What?"

"Do you think you can sleep?"

"I'm going to try."

He chuckled and shook his head, "You are an odd woman."

"Why do you say that?"

He blew the candle out, then settled beside me, propped up on his elbow. "Because you have all this," he motioned to himself with his free hand before placing it on my belly, "in your bed, and you want to sleep."

I groaned, "How can you be so full of yourself? You are attractive, but you- no. No. Get that look off your face."

The gleam in his eyes changed the moment I stated he was attractive. His hand began traveling, and he leaned over me.

"What look?"

He might as well have been purring with the way he said those two paltry words. "That look." I covered my breasts with one arm, "What happened to not acting on anything?"

"That was before I knew you considered me attractive."

"If you had let me finish!" His hand changed direction, trailing down. "I was going to say that your type of attractive isn't attractive to everyone. People like different things."

"Um-hm." His fingers curled over the curve of my hip, "Still means you find me attractive. Besides, I know exactly the things and type you are attracted to."

"Do you?"

"Of course."

"You're so smart."

He chuckled, "Easy or I will take that sarcasm as another compliment and you will be in trouble."

"Two compliments and you melt, is that how you work?"

"Three compliments and I show you how appreciative I am of your appreciation."

I willed a yawn to come along. My body was betraying me. His hand was sliding back, those fingertips brushing my ass. I swatted at his hand from under the covers. "Stop."

He stopped moving his hand. But his lips found my forehead. Some of his hair tickled my cheek and neck. His lips moved to my temple, then my earlobe. He whispered in my ear, "May I taste?"

"Huh?"

Another low chuckle, and his lips trailed along my jaw. He stopped, his breath feathering over my lips. "I would like to kiss you. Allow me?"

I swear they started tingling. Lips, such betrayers. "I…they said we should sleep because they'll be waking us early in the morning unless something happens."

He let out a sigh, pressing his forehead to mine. "Very well, I'll just suffer some more. It's not like I haven't seen you naked. Bathed with you, too. Carried you naked. What's a kiss?"

"Intimate."

He kissed my forehead again, "I understand." He flopped onto his back beside me, "Still think you can sleep?"

I turned to my side, my back to him, "Yes."

Chapter 35

I was up before dawn. I slept, some. Austere had a tendency to roll and grab and snuggle in his sleep. It was all rather exhausting debating on whether he was really asleep or awake and just torturing me.

He was definitely asleep as I got dressed and headed downstairs. I stepped out into the dimly lit world, shrugging on my jacket against the chill morning air. I circled around the house, heading toward the vent we dug out yesterday.

"Hello, human Hero."

I jumped back, my fingers digging at a dagger before I recognized the tinkling voice. "Sorry. Hello, Jingles." He floated level with my face. His limbs folded into his fur made him look like a large white fluff ball with eyes and ears. "How did it go last night?"

"We have most of it out and it did not spread further. You humans can start cleaning the ash around where this mess all started. We have moved our dead and are preparing their rites."

A lance tore through my heart, "I'm sorry."

"Don't be, child. You did not know any better. It was a disgrace for us to keep them like that, but we had nowhere to put them and couldn't care for them properly." Two of its paws slid out from the fluff, and Jingles rubbed them together. *"I have something else to say to you."*

"Go on."

"We will not help. This land is not ours to govern as we see fit. You have your own gods."

I sighed, then my face heated, "You heard all that?"

"I know everything in my purview. I find it angers your kind more than anything else to have private thoughts violated. You have not yet learned to be fully open and honest." Those little paws disappeared back into their fur, *"Your thoughts are written on your face. You think I'm cute. I think you are cute too."*

I laughed, my cheeks still on fire, "Thanks, I guess."

"Another thing. Do not limit yourself. In all things."

I stared at Jingles for a moment. Watching its tail fluff, then smooth as it stared right back at me. In all things? What was I limiting myself?

Those bells on its tail jingled, and I heard laughter. *"You will prove worthy for more than you know."*

"Can you speak in plain speech?"

Another tinkle of laughter, *"That is as plain as I will allow you to hear. I can't hand everything to you. Figure it out for yourself."*

Were gods ever truly helpful? "If I were to start believing in you, instead of the twenty-seven, except for Aul since I met him, would you gain more power and them less?"

"Not in the way you may think."

It paused, and I thought it would be yet another riddle that I would have to puzzle out. But Jingles continued, *"It is not power that belief and prayers give us, but strength and purpose. These gods you have, they are different. One female made them up, and the story spread and evolved to what they are today. They do not live among you, but separate. Your belief in them gives them form, yes, but it also controls what they can do. Unlike us, they are limited to the imagination of those that believe in them."*

I walked toward a stump at the back of the house and sat. I felt pressure building around my temples. "If my companions and I believed that the Goddess Meandria could spray water on the stars she could? But she can't until we believe she can?"

"Yes. That is why there are so many priests and churches for each god and goddess. They have to control what you believe, or it would be chaos."

"How did your kind manipulate what people believed?"

"We don't, for we live among you. We are born to power just as Stygra and Welkan are, developed to tendencies just as Rogues are, and you will be born to powers and tendencies once you prove you are worthy." Its tail fluffed momentarily.

I wondered if it had said more than it had planned with that last bit. "Why did you hide then?"

"We thought it would be best. Humans here believe in the twenty-seven, if we were to make ourselves known, there would be confusion. We may come under attack from the twenty-seven

and that would hurt more of you than it would us. We could not bear that thought. Besides, there are few of us here, only our group."

"The rest of your kind are on islands?"

"Mostly. We have some that have moved to the mainlands, but our numbers remain low there."

"Why did you come here?"

"We wanted a change." His tail flicked, the bulbs ringing hard; *"We do regret we cannot live among you and have often thought of returning to our islands. We love this family. I have had great joy and sorrow with them as they have lived."*

"I could really use your help. The Stygra are powerful. Keandria is… she's… unpredictable."

He held up two paws; the bells jingling continuously, *"No, child. This is between you, your gods, and the evil you must face. I will tell you this, the gods do not know what is going on. They seem as confused as you are. The cycle they created is awry."*

"What are they doing about it?"

Jingles chuckled, *"Why don't you ask one yourself?"*

"I don't know…" the smell of rot wafted toward me as darkness grew from the ground. It rose into a column, filling out and shedding at the same time. The reek of dead things and rot made my diaphragm lunge. I covered my nose.

Orange powders grew along the edges and folds of the shadow, forming into robes and skin. The colors shifted, some turning green, others red, others black, and yet more into the color of pallid flesh.

Jingles moved to sit on my shoulder, folding its paws and arms into its fur again. It trained its eyes on the form. It sighed, *"Dramatic entrances still. Such children."*

"Childlike we may be, but there is a belief we must endure. Humans like this stuff." The figure turned, and in a robe now mostly gray and black with little pieces of orange and reds along the folds, she bowed. "Well met. I am Ocrid."

Ocrid? Now I'm going to die. "I… are you taking me?"

"No, my Hero, not yet. Not for a long while. I am here to talk with you." She sat, a large orange mushroom forming under her bottom. A light cloud of spores followed each of her movements.

"Thank you for your time." I fumbled for words. Should I call her majesty or what? No, she was a goddess, I should call her such. My mind nearly cleared of all thoughts as a tiny paw rested on my hot cheek. It patted me, slow, long pats.

I was a child.

"No, I feel privileged to talk to you. It is rare that I get to interact with humans." Ocrid smiled, the planes of her face fading as spores fogged around her movements. "I will not take up much of your time. I fear this is all wrong."

"That is an understatement, my dear." Jingles stated dryly.

"This was supposed to occur over five decades ago."

"This? this quest in particular?"

"No, all the quests you have taken part in and the ones to come. They have been sitting idle, growing more and more irritated and impatient or lazy for fifty years." She took a breath, another cloud rising before settling around her again, "That is why they are all so... weak, yet potent for others. Once released, these beasts we created or challenges we set feel as if they have fifty years to catch up on."

"I wasn't born... I'm not that old."

"We did not make these with you in mind. A Hero has been skipped. Yours were more strategy based, puzzles and battles. We made these quests for a brute of a woman or man who was to have an alchemist and healer as companions, not for you and your writer, pirate, hunter, princess and prince companions. No Stygra is supposed to be a companion for you either." She shook her head.

"Why are you telling me this now? Why not stop all this?"

"The quests are not with us. Someone pillaged our earthly home. They took these from us and kept them hidden."

Keandria.

"Is it a map?"

"A large platform, some call it a desk, that has a map upon it of the isthmus, yes."

"I know where it is."

"Unfortunately, we cannot hinder this. It is set in motion so it must finish." Ocrid leaned forward, "I am sorry." That is when I noticed her eyes. They were the same color orange as the mushroom she was sitting on. From corner to corner, that orange stared at me. I only knew she was looking at me because of her black slits for pupils. They dilated before she said, "You have died?"

"Yes."

"Maxid did not tell me that."

The god of time? "Why… how did you not stop the pillaging?"

"It is difficult to explain. Time is not linear for us as it is for you. Only Maxid can do well with keeping up with the order of things. For some time now, he has been telling us that the world has been off, but we were slow to react. He is warning us of things all the time."

"*You ignore the one god that can keep tabs on your world and your followers. Brilliant.*"

I wanted to hug the fluffy god sitting on my shoulder.

Spores flared, turning from their gray hue to greens, blues and oranges. Ocrid showed her stumpy teeth in a flash. "By some of us, yes."

"*When did he mention it to you?*"

Ocrid paused, the spores settling back down to gray, "I believe it has been two years."

"Why did he take so long to tell you?"

"Maxid and I do not get along." She bowed her head, petting a small orange growth on her knee, "He thinks I smell too much. My priests do nothing to change that for me."

The pressure building at my temples had turned into a throbbing pain and spread over my brow. I pinched the bridge of my nose, thinking that might relieve some of it. It certainly helped lessen the reek. I didn't blame Maxid. "Even though the quests are not mine, the gods will do nothing to aid me?"

"No."

What use were they then?

"If I finish these, will I be worthy, then? Or since they are not my quests, will you have another set planned for the next Hero?"

"That I cannot say."

I glared at her, "Why did you want to talk to me?"

Her pale hands fisted, "I will rid this land of the death and fungus based virus I created. I will also enrich the soil for the family, so that the growth of their trees will be quick and the fruit the best in the world."

"I appreciate that." At least the innocent family would be taken care of. "What about the other areas the quests have affected more than they should have?"

"We are working on plans for them. We have already set most in motion. The miners will find rich deposits, the fishermen will see more fish in their lifetimes than all their ancestors have combined. This matron is Keandria, correct?"

"Yes."

She muttered something under her breath that I did not catch, but Jingle's ears pricked forward as its tail shook in what I took as excitement. I wasn't sure if one god being excited while the goddess of death talked to herself was a good thing. My stomach lurched, trying to empty, even though it held nothing. For yet another time, I was thankful for skipping a meal.

Jingle's tail curled under my nose. The soft fur smelled of grass, and lavender, and the earth. It was a far better scent than that of the goddess before us. My stomach flopped again, but settled after that last lurch.

Ocrid hissed in a breath, "Some enemies are on the way to your family now. Keandria has no power blessed by us. She is of her own making. Her own evil."

I stared at her. "Who? What do you mean?"

"Your family is in danger."

"Go."

I whirled.

Kodola stood there, clutching a shawl around her body as she gawked at the goddess. "Go. You have helped enough."

I turned to look back at Ocrid, but she was fading away.

Jingles put his paws on my face, those dark little eyes focused on mine. *"I will provide for and aid this family. I will do what I can with your ridiculous gods."*

"They are no gods of mine." My voice sounded like a frog.

"Your family is safe right now. But not for long. You must go."

Kodola walked with me, "thank you for coming. Without you, we would not have been able to help the Natural Ones get rid of that. You helped us see them. Know this, if you are ever in need in a way that I or my children can help, we will."

"Thank you." My mind was already racing through the preparations we needed to make. We were closer to my family than we would have been if in Galanesse, for that much I was hopeful.

"I'll have my kids get your horses ready."

"Thank you."

As we reached the porch, Kodola rang the bell hard and quick. I could hear the ruckus of many people waking up in the house. Feet hitting the floor at a run.

My head rang with each bell toll. My family was in danger again. Because of me.

"What's going on?" Austere had taken the stairs at a run, buttoning his shirt as he did so. How he could move from one point to another so quickly had to be part of a blessing he had painted on him.

"My family… we need to get there. I'll explain on the way."

Austere nodded and bellowed up the stairs to where Spacya stood with spears in hand, Tori had his sword out but no shirt on and barefooted, and Blari rubbing his eyes with a massive yawn, "Move! Pack up, we're leaving!"

His voice was a bark. An unquestionable order like he gave his men on his ship. He looked back at me, then was on me in two steps. He scooped me up into his arms and carried me up the stairs. The scent, the musk of him, pulled the smell of rot from my nose at last. "I can walk." I pushed at him, weakly.

"You're pale. I'm walking for you for now."

I rested my temple against his shoulder and closed my eyes against his movements. His steps, while long, still jostled. I felt him bend, my body leaning out away from his body, and I clutched at him. He chuckled, I smacked his shoulder.

"I've got you. Here, let's sit you down on the bed. I'm going to pack up my room and then I'll be back to do yours." He cupped my face in his hands, "If you move from this spot, other than to lie down, the next time we are alone, I will torture you until you beg for more."

I blinked, and he was gone. "What does that mean?"

"Obviously something humans have always enjoyed doing to each other."

Of course, Jingles was still on my shoulder. I stood and pulled my things from the drawers and shoved them into my bag. We would move quicker if I was ready by the time everyone else was. Besides, Austere would not lay hands on my underthings, too. He had already taken enough privileges.

"Why do humans wear so many pieces?"

"Er... protection and decency."

"Maybe when you prove worthy, ask for fur."

I stared at Jingles for a moment. Was it telling me I was going to be the Hero to prove humans were ready for whatever gift the twenty-seven had in store, or was it just saying that in general? Its tail shook, tinkling like a giggle.

"You moved."

"You take too long."

"You should prepare yourself for the time when we are alone again."

"Do you really want to threaten me like that? I have daggers and I'm rather good with them."

"She is. One of the best humans I have seen with such small blades. I can tell."

I grinned at Jingles, that tail tinkling again.

"I'll take my chances."

I put everything in my bag and slung it over my shoulder. Then stumbled a few steps back as Austere took it from me. "I..."

"Hush and move." He jerked his chin toward the door.

"Horses are ready! We packed meals for you as best we could." Kodola called up the stairs.

Sam Wicker

"We're leaving our rooms in a mess..." Randia looked up at Kodola with wide eyes.

"No problem." She took my hand, "Be safe, and remember what I said. We owe you."

Jingles moved over to her shoulder, "*The road will be clear. I cannot say anything further than that. I have said too much.*"

I nodded and ran out the door, most of my companions already on their horses.

"The quickest route will be over the hills to a path called Hulaniue Road. Due northeast." Tori pointed his horse in the direction we were to go.

"Lead."

He nodded and we pushed into a ground eating canter.

We rode hard for two days. On the third morning, I skidded to a stop within the shadow of the southwestern gate of Owlimount. The guards halted me and one reached up to take the rein of my horse. He tilted his helmet up to see me better, then bowed. "Nadachia, welcome home."

He let go of my rein and motioned for us to go through. "I'll alert the..."

"No need, just passing through for now. We'll be back later. I want to see my family." I called as rapidly as my tongue allowed as I urged Unia into the village.

I pushed my mare into a trot. That was as fast as I dared go. I would have rather avoided it altogether, but the western side of the village didn't allow for paths or roads, as it was a rocky hillside full of thorns and brambles. It was great for rat and rabbit traps. That was about it.

I waved at some familiar voices calling out to me. I called back my excuses, making my way to the eastern gate. Once through it, I kicked her back into a canter. My poor Unia breathed heavily, tossing her head to let me know she was reaching her limit.

"Just a little longer."

I wanted to gallop. But I also didn't want our horses to fall over in exhaustion either. Soon enough, the familiar gate came into view. On the outside, nothing seemed to be amiss.

The garden was heavy with ripening vegetables and some fruit. They had started an addition to the side of the house. New cows mooed in a new pasture at the back of the house. The lantern hung heavy on the tree that made a gatepost, still lit.

I paused, pulling the reins to stare at it.

Father would put it out by now. Saving the oil.

"What?" Austere came up beside me. His large stallion was the only one that didn't seem winded.

"The lantern is still lit."

He frowned at it. "Maybe he leaves it on all the time now?"

"Father doesn't waste things." I turned, "Blari, take Spacya to the Welkans, will you? Tell Taspe to come check on us."

He nodded, Spacya and he peeling off to go back down the road to the larger dock on the border of our property and the farm next door. I moved forward, leaning over my saddle and unlatching the gate to let us through. I left it open. Just in case.

We trotted up the path and I slid off at the front door. Father opened the door, his back rigid, "Daughter?!"

He never called me that. I met his gaze. He widened his eyes, then darted them to the side before looking back at me.

Out of the corner of my eye, I saw a movement between our house and the stables. Next thing I know, Tori launched himself from his saddle at the movement. I heard a half scream, and Tori grunt. The prince had tackled a Stygra and was holding his sword to their neck.

I was up the stairs and pulled Father to me because I couldn't see what was behind him. He wrapped his arm around me and pivoted, putting his back to the doorframe, trying not to let me through.

I saw the shine of silver against the pale skin of CiaCia, another against Moko's neck.

"Don't! you tell that prince to let my boy go." Her thin hand shook, the blade nicking Moko's neck. A droplet of blue blood slowly formed before it trailed down to the flowery neckline of her dress.

"You let them go and he might live." I spat, straining against Father's arm.

"Release him!"

The sink window flew open. Throwing knives flew through it. Father released me and pivoted with me. I grabbed Moko; he grabbed CiaCia, and we pulled them to their feet from their knees. I flung a dagger as I pulled Moko behind me. It sank deep, with a squishing sound in a Stygra eye. His body bowed back from the force of my throw, then crumpled to the floor.

The Stygra mother screamed and lunged toward the body.

Father's boot slammed into her face. The crunch of her nose against leather came seconds before the spurt of black blood over her pale face. She slid off his boot onto the floor beside her friend.

"Stables." Father stated.

I bolted for the back door. The clash of metal on metal rang. The screams of the chickens started drowning those sounds out. CiaCia and Father were on my heels. I flung open the door into the backyard and sprinted for the stables.

Austere's sword crossed with that of another man. One arm hung limply at his side. His sleeve drenched from shoulder down to his wrist. A black thing sticking out of his bicep told me all I needed to know. I threw another dagger, hoping Austere wouldn't move.

It sank into the stranger's cheek.

Austere took his surprise to drive both swords into the slim body. He pushed the strange human down. In two strides, he was at the door and kicked it off its rusted hinges into the stable.

Feathers flew. Chickens screamed. Talons and wings beat at me as I moved in.

"Here!" Vey's voice.

I whirled. His mouth split at the corner, dark red rivulets covered his chin. His claws were deep in the knees of the Stygra female behind him.

The Stygra pulled Vey's head back again, threads forming at her fingertips.

With a scream, I shoved a blade into her shoulder with all my might, following it with my body.

She screamed and fell under me, pulling Vey with us by his hair and Vey's grip. I gained my knees, pulling my dagger out. My back barked in pain as I arched back, lifting my hands above my head before driving the dagger deep into her neck. I twisted and dragged, then pulled it out.

There was some sickening, half gulping, half choking noise, as the black blood dried on my fingers. I wiped the dagger clean. I looked up at the hazel eyes of my father. The ones that matched mine.

I had never seen him look at me like that.

Then he was on his knees, helping Vey free himself of his grip. Those claws of his dragged against the bones of the Stygra's knees as we pulled them out.

Austere was dragging his curved blade out of the side of another human dressed in Stygra robes. Detri held Greta to his side.

CiaCia's wail curled deep in my gut as it keened through the stables. A vine had sprouted from the mouth of a Stygra I hadn't seen in the corner. CiaCia held a body close to her, another hand on a small form at her side. She was curled in the hay. Around the bodies.

"No." Father's whisper made my heart drop. He walked to them, falling to his knees. He touched all three. Fingers gingerly brushing their hair.

My vision turned red.

Footsteps came to the stable door. I whirled, gripping the dagger I had just used.

Tori held up a hand, "I have your Mother and Seaghla, both are alright."

We were missing three.

I looked around the stables.

"They were going out." Detri pointed toward the new pasture.

I ran, shoving past Tori, who bolted after me. He overtook me, and then we split. He circled around a few hay bales and I headed straight toward two robed shapes. I skidded to a stop, my boots sinking into the soft earth, sticky with mud.

"Let them go." I pointed a dagger at the one holding Aber and Tokli.

He laughed, "I'll kill them before you kill me." He pulled them off their feet. They dangled, kicking, their little fingers digging at the slim, unnervingly long fingers wrapped around their throats.

Tokli's lips were turning blue.

My fingers tingled. Everything was still except for my siblings and those horrible grinning fiends. One Stygra. One Welkan. The scars along her shoulders finally drew my attention. I looked into the eyes of the one holding Biobi.

"Hello, Chi." She grinned, pulling Biobi against her with the short sword at his neck, "So nice to see you again."

"Caterwalla." I swallowed. That gleam in her eyes I had seen before. It was the same gleam she had when she stabbed me in the side over the pig carcass I was helping her dress. "I wish I could say the same."

"Aw, are we no longer friends?"

"That's your choice. I've always been willing."

She frowned, her arm tightening. Biobi strained to pull away from the blade tickling his throat.

Tori was to my right. He was the only aide I could get at the moment, but his angle would be off. He couldn't get clear in time.

The power tickled in my veins. I took a step forward. I latched on to that feeling in me. Focus.

"Stay." The Stygra warned, shaking Tokli at me.

I stilled. I wasn't sure how far I could reach with them. How accurate could I be. I had to try. The choice loomed: distraction or harm.

Either way, my siblings could end up dead or hurt worse than they were.

My answer came in an acrid scent that made my eyes water. The air thickened with it. In another breath I knew what it was. I chanced a glance toward the river.

Over the roof of our house, great billows of black and gray rose into the sky. Several of them, grouped closely together. "No!"

Caterwalla twisted and screamed, Biobi fell from her clutches. The other Stygra looked up and around. His arms dropped the children to about his waist level.

Before he could turn, I had two daggers in his chest, in the soft flesh just inside his shoulders but above the ribs. Tokli and Aber hit the ground. Coughs and gulps of air let me know the Stygra's grip had loosened enough for them to survive before I threw another dagger into his left eye.

Tori ran from behind the last hay bale and tackled Caterwalla to the ground. The two were rolling in the mud and grass, slamming fists and elbows into each other with deep grunts. I strode over to them. Tori caught my movement and bucked away from the female, throwing her toward me. She landed a few steps away.

I ran, putting my foot on her neck before she could get up. "We could have been friends."

"Please! The village!"

"I know." I looked up at Tori, who stood on the other side of her. "Can you knock her out and tie her up?"

"Got it. Go."

I lifted my foot just as his sword hilt met her temple.

"Come here." I grabbed my siblings up in a fierce hug. Then pulled them back to check on their necks. The smoke stung tears from my eyes as the wind brought the plumes closer to the ground. "Get in the house, okay. You stay there. You hide until we come back."

"I'll watch them." Tori dragged Caterwalla up onto his shoulders after sheathing his sword.

I nodded, "I'll be right back."

They sniffled, but my little hearts didn't complain.

I stood and ran around the house. I could see Father ahead as he made his way down the path to our rowboat. Austere was leaning against the stable wall, clutching his arm as Moko jerked out the spike embedded in his shoulder.

"I'm going!"

"We'll be fine!" Moko called over her shoulder.

"I'll be along in a moment." Austere grunted, sweat beading off his face and making his hair stick to his neck.

I shook my head at Moko; she nodded. Then I ran off and tried to catch up with my father. I called to him, and he paused, sitting in the raft, the paddles ready.

I jumped into the small boat.

"Detri and Vey are going to hide everyone. Biobi, Tokli and Aber?"

"They're fine. Tori has them. He's staying with them. Clara?"

"She's in Ecia, will be back today." Father looked up at the now black sky, clouded with smoke and ash. "This doesn't bode well, Nada."

The strain in his voice made me swallow the bile rising up in my throat. I had killed. I had killed several.

Instead, I checked my daggers, pulling some from behind me to the empty side sheaths where they would be easier to pull. My crossbow was on my horse. I cursed myself for forgetting it. "They'll be alright."

They had to be. I had to believe that.

As soon as we landed at the dock, we scrambled up it. Father had enough sense to put the rope around a moor. I ran down the path, his heavy-footed run thudded behind me. Before reaching the village's clearing, I jumped into the woods, circling until I found the back of a house not burning. I moved in behind it. Father, right after me.

We looked around the corner. I crouched low; he stood at the ready.

The main hall was on fire in two different places. The doors sealed shut. Five Stygra were on the outside, sloshing oil onto the flames to make the smoke black as night. A small house to the side of it was treated much in the same way.

I pulled back and looked at Father, "There isn't any screaming."

"No, there isn't."

I pressed the scar in my palm. The heartbeat there was strong and steady. I looked back around the corner. Father took a moment to take in a few deep breaths. The smoke hovered over the village, blocking the sunlight. Day into night. The medical house was unharmed, doors open wide. There was some damage to some nearby houses, but nothing that looked too concerning.

Where was my Welkan family?

I heard a morning song bird sound behind and to the right.

I searched every alley, every house window and door to see if I could see any movement. Nothing. Just the smoke. Just the two handfuls of Stygra and a couple of humans with them.

The songbird sounded again.

I straightened, looking back at Father. He looked back at me.

"Did you see any of them?"

"No."

Something nagged at me.

The songbird sounded again. The notes off. I rubbed the sweat off my forehead.

An arrow thunked into the wall right beside my head.

I gasped, falling back on my ass and bumping into Father's legs. I looked into the woods. Taspe's nephew threw up his arms, a bow in one hand. The look on his face called me stupid as he whistled the tune of the songbird again.

I pointed. Father nodded.

Keeping in line with the houses and low to the ground, we kept glancing behind us to make sure the Stygra in the village wouldn't spot us. I slid into place next to Taspe's nephew, Lave, behind a wide tree, as Father crouched behind another one nearby. "You coulda hit me!"

"Are you deaf now or something?"

"Couldn't you have done a hawk?"

"Oh yeah, that would've made you look rather than a bird that only sings at dawn. A sound, I might add, *we* taught you to listen for."

"Hate to interrupt, but where is everybody?" Father gave us a pointed stare.

"Gaming grounds. Come on."

We slunk through the forest behind our guide. My heart was beating faster and faster. My lungs and eyes cleared of the smoke that hung over the village. Didn't they know what kind of white bees' nest they had kicked by attacking this village?

Cresting the hill I looked down at the gaming circle and almost cried. Every Welkan was there. From the kids that always ran underfoot, to the elders that lectured and told stories, to the warriors, artists, and traders. They were all there. Safe.

From the edge, one of them broke free and ran to me.

I grinned, jumping down the rest of the slope. He caught me in his arms. "Gods watch." His lips moved against my ear, then cheek. He then fit them against mine as his arms crushed me to him.

"Is everyone well? Anyone hurt?"

"Yes. No. Are you hurt?" Taspe loosened his grip, leaning back a little to study my face, then my body. He stopped when Father cleared his throat. Taspe dropped me.

I nearly fell against him when my feet hit the grass.

"Rossi, sir." Taspe was stiff against me, his hands pressed to his sides as if his life depended on it.

"Taspe." Father nodded his head.

I caught that glint in his eyes, that little curl to his lips as he took a few steps toward us. "You call that a kiss?"

He walked past.

I covered my mouth with my hands and stepped away so Taspe wouldn't feel me trying not to laugh.

He blinked. Following my father with his eyes, before he turned to raise his brows at me. "Did he... did he just say what I think he said?"

"Yeah, he said you were a weak kisser. That a grandma could do better. That you should step it up." The priest muttered as he stopped beside us.

I grinned and giggled as Blari kept going on and on, his wide hand up on Taspe's shoulder.

Father paused, chuckling as he listened too.

"Gods…" Taspe ran a hand over his hair and looked up at the smokey sky. "After the battle."

"Battle?"

Taspe nodded, "There are about ten in our village, but there are nearly a hundred just around that hill, past that little grove we planted three summers ago."

"Owlimount?"

"Untouched, for now. I sent word to the Captain early this morning to keep an eye out. He pulled the reserves and managed the villagers. All are safe from what my scouts report."

"How did you…"

Taspe smiled, lifting the palm of my hand and kissing the scar. "You were scared. The type of scared you get when someone you love is in danger. It's the exact feeling you had when we got your family out of Galanesse. I mobilized immediately and found their camp. A few scouts heard their plans, but… by then they had already moved in on your family." He cupped my cheek, "I'm sorry. Are they well?"

I shook my head, "Kentrim and Rosen…" was all I got out. What type of person just shared a kiss and a laugh when they had just lost two of their siblings?

I was going mad.

"They are avenged?"

"Yes."

"I shall avenge us soon." He turned to watch his people. He held up a fist.

The warriors peeled away from the rest of the villagers. The blue, yellow and black paint on their bodies made them nightmares walking in daylight. Black went around their eyes, making them shadowed, but it kept the sunlight from blinding them as they soaked it up for the fight. Blues and Yellows formed over their dark tattoos, enhancing their blessings, or their curses.

Taspe looked them over as they stood in rows before him. There were forty-three of them. I knew there were others lying in wait, his scouts who doubled as warriors too. Total, they did not match the Stygra numbers.

My stomach gave its usual unwieldy spin in my body.

Taspe glanced at me. He then smiled, "We've had two sunny days after a week of rain. They should quake in fear."

One warrior chuckled, smacking the flat of his blade with his hand, "Little Stygra rebels will run like rats."

Spacya came to stand beside me. She placed a hand on my shoulder, but kept her eyes on the smoke still curling in long, thick columns over the village. My dear friend, I understood her. "Let's make them pay."

Taspe grinned, "Stay with me. Rossi, my left flank could use your guidance, they are pretty new. We'll be going in heavy on the front, and I would like my flanks to take care of stragglers as they come in to meet me at the center of their camp. Spacya, you mind leading my small group to get rid of those in the camp? Use your spears to pin them."

Spacya nodded.

"Me?" I turned, Austere was at the top of the hill, Taspe's nephew by his side. Looked like he was bringing in all the strays.

Taspe took one look at him, "Healers."

"I can fight."

"You can, but not well enough to survive. If they get past us, you know what to do."

Austere frowned and looked at me. I nodded. He sighed and made his way down the hill to the Welkan camp.

His warriors broke up into their groups, splitting at the forest's edge while we took the path around to the little grove. Some of his warriors picked up their pace, flanking me and Taspe before overtaking us to lead the charge. Taspe frowned at it, but didn't halt them.

His people took care of their leader. He should have been used to it by now. His people had seen more battles in his leadership than they had since the revolution against their slavery. I knew he felt terrible. But they were thriving under his leadership.

So was Owlimount, and my family.

We slowed, crouching to move forward as we neared their camp. They were expecting us. Long black spikes surrounded them, jutting out low and sharp from the ground. Stygra and humans stood behind the spike wall, weapons and powers at the ready.

"Can you feel which one made the spikes?"

I blinked, then stared ahead. I felt the right kind of power. Power like Eilse's that now flowed through me. "There's one. Tall, skinny, shaved head standing in between a human in a black shirt and the one with a yellow cloth over his head."

The new gods I believed in were treating me well. My practice using these powers was proving worth the splitting headaches and impatience I felt every night on the road. I didn't dare practice while we were in the capital.

"I think the other one- no, there might be two together. At the far right, the two standing together closest to the tent with the blue sash hanging from one pole."

Taspe relayed directions in Welkan to his warriors. I was getting rusty with the language I should know as well as my own by now. A couple of warriors broke off, pulling bows from their backs and knocking arrows. They circled and hid in areas they could get an excellent shot off.

Taspe straightened, that songbird sounded again, this time from his lips. It sounded true to the songbird. I would have to tell Lave to practice harder.

His warriors burst forward at once. A solid wall of death heading directly for the Stygra camp. We moved with them.

Bolts of dark green shot forward. As one, Taspe's unit dodged. Moving like a school of fish, absorbing the magic into their ranks until it flew out the other side. Not one Welkan left standing out on his own to make an easy target. Taspe grabbed my waist, moving me with him so I wouldn't be left out of the loop.

Father knew what he was doing, and had moved with the Welkans ahead of him.

I had never seen a Welkan battle.

Four Stygra dropped. Arrows stuck out of their necks, chests, or faces. Half of the black spikes around the camp disappeared.

Two enormous balls of light blazed like fire and hovered over the Stygra. They ducked and cowed underneath the burning spheres like they were burning. All the while, we pressed forward. The Stygra's magical and spear attacks were reflected away at the edges or blocked outright.

" Adelyasv!" Taspe bellowed, throwing me down on the ground with himself.

Welkans stepped between us with one foot as they used their momentum to launch spears into the camp.

The shafts had barely left their hands when Taspe pulled me up again.

I was going to get him killed if he had to keep watching out for me like this.

Several of the Stygra folded over the spears as the blades slid into their bodies. Some spears pinned the victims to another, or threw them into the tents behind them. That's when the stoic warriors of the Stygra came unglued. Screams erupted from their mouths. Gurgles filled their voices as they thrashed in death throes. Somewhere in that attack, or the volley of arrows, the rest of the black spikes disappeared.

Taspe's warriors strode into the camp as if they were walking through a field of flowers.

Taspe formed a ball of light, and it spread and flattened until it was as tall and as wide as his body. "Back to back." He looked at me.

I nodded and pressed my back against his. As his sword swung and the green blood began splattering the ground, I found my folly. He wasn't about to let any of them pass him so I could fight, too. Ass.

So I pivoted to his shield side, I nailed a Stygra running to him in the neck with one of my daggers. "I need it." I moved to press my back to his again, shifting my weight as he moved with each of his strike and block stances.

Taspe chuckled, "Running low?"

His trajectory shifted, as did the line of his warriors. I noticed then; they formed a loose line. There was enough room between each of them for swords to swing freely. A warrior stood at each warrior's back. They moved together and around, attacking in turns, the front one blocking with a shield similar, if not exact, to Taspe's.

The left and right flanks closed in. No escape.

I whirled, throwing another dagger, then another. I caught the Stygra in the thigh, then again in the shoulder. Taspe took his head off with a swipe and stepped over the first body. I dug my dagger out of his neck, then the two out of the next body.

I hadn't thought this through either. I could sheathe them.

I sighed, holding two in my off-hand as I watched all around me and kept up with Taspe's steady movements. We were dancing. We were dancing on a battlefield and not facing one another.

I swung around, barely missing a bolt of green stuff, it sliced my shoulder open. Off balance, but I still landed the dagger into the Stygra's torso. Taspe got his blade caught in the ribs of another. He paused.

Another dagger thrown after switching one from my off-hand. This one landed in the Stygra's eye as he turned toward me. Taspe freed his sword.

I swore to the gods that I saw a spinal column peeking out from the gash that Taspe had made into that Stygra.

"Done!"

I looked up. Some warriors along the lines were making their final kills. The only Stygras that stood were the ones pinned up by spears. The warriors gave a single whoop as their shields disappeared, and they lifted their arms.

Taspe turned and watched me. I looked up at him, green smears were along his sword arm, neck, and chest. Some splatters were on his legs too, but not a drop of blue could be found anywhere. "That was quick."

"It was a good fight."

"Pyres."

"Yes, we will build them." He looked away, watching a runner coming toward them. He tilted his head as the runner stopped in front and caught his breath.

"Village is clear. Only one hurt, one of ours, not Spacya." He grinned, "That woman… I've never heard anyone growl like that."

"Good. Scared you, did she?"

"A little." The scout admitted with another grin.

I smiled and circled around. Father waved from across the battlefield. He looked unharmed.

Another set of warriors went through, gathering bodies and putting them on sheets to be carried two or three at a time to wherever they were going to build the pyres. Taspe wiped his sword off on a nearby tent flap, checking furtively inside as he did so.

"Have them inspect the village. I don't want any surprises. We will build pyres next to the gaming grounds. I think we need to build a new field, anyway."

"Yes." The scout nodded and started back toward the village.

Taspe's arm shot into the tent. There was a startled sound, a sharp yelp, and he dragged a thin Stygra woman out. She thrashed, her claws elongated, and she went to slam them up into his stomach. Taspe threw her to the ground.

Before I knew it, a dagger had left my fingers. It stood in her neck. I gasped. Taspe finished the job quicker with his sword, creating a longer cut across her throat.

"Remind me not to make you mad when you have those knives in reach."

I shook my head, staring at my hand for a moment.

Taspe wrapped his arm around my shoulders, his lips pressing against my hair, "Breathe. If you hadn't taken their life, they would have taken from us a life."

I took a deep breath through my mouth. The stench of vomit, blood and bodily wastes filled the air as the dead began the death processes.

I needed an army of Welkans. I looked up at Taspe, "We've got a lot to talk about."

"I know."

We spent the next few days cleaning up after the battle. The village was our chief priority. Only burned crusts of the larger beams remained of the main hall. Some other houses had a little heat and burn damage, but we quickly mended them.

We built pyres for Kentrim and Rosen first. Moko and CiaCia could not stop weeping. I felt their pain. The past few nights, since arriving home, I had cried myself to sleep.

After the pyres were built, and the remains properly and respectfully taken care of, we focused on the farm and getting rid of the remains of the Stygra camp. The captain came and made his report.

I had a plan.

Along with the captain's report, I sent a letter to Keandria. I would not return to the capital until I absolutely had no other choice. I turned my attention to Caterwalla, who we held prisoner in the stables.

Taspe was going to kill Caterwalla for her crimes. The tribe had already made that decision. She knew she was on borrowed time.

"Who can form a curse like the one Austere has in your tribe?"

"Our tribe." Taspe corrected gently as he swiped the whetstone down his sword he held along the edge of the table. "Mother might. Our best blesser and curser is in another village, though. I can call her, but she might take two days to get here."

I shook my head, "No, well, unless your mother won't do it."

Taspe's gaze flicked to mine after he inspected his sword for the thousandth time. I couldn't blame him. I was just as peculiar with my daggers as he was being with his blade.

Sam Wicker

"It's a waste to use that much magic to curse someone only to kill them."

I sighed, "How else are we going to get the truth?"

"Spacya."

I stared at him for a moment.

"You heard what Mylari said." At my blank blink, he sighed, "The scout that was with them when she led a group to clean out the village. Put them in a room with her. They'll talk. All she'll probably have to do is stand there and stare."

"We'll try that."

"Then we'll try Austere."

I pressed my lips together and bit them for a moment before asking, "Is that to torture him or for Austere to torture Caterwalla or Keandria?"

Taspe smirked, sliding his blade into its sheath as he stood, "Both."

I nodded, and we started out of his village house and toward the new main hall. It was a skeleton of a building. They had erected only the main pillars and supports along with most of the roof, but it was coming along nicely. Just past it was a small home. We stepped inside it.

Spacya had the same idea Taspe had. A whetstone in one hand and a spear in the other, she sat at her table and worked on it. She looked up, gave us a nod, and went back to watching what she was doing.

"Think you can make our prisoners talk?" I asked, leaning against the table to watch her.

"Sure."

Taspe chuckled, "That's my girl."

"Gonna try the pirate next?"

I rolled my eyes to the ceiling.

"Sounds like a plan." Taspe grinned.

Spacya nodded. She stood and set her spear with the others in the corner of her little house.

"Wait. Are we really going to torture Austere?"

Spacya and Taspe shared a look.

"He can't lie to a Welkan!"

"I don't remember that conversation. I didn't know that. Did you, Spacya?"

"No, don't know it at all. What's she talkin' about?"

I threw up my hands and shook my head.

Chapter 36

Spacya was still in with Fornid, one of the Stygra prisoners, when Taspe and I finished taking Caterwalla to her grave. The female had no regrets for what she did. She only hated that she hadn't gotten to kill me.

Austere sat in a chair he had dragged out of the kitchen into the yard. He had the back propped up against the side of the house, leaning it on two legs as he looked out across the garden. Gano had healed his shoulder as much as he could. It was closed, but the muscles were still healing underneath the skin. He just had a small scab.

He gave us a grin as we walked up.

Taspe sat on the stoop beside him, "I hear you like to sleep with my best friend while I'm not around."

Austere snorted, "I made that perfectly clear when you were around."

"She told me you think we could co-exist in some three-sided mating affair."

"She did what? I thought she was jealous? I mean… it could work. In the long run. You'll live longer than me, and so will she probably."

Taspe turned his gaze to me, "This isn't any fun with that curse on him."

I laughed and shook my head. "You're the one that wanted to make this some kind of torture for him. He's just being honest."

"Started without me?"

I felt like I was going to shoot out of my skin. I hated when Spacya went into silent mode when she walked. Especially when she came up behind me. Her grin made me stick my tongue out at her.

"Yeah, he caved easily."

"Fornid too." Spacya was wiping blackish blood from her fingers. "Keandria set this up. He thinks she did it to make us focus on the idea of a war instead of what she was doing with the gods."

"What war idea? Taking her out?"

"Perhaps."

I reviewed everything that Keandria and the Royals had said. "Do you think she is fooling the Royal Family too?"

"Tori!" Austere bellowed.

After a few moments, Tori stepped out from the side of the house. "You know… you can walk to me just as easily as I can walk to you."

"I'm injured." Austere's bottom lip protruded slightly.

"In the shoulder. Nothing wrong with your legs." Tori paused, his lips curling up, "Yet."

"Oooh, that sounds like a lovely little promise. But I must know something first. Do you know, without a doubt, that there are plans for some war?"

Tori leaned against the side of the house by Austere. He took his leather gloves off and ran his hands through his hair. Vey had taken a liking to the prince, and so had Gretta. Currently, they were all working on a contraption Gretta had dreamed up that lifted the milk pails up onto a cart for us.

So far, we had lost five pails. Luckily, she tested with them being filled with water.

"No. All the sources came up empty-handed, except for a few. Those… well, I don't trust those anymore."

"Why?" Taspe craned his neck so he could look over Austere to see Tori.

"They talk with Keandria or one of hers often."

"According to Fornid's recent torture, we think that the war was a ruse."

Tori's brows quirked, "A ruse, sir?"

"Yes, a ruse." Austere nodded.

"Now, what do we have? No war, Keandria trying to keep humans from getting magic from the gods, if that's what they are going to give us, a set of quests that we're not sure when or if they will end now that Keandria has messed up the sequence, and her minions attacked us. Is that it?" Tori ticked each one off on his tapered fingers and held up three. "It's all Keandria."

"We kill the one, and the rest falls into place."

"Except for the quests. We have to finish the ones the gods put forth."

I sat down on the stoop, leaning back on Taspe's torso between his legs. "How do we kill the most powerful in the world?"

"Other than the Natural Ones, who won't help. And the twenty-seven gods and goddesses, who also won't help, I dunno. Now that we found a new species, to us at least," Tori shot a glare at Austere, "We can probably count that if we find another all powerful being, they won't help us either. We have a human who has the powers of two Stygra in her. Doesn't that count as a most powerful being?"

I snorted, "Tori, please. This is not powerful at all. I can barely control them when I'm able to concentrate on them. If we fight Keandria, and all we have to rely on is me, I'm afraid we will lose. Badly."

Spacya sat beside Taspe and me, still rubbing the rag over her fingers, carefully picking off every speck of blood. "I'm wonderin', does she know you hold those powers? If she did, why would she keep magician' another to ya knowin' that you would get powers?"

"She doesn't know. She couldn't. Why would she give me a leg up?"

"So that her victory is that delicious."

All our heads turned to Austere.

He rolled his eyes, "You can't think like yourselves. Think like your enemy when you're trying to figure out what they want or what their next action will be. If she has given you these powers, then her win over you is going to just boost her ego through the roof. If she loses to you, then she still won because she allowed you to win, she gave you the way to win."

"Gods." I closed my eyes, "Does she want me to succeed or not?"

"Not succeed. Again, if you do, she still gets some satisfaction."

Taspe rested his chin on top of my head and sighed. "I'm going back with you."

"No, we're not going back to the capital. If she wants us, she needs to come out here and get us."

"Here?" Tori's voice was gentle.

"No… not… I can't put them in danger again. If we depart, we leave them open for attack. If we stay, we're bringing danger to them." I thought over the same options I had mulled over for the past few months. "I have a few ideas. None of them are ideal."

"Go on."

"We fortify here. Taspe, we could really use your Legacy's numbers. We have the guard of Owlimount. While their numbers are low, they are well trained. Ecia is at our back and we are all good with their royals and commanders, they will stand with us." I took a deep breath in, "Or we move my family, and the Legacy, and Owlimount."

Taspe snorted, "Fortifying it is." His hand slipped down the length of my braid. He started playing with the end, flipping it and twining it around his fingers. "My Legacy is ready. I told them to be ready to gather months ago. Some are still hesitant to come to the aid of a human, but they will obey me. But, don't take this the wrong way, I cannot risk them for nothing. I cannot move them for nothing. Those warriors will leave their villages, and while they won't be completely vulnerable, they will be weaker. Some other Legacies may take advantage of that."

I nodded, "I know. That's why I haven't asked before. If they all fight like we did before… we only need half of your force."

Taspe laughed. "Nadachia," He murmured, kissing the top of my head, "My warriors are the best, but the ones of the rest of my Legacy aren't anything to shrug off either."

"They are impressive." Tori added.

Spacya nodded, finally satisfied with the cleanliness of her hands. "We fortify. We include the village, the farm, and Owlimount. That's too much land to protect."

"Fall backs."

When nothing was said, and all eyes were on me, I explained. "We set up a system of forces and fortifications. Once the first falls, we fall back to the next, and then the next."

"How do we make them attack in that order?"

"Owlimount will be first. They're marching from Galanesse to here, they take Capital road."

"If we think of that, won't they send some to attack from the side?"

"They could." I nodded, "But we can set up to prepare for that too. We will have to have mobility. No heavy artillery except what's already on the walls. We need to be fluid."

"Fight like us." Taspe added.

"Yes."

"But with using fortifications too."

"Yes."

He sighed, "It could work." He dropped the end of my braid, "But I'm not so sure we can get them to come out here. The capital is unbreachable. Why would you leave that for a part of the country hardly any of your army or magic users have ever been to? You saw what they sent to take care of your family and my village. It was easy because they weren't the most powerful or useful. They were throwaways."

"If they don't come here and we don't go there, we will be stalemated." Tori pushed off the side of the house and began pacing. "Is there anything we control that isn't mobile that they want?"

"If we could summon all the gods here." Austere muttered.

Dread curled in my stomach. I hadn't decided on a plan because they were all useless. I just didn't want to accept it. "We're going to go there."

Tori stopped pacing and shook his head. "We can't win on her ground."

"We can… if we make it not seem like an attack."

Taspe's body tensed behind mine, "No."

"Every time we go back, she welcomes us. I've attacked her in her rooms, and yet she still allows me in there. Last time she allowed all of us in."

"No. I can't get you out of there if something goes wrong. She already knows that trick."

"Tori knows the cave system that runs underneath."

"You're wanting one of your best close-range fighters to stay in the caves in case something goes wrong instead of being with you against Keandria?" Austere eyed me.

"There's no one else I trust to help get us out. Do you have someone?"

Austere sighed after a moment, leaning his head back against my house, "Point made."

"What about the other Stygra in the tower?"

"They will either be with her or with us. Most of them have stayed out of the fights we've had so far. We can get a better idea of what we'll be facing inside from Randia."

When no one called out to her, I glanced at Spacya.

"Can we trust her?"

"She volunteered to be tied to me knowing that she would probably die." I had to point out.

Spacya just shook her head.

I rubbed my temples with my fingertips and shook my head, "I know. I know." Was I ever going to trust anyone new in my life? Austere's flashing dimples floated in my mind. I doubted him all the time. Randia I suspected too, but I was nicer to her. Nicer because her life was more in my hands than Austere's was.

"I wish Sterla was still alive." I said out loud.

Tori walked over and poked my forehead until I looked up at him, "Isn't she still here? You're always trying to explain to us what it feels like to hold her powers in you."

"Her powers, yes, but it's not like I can ask her questions and she talks to me."

"Have you tried?"

"That's making my life too simple." I shook my head. As Tori's eyes didn't leave me, I sighed and focused on Sterla's gifts. I knew I could feel others with it. Maybe the power had a memory of the other Stygra in the tower.

The power started weaving. Acting like it wasn't sure where it wanted to go or what it needed to do. I mentally chanted the question: how many Stygra are in the Tower that are with us? Still, it shifted and bobbed.

I tried another focus: how many Stygra in the Tower.

Sam Wicker

Nothing changed in the feeling.

I reached for Eisle's power. Hers became hard to hold on to, my focus fading from it as if it was pushing me away.

I shook my head, "It doesn't work that way."

"Had to try."

I glanced at Austere, "You always know more than the rest of us, what do you think?"

His eyes widened, "Me? Acting like I know everything?" He snorted, "My father used to say I didn't hold a mind to play with. That's why I was so fascinated with using my penis more."

Taspe chuckled, "Well… sounds like you are fond of that too."

"Any way we try, we're going to have a hard go at it. We're talking *the* Matron. She's renowned even on the islands. Facing her alone is asking for death. In her Tower with other Stygra around that support her… I think we might bring on the end of the world rather than magic for us weak little humans."

Hoofbeats sounded on the road. I sat up and watched some dust rise over the hill before the horse came into view. The red cap of a Guard messenger was all I could tell about the rider. I stood, making my way to the gate.

The messenger pulled up to the gate and stopped, her horse pawing the ground and tossing its shorn head. "Nadachia of Silverequis, the Hero?"

"That's me."

She pulled a black envelope out of the bag attached to the back of her saddle. "Looks important."

"Of course it does." I gave her a couple of iron bits for her trouble.

She smiled, saluted, and then went on her way at a gallop.

I looked at the seal. Keandria's fancy K with the word Matron surrounding it in silver wax threatened me. I made my way back to my group and sat down. Father came to the door, Mother crowding behind him.

"Another quest?"

I peeled back the wax, "Let's see."

Inside, I found three folded pieces of paper. I pulled them out. The first was a map with a red dot well outside of Lanpress, and toward the middle of Iethyll. The second was a description of the situation of the quest.

Rogue bandits are creating havoc for many villagers and cities. Local authorities and Guards have no resources nor aid from the current pirate king to protect their people. Go take care of the menace.

Oh, this was going to be great. "Austere, you might want to read this quest out loud for us all to enjoy." I handed him the slip of paper.

Father's shoulders lowered from his ears and he breathed deeply. I had the sneaking suspicion he had been listening to our talk of entering the Capital. Mother swiped at her cheek, then wrapped her arms around Father's thick arm.

Austere took it, eying it suspiciously before reading it out to the rest of them. Halfway through it, he stood. His chair rocking forward with the force of him jumping to his feet, before settling back on all fours. After finishing, he let loose a stream of harsh, guttural sounds that I took to be curses either in the Gods' tongue or in whatever he had grown up speaking.

Tori's hand was over his mouth, and he wouldn't look at Austere, or any of us, for that matter.

"I take it that your father wouldn't allow a band of ruffians to bully his citizens?" Father's voice held a little lilt on each word.

Austere whirled, eyes flashing, until he let fly another guttural word and breathed in sharply through his nose with his eyes closed. "This is a mistake. He wouldn't allow someone to harm his people if he could help it. It has to be backwards. There are still pockets of resistance to his rule. Obviously, Keandria shares views with those people."

"We'll go there and figure it out."

"Where did you tell Pitrini to wait with the ship this time?" Spacya took the note from Austere before he could crush it any more than he already had.

"He's still in Galanesse. We had a few repairs from the river. I'll send word to meet us along the coast."

Sam Wicker

I unfolded the last part.

Hero,
You have done well. The orchard reports you handled the
problem masterfully. I am impressed it was so quick.
I heard of your misfortune at home. Killers and crooks will do
anything to tear down great things. Do not let it get to you. I will
investigate these instances you and your family have suffered
personally. I do hope that the reports I received are true, and that
everyone you care for is mostly, if not completely, well.
Your Matron, Keandria

The audacity. Taspe pulled the letter out of my hands. I shook and heat rose from my belly, spreading all over. Not all were well. We lost two. We had wounded. Our hearts would never heal.

They had killed a young Rogue. A young Stygra, too. They had no shame. Keandria had no shame.

"Be angry, but keep it for her." Taspe wrapped an arm around my shoulder once he finished reading the letter.

Austere looked us both over, "I'm going to kill Keandria if you don't."

I stayed home for another two nights. That was as long as I dared keep Austere away from whatever this farce Keandria was sending us on now. This couldn't be something the gods had planned.

I didn't want to leave my family ever again.

I hugged each of them at least a hundred times in those two days. Taspe never left my side. Even when a contingent of warriors from one of his Legacy tribes arrived to protect my family. They set up small camps just outside the fences all around our property. As well trained as I was, and how well I knew the land, it took me a while to find their camps.

513

I didn't trust them. But I trusted Taspe. The leader of this group had been part of Taspe's legacy since he was born, and had proven himself twice when he saved not only Taspe's life, but that of his Mother.

He also had a human husband.

We left early in the morning, stopping to pick up Blari and Randia at the church on our way before heading south. I missed seeing Clara, and worried at her delay in arriving. It couldn't be helped. We were loaded down with food and supplies, just as much as if we had left from Galanesse.

The fanfare of us leaving in Owlimount was far more comforting than anything Galanesse contrived. I hoped I would see all those familiar, bright faces again upon my return. If I returned.

At least I wasn't heading to a known death.

Taspe rode with us as far as the southern road. "Chi, be careful. Send word as soon as you figure out what's going on." He glanced at Austere, "Give him a chance."

I rolled my eyes, "You two have another talk?"

"A talk."

I kissed him, and we left.

We rode southwest, meeting the Southern Wall that kept the heathens from the mainland out of our countries, and rode alongside it for a while. It was the first time I saw it in my life. I hated how it blocked out the sun. Nothing grew near it except scraggly grasses.

We made camp in the wall's shadow. I was in my tent, not caring who would come in to share it with me, when Austere pulled back the flap and just lay down.

He put his head on my thigh, "You ever going to take that leather belt off tonight?"

"You ever going to not ask me that?"

"It's concerning. You're so happy to dig those daggers out and sink them into things. You talk about it often."

"If someone didn't make rude comments all the time, I wouldn't threaten as much. Would I?"

He sat up and moved to his knees in one fluid motion. He nuzzled between my neck and shoulder, "Since when have I made rude comments? I always speak compliments."

"We're in a tent. Don't start anything."

He pulled back, looking like a child that just had his favorite toy hidden away from him. Then a glint entered his eyes, "Just means I get to make up for it once we are on my ship." Austere slid back out to throw in his gear. He came back in, pulled my covers so they lay flat across the tent flooring before spreading his over them.

"Do you ever sleep?"

He sat and pulled off his boots with a grunt each, "I sleep better on the ship. Out here it feels like naps." He lay his long blade beside his side of the bed and propped his smaller short sword beside his pillow.

I moved from my knees to sit and pull my boots and belt off. I didn't feel like having my sides pricked by my daggers that night, but I kept them close to my side as I lay down.

We stared up at the tent ceiling.

"He wanted me to know what to do in case anything happened to him."

I sat up, "What is he planning?"

"Nothing. He just said something about there being more attacks on his Legacy. He thinks the Matron has something to do with it now. Welkans don't get that angry over a new leader for nothing."

I pressed my fingers to the scar. His heartbeat was steady against them. I lay back down.

Austere's fingers trailed down my arm until they found mine and held,

I sighed. It was going to be a long trip. "What's your country like?"

"Too hot during the summer and too cold during the winter. The people are open. There are more nomadic tribes than there are stationary cities and towns." He chuckled, "Somewhere, there is a party or festival going on for something. Actually, I think I've seen where there was a festival and no one could tell me the reason behind it, other than just for the sake of having one."

"So most are rich?"

He nodded, "But they don't show it. Ieathyll is a land of extremes. One is rich or poor. One either has a vast family or none. You either move around or you plant roots and never move again. But all of them dress in these vibrant colors that flow around them. They learn from one another, teach one another and they flow through each other's lives… it's hard to put into words." He paused, "I believe they came to be that way because of the terrors they had for kings in the past. The last three stole so much from them. They could easily be jaded, but they aren't."

"Sounds nothing like Lanpress."

He snorted, "No, it isn't. Lanpress is stuffy. You have too many rules and rulers to follow. Nothing comes together and fits as one."

My mind shot forward and grappled with that sentence.

The Royal Family and The Matron had always pulled together Lanpress. There were always tensions between the two. The Welkans did their own thing. Always had. What if Keandria not only wanted the humans to stay without magic or godly gifts, but still wanted all the power? If she gained what was supposed to be given to humans, somehow, wouldn't that help both of her missions?

She had stolen the quests from the gods, why not their gift to humans too?

"Austere?"

"Hm?"

"We must win."

Instead of shaking in my boots on this ship, dreading going to another land, I was worried about my family. What we faced once we landed in Ieathyll was what we would face. The thought of being further away from my family than I had ever been before was what made my heart flutter and duck into my stomach. I also knew that I could trust Taspe and his people to help them. I could depend on the people of Owlimount. Not just Doc and the Priests, but most of them. They had pulled together and showed me that in the past few months.

I could stand and fight. Yes, there would be death. My heart was bleeding and broken. At the same time, there was something tickling at hope. We had to win.

"Ready for this?" Blari came to stand beside me.

"As ready as we shall ever be."

Blari chuckled, "You've done better than you thought you would, haven't you?"

"In a way. I'm afraid I might be changing." I looked down at the sun sparkling off the water. Here, the tips of the little waves lapping at the side of the ship sparkled like stars in a moonless night sky.

"I think it's a positive change, if my thoughts count."

"Of course they do."

"Chi..." he started, then rubbed a hand down his beard, "I do fear for your life."

"I do too." My throat burned, "But I'd rather welcome my death than someone else's." The words twisted in my mind and I gave him a small smile, "Besides, I've gotten used to dying. I'm not used to someone I love dying."

"I know. They were young. I was looking forward to how bright their lives were going to be under the loving care of your family. Your father, mother, and you have a knack for bringing out the best in those children. You push them to be great and they are great."

I shook my head, "That's all them. They're resilient. We've just given them food and a place to sleep to feed their dreams."

Blari prodded my shoulder, "Would you take a compliment and listen to what I'm saying?"

I glared at him and kept my mouth shut.

"If this is your end. If we go into this, and come out clean and die when we fight Keandria, then you have lived a life well lived and loved. You have been enough."

"Gods, Blari." I looked away from him, my throat clogging and my eyes spilling hot tears over my cheeks.

"I wanted to say that before I couldn't say it any longer. I don't know what will happen. Gods… we could drown in a storm for all I know. It's been on my mind for a while, and I finally got enough gumption to tell you." His wide hand found my back and rubbed a few circles before he walked away.

"Should I go kill a priest?" Austere moved to my side, wrapping his long arms about me.

"No." I swiped at my eyes, "Yes." I shook my head, "No. No, he was just being nice."

"If making someone cry is him being nice, I think I have more work to do on his social skills than I ever did yours."

"Are we loaded up?"

"The men are preparing to shove out now. Don't change the subject. How was he being nice?"

I shook my head, "He… he said I had done enough. That I am enough. That if I die soon, then I've done well."

"Brilliant." Austere whispered into my hair. "You've done brilliantly."

I shoved at him, "Not you too."

"Look, if he's allowed to get all sappy and poetic, I should, too. Priests get all the good moments." He loosened his hold on me, but didn't let go.

"Blari's sobbing. Nadachia's crying. Austere looks like he's about to cry. What's going on?" Tori set his bag down and glanced between us and Spacya, who was on his other side.

Spacya shrugged, "Maybe the sea ain't got enough salt."

I watched as Tori stared at her for a moment. The emotions in his face shifting from wanting to reprimand her to chuckling. "We're all mad." He shrugged, his hands coming up and out at his sides. "Every one of us, mad."

He turned to me, "Are you alright?"

He knew what it was like to lose a sibling. I felt bad for comparing his loss to mine. They hadn't been with me for that long, but I knew he could understand. "I'm mad."

"Well, at least you can joke a little."

"Even if it's a terrible one."

"I thought it was good."

"You would. Your dry sense of humor has infected Chi."

"I'm going to take her to lie down." Austere announced to them.

"I should stay out here."

"No, rest. You've been through a lot and only had two days to process…" Tori trailed off, "Go lay down." He added.

Spacya gave me a nod.

We walked toward our respective cabins, but Austere guided me to his. I pulled back, he smirked, "I can't sleep alone, remember?"

"You sleep better on your ship."

"Imagine the sleep I will get, with you, on my ship."

I sighed, glancing at my friends disappearing down the hall. Alone with my thoughts, was not a place I wished to be anytime soon. "I would think that you would want your room below decks so no one would hear your activities."

"Ah, that will cause all the vibrations to be felt throughout the ship. Up here, only the rooms below might get an earful now and then." He chuckled, opening the door for me, "Why? Afraid you're going to be loud?"

"I'm supposed to rest."

"You will. We have a few days until we get to the port closest to where the Matron wants us to be."

Plenty of time to worm his way into what he wants. I began unpacking a few things from my bag I needed every day. Everything else could stay in it. He sat in his chair and watched me. His cabin was large, taking up most of the back of the ship. Windows stretched from wall to wall.

His desk was a dark wood, bolted to the floor. On top were a few knickknacks and papers. He was in one of two chairs he had in front of it. His leg was hanging over the arm. "You can put your clothing in with mine in the dresser. I haven't unpacked yet, so take all the room in it you need."

"I'll only unpack what I need."

After I finished, I stood before him, "Waiting for me to bawl like a baby?"

"No, but if you need to do that, you can. I like watching you."

I shook my head, "You're weird."

"Chi take your time." His voice grew soft, his fingers trailing down my arm to the palm of my hand. They stopped along the scar. Could he feel Taspe there?

"How is your shoulder?"

Austere lifted it, "It's still pulling, but not as painful as it was a couple of days ago. That healer lady is amazing. I kind of wanted to bring her along."

I laughed, "The tribe would have killed you."

"Ah, good thing I didn't steal her then."

He stood, "You should rest."

"Probably."

I met his gaze, "Why did you want to become a companion?"

"To become a god."

My brows rose into my hairline. He couldn't be serious. "A god? You want to become a god?"

His grin made those dimples appear, "Yes. Legends say that a lot of the past heroes and some of their companions have become gods. People believed they could do anything. Once people believe…"

I shook my head, "Maybe you need to talk more with your little friends."

"Oh darling, remember? I was raised with them." He dropped my hand as he stood and wrapped his arms around me to rest his hands, folded, at the small of my back. "To have powers, be able to do anything. Help people on a whim and punish people that needed it without repercussion. To know things."

"The god of knowledge and justice?"

He stared at me for a moment, his smile fading briefly before it came back with a laugh, "You are brilliant. I'll keep telling you that until you believe it. That would be perfect."

"You don't think all that power and responsibility would go to your head?" I asked, canting my head to the side a little as the ship began moving. The men were yelling orders and I could hear them running about before settling into their stations.

"I don't think so. Especially if I keep you by my side." He leaned down, resting his forehead on mine.

"I don't want to be a god. I couldn't watch my family die and all their heartache."

"But you could watch your family grow. Take part in all the happy moments of each and every generation to come. Yes, there will be terrible things, but think of all the good things too."

I shook my head, my forehead rolling against his gently, "And with you too."

"Mhm." He flattened his hands at the small of my back, curling them as he slid them down my backside.

I stayed still. I paid attention to the different emotions in me. Not an ounce of repulsion. I still felt guilt. There was a warmth there now too. He had grown on me, little by little. There was still plenty to go for him to be loved by me, but Austere was there in my heart.

I slid my hands along his sides, to his broad back. I rested them under his shoulder blades. He was so tall. As if he was bent double to be this close to me. I felt tiny in his hands, like a child.

I wasn't a child.

He had stilled. Waiting. Watching.

I tilted my head, went up on my toes a little and fit my lips to his.

His body tensed under my hands. Then he moved. He pressed us together, gently folding me up into his embrace. He titled his head and flicked his tongue against my bottom lip. I opened to him.

He whimpered.

A thrill scattered over my body and I knew goosebumps were rising on my flesh. I let him taste me. I savored him.

He pulled away, loosening his hold on me slightly. His pupils were wide enough to swallow most of the red once he opened them. He was smiling.

Chapter 37

We landed on a dock covered in people and streamers. The people were as brightly colored as the streamers. And the buildings on the beach and the road leading to the city of Duar were just as vibrant, too.

The view from the ship was gorgeous.

Duar and its people lived against the sea and along the hills that rose toward a range of snow-capped mountains in the distance. The mountains were young, sharp, jagged peaks piercing the sky, much like the range near Emleton. The air here was all salty sea, but it held something different from the ocean at Lanpress.

Strange trees grew among the buildings, shooting up into the sky, bare until their very tops which sprouted large blue-green leaves from the red trunks. A breeze flicked the leaves of one nearby, and petals of purple fluttered underneath, some coming loose in the wind and floating away upon it.

"Red Empires." Austere stated beside me as I took another deep breath in of the rich scent. "They'll produce a tasty fruit in winter, purple like the petals are." He leaned in close, "They taste much like those petals smell. Rich and juicy."

"You make things vulgar."

Austere chuckled, nuzzling into my neck, "You will get used to it."

"Is there always this much going on at the dock when a ship comes in?"

"No, not usually." He frowned, "Gods no."

Pitrini ran up to us, "They're here!"

Austere had a muscle in his jaw that flicked when he was trying to form words instead of saying what he was thinking. It was a small tell, but once I knew what it was, I looked for it often enough. "You told them we would be here in your last letter?"

"Of course I did!"

"We will talk. Later." Austere clapped his hand against Pitrini's cheek, his teeth gritted.

Sam Wicker

"Who's here?"

Austere heaved a breath out of his lungs, and drew his shoulders back and head high with the next intake, "My parents."

Getting off the boat was like being escorted down the parade through Galanesse. We walked in a line, people grinned, waved, cheered and jabbered on either side of us. Austere led the way. I was behind him. Tori behind me, then Spacya, Blari, Randia and lastly Pitrini and the rest of the crew.

Austere led us down the length of the dock and stopped outside a large tented thing. It rested on two poles that were held up by several burly types on their shoulders. The fabric glistened in the sunlight, casting a red hue on the surrounding area and the people holding it up. Inside were mounds of pillows, a silver tray of food, and four people.

The man was as tall as Austere, or so I gathered, considering the length of his legs stretched out before him and how he was still a head taller than the woman at his side. His skin was dark, as if he had spent every moment since birth in the sun. His eyes, though, were a stark ice blue under thick salt and pepper brows.

The woman was not as ebony as the man beside her. A scar ran along her cheek, from the bone to her jawline. Her face was round, a huge grin showing straight white teeth and nearly closing her almond-shaped eyes. Those eyes were a brown, nearly black color, and a line of coal enhanced their shape and matched her hair. Her lips were a bright red, the color of Mother's roses.

The other two jumped out into Austere's arms as soon as he was within reach.

Their laughter pitched as he nuzzled and kissed each of them profusely, squeezing them hard. Their little hands fluttered everywhere. Pulling at his hair, hugging him, pinching his cheeks and pulling on his ears. It was like they had more than two arms each.

"Welcome home!" The woman's voice was warm, like the breeze off the ocean, it held a deep lilt and her vowels sounded odd to my ears.

The man's voice boomed next, "Welcome Hero and friends. Come! We have food and rest prepared for you!" He motioned to someone.

Another tent came out. Austere deposited the children back into their tent. I turned, but he grabbed my hand before bending to lift me into the one with his family. I gasped, floundering on the bed-like structure I was sitting upon until he came up behind me.

"Is she the Hero?"

The little girl sat in Austere's father's lap. The King's lap. Who I had settled right beside.

I pulled myself up into sitting properly and bowed as best as I could. "I'm Nadachia."

The other little girl was crawling to Austere and sat down in his lap. "She's your new wife?"

The king chuckled, "Yes she is!"

Austere coughed, "Pop, no! No, she's not my wife." He shot a glance at me and mouthed the word 'yet' with a grin.

It was hot in this thing.

I grunted and swayed with it as the men and women outside started moving. People still cheered all around us. I looked out at the colors. Such vibrant colors on buildings. Blues and greens swirled together on one, another building was a rich red with white shutters, and yet another was a dandelion yellow with a mountain painted upon it.

"Soon enough," the king smiled, "You can call me Pop, Nadachia. This is my wife,"

She interrupted, "If he gets to be called Pop, I get to be called Momma."

Pitrini jumped into the thing, grinning as the girls launched themselves at him. He laughed and tickled them after a series of hugs and kisses. I smiled. I knew I liked this family already if those girls treated an adoptive brother like that.

"Ah, there you are! How do you hide so well in the crowd, boy?" The king tossed a small, round red fruit at Pitrini.

"I got tackled by one of the merchants." He rubbed at his cheek and neck, where remnants of red, almost the same color as the queen's lips, remained. One girl picked up the fruit and popped it into her mouth.

"Ah, there's my boy." The queen grinned at him, "Is she pretty?"

Pitrini's face grew redder than the lipstick smudged on him. "She is."

"See, I told you not to teach him much. He has his own charm." The queen waggled a finger at her son.

He lifted a shoulder, "He may do well enough on his own. A prince shouldn't lower to a merchant unless she is pretty, though. And it's love."

I frowned at him, "A prince shouldn't lower to a merchant? Well then, I will not marry you at all."

He sputtered, "You're the Hero, there's a difference."

"I was just a trapper before."

"JUST a trapper?" Austere was fumbling, gaze landing on everything but me.

The king chuckled, "I like her already. I may adopt her so you can't have her at all. A Princess Hero, how's that?"

"Sounds far too impressive for poor little Stere." The queen smirked.

Yes, I liked these people. "I might take you up on that."

As we passed through a few of the streets, we made small talk. They asked how our journey was, and a few things about my family. It wasn't until we stopped that the talking paused. I looked out and up at a large home. It was all round pillars in creamy white that had tendrils of a little green vine with tiny red flowers circling from the bottom to the top.

"This house belongs to one of our lords. He has been nice enough to allow us to stay here while we met you. He is at his brother's house." The King smiled and slid out of the carrier once the men and women set it down on the ground.

I stepped out behind him and found one of the girls attaching themselves onto my leg. She beamed up at me. I reached down and lifted her up to my hip. "Am I to call you, Sis?"

She grinned, "No, cause there's two of us. Call me Ash."

"Oh, manners! Forgive me!" The queen gasped, "That's Ashie, and this one is Bellra."

"Nothing to forgive."

She smiled at me, "I hope you enjoy your stay."

The King looked at me, one foot on the first wide stair that led up to the carved double doors. "Shall we let you rest, or do you mind talking for a bit more until a meal?"

"I don't mind talking." I watched as my companion's carrier was lowered beside ours. It was so smooth, and the people doing the carrying barely had any sweat on them.

"Careful what you stare at. I might get jealous."

I shook my head. They were impressive, though. I had never seen such thick arms and thighs on a person as most of these had.

Austere plucked Ash from my arms and put her on his shoulders. She giggled, both hands fisted in his hair as he took the stairs, one large hand splayed over the little girl's back to hold her steady.

Blari came up beside me, "Well, that was different."

"I prefer horses." Spacya grumbled, eying the contraption she stepped out of.

I laughed, "Come on, they want to talk."

I followed the royal family up the steps and stared at the doors as they were flung wide. They were a dark wood, but carved intricately into a landscape of the mountains behind the house. Unpainted, allowing the rich color of the wood to shine through.

We entered the house, and I tripped into Austere as I tried to look at everything at once.

The ceiling was a dome, pillars holding it up at regular intervals. They made the dome of colored tiles that formed a multicolored swirl that flowed down to the pillars. Each pillar was a different color. The floor was a multi-colored tile-work too. There were too many people to see the design clearly.

He turned, taking my hand with a chuckle, "Need to take Ash's place?"

"No." I nearly pouted, because that would have been ideal to see it all.

The walls were white, but held many large paintings. Most were landscapes. Rolling green fields giving away to colorful villages, a river surrounded by greenery that had butterflies and birds enjoying the paradise, and imitations of the beautiful rugged mountains in all seasons.

"It's beautiful."

"I shall let our host know he has the approval of the Hero once he arrives tomorrow. He would have been here to greet you today, but his brother has been injured in a hunt."

"Bear?"

The king nodded, "That same beast we hunted last fall too."

Austere laughed, "They will never get it. He's too cunning."

"Could be a she!" the queen chimed in. She smiled at me with a wink, "We are often much smarter!"

The king chuckled, "Yes, my love, that you are." He wrapped his arm around her, taking a quick kiss from her lips. They walked together, arms around one another as they led us between the two curving staircases to a wide sitting area.

A fire pit was in the middle. Large pillows and furs thrown around for comfort amid the low, thickly cushioned couches and chairs. Windows made up the entire wall. Outside them stood the tall mountains glistening in the sunlight.

The king and queen took up a couch, and we arranged ourselves around them and the fire pit. Austere kept me at his side, pulling me to a couch. The thing was going to eat me alive until his weight evened the odds.

"I heard that your… Matron… was it?" The queen nodded as the king looked at her for verification, "Said that my people were being harassed by my men?"

I pulled the letters from my pockets and handed them to him after fighting to get up off the couch. Austere helped, in a way, with his big hand on my ass, pushing me up. The king winked, and my face burned even more.

He read the letters and shook his head, "Lovely person, isn't she?"

I snorted and shook my head with a smile, "She is… well…"

"Do not worry." The queen said in her lilting speech, "We know she needs to be gotten rid of."

The King leaned back, stretching out on the couch with his arms flung on either side of him. The queen lay her head on his arm. "Truth is there is still a bit of a rebellion since my take over. There are a few slaveholders, mine owners and the like that don't appreciate being told they can no longer sell slaves or use slaves. In fact, the people are free now. Artists are back."

"Things have gotten worse for some people. Those near the slaveholders, but for the most part they know they are free. Just last month, all those lovely colors on the buildings were faded in hue. It was a forgotten part of their heritage. Now, the old ones are teaching the young to paint again." The queen's voice warmed, "It is beautiful."

I nodded, "The people that met us seem happy. Did you ask them to decorate?"

"Oh no. They wanted to welcome Pitrini and Austere back home." The Queen smiled, "They love their handsome princes."

Austere muttered under his breath about overbearing mothers, and then added, "About the slavers, where are they causing the most ruckus?"

"Here."

Austere's brow twitched, "So you came to live here for a bit, even though you are being threatened here?"

The king leaned forward, "Just because I put my ship up doesn't mean I can no longer take care of matters, son."

"He pulled the son card." Pitrini whispered to Tori behind his hand.

Austere shot him a look as the king smirked. "You're a king now, you're supposed to *send* people to take care of it for you."

"Ah, is that so? What else am I doing wrong? Maybe I should let you be king… son."

The queen giggled and shook her head, "Boys, come now, behave yourselves."

"He used it again!"

"No need for commentary." Austere growled, throwing a pillow at Pitrini. It hit Tori instead.

"No attacking princes!" The king growled right back, waggling a finger at his offspring.

"I didn't attack him!" He swatted the pillow away that Pitrini threw back at him. It bent my nose down when it hit my face. I glared at him.

His eyes widened, "Sorry, darling."

I shoved the square in his face, pushing him down with it. I hit him with it twice before trying to get off him.

His hands gripped my hips and held me on top of him, "Not exactly my ideal place for having you on top of me, but I'll take it."

I pushed the pillow back down on his face. Everything from the top of my head down to my chest burned.

The king laughed, it echoed against the walls, "Oh, she's got you matched! About time there was a woman around that wasn't scared to give it back to him."

The queen got up and moved over to me. She tapped Austere's hands off my hips. "Here. When he gets too riled up, do this."

"No. Back off!" Austere bucked his hips, almost unseating me.

Her hands shot to his sides, inches above his hips. Those long fingers began dancing over his skin there after she jerked his shirt up. He gasped, his abs going so tight they formed ridges and dips on his flat stomach.

He laughed, "Stooooop." He twisted from side to side. I clamped down, releasing my hold on it to place my hands on his shoulders so he couldn't twist out of our grasp.

He flung the pillow off, his legs thrashing. Other pillows tumbled to the floor from his kicking. His laughter was deep, long, breathless all at the same time. His hands pushed and grabbed at his Mother's hands, trying to keep them away. She twisted them out of his grip and began again.

"S-s-s stahp!" He breathed, his eyes finding mine. "Help me not her!"

I couldn't help but giggle and grin right alongside the queen.

The king cleared his throat, "Now, ladies, let's not make him wet himself."

The queen laughed, reaching down to cup Austere's face in both her hands. She kissed each cheek, and then his forehead, "My beautiful boy, still ticklish after all these years..." She winked at me.

Before he could get his wits about him, I stood and picked up a few pillows to toss onto him.

He lay on the couch, rumpled, staring at the ceiling as he tried to catch his breath.

I looked over at Tori, Spacya and Blari, "Guess we know how to threaten him to get our way now."

Tori chuckled, "That we do. Thank you, your majesty." He gave a nod at the queen, who had settled back down beside her husband.

Blari rubbed his hands together, "Wonder what would happen with feathers."

Austere clutched a pillow to his stomach, his eyes flying over to stare at Blari, whites showing around the red irises, "Don't you dare!"

We sat and talked until a maid came in to declare that supper was ready for us. The king stood and patted the maid's shoulder, "Thank you, Celense, how's your baby sister?"

"She is doing well now. Thank you for sending your doctor, King Jaye." She bowed her head.

"I am glad." He smiled at her, holding out his hand to help his queen up. They walked arm in arm in front of us, leading the way to the dining room.

Tori watched the interaction, "You're a good man."

The king looked over his shoulder, "A good man?" He chuckled, "Someone who observes and knows one is probably a good man himself."

I smirked and patted Tori on the arm, "He is. He was raised by royals, so he has a bit of learning to do about how to talk to people without sounding aloof."

Tori sighed, "Well said. Didn't know I sounded any different from the rest of you when I talked. Now I'm going to worry I'm doing more harm than good."

The king chuckled, "You're doing well from what I can tell."

We entered the dining room from a long, brightly lit, narrow hallway. The table was low to the ground, a rich red wood with dozens of plates and platters holding all manner of glistening succulent things. The aroma was Gods' realm delicious and my stomach gave a loud rumble in appreciation.

"Help yourselves." The king opened his arms wide as he sat, not at the head of the table, but toward the middle, on a low pillow.

We arranged ourselves. I faced the king and queen, Austere on one side, and Pitrini on the other. A bare plate sat in front of me. They all picked up a plate or platter of food, picked what they wanted and passed the plate to the next person on their right.

"Is this how everyone eats here?"

"Yes, neat isn't it?" Austere took the plate I handed him, added another piece of the meat to my plate off of it before taking a few for himself and passing it on to Randia.

"It takes a long time to learn. These people have a rich background and culture." The queen smiled, "This is my favorite. The food."

The king chuckled, "You say that about everything, darling. You said that about the clothing, the paintings, the spices, their language and weddings...."

Her full lips pushed out, "All is my favorite then, ball buster."

Pitrini spluttered his drink.

I laughed.

The queen lifted a shoulder, "If they not like a queen who speaks like me, too bad."

Austere chuckled, "If they don't like pirates for their royalty. Too bad." He gave his mother a grin.

"We were not pirates in the pirate way." She shook her head, "No, we were pirates to pirates, but not to sailors or normal people."

"We were pirates, darling." The king patted her shoulder, "But we were nice pirates."

Blari chuckled, "I read some stories about your exploits. You are definitely the nicest pirates I have ever come across on the page."

"Thank you, Priest Blari." The king grinned. I saw where Stere got his dimples from. Everything else about him he seemed to have taken from his mother. She was tall too, not matching the king's towering build, but tall for a woman.

The meats were spicy, burning a little on the tongue and lips, but they were juicy too. They mostly steamed the vegetables with a few spices added here and there. My drink was a tea that had a lemon and sweeteners in it that eased the spice of the food enough so I could eat more.

It sated my growling stomach quickly.

If someone wanted a refill, they asked for the plate to be passed to them. No matter our rank, we were all equal. I liked the companionship of a simple, low table with passing food plates back and forth brought. I wondered if I could bring it to my table.

Soon enough, everyone was leaning back from the table. Satisfied tummy rubs and little burps, signaling the end of the meal. "I had the plan that you all could retire to your rooms for the night. Talk, sleep, settle, and we shall resume talks and plans in the morning."

I nodded, then glanced at my companions. They seemed alright with that plan as well, "It sounds good to us."

"Good." He gave me a small smile, "I have a few maids waiting, they will show you where everything is after introducing themselves. If you have questions or need anything, they will be ready to help. They equip each room with a bell that you can use to signal them."

Austere stood and stretched. He reached down, helping me and Randia up, one in each hand. But it was me who he kissed on the temple before going around to give his mother and the girls hugs. He even hugged his father with a grin.

I watched them; they were as comfortable together as I was with my family.

It said a lot when children liked you. Children have the innate ability to know the hearts and truths of a person. The girls hung on Pitrini and Austere, wide grins brightening their faces and eyes glowing with joy.

"You'll be staying in Prince Austere's room, miss?" A maid came up to me with a wide smile.

"Yes, she will." He grinned, "I'll take Ash and Bell to bed with Pitrini."

I glanced at Pitrini; he smiled at me. His eyes seemed hooded, "Are you alright?"

"I… I am." He nodded.

Austere watched him, waiting for him to get a few doors down the hallway before he spoke, "I think having Ash and Bell around reminds him of what he lost. He had a little sister." He sighed, pressing a kiss to Ash's forehead as she snuggled against his chest, "We didn't know it but the girls chose his little sister's room to be their own."

My heart burned for Pitrini.

"Go on, wash up and get in bed. I'll be there in a little while." He turned on his heel and followed Pitrini down the hall. I started to go after them, but the maid stopped me.

It was only then I realized it was the same maid the king had talked with before. "The prince's room is down the other wing." She led me to the other hall and down a few doors to the end. He had a corner room.

"Were you part of the household before the current king?"

"Oh yes, I've been with Lord Izahdi for three years."

"You're not the king's maid?"

"No, miss. Just Lord Izahdi's. The Lord paid for my little sister to have some treatments, but they didn't work. So the king sent for his personal doctor. He thinks it might be something else, so he's working out a plan to get her well." She smiled, "Both are great men. So kind. I was lucky to get hired here instead of thrown in the mines or slavers' holds."

I wondered what the king would do in Lanpress if given the opportunity. We no longer had slavery, but many of the lords and ladies were not as kind as the two the maid spoke of. I didn't know any royals who would have sent their own doctor to a maid's house. Other than Tori. Tori would do that. And Clara, if she noticed something amiss. Sometimes she was so lost in her own agendas that she rarely noticed anything around her.

"Is there anything I can get you?" The maid opened the door for me with a flourish, bowing.

"No, I should be fine."

"The bath is ready for you behind the screen. I got you a nightgown as yours looked dirty from the trip. If you need anything else, the bell is here." She pointed to a rope by the door.

"Thank you." I smiled at her. When she left, I started stripping. I knew there was no use in arguing over where I slept anymore. I had been with him on the ship, in the tent getting to the ship, and many times before that. Why was I being so stubborn with him?

I'm going to die. That won't be fair to him.

I shook my head as I placed my clothing on a little stool at the base of the inset bathtub. Austere must have told them, at some point, what I liked in my bath.

The tiles were a rich blue with white swirls. The white matched the rest of the area's flooring, which had a light blue swirl, like thick wispy clouds on a dark blue sky. In the steaming water were lavender sprigs. I took a deep breath in; the scent washed through me to loosen my nerves and muscles.

Unbraiding my hair, I carefully picked my way down into the hot water, pausing as the heat was a bit too much on my naked flesh. I knew it would settle down into a comfortable warmth if I was patient. Soon enough, the water was up to my chin, and I was letting it hold me.

From what I had seen so far, the people here were happy. There were always going to be a few negative thoughts, some fears, and dislikes, but that was the nature of a group of peoples. Was it the few that had contacted Keandria about their displeasure? Instead of investigating, she sent us down here to handle it.

Handle it we would, but probably not in the way she wanted.

But why was she determined to undermine a fair king?

Sam Wicker

Slavery. Mines. Was she getting something from that? Was that what she wanted to have in Lanpress when she got her way? We knew she probably didn't want us to succeed so humans could get magic. Was it another ploy or part of her plan to enslave us?

I must have fallen asleep. The door opened, and I heard the patter of bare feet on the floor between the rugs. I sat up. The maid smiled at me, holding two steaming buckets in her hands. "Came to refresh the bath, Prince Austere is on his way."

I nodded, "Go ahead." I yawned, leaning over to pull the plug to the drain so the bath wouldn't overflow when she poured the hot water in.

"Is there enough lavender?"

"Yes, it's good." I smiled up at her as she drizzled the water in at the furthest point away from me. I watched the steam rise from the fall of water into the bath. It must be just off a fire. The warmth spread up my feet and legs as she poured. Somehow, she poured so slowly that the bath was draining quicker than she could pour. I replaced the plug.

As if on cue, I heard the door open and shut as the maid finished pouring the last bucket. She gathered them up. Austere rounded the half wall that separated the bath from the rest of the room. His shirt was halfway open and his boots off.

Her face turned red as she gave him a wide berth, her head down, fingers tight on the bucket handles. "So sorry, Prince Austere."

He smiled, "Nothing to be sorry for, dear. Thank you for your hard work. Go home and get some rest."

She nodded, bowed, and scurried out. The buckets banged against the wood of the door in her hurry to get away.

"I think you make her nervous."

He chuckled, pulling his shirt and pants off and placing them on the stool on top of my clothes. He slid into the bath, "Gods, that's hot," he hissed through clenched teeth. "Are you boiling yourself?"

"Give it time, it'll cool."

He sighed, moving to rest his back against the side of the bath by me. "Are you just going to stay here all night?"

I shook my head; it was before sunset when I came in here. There weren't any windows in this section of the room, "It's night?"

"Has been for about an hour." He turned, resting his elbow along the edge to study me, "You fell asleep, didn't you?"

"Maybe."

He chuckled, "Have you washed at least?"

"Maybe." I answered again, trying not to let my chin jut out like it wanted to.

"Mmm hmm." He eyed me, reaching back into a little tile covered basket at the edge of the bath. He pulled out a cloth and some soap.

I took it from him and lathered them up. He was about to reach for another cloth when I put the soap down on the rim and turned toward him. I placed the cloth on his shoulder and started massaging the lather onto his tan skin. "Turn around, I'll do your back."

He did as he was told, rolling his shoulders toward his chest. I paused, wondering if I should. Now I could trace those tattoos. I could feel the heat of his skin.

Steam was coming off him where the water was so much hotter than the air in the room. I began lowering my hands, washing his hips, his tight buttocks. "You have dimples here too."

He cleared his throat, "Momma used to say she could never tell my face from my ass when I was being mischievous because the dimples were the same."

I laughed, "I'm going to have to remember that one." I began on his shoulders and worked down one arm and then the other. Each time I had finished with an arm, he had dropped it to cover his front with his hand. I started on his chest.

"So you have yet another thing to torture me over?"

I looked up from one of his chest tattoos. His eyes were half lidded, with his gaze down upon me. "Yes."

He took the cloth from me, lathering it up some more. I saw what he had been hiding with his hand. The water wasn't the only thing warming me. He nudged me, turning my back to him. He washed my back in swift, but gentle swipes. As he worked his way down to my waist, he slowed. He handed the cloth to me, his hands covered in suds, and then his hands covered my ass. Those long fingers kneaded, and worked their way over my hips, and down my thighs under the water.

He pulled me back against him. I felt him, hard against my ass cheek and lower back. Stere took the cloth from me again. He began washing my lower stomach with it. He worked his way up in slow, circular strokes.

He dropped the cloth into the water as he placed his hands just under my breasts. Those fingers slid up, squeezing gently. My breath caught, and I lay my head back on his chest. His palms slid up, slick. The callouses on the inner sides of his thumbs raked over my nipples. My body jerked, shoving into his hands.

His cheek pressed to my temple. His hands worked over my breasts, squeezing until he pinched my nipples between his thumb and forefinger. "Will you let me love you tonight?"

I cupped his cheek in my hand and turned to look at him. Those red eyes searched mine. There was hope in them, there was that look that only I got from him in them, and there was the resolve. He would stop if I wanted him to. Those secrets in those eyes made me smile. I went up on my tiptoes, pulling him down as I did too. I kissed his forehead. As I pressed my forehead to his, looking back into those darkening eyes, "Yes. Will you let me love you too?"

The pull on his lips was slow, but soon enough those dimples flashed, "Yes."

He took my mouth with his. Slow, chaste presses as he continued to wash me. Those hands of his made quick work of my shoulders and arms, often sliding back to my breasts.

We rinsed each other off. The kisses growing to sample each other with our tongues. He nipped at my lip with one; I returned the favor on the next one.

His hands skimmed down my back as together we moved to the edge of the bath. The cool tiles pressed against my upper back. He cupped my ass cheeks, then lifted. Those eyes of his were on mine as he sat me down on the edge. I gripped his shoulders. He turned his head to kiss my wrists.

Stere broke the moment when he searched for the washcloth. He cursed once, lathering it back up, and I laughed when he returned to me. "We're gonna have to bathe again in the morning anyway…"

One of his brows cocked up, "I've endured your feet for the past week."

I made a face, my cheeks burning differently than they had been while we kissed and touched. "Yours don't smell like roses either."

He did a quick wash of himself, including his feet, before moving back to me. "Guess I need to build a bath in the room on the ship."

"Sharing one with the entire crew makes the bath water nasty quickly."

He paused, his soapy hands on my thighs, "Did… were… my crew saw you in there?"

"A couple of them did."

A muscle flexed in his cheeks. His hands began moving along my thighs, soaping them up with each stroke, "Naked?"

I had some undergarments on, but the look on his face right now made me think oddly, "Maybe."

"I'm commissioning the build in the morning."

I giggled, then laughed at his glare. "How many people have you been with since we met? How many times have you seen me naked? It's nothing."

His lips pinched, "I…I know. But for now… I… after tonight I want to keep you to myself for a while." His hands worked down each of my calves and over my feet.

It was ridiculous, what he was saying. Part of me knew he was being silly, but it still made me smile. It made me warm inside. I pulled him to my chest, hugging his face into my breasts as I kissed the top of his head.

He moaned, the washing forgotten as he slid his arms around me. His tongue licked the skin between my breasts and my breath hitched yet again. I was never going to be able to breathe properly around him. He turned his head, his mouth found a nipple, and I pressed into him, trying to pull him in, urging him for more.

He pulled me back into the bath. I wrapped my legs around him. He turned again, paying attention to the other breast with that mouth that was hotter than the water. He pulled at my nipple with his lips and I felt it mimicked in my core.

I untangled my hands from his thick hair. I pressed my palms against his back. His teeth scraped, and I moaned, my fingernails digging into his flesh to try to hold on to my control. It was slipping fast.

Why had I waited so long for this?

I pulled my hands back up into his hair and bowed my back. I loosened my legs, slipping down his torso. The head of his cock pressed against my inner thigh and I moaned, lowering myself over it.

His hands gripped my thighs below my ass cheeks and held me still. He walked us to the edge. The sloshing sounds of water overtaking the quick beats of my heart and the panting breaths between our kisses in my ears. The water suctioned at me, trying to pull me off him. I wrapped my legs back around him, not willing to let go of an inch of him even if I wanted to take him in me. He held me steady. The head pressing against each thigh with each step.

Cold tile met my back, and I gasped, arching away from it. He moaned, taking advantage by tearing his mouth away from mine and to a breast. I cried out as his teeth scraped such tender skin, even harder with the shock of the icy wall coursing through me.

He peeled me off the wall. His mouth found mine again. He kissed, twice, swiping my tongue with his before he pulled back to say, "Hold on."

My back hit the bed. I grasped for him, but he had thrown me into the middle of the softest bed I had ever been in. I was sinking into it.

His warm hands came down on my knees and spread my legs. His breath tickled my belly button before his head plunged down. I came up off the bed. Heat flooded from his tongue that had touched something that made my core throb and burst.

My fingers tangled in the sheets, trying to pull them from sticking to my body so I could take more of him, not them. He lapped at me again and my body shook. Little whimpers came from my lips and I could care less who heard because there was no one else. Nothing else except that man with his head between my legs kissing me down there with tongue and teeth.

His hands slid heavily up my stomach. His shoulders pushed my legs up. Those hands gripped my breasts right as his tongue slid into me.

Something burst inside. I thought I might drown him. Or me. Those hands of his couldn't hold me down. I could have stood on my head, but his face in my cunt kept me grounded enough for him to thrust that tongue in again. He had to have felt the explosion, tasted it, because that was all I could bear.

The aftershocks calmed enough that I lay back on the bed. I couldn't fill my lungs enough. I uncurled my fingers from the sheets one by one. It took such effort they ached. I looked down my body at him. His hands on my breasts made me stare for a moment.

His skin was so dark against mine.

Those eyes of his. They were just over the hairs between my legs. The heat and hunger radiating from them made me ache more. Those eyes promised many things. One of them being that tonight was going to have more of that.

He unhooked his shoulders from under my thighs. His body slid up, his hands slid down. He pulled himself up on me, my body arching into him. His mouth met the flesh on my stomach just below my belly button. He kissed, nuzzled there, his eyes never leaving mine.

I took my aching fingers and ran them through his dark hair.

He moved up further, kissing over my ribs up to under my breasts. He nuzzled there and drove a moan from me. I slid my hand to the back of his head, at his neck, wrapping those dark, thick tendrils of his hair around my fingers. I pulled at him gently, trying to get him to come up.

I couldn't reach him to give him pleasure.

My free hand slid along his side, fingertips skimming over the top of his hip. I rocked my hips toward him. I didn't have the words, so I moved instead.

His lips closed over my nipple. I pressed into him and rocked again. What I needed rubbed against my thigh. I twisted my hips, almost there.

He pulled himself up. He freed a hand and cupped my hip, keeping me from rocking.

"Austere…" his name sounded different, rolled differently in my mouth.

His mouth was on mine. We breathed in together. He lowered himself, the hand that was once on my hip guided him to me. The head brushed that nubbin that he had used his mouth on earlier, and I bucked. He sank into me.

I wrapped my legs around his hips, taking more of him. All of him.

It was everything I could do not to make a fool of myself until I let that thought go, too.

His hips rocked, and it took a while for us to get into a rhythm. Once we did, the pace drove him deep, and hard. I had made him wait for so long. Too long. Each thrust drove me up on the bed. His balls smacked against me.

Once that flood came again, all I could do was hold on. The first one hadn't stopped when the second one came, I wasn't sure the second one had even ended when the third had me clawing for an edge that wasn't there. That was the point those muscles of his grew rigid and I welcomed his release into my own.

He lay on top of me, slowly collapsing and loosening each muscle. His body should have crushed me. It felt like he was pressing whatever had shattered in me back together with his pieces added, too. I was never so whole as I was coming down off that beautiful round.

I thought we were both falling asleep when he chuckled at my temple. "Good call with not letting me have you in the tent."

I barely opened my eyes to turn my head to look at him, kissing his chin, "Why do you say that?"

"You, my love, are loud."

"Am not!"

He laughed, curling around me more as he shifted his body around mine, "I hate to hear what you think is loud."

"It was just… it felt…" I clamped my mouth shut.

He pulled himself up on an elbow, looking down at me. He pushed a strand of my hair away from my mouth, "Go on."

"Ass."

He chuckled, "If you want it there so much, give me a moment."

"No! You. Are. An. Ass."

"Aaah, perhaps." He smirked, "Doesn't change the fact that you are loud."

"No, I'm not."

That hand slid between my thighs. His fingers parted me down there and the rough callous circled against that so tender bump. I moaned. I blinked as his mouth didn't move with that sound I heard. And it hadn't come from him.

Heat crept up from my chest to my neck and cheeks. "I uh…"

Austere chuckled, leaning down to capture my lips with his in a chaste kiss. He pressed his forehead against mine, cupping my cheek in his hand. "I love the sounds you make. They drove me wild. I didn't hurt you, did I?"

I snorted, "No, all I felt was orgasm after orgasm."

"Oh?" He pulled back a little, his brows high, "More than one, hm?"

That heat was still creeping over me, "Three I think. Two and three kinda didn't have time in between."

He moaned, "That's making me want to take you more. Right now."

I slid my fingers against his shaft; it hardened and moved against me. "I'm not complaining."

There were two too many hands trying to 'help' me get dressed. We were late for breakfast, but not at all late for the commentary of his family and our comrades.

"How many grandchildren am I to have?"

Her fingers wrapped around my arm instead of a muffin. "Er… Dunno."

Austere leaned over, poking his mom in the cheek with a finger as he leaned behind me, "Eleven Momma, eleven."

She went pale, "From just you?!"

Blari nearly crawled under the table, he started laughing so hard.

Breakfast was not a dull affair. I had a hard time not running toward the front door once they announced our horses were ready. The first one outside; sweat beaded up on my forehead before I could take a breath. I stopped.

Austere bumped into me from behind and chuckled, "Told you not to layer like you usually do."

"I… is the sun closer here?"

"Seems like." He kissed the top of my head, "That's why the roads here have tall buildings or tall trees on either side. The shade helps."

My mare looked like she was about to melt already.

"Don't worry, miss. We covered her in a special oil we have. It cools once the horses move so the air can circulate around the oils. It brings it to the skin and holds it there, cooling them. But if they stand still it's hot."

Taking that as a hint, I mounted. The king and queen each mounted their own horses. Both of them large things like their son's, even Pitrini joined us. The king pulled his big red horse up beside mine, "A few clicks and your little horse will be right as rain." He nudged his into a brisk walk, then up into a canter. My little mare tossed her head, not willing to move, until Austere pushed her with his boot on her hindquarters.

After she started moving, she didn't seem to mind it at all. "Where was the last report of a disturbance?"

"The next town. You see that first row of mountains, the one with the green all over it instead of just at the base like the rest of them?"

"Yes, your majesty."

"That's where we goin'." He shot me a look, "Pop, girl, it's Pop." He looked at me again, a softer expression shifting the panes in his face, "Unless your own father is called pop."

"Oh no, I'll call you pop. I call my Father, well, Father."

"Sounds proper, do ya not have a good relationship?"

"The best kind. He called his Father that and so I called him that is all. When I was a baby I called him Dada, but that seems foolish for a grown woman to call her father that."

He chuckled, "It would be cute."

"Her father is a great man, Pop. I think you'd like him. Her mother too. "

The king nodded, his hand running over his stubble with a scraping noise, "I believe I will. They raised a good woman and if my son likes them, I probably will too."

"She has an older sister. Might make a suitable match for Pitrini."

Pitrini choked, "Huh? What?"

Austere sighed, "Fine. Guess we'll have to settle for that merchant woman."

"Her name is Mara."

Pitrini's face was red, and he fisted his hands on the reins. I giggled and shook my head as the brothers began bickering. It made the ride short, even when Spacya tried to tame them and ended up right in the middle of it instead.

The sun was high in the sky when we rode up to the town at the base of the green mountain. Three on horseback, a Rogue, a human and a Welkan met us. "Well hello, dear king! What brings you all the way out here to Amalin?"

His accent wasn't at all like the King's, nor was it like the people at the docks from the day before. He sounded like Lanpress. Plain and unadorned words with no lilt or change in his cadence. Vey sounded a lot like him. There was something to a Rogue Lizard voice that set them apart from any other race or species in the race. Their lips were hard, barely existed, but they still formed words. Their Bs, Ps and Fs were much harder than ours.

The king smiled and pointed his thumb at me, "This here is the Hero from Lanpress. They have sent her to check out our disruptions and right our wrongs."

The Welkan shook his head with a snort, "We can right our own wrongs."

"Well, she came all this way." The Rogue smirked, his lips shifting under pale green scales, "We can at least show her around." He turned his horse's head, his two companions moving with him in sync. They flanked him as they led us into the town.

Amalin was much like the mining towns around Emleton. They painted the squat buildings in a beautiful array of colors, but they were few and set close together. The main street was the best passage from one building to the next. Houses lined the streets right alongside the shops and eateries. The main road ended in an enormous gaping hole in the mountain's side, covered in trees and flowers.

"I've never seen a mined mountain have so many plants on it. Don't they fall off with blasts?" Spacya asked.

I glanced back to see her eyes roaming over the foliage.

"It's our magic. We don't blast to mine anymore. Soon all the mines in Iethyll will not cause more harm than necessary to the natural environment." The Welkan finally smiled, pride drawing his shoulders back and his chest out.

"Interesting, would you care to share that practice with me?" Tori urged his horse up beside the Welkan's.

"Er… sure, not much a human can do though."

Tori nodded, "I know, but our mines are dangerous. They still cause slides and avalanches."

"I will get with the foremen and see if they have time to meet with you. They can explain it inside and out better than I can." He paused, "The name's Quile."

Tori grasped his wrist across the space between their horses, "Tori."

"You're a prince?!" Quile bowed, nearly sliding off the side of his horse in his haste.

Tori steadied the Welkan with a hand on his shoulder, "Yeah, one of many. Right now, I'm the Hero's companion."

"Didn't bow to either of us like that, did he?" Austere smirked over at Pitrini.

The boy shook his head, but there was a gleam in his eyes.

Quile blanched, "Sorry, Princes." He twisted and bowed.

The king cleared his throat, "You bow one more time and that horse'll throw ya."

Quile studied the ears and neck of his horse, "He's not annoyed or anything, sire."

"No, but I have my ways."

Quile turned red, but smiled, "Just showin' respect, Sire."

We stopped in front of the mine. I dismounted after our three guides did. "Going to shove us into the mine to work?"

"I bet the old men won't mind some extra help, but no." The Rogue motioned for us to follow him, "We didn't have anywhere else to put the bastards. We don't have a dungeon here, and we are still debating on whether to keep them alive and make them work like they did us, or to kill them. A little useless to take them all the way to the next town or to the castle to have a place to lock them up. So we put 'em in here in the old collapsed shaft."

"Smart." The queen nodded with a smile.

"Thank you."

"Here we go again." Quile mumbled, "Another compliment on his fine idea of where to hold them. He'll have to shed again to hold his colossal head."

The human grinned, but still said nothing.

I moved over to him, "I'm Nadachia." I held out my hand.

He grasped my wrist, the grin huge on his pale face and his green eyes crinkled at the edges with it.

"That's Mavi, he had his tongue cut out when he was a boy." Quile explained, "Used to backtalk and sing a lot too."

"Kept our spirits up." The Rogue patted Mavi on the shoulder before thrusting his clawed hand out to me, "Sorry about earlier, I'm Evedaisily, Daisy for short."

The way he drawled his name out was odd, out of the normal for a Lanpress speech pattern, but everything else was definitely Lanpressian. I clasped his wrist and shook, "I understand. I don't think I would appreciate someone coming a long way to tell me what to do either."

"Thanks." He jerked his head toward the mine, "This way."

We followed him into the mine. The collapsed area was to the right of the main tunnel, only about fifty feet in. Boards blocked up the entrance, but there was a slit wide enough to reach through, and a square hole near the ground I assumed was for passing food and water through.

"Asses and rapers, come forward." Evedaisily stopped an arm's length away from the boards. Mavi and Quile moved forward to take down a few boards at shoulder and head level so we could see in.

Two lanterns lit the dark cavern. Piled rocks and bits of other debris caged four men who were crawling from their sitting positions. One had sat on a rock, his enormous belly making him look much like a boulder himself. Another limped forward, dragging a twisted left leg behind him. The bandages on it were dirty, but they weren't too old. The other two looked like hired fighters, their arms were larger than me and their legs looked like tree stumps. They towered over the other men. I glanced at Austere and the King. The men inside were even taller than them.

"Bears." I heard the snick of Spacya pulling a spear free from her pack.

"Easy." Blari's gentle voice whispered along the rocks of the mine walls.

Daisy's sharp green eyes slid toward Spacya. Those slits were the only part of them that didn't catch the light of the lanterns in an eerie gleam. "Move too suddenly, boys, and this lady here will have ya pinned with one of those spears. So behave now. Let us all be friendly like."

"What do ya want now? Who are they?" The man with the twisted leg asked, stopping right behind the wood plank barrier. His eyes squinted and he spat toward the King, "Weren't expecting the mighty Pirate to show up."

"King." Daisy corrected.

I noticed the long slick mint green tail flicking back and forth behind Daisy after I made the mistake of stepping into its path. The tail brushed my knee and the warmth of the scales through the fabric of my pants reminded me of Vey sunning himself. "Sorry." I stepped out.

Daisy lifted a shoulder, his lips pulling back to show his teeth. They weren't jagged, but straight and square like his scales. "Meet a slaver and his henchmen."

I looked at the man with the twisted leg, "How many slaves have you owned and sold or transported?"

He snorted, "Can hardly recall. In fact, I don't recall any slaves."

"Did you send word to Lanpress about your troubles? About being held against your will or being harassed by the King and his men?"

"Now that I recall perfectly. It was a few weeks ago. Thought no one cared about little ole me. Yet, here you are now."

"Yes, here I am. Why don't I help you out?"

He grinned, "I knew you were a woman of sense."

"Where can I find me a couple of people to work for me? You know, won't mind just being fed and watered, maybe some pay, you get me?"

"I get you darlin'. I can get you some, if you get me outta here." He tapped the wooden planks between us.

"I'll do what I can, but ya see… It'll take some time and convincing. Got any friends that can vouch for ya?"

"Sure, sure." He listed out some names and where we could find them.

"Alright now, give me a day or two and we'll see if we can straighten this out. Oh, your property, got any paper to make all your goings on all official?"

He shook his head, "I'm sure these fine folks near you will burn it all down. I ain't tellin' nothing about that. But my buddies, now they can't go killing off people, so that's why I'm willing to share them."

I nodded, "Understand. I'll see you in a day or two." Once we hit the sunlight, I turned my face up to it.

"We know who contacted her. We know a few names to throw in there with them, too. Ready to go get them?"

Mavi grinned from beside Austere while Quile laughed, "Why didn't we think of that?"

Daisy got up onto his horse, "Don't know, but I'm ready."

I glanced at the king. He smiled, "Go. I think the queen and I are going to go back to our guest house and spend some time with the lord there. He should return at any moment."

She turned to Austere, "Are you going with her?"

"Of course."

She turned to me, "Keep him safe. He doesn't realize how loud he steps."

He spluttered as she turned back to pat his cheek. "Mama! I can walk quietly."

Pitrini chuckled, "I think I'll go back with Mama and Pop." He mounted and gave us a wave as we headed off in opposite directions.

"The farthest one away is going to be an hour past the next town over. The other two will be in that town. The next two we'll get from here when we get back." Daisy explained.

"Less to have to watch with so much riding. Good plan." Austere nodded.

Blari asked, "We going to get more names from them before we add them to the cave? There's not much room left in there with those big brutes, will they all fit?"

"They won't have to fit long. Once we get two more of their previous slaves' statements, we will sentence them to death." Quile said.

"I can make it bigger." Randia added softly.

I glanced at Spacya as we rode, pulling my mare closer to hers. "You good?"

"Fine. Been a while since I've run into bears or Rogue Bears is all. Don't trust them."

I nodded, "I know." We rode in silence for a few moments until I could formulate what I wanted to say, "You could have gone back with the king and queen. It would've been alright."

"I know, but if there are more of those bastards around I'd rather be able to protect us than worry in a stuffy house for hours."

I grinned at her, "Careful, you're showing you care again."

She snorted, "I care about you."

"And me?" Austere rode up on the other side of her and waggled his brows with that sly grin.

"Never."

A scream split the air as we made it around a mountain root. It took me too long to realize where it came from. Unia flung her head up as Quile's horse at the head of our column reared. A long spear stuck out from its middle.

Quile rolled as they fell to the ground.

I pulled my crossbow, trying to steady my mare with soft words as I tried to follow the trajectory of the spear. There was little cover. Long grasses and a few trees along the road closest to the mountain we were rounding. The other side was a plowed field with low-lying vegetable plants in neat rows.

The horses danced and pawed, moving away from their downed fellow. Before I knew it, I was out front. Which was fine. I would have a clear shot.

The next scream was close. It rang in my ears. Suddenly I was no longer looking at the treeline, but at the sky. My back hit the road and my lungs emptied, refusing to fill back up. My heart clutched with panic as I tried to work air into my mouth and lungs. They burned, my eyes burning along with them when my airways finally opened. I pulled in a gulp of air and tried to pull my right leg out from under Unia.

Austere was on me, covering me as he grabbed my crossbow and fired it into the treeline. I heard a human yelp, then the sound of something heavy hitting the ground in the direction he shot. "I'm caught."

"I know, just a second." He loaded another bolt as he put his shoulder to my saddle and pushed.

With the weight lifted off my leg a little, I pulled it out. I scrambled to take cover behind my mare as Austere was, crouching. I looked into the treeline, "Good thing they went home."

He shook his head, "Yes, it is." He handed my crossbow back to me.

"Keep it. I'm going to get close enough to throw."

"No don't…"

I didn't give him time to stop me before I was running to a large tree, keeping low to the ground and pulling a dagger into each of my hands. I put my back to the tree trunk as soon as I reached it, making sure my knees and elbows weren't poking out for them to target.

Spacya launched a spear into the trees. I couldn't tell if it hit anyone or not. I glanced around the trunk. Before I could focus on the tree line, I watched two men run across the road further down. I whistled.

Tori and Blari both looked at me after ducking back into the ditch for cover. I pointed to the two men, now weaving in and out of the low vegetable plants on their way toward my comrades.

Tori peeled off to meet them.

The horses were running into the vegetables, Blari catching most of their reins to hold them from running any further. I couldn't imagine walking all the way back on foot.

I tried again to look into the tree line.

Something hard and hot hit the back of my head. My vision narrowed as I turned to see what had hit me. I swung my arm around before the blade of my dagger sank into flesh.

A grunt sounded in my ear. Randia cried out, the pain in the back of my head lessening some. My vision still wanted to darken on me.

I pulled my dagger free and tried for another stab.

A thick hand closed over my wrist and twisted. I dropped the dagger as my bones shifted and strained under the powerful grip before they cracked. I slammed the heel of my boot down on his foot.

Another grunt. Another scream from Randia as pain flashed in my wrist, then calmed.

I looked up into a furred face with a long black snout. Canines glistened too close to my face. That hot breath scented of blood and dried saliva. My stomach lurched. Eyes black and soulless stared into mine as those thick lips pulled back further to show a row of large, jagged teeth.

I kicked out, using his hold to kick with both feet. My wrist popped and pain shot up my arm to my shoulder. I bit my tongue to keep from crying out. They lived on fear. They loved the sound of pain they inflicted.

I couldn't give that to this one.

That large maw closed over my shoulder. The spurt of blood onto my neck and cheek burned before thousands of blades shoved themselves into my body at my shoulder and armpit. The thick fur moved and a second later, I shook. My arm ripped from me.

I screamed, no longer able to hide my pain. No longer able to keep back the utter chaos raging inside at being bitten by a Rogue Bear. Another shake as his maw settled over my shoulder and my vision went black.

Chapter 38

Pain lanced through my shoulder as I rolled into something hard. I had a shoulder? I opened my eyes. Heat hit me. My skin was cold with sweat, but waves of heat rose from the dirt road rolling away under me. Cart wheels squeaked to my right and left. Canvas flapped in the movement above me, sometimes hitting my head. I rolled into the wall of the cart again, pain making me jerk back to the center.

I clenched my teeth together so hard my jaw popped. I looked down, followed the canvas cover with my eyes, and searched the end of the cart. It was longer than I was tall, my feet were at least a foot away from the edge. A few rolls of fabric, too short to be beds, were strapped there, and a couple of squat barrels sat in one corner. Those were the only other things in there.

The one that had been torn off was back. Jutting out of my sleeve were bones, sinew, muscles, and flesh growing before my very eyes. This time when my stomach rose, I had something to spill onto the wood slats of the cart and the road.

I wiped my mouth on my sleeve. My arm grew. Biting back another wave of nausea, I swore I wouldn't look at it again. I pushed myself up on my one elbow and tried to get my bearings.

It was a road. Obviously. Trees lined either side. The light was brighter in the west, the sun would set soon. The mountains were to my right. We were heading away from the port.

I sank back down. My body too weak to hold me up for long. I was empty, in more ways than I dared to explore.

There wasn't any talking. Just the wheels squeaking and making noise against the dirt and rocks they careened over, and the clapping of the canvas above me. I closed my eyes and reached out with that still unfamiliar power in me. Two. Two people were sitting up front, and a single horse pulling us.

If I rolled out… would they notice?

I tested my feet. Untied.

I wasn't sure if they were idiots for that or if I should feel insulted for being seen as not resourceful enough to try to run away. I shifted my legs, my boots were on, my daggers still tucked in them, too.

Had they not checked?

I wormed my way to the edge, rolled on my back and tried not to scream as my shoulder hit the side yet again. I pulled the canvas, trying to look over it. Only the backs of their heads were in my sight. A pale one and the black fur of the one that had bitten me.

I twisted to look back at the road again. No one followed. I reached out with my power. I tried to sense anyone or anything close.

Some birds and rodents.

Now or never.

I prayed to the gods, either set, whichever would listen to me and give me aid. I pulled myself closer to the edge, hanging on to the rough wooden slats with one hand, and then I let myself drop. My back hit the hot sand of the road and I immediately began rolling to the side.

My teeth clenched back a scream each time my mangled, growing arm hit the earth, but I didn't stop until I slammed into a tree trunk. I scrambled around it, stumbling and tumbling deeper into the forest. I stopped, pressing my back to a trunk, my knees to my chest, and listened as the cart kept rumbling away.

Insulted. I should feel insulted.

I still had my belt on, but they had left only one dagger in it. It was the decorative little hilt blade. The most useless one I owned. Some lord had given it to me with a pretty letter.

But it was a blade.

I made sure that the bearings I had gathered while in the cart were correct. I thanked the gods. Off the tree trunk and deeper into the forest, I stumbled, keeping out of sight of the road, but close enough to where I followed the thinner canopy it made in the trees and kept it to my right.

There was orange in the sky by the time I sat down against a tree.

The heat made my skin cold. My mouth felt like moths lived in it. The sounds of my arm rebuilding itself had my stomach heaving up into my throat so many times I lost count. If I found water, it probably wouldn't have done me any good.

I closed my eyes, willing to listen to anything else other than what my body was doing.

Here there were fewer sounds at dusk than there were at home. No frogs chirped in the trees. But there was an odd little brown bird that was loud with cries in the treetops. I concentrated on them.

Until the thoughts hit.

I had been taken. How had that happened? I had moved too far away from my companions. The enemies had pinned them down in the treeline. That was stupid of me. A mistake only rookies made.

They said my friends were all dead. That couldn't be true. No, it wasn't.

My heart grew heavy, and it sank, pulling tears down with it. How I still had tears in this heat I would never figure out.

I pushed off the tree trunk. There was still some light left. I wasn't sure when the two would discover that I was no longer with them and circle back, either. I had to get some more distance.

I also had to see if my companions were still alive. If Austere was still living. Spacya, Tori, and Blari I prayed again to the gods to keep them safe, to have them be alive. Randia too.

At the thought of her name, a coolness circled in my belly.

"No." I whispered, stopping and leaning on another tree trunk.

I placed my hand over my stomach and concentrated on what little I perceived of her and her power. There she was. Circling right along with Sterla and Eilse.

How many Stygra had died at my hands now?

My jaws cracked again as I clenched. I shuffled my heavy feet forward, and I kept my eyes ahead. I steered my thoughts to what I needed to do at that moment. Everything else would come later.

How many more would I have to kill?

Night came quickly. The canopy wasn't thick enough to block out the moonlights, but they didn't give off much light tonight. The heavy, sweet scent of rain hung low in the air. I kept moving.

I had to keep moving, otherwise the sounds of my arm would drive me mad. I could feel it. It was enough to set my mind screaming.

I created a mantra. I counted the calls of the animals of the night. I imagined what the strange calls I heard came from. I thought about anything so that I wouldn't hear bones grinding or flesh slip-sliding against muscle.

I walked into a mud wall.

I held still against it. Listening. The only sounds I heard were the distant calls of the animals in the forest. I was still in the trees, but there was a building here, too.

I almost ran around it, desperate for help.

What if this was an enemy camp?

Biting down on my need for water. For contact. I eased around the wall, going closer to the road. There wasn't a break in the barrier until up ahead. No windows. Nothing.

I stopped at the corner and strained to hear. The noise my arm was making sounded louder than anything else in the world. Even the beat of my heart.

I snuck a peek around the edge and saw that the forest cleared; a small town growing out from the road. I was at the end of the row, facing the street at least ten buildings away along a straight dirt path that was barely wide enough for a cart like they had thrown me in.

On this side, the building had windows, but they were dark. The next building was dark, too. But the one across the path had candlelight shining out of it. I kept as low as possible, moving down the track, ducking lower than the windows just in case there were still people inside the darkness.

I hid in the shadows of the second building. My hand slid along something wet. I pulled away from the wall. It came back a light blue, or green, I couldn't really tell with the moonlights. I looked down. Along the front were jars of liquid, different hues of dark and light I took to be different colors.

Sam Wicker

I now had a handprint in a new mural.

I breathed in deep, filling my lungs until they hurt, and let it out slowly. Painting houses was a good sign. Right?

The next handful of buildings had lights, too. I heard the faint sounds of voices coming from one further down. Some string instrument was being played, slowly, with a screech here and there from the one across the path. Why couldn't they be like the villages of Lanpress and have fountains everywhere instead of paint jars?

I tried to stick to the shadows without pressing any body parts or clothing into a mural. The ground kept wanting to come up and hit me after every time I moved from one point to another quickly. I thought maybe I wasn't breathing properly.

The house I pressed up against next had lights on. It was the one voices flowed out of. Buzzing. All the voices were just buzzing. No words formed. My heart rammed in my chest so loudly.

It started getting louder. I started having more hearts, too. A horse snorted, and I drew my eyes from the swirling lights painted on the path up to six colossal figures coming down off the road. "Search every house." One of those figures parted. Then the others, too. One split into three.

Monsters. I had to take care of monsters. It was my job.

I stepped forward. The first figure stopped moving. I fumbled for anything at my waist because I had to have a weapon there. I was sure I had. Did the monster already take it?

"Nadachia!"

Something grabbed me up. It was so hot. It was squeezing me. I gasped and kicked, pushing. *Why didn't I have another arm? The monster ate it!*

"Nadachia, it's me! It's me. Stop."

The squeezing stopped, only to be replaced with hands covering my face. I couldn't breathe.

Wait. It had said my name?

The smell of the sea filled my nose. Spice and that familiar scent I couldn't name. Austere.

"Gods… her arm!"

"She's burning up."

The world turned. He was so hot against me. The buzzing started all around me again. My vision melted into blackness.

I lay on something soft, a light burning my eyes from above, and cold against my forehead. "How can we make sure there's no infection there when it's… growing?"

"I don't know."

"I found a healer!" Something banged, wood against wood maybe. My head throbbed with it, echoing the noise.

"Gods, what is-what is that?"

"She's feverish."

"Lost a lot of blood too and still is."

"We can't move her yet. She's got to wake up first at least."

Spacya?

"I just sent Randia's body back. There's a ship to Lanpress leaving once it gets there." That voice was familiar, but I didn't place it.

"Hey, darling." His voice was deep and right in my ear. "Gonna wake up for us now?"

I tried swallowing. Nothing moved right. I opened my mouth and tried to get words out. I heard a rasp.

"Water. Here." His arm slid under my head and lifted gently before something pressed to my lips. Coolness coated my tongue. I swallowed. I wasn't sure how much they gave me, but I took it all.

"Stere." The word finally got out of the sand trap that had been my mouth. Now it just felt like moth wings. My eyelids didn't want to move, but I managed to open them. His face was blurry, but so close I saw the trails of tears going down his cheeks.

"Hello, my love."

"What happened?"

"Hoping you would tell me that." He kissed my forehead. "They pinned us down. Next thing I realize, you're running for a tree. You sent Tori after two that were trying to flank us and then you were gone."

"Figured you went stupid and charged." Spacya huffed, "So this big idiot, and that one, did the same thing. Nearly got their fool selves killed."

Austere shot a glare at her before turning back to me, "When we cleared them, set them all to running or dead. You weren't around."

"Followed a blood trail to a shack, then nothing from there." Blari added, "But Daisy, of the ridiculous names, figured they were heading toward another port where slavers still had some ships. They've been waiting to catch them in the act, but they're good at covering their tracks with livestock hauls."

"Pity we still have nothing on them." That was the one that found the healer. "But at least she's safe."

"For now. I'm gonna beat some sense into her once she can fight back again." Spacya said, crossing her arms over her chest as she looked down her nose at me.

"Stand in line." Blari nudged her.

"I'm never gonna be normal again." I tried turning over, but Austere stopped me with a tender hand on my chest. "Stay on your back."

"Why?" Then I remembered the noises of my arm regrowing. I looked down.

I had a fresh shirt. It covered a shoulder, fully formed, and they pulled a sheet up to my elbow. I tried moving it.

"The healer numbed that side."

That's why I couldn't feel anything, but I saw some kind of nub waving at me from under the sheet.

Blari and Tori both looked away. The priest pale. "Where's Randia?"

"She..." Blari motioned to my arm, "It must have killed you."

Right. I knew that. "I'm sorry."

Blari sighed and pulled a little leather-bound book out of his bag, "She wanted me to give you this."

Austere took it and held it up for me. He opened it to the first page. The scrawl ran together, "You need to read it to me."

He cleared his throat as he turned the little book toward him and began reading:

"Nadachia,
I hate to start with the obvious sentence, but here we are. If you are reading this, you have died. Again. Therefore, I am dead, for the first and last time. It's good. My life was to always end in the service of a Hero or in another, less honorable way. I'm glad we have managed to get my death to be honorable, at least.
I have given my powers to you. They are not at all useful to me anymore. I think they will work well with what you have already gathered. In this book, I have written out some practices for you to try. You should be able to get through this entire book in the week it will take you to get back to Lanpress; unless I have survived this first quest somehow and we are on another, closer quest.
My powers are that of shadows. I use shadows as extensions of my body. They do not have more strength than what I do, not any powers of their own, but I can pull them around me and hide in them, or use them as an extra set of hands. I can imagine the fun you will have with these powers already. I know I have.
Sorry Blari, you don't have fleas. It was just me.
Practice up. Get stronger. Kill Keandria for the sake of the world.
Thank you for the opportunity to die honorably.
Randia

He sighed and flipped to the next page. He didn't read it though, but showed me. There were drawings and motions, along with a few words here and there. Practices.

I closed my eyes and hot tears leaked from the corners of my eyes and into my hair. "How is that an honorable death over living a long life?"

"Her life would have been lived with Keandria over her. In that respect, this is far better." Tori answered, his voice soft.

Sam Wicker

Spacya's eyes had been on Blari for a while, "You thought you had fleas?"

"I didn't know what else to think!" Blari huffed, wiping at his eyes.

Spacya chuckled with Austere joining, and then Tori. "Is that why you brought double the amount of beard oil on this trip compared to the others?"

Blari muttered something under his breath as he ran a hand lovingly down his thick beard.

"I am certainly glad that you are safe now." The king, Pop, said again for the hundredth time.

After two more days, my arm had grown back fully. My fingers didn't want to move properly, and it was much weaker than my other arm. But I felt the muscles growing accustomed to what I needed. Slowly. I had read through half of Randia's little notebook of practices and mastered only a quarter of those.

"Thanks."

"I'm going to send someone with you."

I glanced up from Randia's scribbles. The King was staring out the large window of the study we were in. His hands clasped at his back, looking like the king he had become rather than the pirate he had been. I stood, stretched and moved to stand beside him, "You don't have to."

"He's willing. Practically begged."

I leaned back against the little ledge at the bottom of the window, "Is it Pitrini?"

"No, the boy wants to stay here. I think he's ready to accept this family now." He turned his gaze from the mountain scape to look at me, "It's Evedaisily."

"Really?"

"Yes."

I lifted a shoulder, "Sure, but, you should understand, this is probably my last quest."

"He knows. He wants to get a piece of the Matron."

I studied the king for a moment, "Why?"

The king shook his head, looking back out at the mountains, "That's for him to decide to tell you."

I nodded, "I'll go find him."

Pops turned and pulled me into an embrace, "It might be your last quest. It might be the last I see of you once you board that ship tonight, but I will think of you as a daughter and pray for your life."

I hugged him back. Austere had part of his father's warmth. With age, he might gain all of it. "Maybe you should order Stere to stay here."

The king shook his head, "I can order all I want, but you and I both know that he will be by your side."

"I'll try to keep him alive and well." I pulled back, trying to ignore the burning behind my eyes and in my throat at the words I was saying.

"And yourself too." He kissed my forehead. "Send word once you are free. I wouldn't mind taking a visit. I would like to meet your family."

Dread and hope circled one another like wild animals preparing to fight inside me, "I would like that. I will."

"He's probably in the little tavern called Maye's."

Maye's wasn't all that hard to find. I just had to follow the music down the main street. It was morning, about time for the mid-meal of the day, and there were already those that stumbled in Maye's full of drink. I tried not to judge them. Such a beautiful town, freedom given, and all that came with a new regime had just happened. People had to have time to mend and adjust in their own time, in their own way.

Quile, Mavi, and Daisy sat at the bar. I was suddenly reminded of a terrible joke some trader or shipman had told Father when I was barely tall enough to hit his knee. I strode through the mostly empty tables to sit beside them at the bar and waved the bartender off. I had never been a drinker until I entered this job, and only then when I was stuffed into a dress in the capital to play games with the royals and Keandria.

I might need to change that too.

"You're looking better."

Quile leaned over the bar to look at me around Mavi. Mavi nodded his head, his lips curled up at the corners, but both of his hands were wrapped around the pint in front of him. During the fight, he'd had a terrible flashback. No one made sudden moves around him.

"Thanks. I am better."

"Something about that arm. Never seen that before." Quile sat back, picking at his teeth with a short straw. The plate before him scraped clean.

I looked at Daisy. His eyes still caught the light to make them bright in the tavern's dimness. "Neither have I." I added, flicking my gaze to Quile just to see him nod, before looking back at Daisy, "Pop told me you wanted to come with me, is that true?"

He nodded. The other two suddenly found the bar interesting.

"You might not come back."

He nodded again.

"I plan on destroying as much of Keandria as I can once we make landfall. If you survive, and she does too, you will be imprisoned. Maybe worse."

Another nod.

"Is that all you're gonna give me?"

Those scaled lips pulled back to one side, crinkling his eye, "I'm your Daisy now."

If the king vouched for him, he should be a good one to have. There was still something nagging at the back of my head. He had left Lanpress. He came here. Why was he wanting to go back now?

Daisy looked around the tavern. The drunk patrons were sitting at tables, closer to the darkened corners. None of them looked stable enough to walk. His hands folded together, scales scraping in a rasp against the bar as he leaned on it. "You wanna know why, don't you?"

Returning the favor, I nodded.

His lip twitched up to make his eye go squinty again. "Keandria destroyed everything I had as a child. I was ten when the first of her counsel members closed in on my tribe. They burned us to the ground. My sister and I, along with a handful of others, survived by hiding in the swamp." His tail lashed behind him.

"We lived in the Dark Swamps. Now they are all Stygra, aren't they?"

I nodded again.

"We ran to another tribe. I don't understand if we led them there, or if they were just systematically getting rid of us, but not two nights later, history repeated itself. My grandparents were part of that tribe. They were officials, part of the council, treasurers. I watched from behind their burning tent as Keandria herself tried to use her powers on them. When she failed, she had one of her little minions cut their tails off and shove it down their throats until they stopped breathing."

"Gods." Quile breathed. Mavi's fingers and hands shook on his pint.

"We ran again, my sister and I. There were even fewer of us that got away that time. We made it to Faladan. An old man there took pity on us and brought us into his household. We lived with him for five years. He died, heart attack. All that time he fed us stories of jewel mines of Iethyll and how a man could earn a fortune if he found a good vein in the mountains. So we packed up, headed here. I guess he didn't hear that Iethyll had turned into a pit of slavery and whoring." He looked away, at the wall of glass that held the hard drinks, "You can probably imagine what we walked into. All you need to know of that is I finally found my sister two years ago. I should say, I found her skin and eyes, put in a glass like a trophy." His swallow was visible and audible, "She would still be alive if Keandria hadn't started her genocide. Is that a good enough reason?"

"Yes." I managed after a moment, "Yes, I'm sorry I questioned you."

Those eyes narrowed, "No, question. Understand. That's the only way you can learn." He stood, stretched, and moved over to stand behind Mavi. He put his hands on the mute's shoulders and just let them rest there. "I know Stygra attacked your family. I understand if you don't want me along. I will find my own way back, my way to help you kill that so-called Matron."

Something stuck out in his story to me then. "When you said that she tried to use her powers on your grandparents… what does that mean?"

His lips pulled back on both sides this time, "Stygra powers cannot be used against Rogues."

I stared at him for a moment. His words rolling over and over in my mind. Why hadn't I noticed that? Had I known that?

"Now, physical things they throw at us can still hurt us. One of our attackers, when I was younger, made rocks and earth pellets that ripped into our flesh. That still works against us. But mind control, the shadows grabbing us, or anything like that doesn't work. It has to be a physical manipulation of items we are already affected by or use before they can use it against us."

A new plan had been percolating in my mind, as Randia was no longer with us. Now, another one formed. "Do you still have friends in Lanpress?"

He shook his head, "No, not really, but Rogues stick together. Rogues will be ready."

"Most Rogues." Quile corrected softly.

"Bears and some Birds are not Rogues. They are just evil." Back on the ship, the moons were high and bright in the sky. It

looked like daylight, almost, with their glows reflected in the ocean. I didn't think the girls were going to let Austere go. My spirit broke for them. He stood at the end of the dock, one in each arm, as he said his goodbyes to his father and mother, and his adoptive brother. He hugged each of them. Their parents had to peel them off. Their cries made my heart shatter.

Austere came up the plank and stood beside me.

"Are you sure you don't want to stay?"

He wrapped an arm around me, "I could never live with myself if I did."

Ashe tried to hop onto Daisy's back. He smiled at her, whispered something in her ear that made her quieten down. He bowed to the royal family and boarded.

As he passed us to get to the cabins Austere asked, "What did you say to her? To get her to stop crying?"

Daisy lifted a shoulder, "I told her not to spill another tear for a brother that would always be with her, no matter what. She just had to believe, and you'd be in her heart."

Tears ran hot, free and dripped off my chin.

Austere wrapped both arms around me, giving a nod to Daisy, who nodded back.

"You're getting better."

"No, I'm the same." I tried to not picture myself slapping him, but it was too late. A shadow snaked out toward him. I barely caught it and reeled them in so it would disappear. The past two days on the ship, I threw myself into the practices in Randia's notebook. Last night, it took a turn for the worst.

The shadows were now attached to my thoughts.

I wanted water. The shadows reached for my cup or skin. Half the time I would get flustered seeing it there and the shadow would end up knocking all the things off the table. I finally got to sleep, only to have Austere waking me up in the middle of the night with a huge grin on his face.

My dreams had turned from the odd-colored landscapes of me falling through them to imagining his hands and lips on me.

He had obliged, for an hour or two, following the lead of where I wanted him by replacing those shadows with his mouth or hands.

The shadows were out of control most of the time. When I controlled them properly, I was so tired I couldn't tell if it was me, or me not having enough energy to think. I shouldn't have enough energy to consider slapping him.

"Shall I get Austere so you can slap him?"

"No, Tor, I'm fine."

The prince chuckled and moved closer to me. He held out a waterskin, and I took it in my actual hand before the shadow one ruined things. "Need to not be so hard on yourself." When I rolled my eyes he smiled, "I say that too much, but if you would actually start practicing that I wouldn't have to say it again."

"You're going to be a great king one day."

He snorted, "Too many siblings for that to happen." He then looked at me, his eyes narrowed, "Are you saying that all kings do is repeat themselves to their subjects?"

"Yup."

He chuckled and shook his head, "I'll make sure that Father and Mother know they have a speech writer once we get to rest from our quests."

"Oh no, no. I'm not a writer."

"But you know we shouldn't repeat ourselves."

I sighed, "Fine. I won't pick on you ever again."

Tori laughed, "Can I get some bits on that?"

I thought about if I had the ability to refrain from teasing my friends, "No. I'd be in starvation mode within the month."

"At least you're not as bad as Austere."

I looked up where he was talking to his second in command. His hand was loose on it, letting the wheel rock back and forth with the movement of the ship, but never further. Then I looked back at Tori. He nearly had as many siblings as I did. The problem was his were close to the Tower, right next door. If things went sideways, they would be the first to be in danger.

"Tori, if you want to back out, I'm giving you a chance."

He took the water skin from me, leaning in to grin, our noses almost touching, "Not a chance. You're stuck with me trying to protect you till the end. I may not become King, but I am now, and will always be a Companion to the Hero."

He eyed me for a moment, "Chi?"

"What?"

"You're doing good." He put the water skin back on his belt, "We're all here because we want to be." He picked up his sword, running his hand along the flat.

It gleamed in the sun. All the battles we had shone in scrapes and cuts along the shiny blade. Thank the gods that most of the marks on that sword were from practices. "I'm ready."

He circled, sword out and pointed at me. He lunged, low. I blocked his weapon from poking into my stomach with the shadow hands. I held onto the blade, gripping tight. Tori nodded. I released, and he stepped back. He attacked again. This time, I pushed the sword to the side.

"That's all fine and well, but what's going to happen when you're attacked with powers? Or with someone that can't be affected?"

"We're least likely to be attacked by swords when in the tower." I straightened, as did Tori. "But he's the best offensive attacker we have in our group."

"Over Austere too?"

Tori shook his head, "We're about the same, he and I. He has a bit more power in his strikes and longer reach, of course."

"I beat him, once. In a spar." Daisy leaned against the mast nearest to us, his tail curling around the base. "Haven't really had the chance to spar with him again."

Tori canted his head. "We should attack her together, then. She could use multiple attacks because Keandria will not fight fair."

"I'm not good at pulling back." Daisy added quickly, shaking his head.

"Then don't."

"Chi, your arm…"

"It's weak, but it's still an arm. It's not like I can get it all healed perfectly in four days before we see Keandria. I need the practice."

Tori sighed, "Then use all of it. Not just the shadows."

I nodded, then looked at Daisy, "I'm not good at pulling back either, so watch yourself."

"Understood."

I barely had time to pull my thoughts into order when Daisy pushed off the mast with his tail. He aimed all four limbs at me. I pulled up black strands. I didn't have time to make anything solid, but I made a web. One of his feet stuck through and clipped my knee while he hung onto the net.

Tori's sword point flashed, I swatted it away with the shadows. Daisy jumped off the web and tried to run around it. I moved it with him, circling until both Tori and Daisy were in front of me with the web in between.

"Nice! I like this." Tori nodded to the net.

Both males ran in opposite directions. Before I knew it, I had split the web. The pieces were too narrow to block them, especially Daisy. I concentrated on building more to the sides.

Daisy leaped, he pushed off the top of the webbing, and then straightened his legs to hit me as he fell. I dodged, barely, by jumping to the side. I brought the web forward, trying to slam it into him. Tori jabbed at my thigh with his sword, but I pushed the web he had reached through away, dragging his boots along the deck with it.

Daisy made his way around the web. I was so concentrated on Tori, I didn't notice him until it was too late. He knocked my feet out from under me with his tail. I swiped at him with the shadow hands, but they passed right over him. He said they wouldn't work, but seeing it made me pause too long. He pinned me, a clawed foot on my chest.

I passed the shadows back over him. They touched his clothes, moved them. I pulled at his shirt. There was resistance against the pull. "Let me try something."

He nodded and stepped off me. I stood and used the shadows to grab his pants and jerked his leg out from under him. He rolled back to sit on his tail.

"Hm. Guess you're smarter than the average shadow user."

"I doubt it. But how often have Stygra had the opportunity to test something out on a Rogue without having to attack or run or panic?"

He nodded, "True. Most Stygra and some humans still see us as beasts. Only the Welkans have been open." Daisy then snorted, bouncing on his tail a little, "We even treat certain species of Rogues the same way."

"It's difficult to judge if someone is good or bad in the heat of a battle with the bad. Some may just be following orders because they have no other choice. The one beside them might just be evil, wanting to do as much harm as possible. They could have their reason. Maybe a member of the enemy force killed their entire family." Tori lifted a shoulder, "You can't be open during those instances of battle, but we can during times of counsel and peace."

"Just gotta get to the times of peace first." Daisy rolled back to his clawed feet. He tapped them along the deck, "I think you'll be fine. We are fighting Stygra."

"The most powerful Stygras."

"Yes, well, you will not be alone." Tori sheathed his sword.

"Just got word." Blari pushed into Austere's cabin. He paused, "I knew I should have brought a chair."

Tori and Daisy had brought their own. Spacya was sprawled on the floor, leaning back against the pirate prince's desk. Austere and I were sitting on the bed, he sprawling like Spacya, to take up most of the mattress.

Spacya tapped the desk with the tip of her skinning dagger, "Look, desk. Perfect for, I dunno, writing. All open and waiting for you."

Blari nudged her with his toe as he passed. She brandished her blade, and he scurried to sit in the chair. "I got word."

"And?" Tori prodded.

Blari unfolded the tiny piece of paper. A dot of blood was on his temple, in the shorthairs of his scalp, "What happened?" I tapped my temple.

"Taspe probably told it to peck me." Blari grumbled, shifting in his chair as he dabbed at the spot with his robe sleeve. He cleared his throat, and I watched his eyes sweep over the paper. Code. Blari was the quickest to decipher Taspe's codes.

"He has his army at Osprey. They should be at Galanesse in two days' time." He flipped the piece of paper, reading the date. "In a day. He's using teams to infiltrate to be inside, while the majority will hide in the forest and cliff areas. Another portion of his Legacy is in Paradisio and Columbri."

"Taspe? You mean THE male leader of the biggest Legacy ever created?"

His eyes were about to pop out of his scales. I nodded, pride warming my heart.

"He's her best friend." Austere added.

"He trains his warriors personally. He learned from only the best warriors himself, too! They say he knew how to dance and fight right out of the womb!"

I laughed, "Well, his mother is pretty talented herself. His uncle always wins the dance and spar tournaments too."

Blari rolled his eyes, "He's not allowed to meet Taspe."

Daisy whimpered, slumping into his chair, "But why?"

"The ass has a big enough head as it is! Can't have you fawning over him to make it even bigger. He won't fit through doors as is."

Spacya chuckled, "Let the boy meet his idol. He can knock Taspe down a notch or two sparing." She shook her head, "He was holding back each time he sparred one of us on the deck."

His claws raked against the scales at the back of his head and down his neck, "I didn't think anyone noticed."

Tori leaned back in his chair, crossing his arms and his ankles as he stretched out, "We noticed. Honestly, I appreciate it for those two." He nodded toward Austere and I, "But Spacya needs a little take down."

"Speak for yourself, Prince." Spacya eyed Tori down the length of her dagger.

A knock sounded on the door.

"Enter."

"Captain," one of the cabin girls moved into the room with long gangly legs, "Another bird." She held another slip of paper out to him.

"Hand it to Blari, thank you." He waved her toward the priest at his desk.

The girl didn't keep her head down like most young ones did in the presence of elders. She smiled, moving through us with loose movements to hand Blari the note. She then bowed, before closing the door behind her. Pride kept warming me; Austere was such a leader that even his lowest ranks were comfortable and at least content in their lives. I realized as I looked at each of my companions; I had an overabundance of gifts.

"Taspe writes that he's had a few of his messengers watching the Dark Swamps. None of the Stygra there have made a move toward Galanesse. Nor are they gathering."

"That's good. We just have to deal with the Tower and whatever support she has."

My eyes rolled back in my head. *What if all of Galanesse was with her? What if this was a fool's errand, and I was about to get them all killed?*

There was a little length of silence as we each mulled over our own thoughts.

"So... does this mean I get to meet Taspe, or not?"

Chapter 39

Upon disembarking, we were dragged along in the usual parade. Daisy ate it up. He was practically standing on his horse, waving at everyone and kissing those that dared to break through the guards. The people fell in love with him for his antics. It gave me plenty of opportunity to pick out familiar faces in the deluge.

Taspe's nephew was the first. Lave slid up to the side of my horse, I hadn't named the beast yet, and placed a cool hand on my knee. His wink and grin made me grin too. In a blink, he became another face in the crowd. Taspe's mother stood beneath a green awning away from the bustle. Her smile warmed me. Another threw a flower at me. I caught it. Inside was a note with the church and Taspe's name in Welkan scrawled inside. I would not see Taspe yet. It was a good thing, though.

He was far too recognizable.

We made our usual busy, headache inducing circuit around the capital before stopping in front of the castle. The king and queen made their nice speech about how we took care of the bandits wreaking havoc in Iethyll. Little did they know, we did nothing. The King handled that perfectly well. They introduced Evedaisily.

The crowd roared their love for him, as loud as it was for Austere, according to the ringing both caused in my ears. Another enormous meal. Another few hours of mingling with the guests the royals invited or allowed in.

Keandria lurked in the crowd. She chatted and talked lively to all the other guests, but she avoided me. My feelings were not bruised.

I wanted to stuff myself as my companions were doing, but my stomach was like a pool of oil, heavy and burning.

One night. Tonight was all we needed, then we could move. This would all be over, one way or another.

Taspe wore a huge grin as he stood in front of my door in the church. His arms wrapped around me in a cool embrace, soothing away the heat of the crowd we had left. He kissed the top of my head, shook Austere's wrist, and threw a comment at Blari, "Pecked head."

"Ass."

"Is that the best you can come up with?"

Blari's chest puffed up, "Cold blooded asinine, big-headed, skinny ankled, little boy."

Taspe frowned and looked down at his ankles, his arm still around my shoulder, "I have skinny ankles," his voice reminded me of a child's.

"I'm going to bed." Spacya managed out between snorts. She opened her door, waited, and closed it again without entering.

She held up two fingers, then pointed them over her shoulder.

I nodded through laughing, "Come on, let's let Taspe pout in private." I pushed open mine. Ida grinned at me. I motioned for her to move back from the door then whispered in her ear when I reached her, "We have to be quiet and they're all coming in here."

Her eyes bulged, "Baths?"

"Yesssss!" Austere grinned at her.

"Gods." Blari groaned from his room. "No, no baths." He opened and closed his door in the same manner. Together, he and Spacya entered my room, Tori and Daisy close behind.

"Why are we all in here?" Tori asked.

"Plan, less chance of ambush, and baths." Austere ticked the positives off on his fingers.

"Ijustwanttosayit'sanhonor! An. Honor. Sir!" Daisy finally got in front of Taspe.

Taspe's grip tightened as he eyed the Rogue up and down, "Hello... Evedaisily, correct?"

"You know my name!" He folded his claws under his chin and those eyes of his were so wide they took up his face.

I tried pulling away, but Taspe's hold was unyielding. "Daisy, just call him Daisy."

"That's fine, but why is he looking at me like that?" Taspe's voice was low as he adjusted his grip and body so that I was more in between him and Daisy.

"One day, someone's going to look at me that way." Austere murmured with a sigh.

Spacya snorted, "Not doin' yer job in the bed well enough if they don't look at you like that."

His brows quirked, "Oh no, that's a different worship. Shall I demonstrate?"

Spacya nodded to me, "Don't bother me any."

"Stop. Laughing." Taspe hissed in my ear.

I covered my mouth with my hand, feeling the damp spill onto my cheeks above my fingers. I needed this. I needed this last laugh.

I pushed him away with the shadow hands, pulling Daisy forward by his cloak with another. They crashed into each other. Daisy clutched Taspe around the ribs, his head pressed to the Welkan's broad chest. "Oh! Thank you… oh… this… this is…"

As his words kept failing him, Taspe's arms looked like they were being pulled by strings at his elbows. He twitched in his eyebrows and his fingers. His eyes were all over Daisy and his hands followed soon after, trying to find a good place to pry the stranger off him. "Look, I know that I'm attractive, but I will have to admit, I've never acted with a Rogue of your stature before. The little owl I ran into… well, that was different. Aren't you supposed to be warm? You're getting cold hanging on to me like this."

His eyes met mine, and he mouthed, 'what am I supposed to do here?' I shrugged. He frowned.

We spent the next few hours planning and sneaking instructions to Taspe's Legacy, and receiving updates via a broken window I was loath to do, but it was the only way. The blue birds and doves were getting extra workouts today as they flitted back and forth. They were also getting many treats. I was worried that after today they would be too fat to fly.

Six groups of eight warriors had already set up in the capital by the time we finished breakfast the next morning. Four were through the night, finding cover in the darkness and staying there. Taspe was waiting on word from two more groups before he would leave to join yet another, that would find a way into the Tower via the caverns below. Two other groups were down there, each one tasked with blocking incoming attackers from entering the Tower from either the Castle or the cliff path.

Tori had finally found a map drawn well enough for Taspe to see in the dark.

I just hoped that the Welkans didn't have to stay down there too long. A lot of his warriors had been slaves. I could see Taspe's concerns about them having flashbacks. They had assured him they would be fine. Still, he gnawed on his bottom lip as he waited for the last two birds to arrive, stating everything was in place.

I sent word via a priest that I was ready to see Keandria to learn of our next quest after going over the plan multiple times. All my companions would be with me. Once the priest came back and stated she was ready to see us, we made our way to The Tower. Taspe already left to meet with his team in the caves. He was to give us fifteen minutes, or if he heard a ruckus start, before he was to act.

Blari prayed over each one of us. I wasn't sure if I wanted to pray again. But, for the sake of my friends, I started praying too.

Each step I had to make myself take. The air grew heavy, my lungs wrestled it into them and I found it useless, as it only caused my heart to pound in my ears. All the sounds were too loud. The gravel of the path to the Tower echoed, the sounds of our boots and Daisy's claws on the marble flooring of the tower threatened to give me a headache as the echoes bounced back and forth on the walls.

We entered her office. She was behind the desk with the map. The thing she stole from the gods. "You're back early." She stated, standing from her leaning position over the design. A single small purple vial rolled between her slender fingers.

"The task was simple enough. We set up procedures." I got out of my dry mouth. Why hadn't I brought water with me?

"Before, you left the orchard early too."

"We completed it."

That vial tinked against her fingernails as she kept rolling it.

My companions spread into the position we had planned on. There were six other Stygra in the room. Two I recognized from some meetings from before. Council members. One was another young female. She trembled, her arms folded against her stomach as she curled inward. I couldn't allow her to be the next victim.

These young ones should have their heads held high. They shouldn't be shaking just by being in the same room as someone who led them. They shouldn't have thoughts of dying running through their little heads.

"So efficient now." Keandria sneered, "Shall we get started on the next one?"

I nodded, "Let's." Had it been enough time?

Keandria reached out her hand toward the youth, the other toward me. The vial had disappeared. I lunged for her. One of my shadows smacked her hand away from the child.

She recoiled, her eyes growing wide as I slid across the map to her. I formed a net, wrapping it around her. Some strands bit into her cheeks and forehead and the green blood oozed in droplets before flowing down her pale skin. "You use Stygra magic?!"

Something slammed into my side and I skidded across the room on my hip and shoulder before I could reach Keandria. I looked up. A dark, thick ooze coated my thigh up to my ribs. A Stygra created another ball of the stuff next to Keandria.

Daisy swiped the goo off me with his tail, flinging it back to the Stygra as she hit him with the ball she just formed. It stuck to him, but he didn't falter. He launched at her from all fours, tackling her to the marble floor. Her blood was a pool underneath her as Daisy moved to focus on Keandria.

Cries echoed in the room. Chairs and other smaller pieces of furniture shattered. The ring of metal against metal overpowered the slick noise of blade into flesh. Daisy clutched Keandria, hauling her to her feet, then dangling her to where her toes barely brushed the marble.

I was at his side, holding a dagger to Keandria's throat, "Those children you killed through me, they gave me their power to use it against you."

Her eyes bulged. "No." Her words were a whisper, and she grinned, "How interesting! You'll do wonders with me!"

Daisy huffed, "She's a lunatic."

Keandria laughed. Somehow, she freed one of her arms and threw something. The vial. It shattered against the floor right at Spacya's feet. My friend jumped free, tossing the Stygra she had been fighting in the purple and gray smoke that erupted from the broken glass.

Her scream ended in the cloud.

The smoke formed into… more smoke? I blinked, trying to get my eyes to clear. The form had a dark hood, held close to where the neck should be by a gold and bronze clasp shaped into the two moons shifting through their phases. The cloak flowed in place. It reminded me of when the wind pushed on the chimney smoke so much it slithered down the rocks like a slick fog.

Something glinted where arms should be. I glanced down. Six silver glowing metal pieces curved in a half moon on each side, thin and long. They tinkled together, sounding like Jingles' laughter. The sound didn't spread warmth. It ate through me and left nothing but icy fear.

It dissolved. It reappeared in front of Spacya. Those curved metals curled through her neck and into her scalp at the base of her skull. Blood hadn't had time to form by the time it disappeared again.

She hit her knees. Her eyes rolled back. Her spear dropped to the marble floor before she did. Blood oozed from her neck to her lips.

Papers flew into the air as the thing grabbed Blari's satchel. The priest kicked. His leg went through it.

"It's called a Pariaper. Beautiful isn't it?"

Keandria's voice was a hiss in my ear. It made the emotion come back. Anger slicked through me at the pool of blood on the floor underneath my dear friend. I slid the dagger across Keandria's throat. Green slid over my fingers.

"Your blood is prettier." Evedaisily crooned, before he dropped her to the floor like she was a sack of refuse.

I moved, my back pressed against the wall as I tried to get a bead on the Pariaper. A shadow loomed taller in the right corner, the clicking of those claws echoed in it, but then it was gone. Daisy set fire to the only set of curtains in the room with a candle from the desk. Orange flames licked up the edges of them before spreading to the top and into the middle. The chamber grew brighter and brighter.

Smoke curled to the high-vaulted ceiling.

Keandria choked. I glanced down, her lips covered in green; she was still smiling. "It's a beautiful creation. A culmination."

The girl screamed as it lifted her off her feet. She kicked, clawing at the claws surrounding her slender neck.

"Sssssisssster…" the thing hissed before ripping its blades through her chest. Her sternum slid down her dress to splatter on the floor along with bits of her lungs and heart.

I threw my new daggers at it as fast as I could. Each one slipped through the smoke. I stopped at five. The next two in my palms. Those five tinged against the marble as they hit the floor.

He lowered the little Stygra until her feet brushed her pool of blood. I threw a dagger where the claws met smoke. It sank in, held.

The Pariaper hissed. Dropping the girl as he used those claws to scratch at the dagger in his arm. The dagger dropped with a clatter. Smoke whirled, a tornado of purple, gray and black. Only the clasp remained steady, moving in circles.

The smoke became solid, slamming me back against the wall I had barely moved from. I felt my spine creak like it was about to break. Needles were in my hips and I cried out at the onslaught of pain as they pulsed or grew in my skin. I couldn't tell, all I knew was they hurt far more than a blade somehow.

I slashed and slapped. Bits of the smoke cloak fluttered away.

"Sissssterrrr." It hissed in my face without breath.

Silver glinted in my peripheral before it shot through the hood. Tori's sword. It pierced through and through. The hood fell away, revealing a plume of smoke.

The needles disappeared, so did the Pariaper. All but the moon clasp. I could see it, a little, floating on its own through the middle of the room. Fast like a rabbit.

I fought to keep my feet. I knew if I fell, I would never get back up. "Clasp." I thought I yelled it, but it sounded like a whisper in my ears. Tori nodded.

Daisy turned from killing another Stygra to look at me. His enormous eyes scanned the room. His scales raised like hackles as he stood so still when his pupils narrowed.

"So many to make it. So many pretty little children. Migarins."

I looked down. Keandria was still alive. "You mean... you made it? You made it with Migarins? With the children of your own kind?"

"Oh yes. You were to give it form. Give it flesh. But I like it better this way."

"Why?"

"Stygra over all. Stygra bow to none. Humans shall not know the blessing of power. No, never."

I gritted my teeth. I flung the blade so hard my elbow and wrist popped with the effort. Her head was near my foot. The dagger, my dagger, slid into her eye, through it, and I thought I heard the tip tink wetly against the marble. "We will keep the peace, thanks." I spat at her other eye. Barely missing my mark and hitting her cheek instead.

I turned in time to see Evedaisily leap into the air. He wrapped his claws around something solid in the smoke. The

Pariaper formed in his grasp. Daisy grinned and ripped the moons from the neck of the cloak.

The vapor of it faded. A solid dark purple and black cloak around a slender pale body formed as both the Pariaper and Daisy fell back to the floor. Daisy had smoke formed scales now. His eyes glowed in them like green embers.

Shouts were bouncing off the walls of the hallway. Taspe had come.

Austere threw his blade into the Pariaper's middle. Tori rolled across the desk and stabbed the neck.

A hundred screams filled the room. Glass that remained whole shattered. Ash swept down over the blades and spilled into the floor as the screams stopped.

The doors flew open. Taspe and Lave, drenched in green and spotted with blue blood, stood side by side as they surveyed the room.

"Little late." Austere rasped, falling to the floor. His leg was in shreds from knee to hip.

I whimpered, wanting to go to him. I tried to take a step and managed a shuffle. Needles of pain lanced up and down my legs and halfway up my back. Tori caught me against his side before I fell face first into the desk.

"Look." He pointed to the map.

Five large dots of different colors had formed on the map. Some were in the mainlands, but two were in Lanpress. One rested right on top of Galanesse. I leaned against the desk with both hands. My back muscles strained to pull my legs forward. I tasted metal in my mouth as I clenched my teeth to keep from crying out.

"Healer!" Taspe barked into the hallway. "Now!"

A few Stygra shuffled in. One checked Spacya and shook her head. Another to Austere, while another came toward me. Her eyes shifted white as she spotted Keandria, but she began her work.

"What… what is that?"

"Didn't the orchard have a spot on it the last time we were here?" Tori asked, wiping sweat from his chin and brow.

Daisy moved over, fluid and smoke. "What do you mean?".

"We have trouble!" Another Welkan barged in, I knew him to be a scout or runner. "There's a… well, it's a… er… thing. Big. Big thing crashing through houses and eating people." He pointed behind him, toward the capital proper.

Blari pulled himself up on the desk. The robes at his side were dark with blood, and he had torn his sleeve to wrap it around his arm. That sleeve was growing just as wet. He looked at the map, then at the scout, then back at the desk. "Quests. The remaining ones."

I had full control back in my feet. The healer was working wonders with her magic even as tears slid down her eyes. She kept glancing at Keandria's body.

I called the Commander of the royal guard and the head of the capital guard. The capital guard I tasked with getting people out, quickly with help of the Stygra still alive in the tower so they could heal the wounded as they moved or use their magic in some useful way. Only half of the ones had believed the same as Keandria. We were lucky.

The Royal guard was useless. Only making sure the lords and ladies could flee. They had already put the queen and her royal family upon a ship which was now floating a safe distance away. They could still give orders via their dyed green doves and songbirds. Tori's face had become a mask when he asked if his able siblings were fighting and the commander scoffed at him.

Taspe and his warriors were herding the beast, trying to keep it away from the most populated areas. That meant they headed here, to the empty plaza with three large buildings to box it into.

If the buildings failed, then the cliffs and the ocean underneath them would serve the purpose too.

The tower rocked after crashing thundered from somewhere in the capital.

Austere was standing now. Daisy had followed Taspe. I could imagine him proving to be quite useful in distracting the beast and leading it here with that clasp. What kind of magic had that been?

How many had she killed to make that thing?

"Are we sure she's dead?" Austere leaned heavily on the desk as the healer fussed at him to sit or lie back down so he wouldn't undo her work. He waved her off. His face, nearly as pale as hers, was turned toward Keandria.

I glanced down. None of the wounds were healing. "By now I think something would have healed if she tied another to her."

He nodded, "Still...." he slid his short sword to Tori.

Tori took it by the hilt and ran it through Keandria's neck after picking out a swath that wasn't covered in my net. He grunted as he sawed through the vertebrae, then put his boot on the flat to push it through. Her head rolled slightly, held to her body by my threads. I wasn't about to let those strands go.

Who knew if she could come back alive? At least she would still be bound.

The Stygra at my side turned abruptly to empty her stomach onto a pile of what used to be a chair and ashes from the curtains. She wiped her mouth off on the robes at her knee as she crouched to get her breath. I kept my head turned slightly so I could watch her in my peripheral.

Tori handed a clean sword back to Austere, who slid it back in its sheath at his hip. He propped his longer blade against the desk within arm's reach. "What's the plan?"

"Drive it here."

"Know that already." Austere grunted.

"Impale it on one of the castle spires."

He blinked at me, "H-how do you know it's that tall?"

"If it isn't, we're going to make one fall on it."

"The east one." Tori stared at me.

I nodded. I had noticed in my many voyages to the castle because of the parades that the east and north towers had not been repaired in years. The south was currently being finished. The east faced the courtyard the three buildings shared. The same courtyard I hoped Taspe's warriors and Daisy were leading the beast to.

"Liogonee."

"What?"

Blari had a shard of a golden vial in his hand. "The name, I'm guessing. Liogonee. Leeongoneee?" He shrugged, placed the piece on the map next to the dot that was creeping closer to the ocean. They were the same color.

"Liogonee it is." I slid my gaze to the floor, toward the middle of the room. Spacya's pool of blood had stopped spreading, from what I could tell. It created a half moon of dark crimson around her. The furs at her neck, once a clean brown of fluff, were now black with it and clumped together.

"Let's drop the largest spear I know of on the thing," my voice cracked, "For her."

A troubling task for two of us, the east tower stairs, wound round and round. I lost count of the steps only a third of the way up as Austere and I leaned on each other, and the wall to get up it. Blari, Tori and a few of the royal guards that didn't mind breaking their orders were already at the top, on the roof, seeing if they could dislodge the long lance shaped piece of metal there.

"It's here!" Tori bellowed down.

Seconds later, a thunderous crash followed by smaller ones shook the tower. Austere pushed me against the wall, covering me with his body as he covered the back of his head with his hands.

"Thanks for the warning." He muttered once the building settled, and he turned to start up again.

We were almost there, I could see the sunlight filtering through a hole in the tower's roof between two rafters. Rafters?

"Hold on to me."

"Yes, my love?" Austere turned back, and those arms curled around my waist. He was looking at me with that look, that smirk.

"No. I have an idea."

"Why tell me no?" He leaned in.

I covered his face with my hand, palm slightly bending the end of his nose down. "Hold on."

I stared at wood beams and pooled Randia's power into a spool I envisioned in my mind. I let it shoot out. The shadows stretched like ropes, looping around the rafters and then coming back to wrap around us. I grinned. "Now, let's see if…" I yelped, my feet dragging the steps until I made the shadows haul us up higher. Austere had hissed, his face getting even paler against my hand.

He shook his head, getting my hand off his face as he watched the tower roof get closer to us. He sighed, "Why didn't you think of this sooner?"

"I'm in pain and putting all my thoughts into figuring out if this is going to work or not."

He groaned, "It'll work or it won't. Figure out our next one if it doesn't."

"Already have."

"What is that?"

"I'll tell you if this doesn't work."

He grunted as his back hit the rafter. "Got one for after that?"

He pulled himself up. I loosened the shadows until I let him go completely after he was safely on the roof. I pulled myself up, "Yes." I said after I had to grunt to get my ass up onto the roof with just my arms.

Tori reached down to pull me up after I got my torso onto the roof.

"How many plans do you have?" Austere stood, looking down off the edge of the narrow square roof that held the spire in the middle of it.

"Five so far."

He turned his gaze back to me. "You're gonna need to look at that beast."

I moved toward him, feeling as if I had to sling my legs forward with each step. The pain made my stomach churn. I looked over the edge.

Beneath was a bunch of white fluff between thicker golden fur with white tips behind an enormous pair of rounded ears. The face was broad; the muzzle squared. Its eyes were large platters of brown. It was up on its hind legs, which were gold and white scales, as thick as the tower we were on. A tail covered in the same scales lashed, rubble skittered back and forth along with it, which created more rubble as they cracked against buildings and the once smooth, stone courtyard. On its tip was a tuft of the golden fur with a white end.

"Lion. Dragon. Bees." Blari spat over the edge.

"Bees?"

The white tips exploded off in a flurry of movement. They gathered and swarmed, moving as one as they surrounded the Welkans nearby. Shields were put up, and most of the white bees bounded off, but some found their marks as wails echoed up to us.

Satisfied with the strikes, or as a tactic, the bees returned to the golden fur. The beast was white tipped again.

Spears, arrows, daggers, and swords bounced off the scales of the legs. It swatted away some. While yet others were swarmed and the aim thrown off before the spear fell harmless to the stones.

The beast had its scaled front claws up on the garden wall that separated the castle from the church. The claws were a long way away from the top edge of the wall. It scraped those large black things into the rock, dislodging some, but the wall was holding. Not for long.

"Can we take it up?" I motioned to the spire.

"It's loose, we can do it." Tori answered.

"Now how are we gonna get it over…"

I let out a long pulse of a whistle, then two short ones, and repeated it.

A shield flashed. From this height, he could have been an ant. I waved my arms, letting out the pulse again.

The shield flashed.

We repeated the process until, finally; the shield waved. "Good, he sees us." I glanced around. Picked up a brick and dropped it off the side, just using the long pulse of a whistle this time.

Taspe's shield waved again.

The Welkan's massive army shifted, cornering the beast, but not just against the wall. They became fewer on the side closest to us, but kept up a wall of themselves so it wouldn't find an opening back out into the city.

My heart swelled, and I felt the tears prick at the corners of my eyes. He understood. I grinned.

"Trying not to be jealous over here."

I shoved away the bricks lined up along the edge, tossing them over the side of the tower. The beast looked over, then up, watching them fall with those rounded ears pricked. A sword landed in its far side. It flinched, jerking toward us. Then it turned toward the mass of Welkans.

"No!" I waved my hands, trying to catch those large brown eyes.

Something green flicked and shifted up on the top of the wall. It jumped, flicked again. The Lioganee stopped, those eyes locked on the green thing. It moved along the wall, toward the east tower. It flicked and jumped, shifted, and those brown eyes followed its every move.

Finally, it came to the tower, where the wall met it below. They fit a slender ladder against the rocks. The green thing jumped onto the ladder, then off it again. The Liogan turned fully toward the tower.

The green smoke flitted halfway up the ladder. As he became solid, Daisy grinned up at me. I grinned back.

The muscles in the Lioganee's back bunched.

"Steady." I waited, watching what Daisy and the beast would do.

Daisy flicked in and out of smoke and some glittering form I hadn't seen the Pariaper do at all. Steadily climbing up the ladder. The Lioganee kept following with its eyes, that great colossal head tilting further and further up.

The nose and eyes looked so soft compared to the rest of it.

Those muscles twitched, and it was up on its hind paws, those front paws reaching toward the green smoke on the ladder.

"Now!" I helped the men push. The spire toppled forward. The base was heavier than the point. It fell end over end. The green smoke caught the end, somehow, and it stopped flipping. The green smoke jumped back, barely missing a paw that was reaching for him.

The end of the spire sunk into the slightly open mouth of the Lioganee.

It stopped moving. Those claws hung in midair for a breath until they crashed into the tower. Austere grabbed me, hauling me to the narrow square floor of the top of the tower. Tori and Blari were lying there already, clutching at the stones beneath them as the tower swayed.

Another crash followed, the tower made a cracking noise, and jerked to the side, then held still. Too still. I whimpered, hurriedly pulled into my borrowed power and began forming a net all around us with both the shadows and the unbreakable threads. It wasn't anywhere near becoming solid when the rocks crumbled beneath us in the growing roar of collapsing stone and wood.

Chapter 40

You are damned with the power of all and none, Hero.
Your journey has barely begun.

Darkness gave way to sound and light.

I jerked up as pain slashed my hips. It followed suit in my shoulder, and then my head. The brightness made my eyes water as I fell against the softness at my back. Something smelled of lavender. Was there this much pain in the realm of the dead?

"Easy, love. I have you." Hot breath blew away the sweetness and replaced it with mint and tea. Warm lips pressed to my temple and the light against my eyelids faded to a soft, red glow. My eyes were like sandpaper as I opened them.

His dark, smooth skin met my gaze before I switched to his red eyes. His pupils were huge. My vision grew blurry, "You're… we're…"

"You're fine. I'm fine. We're all fine… well, other than…" he looked away. "They loaded her into a cart yesterday. Many from the capital are making a procession to deliver her back to Dragotown, where she will have rites once you are ready."

The bed shifted on my other side. Cool skin slid against my arm before his fingers twined into mine. I turned my head to see Taspe sharing my pillow. His face was ashen, his eyes had a dullness to them. "What's wrong?"

He smiled, "A lot of bee poison."

"How many?"

He sighed, "We'll talk about that later. Blari, Tori, and Daisy are fine. So is Ida. She got on the ship with the royals. Focus on the good."

I looked back at Austere, "Your leg?"

"Hurts. But they have an amazing drug." He chuckled, and lay down to nuzzle into my neck.

I breathed in, the lavender scent returning with it as I stared up at the ceiling. My room in the church. With my best friend and my lover. That breath I had taken in became caught in my throat.

Taspe pulled away as Austere sat me up. Taspe gave me a cup, and I drank. I coughed again, drank some more, until I could form words, "We survived."

"Yes."

I choked again. Taspe refilled my cup, spilling some as he laughed.

"Hero Matron Nadachia Wanya Dietra of Silverequis. You're gonna have to change your name."

Austere chuckled, "Wait until she becomes queen."

Taspe groaned, "Gods, she's the same level as me. More. No stopping her now."

I frowned, "Matron?"

"You killed Keandria and have Stygra powers. The remaining Council of Stygra claim you as their Matron." Austere's voice tumbled like a summer storm.

The pain in my hips and shoulder lanced again as he lowered me down to my back. I sighed as both males snuggled against my sides. "Is this how it's going to be from now on?"

"Until you tire of me," Stere murmured, then yawned.

"What about—"

"Shhhh." Sounded from both sides.

"But—"

"Just go back to sleep." Taspe's low chuckle in my ear drew a sigh from me and I closed my eyes to try to sleep.

I stared at the pile of letters on the kitchen table. Then I glanced at the fire. It had burned down to coals and needed refreshing. Out the window, the bright sun blazing low in the sky made the dew drops gleam, and I was sweating already.

Sam Wicker

I sighed and pushed the letters together in one hand while I drank down the rest of my coffee with the other.

"Where's your pirate?"

"In bed probably."

Father grunted as he took off his boots at the door. A pail of fresh milk beside him. They couldn't keep up with the new cows. He could milk one before breakfast and the other two after. I wanted to tease him about becoming a lazy man by getting up so late now, but I didn't.

Teasing these days only meant I would be teased right back about how I had titles.

"Your mother and Seaghla are already at the new house. Doing something with frilly things."

I grinned, decorating was never Father's interest. "Sure you don't want to help them pick out some colors?"

He shot a look at me, then his eyes drifted down to the letters tucked against my side, "Ever going to read those?"

"Maybe we should go for a walk."

"Maybe we should." He grinned before pulling his boots back on. We walked around the property. We had hired help. Not that they got to help much. The children were playing and studying under Moko's watchful eyes.

Builders were working on the new house. The old one we were giving to Moko and Lave whenever they decided they were going to bond.

Father and I stopped beside the garden. We were in the small grove of trees between it and the river. There, we had erected a small fence to protect the two small mounds of stones. Moko hand painted one stone on each with their names. We put flowers among them each day.

Tears still burned my eyes each time I came here.

A month, and I was feeling everything I had lost anew. Perhaps, for the first time. Each day my shoulders agonized under the weight that others wanted me to take. But this moment was for them. Nothing else mattered. This quiet moment was for my little siblings, remembering them. Remembering Jahni, Spacya, Joni, Sterla, Eilse, and Randia too.

Father wrapped an arm around my shoulders, "My heart is your heart. Feel it. My blood is your blood. Know it. We are alive because of you. Many are alive because of you. Many more will owe you their lives. But now, you take your time. You need this time to heal."

I nodded, knowing his words were true, but I still ached with a stone in my heart, cold and dead. It tried to swallow me whole. My family wouldn't allow it, nor would Taspe or Stere.

The salt of the sea tickled my nose with the breeze before another heavy arm slid around me. He hugged my father and me from behind. "Strength is knowing that you carry the rest of what their lives could be with you."

Dear Reader,

I'm proud of you for slogging through this book. It's my first one, and I'm only going to get better from here. As I write this, I've already witnessed the improvement in the five other novels I've written.

Trust me, they aren't as beastly as this one. There is hope! Continue on this journey with me and Nadachia?

Thank you,
Sam Wicker

Follow me and my other books!
https://linktr.ee/writersamwicker
www.carderwickerwriting.com

www.ingramcontent.com/pod-product-compliance
Lightning Source LLC
Chambersburg PA
CBHW011312310726
48973CB00011B/2891